the Hidden Guardian

RANGER OF THE TITAN WILDS

BOOK THREE

J.D.L. ROSELL

Cover illustration © 2023 by Félix Ortiz
Cover design by Shawn T. King
Interior illustrations © 2023 & 2024 by Félix Ortiz
Interior illustrations © 2024 by Joemel Requeza
Book design by J.D.L. Rosell
Map © by Keir Scott-Schrueder

ISBN 978-1-952868-43-6 (hardcover with dust jacket)
ISBN 978-1-952868-42-9 (IngramSpark paperback)
ISBN 978-1-952868-44-3 (BookVault paperback)
ISBN 979-8-321418-03-1 (KDP paperback)
ISBN 978-1-952868-36-8 (ebook)

Published by Rune & Requiem Press
jdlrosell.com

A NOTE ON APPENDICES

You can find appendices on the characters, creatures, and world of Ranger of the Titan Wilds located near the end of the book.

All series lore and commissioned art also appear on my website, jdlrosell.com.

UNERA
SIN
FORSAKEN ARCHIPELAGO
THE BARREN
ORSARR
THE FINGERS
SILVERTUSK SIERRA
THE TITAN WILDS
IRON WOODS
THE GREATHOUSE
HELNIST
ONGUL PEAKS
THE TUSKS
WILDS LODGE
ALTAN-GAZ
CROFT
FOLLY
GORGE OF OXEN
SAINT'S CROSSING
BALTESI
FORSAKEN BAY
ORILLE
LAMAYO
STORMHOLD
SOUTHPORT
THE RADIANT SLOPES
RASPUTIN'S BLADE
MOSLANAT COAST
THE TEARS
KUALA
OCULAR OCEAN
THE VEIL
TORRENT SEA
KEIR 65

N
W
E
S
REFUGIO
TIBERIA
VASRRA
THE ANCESTRAL LANDS
EYT
KHIRM
THE SKY SEA
MUMSI
THE EYRIE
GALKHIR
KALGA
DETGOL

*To Luca and Evie,
my favorite nephew and niece.*

*May you never have to hide
who you are.*

"Life has its own hidden forces which you can only discover by living."

—Søren Kierkegaard

PROLOGUE

She smiled as the ruins' song filled the air.

To mortal eyes, it would seem like mere broken, cold stone. But Atastimina felt its warmth. The wooden beads buried within the blocks kept their sparks, memorials to minds long departed.

Yet their memories lingered. To those who heard, they would never die.

For a time, Ata stood and listened. When she opened her eyes, the day had passed and night had fallen. Guilt stirred in her. Time had once been as abundant as leaves of grass; she had grown used to spending it in idle freedom. Now, eternity had contracted into moments, each as precious and vital as those of her infancy, centuries before.

"We are reborn..."

Cackling to the unhearing castle, Ata strolled through its rubble-strewn corridors. She sharpened her senses as she probed the tumbled stones. Most of the world yielded to her touch, but there was resistance here.

A barrier. Nearly imperceptible, but plain as sunlight to her keen senses.

Ata caressed it with her heritage. Like light reflecting on the surface of water, the magic made the barrier discernible. She pressed harder; the barrier yielded a measure. She thought it might soon give.

Then water hardened to glass, then stone, then diamond. She could press no further.

Ata relented with a sigh. Few things could resist her, and those that did posed a grave threat to the Kin. But she had lived too long to heed fear.

"Even if I should..."

Lifefire flickered above, drawing her gaze. In the sky above the ruins, clouds swirled, forming a towering column, gray and tumultuous. Within it, energy was building and taking shape.

Ata grinned up at the storm.

"You are not the only one who hides, my little friend," she murmured, pressing a hand to her chest. Her talons pressed through the silver fur to touch the beast nestled within. "They were here all along, tucked in their den. I wonder if you knew it. And here I thought your loyalty was to me and our mutual friend!"

The thunderhead flickered with lightning. The sky rumbled. Clouds spilled over the jungle beyond the ruins.

Ata sighed and lowered her head. "But I'm afraid you must leave me now. We each have our duties."

She pressed her nails in harder until amber ichor stained the fur. But that was only a slight pain next to that from the other creature peeling off her soul.

As the silver fox departed, Ata shed her fur. It fell in a shimmering cloud around her feet, and she shivered. Only in moments of transition did the cold touch her.

Then it was done, and he sat before her. The fox's fur shone as bright a silver as the coat she had discarded. His sunset-orange eyes stared up at her. She might have thought him reproachful but for the flick of his tail.

"Why must you make the parting so difficult?" she chastised. "You're as eager to be on your way as I am."

A peal of thunder drowned out the ruins' singing. Ata glanced up to see a shadow against the belly of the clouds. It was wide as the ruins themselves, looming and formidable as few creatures were.

The shape tilted to plummet toward them.

"Watch over her, little one," Ata said, looking back at her companion, "and watch well. I think her time of awakening is not yet complete."

Pausing a moment longer, the silver fox darted away, fleeing the storm.

Ata remained where she was. Anticipation burned through her. Death descended, yet a laugh stole free as power rippled across her wooden flesh.

Lightning struck where she stood.

Stones shattered. Ancient ruins broke apart. Powder rose into the air, shrouding all in dust.

The clouds flew back up from the desolation, spinning in a circle before spreading across the sky. As quickly as it had come, the storm departed.

The dust settled in the courtyard below. Empty of intruders once more.

Ata, unharmed beyond the entrance archway, smiled up at the sky. "Next time, perhaps, my old enemy."

With a flourish of her feathers, she stepped through the world and vanished.

PART

I

THE FACE OF WAR

1

SACRED

*L*eiyn closed her eyes, tilted back her head, and breathed in.

Spring was in the air. Though the stiff breeze nipped her nose and chapped her hands, it brought with it scents sweet to behold. Of new leaves, and the promise of grass. The prelude to all that would soon arrive.

What stirred underground spoke even more of the changing season. Though the grass remained yellow, her lifesense detected the pops of life as seeds broke free of shells to grow roots and seek sunlight. On the broadleaved trees, buds made the branches spark as if they caught flame.

Home—it inundated her every sense.

For a moment, her vigilance eased. The urgency to return to Baltesia and defend her homeland receded. Even the pestering thoughts over Sharo's schemes and if Ata had yet tracked him down faded to the back of her mind.

She only inhaled and exhaled. Appreciating this fleeting moment. When even Feral's stench, cultivated over weeks, had a comforting edge.

"You stink," she muttered to the horse.

The mare huffed and tossed her head. Smiling, Leiyn reached out to stroke her mane.

And froze.

Leiyn sniffed the air. Something lurked beneath the fragrant bouquet of the wilderness. A sign of danger. Hoping she imagined it, Leiyn inhaled deeper. There it was again—a caustic warning to nearby creatures.

Smoke. Must it be smoke?

It could mean nothing. Foolhardy hunters, young or desperate, might venture up this way from around Folly, risking titans and wild beasts to earn their next meal. Or perhaps conditions in the south had driven folks north to try their tools at taming the land. The frontier resisted such efforts at every turn, yet it had not stopped hopeful colonists from making the attempt each spring.

But it could be an omen. The specter of war hung heavy over the lands, even this far into the Titan Wilds. Instead of settlers, enemies might linger near. A ranger did not ignore a potential threat. Especially when they were the last one.

In the north, at least.

Exhaling, Leiyn expanded her awareness through the wilderness. Though her mahia always lay open, it contracted to half a league around her when she was not embodying it. Now, she reached across dozens of leagues, searching for the source of the fire.

It took moments to find the intruders, and a moment more to fan suspicion into flame. The hill on which they camped was distinctive. Though she had not often experienced the Titan Wilds through her mahia, she knew this land too intimately to mistake it.

Thirty humans squatted amid the ruins of the Wilds Lodge.

Leiyn held little as holy in her life. Though she paid homage to the Saints and beheld Almighty Omn with wary respect, they were distant beings, their sanctity disconnected from the day to day of living. It was the same with Refugio, the island central to the Catedrál, despite the claims of its priestesses that it was the place closest to the divine in all of Unera.

Now, for the first time, she understood sanctity. For these trespassers trod on her hallowed ground.

She did not know who they were, but where they walked was cause enough for anger. Yet she did not storm off in pursuit as she might have a year before. Experience had hammered home Tadeo's oft-repeated lesson. She could not afford to be rash.

Neither could she ignore it.

Dismounting, Leiyn took her longbow in hand and slung her quiver of broadhead arrows across her back. Her remaining long knife was sheathed at the back of her weapons belt. The pouch of amber beads, gifted by Mother Xepi and brimming with esse, were tied to the front. The titanbone falchions she had claimed from the Iritu ruins of Qasaar hung from either hip. She had not tested them against ordinary steel, but if they could slay lyshans, she suspected they would suffice here.

Her clothes were less satisfactory. Though imbued with an ancient mahia—Inheritance, as Ata called it—they would defy a killing blow as handily as plate armor, but the aqua-and-gold tunic did not blend in among the spring-green woods. Still, if a battle lay ahead, she would need the protection.

"Stay," she murmured to Feral, reaching out with both her hand and magic. The horse flinched, but settled as the calming touch took effect. Leiyn smiled grimly. Xepi's trick had worked this time; with the unruly mare, it was always uncertain.

Turning, Leiyn pulled her cloak tight about her, then slunk into the shadowed boughs.

～ ～

A dozen signs betrayed them. The glint of sunlight on helms. The regimented fortifications ringing the camp. The color of their coats. The style of their tents.

But most telling was the flag that flew above the ruins: a yellow orb arrayed against white fabric.

Suncoats.

Leiyn tightened her fist on the bow stave until the ashwood creaked. She tried to draw a breath and calm her racing pulse. Her chest felt enwrapped by a coil of rope.

Suncoats had burned her home. That they would defile it a second time was one insult too far.

Breathe. Air does not know worry.

She held back, not from the daunting odds alone. Should it come to that, she suspected she could more than match their force. Reaching the edge of the forest encircling the Wilds Lodge, she sought after the faint connection ever-present in the back of her mind.

The thread had frayed from time and disuse, but enough remained that she could feel the ash dragon swimming through the molten rivers far below. He had kept near her, even as she left the mountain from which he had first erupted, which she had taken as inspiration for his name.

Clouded Fang had taken a shine to her, it seemed.

Noticing her attention, the ash dragon turned one burning eye upon her. Her impression of him was too vague to be called sight, yet somehow, she knew he beheld her. Leiyn stiffened at his attention. Before, he had been her salvation, filling her with lifeforce so that even Man'nah, lord of the lyshans, could not kill her.

Yet Leiyn doubted she would ever feel easy before titans. Their minds were too strange, their motives uncertain. Did they have thoughts like humans, or act by pure instinct? Though she had named the dragon, she was not so certain of him as to depend on his mercy.

The titan lingered a moment, then moved on, his presence fading from her awareness.

Air whooshed from Leiyn's lungs. She took a moment before focusing back on her surroundings. The titan's inconstancy was only the first complication. The second lay to the south.

She and the Suncoats were not alone.

On the south side of the hill she sensed another score of intruders. Though she had yet to travel around the Lodge's ruins to see more, she doubted they were more Suncoats. Holding the advantageous position atop the highest point, there was little reason to split their forces. More likely was that this was an opposing faction; a militia from Folly, perhaps, or a force mustered from the few farms this far north. But she would not pin her life on that hope.

All too easily, she could imagine Isla's expression at her plans. How Batu would shake his head, and Acalan would frown. Teya, at least, would smile and call her "Redlock."

For their sakes, she could not throw away her life after a notion of vengeance. Not when she was one of the few Baltesians who could wield mahia, an ability sorely needed in this war. Nor were these men the true object of her hatred. They were pieces in a greater game, moved by players Leiyn had only just begun to identify.

With a last glance at the Lodge, Leiyn sighed and melded back into the woods.

She gave the Ilberian soldiers a wide berth as she made for the second camp. Evening was swiftly falling; the forest grew dark and still.

All the better.

By her lifesense, she could see all that was alive—and in these woods, that was most everything. The roots that might have tripped her. The branches that could lay her low. Ferns, flowers, and shrubs lit the forest floor, guiding her through with scarcely a sound. Even dead leaves were outlined by feasting bugs and a shimmer of infinitesimal life.

This was her territory. Her sacred land. She was a predator prowling through the shadows, prepared to defend it.

Dusk had set in as the camp came into view. Noting the positions of the four sentries posted around the edges, she subdued her magic and observed what she could with her eyes. No fire lit their camp. They were sheltered among trees rather than in a clearing. Despite this and the gloom, she could pick out enough details from the nearest watcher to draw her conclusions.

Plainsriders.

Their leather lamellar armor, horsebows, hair pulled into topknots and bound with red fabric—all signs pointed to the Gazian counterparts to the rangers. The realization brought a fresh flush of anger.

Leiyn fought it down. To reason out this mystery, she needed a clear head.

Think, Firebrand, for one Legion-damned moment.

She came up with three explanations. The first was a stretch: that this was another attempt by the Suncoats to stage an incident. The Ilberians who had attacked the Lodge had dressed as Gasts; perhaps they now attempted a similar ruse. But who would it be for, and what would they stand to gain? Their allegiances were already out in the open.

The second thought seemed more likely. Taban, the snake who had seized the Gazian Greathouse for his own, knew the Wilds Lodge had fallen. By his prior actions, he appeared aligned with Ilberia. Thus, he might have brought his plainsriders to bolster the Suncoats' position but did not trust his allies enough to camp directly with them.

There was a third possibility: the moorwarden was seizing land for Altan Gaz, taking advantage of the vacancy left by the rangers. Taban's ambition was certainly sufficient to the task.

None of these scenarios left the Gazians as allies. Considering plainsriders had tried killing her and her friends in the recent past, she doubted they could be.

Leiyn flared her lifesense and sat back on her haunches, gnawing her lip. Two groups of enemies, and she could do nothing about either of them—not without significant risk.

The prudent ranger would continue south to report it to Mayor Itzel, then leave her to handle them. She had an urgent mission of her own: conveying tidings of the Gast alliance, then standing by her friends and Mauricio as the Ilberian Armada landed on their shores.

But she could not leave. These raiders trampled her home. How could she not come to its defense?

She felt for Feral, left behind with her saddlebags. Unsure how long she would be gone, Leiyn had supplied the horse with water and feed. She would not suffer from neglect. For herself, however, it would make for an uncomfortable night and a likely pointless vigil. But her mind was made up.

Stubborn fool.

Leiyn leaned back against the tree, laying her bow and its nocked arrow across her lap. Settling in for the long watch.

Her opportunity took mere minutes in coming.

She sensed him: a man moving beyond the periphery of the scouts, then squatting. Relieving himself, she guessed with a grim smile. He was far enough away from their camp for a quiet conversation to go unheard.

Like a jaguar in the night, she closed in on her prey.

2

TRANSGRESSIONS

As the plainsrider pulled up his trousers, Leiyn stepped out from behind the tree, an arrow trained on his eye.

The man jerked around and went still at the sight of her weapon. His hands still clutched his unfastened pants, long tunic bunched around his arms. His weapons belt lay out of reach on the ground.

"Not a sound," she said in Kalgan, loud enough to carry across the ten strides between them. "No more than you have already made." Her lips quirked in mockery.

To the man's credit, a hard stare swiftly replaced his surprise. "Ranger. So you survived."

He spoke back in Baltesian, and spoke it well, though with enough of an accent she had to concentrate on his words.

"No thanks to you lot," she said in her own tongue, then nodded toward the camp. She had positioned herself so the trees hid her from the closest scouts. "Come to pillage what's left of the Lodge, have you?"

"We are not pillagers, Ranger Leiyn."

He knows me. Simple enough to guess how. She and Isla had been more than a little conspicuous during their recent stay at the Greathouse.

"Invaders, then," she amended. "Seizing land not your own."

"We take it not for ourselves, but for your people."

Her patience frayed to its last strand. Leiyn had to stop herself from pulling the bowstring taut.

"Help me understand." She bit off each word. "You mean to fight Suncoats for Baltesia?"

"Our alliance says it will be so."

If the plainsrider was lying, he did it well. His gaze never wavered, and he showed few signs of nervousness, despite remaining in a compromising position.

Iron nerves. A reluctant admission, but no less true for it.

Tempting as it was to see if he would hold steady before a drawn bow, she knew better than to draw unless she meant to loose. For the moment, he remained under her control. His fellows had noticed nothing amiss, judging by their stationary esses.

"Ranger Leiyn," the plainsrider said, "I understand your mistrust. When you visited, our position was different."

"Your position. The one where you tried killing me and my friends, you mean?"

"Yes. An Ilberian conqueror offered an alliance. Altan Gaz saw an opportunity for expansion." The man shrugged. "We had our orders. Would you not obey yours?"

Leiyn flashed him a tight smile. "If it meant butchering innocents? No, I don't think I would."

To her surprise, the plainsrider smiled as well. It was far from a pleasant sight. Gaps showed between his teeth, and scars across his lips pulled wide.

"You always stood up for innocents—I remember that well."

"Do you?" An odd thing to say, but she considered it from a wary distance. Refused to let it tip her off-balance.

"You do not remember me? The boy you fought in defense of the Wilds bastard?"

The memory rose with his words. She had to hold back a laugh.

"Altun, wasn't it? Yes, I remember you. Weren't so brave

back then. Even with friends at your back, you still slunk away after the beating."

"You are right." Altun spoke without a trace of defensiveness. "I was a coward and a bully. But experience can change a man."

She cocked an eyebrow. "Don't seem much like a new man from where I'm standing."

"Ranger. We need not see eye to eye—only listen to what I say. Your governor, Mauricio di Siveña, requested of Taban Khyan that we plainsriders secure the frontier. Premier Itzel welcomed the aid."

"Premier"? Leiyn was vaguely familiar with premiers, officials placed in charge of swaths of land back in Ilberia. Used here in Baltesia, it was certainly an elevation from "mayor." She wondered at all that had occurred in her absence for Itzel to rise so high.

And what she might have compromised to gain it.

"The Ilberian Union lands upon your shores," Altun continued. "Altan Gaz now stands with Baltesia. We are your allies, not your enemies."

Memories of fleeing the Greathouse flashed through her mind. The nighttime flight across the shadowed plains. The arrows falling. The fiery pain of one piercing her leg. The titan rising from the river and overwhelming her.

"But if we were not," the plainsrider pressed, "what would you do here? Fight both us and the Ilberians? Leave them to terrorize your people? You cannot kill us all. I would welcome your bow in our raid, but if you do not trust us, then I ask that you stay out of our way."

She bared her teeth, but before she could spit another insult, her lifesense alerted her to movement. A scout headed their way.

"Fesht," she muttered under her breath, then spoke loud enough for Altun to hear. "I'll be watching. If everything isn't as you say, then know I'll hunt you down. Every last one of you."

The approaching watchman shouted something in Kalgan,

still too far for her to make out. Leiyn backed away, lowering her bow as the distance widened between her and Altun. The plainsrider watched her depart, calmly tying his pants.

"At midnight," he called after her. "You will see we are true then."

Cursing, she retreated into the forest, feeling like a fox fleeing before a hunter. But come midnight, she would hide no longer.

3

UNDER A MOONLESS SKY

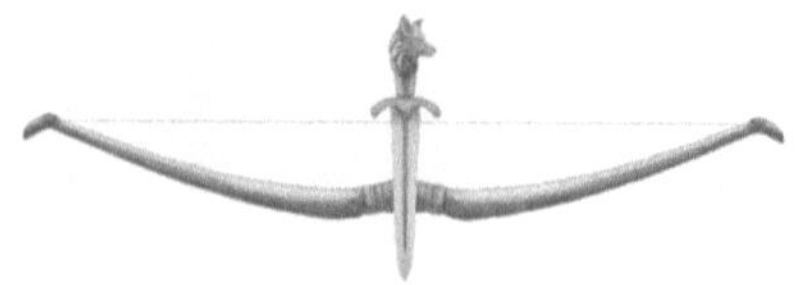

*T*he moons peeked through the trees. Leiyn watched their progress as she tracked Altun and the plainsriders through her lifesense. The Catedrál had little to say on the moons, far more concerned as it was with the sun, but Tadeo had told her of the Gasts' perspective. Great Teyao and Young Chiuni, the natives named them. They were called the guardians of the night, seen as the counterpoints to the titans of land and sea.

It was never a belief she had bought into. But knowing that titans could be allies as well as antagonists, she wondered if any truth lay in it.

Chiuni set first, then Teyao. Dawn was still far off, yet Leiyn had expected the assault to begin while there was still light to see by. She suspected that, despite Altun's sincerity, there would not be an attack at all.

Yet the plainsriders had not settled down to sleep. They sat or moved about tasks she could not discern by mahia alone. She tracked Altun as he moved from warrior to warrior, like he refreshed them each on a plan.

Feshtado *fool, believing that man.*

She had been as far from trusting Altun as she could have been upon their first encounter. The altercation had arisen during the summer she and Isla had spent at the Greathouse. Altun, then a young man come early to his strength, had tormented Batu, a scrawny boy still far from his own growth spurt. Leiyn had been keen to brawl in those days. She had given the bully a sound enough beating that he and his friends had given Batu a wide berth for the rest of their stay.

She had always wondered how the young plainsrider had survived after they departed. He had given her the credit when the matter resurfaced, but she doubted fear of her would have lasted long.

Life had clearly left its mark on Altun. He moved with a limp, favoring his right leg. The old wound seemed high on his leg, judging by his gait and where he pressed a hand to it. Scars aplenty had marked his face as well. Most telling of all had been his composure at the pointed end of her arrow. A hard lesson had taught him to control his emotions, forging an angry boy into a formidable foe.

Or ally.

Though she did not wish to, she had to consider the idea. Once, she had believed Gasts to be her enemy through a tragic misunderstanding. It was conceivable that the same had happened here. Still, it felt less likely. She had only heard of the circumstances of her birth from the biased and grief-stricken viewpoint of her father. Taban had betrayed and hunted them down, making his position unequivocal.

Yet Baltesia needed allies in their war. She would not put it past Mauricio to bury the hatchet if it meant bringing Altan Gaz into their fold.

A sigh hissed between her teeth. *I'm trying not to be rash,* she thought to Tadeo. *But must it be so egreshti hard?*

As time passed, Leiyn's expectations sank lower. Yet, waste of time or not, she had already made her decision. Relenting from her watch only to relieve herself—and keeping a careful eye out for ambush—she had just pulled up her trousers when the plainsriders finally congregated.

Hurrying back to her post, she kept her hand on her

bowstring and peered in their direction. It was the night's darkest hour. By her eyes, she could detect little more than movement among the shadows. Her lifesense, however, tracked the twenty men as they went silently up the hill. Only one remained behind, watching over their horses. Their hunched approach bespoke of sneaking up on an enemy, as did the hour. All was as Altun had said it would be.

Leiyn tailed them as she chewed through the decision. Isla would have told her to stay out of the fight. Batu would have remained silent, torn between loyalties. Teya, however, would have been by her side, no matter what.

If there is a fight, the scout might have said, *choose the winning side.*

The plainsriders split into several groups. Four moved around to the east of the hill atop which the Lodge's ruins sat, staying within the shelter of the woods. Another four did the same to the west. Of the remaining company, Altun and three others moved from the forest cover out onto the open plains.

Leiyn had to admit it was the correct move: sending a split vanguard to remove the sentries before they could sound the alarm was prudent. Should the plainsriders gain the advantage of surprise, their superior marksmanship would cut down the drowsy Suncoats without weakening their own company.

She tensed and untensed the bowstring as each group moved into position, spaced more or less equally around the perimeter. Then, by an unseen signal, they advanced up the hill.

Leiyn looked at the hilltop camp and noted the Suncoat sentries by their esses. They had posted a single man in each direction. A testament to degrading discipline? Or did their company have enough wounded to make the unwise course necessary?

Whatever the cause, this was likely their last watch.

The thought should have brought her vindictive satisfaction. Instead, she dreaded it. She would feel every lifefire being snuffed out. Sense every death like a shadow of her own. As her mahia grew, her weakness matched it in proportion.

It was not noble to be callous to killing, yet part of Leiyn wished she could return to the numbness of before. When she had buried her mahia deep. When violence did not cut her to the quick.

No. Never again.

She could not return to the woman she had been. The devil who could have killed an innocent Gast and thought herself justified.

If this was the cost of atonement, she would pay it thrice over.

Leiyn bared her teeth at the darkness, then crept closer, stopping at the edge of the field. There, she watched the scene unfold.

The plainsriders closest to her had paused. Though specific actions were difficult to discern by lifesense alone, they were close enough to mark their targets. She saw no sign that the Suncoats knew what was coming. Though they were the more certain of her enemies, it was enough to almost pity them.

Bows thrummed as arrows flew.

One sentry collapsed, his esse falling dark. Then a second. A third. The fourth's light darkened as he sustained a grievous wound, but this one did not entirely fade.

A scream pierced the night, scraping shivers along her skin.

The camp roused at once. Leiyn heard a plainsrider curse as Altun led a charge up the hill. The other two groups also spurred into a sprint, as did those warriors left in reserve. Their charge went unopposed but seeing the Suncoats form lines, she knew that would change once they passed the barriers.

Altun reached the ashen walls of the Lodge and leaped over them to meet the Suncoat line. Three of his men were beside him a moment later. The reserves, holding a mixture of bows and other weapons, remained a little way back.

Dark slices through lifeforce showed the wounded multiplying on both sides. Bellows of pain and rage broke the peaceful night.

Leiyn squeezed the wood of her bow until it groaned. The

moment had come. She had to decide. Would she do as Isla would and stand to the side? Or go Teya's way?

As if that was a choice.

Scarcely had the resolution formed than Leiyn was running up the hill toward her old home.

4

BLOOD & ASHES

air hissed through her teeth as she raced through the tall grass. Her bow, nocked and ready to draw, swung side to side with every stride. The evidence of battle grew; the screams and stenches that haunted her nightly.

Drawing on her amber beads, she drew out the esse from two of them and channeled it into her body. The hunger and aches from the long vigil faded, and an insistent vigor rose in their place.

She pressed on faster.

Deep below, a dragon roused and aimed its burning eye at her. She longed to reach for Clouded Fang but blocked him out instead. She had to keep him at a distance. She was being rash enough without relying on an uncertain titan.

The fallen watchtower loomed from the shadows, backlit by fires spreading through the camp. Shadows danced across the grass as warriors fought and slew each other. Stop to consider them for even a moment, and she feared icy death would inundate her lifesense.

Leiyn surged up the ashen mound, then skidded to a halt as the battle came into view.

A stalemate had blossomed. Though most of the Suncoats

were half-dressed, their numbers surpassed the plainsriders, and they attacked with equal measures of discipline and savagery. Their line, though untidy, held against the plainsrider push. An underfed and unshaven lot, they fought with the ferocity of cornered beasts, knowing they would live or die this night.

The element of surprise was not Altun and his men's only advantage. Spry and experienced, they wielded assorted weapons against the soldiers. For every fallen plainsrider, three Suncoats lost their lives.

But the night was far from determined. Entrenched behind shields, spears, and a stake barrier, with crossbowmen providing support from behind, the Suncoats had halted the advance. Drill and coordination compensated for what they lacked in individual skill. Plainsriders, like rangers, trained for solo combat. Though Leiyn's concept of military strategy was basic, she knew enough to realize if the Ilberian line was not broken soon, the Suncoats would likely repel the assault.

Wincing, each fresh wound among the warriors grating against her lifesense, Leiyn climbed the ruins of the wall next to the fallen watchtower. From there, she had a view of the soldiers sheltered behind their shields. Raising her bow, Leiyn sighted her first target along the back of their rank, an arbalist aiming at Altun. Anchoring her hand at her jaw, she held a moment to judge the angle, then loosed.

The arrow flew, barely visible until it sprouted from the Suncoat's chest, punching through coat and steel. The man spun to the ground, black staining his lifefire.

Death reached into her mind.

"Fesht!" She staggered, nearly slipping off her precarious perch before withdrawing her mahia from the dying man. Gasping, Leiyn tried catching her breath as she shook away the creeping sensation. Surrounded by death, it felt all but impossible. Her magic flitted to each snuffed life as if she might fix it—or consume its fading succor.

What's wrong with me?

Surging to her feet, Leiyn pulled back her mahia as much as

she dared, limiting her focus to dozens of paces around her. Nocking and drawing, she sighted a second marksman and exhaled, trying to steady her shaking hand, then loosed.

Her arrow shot past her target, a tremor sending it too high.

Startled, her target ducked for cover behind a tent. Leiyn cursed under her breath and tried to force herself to calm. As if that would work.

Not now, Firebrand!

No time for frustration or bafflement—she had to keep dismantling the Suncoat back line. The plainsriders had gained momentum; lose it now, and they would be driven back. The Lodge would remain in Ilberian possession.

She could not allow that. Tadeo's bones and those of the other fallen were littered across those ashes. Trampled by the boots of their killers, or those like them.

She would be their revenant. A ranger returned from the grave, come to avenge them. A revenant did not suffer from the death it dealt. It killed without mercy.

Don't feel, she told herself, drawing again, limbs trembling. *Don't feel any of it.*

Only a few crossbowmen remained. As she sighted one, two turned, quarrels pointing at her. A third—the man who had evaded her before—emerged, his weapon loaded and leveled.

"Shit!"

Leiyn pivoted back around the fallen watchtower, sliding on the detritus as she went. Three cracks cut through the din. Bolts flashed through the air where she had stood a moment before.

She was already scrambling back up. With their quarrels loosed, she had the advantage; a bow was quicker to reload than a crossbow. All three men had bent out of sight to load fresh bolts, but she spotted another cradling his for a shot.

Moving quickly, she loosed. As her arrow flew, she heard his weapon release.

A plainsrider spun to the ground. A split moment later, her arrow caught the Suncoat in the neck.

Leiyn rocked back, mahia reaching for both dying men at once.

"Legion take it all!" she spat as she clawed back control. "Focus, damn you!"

Even with her magic flitting about the battlefield, she sensed the trio of crossbowmen emerging from cover. Aiming for her. She had seconds to decide her course.

Leiyn raised her bow, then blanched before their lifted weapons. She spun away.

A quarrel whished by, close enough to rob her of breath. She waited for the second and third to follow.

They never came.

Silently railing at herself, Leiyn slid down the ashy slope and ran around the tower, searching for a fresh vantage point. The Suncoats had her previous location pinned. A new one could buy her the time needed to take them out.

If I could steady my damned aim.

She went a score of strides away from the brunt of the fighting, the darkness hiding her movements. As she moved from the fight, her mahia seemed to settle. Cautiously, she extended her lifesense around her, watching for ambush.

Staked barricades remained in her way, but the arbalists' previous positions came into view. By both eyesight and magic, she detected one marksman still aiming at where she had been, waiting for her to emerge.

Don't botch this, Firebrand.

She held her breath as she rose, arrow trained on the Suncoat's eye. Letting the air out in a steady hiss, she quieted the clamor inside, then loosed.

The man's head rocked back, his crossbow cracking as its quarrel thudded uselessly against the ground.

Her mahia kicked like an overeager hunting dog, but Leiyn was ready for it. Reining it back in took only moments. She had grown too used to the quiet. Battle calluses had peeled and torn away.

No longer. Once more, she had to numb herself to all she did.

Weaving between the spikes of the barricade, Leiyn advanced on the remaining Suncoats with a nocked arrow, life-sense picking out the two crossbowmen left, crouched and reloading. Moving behind a tent, she kept her bowstring loose, waiting for her moment.

The plainsriders stole it from her.

The Gazians roared as they broke through the Suncoat line and flooded into the camp. Altun led the charge, his limp disguised by his quick stride, his scarred face lined with fury. She watched his hammer rise and fall, crunching through the head of the first arbalist and sending a wave of darkness through the Suncoat's lifefire. Then he charged the second, round shield lifted as the man rose and aimed, a mere dozen paces away. Close enough for the quarrel to pierce a compromised shield and kill the man holding it.

Leiyn had drawn and loosed before she had time to think.

Her arrow caught the Suncoat in the throat. He fell, limp as a strawman, his life bleeding into the ground. Taking a moment to steady her reaching mahia, Leiyn turned to find Altun's gaze on her. He nodded.

Despite the reluctance plucking at her chest, she returned it.

Turning to scan the area for any foes, she found the battle was quickly concluding. With their defenses dissolved, some of the Suncoats had run, but to no avail. Their own barricades slowed them enough for a group of plainsriders to cut off their escape. Those who did not keep fighting threw down their arms and fell to their knees, hands raised in surrender.

Leiyn lowered her bow and retreated beyond the Lodge's borders. Altun had been true to his word, but there was still opportunity for treachery. Standing amidst the tall grass covering the hill, she watched as weapons were collected and hands were bound. Less than a dozen Suncoats remained, and all looked to be wounded. She grimaced as she noticed how young some of them were, scarcely old enough to be called full-grown.

War spares none, Tadeo had said one night as the rangers prepared for potential dangers. *The young least of all.*

The plainsriders had suffered as well. Only three lay still, but a dozen had taken dire injuries and were being tended to. This victory had come with a great toll.

But whose victory is it?

She could help those suffering. Xepi had taught her enough of healing that she was confident she could keep all but the most grievously wounded alive.

Yet Leiyn kept her distance. None were dying, and it would put her in a compromising position, besides.

There was a deeper concern. Little as she wished to admit it, her mahia had been a liability during the fight. Until she mastered this newfound sensitivity, she could not risk using it unless there was no avoiding it.

At length, Altun turned and, spotting her, picked his way across the battlefield. When he came within a dozen paces, Leiyn half-raised her bow in warning. He halted. Blood covered the leather plates of his lamellar armor and dripped from his hammer and domed shield. He stood with the sloped shoulders of the weary. Yet it spoke to his skill that his esse showed only the slightest wounds taken.

"I have done as claimed, Ranger," he said in Ilberian. "Do you trust me now?"

Leiyn forced a low laugh. "I'll wait to hear what the Lord Governor has to say first."

The plainsrider nodded, seeming to have expected no less. "If you have an audience with Lord Mauricio di Siveña, tell him what happened here. Altan Gaz keeps her promises, as does the *Baishin.*"

Her lips curled. After all she had suffered at the hands of plainsriders, the words were too ironic not to sneer.

"And tell Premier Itzel of Folly as well," Altun added. "She requested a report."

"Never fear. She'll know."

Leiyn backed up a step. It would be better to leave before more plainsriders were freed from their duties in case they meant to pursue her. Before she had taken another, though, Altun spoke again.

"And Ranger, if you see Batu Khatas when you travel south, give him my best."

She bared her teeth, then turned and fled into the night.

THE PREMIER OF THE FRONTIER

The leagues to Folly passed swiftly.

Leiyn had much to keep her mind occupied. The events at the Lodge spun through her head, their implications even more prescient than their horrors. The significance of the Suncoat occupation, the trustworthiness of the plainsriders, the possibility of an alliance with Altan Gaz—questions crowded her head, and she had answers to none of them.

Only that Itzel might have explanations and the prospect of seeing long-absent friends kept her sane. Soon, the mysteries would be cleared away, the mayor's promotion included.

When she could no longer endure idle speculation, Leiyn set to practicing her mahia. The battle had revealed its deficiencies in stark detail. She could only imagine Mother Xepi's disgust had she borne witness. The shaman had already been reluctant for Leiyn to depart, claiming she still had too much to learn.

"Attend to it each day," Xepi had said before Leiyn left Qasaar. "*Semah* is not unlike a muscle. Neglect it or use it poorly, and your control and power will fade."

Leiyn had promised the irascible woman as much and committed to memory techniques designed to improve her control and capacity. Yet, though she had touched upon them each day, she had not pursued the exercises with much enthusiasm.

The battle at the Lodge had changed that. Now, each day as she rode atop Feral, whether the spring rain fell or Omn showed Its blinding face, she committed herself to her training. She stretched her seeking to its limits, then sought to divine as many details about a remote lifefire as she could. Distance became murky when experienced through the magic, but from her estimations when atop a hilltop, she guessed she could sense creatures as far as three dozen leagues away, if only vaguely.

When beasts strayed nearer, she practiced manipulating their lifeforce. Confounding their senses as she had once seen Zuma do to Suncoats, she tested her abilities on deer, birds, and other critters. Once she was sending squirrels walking drunkenly along branches and deer bumping into trunks they had not seen, she put it to a more practical application by luring and dazzling a rabbit only to take it down with her bow. Though it saved precious time otherwise spent hunting, Leiyn could only bring herself to use it once. The trick made her feel guilty, as if it broke an unspoken vow between predator and prey.

She was still becoming sure of her magic, yet she judged her progress might have won a nod from Xepi. Though the shaman would no doubt have followed it up with a reminder.

Beasts are one thing, she imagined the shaman saying. *Humans another. And the* sach'aan *another realm entirely.*

The specter of their enemies haunted both her waking hours and her sleeping ones. Dreams of lyshans came nightly. Sometimes, Man'nah battered her, and Clouded Fang was not there to help her mend. Others, she would find herself in the Iritu halls to be ambushed and torn to pieces, no Ata present to rescue her.

Those moments reminded her how frail her body was, even when supplied with mahia. How vulnerable she was alone. She had only come this far through others' aid.

A sore reminder while she traveled the Titan Wilds with no one but Feral for company.

Sharo figured prominently in her dreams as well. Often, he

stood to one side, laughing as she was slaughtered. Sometimes, he would taunt her with cryptic warnings. *"Ware the Wither, Oldsoul. Your weakness is my strength."* The words needled her even upon waking, and though she saw little wisdom in them, she could not seem to shake the omen.

She had some thin reasons for reassurance. Ata had mentioned that lyshans would not dare cross the Silvertusks. Perhaps that remained so. Perhaps some enchanted barrier, like the one that protected Qasaar, prevented them from coming over the mountains.

Yet Sharo was devious. He might have found a way around such protections. After all, he had influenced the Caelrey and Altacura to do his bidding—at least, she assumed he had from all he had claimed. That meant he either had the means to leave the Barren, or his sorcery reached far beyond his body. Not such a far-fetched prospect considering the depths of his Inheritance and the years he'd had to expand its capacity.

Still, that she had made it this far suggested that Sharo did not wish to hunt her—or that he could not. The lyshans had suffered a grave blow, their scarce numbers decimated. Even beings as ancient as they would require time to lick their wounds. Or perhaps Sharo bided his time, allowing Ilberia and, if they were unfortunate, the other Ancestral Lands to grind down the Tricolonies before he swept in to stamp out any remaining resistance.

Driven by her fears, Leiyn remained dogged in advancing her martial magic as well. She practiced drawing on her esse to fuel her strength and speed. She grew accustomed to fighting while augmented, honing her skills to deadly efficiency. When she sustained minor injuries from wayward branches or bumping into obscured roots, she practiced healing. Her fight with Man'nah had demonstrated the swift strain from which her mahia suffered in battle. Clouded Fang could not help her if she lost the willpower to wield his font of lifeforce.

Of equal importance was her study of the scavenged Iritu artifacts. She delved into the enchantments imbued in her clothes, swords, and arrows, seeking to understand them. Even her bowstring drew her attention, having replaced the worn one on her longbow with one supplied by Qasaar's hidden barracks.

Slowly, she identified the weaves in the lifeforce. They were remarkably similar to the knotted nature of infected wounds, though constructed in a rigid and orderly fashion. Some weaves appeared to be for toughness; these she could tell by the thickness and tightness of the pattern. Others, like in the arrowheads and sword edges, possessed killing intent. They resembled barbs in the arrowhead, the frayed tips of the weave sharp to dig in and tear. The swords were less chaotic, but still looser and more flexible than those in the clothes. Waving the blades around, they seemed to have the amplifying effect of a whip with each slash, making each strike deadlier still.

Other weaves, such as those in the talismans, defied her comprehension. Though she studied them in the darkness when dreams had denied her sleep, she could not understand how each motif created its effect. They remained as mysterious as magic was to those devoid of its touch.

Her most vital artifacts were the amber beads Xepi had gifted her. Filled with esse, they provided a source of lifeforce when all others failed. Despite their small size, Leiyn had been surprised by how much esse they held, the ten together containing as much as an entire tree.

Even with all these tools, she feared it would not be enough to win the wars she was caught up in. Soon, she would have to confirm she could draw upon Clouded Fang—or other titans—as she ought to be able. For the moment, she was spared the necessity, and her journey proceeded swiftly.

Following the old ranger paths, she noticed how already they were becoming overgrown. Grass sprouted where hooves and feet had once trampled the ground to dirt. Leiyn paused at parts, taking in the slow decay. Yet another reminder that, even after the wars were through, life here would never be the same.

Nor would she.

After a week of travel, Folly's walls came into view. The guard admitted her on sight with a gap-toothed grin. Leiyn returned it hesitantly as she led Feral inside.

She braced herself for the press of lifeforce, but after her time at Qasaar, Folly's population was easy to bear. Perhaps, in time, even Southport could become endurable. Not that she ever wished to spend enough time in the capital to find out.

She went straight for the town hall, where a groom took Feral to the stables. A servant ushered Leiyn to the parlor and poured her a glass of brandy before departing.

Barely had she had time to fidget before Itzel walked in. Leiyn turned and raised her glass toward her.

"I hear you deserve a toast, Premier."

The former mayor paused, eyes flickering from the cup to Leiyn's face. "I would accept one. Though I'm surprised you've already heard the news."

Leiyn took another swig of brandy. The alcohol burned as it went down. After months of Gast liquor, it was a delight to indulge in Baltesian brandy once more.

"Rangers hear everything," she said with false cheer. "I thought you would remember that."

A smile flitted across Itzel's lips. She moved to Leiyn to press her arm, firm but friendly. "I do. And I'm sure you have questions for me. First, let me say how glad I am you survived your trip north. From Isla's report, it sounded a... laborious task."

All she had suffered at the hands of lyshans flashed through Leiyn's mind. Though her broken bones and torn flesh had healed, each injury remained in her memory. Wounds of the mind were ever slower to heal.

She drained her glass and set it down hard, then began pouring another.

"You could say that," she said. Setting down the decanter, she straightened with her cup in hand and met Itzel's gaze. "So Isla and Batu made it this far, at least?"

"You need not fear for them—I've report they arrived at

Southport. But please, sit. There's much to tell you, and I would hear what you have to say."

Leiyn glanced at Itzel sidelong. "A report for my premier?"

"For a friend first, I hope."

Smiling, Leiyn sauntered over to the chair and slouched down in it, watching the amber liquid as she swirled it around the glass. "I'm glad the position hasn't gone to your head yet. Care to explain how you were promoted?"

Itzel pursed her lips. "There isn't much to say. Lord Mauricio heard of our efforts here and wished to express his appreciation. My elevation to premier formally places me in charge of all the land beyond the Gorge de Omn within our borders."

"Quite the responsibility." Leiyn looked at the premier over her glass. "That's more land than lies to the south of the canyon. How far does your ambition extend, Premier?"

"Please, Leiyn." The older woman's face grew serious. "I know you enjoy needling figures of authority. But, for this night, I'd appreciate if we pretended like these were old times. If we were like before all this began."

Sometimes, Leiyn forgot Itzel's age. For a woman in her late forties, she seemed to possess as much vitality as Leiyn. Her esse certainly burned strongly enough. Yet her years showed in her furrowed brow, in the gray along her forehead and temples, the pinch around her mouth. The realization softened Leiyn's suspicion—if only slightly.

"Sorry. I heard about you becoming a premier from the last people I wanted to come across." She watched the premier, gauging her reaction. "From plainsriders."

Itzel did not flinch or show other signs Leiyn would take for duplicity. Instead, she sighed.

"I wondered if that was it. Explains your attitude, at least."

Leiyn bit back a retort, refusing to act as combative as the premier made her out to be. "It's true, then? That they're fighting on our behalf, at your request?"

"Yes. I know, Leiyn," Itzel rushed to say as Leiyn stirred.

"Don't think I've forgotten what they did to you. But Baltesia needs allies. We need Altan Gaz. I'm sure our Lord Governor is keenly aware of that fact. The Greathouse moorwarden is in Southport even now, negotiating for acceptable terms for an alliance. Last I heard, the prospect of a unified Tricolonies looked promising."

Leiyn forced her jaw to relax. "I understand that. But an ally you cannot trust isn't worth much. I'm guessing this 'moorwarden' is named Taban? Taban Khyan?"

"Yes." The premier read the emotions flitting across Leiyn's face. "People come into power in many different ways, some right and some wrong. But when we need their cooperation, it won't do to dredge up the past. We must look to the future."

"If you say so." Bitterness laced her every word. "And what of their previous agreement with Armando Pótecil? Or has that, too, been swept under the rug?"

"No. We have not forgotten, nor will we. But with the conqueror's fall, it seems Master Taban has reconsidered his options and been swayed by our offer."

An edge gathered in Itzel's voice. Better than the weariness, to Leiyn's mind. Even if it threatened to cut.

"And what exactly is that?" Leiyn pressed.

"Concessions of land. Gifts of coin. Special trade agreements." The premier waved a hand like banishing an unpleasant odor. "I'll spare you the details. From what I understand, the governor strives to give as little as he can. But for Altan Gaz to defy the Ancestral Lands, some sacrifices must be expected. As Tadeo used to say, 'The least given for the most gained.'"

Thinking of Tadeo—killed and burned on the orders of the same conqueror with whom Taban had briefly allied—soured Leiyn's mood further. She downed the rest of her second glass and stood to fetch a third, striving to leash her temper.

Itzel spoke into the silence. "Of the plainsriders' task—do you know if they succeeded?"

"If you mean clearing out the Suncoats from the Lodge's

grounds, then yes." She cast a rueful smile in Itzel's direction. "In fact, I helped them."

"Did you?" The premier narrowed her eyes. "Without killing Gazians, I trust?"

"None this time. The Suncoats were the more obvious enemy." Her glass full, Leiyn moved back to her chair and perched on the edge. Though she had traveled all that day, she was already beginning to twitch with restlessness. All this talk of war had her itching to return to the road. The only way she could ensure her friends were safe was if she was back in Southport herself.

Itzel took another sip of brandy. "Very well. You have my thanks for lending your aid. With those Ilberian soldiers gone, the borderlands are clear of their presence."

Her chest loosened. "That's welcome news," she admitted.

"If only the war proceeded as well on other fronts."

"The coast doesn't fare well?"

"Not nearly as well. At last report, Ilberians have made landfall at several locations along our coastline. Each will be heavily fortified and backed by enough manpower to be impossible for us to rout. Yet, at least." Itzel took another long drink. "From these, they'll have access points to march deeper into our territory—or the other colonies, should it suit their strategy."

"Marvelous," Leiyn said. "And the cities?"

"Southport suffers an embargo. Most of the Armada surrounds Anchor's Refuge. They say the sea is so dark with them the sun no longer touches the waves."

Leiyn snorted a laugh. "What poet said that?"

"The governor, actually. He's always had a floral hand."

Despite her doubts to its truth, Leiyn could not help picturing the scene. Were they a score? Two score? A hundred? The Ilberian Armada was famed across Unera for its might. The Tricolonies could not hope to match it.

A titan could even the odds.

Trepidation trilled through her. Though she had located a kraken in Southport's bay and controlled it enough to kill the treacherous conqueror, that scant victory had ended with Zuma's death and nearly destroyed every Baltesian ship in the harbor. She had progressed much since then, but even now, could she leash it as she had Clouded Fang? A spark of the shaman might still be with her, but Zuma could not save her if she failed again.

Ignoring a thing does not make it go away.

Tadeo's old words came to her, as they so often did. *Face it head-on.* Normally, the memory of his advice brought comfort. Now, it only awoke the terror of letting him down.

I'll try, Tadeo. I'll try my damnedest.

Itzel heaved a sigh, drawing Leiyn from her thoughts. "And then there's the trouble between our people."

"Between our own? What now?"

"A division of loyalties." The premier eyed her with pursed lips. "You didn't think everyone would forget our Ilberian roots, did you?"

Leiyn shrugged. The night the Lodge fell was burned into her mind. Where her loyalties laid was never in question.

The premier seemed to glimpse her thoughts, for she shook her head with a small smile. "Why am I not surprised? Since you'll be riding through the thick of it, allow me to appraise you of the situation. Here on the frontier, those most loyal to Baltesia have started calling themselves 'Freefolk.' They're no more than a loose coalition spread across the territory, but they're aligned in their purpose: rooting out and opposing the Unionists, or 'Goldbloods' as they call them, those still outspoken in their support for the Ilberian Union."

Leiyn sipped her brandy. "Doesn't sound like such a bad thing. Can't have traitors in our midst."

"Ah, but that is precisely the question: *Are* they traitors? How should they be punished if they should? Who should administer the punishment? If the law is in the hands of every man and woman, the tyranny of mobs is not long in following. It is no longer Gasts who suffer hangings without due process and judgment, but anyone deemed disloyal to our cause." Itzel raised her gaze to the mantelpiece above the fireplace. "That is not the freedom I am fighting for, nor the country I wish to create."

Leiyn followed the premier's gaze to the mantel to see a wooden carving centered atop it, one of a howling wolf. She would have recognized its carver's style anywhere.

Tadeo.

Little wonder why Itzel looked to him in this moment. The lodgemaster had possessed an unwavering sense of justice, even in cases where the lines between truth and lie became blurred. He had done his best to instill those same lessons in his rangers, and Leiyn liked to think he had succeeded with her. Even if a few of them had taken a long while to sink in.

Justice must not fall so swiftly it was uncertain. It should be decided by the weight of evidence, not by the noose or knife. The times her arrow had flown in the face of those principles cut her now. Her errors only hardened her resolve to correct them moving forward.

Leiyn looked back to the premier. "Nor I," she murmured. "For my part, I will make sure our codes of law are upheld."

Itzel smiled at her, a fond crinkle to her eyes. "I know you will. But enough about Baltesia. Tell me of your mission beyond the mountains. Isla was vague on the details, though I understand there is some... greater threat?"

"There was." *Is,* part of her pointed out, but Leiyn ignored it. "It's taken care of. And the Many Tribes are now our allies."

Itzel stared at her a moment longer before loosing a surprised laugh. "You should have said so from the start! Never thought I'd see the day that Leiyn Firebrand would negotiate an alliance with the Gasts."

A reluctant smile won free of Leiyn. She wondered what the premier would say at her having an intimate relationship with a Gast. For the moment, she kept it to herself. Perhaps later, she would feel comfortable bringing those personal matters to light.

"Nor I," she said.

"When will they march? In what numbers? How many

shamans will they bring? Lord Mauricio is eager for these details. I'll send the postriders ahead of you with a summary so he may know what to expect as soon as possible."

Leiyn opened her mouth to answer, then was surprised she could not. Only then did she realize how many of the specifics she had overlooked in the final negotiations with the Tetrad. She remembered Acalan mentioning Qasaar housing two thousand warriors and scouts, but she did not know precisely how many would come to Baltesia's aid.

However many they were, she knew they would come. She trusted Acalan—to make no mention of Teya—too deeply to believe they would not honor their word. It helped that they stood to gain from complying with their agreement.

The mayor watched her, impatiently awaiting her answer.

"Five hundred," Leiyn settled upon. Better to promise less than more. "They'll arrive by autumn."

Itzel waited a beat before prompting, "And the shamans?"

"Ah... none."

"None." The premier's eyes went flat. "They believe they can claim part of the Titan Wilds for five hundred warriors alone? And you made this promise, Ranger Leiyn?"

"Don't 'Ranger Leiyn' me." Leiyn held her cup tightly enough that the glass protested. With an effort, she set it on the table between them. "The enemy beyond the mountains decimated their shamans, even more than we did during the Titan War. They have none to spare. And the Many Tribes bring more than just warriors. They wield artifacts imbued with ancient magic. Artifacts such as the ones I wear."

Itzel scanned her Iritu garb with a hard gaze. "Those? They appear ordinary to me if a touch outlandish."

"But you don't possess mahia, do you?" Leiyn exhaled, trying to rein in her temper. "There's more. I received training while I stayed in their city. I can"—she tried to find the right words—"do as their shamans have done in the past. I can command titans."

It had been uncomfortable to first reveal she possessed Wilds magic to Itzel. Knowing the news would reach Folly eventually—Leiyn's role in the revolution had been too prominent to hope otherwise—she had broken the news herself on the journey north. The then-mayor had accepted it calmly, devoid of any astonishment. It made her wonder if Tadeo had known more about her magic than he had let on and confided those suspicions in his beloved.

The skepticism Leiyn had expected then now showed on Itzel's face. "You have a shaman's abilities?"

"Yes." Leiyn did not let her gaze waver. She refused to show the premier her doubts. She could still command titans. She had to.

"Very well." Though she plainly did not believe it, Itzel waved a hand. "But you are only one, Leiyn, and new to these... abilities. The Union has hundreds of odiosas, and Saints only know how many priestesses possess similar powers."

Leiyn could tolerate it no longer. Draining her glass, she stood. The brandy had gone to her head, but she made sure to appear steady.

"I know, Itzel. I know the odds are poor. But this is all we have."

The premier stood with her, leaving her glass on the table. The tension seemed to have left her shoulders as she stepped closer and rested her hands on Leiyn's forearms.

"I know you did all you could. Never doubt that I know that. I have seen enough of you through Tadeo's eyes to know you would never give less than your all."

Leiyn met her eyes. A mistake—her own began stinging. Looking aside, she blinked rapidly. Part of her longed to pull away. Another part wished Itzel would hold her like the mother she had never known.

The premier did neither. Instead, she released Leiyn's arms to grip her hands. "I expect you'll be leaving soon."

"Yes. In the morning."

"Then come and eat with me. We'll speak of happier things. But before we do, Leiyn, make me a promise."

The woman's words drew Leiyn's gaze back to her.

"For Tadeo's sake—and mine—don't fight this war on your own. I know how you can be. How you believe you must bear your burdens alone. But you're *not* alone. You have your friends, the governor. You have me. Accept help when it's offered."

Though she had longed for motherly comfort only moments before, Leiyn hardened to it now. Squeezing the premier's hands, she pried hers away.

"Don't worry about me, Itzel. I've stayed alive this long."

Itzel only gave her a long look before leading her out of the parlor.

6

FREEFOLK

The jays still chirped their morning songs by the time Leiyn rode Feral out of Folly's south gate.

"Kill a Suncoat for me!" the young guard posted there shouted after her. "Or two, if you can!"

"I'll make it three!" With a last wave, she turned and coaxed her mare to a trot.

Her head still ached from one too many brandies with Itzel the night before, but the fresh air soon settled it. With her mahia open and aware of lifeforms leagues afar, Leiyn rode Feral at her ease. Even the irascible horse was mild-mannered, not making a single attempt to unseat her rider.

It being early in the season, she encountered few passersby that first day. Only the most enterprising—or deluded—of merchants braved the trip north when chance snows might fall. As a second and third day passed, the traffic grew thicker. Leiyn admired the folks trudging over the muddy road, mules and wagons in tow. By their looks, few were trained to defend themselves, yet they persisted in their livelihoods, war and weather be damned. It was for that Baltesian spirit that she pushed south each day.

On the fourth day, a glimpse of bushes alongside the road

caught Leiyn's attention. Smiling, she dismounted and led Feral over.

"See what we have here, old girl? Crebberries!"

To the untrained eye, the fruit looked far from ripe. But that shade of deep green was exactly how crebberries were supposed to be.

She popped a few of the berries off and held them out to the horse, keeping her fingers straight to avoid tempting the mare to bite them. Feral was suspicious, snuffing the emerald orbs before slurping them up.

With a wry chuckle, Leiyn rubbed the horse saliva from her gloves onto her trousers—the Iritu magic would soon take care of the mess—then picked off some for herself. Sour, spicy, and sweet all at once. Her eyes watered from the first mouthful.

The mare nudged her for more. Yet halfway through another helping, Feral raised her head and skirted sideways. Leiyn stiffened, scanned their surroundings, and reached for her bow. For all Feral's faults, her mare was not skittish. Even if she had not sensed danger herself, she heeded her horse's fears.

Only then did she see him.

Dead—she could readily see that without mahia. Swinging from the tree positioned at the crossroads ahead, crows had already plucked out his eyes and were working on the rest of him. Flies buzzed about the body, loud and busy to both ears and lifesense. Judging by his state, he had been recently killed; a few days gone, at most.

Leiyn checked with her lifesense, but the nearest esses were a league down the road. A small village, she guessed. Still, she moved with the same care as if predators lingered out of sight.

"You can stay," she murmured to Feral, giving the horse a comforting nudge with her mahia before padding toward the corpse, unstrung bow in hand.

Reaching the spot, she stood before the gently spinning cadaver. He looked to have been a young man, well-built and tanned from a life spent outdoors. His clothes, simple and homespun, showed him to have humble origins. Wet as the spring had been, the body reeked with rot.

A sign hung from his neck, looped over the noose. Painted upon it in a scrawling hand and with poor spelling were two words: *Goldblud Pyser*.

Goldblood pisser. It should have been reassuring. A show of loyalty to the colony winning out over allegiance to the Crown. Yet Leiyn's frown only deepened.

She studied the body. His clothes bespoke of field labor rather than travel. No rifled belongings spilled at his feet. He had not gone far from his home before meeting his end. Unless roves of Baltesian fanatics roamed the Frontier Road that she had not heard tell of, it left one conclusion.

This had been a local boy. A farmer's son. And his neighbors had killed him.

She stared at the corpse, mind turning as slowly as his body. No doubt the so-called "Freefolk" that Iztel had told her about were behind this. She wondered what the boy had said or done to warrant his fate. Surely, it took more than conviction to condemn someone you had known your whole life.

Back on the road north, Feral shifted, impatient to leave the morbid scene. Still, it was a long time before Leiyn sighed and turned away. Much as she wanted to cut the boy down and bury him, reason prevailed.

Best not to piss off the locals yet.

She was comforted that Gast custom was to let bodies lie out in the wilderness, to give of their flesh to the world that once sustained them. It was the best good his body could do now. Enough of her remained an Omnist, though, to be uncomfortable at leaving the dead to rot.

Leiyn mounted Feral and kept moving south, but her thoughts remained on the swinging corpse. This was where wars began and ended: neighbors pitted against one another. Lives and homes destroyed over ideas. All of them pieces moving to strings, never seeing the hands hovering over them.

Another tally against you, Sharo. Her hands clutched Feral's reins. *Another debt you'll pay in full.*

The threats rang hollow even in her head. After all, a ranger could not hit a target that never showed.

——— ~

She meant to pass through the nearby village—Carmenar, according to its entrance archway. But with a fresh drizzle starting and evening creeping closer, she resigned herself to entering the single inn whose weathered sign declared it to be "The Gourd and Corn."

Just to sleep, she told herself as she handed over Feral to the stableboy. *I'll keep my nose clean.*

Stepping inside, Leiyn found the inn's name to be fresh paint on a rotten interior. The stink of it, sour and acrid, almost drove her back into the rain. A banked fire was the only light with the windows boarded against the weather. Water had stained the wooden walls, a promise that rot had long set into them. A drip fell in the far corner, a bucket positioned to catch it. As Leiyn moved to the counter, the planks creaked with each step, even with her light footfall.

It was a wonder the place remained standing.

"Small beer," Leiyn asked of the barkeep, a skinny man with a miraculous head of hair for his age. After she handed over Union coppers, the man stared at them, then scooted them back across.

"Colony coins only."

Leiyn studied him. His manner remained mild, but there was a determined cast to his lifefire. He was serious.

"Coin is coin, isn't it?" She took one copper and tapped it on the counter. "Made of the same stuff."

"Colony coins or nothing."

"Here, lass. I'll trade you."

Leiyn tensed as the man seated at the table behind her stood and made his way over. A rancher, telling by his wide-brimmed straw hat, though farmers had also begun adopting the fashion. He was fine-featured for his profession, hard labor only roughening him around the edge. His eyes were bright in the firelight.

Thinks himself pretty, no doubt.

The man withdrew a few coppers of an unfamiliar design. Leiyn peered at them, ensuring they were of similar thickness, before shrugging and making the trade. The barkeep accepted these new coins without comment, then fetched her drink.

"Join me," the man said as he returned to his table. "It's too gloomy to sit alone."

Leiyn thought of refusing. She guessed his intent and doubted she would have been agreeable even if she was inclined toward the male persuasion.

But the dead youth swung in her mind, hollow sockets staring. Accusing.

She sat at his table, setting down her saddlebags next to her. The man raked his eyes over her for a long moment before speaking.

"The name's Emilio. Yours?"

Giving her name went against both her mood and purpose. Still, if she meant to coax him into conversation, she had to give him something.

"We'll see if you earn it."

It snagged him like a hook would a hungry fish. Grinning, he leaned forward. "I bet I can. Well then, what brings you to Carmenar? Few like you pass through."

"Wouldn't think many pass through, these days especially." Realizing she had to give some straight answers, Leiyn added, "I'm coming from Folly."

"Folly? Right at the edge of nowhere, that town. Never been, though you hear tales. Do all ladies there wear such odd clothes?"

"Some."

Emilio eyed her. Hungry still but growing wary. "What were you doing up there?"

Leiyn sipped her drink and forced herself to swallow. Weak

as the flavor was, it left behind a vile film in her mouth. But it would not kill her—which was more than she could say for the water, had she chanced it.

"It's my home," she lied. "I'm south on an errand for my aunt."

"Must be some errand to send a young girl all this way on her own."

Young girl. Leiyn would have snorted at that any other time. Instead, she forced a smile and hoped it did not look as brittle as it felt.

"It is. Came across a sight that gave me a startle a league back, though. Someone left a man hanging."

The rancher leaned back, his smile disappearing. "Serves him right. Goldblood pisser."

Her pulse quickened. She had only thought to squeeze him for information. She had not expected to find herself sitting across the table from one of the murderers.

"You knew him?" she asked.

"Knew him?" Emilio harrumphed and looked about to spit on the floor, then swallowed with a look at the inn's proprietor. "Francesc lived next door."

"What happened?"

The rancher opened his mouth to answer, then his eyes narrowed. "You came here with Crown coins."

Leiyn kept still. She did not fear him. Not only did she doubt his martial prowess, but her magic would be more than enough to overwhelm any he might possess. Even the half-dozen others in the room were of little consequence, though their attention made the hair on her neck stand on end. Still, it was instinctual to brace before a larger creature's ire.

"As I said, it's all I had. Not from lack of loyalty to the colony —we haven't gotten any others so far north." She forced her rigid shoulders into a shrug. "I'm Baltesian, through and through."

The rancher did not move for a moment longer, then he smiled and leaned forward. "'Course you are. Didn't mean to imply otherwise."

His hands shifted to lie in the center of the table. Leiyn

moved hers away from her cup. She wanted to appear friendly, not give him hope for intimacy where it could only founder.

"The Goldblood pisser?" she prompted.

The man cleared his throat. "Bastard set to sabotaging the town like a damned *ferino*. Set my cattle free. Spoiled Teppo's larder with rats. But the barn was the last straw."

It was growing harder to pretend affability with this man. *Ferino* had once rolled off her tongue as easily as any curse. Now, it stank as the foulest of insults. But for the moment, curiosity triumphed over distaste.

"The barn?"

"He burned it. Burned it even with all Ruy's livestock in there. Can you believe it? Stole away the goodman's livelihood in a night. Damn near burned down his house, too, and his family in it, on account of the sparks. If the rain hadn't come..."

"How'd you know it was him?"

The rancher stared at her. "We knew, alright? He was always going on about 'Union' this and 'Union' that. And we'd caught him at stuff before. The boy had it coming. Even his parents must've seen that."

Leiyn imagined the parents. How it must feel to know their son swung in plain sight of the open road and be able to do nothing about it.

"We?" she repeated. "So it wasn't just you?"

It was a question too far. Emilio stared at her, shallow charisma melting away. "What's it to you? You ask a lot of questions, girl. And you still haven't given me your name."

Leiyn placed her hands back on the table, flat against the wood. She sensed the stares of the others in the room. If her time as a ranger had taught her nothing, it was that resistance was best nipped in the bud.

This called for a show of force.

"Who I am doesn't matter. It's who I know that should make you worry."

"Is that right? And who's that?"

"Premier Itzel." She let the name fill the room. "Surely you've heard of her? All that happens here is within her jurisdiction. The murder of one of her citizens would greatly interest her. As would the name of the man behind it."

The rancher jolted to his feet, looming over her, calloused hands bunched into fists. But though his esse writhed with anger, she knew the fear that fueled it.

"Don't make threats you can't keep, girl," the man growled. "We don't abide by Goldblood pissers here."

"And I don't abide by murderers." Slowly, Leiyn rose as well. The other villagers were standing, too, though none came closer or took up weapons. She rested her hands on the hilts of her falchions. "I meant what I said: I'm loyal to Baltesia. But I also carry out her justice."

"Is that right?" Emilio sneered. "Think I should fear a young girl's knives?"

"You would if you've heard of rangers."

"Rangers!" The rancher barked a laugh. "They're dead, you dumb chit! Suncoats burned them all. You won't pull the wool over my eyes with that Legion-shit lie."

Once, his words would have been enough to incite her to violence, or at least the threat of it. But Leiyn had seen enough death this day. And she remembered all too well the pain of each life being snuffed out on the ashes of the Wilds Lodge.

"You and your comrades are in luck," she said, each word measured. "I'm in a hurry at the moment. But once I come back through, I wouldn't count on being so fortunate."

"You think you'll come back through?" But even the outraged rancher seemed to have caught on to his peril. His eyes flitted over her figure once more. This time, he seemed to notice all the weapons she bore and the familiar way she carried them.

"I do." Leiyn cast her gaze across the room. "If those behind Francesc's killing are still here, it'll be their bodies hanging at the crossroads."

If there was going to be an attack, she expected it then. But though Emilio panted with rage, and the others across the room stared resentfully at her, all remained where they stood.

Cautiously, Leiyn bent to pick up her saddlebags and bow. Channeling a bit of her esse for strength, she showed the ease with which she carried them, reinforcing the impression that she was not one to be trifled with. Then, drink mostly untouched, she walked unhurriedly toward the door. Her lifesense tracked the men even as her eyes left them. None moved to assault her back.

"Clear out!" she called over her shoulder before stepping out into the rain.

PART II

THE BURDEN OF POWER

7

ELEVEN YEARS BEFORE

There," Tadeo breathed in her ear. "Do you see her?"

Leiyn nodded slowly, not wishing to alert the spotted doe grazing in the small glen not ten paces before them. They had approached from the west to avoid the wind and kept to the shadowed cover, but the slightest sound or movement might still send the beast darting into the woods.

"Note your mark," Tadeo continued. "When you are ready, take the shot."

She did as directed, marking where her arrow should pierce the deer's heart. The lodgemaster had guessed her age to be under two years old, ideal for their purposes. She had a warm glow to her coat and a plumpness that spoke of good health.

It seemed a shame to steal away the rest of her life. But with mouths to feed back at the Lodge, there was no room for compromise.

Breathing through her mouth, Leiyn raised her bow. They had chosen their spot well, a place where the brush was thick in front, but thin enough not to catch on the stave. She had to hold it sideways, a position she was less certain of, but had practiced for such occasions as this.

Her arrow was already nocked, so she took aim and drew. The draw weight of the bow was more than what she was used to, and her muscles trembled under the strain. Still, she double-checked her aim as the doe bent its head to take another bite of meadow grass.

She released.

The bow jerked in her hand, the noise of release quieted by the cloth wrapped along the stave. The arrow cut through the brush—

—and pierced the beast's side.

The doe stumbled and shrilled, yet she did not fall. Still alive, she bucked and dashed away.

"Shit!"

Leiyn stood and fumbled for another arrow, but before she could take one in hand, movement flashed in the corner of her eye. She barely saw Tadeo's arrow before it sent the doe's head lurching back.

Their quarry fell.

The forest quieted but for the flapping of wings as birds scattered from the boughs. Glancing back, Leiyn saw Tadeo lowering his bow, mouth pressed in a thin line. She looked back at the deer, cheeks burning.

"Sorry," she muttered. "Guess I missed the heart."

His hand settled on her shoulder with a slight squeeze. "No, you did well, Leiyn. I only intervened so she wouldn't suffer."

Daring to look around again, she saw the displeasure in Tadeo's face had faded. The pressure in her chest eased.

"Speaking of which," she said, nodding toward the clearing, "shouldn't we check on her?"

Tadeo led the way forward. After the time spent in the shadows, the sunlight on the meadow knifed into Leiyn's eyes. Squinting, she kept her gaze on the dark, still form on the ground.

The doe had flattened the grass where she fell so it fanned out around her body, like the petals of a macabre flower. Reaching it, Leiyn stared down at the deer. Tadeo's arrow had caught it in the eye, giving it a quick mercy. Her eyes traced the blood leaking from the arrows, noting how it matted her handsome coat.

She had killed animals at her father's behest when she was young and her mahia was still open. She knew how the creature's lifefire would fade, then disappear entirely. And though she did not feel it now, an echo of remorse still haunted her.

Tadeo kneeled near the doe's head, checking for signs of life. When he shifted back, he motioned to Leiyn. She kneeled next to him. The deer smelled less fair than she looked, a musty odor to her fur that the blood did little to improve. Leiyn made no objection.

"Your spirit touches mine," the lodgemaster murmured to the deer. At his look, Leiyn repeated the words.

"Your spirit touches mine."

He nodded. "We must always speak the words after a successful hunt. To honor their sacrifice."

"Even though she didn't have a choice?"

Leiyn did not know where the words came from. She could not say she regretted what she had done. They had to bring back food for the others at the Lodge; they could not survive on their livestock and gardens alone. Yet the question needled her all the same.

Tadeo did not seem bothered, his expression placid. "Especially then. If the kill was by your hand, it is your burden."

"What kind of burden?"

Tadeo pursed his lips, gazing off into the forest. "A debt, perhaps. An owing to the world. You have taken a creature from its bounty, robbed it of the life it had yet to live. All its pleasures and terrors."

"You make it sound as if it were human."

"No, not human. But can you know what a deer feels? Or any other creature? Just because it is not like us doesn't mean it is lesser."

Leiyn considered his words as she lowered her gaze to the deer. All creatures contained lifeforce, and some held more than humans. Before she had recognized her mahia for the curse it was, she had felt their pain as poignantly as if it were her own. Something in the thoughts seemed to confirm the lodgemaster's words.

Tadeo drew his belt knife. "We must eat meat to live and be strong. It is our way. But know that every act of violence echoes across the world. A ranger must be judicious in how they mete it out lest it spread."

Leiyn unsheathed her blade. "You make it sound like the world is alive."

He glanced up. "Is it not?"

Before she could respond, he pointed at where her arrow had lodged in the deer's side. "First, we remove the arrow to keep it out of the way."

She set her free hand to the shaft and tested its hold, reticence gone with the animal's life. It was lodged firmly in its flesh.

"You likely hit bone," Tadeo observed. "Break it off and we'll recover the head as we clean it."

As she obeyed, he touched the tip of his blade to the deer's lower belly. "As your father likely taught you, we must remove the innards at once or it will spoil the meat. Make the first cut here."

Leiyn obeyed. As much hesitancy as she had around the killing, she was familiar with gutting animals. Following Tadeo's directions, she carefully sliced up the belly.

"Now," he continued, "we cut the intestines and organs away from the sides, then sever the anus and windpipe. Watch for the arrowhead—don't need that complicating matters. If we do it right, its innards should slide out the back and barely stink."

"How do you always know what to do?" she teased as she reached down to do as instructed.

Tadeo paused and looked up, so she followed suit. For a moment, he seemed as though he had transported away from their bloody task, knife tilting downward.

"Teaching is not always easy, Leiyn. There are many moments when I don't know the right path forward. But those who don't act can never truly be. Do you understand what I mean?"

She had only meant it as a jape. But like in most things, Tadeo had uncovered a lesson. For him, mentorship seemed to come as naturally as breathing.

Leiyn rolled her eyes. "Yes, Master Tadeo," she droned as she sawed into the bone.

He smiled, then grew somber. "You will have many apprentices of your own, Leiyn, in time. Be sure of what you know and what you do not. Nothing loses respect faster than insincerity."

"And nothing makes me more nauseous than this smell." Withdrawing from the doe's belly, Leiyn waved her knife over the partly eviscerated body. "Can we keep going?"

Tadeo chuckled and set his knife back to the task. But before he made the next cut, he paused again.

"You're a fine student. You'll make a fine teacher as well."

Leiyn had her doubts about that. She had a fire in her, and it burned with a haste she could not contain. But she hid her true feelings behind a snorted laugh.

"You always get this weepy over gutting?"

He glanced at her sidelong. "Only with my favorite apprentices."

Leiyn looked back down at their task so he would not see her smile.

8

A SILENT SIEGE

The night spent in the woods outside of Carmenar was wet and uncomfortable, but nothing Leiyn had not suffered through before. Feral was less forgiving. After being interrupted during her meal of oats and dragged back into the damp, her short-lived mildness abruptly ended.

Leiyn scarcely noticed. "Your spirit touches mine," she murmured to the dark, hoping she had done enough that the boy Francesc could rest at peace.

During the following days and weeks, she bore witness to more injustices, large and small. Quarrels between neighbors. Beatings. Even town-wide conflicts. Yet her experience at Carmenar kept her wary of engaging with them.

Perhaps she had made a difference by holding Francesc's murderers accountable. Perhaps it only entrenched them further in their justifications and would make her life difficult when she came back through. Try as she might, Leiyn could not bring justice to the entire colony. She served a greater purpose.

Yet, for all the tragedies she witnessed, Baltesia was uniting behind their governor's revolution. Colony blue trailed from doors, wrapped around lampposts, hung from village archways. She even saw a new flag, blue with a white kraken over it.

This was the Baltesia she had fought to make. Yet, returning to it from beyond the Silvertusks, she wondered if she knew it anymore.

———

Leiyn summited a final rise to find Southport spread out below.

It was almost a relief to see it. She had grown no fonder of cities for her time spent in Qasaar, but only in the capital could she find answers to the questions piling up in her head.

Glimpsing the Ilberian Armada curbed any comfort. Itzel had exaggerated its size, but not by much. The number of ships was impossible to tell at the distance, but there were enough to darken the sparkling sea at the mouth of the bay. It would be all but impossible to slip a boat through the tight net they had woven. The maritime trade the city relied upon was utterly throttled. But fretting would not solve anything.

"Come on, old girl," she said, coaxing Feral down the hill.

The gate was crowded, and not with folks coming to market. People wearing tattered clothes, vacant stares, and carrying limp packs looked up as she passed. Hunger and other ailments made their lifefires burn low. Their bodies reeked of despair. Some loitered by the road outside the queue to enter. She wondered if they might be refugees from the coastal towns where the Suncoats had made landfall. Even here, where they should have found shelter, there was none.

Where will they go when the Suncoats march?

Leiyn firmed her jaw and drew her mahia in close around her. It did them no good for her to feel their suffering as well as see and smell it. All she could do was keep pressing forward.

The sun stretched far across the sky before she reached the gate. There, Leiyn startled at a familiar face: the same wall captain who had admitted her last time she visited Southport.

The blonde woman had a pinched expression as she watched over the fretful crowd. A new patch embroidered her gambeson, white with three blue wavy lines across it. A symbol of her rank in the new government, Leiyn had to assume. Her complexion may have suffered for her duties, but her esse had not. Leiyn was surprised at the alluring brightness of it, the vivacity of its emerald hues. Thinking of Teya, she pulled her gaze away before she indulged the temptation to read her lifemark.

The captain's eyes alighted on Leiyn as she approached. The creases smoothed from her brow. "Ranger! Survived your journey north, did you?"

Leiyn held up a hand in greeting, trying not to squirm under her appraising gaze. That her heart belonged to another only made her shyness prick the sharper.

"Looks like you have your hands full," she offered.

The wall captain's grimace returned. "I'll say. Nothing to be done, though. Southport will become a breeding ground for disease and crime if we let anyone else in. Not meaning you, of course, Ranger Leiyn."

A flutter awoke in her stomach. "You know my name."

The woman's smile reappeared. "That I do. You made quite the impression when you were last here. Or hadn't you noticed our new flag?"

Leiyn looked up at the banner waving over the guard station. At the white kraken set on the blue sea.

Her throat went tight.

The wall captain laughed. "As I said, *quite* the impression!"

Saints. She was at a loss for words.

"You know my name," she said, trying to keep her tone light, "but I still haven't caught yours."

"Captain Belen." Belen gestured toward the guardhouse behind her. "Ask after me sometime if you have the chance. I'll tell you the story behind that flag."

Hard to miss the invitation in her offer. Heat flushing her face, Leiyn restrained herself to a nod and a quick, "Until then."

Proceeding onto the main thoroughfare of Southport, Leiyn was glad when Feral forged her a path forward. The mid-afternoon city was even more crowded within its walls than outside its gate. The clamor of sound, stench, and sight dizzied her and made Leiyn wish to hunch down in her saddle. An ache in her head rose to match the pulse of the city. The desire to close her mahia's walls was almost irresistible. Her heart thrashed like a squirrel caught in a snare.

"It's the ranger! The ranger's returned!"

Leiyn snapped her head up, looking for where the shout had come from. A man stood at the edge of the street, waving an arm above the masses. Despite his emaciation, a grin stretched from cheek to cheek.

"The ranger Leiyn!" the man shouted again. "Look! There she is, come to liberate us!"

Others turned toward her. The surrounding traffic slowed, then stuttered to a stop. Murmurs rose until they formed a chant.

"*Ran-ger! Ran-ger! Ran-ger!*"

Leiyn froze. Where could she flee? Did they expect her to say something? Speeches had always frightened her more than fighting. And this attention, this *adoration*... She'd had a taste of it in Qasaar, and found it bitter then, too.

I don't deserve this.

Her chest heated. Her throat swelled. Only as she spoke did she realize it was anger coursing through her veins.

"Move!" she called above the chorus. "I must reach the governor!"

She repeated her demands with rising urgency, again and again, until the crowd parted. She tried not to look at the confused expressions as she passed through. But it was only after she had left behind the gathering and the last of the cries died away that the blaze inside her sputtered out.

She was not worthy of their hopes, their chants, their *flags*. Whatever they believed her to be, she was far less. All she had done was take vengeance and get a friend killed. She had started a war, one architected long before, and destined to kill hundreds, thousands.

She was no liberator. No savior.

Leiyn clenched her fists around the reins and pushed Feral forward as fast as she dared.

⁓

Her head throbbed by the time she reached the gates to the governor's villa. The guards admitted her without even asking for her name, much less her ranger's seal. When she questioned it, they gave her queer looks.

"Of course we recognize you, Ranger Leiyn," the older of the two said. "After what you did for us, how could we not?"

Leiyn repressed a grimace. Infamy, at least, had its perks.

The mayordomo, Dinis Sorje, met her before she could even relinquish Feral to the stablehand. "Envoy Leiyn of the Titan Wilds," he said with a deep bow. How he kept the white hairpiece atop his head was beyond her. "I must offer you my most sincere apologies, for I am obligated to request that you come with me at once. The Liberty Council confers at this hour and requires your report, now that you have arrived to administer it."

"Nice to see you, too, Dinis." Leiyn smiled at the manservant's scandalized expression. "Care to explain what's going on?"

"Along the way, Envoy, if it pleases you. Do not fear—your belongings will be handled with the tenderest of care and sent to your accommodations forthwith."

"Then this council meeting is a casual affair?" Even with Iritu magic keeping her garb clean, she knew she reeked of sweat and horse, a perfume no doubt unpalatable to the governor's councilors.

"Formalities, I am afraid, must be set aside for expediency in times such as these." Dinis's tone made it clear how woefully tragic he felt that to be.

Seeing no graceful way out of it, Leiyn relented, sending her bows, quivers, and saddlebags along with Feral. The mare bared her teeth, but only snapped at the stableboy once as he took her reins.

Leiyn turned to follow the mayordomo, but the servant

remained where he stood. "I am afraid I must insist upon the surrender of your swords as well, Envoy."

She smiled, feeling it a match for Feral's worse bite. "Try your luck elsewhere, Dinis. Or don't you remember what happened the last time I was here?"

A pitched battle crossed the man's powdered features, severe enough that Leiyn almost pitied him. Her mahia would likely prove sufficient for protection, but she was still reluctant to part with her falchions. When lyshans, titans, and odiosas could threaten them at any moment, a ranger had to remain ready for war.

"Very well," the serving man relented. "If you would allow me the honor of escorting you..."

The mayordomo led her away from the governor's villa and across the grounds to a building Leiyn had yet to enter. White stucco walls rose to a dome of copper shingles touched by green patina. Marble columns veined with pink framed a vast portico atop a flight of broad stairs.

"The council is humble in their accommodations," Leiyn noted.

If the white-wigged servant caught her sarcasm, he did not show it. "The Council Domo," he droned, "was built in 731 EE as an entertainment hall for dignitaries come to visit the colony from the Ilberian Union. Its grandeur now reflects the importance of bringing us through these tumultuous times to a brighter future for all the Tricolonies."

Leiyn barely refrained from rolling her eyes. "I'm already fighting this war, Dinis. You don't have to convince me."

The mayordomo's only reply was a sniff.

Despite her best intentions, as they ascended the Council Domo's stairs, Leiyn felt the awe of the place seeping into her. The doors, thrice her height, were impressive in their own right. In homage to the Veiled Lands, titans had been carved upon their face. Topping the rounded doors were the five Sacred Saints and Omn Almighty. The effort must have cost hundreds of gold cimas and thousands of hours of labor. It easily rivaled the expense put into the First Temple, and that was no mean endeavor.

What a waste.

At their approach, a guard bowed and opened one of the grand doors, allowing them to slip inside. The atrium was no less impressive. Marble tiles spread across the floor, glittering in the sunlight that streamed in through the tall windows lining the way. Frescos adorned the sloped ceiling depicting the World Kings of yore. Seven of them fanned out in all their painted majesty, rising from a disc representing Unera.

"The Freedom Chamber," the mayordomo announced as they reached the doors on the other end of the entrance hall. These were not as grand as their outer counterparts, but appeared nearly as heavy as a guard heaved them open.

A hubbub came from within, many voices speaking over one another. Only then did Leiyn stop to think of what she walked into. The councilors might appear a spattering of old men and women in frivolous wigs, but they held the reins to Baltesian power. To act with her usual defiance might have grave consequences—for herself, her friends, and their cause.

Don't be rash, Tadeo whispered in her head.

Leiyn firmed her jaw and followed Dinis inside.

The dome rose twice as high as the atrium, giving the chamber an airy feeling not unlike being under an open sky. Leiyn glanced around the edges of the room at the bronze statues and marble busts before settling her gaze on the people at its center. A long table that seated two dozen occupied the space before them. Rising around it were rows of stone benches arrayed like an amphitheater. These benches were sparsely occupied, so even though there were thirty-some people to scan, it was easy to pick out the familiar face among them.

Isla flashed her a wide smile before comporting herself. Her friend looked hale, if garbed strangely.

For she wore a dress.

Leiyn had never seen her in one. Nightgowns were the closest they had come, and those were nothing like the dress she had on now. Made of emerald wool, it hung flatteringly on her lithe frame and exposed the slenderness of her neck as it dipped down toward her laced bodice. She also wore jewelry, silver spirals falling from her ears. A silver pendant hung from her neck to nestle against her sternum.

Despite her unsettling appearance, seeing her friend alive and well was comfort enough. Leiyn straightened, glad not everyone here would look down on her.

Isla was the least ornately dressed among the assembled. To a one, the councilors and other personages fashioned themselves in bright cloth, delicate lace, and frills erupting from sleeves and chests. Most every head at the table was white with wigs.

There were a few notable exceptions. Leiyn's attention was drawn to the most outlandish man among them. Judging by his features, the austere patterns of his robe, and his beaded head-dress, he hailed from Altan Gaz. Despite the warm day, fur trimmed his shoulders in a short mantle. He lacked the scars and chiseled strength of a warrior, yet his dark eyes were unyielding as stone.

If his appearance was not enough to clue her in to his role, his esse was confirmation. Like others possessing mahia, his life-force drifted outside the boundaries of his body and shone a shade brighter. He did not seem as powerful as Xepi or Zuma, much less herself, but his control was admirable.

A wiseman.

Batu had mentioned the magic wielders of Altan Gaz and Kalga. This man had to be one of them. She wondered what his role was here. Though Altan Gaz was supposed to be Baltesia's ally, she could not stifle her distrust toward them.

The wiseman's eyes flickered to her. By instinct, Leiyn almost threw up her walls. Though she might possess more power, he had decades of experience over her. If he was anything like Xepi, he would have more than a few tricks up his sleeves that would make him difficult to contend with.

She looked away. A ranger always sought to be prepared, but preparing to fight her allies was not what she needed to concern herself with. Her lips quirked as she imagined what Isla would have said.

Focus, Firebrand.

One person continued speaking as she and Dinis entered, their words echoing throughout the vast chamber. Most, however, shifted their attention to Leiyn. The mayordomo halted a dozen paces back from the table. Leiyn stopped next to him.

When the speaker paused, the mayordomo spoke into the gap. "Please accept my deepest apologies, members of the Liberty Council. As I was bade to do, I present to you Envoy Leiyn, ranger of the Wilds Lodge."

The room's attention shifted to her now. Leiyn tightened her jaw, knowing she could do nothing but tolerate its hefty weight.

"Ah! And here she is, at last!"

Leiyn looked over to see the man at the head of the table standing with a wide grin. Mauricio di Siveña had scarcely changed in the past few seasons. His vestments were as spruce and overstated as ever, sporting a bright blue vest over a silken shirt with a gold coat over the ensemble. Only in his mess of curly hair was there any sign of the pressure of his position, his brown locks struck through with gray.

Ignoring all manner of decorum, the governor strode to Leiyn. But instead of greeting her in the personal manner she expected, he turned back to the assembly and swept an arm grandly toward her.

"At last, I can introduce to you the full breadth of our plan. For here stands our Prima Maha herself!"

9

THE ORDER

Those gathered erupted into whispers in the wake of Mauricio's ringing words. All eyes turned to Leiyn, expectant.

She wondered if they could smell the month of travel layered over her.

Her mind snagged on the governor's words like a boat on a hidden rock. *Prima Maha.* A title, clearly, but it meant little to her. Still, it reverberated with veiled meaning, all the more since it plainly had to do with her magic.

Isla stood and spoke over the susurrus. "Forgive me for speaking out of turn, Lord Governor, but perhaps Envoy Leiyn could be apprised of the situation before making any decisions?"

Gratitude swept through Leiyn. Though everything had changed, some things never would. Isla always came to her aid when she most needed it.

"Of course, of course. It is I who should ask forgiveness." Mauricio turned to Leiyn, smile never faltering. "Shall we find you a seat, Envoy, or would you prefer to stand?"

"I'll stand." Her tongue was too clumsy and her thoughts flowing too sluggishly for more elegant words.

The governor only chuckled. "Then so shall I! It is an invigorating idea, after all. Now then, where to begin... Ah, perhaps with my own decree!" He held up a finger. "By the power vested in me as the Governor of Baltesia, and with the blessing of the Liberty Council, I have established a new branch to our government: the Colonial Order of Mahia."

Mahia. Now, the truth showed its ugly face.

"You what?" she could not help but blurt.

Isla winced as she sat again. Leiyn knew she was acting the fool. But with her head splitting and events flitting around like hummingbirds, she could not think straight.

Mauricio ignored her poor manners. "During your last visit to our fair capital, Envoy, you demonstrated the potency of this power. You raised a titan from the sea itself, like one of the Gast shamans of old, but in our defense! It opened my eyes to how sorely we have neglected magic and mistreated its wielders. Those injustices were perpetuated under the cruel Ilberian law and corrupt Catedrál, 'tis true. Yet the duty still falls to me—to *us*—to set it right. Hence my gubernatorial ordinance for the Order, and naturally, putting you as its leader as our first and mightiest maha."

Maha. Another title, and somehow one that weighed heavier. Always, she had been a ranger first, even when compelled to masquerade as an envoy. Now, the governor wanted her to own up to her magic like a shaman or a wisdom.

Ranger. Envoy. Maha.

Leiyn fished out her most pressing question. "And what is this Order supposed to do?"

The assemblage began to mutter. She was putting on a boorish show for someone who was supposed to lead this strange new branch of government. Blindsided as she was, Leiyn could scarcely help it. Only Isla's encouraging look kept her from sprinting from the chamber.

Mauricio's voice turned low and inviting, a grandfatherly figure by a warm fire on a cold night. "You will be to Baltesia as the wisdoms are to Altan Gaz, the *eesuwé* to Ore-Ofe, the shamans to the Gasts. You and your mahas will defend us against odiosas and titan attacks, and any other threats of mystical origin."

His condescension, intended or not, ignited the coals of her anger. She had always been bravest before a fight, and his tone promised one.

"I'll do what I can," she said shortly. "But I cannot guarantee the same for others."

The governor turned conciliatory at once. "That is all I could ask. But I assure you, Prima Maha, we've selected only the most promising candidates. Your mahitas, shall we call them, are all eager to learn what you have to teach them and to embrace the magic so long denied by our oppressors." Mauricio paused, then continued almost contritely, "Of course, it is only possible should you agree to lead it. There is no other."

Leiyn stared hard into his hazel eyes. Behind the artifice—and exaggeration, if her suspicions proved true—lay something jagged and sharp. *Desperation.* The governor needed this victory. Without it, she wondered if he would remain their governor for long.

"I'll consider it," she said at length. "But I'd prefer to know our standing in the war first."

"At once! Though we prefer to call it a 'secessionary conflict,' if you please." Mauricio's lingering gaze showed he was not the fool he sometimes pretended to be. A glimmer of derision peeked through. "Lord Conqueror Luca, if you would appraise the Prima Maha of the situation? Briefly, for all our sakes."

A tall man at Mauricio's right stood, drawing Leiyn's gaze. He was the other Baltesian neglecting to wear a white wig, so his oiled blonde hair shone in the sunlight. The rest of his uniform was as expected of his position. A polished steel breastplate, a blue sash draped across it. A longsword with an ornate hilt buckled at his hip. Unpretentious breeches that could easily slip under an armored skirt. He had an odd way of carrying himself, at once soldierly stiff and distracted. His eyes did not land on her, but wandered across the wall, as if they could not stay focused on one spot for long. His powerful jaw, stubbled with an afternoon shadow, and strength in his tall frame spoke of the discipline necessary for his station.

Yet that word, "conqueror," stuck in her mind like a barbed arrowhead. She had hated the mere thought of it for months. A conqueror had stolen away her frontier family, her home. Her life.

Yet this man before her was not her enemy, as Armando Pótecil had been. He was a general for Baltesia, the leader of their forces. An ally.

Listen first, for once.

Lord Luca cleared his throat. "At present, we have eleven thousand five hundred and twenty-three soldiers trained and in active duty. Eight thousand two hundred and eleven remain stationed here in Southport. The other three thousand three hundred and twelve advance north to..."

Already lost in the figures the strange conqueror rattled off, Leiyn's mind drifted to more immediate concerns. *Prima Maha.* She knew Mauricio would force the decision before the meeting was over. His intention to ambush was plain. And the trap was sound—not even her natural obstinacy would allow her to compromise their standing in the war.

Yet could she do it? She did not want the responsibility, nor was she ready for it. Only months before, she had been a pupil herself. Far too much remained for her to learn to teach others.

And she had not returned to Southport to be a teacher. She came to fight.

Leiyn looked to Isla. Her friend watched her, a sympathetic tilt to her head. Isla knew her, inside and out. Knew how diffi-cult of a role this would be for Leiyn to take on. When the Wilds Lodge had stood, all had expected Isla to take Tadeo's place as the lodgemaster. Far from jealous, Leiyn had been relieved the duty would not fall her way.

But there was Isla, firming her jaw and nodding, her message clear. *Do it. Teach them. Become what they need you to be.*

Leiyn wanted to shake her head, throw out all the reasons

she should not. How could training a few stunted mahas change the tide of the war? How could they learn enough to fight odiosas and lyshans and leash titans? Even Xepi, with her lifetime of experience, could not do all Leiyn could. Some things could not be taught.

Each excuse fell before the arrows of necessity. No matter her objections, she had to do it. Distasteful and tedious as the task would be, Baltesia needed more than her defending it against magic. Qasaar had shown Leiyn she could not fight alone and expect to succeed.

Time to be like you, Tadeo, she thought to her long-lost mentor. *If I can.*

Mauricio cut into the conqueror's droning, drawing Leiyn's attention back to the room. "That will suffice, Lord Conqueror. Thank you."

With a jerky nod, the conqueror sat. Leiyn drew her gaze away as she felt the governor's attention return to her.

"So?" Mauricio prompted. "What do you say to my proposal? Will you lead the Colonial Order of Mahia on behalf of our people?"

Leiyn opened her mouth to speak, but the words stuck. But thinking of Qasaar gave her one way she could be happy agreeing.

"So long as the terms of the Gast alliance are honored, I'll do it."

Fresh murmurs erupted around the Council table. She guessed they had all heard the report she had sent ahead. Some of the councilors did not bother to hide their scowls.

The governor studied her for a long moment, lips pursed. If she was not mistaken, wary respect had bloomed afresh in his eyes. But only a beat passed before he seized her arm in a hearty clasp.

"But of course! We had no intentions of doing otherwise. This is excellent news, Prima Leiyn, quite excellent! Today, we shall let you settle in. Your pupils will join you in the chapel for their first lesson tomorrow. At noon, shall we say? Rest assured, you shall remain undisturbed—all shall be forbidden entrance while you train. But I won't keep you any longer. I'm sure you'll be happy to kick the dust from your shoes!"

Mauricio had released her and was striding back to the table before she could say a word. Leiyn pursed her lips. *More theater.* The governor had made a favorable impression before, but the way he conducted his affairs now grated on her.

None of that changed what had been decided. Leiyn gave a curt bow, then Isla descended the benches and, taking Leiyn's arm, they strode from the Freedom Chamber together.

"What in all Legion's hells happened?"

Having cleaned, eaten, and tracked down her belongings, Leiyn sat in her appointed room, sinking into her too-soft bed. Isla and Batu occupied the elegant furniture opposite her with far more familiarity.

Luxurious as her surroundings were, she could not relax. The chamber was even finer than her previous stay. According to Isla, it reflected her rise in station.

Leiyn wished that was not the case. The chairs almost glowed with their shiny stain under the sun's dying light. Naught but air filled the garderobe, though the mayordomo had promised to replace that with clothes no doubt equal parts impractical and uncomfortable. She wished she had a starry night sky overhead, Feral fuming nearby, the world open and welcoming to her mahia. It would be far preferable to the lifeless stone and wood that surrounded her.

Her friends went some way to easing the discomforts, having joined her after finishing the day's responsibilities. The former plainsrider had yet to wash after training with Baltesian soldiers, but she did not mind the ripeness. He looked stronger and more mature than even a season before, and more certain of himself as well. Gone was the apology in his eyes, and his incurable stoop had been replaced by a warrior's spine.

Isla crossed her legs and leaned back. "It cannot have been unexpected."

"You thought I'd expect this?"

"Teaching." Batu teetered on the edge of laughter. "Doesn't quite suit you."

Leiyn glared at him. "I came to fight, not pretend to be a shaman."

"Leiyn," Isla sighed. "Mauricio needs magic. Surely, you see that. You heard the conqueror—even with the warriors of the Many Tribes, we're outnumbered two-to-one. And that's by optimistic measures."

"Actually, I didn't hear." She grimaced at Isla's exasperated look. "Come on, how could you listen to that man? But it doesn't matter—we always knew the odds would be long. If I summon a titan or two, they'll be shorter."

If you still can.

Even as she asserted the words, doubts bubbled up in the back of her mind. She had to believe that, even after months without mustering a titan's strength, the ability remained with her. She had never lacked force of will before. Why should it fail now?

"Maybe so," Isla conceded. "But Mauricio thought he'd get further with Altan Gaz and Ore-Ofe, not to mention the Gasts."

"You told him how few shamans remain?"

Her fellow ranger nodded. "I couldn't let him have false hope. You did much the same, from what I heard of your report."

Leiyn looked out one of her room's many windows, staring over the dark sea. While it was their duty to report all information to the governor as Baltesia's envoys, Leiyn was not sure either of them had done the right thing. The information could be used against the Gasts all too easily. She only hoped Mauricio would value the Gasts' friendship more than the land she had bound him to concede.

"Still," she murmured, "me as some 'Prima Maha,' teaching others about mahia..." Leiyn shook her head. "I barely know what I'm doing."

Batu leaned forward, his expression earnest. "But you've made miracles."

"Miracles." A bitter laugh escaped Leiyn. "Is that what you call rousing titans to kill?"

His eyes hardened. "Against those who mean us harm, yes."

She bowed her head to stare at her hands. He was right. Of course, he was. Surely, she believed the same. Yet somewhere along the way, her resolve had wavered. Each killing blow dealt her damage back.

She needed to be strong, yet she scarcely knew how.

Isla rose to sit on the bed next to her and rest a hand on her arm. Reluctantly, Leiyn looked up into her friend's eyes.

"You can do this," Isla said. "We had the best mentor, didn't we? Just teach them the way Tadeo would have."

"And teach these 'mahitas' to take on odiosas in weeks?" Leiyn shook her head. "Even for Tadeo, that'd be impossible."

She glanced toward Batu. *Miracle*, he called what she had done. He and Isla both expected the world and more of her. Never doubted her for a moment.

She firmed her jaw. "If I'm doing this, I need both of you there."

Isla winced. "Sorry, Leiyn. I have to attend Council sessions, and they come about every day now."

It was as much as Leiyn had expected. Little by little, Isla slipped further into her role and away from the ranger she had been. But that was a pain for another time.

Leiyn looked at Batu. "Then I'll settle for you."

"What an honor." He grinned, but his smile swiftly slipped. "But I'm not sure I can. I'm conscripted now—a condition for my citizenship."

"You're Baltesian?" Despite the other news, Leiyn had to laugh. "Just in time to sink with the rest of us."

"We can hope not."

"Don't worry about all that, though. I'll ask Mauricio to station you with the Order as a protector. Saints know we're bound to need it."

Batu hesitated, but at a meaningful glance from Isla, he nodded. "So long as you agree to train with me in your free time. We both have to stay sharp."

"I wouldn't dream of doing otherwise."

Leiyn smiled at her friends. It felt brittle, a thin layer of ice over a tumultuous sea. But it was not the first time she'd had to quiet a storm.

"Now then," she said, standing and stretching. "Where would the brandy be? After leaving me in Qasaar, you both owe me at least a drink."

"Or two," Isla countered with a smile.

10

A RANGER OUT OF THE WILDS

*L*eiyn strode through the halls of the governor's villa feeling as if she went to battle.

She was certainly dressed for it. Though Mauricio had gifted her fresh tunics, trousers, and other garments, she had spurned them in favor of her usual Iritu garb. With the governor's blessing, she continued wearing her falchions along with her remaining long knife. The artifacts were a comfort not only for their protection, but from their soft diffusion of esse. In a way, they made her feel more like the Prima Maha she was supposed to be.

It was a far cry from how she had felt the previous night. Tossing and turning, she had lain sleepless until sunlight peered across the Torrent Sea, plagued by thoughts of what awaited her. It was also the first night in Southport that she had left her mahia open, an irritant in itself, like walking with pebbles in her shoes. Though the city did not whisper as Qasaar had, its population was far greater and proved the more vexing for it.

She had never been one to eschew a bed, but as she turned from side to side, she would have far preferred her bedroll and a campsite back in the far wilderness of the north. But there were no woods to escape to, no place her duty would not follow. One way or another, she would have to remember how to sleep in a city.

Yet another thing to stomach.

Dragging with exhaustion, yet jangling with nerves, Leiyn dealt with her problem the only way she knew how: a morning spent in physical training. Finding the guards' training yard, she staked out an unoccupied spot, assuming her position gave her a right to it. A sparring partner would have been welcome, but with Batu not yet released from his duties as a common soldier and Isla occupied by Council business, she was left to practice alone.

Few men and women populated the courtyard at the early hour. All of them stared at her as she readied her equipment. Leiyn ignored them as she moved through her modified flows with her mismatched falchions. She had spent enough time with them that the movements felt natural, though having tested them in a single battle, she knew kinks remained to be smoothed out.

As she worked up a sweat, her mind turned over how to approach the afternoon's lesson. She wished her friends were around, Teya and Acalan included. Both Gasts had years of experience as leaders. Even Xepi's advice would have been welcome.

If only you spoke, she thought to Zuma's spark.

The shaman's guidance would have been best of all. He had been as patient as Tadeo and as knowledgeable as Xepi in matters of mahia. But Zuma's soul remained dormant to her touch, burning with a small, steady light, as he mostly had since Qasaar.

Leiyn cut both falchions in front of her, then paused to cuff away the sweat from her brow. Devoid of mentors, she was left only with their memories. And of those, Tadeo's lessons suited her best.

Be sure of what you know and what you do not.

She knew little, and still less of how competent her students might be. That was where she needed to begin. Only once they established a foundation could they build up any knowledge.

At least one thing's decided.

"Pardons, my lady."

Leiyn hid her surprise. She had not noticed the approaching pair of soldiers. Turning, she lowered her swords and looked around. A man and a woman stood together, both taller than her, yet there was a certain deference in the way they held themselves.

"What is it?" The words came out brusquer than she meant. She had always been pricklier after exercise.

The woman who had spoken cleared her throat and flashed an apologetic smile. "My idiot friend here was doubting what they say about you is true."

"That's nice, Siany," the man retorted. "Really representing me well."

The female guard, Siany, ignored him, her eyes earnest. "It'd be a great favor to me if you'd prove him wrong."

Leiyn shifted her balance, an uncomfortable feeling threading through her. "That depends on what they're saying."

The male guard broke in. "That you raised a kraken from the sea. That you told it to strike down that traitorous conqueror. That you've returned from the north and won the Gasts as allies." He paused, watching her while his companion rolled her eyes.

A flush threatened to spread across Leiyn's cheeks. "All true enough."

Siany laughed and elbowed her comrade in the ribs. "Didn't I tell you, Tiago! She's not called the bloody Tideraiser for nothing."

Tideraiser. Simple enough to guess what the title referred to. Though she had indeed commanded a kraken, it was a name better fit for stories than her. The truth was not half as heroic as they believed. But it would do neither of them favors for her to explain that.

The male guard, Tiago, remained skeptical, but awe was

quickly replacing his doubt. "Well, Saints damn me to the hells. I stand corrected."

His companion flashed him another triumphant grin, then turned back to Leiyn. "Thanks, my lady."

"Happy to help. But I'm afraid I have to be going."

Turning her back on the pair, Leiyn tried not to make it seem as if she fled the yard. The excuse was not wholly untrue; she had to clean up before meeting the Order. Though she would remain in her martial outfit, she saw no need to stink like swine as a first impression.

But once she had cleaned up and eaten, there was little reason to delay. Heaving a sigh, she made for the First Temple.

She neared the exit to the villa when three men entering brought her up short. All were dressed in leather lamellar armor. Red sashes decorated their arms, and horsetails sprouted from the helms carried under their arms.

All telltale signs of Gazian plainsriders, even if their features had not differentiated them.

Leiyn's stare was inevitably drawn to the man standing at their center. Fury blazed at once. She clenched her hands into fists. Her mahia burned hotter, yearning to strike.

For the moment, however, Taban Khyan was beyond her reach.

As the moorwarden and his lackeys neared, she could not make herself take an alternate route, nor simply walk past. The man's eyes had locked on her as soon as he entered, and like a hound hunting a hare, he did not appear easily deterred. With a thin smile, he continued their approach to within a few paces. Her glare challenged him to do more, but he remained as prudent as before.

The bastard was nothing if not an opportunist.

"Ranger Leiyn," Taban said. "Or should I say 'envoy' or 'Prima Maha,' now? Perhaps 'Tideraiser' is what you prefer?"

"Call me what you like." Leiyn kept her temper tightly reined, her voice flat. "Won't change anything."

"I disagree. Titles tell others who you are. They shape your standing in the world. Your power."

"Only you would believe that." She said this in Kalgan. Despite her best efforts, the words came out halting and stilted.

Taban let out a humorless laugh. "Believe what you will, Ranger," he said in Ilberian, speaking more fluently than she had in his tongue. "It does not change the order of the world."

The conversation could lead nowhere productive. Their last clash had resulted in a moonlit flight across the plains and the deaths of several plainsriders. Baltesia could not afford another catastrophe like that, even if the moorwarden made for a poor ally in her estimation.

"Step aside," she said, returning to Ilberian. "I have duties to attend to."

Taban studied her, then motioned to his men. All three moved aside to admit her passage.

Leiyn pressed past, but before she made it through, Taban's hand snaked out to encircle her arm.

"Take care," he whispered. "Your enemies are legion. I would not wish anything to happen to you or that traitor you keep as a pet."

He was not a large man, but the power in his grip spoke of years training with the bow and saber. Leiyn met his eyes. She possessed more than the strength of her body. She could tolerate threats to herself.

But she would not overlook them toward Batu.

In a scalding wave, she flared out her lifeforce. The moorwarden snatched back his hand, grimacing.

"Witch," he hissed, then turned and strode off. His men stared at her before following.

Leiyn could not help herself a light laugh, even as his words continued to jangle inside her head. "*Feshtado* bastard," she muttered loud enough that he might hear.

Taban Khyan kept walking.

Her mood fell lower still as the temple came into sight.

The First Temple of Baltesia remained an impressive sight, as opulent in design and decor as the first time she had laid eyes upon it. Yet, robbed of its holy veneer, Leiyn could only remember the dungeon that lay in its underbelly. Her stomach turned as she recalled the days of starvation spent in the dark, lonely cell beneath its oubliette. She licked her teeth, the feeling of rat fur stuck between them.

Breathe, just breathe.

By her lifesense, Leiyn could feel the people waiting within. She could not fail them before they had even started. Taking measured breaths, she mastered herself, then lowered her gaze to the doors and strode forward. She had to be in control, now more than ever. She was the Prima Maha.

Taban was wrong about titles. They did not confer power alone; they were tethered to responsibility. Hers was a privilege she would take seriously.

Though not without a few hearty curses thrown Mauricio's way.

Pressing open the doors, she entered the nave and looked upon her students. A dozen in total, some milled about the chamber, staring at the busts of the Sacred Saints, the stained glass windows, or the golden orb of Omn. Others sat on the pews, waiting with varying degrees of patience.

The only thing they had in common was their dissimilarity. Leiyn had expected her mahitas to be children, still new to the idea of their magic and less convinced of its wickedness. Instead, only two or three were young enough to qualify. The rest ranged from young adults to the elderly. One woman appeared old enough to be a grandmother twice over.

Mauricio had claimed them to be choice candidates, hand-picked to train under her. Her lips tweaked, though the situation was far from amusing. These were not mahas, much less mahitas.

Tadeo would say to work with what you have, she reminded herself. *And not jump to conclusions.*

Her students turned at her entrance, expectant looks in their eyes. Leiyn wondered what she was to do with the motley assortment. How could she teach people of such divergent experiences, both in their lives and their magic? Yet she remembered how Tadeo had carried himself. Somehow, he had always made it seem as if he was confident in his decisions, even when Leiyn knew he had felt anything but.

She drew herself up straight and managed a little smile. She had often had to dredge up confidence in the direst of situations. The stakes were not so high to prevent her from fabricating it now.

The students drifted closer, but the youngest among them, a girl barely coming into womanhood, spoke first. "Are you the Prima Maha? Prima Leiyn?"

Leiyn nodded. "I am."

Some of the older students exchanged looks. The grandmotherly woman, who still sat on a pew, hummed a note in contemplation. Perhaps they had expected something different from her. Someone older, to start.

Irritating as their skepticism might be, Leiyn did not let it show. "Stand and line up here, before me."

She tucked her hands behind her back to hide her fidgeting as she waited. Though they took their time, her students obeyed.

I have that much authority, at least.

Once they had fallen into a haphazard line, Leiyn started down it in silence. She thought of having them make introductions, but doubted she would remember their names that way. While her eyes brushed across their faces, her mahia probed deeper, examining and touching their esses. For the moment, she did not concern herself with their lifemarks. They might hold keys to who they were as people, but they would tell her little about their capabilities.

Instead, she examined the brightness of their lifefires, how much they left their walls open or closed, how responsive they were to the touch of magic. Half of them flinched. The more promising ones rebuffed her probing. Most curious of all was a fit young man who held himself with a soldier's stiffness. He did not respond to the contact either way, his esse remaining as placid as an undisturbed pool. While the older candidates seemed to burn dimmer on average, age did not always correspond with potential. Two of the eldest, spouses by how closely they stood together, were some of the liveliest of the lot.

Reaching the end of the line, Leiyn paused before the last pupil, a prepubescent girl. Before she could speak, a woman slightly older than Leiyn cut in.

"What, precisely, are we supposed to be doing?"

Leiyn met the woman's gaze. Judging by the ostentation of her dress, she was an offshoot of Ilberian nobility, or perhaps part of the rising merchant class. Cloth of silver lined her dress, and gold ornamentation flashed on her ears and above her low neckline.

Leiyn kept her tone flat as she responded. "I'm judging if any of you have talent."

At once, she regretted her words. A tall, gangly girl, who looked to be at the upper end of adolescence, flinched and looked to her feet. Her garb was far homelier than the merchant lady's, a homespun, undyed dress suitable to hard work, and her shoes sported more than one patched hole.

Pitiable as she looked, Leiyn tried to harden herself to the girl's temerity. If a few hard words broke her, she would never survive war.

"Take your time," said the older man of the couple, his face creased in a kindly smile. "We're grateful to have your instruction."

The woman next to him—his wife, Leiyn assumed—nodded and smiled. Leiyn returned it, if briefly. Though she knew it ill-befit her position, her spirits lifted with their support.

Turning back to the youngest girl, she considered her for a long moment. "What's your name?"

This girl, at least, was not intimidated by Leiyn. "Evie," she said. "Well, Genevieve is my full name. Genevieve of Orille."

It felt as if all the air was sucked from her lungs. She stared, knowing how she must look, but unable to help herself.

Orille.

How long had it been since Leiyn stopped to think of her first home? While traveling the Frontier Road, she purposely kept her thoughts from drifting down the lane that led through the forest to the town. And though she treasured the time she'd had with her father, the lies he had instilled in her had tainted those early years.

But peer into that well too long and she would drown. Piece by piece, Leiyn put herself together and scrambled for the next step.

Test her. See what she's capable of. The instructions came to her almost like Tadeo spoke them. Or could they come from Zuma's spark?

Focus, damn you!

"Genevieve," Leiyn said to the girl. "I want you to try something for me. Reach out and nudge me with your mahia."

Genevieve scrunched her brow. "Nudge you with magic? But how would I? Do you mean...?" She held out a hand, reaching toward her.

"Not with your hand." Horror crept over Leiyn as she looked down the line. "Who knows how to reach out with mahia?"

Only a few nodded: the teenage boy with a bored affect and the older couple. Unsure yet how to deal with the youth, who had the rough look of one making a living on the streets, she moved to stand before the couple.

"Your names?"

"Reyna," the woman said, smiling again. "This is Izan, my husband of thirty-four years."

Leiyn nodded, noting they did not give the rest of their names. Their oft-mended clothes told of those who had learned to fend for themselves. The potent presence of their esses suggested they had not restrained themselves, but been allowed to flourish. They were cautious, even though they had answered

Mauricio's call, and old habits died hard. But caution might serve them well when the battles began.

"Reyna, Izan, raise barriers around your mahia. Seal them as tight as you can."

The woman glanced at her husband, understanding passing between them. "You must mean hiding."

Before Leiyn could ask them to clarify, both of their lifefires disappeared—or nearly so. Their walls were not as secure as she might have hoped, allowing the edges of their esses to leak through. Yet when she tested them with a few prods, there was force behind them. Enough to work with.

"Good. We'll start here." Leiyn took a step back and gestured to Reyna and Izan. "You all can see what they've done? Try to replicate it. Protecting your esse is vital for a... a maha." The word still stuck like a bone in her throat, but she choked it out all the same. "Control is vital to wielding mahia. Walls keep out your enemy. I'll make sure you have strong enough ones to resist any attack."

"Why?" It was the teenage boy who spoke. As Leiyn turned to him, he added, "Prima Maha."

She ignored his insolence, knowing no good could come of acknowledging it. "Your name?"

"Simó. Of Lake's Edge."

A lie. Judging by his poverty, he could not have come from so far. Perhaps he had once lived there, but Leiyn knew a sewer rat when she saw one. Yet, that he might hail from the same town as Tadeo and Patli, and be an orphan as well, compelled an irresistible kinship from her.

"What do you mean, why?"

"I mean, Prima, what are we supposed to be doing here?"

"Learning to fight." The soldierly man snapped out the words toward the boy. "This magic is a weapon. We will learn to fight the Suncoats with it."

As a riot of expressions rippled across her students, a realization pricked at Leiyn. Tadeo had once said, *Those who do not understand cannot learn.* She had missed a foundational step in this lesson. The only thing for it was to return to the beginning.

"Sit. All of you. We have to talk."

Her students quickly complied. Though they seemed more leery of her than she preferred, Leiyn tried not to let it hurt. Swift obedience was necessary in warriors. Even if they would not hold steel or bows, they would need that same martial discipline.

Once they were seated among the pews, Leiyn stood before them, sorting through her thoughts until she found the right thread to pull.

"I don't know what you've been told about your mahia or what you think about it. But if you're like me, you grew up believing it was a curse. Perhaps you thought it came from Legion, as the Catedrál would have you believe. Perhaps you thought, as I did, that it was a magic born of the Gasts. You knew it was something to be hidden, or witch hunters would steal you from your home, never to return."

Some looked away as Leiyn's gaze raked across them. Others, like the older couple, nodded. She pressed on.

"But through my travels, I've heard other perspectives. The Gasts believe it to be a blessing bestowed upon a fortunate few by the spirit of Unera itself. The dryvans—the witches of the woods—believe it to be an inheritance, and like any noble or merchant who has amassed wealth, it is to be hoarded by the chosen."

Now, she saw awe appear in some of their eyes, disbelief in others. The teenage boy, Simó, looked as if he was about to spit, but swallowed at her glance. She could not blame him. In his place, she would have felt much the same.

"I don't know which is right," Leiyn continued. "But I know that shame poisoned my life for too long. This magic isn't evil. It can be used for evil, yes. But it can also better our lives and world."

She paused, letting the admission sink in. Honesty was a risk as a leader. It could undermine her authority as easily as gain their trust. But it had worked for Tadeo. She had to hope his lesson would ring true once more.

Not all were convinced, but some wavered. She could only hope she would break through to them soon.

"That's what I'll teach you. To wield mahia not only as a sword, but also a shield, and a balm. You are capable of attacking, protecting, healing. And some of you may be capable of commanding titans."

All were silent now, hanging on her every word. Even the teenage boy looked impressed.

Leiyn repressed a smile, keeping her tone stern. "But to do that, you must learn control. Stand."

There was a pause as the spell broke, then a scramble to obey. As they moved, Leiyn raised her voice above the din.

"We'll practice those walls first. See if you can keep me out."

With a grim smile, she moved back to the beginning of the line.

11

ECHOES OF THE PAST

The lesson lasted long into the afternoon. By the time Leiyn dismissed her students, their eyes had glassed over and they sagged with exhaustion. Yet something new hummed in the air, something that had not been present before.

They were beginning to believe. In her. In themselves. In the magic that united them.

Maybe I can do this. Be the Prima Maha, rather than pretending.

Leiyn had grown weary herself, though she endeavored not to show it. She stood as tall and proud as at the start while the mahitas of the Order streamed past her. Over the hours, she had learned their names, their capacities, even vague details of their lives. The young man with the background as a soldier was Nestor. Estel was the merchant lady, and her self-absorption did not lessen throughout the afternoon. Naia, Celia, Sergi, Noemi, Carles, Tecla—each had a story she had only started to uncover.

But this was only the beginning. And judging by how the afternoon had gone, they would have plenty more lessons together to become acquainted.

It started with Leiyn testing their walls and showing them their flaws. Most had known how to obscure their lifefires, though only as a prey's instinct to hide. Once Leiyn showed them how weak their barriers were, they soon learned to throw more force behind them. The girl, Genevieve, had shown surprising vigor in the exercise, and she and the soldier had the stoutest defenses. But all showed progress and formed walls by the end.

Once she had broken through each several times over, Leiyn led them through the basics of using lifesense. Few had as sensitive of mahia as hers. Those with the dullest had to concentrate to distinguish a human's esse from anything else. For others, like the teenage boy Simó, it came so naturally she had to find additional ways to keep them occupied. Simó in particular, lest he wander off and cause trouble around the temple.

Their progress had been marginal, but Leiyn felt something important had built between her dozen students and herself. The Colonial Order of Mahia was nothing like the Wilds Lodge had been. Camaraderie was lacking, these people so different from each other, and not keeping one oath and one livelihood, as the rangers had.

But they shared a purpose. They knew what was possible and what was at stake and tried reaching for it. For now, that was enough.

"When would you like us to return, Prima Leiyn?" Izan asked after she had dismissed them.

Only then had Leiyn realized she did not know. What these people's lives were and the extent of her authority remained vague. But knowing lessons faded quickly from the mind if they were not reinforced, there was only one answer she could give.

"Tomorrow at noon."

"Tomorrow?" the merchant, Estel, protested. "I have a business to run! I cannot spend my entire day at this. My clients will think I've cheated them. I'll be ruined!"

Others murmured affirmations. Leiyn looked around, realizing she did not know Mauricio's intentions for supporting them, either. Were they meant to stay in their own homes? Did he give them stipends to support them while they learned and, eventually, fought on Baltesia's behalf? In many ways, they were soldiers like any other, or like the rangers on the frontier. They deserved fair compensation.

But right then, all she could offer were words.

Leiyn pointed out one of the west-facing windows and met Estel's stare. "Look at the horizon. Do you think the Ilberian Armada gives a damn about your livelihood? Your lives? When they tire of blocking the harbor—and they will, sooner or later— we may be all that stands between them and Baltesia falling. Are a few failed contracts worse than that?"

She had meant to inspire them, but other than the soldier Nestor, most seemed to wilt. Only Naia, a serving lady in a nobleperson's manor, stood up straighter, her face set in a deter- mined grimace Leiyn had to admire.

Though her words did not have the effect intended, Leiyn resisted the urge to qualify them as her disgruntled students left. If they did not have the grit or desire to learn magic, she could not change that. Far better to cull the herd than draw things out.

Leiyn waited as they disappeared through the door until only one person remained. By her lifesense, she felt Genevieve shifting where she stood. A strange reluctance filled her, yet Leiyn knew she could not show fear to any of her students. Clenching her jaw, she turned to meet the girl's wide, brown eyes.

"Pardon me, Prima Maha," Genevieve said. "But are you really from Orille?"

The invisible hand returned, squeezing tight over her heart. For several long moments, Leiyn only stared at the girl. Genevieve's gaze was so innocent Leiyn knew she could not mean her harm.

Yet her mind filled with her final experiences in the village. The corpses of the livestock spread across the barn floor. Licky, her hound, loyal to the last and still lying beside her. Her home burning, having struck the flame herself to hide her sins.

She had accepted her mahia, and Baltesian law had legit- imized it. But it did not change the horrors of what it had done. What she had done with it.

I did what I had to.

A new thought, bright and shining among the gloom. Leiyn held it, turning it over. Could it be real? Could she justify the things she had done? She had been a child with no training in her magic, only the repeated warnings of her father to repress it. What could she have done to stop it?

She was not ready to accept it as true. But maybe it was time to stop denying her past.

"Yes. I am."

Under her silent gaze, Genevieve had been shifting uncomfortably. Now her expression brightened. "Oh! So the rumors are true! Back home, they talked about a Leiyn who died with her father in a fire around the time of the Blush. I'd just been born, but it was so mysterious, people talked about it all my life! But when we heard of another Leiyn who raised a kraken from the sea, an orphan who had hidden her power by becoming a ranger... well, I knew you must be her."

Leiyn tensed with each word. She never wanted this... notoriety. This attention. She belonged among the quiet hills, the verdant forests, patrolling the Titan Wilds to watch for threats and keep the colonists safe. She had always felt more comfortable out of sight and in the presence of her frontier family at the Lodge.

But they're gone. And I'm not hiding anymore.

Leiyn struggled to comport herself. She could not stop from biting off each word, though. "That Leiyn is gone. She burned with the barn."

The girl's smile melted away. "How can you say that? I had to leave Orille, too, but my home is always a part of me."

"Orille's not my home any longer."

"Oh." Genevieve turned away. "I... I'm sorry."

Leiyn could only watch as the girl shuffled out of the door.

Damn it, Firebrand, a part of her railed. *You're the one who should apologize!*

But her feet remained planted where she was. She had

spoken true. The girl she had been in Orille was gone. She was a ranger now, a maha. She was a child no longer.

She needs to toughen up. Like I did.

Waiting until Genevieve was well on her way, Leiyn finally left the temple.

———

Teaching left her drained, yet Leiyn's obligations continued. She needed to speak with Mauricio regarding the logistics of her students' schedules and lodgings. Instead of heading for the governor's solarium, however, she found herself moving toward the villa's feast hall.

The room was every bit as grand as the villa's atrium. Three rows of tables, sparsely occupied for the moment, promised to seat a hundred. Baltesian blue drapes were tied back from ceiling-high windows. Suits of armor stood at attention along one end, backed by walls of bright stone. Dark beams bisected the stucco ceiling.

To her relief, Batu and Isla were already seated at the far end. Leiyn waved down a servant, who bowed and went to bring her food and drink. Being served was a concession to formality she had to swallow. Fetching them herself would be cause for scandal, a notion Leiyn still struggled to grasp.

"So you survived," Isla said as Leiyn slumped into a chair beside Batu. "And here I wagered the students would chew you into cud."

Leiyn cast her a droll look as the servant returned bearing a pitcher of wine. Refusing the woman's offer to water it down, she drank greedily of her goblet. It had a boozy undercurrent and tasted as strong as a port. Just then, she was glad for it. The numbness would bring welcome relief.

"Looks like it was a near thing," Batu commented.

Setting down her cup, Leiyn looked at each of them. "And I'm doing it again tomorrow."

They winced.

"By our governor's request?" Isla queried.

"No. My own damn fault."

Batu sipped of his chalice, which was filled with some manner of ale. "Sounds about right."

"Playing the common soldier cannot be much better."

"Probably not," he admitted. "My sergeant isn't fond of having a former plainsrider among the ranks."

"You won't have to tolerate it much longer. I'll speak with Mauricio soon." She glanced at Isla. "Would that you could join us."

The serving woman returned with Leiyn's meal. As she set the steaming bowl before her, Leiyn breathed in the fragrant mix of spices. A seared fillet of fish—cod, by its color—laid atop a bed of paella, a rainbow assortment of vegetables adorning the rice. She tucked into it with ill-mannered haste before the servant had gone two steps.

Isla sniffed with pretended affront before speaking. "It won't be like this forever, just for now. I need to attend every Council session. Matters are moving so fast skipping a single one might mean missing something crucial."

Leiyn waved her free hand, not bothering to pause her feast.

"If you think the Lord Governor will acquiesce," Batu said between bites of rice, "I'll agree to it. Though I'll still need to train."

Leiyn swallowed a large mouthful and had to cough to keep from choking. "So do I," she gasped. "We'll have all morning for it."

His lips quirked. "Get his permission. I'll come."

The rest of the meal passed with catching each other up on their days. Leiyn confessed to her run-in with Taban and endured the inevitable chastisement. She kept the threats he had aimed at Batu to herself, seeing little good in breaking open old wounds. Isla prattled on about the latest developments in the political arena—which, to Leiyn's ears, sounded like a lot had been said with little done. Then they moved to more pleasant conversations—as pleasant as any could be just then.

When Leiyn had stuffed her belly with as much paella as she could stomach and guzzled two glasses of wine, she followed the others to their rooms. But as they turned the corner and their doors came into view, Leiyn saw a manservant in a formal coat waiting outside her room, hands clasped behind his back.

"Guess I'm discussing things with Mauricio tonight," she muttered.

As she had guessed, the man issued her a summons from the governor. Leiyn bade farewell to her companions before following the servant back down the corridor.

When they reached Mauricio's solarium, the attendant opened the door, announced her presence, then bowed his way out.

"Ah, Prima Maha!" Mauricio did not look up from the document before him, his quill scratching across its face. "I'm pleased we have a moment to speak alone."

"Likewise, Lord Governor." She barely disguised her sarcasm as she sauntered in, the servant sealing the doors behind her.

After several moments, Mauricio finished writing, set the quill back in its holder, and looked up. He bared his teeth in his usual wide smile, but there was a tightness about his eyes that had not been there during her first visit.

"I believe I owe you an apology, Leiyn—if you'll forgive me for speaking so familiarly."

"You know I prefer it."

"I do," the governor agreed. "I realize that this responsibility may not be one you embrace."

Leiyn crossed her arms and set her feet wide. Her silence and posture spoke as plainly as words.

Mauricio drummed his fingers together, considering her. "You must understand, our present position leaves me with little choice. An underhanded tactic, perhaps, but necessary all the same. And while I will apologize for the manner in which I sprung it upon you, I cannot withdraw my ordinance."

"Not sure that qualifies as an apology."

"Very well." The governor stood with a stifled groan, moved

around to the front of his desk, and bowed deeply. "You have my sincerest apologies, Leiyn of the Wilds Lodge, for all I have and will force upon you."

The hair on her neck stood up. "Will?"

"I'm afraid there's more." Mauricio waved a hand before his face and leaned back on the desk. "But first, take some brandy and tell me of all you've seen since you were last in our fair capital. Envoy Isla told me all she knew, and Premier Itzel's letter said more, but I'm sure you have a fair few explications."

Leiyn took the offered cup—unwisely, as her head already simmered from the wine at dinner—before setting into her narrative. She held little back; there was scant reason to. She was proud of what she had done in Qasaar. And with Isla having already divulged the shamans' sparse numbers, she had no reason to lie about them.

But she did not tell him all.

Three things she kept to herself. Her relationship with Teya was the first of them. Not only irrelevant, but it was also none of the governor's damned business.

Second, she gave few details regarding Ata. The dryvan had trusted Leiyn with her true name and more. She would not violate that, even if it flirted with treason.

And she said nothing of Sharo.

Why she refrained from speaking of the conspiracy—which had spawned their secessionary war, if the lyshan was to be believed—she was not certain. She trusted Mauricio as much as she would anyone in his position. But with how subtly Sharo pulled his strings, she could not dismiss the idea that even the governor was within her enemy's power.

When she finished, the governor polished off his brandy, then offered the decanter. Tempted as she was, Leiyn shook her head and set down her cup.

"You might regret it," Mauricio warned, "with what I have to tell you."

Her stomach clenched but she had never been one to shy away from unpleasant truths.

"You believe the Order is essential," she guessed.

The governor sighed and poured out another measure of liquor for himself. "Southport is protected in the immediate term. The Gazian wisdoms present in the city—half a dozen of them, to be precise—are reputed to be skilled at warding off magical attacks, be they titan or otherwise. So long as that holds true, Southport should be able to weather any initial assaults."

Mauricio sipped from his cup, then leaned forward. "But we cannot always rely upon our neighbors. We must become strong and self-reliant. We *must* have our own mahas. Capable as you are, you cannot hold back the whole of the Union. And the Crown and the Catedrál's repression of those with your gift have put us far behind where we need to be."

Leiyn pressed her arms tightly to her middle. "You're right. I do wish I'd accepted that second cup."

He chuckled, but quickly sobered. "Tell me, what is your initial impression of your new pupils?"

She pursed her lips, deciding how to frame her thoughts. "It's only the first day."

"Your initial impression, I requested."

"If I must, then... I doubt they'll be able to fight anytime soon."

She had hoped to feel relieved by the confession. Instead, the truth only weighed heavier for being spoken.

Mauricio frowned, swirling the brandy in his cup. "Is it because of a lack of ability?"

Yes, she was tempted to say. It would not have been an inaccurate assessment. All lacked the vigor of her own mahia even before she had begun actively using and training it. Whatever the reason, hers seemed to be a rare strength.

"Temperament, more like," she said. "With one or two exceptions, they aren't fighters. I see little sign of them having the instinct. Even if I can train them to use magic as I do, they cannot match odiosas."

The governor stared into his cup and its swirling liquid. The silence stretched on. Leiyn shifted, wondering if this was a tactic to draw out an answer he liked better.

Then he's about to be sorely disappointed.

Abruptly, Mauricio stood, drained his cup, and set it down on the desk with a firm clink. "Come. There's something I'd like you to see."

Not waiting for a response, the governor rolled his shoulders and strolled to the solarium doors to heave them open. Mystified, Leiyn trailed after Mauricio as he led them through the corridors to the front gates of the compound. When he said they would be gone for some time, the guards posted there asked if he required an escort.

"Of course not." The governor gestured to Leiyn. "I have the Tideraiser accompanying me."

Leiyn kept her expression placid before the guards' scrutinizing stares. Though both were larger than her, she suspected her abilities far surpassed their own. Yet she could not help a sliver of doubt as she and Mauricio exited alone onto the cobbled street. She had never acted as a bodyguard before, nor did she relish the opportunity.

Bit late to refuse now.

Mauricio led them toward the bay. Without the walls impinging on their view, the lanterns burning on the decks of the Armada ships sparkled along the horizon. Leiyn tore her gaze away to pay attention to their immediate surroundings. The crowds had thinned with nightfall, yet there were enough people about for Leiyn to track with her mahia that the task took most of her concentration.

The governor's villa was close enough to the bay to smell brine on the wind, but far enough to keep out the stink of old fish. As they neared the docks, the stench of fisheries inundated Leiyn's senses and turned her belly. She swallowed the taste of sick, hoping the brandy and wine would stay put.

Traveling along the boardwalk, they passed a few night vendors and their dubious wares before Mauricio halted before a wide, squat building. A warehouse, Leiyn guessed, not only by its size and location, but the doors designed to admit crates and barrels.

"It's just within," the governor said before approaching a man dressed in a sailor's tarred attire standing at a side door. After a swift exchange, the man bobbed his head, then unlocked the door to admit them. Leiyn's apprehension rose as stale air rushed over them.

The sight that greeted her was unexpected. Illuminated by the oil lamps lining the walls were dozens upon dozens of racks and crates filled with weapons and armor for as far as she could see. Leiyn guessed there to be enough equipment for a thousand soldiers.

A secret armory.

Her attention only lingered on the armaments for a moment. Looking beyond the few workers milling between the aisles, she sensed another lifeforce unlike the others. An esse that extended beyond the boundaries of itself.

One eerily familiar.

"This way," Mauricio said, heading toward the presence, "though I believe you've already guessed that."

The bars came into view first. It looked to be a cage wagon designed to transport criminals but unmounted from its wheels. Within, a man sat, head bowed, wrists and ankles chained. A hood obscured his face, and a tattered gray robe covered the rest of his body. If his possession of magic had not been sign enough of what he was, his appearance was sufficient.

Leiyn stopped two dozen paces off, drawing Mauricio to a halt beside her. Her accusation came out in a hiss.

"Why do you have an odiosa?"

12

INSTRUMENT OF WAR

*H*er question hung between them, suspended as if on a taut rope. The governor snapped it with a smile.

"Have faith, Prima Maha. Lord Luca trusts the men and women working here. This is the least of the secrets they keep."

Slowly, Leiyn faced the witch hunter again only to find he had raised his head. Eyes devoid of emotion stared up at her from beneath hooded lids. Memories flashed through her mind of the last time she had looked into those eyes.

"I know him," she muttered. "He interrogated me below the temple."

"Truly?" Mauricio's eyebrows flew up. "A vagary of irony, would you not say? Come, my dear ranger. You need not fear him while he remains behind bars."

I'm not afraid.

She trapped the words behind her teeth. In silence, Leiyn followed the governor forward, halting not three paces away from the bars.

The odiosa watched their every step. She wondered how she had recognized him as she studied his features. His face was ordinary, more than seemed possible, as if it were every bit as anonymized as his fractured mind. Yet his esse, which had once violated her soul, felt familiar enough.

Sensing another's gaze, Leiyn glanced over to see Mauricio watching her. Hoping she had kept her thoughts from her face—suspecting she had not—she tightened her jaw and hid her fear.

"You need not stand so far away," the governor murmured. "He does not bother those who work here. Perhaps his magic requires touch?"

She shook her head. He had not needed touch when he had assaulted her. And distance did not keep her from affecting others. Still, a pace closer would scarcely make a difference.

I'm not afraid.

She advanced to the edge of the cage, close enough that, if the odiosa's chains allowed him, he could reach out and grab her. Mauricio stepped up beside her.

She kept her eyes on the man huddled before her as she asked the governor, "Why did you bring me here?"

"Why? That is simple enough to answer. I wish you to break him—or save him, whichever proves feasible."

His tone remained light, yet she felt the hidden blades in his words.

Break him. Save him.

In a burst, Leiyn raked her awareness across the odiosa's esse. She could often see lifemarks at a glance, but his seemed murky and ill-defined. Concentrating brought it into focus: a hand set aflame. As she beheld it, the hand seared into her mind with true heat.

Driving her lifesense forward, she tried to see beyond it to the rest of his marks, but the hand obscured them. All she perceived was the silhouette of a person wreathed in smoke—the one thrusting forward the burning hand.

The truth made her recoil. This mark was not the odiosa's own. Like a slave inked with her master's sigil, another had branded his soul.

Leiyn withdrew and stared at the odiosa. He had not moved from the cage floor, nor shifted his gaze from her.

"I think he's beyond saving," she said slowly. "And I'm not

sure I can break him. His inner core is sealed and branded. Like... like someone has leashed his mind."

Her thoughts flitted to Sharo. *Puppets,* he had implied of the Caelrey and World King. Had he strung up more than those two marionettes? Did every odiosa serve his will, just as he had forced poor Patli to? But though she had detected little of note about the brand, it did not feel like a lyshan's touch. Even if the plot was Sharo's, the immediate blame belonged to another.

"I understand." Mauricio's voice held a smile. "Yet you must either succeed here or with your students, Prima Maha. I need an edge with this magic. I refuse to let Baltesia fall to Ilberia's greed, as the Gast nation did before us."

Leiyn turned back, comprehension dawning at last. "That's what you want. Their secrets to mahia."

He nodded. "Or to have him wield them on our behalf, yes. How much do they know? Have they learned to command titans, or only repel them? How might we foil their tricks? With odiosa magic on our side, we stand a chance of survival."

And without it, we fall. The implication echoed in his words and rang true in her. She had slain Man'nah, but this was the force of an entire empire. As the governor had said, Leiyn alone could not turn the tide of the war.

"Fine. I'll do what I can."

"That's all I ask."

Resigned, Leiyn exhaled her doubts and turned back. Before she faced the cage, though, the odiosa moved.

She jerked back as the man stretched forth his arms. She need not have—his reach fell inches short of the bars. His chains rattled, but not as loud as her thumping heart. She sensed the attention of the warehouse workers settle on them. An audience —the last thing she needed.

Leiyn pushed down her rising fluster and stepped forward again. She stood bare inches from the bars now, inches from his grasping fingers. Tremors worked through her muscles. She tried not to show any sign of weakness.

The huntress. Be the huntress.

"Do you remember me?" she asked, each word an arrow.

The man's dead eyes followed her every movement. His chapped lips curved in a smile.

"An Instrument must always remember."

Instrument. She had forgotten that was how they referred to themselves. Like they were not human even to their own minds, just tools to be used.

But he was not just that. Despite his lifemark being obscured, despite his peculiar behavior, he *was* a man. His life-force burned the same as hers. He spoke. He remembered. If he appeared an empty vessel, it was because someone had damaged him. That which was broken might still be repaired.

If San Inhoa is feeling merciful.

"What's your name?" She waited for an answer, but when the odiosa continued to smile, her patience ran thin. "Who were you before you became an odiosa?"

Again, silence.

"How were you taken? Do you remember your childhood, your family, your home? Or were you born to this?"

She could have been speaking to a wall for all the reaction her words stirred. Leiyn gritted her teeth. She pressed forward so close she almost touched the rusted bars.

"Who do you serve?" she said in a harsh whisper. "Are you a tool of the Catedrál? Or the World King? Or do you belong to another? A... higher power?"

She expected a stir in those eyes if she struck near the truth. If she did, any sign of it remained hidden. The odiosa was as devoid of emotion as a statue. Only in the trembling of his body as he strained against his chains did he show signs of life.

Abandoning the course, Leiyn quested forward again with her mahia. She examined the colors of his esse, hoping they might give some hint of the man behind the brand. There was only a hint of pink to it, diluted like blood in water, so faint she wondered if she imagined it.

The odiosa surged forward again, or tried to, but his bonds held. Leiyn flinched, then bared her teeth.

"Remember who won our last encounter? I wouldn't be eager to repeat it if I were you."

Though her goad yielded no more than her earlier words, an insight came to her. *He's sensitive to magic.* The examination of his lifeforce was the only thing that had provoked him thus far. Perhaps he feared her exploring it.

She knew well how weakness could spawn for fear.

Leiyn blew out a breath. As she did, she flared her mahia within her body, burning away the remaining alcohol running through her veins. Clarity, sharp and unpleasant, crawled back in. She did not let herself focus on it.

Darting out a hand, she grasped the odiosa's wrist.

He tried wrenching away, but her grip was too strong. Her mahia surged, barbed as nettles. She had only won their previous encounter through trickery. Now, with experience and training, Leiyn swiftly overwhelmed him.

The odiosa railed against her invasion, but she repelled each attempt to dislodge her. She was as relentless as a hound at the hunt, jaws locked on its prey.

"Release me!" the man shrieked. "*Release me!*"

Ruthlessly, she clung on and attempted to rifle his soul. Each barrier he erected, she tore down to bore deeper into his esse. The further in she went, the more the flaming hand pressed back, blistering and unyielding.

A grunt escaped her as Leiyn drove against the brand. She struck at it directly, then at its peripheries. It felt like punching a rocky cliff with her bare fists. Worse, each attempt left a singed feeling behind like she had been burned. Smarting, she tried to circumvent it, but the lifemark was sealed as tightly as her walls. Impervious.

Leiyn released him. The odiosa scrambled away to huddle against the far side of the cage, banging his head on the bars in his haste. Before the pitiable sight, she could not help feeling disgusted with herself.

I'm not the true culprit.

It had not been she who had branded and broken him. She had not stolen his humanity.

But she might still free him.

Stepping away from the cage, she turned back to find the governor watching with interest. As she swept her gaze across the warehouse, workers hastily busied themselves and pretended they had not been spying as well.

"Well?" he prompted. "Did you learn anything useful?"

"Not exactly." Leiyn wiped her hand on her breeches. Her skin felt filthy from even that brief touch. "His mind is... locked away. Anything that remains of who he really is lies behind it. I suspect the secrets of his order are there as well."

"A lock. Then perhaps there is a key?"

She shrugged. "Maybe. But for now, I don't have it."

Mauricio smiled, but it was limp and false now. "If you cannot unlock him, you understand what this means. The Colonial Order of Mahia must succeed. One way or another, you will gain Baltesia the advantage it so desperately needs."

For a moment, her rebellious nature flared, and sharp words tipped her tongue. Prudence won out in time. No matter the power she had gained, she was still a subject of Baltesia, a ranger in service to her country. She was sworn to obey her governor.

Even if it killed her.

"As you wish, Lord Governor." Less than graciously said, perhaps, but it was all that was required of her.

Mauricio loosed a little laugh. "The best I'll get, I suppose. Now, let us leave this putrid place and retire for the night. Tomorrow no doubt holds more trials and troubles for us both."

Leiyn cast a last glance over her shoulder at the caged man, then followed the governor from the warehouse.

13

CHAINS OF COMMAND

For a city under siege, the following months in Southport passed in relative calm.

Mindful of her duty and Baltesia's need, Leiyn threw herself into her teaching. The initial sessions remained as awkward as the first, but by the time the second week rolled around, she and her students had become familiar with each other. Leiyn slowly let more of herself peek through the hard mask she had donned.

She ribbed the vagrant youth Simó when he made a mistake, provoking grins. When the merchant Estel or the soldier Nestor grew impatient, Leiyn did not hold back a sarcastic reply. A colorful curse or two slipped between her teeth, eliciting blushes and chuckles in equal measure.

Positive or negative, their interactions became genuine. And, like Tadeo had always claimed, it drew her students closer.

Only around Genevieve did Leiyn remain stiff and formal—a fact not lost on the girl, judging by her glumness. She despised what she did, yet Leiyn could not help but push her away. Each time she looked at the girl, memories of Orille rose within her, pustulant and withering.

Even with her victories, though, the role of the Prima Maha became increasingly stifling. Having pried Batu from his soldierly duties, Leiyn drove hard against him on the courtyard in the mornings before lessons. He had never been an easy opponent and had become even less so since Qasaar, adding the cunning of a Gast *situal* and the discipline of a soldier to his training as a plainsrider. Their bouts ended in his favor nearly as often as in Leiyn's. Only when she practiced drawing upon her esse for speed and strength did she prevail.

So fierce was their training that they began gathering spectators. Some were villa guards, interested in their techniques. Others were servants or dignitaries seeking a spectacle. Leiyn did her best to ignore them.

Mostly, she succeeded. Her reputation around Southport had garnered enough attention that she had quickly grown used to being stared at wherever she went. The watchers had a worse effect on Batu; naturally shy, his performance suffered the greater their audience. Yet even he was growing accustomed to it.

She was doing everything she could to further Baltesia's cause. It never seemed enough.

Leiyn spent the evenings slumped in her, Isla, or Batu's room, drinking wine and brandy. Though she knew it was the last thing either of them wanted to hear after their own exhausting days, she could not help but vent her frustrations.

"Relax, Leiyn, for once," Isla tried reassuring her. "You're doing enough. Saints, you're working wonders, from how Batu tells it. Haven't you said yourself how far your mahitas have come?"

"'Wonders' might be generous," Leiyn replied. "They're still learning things I grasped before my first moonblood."

Yet the fledgling members of the Order had come leaps and bounds from where they had started. Izan and Reyna, the older couple who had spent most of their lives isolated in the woods west of Southport, expanded on their foundation. Genevieve, despite her gloomy manner, remained eager to learn and quickly mastered each lesson. Simó struggled to maintain focus, yet when he applied himself, his progress surpassed even Genevieve's.

Most surprising of the promising pupils was Naia, the middle-aged servant to a merchant lord who sat on the Liberty Council. With middling control to start and difficulties grasping even the most basic of lessons, Naia had met each failure with renewed determination. Her quiet fierceness reminded Leiyn of herself—though her own determination had rarely been quiet.

Not every sign was auspicious. Estel tried abandoning the Order after the second lesson. When she returned the next day with an expression that could curdle cream, Leiyn suspected only the governor's intervention kept her there. Nestor had a different sticking point. Despite his best efforts, his drive to learn mahia was proving shallower than his capacity. As he struggled in silence, she wondered if he would not be more useful among the army's ranks.

But not every lesson was learned by her pupils. As Leiyn led the mahitas through one of Mother Xepi's exercises designed to expand the reach of one's lifesense, she noticed Reyna and Izan failing to follow her instructions. Unfailingly kind as the older couple was, Leiyn dragged her feet each time she needed to chastise them. For the moment, she contented herself with watching and understanding what they were doing.

The rest of the mahitas stretched their mahia toward a point at the southern end of the city, one of the towers where the Gazian wisdoms would go in the event of a titan attack. She could feel their strain, see the wispy clouds of their lifesense reaching across the leagues between them and their destination. Most fell short.

Izan and Reyna, however, did not spread their mahia in one direction: they spread all around them. Their touch was gentle and light and thin as air. Leiyn could only detect its presence by a slight shimmer against her lifesense. How far they reached, she could not say, for with any distance, her awareness of it faded.

Feeling she would be doing them a disservice to delay longer, Leiyn slowly approached the pair. "How's it going for you two?" she asked lightly.

Their eyes, before closed, fluttered open at her question. Reyna cast her a beatific smile.

"Very well, dear. We have never had much trouble with sensing."

"That so?" Leiyn turned to Izan, hoping he would give her more to work with. "Same for you?"

"Very much so, lass. Though Reyna always was the more gifted between us." He pressed his wife's shoulder fondly, at which she turned her smile on him.

Seeing no other choice, Leiyn opted for her usual tact: blunt honesty. "You remember the task, don't you? You're supposed to reach toward the tower. Can you sense it?"

"Of course, dear." Reyna's smile slipped. "Have we done something wrong?"

"Not wrong," she hedged. "It's your mahia—it's spread out all around you, not in one direction."

Izan cocked his head. "Well, no, lass. Why look in one direction when you can see all around?"

"Not just around," Reyna scolded. "*In* and *through*, that's the way of it. Leastwise, we thought so," she said, turning meekly back to Leiyn.

She was too perplexed to pay it much heed. "What do you mean, in and through? I'm not doubting you," she added. "I'm curious. It sounds different from what I know."

The older man furrowed his brow. "As you say. Dearest, would you care to explain?"

"Certainly, love. It's how we always did it in our little cottage in the forest, feeling the plants, the animals, everything in the good ground and on the breeze. It—well, it made us feel a part of it all. Connected, like we are. All one."

All one. Leiyn knew that feeling, to some extent. Back when she had repressed her mahia, the times it broke through had felt like reunion, even if guilt spoiled the moment. Like being welcomed into a home she had been long away from. And she had always felt her mahia was at her most potent when it connected with Unera and its inhabitants, and not existed in herself.

She did not know if it would help with Clouded Fang. But it was something to consider.

"Thank you," she said with feeling. "So long as it does not limit the range of your lifesense, I don't see a reason you shouldn't keep doing it that way. It might even be the better path."

"You are too kind, Prima Maha!" Reyna exclaimed. "A better path, Izan, did you hear?"

She spoke loud enough that her husband hushed her with an embarrassed look. Soon, they lapsed into a hushed conversation.

With a rueful smile, Leiyn turned to check on the others.

⁓

Neither successes nor setbacks in the Order could banish Leiyn's disquiet. During restless nights, she visited the nearest balcony to stare over the ships dotting Anchor's Refuge. Visible by the watch lanterns, they haunted the sea even at night. She counted them like her father had once advised she count goats when trying to sleep, but it only heightened her anxiety.

How in all the black hells can we beat them?

She already knew the answer: Titans—they were the only solution in sight. For two full weeks, she had buried that private worry, but it inevitably rose again. In serving her country, Leiyn avoided the thing she should be focused on:

Her mahia.

During spare moments, she continued to practice Xepi's exercises on her own to deepen her understanding and control, but her physical training claimed more prominence. There, alone but for the lantern lights and the brisk ocean breeze, she could not deny what held her back. When she reached for her connection to Clouded Fang, it felt so brittle she scarcely dared touch it.

With their bond so feeble, how could she summon the ash

dragon, much less draw upon his strength? Was it her fault for not reinforcing the connection? Or was this a natural decay? She had long ago left the environs in which she had encountered the titan. Perhaps, here by the shore, it was simply too much to ask for one of his kind to rise.

Following this line of logic, Leiyn spent some of those sleepless nights searching the bay for the kraken that had made her notorious. To her relief, it remained hidden in the waters, slumbering as it had before she roused it. When she tried inhabiting the world as Reyna and Izan had described doing so with their mahia, the titan felt even closer, its dormant presence inundating her every pore like calm, lukewarm water.

Leiyn did not try to draw it out. Doing so had gotten Zuma killed and nearly destroyed every ship in the harbor. Though the shaman remained a spark within her, he might not be able to save her next time. Until it was their last resort, she had no intention of trying to raise it again.

Mauricio, Isla, Batu, all of Southport—they had seen her perform miracles and expected them from her again. "Tideraiser," they called her. As if she commanded the ocean itself.

All she had were doubts. She had possessed the power of titans and killed the strongest of skin-walkers. Now she wrapped her arms about herself, the wind cold on her face. Never feeling more frail.

I will be enough. I must be.

She missed Teya most in those moments. The scout would not have had a solution any more than Leiyn did, but her presence would have lightened her load. Leiyn closed her eyes and imagined the scout's arms encircling her, their esses twining. The boundaries of their bodies falling away.

Until autumn arrived, it could only remain a dream.

～

Two months on, Leiyn exited the First Temple to find Isla and Batu waiting outside.

"No Council session today, eh?" Leiyn glanced at Batu. "You, I'm not surprised to find here. What else would you have to do but bother me?"

Ignoring her teasing, the two exchanged a look.

"Do you want to give the news," Isla said, "or shall I?"

Batu gestured her forward. "You'll enjoy it more."

"What now?" Leiyn's smile slipped.

Her fellow ranger winced. "Another appointment. Lord Luca has requested an audience. I believe he wishes to apprise you of your duties as the Prima Maha should Southport suffer an invasion."

"By 'requested,' you mean 'commanded'."

"He *is* a conqueror."

As if I needed the reminder.

Heaving a sigh, Leiyn drew herself up straight. "Ready when you are."

The trio headed out of the villa gate and down toward the docks. The route stayed the same as the one Leiyn had taken with Mauricio several weeks before, only deviating once they moved past the disguised warehouse. Leiyn could not help her lifesense lingering on the odiosa locked inside. She did not think she imagined it when his mahia drifted against hers for a moment. She felt soiled imagining his touch.

The visit with Mauricio had not been her last to the prisoner. Four more times, she had returned to see if she could make progress in unlocking the odiosa's mind. For all her efforts, for all the tricks she tried, she could not move beyond that lifemark. Perhaps it was impregnable; perhaps the issue lay with her. Either way, the possibility of gleaning information from him grew more distant with each passing day.

Not wanting to dwell on her shortcomings, Leiyn turned to Isla. "So what's a conqueror doing fighting for Baltesia, anyway?"

"Lord Luca?" Isla shrugged. "Do you want to question what's going on in his mind?"

"He seems a bit odd."

"A bit?" Batu, a step behind them, let out a quiet laugh.

Leiyn smiled over her shoulder before looking back to Isla. "Seriously. He's got to have some reason for it."

"All I know is what Mauricio told me." Isla stared ahead of them with pursed lips. "Luca di Eño Vasara. He wasn't a conqueror until recently, though he was born and raised in Ilberia. He was a captain stationed here, I believe, when the war broke out."

"A captain for the Union? So he's a turncoat?"

Her fellow ranger looked sidelong at her. "Would you prefer he wasn't?"

"I suppose not. But how'd it happen?"

Batu was the one to respond. "He delivered his commanding admiral, bound and tethered, to the governor, offered along with his hat."

Isla cast him a long-suffering look. "Was this your story?"

He grinned. "Apologies, *kha-ir*."

The Kalgan endearment was only vaguely familiar to Leiyn, but she rolled her eyes at it all the same. "That doesn't explain *why* he's fighting on our side," she pointed out.

Isla finished her mock glare at her beloved before answering. "'Conviction,' was the best answer Mauricio could give, but I think there's more to it than that." Her gaze turned pensive as she turned to stare over the sea. "You've seen how he is. He'd managed to climb up the ranks, and for good reason, but I don't think he felt he ever belonged in Ilberia. Here, he does. Baltesia can be a refuge for many people of different kinds, don't you think?"

Leiyn thought of her ostracization. The magic that had been a sentence of death or worse. And how Mauricio had freed her from that burden.

"Yes," she murmured. "I could agree with that."

Conversation ceased as they drew abreast of the official base of operations for the Baltesian military. Lord Luca and his officers had moved into the abandoned Ilberian barracks and adopted it as their own. Leiyn had never come near it before, much less entered it, and was taken aback by the bustling activity she sensed within. People moved back and forth in its halls, as industrious and ceaseless as ants. Bracing for the onslaught, Leiyn trailed Isla and Batu as they approached the guards.

Their names and positions proved sufficient to be escorted inside. Leiyn turned this way and that as she took in their surroundings. The building was as austere as expected. Baltesian blue came in ample supply, from simple arrases on the walls, to window curtains, to the cloth kerchiefs tied around every arm. Uniforms were scarce, and the boys who ran back and forth clutching sealed scrolls appeared little different than the rest of the citizenry. Only the officers wore anything resembling military regalia, and even these lacked the uniformity of Suncoat livery. Leiyn put little stock in decorum, but small things spoke volumes about an army.

A soldier at the door ushered them through the crowded main corridor to a solarium at the far end. There, an impressive set of double doors opened into a room slightly more ostentatious than the rest. The ornamentation consisted largely of gleaming armaments and military maps rather than more frivolous displays of wealth. The chamber was less crowded than the hallway leading to it, only officers appeared more frequently. The exception lay at its center, where a tall man with shining blonde hair leaned over a large, mahogany desk with no others crowding him.

"Lord Conqueror," their escort said with a quick bow, "the envoy and Prima Maha have arrived."

Luca di Eño Vasara took several moments to look up. When he did, he blinked as if startled to see them standing there. Once more, Leiyn wondered at this odd conqueror of theirs.

"Envoy Isla Ogbi. Prima Leiyn of the Wilds Lodge." Lord Luca stared at Batu for a long moment. "I don't know you."

"Batu Khatas, my lord." Batu gave him a deep bow. "A former plainsrider now serving Baltesia."

The conqueror stared at him a moment longer before looking away. Leiyn frowned at him, yet something in Luca's expression seemed more perplexed than dismissive. Like Batu was a piece that did not fit into a puzzle.

Isla seemed more certain about how to deal with the conqueror. Firmly, she said, "I believe, Lord Conqueror, you wished to inform the Prima Maha of how you would like the Order of Mahia to operate within the greater strategy."

"Yes, yes, yes." Luca bobbed his head. "To know the part of the Order requires knowing the greater strategy. In the eventuality of an invasion by sea, it is likely fifty-eight of the one hundred and twelve ships in the Ilberian Armada will attempt to disembark directly on Southport's docks. The other fifty-four may maintain the perimeter to negate any possibility of Baltesian ships escaping."

The words spilled off his tongue, tumbling into one another. Leiyn had to concentrate just to parse them.

"Our soldiers will likely be able to hold off any landing parties," the conqueror continued. "The eventuality for which I cannot account are the odiosas aboard their ships."

"Which is where I come in," Leiyn supplied.

If Luca heard her, he gave no indication of it. "Lord Mauricio has reported the Order of Mahia is unlikely to be proficient before Ilberia presses forward with an attack. Thus, the Prima Maha is to coordinate her efforts with the wisdoms of Altan Gaz, led by Wise Jegu Qayag."

Am I invisible? Instead of growing irritated, however, Leiyn found she was beginning to understand the man. Foreign and strange though his behavior was, she could identify the logic his mind followed. It made it easier to swallow the rest.

"Perhaps I should speak to Wise Jegu," she said.

The conqueror looked at her, eyelids flaring, as if he only now saw her. After a pause, he answered, "He will be here soon."

Resisting the urge to exchange a glance with Isla, Leiyn nodded.

"It is my understanding that the Prima Maha can command titans. Without intelligence regarding the extent of Catedrál power, we must assume the least favorable externality: that odiosas can also command titans."

Leiyn opened her mouth to protest, then paused. She had only come into conflict with odiosas twice throughout her life. One of those occasions had been while facing off against titan trappers, a group of poachers that had somehow subdued a hill tortoise and were mining stone from it when she caught them. It only stood to reason that the odiosa had been responsible for the docility of the spirit beast. Yet, until that moment, she had never fully formed the realization.

A commotion behind them compelled Leiyn to turn around. The same wiseman she had seen in the council chamber made his way toward them, soldiers parting before him with respectful speed. Unlike her esse, which she held tightly within, the Gazian's spread out to touch those surrounding him, like the legs of a cautious spider feeling his way through an enemy's lair.

Leiyn marveled at his control, though she wondered why he did it. To track every movement around him? Or did he manipulate them somehow—perhaps inspiring such careful respect?

If the conqueror was touched by Jegu's influence, he showed no sign of it. His gaze lingered on the wisdom as little as it had Leiyn and her comrades.

"I have been informing the Prima Maha of her duties," Luca said without preamble. "And that she is to submit to your counsel."

Submit was not a word Leiyn was used to swallowing. At a look from Isla, though, she held her tongue and gave the wisdom a respectful nod. "I look forward to working with you, Wise Jegu."

"And I you, Prima Leiyn." The man's voice was deep and rich, the effect accentuated by his accent. "Many whispers fill my ears of your deeds here."

Her cheeks warmed, but Leiyn fought down the flush. "I've done what I could."

The wisdom's gaze lingered before he turned to Isla. "Envoy Isla."

"Wise Jegu." Isla bowed, achieving a more graceful and proper showing than Leiyn.

"And one of my former countrymen." Jegu spoke this last to Batu. His expression remained placid, yet Leiyn felt hostility radiating from him. She longed to step between them, but Isla had already angled her body to be in her way, anticipating her protectiveness.

Batu remained impassive before the accusation. Bowing stiffly, he spoke without a hint of resentment, "Wise Jegu, you honor me with your attention."

The wisdom studied him, the corners of his mouth pinching, before turning back to the conqueror. "I understand you had a request of me."

Luca's gaze had already wandered back to the charts he had been studying before, either oblivious or unbothered by the tensions playing out before him. "Yes. Please explain your expectations for the Prima Maha in the event of an offensive on Southport."

"As you wish, Lord Conqueror." Jegu turned back to Leiyn. "I have been privileged with leading my fellow wisdoms in the defense of your city. Five others have accompanied me here. While the Gast secret of commanding an *avaga*—a titan—is beyond our knowledge, each of us is skilled in repelling them. I assume you have this capability in addition to your other talents?"

"I do."

The wisdom's disrespect toward Batu cooled Leiyn's opinion, little inclining to confess the full extent of her abilities.

The wisdom nodded, looking thoughtful. "Very well. We shall rely upon your skill, should an invasion come."

"Then I hope to never work with you." She smiled, disguising the insult as a joke.

"The Prima Maha will cover the area closest to the Lord Governor's villa," Luca said, barreling forward like a bull into a rotten fence. "This will shield a portion of the docks and surrounding estates. Wise Jegu and his wisdoms are to protect the rest of the city and bay."

Jegu bowed. "We shall fulfill this expectation to the fullest extent of our ability."

"Good, good." Luca's gaze lingered on the maps. After a disjointed pause, he jerked his head up and blurted out, "Thank you, Wise Jegu."

"In the gods' eyes." The wisdom's eyes swept over them all one last time before he turned back the way he had entered.

"Must you make enemies of all our allies?" Isla muttered as they watched the wisdom disappear among the soldiers.

"Not all of them." Leiyn glanced at her friend. "I won over the Gasts, didn't I?"

Isla let out a disbelieving huff.

"The others in the Order of Mahia," Luca interjected. "The... mahitas. They can direct titans as the Prima Maha can?"

Leiyn tried remembering where they had left off. "No. And it'll be a long time before we know if any are capable of it."

Only then did the conqueror stare at her. "They cannot command titans?"

"They're new. Fresh recruits," she added, thinking it might make more sense to him. "Using magic is like learning to fight as a soldier. They're at the beginning of that training."

Luca's brow wrinkled. "Baltesia must have titans on our side. If the mahitas cannot help, the responsibility falls to the Prima Maha alone."

Leiyn flashed him a bracing smile. She felt her companions' gazes on her. Both knew how this would weigh on her.

I can bear it. I must.

"I'll do what I can," she said.

The conqueror stared, but finally his gaze drifted back to the papers on his desk.

"Are we dismissed, Lord Conqueror?" Isla asked.

"Yes. You are dismissed." He never looked up.

They gave their half-hearted farewells, then found their way out of the barracks.

14

RISING TIDE

As she often had at the Wilds Lodge, Leiyn sought solace on the bow range.

Placed adjacent to the guards' courtyard, she had become familiar with the small range over the past months. She made her way there directly after returning from the visit with the conqueror.

"You sure you don't want us to wait?" Isla asked as they split to go to the feast hall. "Batu's always ravenous, but I can hold off."

"I'll be fine."

More talking was the last thing Leiyn wanted. Sensing her mood, her friends departed for their meal while Leiyn fetched her bow.

To her relief, she had the range to herself. As she set her feet shoulder-width apart and nocked a practice arrow, Leiyn felt the tension ease from her shoulders.

This was what she needed. The strain of the bowstring. The pointed focus. The guiding of the arrow's path. Long had she tired of her other burdens, her weighty concerns. Being the Prima Maha. The only Baltesian who could raise a titan.

The hills, the forests, the rivers, the beasts—these were the poultice to the malaise spreading through her. She needed time among them to find herself again. Time to wander.

The very thing denied by her duties.

She was a ranger at heart. She longed for those days when that was all she had needed to be. Yet they were no more. And, staring down her path, she saw no end to unwanted duties.

The sky burned vermilion when she sensed someone approaching, their esse bright and distinctive. Reluctantly, Leiyn lowered her bow and turned.

"Hello, Genevieve."

The girl flinched. At once, Leiyn regretted her stiff greeting. Try as she might, she always acted distant toward the girl.

Leiyn forced a smile and gentled her tone. "Is there something I can help you with?"

Genevieve stopped several paces away. One of the few mahitas to take Mauricio's offer to stay at the villa, Leiyn had done her best to avoid her while moving about the compound. She wondered if that had not gone unnoticed by the girl. Her usual cheer was absent, her small hands clenched into fists. Her warm eyes never wavered from Leiyn.

Then tears began streaming down her cheeks.

Panic rustled through Leiyn. "What is it? What's wrong?" Setting down her bow, she stepped forward before stuttering to a halt.

"Why don't you like me?"

Leiyn had not known what she expected. But it was not this.

"Who says I don't?" Realizing how that sounded, Leiyn added, "I like you, of course I do."

"You don't. You barely look at me. You never say I do a good job. You don't call me 'Evie' even though I asked you to. Even though everyone else does." The girl stared at her feet. "But you're right. I'm not good enough. I cannot do this. Maybe... maybe I should go home."

Toughen up. The words pressed behind Leiyn's teeth. It was what her father would have told her, *had* told her many times throughout her childhood.

But that had been what Leiyn needed to hear. She had always been resilient and stubborn. Under her father's guidance, she only became more so.

Genevieve was molded from different clay. She was kind. Open-hearted. Soft, yes, and perhaps unsuited to the role into which she had been thrust. But Isla had shown Leiyn there was strength in gentleness. She tried to think of what her friend would say.

"Gene—" Leiyn swallowed, then pressed on. "Evie. I'm sorry."

The girl looked up. Her eyes still shone with tears, yet sparks had ignited behind them.

"What do you mean?" Evie whispered.

Leiyn fought a grimace. "You're right. I've been distant. But it's not because of you. It's our home."

"Orille?"

"Yes. I try not to think about it. The memories are..." She gestured, grasping for the right words, but they eluded her. "Still painful."

Evie nodded solemnly. "I understand."

Leiyn started. "You do?"

The girl tilted her head to the side. "I think so. I have mahia, too, remember? I had to hide myself like you."

How could she have forgotten? It would have been no easier for Evie than it had been for her. Leiyn wondered what her parents had told her. If she had even shared it with them. Though, knowing the girl's outspoken nature, she had to have shared it with someone.

Still, they both knew the isolation of being different. Of having a stain upon your soul.

Leiyn advanced as if toward a wild animal caught in a trap. She halted an arm's length away.

"I'll do better. I promise. So no more talk of leaving, alright?"

Evie's eyes sparkled afresh. She nodded. "Alright."

Before she could reply, the girl rushed forward and threw her arms around her.

Shock stiffened Leiyn before she relented to the embrace. No more remaining aloof. Evie squeezed her tight, and Leiyn held her back. Their esses, open to one another, touched tentatively. Warmth grew between them. She wondered if this was what it would have been like having a little sister. Or a daughter.

One hells of a mother you'd make.

After a time, the girl stepped away, sniffing and cuffing her nose. "Sorry. I didn't mean to—"

"It's alright." Leiyn smiled. "I think I needed it, too."

To her relief, Evie's usual wide smile awoke. Wiping her eyes dry, she brought herself up straight again.

"See you tomorrow, Prima Maha."

"Tomorrow then, Evie."

That night, Leiyn lay awake in her bed.

She stared at the ceiling, unseeing, thoughts wandering. Renewing Evie's spirits had heartened her for the rest of the evening, banishing her own worries and doubts more thoroughly than the bow practice had. She had eaten a healthy meal and indulged in less alcohol than had become her habit. Upon visiting Isla and Batu, they had noticed the change. Isla teased her, asking if she had found another woman to lift her spirits, drawing Leiyn's mock ire.

But the consolation had not lasted. Alone in the dark, her fears returned twofold. She'd had a small epiphany in her teaching, but what did it matter? It would not prepare Evie any faster for the horrors she was doomed to face, nor any of the other students. They were too inexperienced, too far behind. They would never be ready in time.

Is that truly what worries you, Firebrand?

Gan had once said something that stuck with her, a rare moment of poignancy for the jesting ranger. "That's the problem with forging people into weapons," he had mused. "Even among friends, their edges cut."

She had made herself into a weapon long before Tadeo had honed and polished her instincts. Anger and deep-rooted hatred had been like oil on the blade, readying her for the killing stroke.

But with the old wounds healing, Leiyn felt like a sword exposed to the elements. Rust had settled in and remained, no matter how she scrubbed at it.

I'm not meant for this.

Life had been simple once. She had been responsible for herself and her friends, and that was all. She wished it could be simple again.

Wishing for something makes it grow no nearer.

Tadeo's words, sighed by ghostly lips, counseled her yet again. She pulled out his fox figurine and clutched it tight. The lines had dulled, yet they dug into her skin. He would have meant the words to comfort her, a balm to ease the surrender to sleep. But Leiyn saw a different lesson in them now.

Rising, she removed her nightgown—a necessary capitulation to propriety while in the governor's home—then drew on her Iritu garb and fastened on her weapons belt. Fully clothed, she exited the manor and compound. The guards on watch gave her odd looks, but upon her request, they opened the outer gate. She felt their eyes on her back as she strode down the street toward the harbor.

"Stay safe, Prima Maha," one called after her, a man with closely shorn dark hair and dark eyes.

She acknowledged it with a raised hand.

At the warehouse, too, she was swiftly admitted. Few workers were in at the late hour, though the storehouse was rarely without activity in these days of war. She ignored those present as she crossed the cluttered space to the cage on the far end. A guard, a young fellow with glossy chin-length locks Isla would have thought handsome, sat at on a stool nearby, idly popping grapes into his mouth. At her look, he gave her a nod. She returned it.

The odiosa raised his head as she neared. His robes hung more off his thinning frame with each visit, despite the platter of food sitting in one corner. Leiyn had heard from Mauricio that they had begun having to forcibly feed him. His will to live had died with his capture, it seemed.

Leiyn stood close to the cage with her arms crossed. She had grown callused to her initial fear, yet each time she laid eyes on the husk of a man, a fraction of it resurfaced. But she was a practiced hand at shoving down her feelings.

"Odiosa," she said to him. "Come here."

The enslaved maha only blinked slowly at her. His eyelids appeared heavy as rain clouds about to spill open.

She sighed. "Instrument. I command you to come here." She hated referring to him that way, but it was the only way she could provoke a response.

A wheezing breath issued from his chapped lips as his chest rose and fell. "You are not Master," he whispered. "You do not serve Master."

"And who is your Master, Instrument?"

Again, she received only silence.

Leiyn had harbored scant hope for the attempt. Distaste for her next measure had forced her to it.

There was no stopping it now.

She turned to the comely guard. "I need to enter."

"Now?" Finishing the grapes, he tossed the remaining stem on a small sack at his feet and stood, brushing his hands clean. "As you wish. Me, I wouldn't get my hands dirty if I didn't have to."

She gave him a thin smile. "That's assuming I have a choice."

With a shrug, the guard ambled over and retrieved the ring of keys from where he kept it tucked beneath his gambeson. Fitting a large rusted one into the lock, he swung the door open and swept a gallant hand forward. "Prima Maha."

Leiyn nodded her thanks and stepped inside. She flinched as the odiosa slid to his feet, but he made no move toward her. Even if he did, she was more than a match for him.

But the fear in his eyes—that, she had not prepared for.

It only lasted a moment before the blankness returned, but

Leiyn knew she had not imagined it. Fear was in his posture, how he pressed his back against the bars. Some part of him remembered her, even if he did not show it. He knew what she was capable of.

Firming her jaw, she approached him. "Don't resist," she advised him. "It'll be easier for us both."

At the final step, she lunged and seized his arms by the elbows, then thrust her mahia within.

He struggled, body and mind, but both had weakened throughout the spring and early summer. Leiyn overwhelmed him in moments, yet it took longer to break his will. Even when his rebellion subsided, she felt his presence hovering at the peripheries, waiting like a wolf in the shadows for the first sign of weakness to pounce again.

Ignoring him, Leiyn focused on his branded lifemark. Once more, the burning hand presented itself to her. The shadowy figure holding it up almost seemed to mock her as its impervious defense continued.

She stood there, considering it, as it smoldered against her lifesense. She had tried every trick she could think of to break it. Pressed against it with all her will and strength. Tried circumventing it with guile, speed, and distraction. Even implored the odiosa with reason and bribes.

Nothing had lessened the vivacity of its defense. It burned as furious and frenzied as ever, even as its owner's lifefire dimmed. Almost as if it leeched its strength from his.

Only then did she realize there was one avenue she had not tried.

It's a scar. A wound. One that always festers.

A wound—seen that way, there was only one thing to be done for it. Leiyn drew in a deep breath, exhaled it. Then she filled the odiosa once more with her esse.

This time, she did not come to harm, but to heal.

Her touch was gentle as she offered her essence to the burning hand, cool and inviting as an oasis to the thirsty. The brand did not take her offer, but the odiosa did. Ingesting it like parched earth would fresh rain, he absorbed her strength and began brightening his own.

Abruptly, she cut off the stream. It would not work that way. Strengthen the odiosa, and she would only bolster the brand's resistance. A parasite only benefited from gifts to its host.

She did not need to be gentle to heal.

Treating the brand like she would an infection, she formed her mahia into a substance akin to cleansing water. Inundating the hand with it, she tried to burn as cold as it did hot.

She heard the odiosa gasp, his filthy fingers leaving trails of grease on her sleeves. She paid him no heed; she could not afford to. The brand refused to yield. Every ounce of power thrown against it was matched.

Yet like any injury, she felt its resistance waning before the healing. It was strong and drew on the odiosa's lifeforce, but that was swiftly reaching its limit.

More, Firebrand!

She drew on Xepi's amber beads, ever kept at her hip, guzzling down lifeforce like Feral at a trough after a hard ride. Draining one bead after another, she surrounded the brand with healing power. There was nowhere it could escape the flood.

Its flames dampened. The tips of the fingers curled downward. Sensing it weakening, Leiyn drew from the last of the beads and summoned her mahia into a tidal wave. The odiosa shrieked, but with the roar of the clashing lifeforce filling her being, she barely heard it.

The wave crashed into the hand—and the brand extinguished.

Suddenly, Leiyn was rushing past. The shadowy figure came into focus. An aged woman stood with her arm outstretched, white-robed and elegantly decorated. A tiara of gold set with topaz rested on her brow. Gray hair was carefully braided into a crown, then tucked under a thin, silk hood, only halfway covering her head. Her eyes were cold and imperious, but not in the way of odiosas. Her cruelty was a thing alive, a fire eager to consume, always hungering for more.

All of that might not have been enough to know her, but the shape of her golden medallion was. The sun. The sign of Omn Itself.

The Altacura.

Words reverberated through Leiyn as the leader of the Catedrál—or the memory of her, at least—spoke. *"Submit. Become the Instrument of thy Master. You shall serve me and mine until death doth part thine spirit from thine flesh. Submit!"*

Leiyn braced, expecting the branding to flood forward. Even recalled, the agony would be unpleasant to endure. But no blistering power issued forth.

Instead, something else behind the Altacura rose, so enormous it blotted out all hint of light.

With the aged woman taken for scale, this creature was larger than any titan she had encountered. A dozen or more hill tortoises could have fit in its shadow. Still, it loomed ever larger, and where its influence stretched, esse went dark.

Leiyn almost fled. But this was only the odiosa's lifemark now, a core memory. It could not truly harm her.

The shadow fell over Leiyn.

She felt it as if she had been present at this memory's formation. Its consideration was heavier than the sky, heavier than all of Unera. It dragged her down, a tide more irresistible than the kraken's. She could not breathe, could not think. Only panic and the need to flee remained to her.

Leiyn wrenched free.

Tripping on the food platter, she went sprawling. Leiyn cursed every vile profanity she could think of as she scrambled back to her feet and waved away the guard, who hovered nearby. She had eyes only for the odiosa still crumpled against the opposite end of the cage.

His eyelids fluttered, half revealing his eyes. Then they fully opened and focused on her.

"Where... am I?"

She could only stare. The quality in his voice had shifted.

Where only flat intonation had existed before, now emotion had returned. Not only that—*life*.

He had said *I*, not *Instrument*. That alone was proof enough.

Leiyn held up her hands and approached as she would an injured wild animal. "Don't worry. You're safe now."

"Safe..." The man groaned as he dragged on the bars to sit up straighter. His gaze remained vague, but it sharpened with each passing moment. "Am I your... prisoner?"

"You were," she admitted. "But I don't think you need remain so. You were an odiosa—do you remember?"

"Odiosa... Yes." His gaze grew distant, his brow furrowed. "Yes, I remember. But it is like a dream." He looked up. "How long?"

Leiyn grimaced and crouched so she was eye level with him. "I don't know. Too long."

A rattling laugh issued from the freed man. "That's for certain."

"Do you have a name?"

The amusement faded. "Yes. I think I did." His eyes widened, his mouth falling open. "I *do*. Wynn. I am Wynn of Saints' Crossing."

She gave him a small smile. "Nice to you meet you, Wynn. I'm Leiyn."

"Leiyn..."

The former odiosa's eyes crossed even as her name passed his lips. She winced as she watched him slump back to the filthy bottom of the cage. The momentary clarity fled along with consciousness.

Cautiously, she edged over to him and pressed her fingers to his neck. His pulse was light but steady. She pressed her mahia into him and found the same of his lifefire.

He would live.

Sighing, Leiyn rose and left the cage, then faced the guard, who watched with wide eyes outside the door.

"Keep him here for the moment," she told him, "but see to it that he has food and clothes for when he awakens. And fetch me as soon as he does. I don't care when it is—day or night, you send someone for me at the Lord Governor's villa. Understood?"

"Yes, Prima Maha." The young man had lost all color to his face. He seemed even more deeply shocked by what had occurred than she was.

"Good." She started to move past him, then paused. "Take care of him. Please. He could signal the turn of the tide."

Only once the guard nodded did Leiyn turn and stride from the warehouse.

⁓ ⁓

Back in her bed, sleep kept far out of reach. She hardly minded. Too much remained to be sorted through for her to feel the need for rest.

Odiosas can be saved. We can save them.

She had not exaggerated her declaration to Wynn's guard. The former odiosa—so long as he remained so—showed a future none of them had dreamed possible. Freeing those enslaved to the Union and the Catedrál. Righting a centuries-old sin while gaining an advantage in the war.

Ending the horror of people being caged in their own minds.

And that was only the start of what she had learned. The Altacura, from what she could tell of the branding memory, was a maha. That Gran Ayda possessed mahia did not come as a surprise. The presence of priestess mahas—like the one that had tricked Leiyn before the start of the war with the Union—had been an indication that not all was as it seemed with the Holy Catedrál. But to confirm the head of the institution was a maha was still disquieting.

Most perplexing was what had come after: the menacing presence behind the Altacura. She could only guess at what it was. Titans came as close to what she had sensed from it, both in size and sorcery, but not even they could match it. And she could not imagine it could ever be leashed.

Even in memory, it had felt like standing in the presence of a god. One as full of death as it was of life.

She longed to discuss it with Isla and Batu, but for once, the prudent side of her reigned supreme.

Breathe, Firebrand. Just breathe.

Exhaling, Leiyn let it all go. At last, sleep bundled her into its folds.

—— ⁓ ——

She woke to drowning.

Weight pressed on her, crushing. She tried to rise, to prove it was only a dream, but the swell sucked her back down. It was a rising tide, its pull building with every passing moment. She flailed against it, fighting with all her strength, but it was as if she struggled against the entirety of the ocean.

Swim, damn you!

Panic gave way to fury. Summoning her every scrap of energy, she formed walls around herself and drove against the current. The sea could not prevail. Like waves before a sharp rock, they broke and parted.

Leiyn gagged, gasped, and finally drew in a ragged breath.

She was not in water; she still lay in her bed, drenched only with sweat. She had not been drowning—it was her mahia, inundated with lifeforce.

Only one being could do such a thing.

"Titan." Her tongue was clumsy. The word sounded distant to her ears. Her lifesense quickly found the kraken at the center of the whirlpool welling in the bay. But others might not sense it in time.

She had to warn them. She sucked in a deeper breath.

"A titan's rising!"

Too quiet. Would anyone hear through the walls? Leiyn levered herself upright. She would have to run in her shift through the halls, screaming the alarm. Undignified, but war left little time for propriety.

Her feet never touched the floor.

A flash of movement, a blur of esse—her only warnings.

Something slammed into her sternum.

She fell back, stunned, limp. The cold of shock. The fire of agony. Strength drained from her body. With its last vestiges, she raised her head.

And saw the knife buried in her chest.

15

CLINGING

*G*et up! a voice prodded Leiyn. *Fight back!*

She tried. Instead of rising, her head fell back. Her heart flailed against the steel nestled in her flesh, dangerously near. Consciousness leaked out as swiftly as her blood.

Fight, Firebrand!

Leiyn felt the slither of the knife as the assassin drew it out. Would he stab again? Ensure the task was finished? She could not worry about that. It was almost too much effort to follow the movements of his lifeforce.

FIGHT!

The old anger roused. Just a candle's flicker, but in the swallowing darkness, it was all she had to follow. Leiyn summoned her mahia and pressed it against the wound. Like trying to dam a river with only her hands. Icy death flowed in, suffocating her dimming esse.

Xepi's beads!

But even as she had the thought, she remembered she had emptied them of esse healing the odiosa's brand. They lay as dead and drained as she was quickly becoming.

That left only one nearby source: her assailant.

He stood over her, watching her die. Leagues away, for all

she could reach him. For a living being, contact was often necessary to draw out their lifeforce.

She would have to hope she remained strong enough still.

Straining, she sent out her mahia to tug at his vitality. It was like a breeze stirring a bonfire. His lifefire bent toward her supplication, but only sparks crossed the gap between them.

Leiyn lapsed, the agony growing too great. Darkness seeped in, frigid and numbing. Almost welcome in the wake of her pain.

She clung to her fury, the mortar that kept her mind whole.

By her lifesense, she felt another presence nearing. The door to her room banged open.

Someone had come for her.

Her assassin turned to engage them. The newcomer's voice was a distant roar as they clashed. She felt the vibrations of their struggle, but she could not see them, much less act. The best she could do was survive, and even that felt beyond her.

Don't bleed out—stem the wound!

Drawing on her own feeble esse, she started to knit her flesh back together. The ebb of her blood slowed. Too little—death crept closer, its talons tearing deep into her chest.

More. I need more!

The assassin and her would-be savior continued to fight, too far away and moving too fast. But she remembered another source that could provide her enough life. The ally that could save her.

Leiyn reached for Clouded Fang.

Finding their connection felt like trying to locate a gossamer thread in the dark. The bond had been so frail when she last plied it, she was afraid the slightest pressure would snap it.

But she found it, still present and unsevered. With fleeting strength, she followed it down. She could only go so far. She sensed the ash dragon now, but he was so far away, so dim. Out of reach.

Desperate, she called across the fathomless leagues, hoping that her pleas would reach his molten den.

Clouded Fang! Come to me! Please, you must come...

Nothing came in return. Not even a tremor of recognition. Despair swallowed her cries. The titan could not hear her or refused to.

She was going to die.

Almost, she relented to the corpse tide washing over her. Why fear death? She had been promised to it since the day she was born.

But she had never been one to surrender.

Leiyn strove toward the surface. Inhabited her pain-wracked body again. Clotted the blood. Stretched the skin back over the gash.

She clung to life.

As if from nowhere, someone appeared by her side, their body bright with esse. Hands pressed hot against her chilled flesh.

"Leiyn! Wake up, *wake up!* Don't you dare let go. Heal your-self—*you have to heal!*"

Isla. She knew the warm gold of her lifefire. She was glad she was there. Glad she would not die alone.

"*Take it*, Leiyn! Take my strength. Let me help you heal!"

Instinct asserted itself with the invitation. Hungrily, her mahia tried seizing upon the suggestion. Leiyn barely had the strength to hold it back. Begin drawing on Isla's life and she doubted she could stop. She would leave her friend a husk, as she had left others many times before.

Another person, a steady force of green fire, stood next to Isla and pressed a hand over hers.

Batu.

"Use both of us, Leiyn. *Now!*"

Revulsion rose, but the temptation proved too strong. Leiyn tried pulling her hand away, but her friends' grips were too much for her feeble will.

She could not hold out any longer.

As she relented, fire seared up her arm, collecting in a bonfire around the hole in her chest. A scream welled up in her throat. She had no choice but to relent. Now that she had begun, she had to heal quickly. It was Isla and Batu's only chance at survival.

The influx of esse thawed her mind and freed her focus. Taking an active hand, Leiyn guided the healing through the worst of the damage. As she stole yet more life from them, her friends' esses dimmed. She felt them sag over her bed.

Slowly, the darkness receded from Leiyn's chest. Her senses asserted themselves. She inhaled, and there was only a hint of wetness in her lungs.

As soon as she could, Leiyn jerked away from her friends, managing to break free this time. Isla and Batu sank to the floor, gasping for breath.

"Leiyn?" Isla sat up. She had to lean on the bedframe to remain upright.

Leiyn forced herself onto her elbows. No longer fighting to stay alive, her awareness expanded beyond their struggle. The titan in the bay was a blinding, writhing force. For the moment, it was stayed. Six figures across Southport radiated clouds of magic, all pressing toward the spirit beast to hold it back.

Blinking away the scene, Leiyn looked at her friends, then at the body lying still on the floor. Its lifeforce had dimmed to darkness. She tried studying Isla and Batu but could make out little of them. The room was dark and her vision remained uncertain.

"Are you alright?" she croaked.

Isla stared at her before barking an incredulous laugh. "Are *we* alright? Leiyn, that man stabbed you in the chest!"

"I almost killed you."

"We're fine." Batu clambered to his feet. Though she had drawn as much from him as Isla, he barely swayed as he moved toward the door. Only then did she notice the axe in his hand, its head dark with blood.

Leiyn caught Isla's gaze, her vision settling. "Batu killed him?"

Isla nodded, her eyes unfocused. "Before I arrived."

Gratitude washed through her. She had never felt less

deserving of her friends. But she pushed it down. Now was not the time for tender feelings.

Reaching for the bedside table, Leiyn grabbed the pouch of amber beads. They would not do her any good as they were, but it would be better to have them on hand, just in case.

"What are you doing?" Isla clung to the bedframe, eyes wide, still unable to rise from the floor.

Standing, Leiyn was gratified her legs did not give way. "Helping the wisdoms."

"Leiyn, stop! They've held out this long. Take a moment to rest!"

Ignoring her, Leiyn moved to collect her gear, then disrobed. Only a sliver of self-consciousness rose at stripping naked when a corpse lay mere feet from her and Batu stood outside her open door. This was no time for modesty.

"You never change," her friend moaned. "You never will."

"Didn't I just?" With a bleak smile, Leiyn secured her weapons belt around her waist, then let the Iritu artifact make the final adjustments as she kneeled next to the assassin. Little placed him apart. He was dressed in dark clothes suited to his work. His dark hair was shorn short. Blood splattered his face and stained his clothes a darker black. Batu had dealt him the killing wound to his collarbone. Beneath the stains, she detected hints of scars by the scant light.

With a start, she recognized him: the guard at the gate. He had spoken to her that night and wished her safety. He had existed within Mauricio's own household, passing innocently by on countless occasions.

Had he plotted her murder the entire time she had been here? Why had he chosen now to strike?

It also put the other guards under suspicion. How many more among them were Goldbloods fanatical enough to kill? But there was no time to worry about it now.

Stifling a groan, Leiyn rose and made for the door. "Stay here," she told Isla before exiting.

"Where are you going?" Batu leaned against the wall outside

her door. The commotion had brought others out of their room. More lamps brightened the corridor with each passing moment. Other guests of the villa gaped at them, clad in nothing but their bedclothes, before retreating behind their doors. At the far end, two guards headed toward them, faces set in hard grimaces.

"Handle them." Leiyn nodded toward the pair before staggering off in the other direction.

"Leiyn!"

She ignored Batu's call and compelled her legs into a long stride. Her body threatened to tumble sideways with each step, but she managed to keep her balance. Running was out of the question. Just a glance at the trembling light of her esse told her she was already pushing toward her limits.

What choice do I have?

She made for a sea-facing balcony, ignoring all she passed. When guards tried to stop her, she ordered them aside, and they obeyed. Every person in the villa recognized the Tideraiser. With blood splattered down her neck and speckling her face, few dared question where she went.

At last, she reached the balcony doors. Throwing them wide open, Leiyn stepped out into a storm.

Rain lashed her face. A gale howled in her ears. Trembling with the cold, she leaned into the wind and fought her way to the balustrade. When she reached it, she clung to the stone railing to remain upright.

Then she caught sight of the creature in the bay.

She had once summoned this same kraken, but she had caught only a glimpse of it outside her lifesense. Now awe shivered through her as she beheld its full majesty. The colossal titan loomed over her and the city both. Rising from the sea, it was several stories tall, eclipsing even the generous height of the villa. A bulbous body emerged from the center, while a litany of limbs waved in the sky above. Seawater composed its form. Foam from the lashed water and trails of seaweed and debris outlined its figure. Waves and ripples ran along it like it possessed a tide all its own. Even more imposing was the esse, billowing outward like sea spray against a rock, blistering like salt in a wound.

The Wight on the Tide, sailors called it. Now, beholding the sea titan, she understood why.

The irony of a kraken attacking Southport did not escape her. Ilberia had taken the symbol of their resistance and turned it against them. But it was hardly her greatest concern. Unless it was driven back, no one would remain in Southport to lament that loss.

Striving to remain upright, Leiyn rallied her spirit and dredged up the last vestiges of her lifeforce. All along the city coast, she felt the bright spots where the wisdoms stood throwing their magic against the titan. They had held so far, but she did not know if they could do more than that.

She had turned back a titan before. They might need her guidance.

Leiyn reached out with her mahia. Among the ships beyond, withdrawn a safe distance from the titan, she could sense the odiosas who controlled the titan. They were many leagues away, farther than Patli had been when he had commanded the sand stampede against Qasaar, and they appeared to be pooling their power together. Yet, if she began striking them, perhaps she could stop this at its source.

Before she could make the attempt, a shift in the air gave her pause. Leiyn gazed upon the titan, only to see the top of it fall away. Like an axe had split it open, water fell to either side, disintegrating its form and dispersing its esse.

The titan returned to its slumber.

Leiyn clung to her power until the kraken was halfway gone. Only then did she relax her mahia and sag against the railing to watch the rest dissipate. On the ships, the flames of the odiosas faded back to their normal luminosity: brighter than average, but not the bonfires they had been moments before.

It was over. Southport had survived a titan attack.

Yet the city had not gone unscathed. Ships lay in wreckage, including a dozen of the larger ones. Half the docks had been torn apart. A single section of the harbor appeared to have been lashed by one of those watery tentacles. Suspicion rose in her as she identified the affected area. The absence of the caged odiosa's presence confirmed the target.

The kraken had destroyed Mauricio's secret warehouse. It had killed Wynn and the promise of all he represented and knew along with him.

Leiyn rested her head on her arms, taking in breath after breath. She knew she should remain vigilant, but weariness hung too heavy on her limbs. Her mind whirled on, turning through what had happened and what it all meant.

An idea struck her as hard as the knife had her chest.

It's him. All of it, him.

This assault had been devious, meticulous. The assassin had struck her at the precise moment her mahia was most blinded by the titan's awakening. The kraken had attacked where it would hurt most, robbing Baltesia of the chance to learn Ilberia's secrets and hampering its military capabilities. Even with Jegu and his wisdoms turning back the titan in the end, the attack had cost their enemy nothing while dealing Baltesia a grave blow.

A plan of this sophistication and foresight reeked of one individual. The invisible hand guiding this war.

Damn you, Sharo.

Leiyn raised her head to stare blearily over the bay. The waters grew calmer with every moment. The horizon was brightening to gray with the coming sun.

It should have reassured her. Instead, she shuddered and clutched at the railing. Only her friends' swift intervention had prevented the lyshan's scheme from succeeding. She had come within a breath of death this night. And still, she had no clear way forward.

I won't stand by any longer. I can't.

She had acted the loyal subject long enough. Being an envoy. The Prima Maha. The *Tideraiser*. None of those roles would put an end to the war. None would do more than make a dent in their true enemy's ambitions. She had to strike directly at Sharo.

If the feshtado *coward will show his face.*

Stone creaked in her hands. Leiyn released the balustrade to find cracks spiraling away from where she had gripped it. Inadvertently, she had channeled her precious esse to strengthen her limbs. A waste her frail body could scarce afford.

A bitter laugh escaped her as she swayed where she stood. Still, she acted the fool. Ata had set off in search of Sharo. Surely, if she had found him, the dryvan would have come to Leiyn to let her know. And if Ata had not located him, what chance did Leiyn stand?

Yet one fact remained: Leiyn could not remain in Southport.

Wherever Sharo was, she would not find him here. While in the city, she was vulnerable, and not only to further attacks. Perhaps Clouded Fang did not keep away by choice. Perhaps, somehow, Sharo had discovered a way to come between them.

Out there lay answers. Paths forward. Beyond Southport's walls waited the enemy of all. The target at which her arrow must point.

And there was a chance she would not need to hunt Sharo down herself. Given the right circumstances, the lyshan might come to her.

It was not a plan. She had nothing at which to aim. But it was a step forward.

Far better than staying here.

Turning from the balcony, Leiyn wove her way back inside.

PART III

A TRAIL OF AIR

16

FOUR YEARS BEFORE

Feathers fluttered against her skin.

Leiyn jerked her head up and scanned for the offending creature. As she peered into the swampy overgrowth looking for a bird or bug camouflaged against the brown and green, her task of restocking Shelter Swallow was forgotten.

A brush pheasant, perhaps?

But as she felt the soft brush of wings once more, she realized they had no external source. Disquiet filled Leiyn as she stood and lowered her hands to her knives. Her gaze traveled in the direction she had felt the sensation.

"Leiyn? What's wrong?"

Isla approached from behind. As stocking shelters was typically a two-person job, her closest friend had been the first to volunteer with her. Usually, Leiyn would have been glad to have her nearby.

But not when it came to magic.

"I felt something." Leiyn carefully phrased her words. She had hidden her curse from Isla for too long to confess it now. "Might be nothing."

"But it might be something." Isla stepped next to her and squinted west, the direction in which Leiyn stared. "What do you think? A creature we haven't encountered? Or..."

"...a titan." Leiyn nodded. "It doesn't feel dangerous. But we should be careful."

Isla had already turned to fetch her bow and spear from where she had leaned them against a nearby tree. "After you."

The trek took them far beyond their route, out of the Coyote Fens to the edge of the tree line. Hurrying so as not to miss their quarry, Leiyn and Isla drove their horses fast down the paths. Steadfast and Gale were more than a match for the challenge. Their passengers suffered more; rumps battered, legs wearied, and assaulted by the insects rampant throughout the swamps, the ride was far from pleasant.

Yet, as they stepped free of the tree line, all other concerns fell away.

Tadeo had taught them to always be wary of titans, and Leiyn's experiences with their awakenings had cemented the lesson. Yet, looking upon the creatures below, she found herself wishing to throw away all caution.

Never before had she seen titans quite like these.

Two swans, they appeared as, though of gargantuan proportions. The pair swam atop Storm Lake below, their long, sleek bodies shimmering like light dancing upon a pond's surface. Though the lake was long and broad, these titans occupied nearly an eighth of it as they slowly circled its shores.

Her breath caught. The fluttering against her mahia's walls grew as they came into open view. Leiyn scarcely minded. The sight and sense of them were so soothing she could scarcely believe they were titans at all.

"They're beautiful," Isla breathed. A glance showed her to be slack-jawed, eyes wide as a toddler staring at a new toy.

"Suppose they are." Leiyn found her caution returning with Isla's slackening. She peeled her gaze from the dazzling swans to scan the surrounding area. Nothing looked disturbed by the titans' awakening. It had been as gentle as they appeared to be.

"Do you think any of the rangers have seen this before? Surely, they would have told us!"

Leiyn shrugged. "Even if they had, would you have understood if you hadn't seen them?"

"Never." Isla smiled. "I'm glad we got to be here."

"Me too."

Her eyes kept drifting back to the swans, like they were a current she was caught up in. When something moved on the far shore, however, alertness stole back in.

"Isla. Look at the opposite ridge. Do you see them?"

Isla shook her head before squinting. "Your eyes have always been better than mine. What do you see?"

"People. They're watching the titans. Maybe us as well."

"People..." Isla laughed. "That's two rare sights today! They must be skystriders, don't you think?"

Leiyn nodded. Skystriders were nearly as elusive as titans. Ore-Ofe's counterparts to the rangers, they shied away from close contact with the Lodge, preferring to keep to their own in the "Stormhold," as their bastion was called in the Titan Wilds. Ostensibly, they would act peacefully toward them; no colony wished to provoke conflict with another. Yet tension still spread through Leiyn's shoulders.

The arrow is the last resort. Tadeo's words drifted into her mind, and she saw the wisdom in them. Cautiously, she raised the hand that did not hold her bow.

A beat passed. Then two.

One of the figures raised a hand in return.

It was a silent greeting across the half-league separating them. A smile stole free of Leiyn as she let her hand fall. She exhaled her remaining tension with a breath. "Guess they're enjoying the oversized swans, too."

"How could they not?"

They stood there, watching the pair of titans swim about the lake. A rare sense of peace filled Leiyn. Often, the Titan Wilds seemed ferocious and untamed, a place beyond civilization. But it was not wholly one thing. Perhaps nothing ever was.

The world was perilous; that was never in doubt. But it did not mean it was not also full of beauty.

She sucked down another deep breath of clean mountain air, then turned to Isla. "Hold my bow. I need to fetch my sketchbook."

"Hurry!" her friend urged as she shifted her weapons to accept it. "Or you'll miss them leaving!"

Leiyn sprinted for their horses, reveling in all the wonder of the world.

17

MORE

You wish to leave."

Leiyn met Mauricio's placid gaze as he leaned onto his solarium's desk. She hid her hands behind her back so he would not see how tightly she clasped them.

"Not wish," she corrected. "Have to."

For a long moment, the governor beheld her. Eyes heavy from lack of sleep, Mauricio appeared as weary as she had ever seen him. Almost as weary as she felt. Even after the kraken had subsided back to the sea, she had not been able to sleep.

Every time she closed her eyes, knives flashed behind her eyelids.

When he spoke, he sounded as if he chose every word with the utmost care. "I know you have undergone a traumatic experience, but as I have told you, we are ensuring Unionists never again infiltrate this compound."

"This isn't about him."

Rúben, Mauricio had told her his name was. Rúben of the Docks. Strange to put a name to the man who had nearly murdered her.

Yet who he had been did not matter. None of the Goldbloods in their midst did. The true enemy still lay out there.

She had to find him.

"Please, Prima Maha—"

"I cannot be your Prima Maha anymore, Lord Governor."

Slowly, he straightened. The governor of Baltesia was hardly of an imposing height, yet she had the impression of him drawing on every scrap of his authority, as she might with her mahia.

"Our fledgling country has suffered a grave blow. We lost seven frigates and five galleons, not to mention the weapon stores and the odiosa in that warehouse. An odiosa you claim to have freed from his horrid condition." He paused, as if considering the importance of that lost opportunity, then shook his head. "The symbol of our resistance has been stolen from us. Now, you wish to inflict a further setback by robbing the city of its sole competent wielder of magic."

She kept her expression as smooth as stone. A difficult task, given that her restraint lay in shambles since her latest brush with death. "You have Wise Jegu and the wisdoms still. They'll protect Southport as they did last night. I have to go."

"So you have said." Mauricio crossed his arms. "But you have yet to say precisely why."

Leiyn considered the governor. Head still muddled from the battles and the conversations and bustle that had followed them, she was not prepared to make irrevocable decisions. Yet the moment for them had come.

Can I trust him?

The truth—of Sharo, of his plans, of the real reasons they fought this war—was the only explanation she could expect Mauricio to accept even halfway. While she had a chance of forcing her way out of the city if necessary, she remained a Baltesian to her core. She wanted to be loyal and strove to remain so, as circumstances allowed. She did not want to defy Mauricio unnecessarily.

Yet she still had too many questions about the governor, too much she did not know. He could be Sharo's pawn, perfectly placed at the center of this "rebellion" to play both sides of the war against each other and root out any resistance to the lyshan's ultimate conquest. Leiyn knew too little of Sharo's schemes to understand where his puppets lay or the extent of his reach.

The question emerged of its own accord. "Why do you fight?"

Mauricio's eyebrows shot up. "Pardon?"

"Why are you doing this? Any of this?" Leiyn waved a hand around the solarium. "You came here from Ilberia. Studied in Ilberia. As far as I know, your family is back there. Why throw all of that away to lead a revolution?"

She finished, breathless, her stare challenging. The governor's expression spasmed, but he held her gaze.

"You are correct on all counts. I have many ties to the Union that I must assume were severed when we stood against Lord Armando. My father and mother, my sisters and brother... I wonder if I shall ever communicate with them again." Mauricio fell quiet, his gaze dropping before it rose to her again. "But there is one question you failed to ask: how I came to govern Baltesia."

Leiyn crossed her arms and raised an eyebrow.

Mauricio leaned back and waved a hand, as if warding off a foul scent. "As you might have guessed, I was born to wealth and noble heritage. Yet, as the third of five children, I stood to inherit very little of my family estate. The Ancestral tradition is for the eldest daughter to receive the majority of the holdings to keep them intact, and the eldest son be bequeathed a substantial dowry to expand the family connections."

She repressed a snort. A dismal system all around, with children treated unequally and used as pawns to expand power. But, wanting to hear more, Leiyn held her tongue.

"I knew early in life," Mauricio continued, "that I would have to find my own way in the world. So I did. I excelled at my boarding school and in university. I caught the eye of the headmistress, who recommended me to the Caelrey's own staff. From there, diligent work and, if you'll excuse me for saying it, a charming disposition won me into the good graces of His Imperial Majesty."

The governor chuckled and took a drink of his brandy. "All this should only increase your suspicions, of course. If I have a relationship with the World King himself, why would I defy him? But there is a thread of which I have yet to inform you, which has intersected my life to inform my most every decision."

Mauricio moved from his posture of repose to lean onto his desk, eyes bright with yen. His lifefire burned a little hotter. Leiyn held steady before this change, though part of her wanted to take a step back.

"And that is?" she prompted when the silence stretched.

A smile curled his lips. "That I despise the entire system. I always have. My disdain for it has only matured with growing familiarity. From a young age, I questioned and searched for an alternate way of governing a state. My inquiries grew quieter when I realized the damage they might do to my career, when a curious mind is seen as sinister rather than merely inquisitive. But the questions never faded.

"When the Caelrey requested I fill the vacancy left by the former governor's death, I saw my opportunity. The chance to create something different. Something better. A government that ruled justly and with equality. Baltesia was the castle I would form from sand, if you will, and I was eager to dirty my hands."

His hands clenched into fists, but as Mauricio sighed, he loosened them and sank back into his chair. "But governing is trickier than it seems from the outside, I imagine. Ideals are swiftly compromised in favor of results. You've seen my council: in place of landed gentry, we have merchant lords pursuing their interests over those of the territory. I have not always ruled as righteously as I wish." The governor paused and sipped again from his brandy. As he set the glass down, his eyes recaptured Leiyn's gaze. "But I have kept sight of my ultimate aim. To create a nation unlike any other."

She had to admit his vision resonated with her. Leiyn had

no desire to rule, but justice was a thing the world sorely lacked. If Mauricio could bring a measure of it to Baltesia, it would be a start.

But she did not relax yet.

"So that's it? You had a dream and gave up everything to see it through?"

Mauricio spread his arms. "That's it. Just a man keeping true to his convictions. Alas, no melancholic story spawned these drastic actions. My insanity is of my own invention."

Leiyn let her arms fall to her side and afforded him a small smile. "I wouldn't have trusted a tragedy if you had fed it to me. Stories are the worst sort of lies."

"Quite true, quite true!" The governor laughed and drained his glass. "Now that I've won your trust, you must answer my question. Why must you leave? What do you seek out in the Veiled Lands that you will not find here?"

"Peace of mind," she quipped. Despite her earlier reservations, she believed Mauricio's explanation. He might be wily and suave, but he was also genuine. And if he was Sharo's tool, could letting him know she knew of his master's plans make anything worse?

She needed allies in this war, and the governor of Baltesia would make for a powerful one.

"You remember the enemies I fought beside the Gasts. The lyshans."

"Difficult to forget them." Mauricio feigned a shudder. "Dryvans are frightening enough. Malevolent ones may give me nightmares."

"I didn't tell you everything about them. There was one among their number different from the rest. He's sly and... zealous. I don't know his motivations or how far his reach extends. But he knows too many things that he shouldn't."

The governor held still, transfixed by her words. "And what is he doing?" he asked, hushed.

Leiyn grimaced, hating to admit the truth. But keeping it unspoken made it no less true.

"Destroying us. The Tricolonies. The Ancestral Lands. The dryvans." She swept a hand out. "He implied that he's behind this... 'secessionary conflict.'" She smiled despite herself. "Though he claims it is because he wants to rule, that he desires power for power's sake, the result is the same. Death follows in his wake."

Mauricio wrinkled his brow but accepted the damning news with remarkable calm. Too much calm?

No. Don't doubt him now.

"This... enemy," he said after a long pause. "Does he have a name?"

"Sharo is the only one I know."

"Sharo..." The governor nodded. "Am I correct in assuming you believe him to be behind the assassination attempt?"

She hid her surprise poorly. It was a leap of logic that she had not expected him to make. Again, Mauricio showed himself to possess an incisive mind.

"Yes," Leiyn admitted. "I cannot imagine Suncoats being clever enough to think of it on their own."

"I wouldn't say that. You met Lord Armando. Rigid and inflexible though he may have been, he was damned clever as well. They know what you mean to Baltesia, and not only for your power." He waved a hand at the kraken-emblazoned flag hanging in his solarium. "You're a symbol, an... inspiration. They would want to take that away from us if they could."

She remained unconvinced but saw little point in arguing. "Still. I cannot ignore him any longer. I must find and fight him if I can. Only then can we hope to win."

"Then I trust you have an idea of where he might be? Surely not beyond the Silvertusks?"

"No, not there." But what else could she say? Where could she find him? She could travel to Glade hoping Ata or one of the other dryvans might lead her to Sharo. But if Ata had found him, surely she would have fetched Leiyn.

Or would she?

The dryvan had always been unpredictable. They called

one another "friend" now, but could she truly say she knew what Ata would do?

Mauricio cleared his throat, breaking the silence. "If you do not know where you must go, I must implore you once more to stay, if only to train your mahitas. Perhaps by the time they are fit to fight in your stead, you will have some better idea—"

"No. I cannot stay." She fought against the despair welling up in her, clinging instead to her hatred for the lyshan responsible for it. "I cannot do what I must within these walls. If I'm to be useful in this war, I must learn more. Reach for more. *Be* more. Pretending to be the Prima Maha will only hold me back."

The governor's expression tightened with her every word. "Then we must depend upon Wise Jegu's generosity. Perhaps if he or one of his wisdoms consents to training the Order in your stead, we will not lose too much progress."

Leiyn's chest loosened at the suggestion. "That would be best, if they're willing."

"But," Mauricio continued, "since you seem to have little sense of direction, forgive me for making a second suggestion. I was intending to send Envoy Isla to Ore-Ofe to win over their mahas to our cause."

Just like that, it became difficult to breathe again.

"You wouldn't send her on her own," she said in a low voice.

The governor raised an eyebrow. "Not unguarded, if that's what you mean. I expect her not-so-secret beau would wish to travel with her. But if you mean to leave the city, you might go with them and provide additional protection."

It represented an obligation of a different kind, one that restricted Leiyn's options. Yet, though she was loath to admit it, she was an eagle flying in circles with no better direction to move. Letting Isla and Batu travel across perilous territory, headed for a place that could be hostile to them—Isla especially, with her heretical background—was unthinkable. She had worried enough when they traveled through the heart of Baltesia, and that had been before the war began in full.

Taking her silence for hesitation, Mauricio pressed his

argument. "The mahas there call themselves *eesuwé*. All belong and are loyal to the *Kekére*—the 'Coterie,' in translation. I believe their order lives in a tower in their capital, Kunu. These *eesuwé* are said to be more powerful than the Gazian wisdoms by benefit of their formal, rigorous training. Having failed to bring Ore-Ofe into an alliance, I must hope we can convince the Coterie to come to our aid." The governor leaned forward onto his desk with a smile. "Perhaps you'll have a similar effect on them as you had on the Gasts. If you can bring back an *eesu*, or learn some of what they know, perhaps that could change the tide of this war. And, for your purpose, you might learn a trick to use against this Sharo whenever you find him."

Only the last part of his appeal left an impression. If the *eesuwé* were as skilled as Mauricio made them out to be, they might know what was going wrong with her connection to Clouded Fang. As far as she knew, none of the colonies' magic wielders had commanded titans back when they first landed upon the Veiled Lands' shores. But seventy years and war with the Gasts could have changed that.

It was not an ideal plan, but it was a path to follow. One preferable to staying in Southport.

Leiyn sighed. "Fine. I'll go."

"Good, very good." Yet the governor only looked graver for her assent. "There is one additional thing I must say. I've given you plenty of leeway, both now and before. This freedom is far more than I award any other. Please, do not take my generosity for granted. Baltesia needs you, but it cannot stand for you to defy your governor. I feared what you would have forced me to do had you not accepted my second proposal."

Leiyn did not need Isla's political acumen to understand a thinly veiled warning. Even from such a mild-tempered man, she should have expected it. She had defied the governor in saying she would leave her post. All her mahia could not prevent him from condemning or exiling her, should it be his wish, and separating her from her homeland.

Yet instead of apologizing, her spine stiffened and her jaw clenched. Even Mauricio's displeasure could not cow her.

"With all due respect, Lord Mauricio," she said, "I'll do what I must to protect our home."

Not waiting for another censure, Leiyn turned on her heel and strode from his office.

<h1 style="text-align:center">18</h1>

<h2 style="text-align:center">A PATH FORWARD</h2>

Though Leiyn wished to depart Southport the moment she left the governor's solarium, obligations and preparations delayed the outset of their journey.

She found Isla and Batu in Isla's room, but news of their trip had already been broken by Mauricio's messenger, who had brought Isla a writ of diplomacy in an oiled case before Leiyn even met with the governor. Her friends were delighted when she announced she was coming with them.

"I wasn't sure I should even ask," Isla admitted. "I know you hate it here, but with you being the Prima Maha and all..."

"They'll make do," Leiyn replied. It was a sour reminder of the arrangements and farewells still to come.

Packing ate away the rest of the morning. All too soon, she was striding across the courtyard toward the First Temple of Baltesia. Her mind spun with all she must do, and she remained weary from the previous tumultuous night. It felt a near insurmountable task to don the mien of the Prima Maha as she stepped through the doors.

Her students crowded around her before she even stepped inside. "Prima Maha!" Evie said, squeezing ahead of the rest. "Prima Maha! Is it true? Did someone try to kill you? They say you were dying!"

"How could that be?" Estel snapped. "She's up and walking, is she not?"

Leiyn held up her hands for silence. "It's true. An assassin stabbed me through the chest." She cocked an eyebrow at the merchant lady. "I'd show you the scar if it wasn't indecent."

The mahitas shared looks among each other. Before the absurd claim, she could scarcely blame them for doubting, even though every word was true.

"You healed from that?" Reyna shook her head with a slight smile. "My dear, you are a miracle!"

"Not a miracle," Leiyn corrected. "If you work at it, you'll all be capable of doing the same." She let her words sink in, hoping the praise might soften what came next. "But that's not what I need to talk to you about. I've been called away to another duty and can no longer teach you."

The mood in the temple shifted.

"Called away?" Evie exclaimed. "You're leaving?"

"You're the Prima Maha." The look in Nestor's eyes was that of a soldier abandoned by his captain. "You cannot leave."

"I must." Unflinching, Leiyn faced the pain and confusion in her students' eyes. "I know it's not ideal or what you expected, but you will still be protected. The wisdoms of Altan Gaz drove back the titan last night, not me. You remain in good hands."

They were reduced to muttering among themselves. If her words brought any comfort, it did not show on their faces. But time was too short to worry about that.

"Speaking of the wisdoms," Leiyn continued, "Wise Jegu has agreed to send one of his comrades to continue your training. You'll learn as much from them as you would from me."

"I should hope so."

Leiyn jerked around. Absorbed with delivering the news to the Order, she had not noticed the pair approaching from behind. Jegu, who had spoken, stood with a woman in a similar garb. Another wisdom, Leiyn could only guess. She possessed a mature beauty and a piercing dark gaze that seemed to absorb the proceedings with a single look.

"Thank you for coming," Leiyn said, hoping they had not noticed her alarm. "Mahitas, this is Wise Jegu. And you are?"

"Qara Gegeen." The wisdom's answer was smooth, despite Leiyn's abruptness. "Divinities smile upon our meeting, Prima Leiyn."

The generosity of the response put Leiyn to shame, especially when she failed to muster any in return.

"Wise Qara is as skilled as any in Altan Gaz," Jegu said to the members of the Order. His pinched eyes showed he had noted Leiyn's lack of response, but he kept it from creeping into his voice. "She has agreed to take your Prima Maha's place as your instructor."

There was a moment of silence as the mahitas processed this news. Then Reyna and Izan stepped forward and bowed toward the wisdoms.

"Thank you for sharing your knowledge with us," Izan said, grinning as he rose. "We'll be most eager and grateful to learn from you."

Reyna bobbed her head, appearing as sanguine as her husband.

The other students followed them in thanking Qara. Leiyn knew she should be grateful to the couple for being the first to accept this sweeping change, yet she could not deny that it stung. How easily she had been replaced.

"You are too kind," the wisewoman said in reply, her smile at once composed and warm. "It will be an honor to be your teacher. I pray you will learn much from me, and I swear by all the gods I will do my best to teach you."

The students' responses were warm in turn. Qara glanced at Leiyn, a tacit request for permission. She had no choice but to nod back, then watch as the wisdom won the trust of the group in a matter of moments.

This is for the best, Leiyn scolded herself. *For all of us.*

"Wise Qara is a fine instructor." Jegu spoke low so only Leiyn could hear. "You should be grateful she agreed to this."

She met his disapproving gaze. "I am. You must excuse me. I depart today on a pressing errand."

The wisdom's mouth tightened. "So I have heard. Tread lightly among the Ofeans, Prima Maha. I do not think they are as enamored with independence as our peoples."

"Don't fear for me, Wise Jegu. A ranger always treads lightly."

Leiyn afforded him a curt bow, then turned and strode from the temple without a backward glance.

Leiyn had nearly finished saddling Feral by the time Isla and Batu joined her in the villa's stables.

"Someone's eager to be off," Isla noted as she moved to the next pen where her horse, Mottle, was being kept. The gelding practically danced as his mistress neared, displaying far more excitement than Feral ever would for Leiyn.

"Not just me, then," Leiyn replied wryly as her mare fought against being led out.

Batu chuckled and moved to his horse, a spotted blonde. Isla teasingly called him Saikan—"Beauty" in Kalgan—after Batu refused to name the gelding himself.

"Still have to wait for the rest of the company," the former plainsrider pointed out.

Leiyn stopped wrestling against Feral to stare at him. "The rest?"

Isla stepped back out of Mottle's stall wearing a nervous smile. "Ah, yes. Lord Mauricio insisted we bring additional protection."

"Did he forget we're rangers? Or close enough," Leiyn amended with a glance at Batu.

Isla shrugged. "These are dangerous times. A little help cannot hurt."

Leiyn stared at her friend a moment longer. She suspected Isla had not accidentally concealed this bit of information.

Given Leiyn's temper the day before, however, she could scarcely blame her.

"Fine. Where are we meeting them?"

Isla shared a relieved look with Batu. "At the north gate. I'm sure they'll be there as soon as we arrive."

Before long, they had tacked up their horses and rode for the villa's gate. Leiyn tried to ignore the questioning looks of the guards, though she felt their eyes on her as they rode away. She recognized a pair of them—Siany and Tiago, the two who had questioned her in the training yard about her infamy. No doubt they now wondered why the Tideraiser had done so little to protect them. Why she now abandoned them.

She rubbed at the scar bisecting her chest. The mystique surrounding her had likely been shattered. All the better—she had never wanted it to begin with.

After wading through Southport's bustling main promenade, the northern gate of the outer wall came into view. True to Isla's word, a small band of soldiers awaited them, a dozen in total. They wore light armor suitable for travel with blue sashes tied around one of their arms. Their horses appeared loaded for a long journey.

Among them waited one further surprise. Leiyn startled as she recognized the woman standing at the front of the company. It took a moment to repair her composure.

"Captain Belen!" Leiyn called with forced cheer when they came within earshot. "How'd you wind up with the short straw?"

The wall captain smiled, the red scar on her cheek pulling into a crescent. "Had to track you down when you didn't meet me for that drink."

A lump lodged in Leiyn's throat. She had hoped to avoid the matter altogether, but with Belen accompanying them, she would have to address it eventually.

Though not yet.

"Plenty of time for a drink on the road." Leiyn surprised herself with how easy she sounded. "Shall we be off?"

While Isla and Batu exchanged greetings with Belen and

her crew, the gate guards opened the way for them. Feral shifted, displaying every bit as much eagerness to be off as Leiyn felt. She looked over the verdant hills beyond the rising portcullis and homesteads spread across them. The sparkling sea, a stretch unmarred by the Armada, lay past the shore.

In that moment, the scar on her chest did not pull so tightly.

"Let's go, old girl," Leiyn murmured, pressing in her heels. Feral scarcely needed the encouragement. At the slight pressure, the mare surged forward in a trot. Only Leiyn's firm hand kept her from moving faster.

"Best not delay!" she shouted over her shoulder, not caring how she sounded. For the first time in a long while, she could breathe.

⌒ ⌒

Captain Belen fell in next to Leiyn as the road wound through the first village outside of Southport.

"Wharfhaven," she named it. "I was born here, if you can believe it."

"I can," Leiyn quipped. "You've always had a fishy scent about you."

A surprised laugh stole free of the captain. She gave Leiyn a ponderous look. "A lady might be offended by that."

"Ladies don't become captains."

"Nor rangers."

They fell into companionable silence. Leiyn looked around the village. Like most towns devoted to the ocean, its aroma left much to be desired. The catching, gutting, and smoking of fish was rarely pleasing to the nose. But the houses were clean and kempt, and the villagers were warm in their greetings. Despite the war, life continued here much as it always had.

She wondered how many of these towns would remain standing afterward. No matter which side won, those living on the outskirts of a capital city were likely casualties.

In the corner of her eye, she saw a girl scurrying after a

young boy. Her misbehaving brother, most likely. Leiyn imagined the girl as a young Belen and smiled.

"One of my students is from here," she found herself saying. "A sailor's widow by the name of Tecla."

"I know Widow Tecla! She's your student, is she? One of those you teach magic to?"

Leiyn tensed instinctively, but times were changing. She forced herself to nod.

You don't always have to hide.

"Widow Tecla." Belen shook her head with a bemused smile. "Of all the people to possess mahia, I wouldn't have thought it would be her."

The captain's quick acceptance put Leiyn at ease. "When your life depends on you hiding something, you get good at it."

"I suppose so."

They lapsed into silence. With her lifesense, Leiyn sought after Isla and Batu and found they lagged a dozen paces behind, the rest of the company trailing after. It was not that she disliked Belen's company; to the contrary, they shared an easy rapport. But anytime she thought of Teya, guilt stirred in her gut.

Almost as if she glimpsed Leiyn's thoughts, Belen asked, "Why didn't you come for that drink, anyway?"

Leiyn kept her eyes forward. The captain did not speak accusingly, yet Leiyn could not help but feel a sharp edge in the question. Desperately, she tried to think of a suitable reply. But all she could do was speak the bald truth.

"I'm bound to another."

When Belen did not immediately respond, fear that she had misread the situation awoke in Leiyn. She risked a glance at the captain and found, in defiance of her expectations, the woman was smiling.

"I thought there might be someone. Not her?" Belen jerked her head backward.

"Isla? Never!"

"She does seem tied at the hip to that young Gazian. Batu Khatas, wasn't it?"

Leiyn could only nod, her mind still racing to catch up.

The captain raised an eyebrow. "Oh, don't worry. I'm not a damsel to go off sobbing at being snubbed. There's too few of us to be like that, really."

Too few of us. Only then did it register how much she and Belen had in common.

A smile stole free of her. "If you say so."

The captain's expression turned coy. "So, are you going to tell me about this lucky lady?"

"No."

Belen laughed, the sound of it ringing up and down the village road.

19

CATCHING SMOKE

The next few days down the Via Austral unfolded with pleasant swiftness. Leiyn had felt as tightly bunched as a sailor's knot during the weeks in Southport, but the tangles smoothed out as they left behind the mass of people and responsibilities. Conversation among the company grew friendlier.

Surrounding Southport were villages and homesteads that supported and profited off the city. Traveling through civilization made Leiyn almost feel safe. Only at night did she fret, visions of assassins in the dark keeping her awake and alert into the early morning.

After three days, they passed through the last of the fishing villages. Beyond them lay a wilderness that stretched until the border between Baltesia and Ore-Ofe. In that wilderness, if Belen's reports were accurate, camped a host of Suncoats.

Just like to the north of Southport, Ilberian soldiers were rumored to have made landfall somewhere along the coast. Their precise location varied by the account. In moments like these, Leiyn was grateful to have her mahia. She could at least rely upon not being ambushed, her lifesense able to pick out danger from leagues afar.

But her magic brought its own host of problems. While surrounded by people, she'd had reason to delay investigating her feeble connection to Clouded Fang. Departing society removed the last of her excuses.

She hoped the *eesuwé* could help with it, as Mauricio had suggested, but a hope was no guarantee. Sharo might hunt her down at any moment. Why he had only struck after she had been months in the city remained a mystery, but it had awoken renewed determination in Leiyn. She had grown complacent during the quiet, assuming retaliation would never come.

No more.

On the fourth night of their journey, Leiyn excused herself from camp and headed for a nearby clearing. Her comrades' spirits remained high, the excitement at the outset of a new journey spreading among them like a plague. She was loath to leave; losing the Wilds Lodge had taught her such companionable times were precious. But duty called louder.

Moving far enough away that their voices grew muted and the light of the campfire dimmed, Leiyn sat cross-legged on the ground and tried to focus on the thin thread linking her to the ash dragon. Inhabiting her mahia made her especially attuned to her lifesense. Her attention drifted back to the camp, then the surrounding forest to check for danger. A fruitless task. Though she would sense human assassins that way, lyshans could appear anywhere at a moment's notice.

Leiyn exhaled and attempted to concentrate once more. Finding Clouded Fang's thread came easily enough. Trying not to remember the last time she had tried calling upon it, she directed all her attention at the connection, then sent her awareness down beneath Unera's surface.

Ash dragon. Clouded Fang. Come to me.

She could sense the titan, curled up in a lava flow. Reinforcing the words with a pulse of lifeforce, she surrendered a part of herself to him as she had done at that first summoning.

Clouded Fang, come. Please.

The titan did not rouse. Leiyn dove deeper, straining the limits of her mahia. The pocket of fire where the ash dragon slumbered was far enough that she felt her body tremble with the strain it took to reach it. But driven by desperate abandon, reach she did, until she touched upon the titan himself.

Titan! Heed me!

Leiyn pressed all of her sense of purpose into that shout, pulsing esse again as she did. Feeble though it was over the great distance, it should have been enough to at least rouse the dragon. Yet all it afforded her was a pulse in return, so small as to mean nothing.

She tried seizing him then, to hold him with her mahia and compel him to attention. It was like trying to capture smoke with her hands. Either the distance was too great, or she was too weak to command a titan that way.

She continued to prod the titan for several minutes before the strain became too great. Relenting, Leiyn retracted her mahia and returned to herself. Already, her head throbbed and her muscles felt worn and shaky. Swallowing a hint of sick, she stretched her limbs and wondered if she had grown so weak, or if the sleepless nights were taking their toll. Leiyn rubbed at the scar on her chest, the seam of flesh also renewing its ache.

Old at twenty-six.

The wound was the least of her concerns. Plainly, she would not awaken Clouded Fang as easily as she had before. Perhaps he truly did slumber, and he would not awaken for another decade. But their connection remained. She remembered how it had felt to be flooded with a titan's vitality. Having one ready to draw upon was too keen an advantage to surrender.

"Wishing for something makes it grow no nearer," she muttered, thinking of what Tadeo would do in her stead as she spoke his oft-repeated words.

The answer came at once. Tadeo had not been her only mentor. Another laid dormant within her soul. Ignoring her body's complaints, Leiyn reached for the brighter of the sparks nestled within her esse.

Zuma, please. I need your help.

She felt a growing warmth in response. Heartened, Leiyn pressed her question upon him.

Guide me in binding a titan, as you did before. Help me understand what I'm doing wrong.

No sooner had she formed the question than visions flashed through her mind.

Darkness, then walls illuminated by light. She quickly recognized it. *Qasaar's barracks.* After her disorienting journey into the hidden grotto, it was hard to forget.

She watched through Zuma's eyes as he stumbled down the hall, opposite the way she had gone. Then the scene stuttered, and he was in a different place in the grotto, his journey there missed.

Panic threatened to rise, acrid and bubbling. Did the shaman truncate the memory for her? Or was it being eaten away, his spark fading with time? Xepi had not mentioned sparks fading, but there had been many things she had not said.

Don't think about that now. Focus.

The memory skipped again. Abruptly, Leiyn found Zuma stumbling into the bright wastes of the Barren and looking around, as dazed as she felt. The flickering vision was making her sick but Leiyn gritted her teeth and endured. There was no closing her eyes to this even if she had wanted to. Zuma was trying to show her something. She would be damned if she missed a moment.

After glancing back toward the cliffs, they moved forward, deeper into the wasteland. Leiyn felt Zuma's awareness expand around him, his lifesense seeming to search for something.

Titans. He's showing how he first connected with one.

Swallowing her nausea, she leaned forward, as if to peer deeper into the memory. Zuma came to a halt and stared toward the dusty horizon. There, one of the wardstones towered, black and bold against the dun surroundings. She felt him consider it.

Wondering how to reach titans within the wardstone barrier.

He seemed to decide the walk—which would have taken well over a day on foot—was not worth it, for she felt his lifesense once more expand. This time, Zuma surged down, searching as she had for titans among the stone and earth. Deep he went, then deeper still, well beyond the minuscule life that occupied the upper layers or the waters between layers of rock. Only as he neared magma did his advance falter, then halt. He had reached the end of his limitations.

Yet her anticipation grew. This was the moment. The one he had shown her before she bonded with Clouded Fang. His mahia wavered, then retracted, but she knew it was only the prelude to victory. Failure was a necessary sacrifice for success.

Before Zuma's strength failed, something stirred before him. Burning eyes opened. Inert stone took shape; first a shell, then four legs. A tail and head emerged from the shell.

A hill tortoise, buried deep in the world, awoke and gazed upon Zuma.

The shaman's remembered elation filled Leiyn. He reached for the tortoise, seeking to hold to it. But unlike Leiyn's attempts with Clouded Fang, he gripped it at once. The tortoise seemed pliable and willing. Substantial in a way her ash dragon had not been.

Doubts plagued her, but she stifled them, determined to see the memory through. Another skip, and she witnessed Zuma gasping from his efforts. He clung to the titan like he would drown down there in the earth. She felt every manner of compulsion at his behest be used, then discarded. Then, at last, came the moment she had known must.

Zuma surrendered to the titan.

The hill tortoise rose. Its power trampled the shaman. Zuma collapsed even as the titan took shape in the desert before him. It was unlike any hill tortoise she had seen. In place of trees on its back, the black outcroppings of the Fingers bristled like spines. Its body was orange and red rock, its eyes liquid sand.

It loomed over Zuma, as if contemplating whether or not to crush him.

His fear and doubts made her heart race. Leiyn clutched at the dirt, feeling his agony as her own. Yet she did not pry away, but clung to the memory. She needed to witness every moment. To see how he had succeeded.

Zuma did not dominate it, nor compel it as other commanded titans. He gave of himself willingly. Yet she felt some part of him hold back. The fearful part that did not want to die.

The hill tortoise, three stories tall and twice as many wide, bent its head closer, its nose almost touching the shaman. Almost, it seemed to sniff him, like a dog would a carcass to ensure it was dead. Its esse, pounding and pulverizing as boulders, never ceased to batter Zuma.

She felt a part of him break. Crack. Shatter. His heart thumped in his chest so fast she wondered how it did not burst.

Then, all at once, the world stilled.

As it withdrew its magic, the titan lifted its head. With one last lazy look down, it retracted into its shell. The legs and tail followed until it seemed little more than an oddly shaped piece of land.

Then the tortoise sank back down into the desert.

Leiyn watched, her bafflement and despair a match for Zuma's. *No. That cannot be it. He did it, damn it! He bound it to him!*

But had she seen him succeed before? Her previous experience had only shown to the moment when he had surrendered, not beyond. And had not Xepi said Zuma was unable to leash a titan, even after he had discovered the secret of it?

She thought the memory would end then, but it lingered, then skipped. It resumed sometime later in the day, the sun having dipped toward the horizon. Zuma was rising from the ground. His shame was unabated.

Slowly, the elderly man found his feet, then tottered back toward the cliffs. There, the vision closed as Zuma's spark retreated to an ember's glow.

Leiyn opened her eyes. A splitting pain worked through her skull. Her heart still raced as if she had been running at a full sprint.

She tried not to jump to conclusions, but they seemed all too clear. Zuma had failed. What was more, he had been rejected. The titan had peered into his soul and found him unworthy.

Just as Clouded Fang now rejected her.

Is that it, Zuma? Is that why he won't come?

She waited, hoping for further answers. But Zuma's spark did not even warm to her thoughts.

I need answers, Zuma. Answers only you have. My life—our lives—depend on it.

Before her growing desperation, the shaman's gleam only waned. No matter how she tried to spawn him to action, Zuma faded back to his normal dullness.

"Damn it all!"

Tearing her focus away from the task, Leiyn slammed a fist into the ground. Dirt spat up with the impact. Once again, she had channeled esse into strength in her tantrum.

Disgusted and deflated, she leaned back and looked up through the canopy at the constellations displayed in the sky, letting the residual pain roll off her. "Would that you had answers," she muttered as she picked out the shapes of stars she knew. Tadeo had taught her most of them, but she recalled some that her father had first shown her, and others pointed out by Teya.

What would you tell me to do? she asked of her absent lover. Teya had a way of guiding her as no one else could, even Isla. She wondered when she would see her again, and what she would say about her new scar.

Sighing, Leiyn picked herself up off the ground. Another night of failure. A theme she was becoming far too familiar with.

Maybe I need sleep. Maybe I'll know in time.

Even in her head, it seemed a vain hope.

～～

Her attempts to compel further answers from Zuma failed over the next several nights, as did her outreach to Clouded Fang. Despair dogged her waking hours; the fear of an assassin's knife haunted her slumbering ones. She began feeling as insubstantial as a ghost, drifting along the high road toward their far destination with as little will as wisps in the wind.

Her speculations on the problem grew increasingly wild. Perhaps Zuma merely tested her. Perhaps he *had* reached the hill tortoise but wanted her to figure this out for herself. Or maybe she had truly surpassed his experience, and he had offered all he could.

In her darkest hours, she wondered if he had abandoned her as Clouded Fang did. If, seeing into her soul, he had grown ashamed of what he beheld.

No. He opened to me. He never judged me while alive. He still cares. He must.

She clung to her justifications with the stubbornness she was known for. They were all that kept her from drowning.

Leiyn's mood proved as infectious as the initial excitement. Soon, their camp conversations were muted and cut short in favor of more tossing and turning in their bedrolls.

When she confessed the problem to Isla and Batu, they tried their best to comfort her. "You did it before," her fellow ranger pointed out. "That means you can do it again."

"But I can't. It doesn't work." Her whining annoyed even herself, but Leiyn could not seem to cease it.

While Isla fell silent, Batu said with quiet confidence, "If anyone can figure it out, Leiyn, it's you. You've never given up before."

People change, she wanted to say. And she had, but not enough to relent.

So she persisted. Tortured herself, night after night, even as she arrived at the same results. Zuma stayed silent; Clouded Fang, distant.

I'll find a way. Legion damn me, I will.

Two weeks into their journey, Belen fell back to where Leiyn trailed at the rear of their company. She had grown wary before Leiyn's dourness, dampening their camaraderie. Much as she regretted it, Leiyn saw little to do about it. Not while her failures continued to pile, one on another.

"We're nearing the Radiante," the captain said. "Should reach it tomorrow. To cross it, we'll stop in Fort Ribereño. The captain stationed there might have a better sense of where those Suncoats are hiding."

"As you say."

Reaching the River Radiante, the border between Baltesia and Ore-Ofe, brought them one step closer to their destination. The changes in the surrounding land showed that they were leaving familiar territory behind. The wooded landscape became increasingly hilly as the foothills of the Radiante Slopes infringed on the Via Austral. The trees in the forest changed to unfamiliar ones. Their canopy thickened and blocked out the light. Despite that, the underbrush proliferated.

The land was not the only thing to undergo changes. The weather grew increasingly wet, with rain showers descending every afternoon. Even Leiyn's Iritu garb, which absorbed excess moisture from her skin, and ranger cloak, waxed to repel the rain, could only do so much to ward against incessant dampness. They were of even less help when they slept on the wet ground. Her companions fared worse, lacking both enchanted clothes and mahia to keep them warm. Leiyn often caught Isla shivering during a downpour, as did many of the soldiers, Belen included. Only Batu seemed unbothered, his esse burning with the same steady green as he remained erect and alert in Saikan's saddle.

Under such duress, the shelter promised by Fort Ribereño became a thing often dreamed of. When its bluff wooden walls loomed out of a drizzling afternoon, Leiyn was as eager as the rest of her company to hurry toward it.

The highway led directly to its front gate. Its walls extended for two hundred paces in either direction, far larger than the Wilds Lodge had been. By habit, Leiyn quested within the walls with her lifesense. Roughly a hundred soldiers were garrisoned there. A significant force, though given the stronghold's strategic position, it only made sense. Not only did it guard the colonial border, but it oversaw the only bridge over the Radiante, opposite an Ofean fort on the other bank. No traffic crossed the river or moved in or out of Baltesia that did not pass through its walls.

She noted the soldiers' positions. Some occupied the walls. Others moved about the interior with determined purpose. Still more appeared to be mounting horses in the central courtyard.

To meet us? Or to go on another errand?

Leiyn had taken to riding at the rear of their party. Now, she spurred ahead to join Isla, Batu, and Belen at the front. Isla already had the oiled writ case in hand, ready to present it to the guard at the gate for swift admission.

"Strange," Belen said as Leiyn approached on her right. "The kraken doesn't fly above its walls."

Isla frowned up at the battlements. "Perhaps because of the rain? It wouldn't fly well in this weather."

"Perhaps." Belen looked unconvinced. "The principle remains unchanged. I'll have words with their captain. And where are their sentries?"

Leiyn found herself scanning the soldiers' esses again with growing alarm. Though she could not see the sentries, she sensed them crouched atop the wall just out of sight. Though her lifesense could distinguish certain traits, it could not differentiate allies from enemies. If there was cause to worry, she could do little to confirm it.

She leaned on her other senses. The patter of rain disguised any noise coming from the fort. Peering at the walls, she saw furrows in the logs. From battles past, perhaps? Without moving closer, she would not be able to tell if they were recent or old.

She held her tongue as they drew nearer. Leiyn repressed a shiver as they crossed within bow range of the walls. Still, the sentries did not rise. As if to give the impression that the fort lay abandoned.

Her suspicion became too much to ignore. Leiyn pulled Feral to a halt. The others continued a few paces before drawing to a stop as well.

"What is it?" Isla asked, eyes pinched. "Did you sense something?"

"Nothing in particular. Just—"

Leiyn had not finished speaking before archers rose on the battlements.

She had faced drawn bows before. Though two dozen of them lined the walls, each prepared to loose death upon them, it was not the dull flash of the arrowheads that made her flinch. It was the symbol emblazoned on their tabards.

The golden sun of the Ilberian Union.

"Suncoats!" one of their company shrieked as the first arrows fell with the rain.

2O

AN END TO MERCY

*T*he arrows descended. Their company rippled and split as panic spread. Feral neighed and danced back, alarmed by the tumult.

Leiyn wound the reins tighter around her hands and wrestled back control.

"Ride!" she roared as her companions struggled to turn their mounts. "Ride for cover!"

Feral had barely kicked into a gallop before the first volley fell. A few arrows thudded into the mud at her hooves. The screams of humans and horses told of others finding flesh. Several of her comrades' esses darkened with wounds. One soldier's lifefire winked out completely.

Even braced for pain, Leiyn flinched at the death, blasting like winter winds against her lifesense. But she did not freeze before it as she had at the battle at the Lodge. Her preparation had not dulled the pain, but it helped her move in spite of it.

Leiyn glanced around to confirm what her lifesense had already told her: Isla, Batu, and Belen all remained unharmed.

For now.

"Go!" the captain shouted. "Back down the road!"

Feral scarcely needed the encouragement, already carrying her away. The rest of their company was slower to turn; with their horses submitting to the panic, they blocked the way back up the road. Leiyn pulled Feral short as they nearly collided with the mounted soldiers.

Gritting her teeth, Leiyn cast a glance over her shoulder. The riders she had sensed before became visible as Fort Ribereño's gate cranked open. Their mounts danced in place, eager to be the first through the gap. Soon, a score of riders would be upon them.

She turned back to see the company moving, though sluggish and haphazard. "Move, Legion damn you!" she shouted at their backs, halfway ready to barrel aside those in her way.

As the first Suncoat rider passed through the gate, the Baltesian soldiers finally recovered. Feral spurred into a gallop as a second wave of arrows spat at the ground behind them. The horse was a whirlwind underneath her; Leiyn struggled to remain mounted. She squinted through the rain and flying mud at the road beyond the rest of her company but could see little. By her mahia, she sensed no more soldiers waited in ambush, at least.

They labored up an incline, the muddy highway making the ride difficult and dangerous. They had left the archers behind, but a different worry pressed in now. Her company and their mounts were weary from travel and laden with their belongings. They would not outpace their pursuit for long.

Already, she sensed the Suncoats closing the gap between them. Leiyn shot a look over her shoulder to see the riders pressed low over the backs of their horses. Their steeds were bred for speed and courage, and it showed as they barreled after her motley company.

They had minutes before the enemy caught up to them.

She should have been afraid. Instead, anticipation grew within her. An adversary finally stood before them. One she knew how to fight. This was a battle she could win.

So long as the cost was not too high.

"Turn into the forest!" Leiyn shouted. The wind stole the words from her mouth, but Isla, Batu, and Belen looked her way, indicating they had heard part of them. She waved to the trees to their left, hoping to make her intentions clear.

"Turn *now!*"

Isla obeyed. When she peeled away, others began to follow. Belen repeated the command. With her voice lower-pitched and louder than Leiyn's, most of her soldiers seemed to hear. Only two kept riding down the road, ignorant of the plan.

Leiyn braced against Feral's back as they barreled beyond the tree line. The thick vegetation made for uneven footing, and the closeness of the trunks conspired to slow their pace. Minutes had shortened to moments before the Suncoats were on them.

"Where?" Isla called from the front.

"Deeper!" Leiyn bellowed back.

Feral, panting hard, carried her on as swiftly as she could, but they had barely moved thirty paces into the forest before the Suncoats entered it. They called taunts and insults at their backs as they followed.

"They're closing in!" Batu shouted, voice cracking with strain.

"Keep going!"

Even as she spoke, Leiyn reached down, freed her warbow from the saddle, and pulled her feet free of the stirrups. Feral, sensing the shift in her weight, whinnied in protest, but Leiyn was already sliding off the mare's rump. It was not a movement she had practiced often, but as she pushed free, Leiyn managed to keep her feet under her.

She had barely jolted to the ground before she had a bodkin arrow nocked and drawn. The warbow was less powerful than her longbow, but with the Suncoats twenty paces away and closing, it scarcely mattered.

Leiyn loosed.

Her arrow flew true. The leading Suncoat slumped back in his saddle, the armor-piercing arrow punching through the mail over his throat. His horse neighed and turned aside, temporarily barring the way forward for the others.

Leiyn nocked another arrow. Even as she did, she lashed out

with her mahia, seizing the esse of the riderless horse. As Xepi had taught her, she confounded its senses and sent it into a frenzy.

Suncoats shouted as the horse reared, hooves knocking another rider to the ground.

Leiyn's arrow followed a moment later, taking the stunned rider in the shoulder. She struck indiscriminately with her magic, lashing humans and horses alike. Confused and entangled, they fell to each other's thrashing as often as the sharp death she launched into their midst.

A pair of dismounted Suncoats broke free of the mass and rushed her, bucklers raised and swords in hand. Leiyn slowed them with a wave of magic, then loosed one last arrow.

Throwing aside her bow, she drew her falchions.

She had tested the titanbone swords against steel, needing to be sure they would not splinter at the first strike, and had been pleased with the results. Feeling the esse resonating within them, she trusted they would hold true now.

Despite the chaos she had caused, the pair of soldiers remained coordinated in their attack. Keeping their small round shields up, they herded Leiyn back to ground more advantageous for themselves. Only her lifesense kept her from tripping over roots as she retreated. She tested their guards, but they showed some skill, their bucklers deflecting her every blow.

Each moment of delay was another for their fellows to recover and close in. She had to strike, and strike so they would not rise.

Drawing on the esse in the amber beads—which she had replenished in the prior days—she flooded her body. Heat blossomed throughout her, carrying with it a heady strength. A wild grin appeared on her lips.

She knew the way forward.

Ceasing to retreat, she let the soldiers close in before she raised her falchions. Their eyes flickered at her smile, but they did not slow their advance.

With every ounce of her strength, Leiyn struck.

The soldiers raised their shields, as she had known they would. Titanbone met steel. The blades flared with distress.

Then, like a razor dragged over skin, the falchions sliced through, severing steel and bone alike.

The Suncoats screamed and stumbled back, holding up the stumps that remained of their shield arms. Leiyn felt the blackening of their esses, but the splash of pain did not give her pause.

They had threatened her own. This was their just reward.

She closed in to finish them, but more Suncoats were joining the fray—seven more, and those quickly surrounding her. Three held shields paired with swords and axes; the other four had poleaxes that could strike her from a safe distance. For any other, they were hopeless odds.

Shrieking without words, Leiyn drove at her closest three assailants.

Her attacks were graceless, but fueled with lifeforce, they did not need finesse. She lopped off the end of a poleaxe, then spun in close to take the head of the soldier who had carried it. Another Suncoat tried striking her with a sword, but the blade shattered beneath a parry from her falchion, sending him stumbling back.

The third man backed away before he could come within range, staring at her as if she had transformed into Legion himself. Leiyn sniffed, catching the stench of urine, then laughed as he turned tail and fled.

The others, seeing their comrade run, stuttered to a halt and took in the carnage. Leiyn advanced a pace.

They retreated, fear written in every movement.

"Curs!" she spat. "Cravens! I'm one woman! Come and fight me!"

She held her falchions aloft, taunting, daring. Blood dripped down the blades to stain her hands and arms. She scarcely heeded it. At last, she knew how Ata must feel before mortals.

Invulnerable. All-powerful.

Goaded by her words, the Suncoats advanced. Leiyn moved to meet them, falchions pointed forward.

Before they could clash, one soldier's head jerked back. Only as he fell did Leiyn see the arrow that had pierced his eye.

The archer did not remain mysterious for long. By her life-sense, she felt Isla and Mottle emerge from the forest. Behind them returned the rest of the company, discovering at last Leiyn's foolhardy stand.

It was too much for the remaining Suncoats. Shouting, they fled for their mounts, crowding behind the few holding shields. Isla and the others loosed a steady hail of arrows, all but assuring their retreat.

Leiyn let the falchions fall back to her sides. She should have felt relieved, but fury still smoldered through her. It had not yet been sated.

Then she noticed not all her enemies had gone.

One of the soldiers whose arm she had severed had ceased to move, but the second slithered through the underbrush, trying to reach his comrades. Leiyn closed in on the survivor, her stride faster than he could crawl.

He twisted around at her approach, eyes wide and showing the whites. With his helm removed, she saw he was young—seventeen, eighteen at most.

Standing over him, she watched as he stopped moving and slumped against a tree. His eyes were vacant; blood loss, pain, and panic conspired to overwhelm him.

Leiyn had felt it all before. That fateful night, when a different Suncoat had stabbed her through the belly, while his comrades burned her home and her friends with it.

This man, young as he was, would have killed her. Her, and Isla, and Batu, and the rest of their company.

All to follow orders.

Leiyn sighed. The flames inside her sputtered, then blew out. Kneeling next to the soldier, she set down one falchion, then reached out and took his bloody stump of an arm in hand. The young Suncoat wheezed, agonized by her touch, but too weak to resist. Holding him firm, Leiyn closed her eyes and reached for her mahia.

She pushed lifeforce into him.

The amber beads had filled her to excess. Though the wound was severe, she had more than enough to scab it over and keep him alive. When it was done, Leiyn opened her eyes and released him. The soldier had fallen unconscious, the healing too much for him to withstand.

But he still lived.

She picked up her weapon with a blood-coated hand and stood. Without the surplus esse, she felt weary and sickened by the slaughter. Death once more clawed at her lifesense.

"Leiyn?"

She looked over to see Isla standing nearby, eyes flickering between Leiyn and the Suncoat she had spared. The question in her eyes was plain.

Why?

Leiyn shrugged. She could think of several reasons. He might give them critical information. Or act as leverage if the Suncoats pursued.

But those were mere excuses. Lies to hide the truth. She had buried the truth too often before. Knew it only allowed wounds to fester and spread.

"I don't know," she murmured. "I guess I'm tired of hating."

Isla's lips parted, then paused. Before her friend could respond, Belen strode up to them.

"No time to linger. They'll have five times that back at the fort. If they mean to follow, they'll be on us within the hour." The captain's eyes fell on the Suncoat, noticing the rise and fall of his chest. "A survivor?"

Leiyn shrugged. "For now."

"We should take him with us," Isla said. "He could be useful."

The captain crossed her arms. "He'll slow us."

"There's an empty horse. We can put him on it."

Before Belen could object again, Leiyn decided for them.

Sheathing her filthy falchions, she bent down and drew on the esse in another bead. It was enough to fuel her body so she could lift the unconscious, armored Suncoat on her own.

The captain blanched at the display of strength, but quickly recovered. "You two better look after him, then. Zezé! Bring Mona's horse."

Leiyn walked over to the soldier approaching with two horses in tow. Ignoring the man's baffled look, she hefted the unconscious youth onto the saddle. Even with her augmented brawn, it was barely feasible.

"We need to bind him," she called.

No sooner had she spoken than Isla was next to her, a coil of rope in hand. Nodding at her, Leiyn held the youth in place while her fellow ranger bound him to the saddle.

When it was done, Belen snapped, "*Now* we ride!"

Leiyn did not argue. With her lifesense, she sought Feral and was relieved to find Batu leading the mare toward her. The former plainsrider gave her a nod as he handed over the reins, one she returned.

"Thanks for staying, old girl," she muttered as she lifted herself into the saddle. Turning, she accepted the reins from Isla to the horse carrying the bound Suncoat.

Feral responded with a half-hearted neigh as she carried Leiyn deeper into the forested hills.

21

IF YOU CAN

They marched until dusk.

"Here," Belen declared. Halting with her hands propped on her hips, she breathed hard as she looked around the clearing. "This should do for the night."

Leiyn wiped the sweat from her brow and inspected the campsite. Positioned on a cliff overlooking the River Radiante, the views it afforded would have been striking at any other time. Just then, the cliff and river were solely strategic elements to protect their flank. The ground was rocky and uneven, but it was level—more than could be said for the wilderness they had been traveling through since the Suncoat ambush.

With no better plan than to put as much distance between them and their enemies as possible, they had labored up the forested hills, which proceeded at a steady incline toward the Radiante Slopes. Already exhausted from fear and fighting, their party's moods had plummeted further.

They had long ago left behind Fort Ribereño, yet the ghost of pursuit continued to haunt them. Leiyn had sensed no Suncoats following them into the forest. If she concentrated, she could even reach her lifesense back to the river fort, where the Ilberians had returned to lick their wounds behind the stolen walls. A glimmer of anger returned each time she examined them.

But she had only to examine their captive for her feelings to cool. The young soldier had largely remained unconscious throughout the hike, never coming awake enough to recognize his change in circumstances. Isla had taken to looking after him. With him bound to a tree, she tried to dabble water onto his chapped lips, giving him the moisture he badly needed. Batu stood nearby, frowning at the pair. No doubt he worried, as Leiyn did, what would happen when the soldier awoke.

Leiyn turned away. She would deal with that once she could no longer avoid it.

In the meantime, she helped set up camp, then spread out her bedroll and sat atop it. Her eyes fell on Feral, where she attempted to graze with the other horses. The mare examined the sparse pickings with a dissatisfied air before nipping at another patch of wiry grass.

"Sorry, old girl." Leiyn dug around for the feedbag. As she filled it with oats, she stood to offer the horse a handful. "This should go down better."

Feral eyed her reproachfully, but it did not stop her from gulping down the grain. Leiyn wiped the slobber from her hand before fastening the feedbag over the horse's head. Once it was secured, she returned to her bedroll.

"No fires," Belen reminded the soldiers. Then Leiyn felt the captain approach until she stood behind Leiyn. Repressing a sigh, she found her feet and faced her.

Belen's expression was pinched. Leiyn suspected why even before her eyes flickered to the Ilberian. "We lost three of mine. Two horses as well." The captain shook her head. "Good men and women."

Leiyn tensed. She knew who was to blame. She extracted each word like they were rotten teeth.

"I should have stopped us."

"Don't." The word fell like an arrow between them. "We

cannot wallow in regrets, not now. I noticed the missing flag, but I didn't stop our approach, either. What's done is done."

Leiyn found she could not agree. There had been too many warning signs she had failed to heed. But the captain was right on one point: indulging in her guilt was a luxury they could not afford.

"What's done is done," she murmured.

The woman sighed, some of the tension leaving her shoulders. "Best we focus on what's coming. Still no Suncoats on our trail?"

"No. We're safe for now."

True words on their face, yet Leiyn wondered how long they would remain so. Suncoats might not assault them this night, but if they had a way of contacting Sharo, the run-in might invite him to send a lyshan henchman. Until the danger had passed, she had to keep watch.

Another sleepless night, then.

Belen stared off into the woods. "Lord Luca must know of this. Fort Ribereño falling means the Ofeans have no safe route by which to reinforce Southport. We must retake it at once."

"What are you suggesting?"

The captain caught her gaze. "I think you know."

"Turn back?" Leiyn shook her head. "No. Not an option. Not for me."

"Nor for me." Isla approached from the gloom, Batu by her side.

Leiyn turned toward them, grimacing. "Wait a moment, Isla. Think about what lies ahead."

Her friend gave her a small smile devoid of joy. "We've survived worse. I have to reach Kunu. As Baltesia's envoy to the *eesuwé*, I must plead our case to them. You heard the Lord Governor, Leiyn. We need this alliance."

There was a finality to her words that Leiyn found hard to argue with. As ever, the best she could do was accept her friends placing themselves in peril.

"I understand." The captain glanced at Leiyn, a question in

her eyes. Aloud, she only said, "My soldiers and I will continue with you, all but a pair that I'll send back to Southport. The Via Austral was clear up 'til now. They should be sufficient to carry the report." Belen looked at Isla, then Batu. "If today was any sign, you'll need all the help you can get."

"Maybe." Batu nodded at Leiyn. "But we still have her."

The three of them looked at her with strange expressions, an awe that was becoming unsettlingly familiar. She felt she must wilt before their attention.

Instead, Leiyn drew up straighter. Perhaps she could use it to dissuade them still. Before she formed an argument, however, a cry split the gray evening.

"Wha...? Where am I? What did you—?" Another scream interrupted the incoherent questions.

Leiyn was running toward the captive Suncoat before the others moved. Halting over him, she saw the young man was staring in horror at the bound stump where his left hand had been. Stifling her boiling guilt, she fell to one knee and tried to catch his gaze.

"Shut it!" she hissed. "Not another Wilds-cursed sound, hear me?"

The threat drew the soldier from his stupor. He stared at her dumbly before fresh horror washed over his expression.

"Y-you're that she-devil. The one who..." The young man trailed off, eyes falling back to his crippled arm.

Leiyn's chest wrenched. She had no choice but to callus her heart.

"Yes, I am. So you'll listen to me, won't you?"

A heartbeat passed before the Suncoat bobbed his head.

"No screaming. No speaking unless spoken to. And you'll answer my every Legion-damned question."

She did not need to explain the threat. His eyes showed he understood the price of failure. Again, the young man nodded.

"First, tell us your name." Isla had come up behind Leiyn, accompanied by Batu and Belen. Her tone was gentler than any Leiyn could muster.

The Suncoat turned to her, his expression as insensible as a cow's. Isla had wiped the blood from his face, but he had suffered bruises as well, adding to his pitiable appearance.

"Arias," he whispered. "Di Carille."

"Arias." Isla spoke like she addressed a boy rather than a man grown. "I know Leiyn is frightening, but she won't harm you. Please, answer our questions."

"Leiyn..." Arias's eyes widened. "You're the Wilds Witch?"

Wilds Witch. She might have laughed at the title, but for the sight of what she had done to the young man.

"I suppose I am," she answered.

Belen stepped forward, looming over the Suncoat. "How did you take Fort Ribereño? How many soldiers hold it? Are more in the area?"

Her breath was wasted. Arias's eyes were already rolling up in his head, his overwrought mind folding in on itself. Soon, he would lapse back into unconsciousness.

Leiyn reached out and grabbed the side of his face. Holding him upright, she gave his esse a sharp prod.

Arias gasped and jerked awake. As his gaze refocused, his horror waxed greater than before.

"Don't." The word came out as a growl. "Don't die on us. I won't have you saved for nothing."

Leiyn held him there until she could no longer stand it. Releasing his head, she rose and stepped back, wiping the hand that had touched him on her trews. Even with his face cleaned, touching him felt as if it soiled her.

Isla stepped closer, angling her body before the captive. "Captain Belen, I'd request that you ask your questions in the morning. Give him the night to recover."

Belen glared at Isla. "We may not be able to afford a night. But if you insist, Envoy, any consequences are on you."

She turned on her heel and, stiff-backed, strode away.

Isla gave Leiyn a lingering look, then kneeled next to Arias, her voice soft and comforting.

Batu drifted closer to Leiyn. She feared his words as his mouth parted, but all he said was, "Are you alright?"

A bitter laugh escaped her. "Terrific. You?"

"Been better."

They stood in silence for a moment longer. Leiyn wanted to flee to her bedroll, but with a long night of watch ahead, she saw little point in it.

At last, Batu spoke again. "I heard what you said before, after the battle. About being tired of hatred."

Leiyn wished she had more laughter in her. Anything would have been preferable to the ache in her chest.

"After all the hating I've done," she muttered, "who wouldn't be?"

He nodded. "Among the plainsriders, there's a saying: 'Save if you can. Kill if you must.'" Batu paused, then shrugged. "I think it's good that you spared him."

"You and Isla both."

"Don't you think so?"

Leiyn tilted back her head. As the last of the sunlight faded from the sky, the stars revealed themselves from behind the gray veil. Tiny sparks of light, swallowed in the great darkness.

"This is war," she said at last. "How can we save anyone?"

"We can. We will."

His confidence was rife with naivety to her mind. She marveled at Batu keeping it after all he had seen. Some part of her even envied him.

After a moment, Batu reached out and squeezed her shoulder. His large hand was comforting pressure, the touch of his steady esse even more so. With a nod, he turned back to Isla, kneeling next to her and the captive Suncoat.

Leiyn resumed looking at the sky. The plainness of Batu's philosophy held some reassurance, however slight.

Save if you can.

Nodding to herself, Leiyn moved over to the edge of the camp and set her back to a tree for the long watch.

22

CROSSINGS

The night passed, slow and uneventful. Neither Iyshan nor Suncoat came sniffing after them. The most Leiyn saw was a pair of raccoons, curious and eager for any scraps their company might have discarded. The worst enemies she faced were her thoughts.

The morning brought its fresh share of troubles. After selecting and sending a pair of soldiers back to Southport, Belen gathered the remaining half-dozen soldiers along with Leiyn, Isla, and Batu. They left Arias tied to his tree and spoke beyond his hearing.

"If we're to continue to Kunu"—the captain's tone made clear her opinion on that plan—"we must cross the Radiante." Belen pointed south. "I've seen no likely fords since we've come alongside it, and none are shown on our maps." She indicated north. "I propose we continue toward the Slopes. The river should grow shallower and narrower as we move higher, perhaps enough to cross."

No one had a better suggestion, so they moved according to the captain's plan, laboring up the hills once more. Ordinarily, a hike would have posed Leiyn scant issue. But between the sleepless night, the expenditure of mahia, and the drizzle that started up mid-morning, she depended on Feral to drag her uphill.

The mare was less than pleased with this turn of events. Tossing her head, Feral tried to jerk her reins free.

"Shove it," Leiyn wheezed, tightening her grip. "And quiet down."

The horse neighed louder, eyes flared in defiance.

Their progress slowed, and not only because of the conditions. Traveling without a path, they had to backtrack often as they encountered one dead end after another. The thick vegetation proved another challenge, one they were ill-equipped to meet. Even if they had carried machetes such as the rangers had used for forming new paths around the Lodge, Leiyn would have scarcely had the energy to swing one.

She suffered less than some in their party. Leiyn often found her gaze drifting back to the captive Suncoat. Though they allowed Arias to ride on the additional horse much of the day, there came parts too treacherous to remain mounted. Then, he was forced to stumble along behind the horse, mutilated arm clutched to his chest, his expression that of a man tortured by Legion's thousand demonic voices.

Leiyn wondered if it had truly been a mercy to spare him.

Despite it all, they ate away leagues that day, though their labors gained them little. When they stopped for the night, the River Radiante had grown more foreboding rather than less. Cliffs rose from either bank, climbing higher with every league, impassable for their horses and prisoner. With the rain unrelenting, their camp was as dismal as any Leiyn had seen.

Isla was never one to be deterred. "Leiyn!" she called after Leiyn had finished settling a foul-tempered and damp Feral under a tree's inadequate shelter. "Come help us lighten our supplies!"

Guessing what she meant, Leiyn picked her way across the campsite, a root-filled clearing that promised another poor night of rest. She confirmed her suspicions as Isla took a hearty pull from a flask, then offered it with a limp smile.

Sighing, Leiyn accepted it and put it to her lips. The taste of the liquor filled her mouth, sweet and pungent at once. Heat spread down her throat to settle in her belly. She took two swallows before surrendering it to Batu.

"What's that you have?" Belen had made her way over to them, forced cheer in her voice.

"Apple brandy." Batu took his fill and offered the flask to the captain. "Have you had it?"

Belen snorted a laugh as she took it. "Had it! Lad, I suckled it from my mada's teat." With a fresh laugh at Batu's expression, she tilted back the flask and gulped down the liquor.

They continued passing the apple brandy around until it was nearly gone. With every drop imbibed, their moods lightened that much more. Leiyn's head ached and her body dragged, but the easy camaraderie was almost a balm to her ills, physical or otherwise. Belen's soldiers had taken inspiration from their captain and indulged in their own supplies, though they stopped short of recklessness at Belen's sharp reminder.

As Leiyn accepted the drink to polish it off, a thin voice called across the camp. "Could I have a taste?"

They quieted and turned, smiles fading. Leiyn lowered the flask to stare at the prisoner. Anger spiked through her, but vanished almost at once. Even from across the camp, she could see Arias shivering, arms clutched around his body. He lacked their weatherproof clothes, having come equipped for battle rather than survival. His esse burned as low as one could while remaining alive.

"Leiyn," Isla said. A soft warning.

Leiyn stood and strode over to him. She crouched before the Suncoat, staring at him for a long moment.

Then she held out the flask.

Arias hesitated, but only for a moment. Unfolding his arms, he accepted it with his remaining hand. When Leiyn did not take it back, he put it to his lips, closed his eyes, and gulped down all that remained. His youthfulness was further illustrated when he coughed on it, some of the liquor dribbling from his mouth. Leiyn bit back a reproach and waited for him to recover.

"Thank you," the young Suncoat gasped when he could. "The pain, it... if it helps even a little..."

Leiyn huffed a sigh and gestured with a hand. Arias flinched back, eyes flickering.

"Let me see it," she grunted. "Your stump."

Either her brusqueness or the kindness proved sufficient to convince him. Hesitantly, Arias extended his injured arm. Leiyn studied it with her lifesense. Black threads shot through it, signs of lingering injury and infection. She had mended the wound before, but the tender flesh had broken open and bled, turning his moist bandage pink.

The stench of the wound turned her stomach, but Leiyn had never let queasiness put her off for long. Quashing it, she reached out and took the stump in both hands and, ignoring Arias's pained gasp, she drew on her mahia.

Lifeforce poured through her fingers and into the soldier.

Leiyn did not bludgeon the disease into submission, as she had once attempted with Isla's. Instead, she guided the esse with the precision Xepi had taught her, concentrating it into a sharp instrument. Infection was no weed; it was best burned from the top down to the source. Free it first, and the Suncoat would likely succumb to it.

Leiyn tracked the infection into his shoulder. Once it became so thin she could barely detect it, she directed her mahia at it with an intense, sustained battery. Distantly, she heard Arias cry out from between clenched teeth.

She did not relent. As carefully as Surgeon Arlo would have tended to a wound, she eradicated the infection until she reached its origin at the end of the arm. Only once it was gone did she mend the skin of the nub. An extra push ensured it would callus and protect it from breaking open afresh.

Releasing the youth, she nearly fell back on her rump. A profound weariness filled her, tempting her to draw on the final reserves in her amber beads. Too weary to fill them throughout the day, she had precious little remaining.

She resisted the impulse. The prospect of an attack still

loomed large. If one came, she would need every scrap of esse for it.

"You healed me. Again."

Leiyn looked up at the young man. There was something in his voice, a note of wonder she was tired of hearing.

She swallowed a sigh. "I did."

The youth looked at his bandaged arm, eyes raking over it. "With your... magic?"

"Yes."

"Were you an odiosa before?"

"No."

The soldier fell silent, eyes downcast. "You could have left me to die."

Leiyn shrugged. "I could have."

"Why didn't you?"

"I'm getting tired of people asking that."

When Arias did not respond, Leiyn noticed her companions' muted conversation at her back. Something in their esses made it feel as if they watched her.

At length, the youth spoke up again. "You're not like how Captain Ranen said you'd be, Baltesians. He and the other soldiers called you bloodthirsty *ferinos*. As uncouth and uncivilized as the natives."

Ferinos. She tensed at the word, unable to help but remember all the times she had spoken it herself. She wondered how Teya would react had she heard her say it then.

She stared at Arias until he met her eyes.

"Don't make assumptions about others. Don't think you know someone until you've taken the time to understand them." Her voice sounded as rough as quarried stone to her own ears. "I had to learn that lesson myself. Took too damn long."

The young man's gaze lingered. Then he flushed and looked down.

A sigh wheezed through Leiyn's teeth. "You want to know why I saved you? Truth is, you and I aren't that different. Maybe we're on opposite sides, but we're both fighting for our people. For something we believe in."

Her words drew the youth's gaze back to her. Almost, he seemed transfixed.

"We're not enemies," she continued. "Not really. We're pawns. Greater forces move us in their games."

"What do you mean?" Arias whispered. "What... forces?"

Leiyn shook her head. She doubted she could explain Sharo and his role in all this even if she wanted to.

"The Caelrey and Altacura," she said instead. "And on my end, the governor and his Liberty Council. They each stand to benefit from this war. But their lives aren't on the line."

She had not realized the extent of her disdain until then. Yet, having spoken it, she would not take back a single word. Whatever the governor's intentions, Mauricio stood to benefit greatly from this war.

If we win.

The Suncoat's head fell. For a moment, she wondered if he had lapsed back into unconsciousness. As she made to leave, Arias spoke again.

"Back downriver. When taking the fort, Captain Ranen had us build a ferry so we could attack from both sides. We left it up in case we needed to retreat."

She considered it. Plausible, perhaps, yet Leiyn doubted every word. Barely a day had passed since they had taken the youth prisoner. They had killed his comrades and lopped off his arm. Surely, these small kindnesses could not be enough to compel him to betray the Union. But caution bade her to keep the suspicion from her face.

"We'll think on it," she said, rising. "Sleep. Healing takes a toll on the body."

Arias was nodding off even as she turned away.

23

ON AN OATH

"C an we trust him?" Isla gnawed her lip as she glanced toward Arias.

Leiyn shrugged. "Don't know. But the other option is to keep going uphill on a hope."

"I'd rather not," Batu muttered.

They all wore haggard smiles at that.

It was the same debate as they had the night before when Leiyn reported what Arias had said. Though the boy was amiable enough, it seemed unlikely he would turn traitor so soon. Even if she had detected no lie in his confession.

Lingering guilt did not keep her from slumber. Knowing she could not last many more sleepless days, she had slept the night through, lulled into a dreamless state by the rush of the Radiante below their camp. By some turn of fortune, nothing ambushed them in the dark. When she awoke, she felt as rested as one could after sleeping on hard, damp ground.

Belen interrupted their fretting. Striding over from where her remaining soldiers hunched over their morning meal, she stood there, staring down at Leiyn. It was not difficult to guess her thoughts.

"You want to try it."

The captain grimaced but nodded. "So long as you sense nothing amiss, it's worth the risk."

"And if he's leading us to an ambush?" Isla questioned.

Belen jerked her head at Leiyn. "Then it's a damned good thing we have her."

All three stared at Leiyn. Under their gazes, she could only turn to look over the river canyon, cheeks warm despite the chill day.

"We're only a day out," the captain continued. "And if the Radiante keeps on like this, we'll have scant opportunity to cross. This may be our best chance."

Leiyn, cooling under the morning drizzle, met the captain's gaze. "I'm willing to try it."

Agreed upon their route, they wasted no time in setting back southeast. Moving down the slope and over ground they had already trod made their progress swift. As poor-tempered as Feral was, she proved more willing to move downhill rather than up.

"You always prefer the easy path, don't you?" Leiyn chastised the mare, at which Feral tossed her head.

She glanced back often at the prisoner traveling in the center of their fellowship. Arias looked more alert and healthier this morning, though a feverish flush still spread over his features. She sensed nothing with her mahia, yet she could not ignore the itch between her shoulders every time she turned her back on him.

You're paranoid. There's no one around. We'll find this ferry, cross, and be on our way.

The assurances sounded hollow even in her head. If experience was any guide, things could never be that simple.

They proceeded alongside the river, not wanting to risk missing the ferry. As the march took them toward the afternoon, Leiyn quested out with her mahia until she reached Fort Ribereño again. Most of the human lifefires she sensed were there, but not all. Farther up along the river stood four men, nearly hidden among the smoldering esse of the vegetation. On the opposite bank stood another four.

Drawing back, Leiyn turned on her heel and stalked up to Arias. The young man flinched, though he tried to hide it.

"What is it?" Belen came over, brow creased, blonde hair turned dark as rain plastered it against her skull. "Did you sense something?"

Isla and Batu drifted near. With the march halted, the other soldiers crowded close as well.

Leiyn kept her eyes on their captive. "If my guess if correct, Suncoats guard the ferry."

Arias's eyes flickered to either side. "I didn't know that. Captain never mentioned duties near the ferry."

"Maybe your captain didn't," Belen said, "but your fellow soldiers must have. There aren't enough of you to miss that, 'less you're simple in the head."

The young man cast down his eyes and kept his silence.

Leiyn turned to Belen. "There's only four on this side, though. Isla, Batu, and I can take care of them."

"Just you three?" The captain jerked her head toward her soldiers. "It'll be an easier fight with all of us."

"And a noisier one." Leiyn pointed across the river. "There are guards on the other side as well. If they realize something's wrong, it'll make it trickier to cross."

Belen grimaced. "On the Ofean side? How have they not been discovered?"

Leiyn shook her head. It was a poor omen. Ofeans were supposed to hold their fort on the opposing shore of the River Radiante. That Suncoats would infringe on their territory implied it had fallen as well. Or, worse still, that the Ofeans had willingly allowed them through, a sure implication of an alliance. At best, they were holed up within their walls, unable to drive back the intruders.

Isla stepped closer and pitched her voice low. "Let's worry about that later. Leiyn's plan is good. We'll manage between us." She gave Batu a nod. He returned it with grim determination.

"I suppose you know what you're about." The captain glanced back at Arias, who studiously avoided her gaze. "So long as we reach the ferry, I don't care how."

Their party proceeded in silence for the remaining league between them and the Suncoats, Arias made to comply by Belen's deadly promises. Leiyn kept her lifesense wide and her senses sharp, as keenly aware as a fox approaching a trap. She sensed nothing more amiss.

When they verged on being within earshot, Belen halted the company, while Leiyn, Isla, and Batu continued on. The three crept forward, bows nocked and eyes peeled ahead. Her friends' eyes darted about, looking for the Suncoats they knew to be hidden nearby. Leiyn whispered guidance as best she could.

"There. Behind that tall pine by the small clearing. You can just see his face."

After several moments, Isla breathed an assent. "I'll flank him. Where are the others?"

Leiyn pointed them out. They each occupied a different post around a flat part of the riverbank among the vegetation. Though the forest obscured their view, Leiyn assumed that section of the river was where they had tied up the ferry.

"I'll take the far two," she murmured. "Batu, take the one closer to the river."

The former plainsrider nodded. His hand tightened over his bow, but his expression held only stolid determination.

"On a signal?" Isla queried.

Leiyn considered it. Tadeo had devised several methods of signaling among the rangers. Whistles imitating birdsongs. Flashing metal in sunlight. But while they could help coordinate an attack, none of them were without risk of discovery.

"Loose as soon as you hear the first fall. That will give me time to reach the second guard before they're alerted."

"Alright." Isla reached out and squeezed Leiyn's shoulder. "Stay alive, would you?"

Leiyn gave her a grim smile. It was not for herself that she was concerned. "You, too."

With a nod at Batu, she split from her companions to ghost through the forest. Like she used to when stalking beasts in the Titan Wilds, she veiled her lifesense, leaving it open only enough to track her and her comrades' quarries. Most beings seemed able to sense mahia to some extent, if only as a distant itch. She meant to risk as little as she could.

Flanking the two soldiers, she found a position among the brush between them. Only one was in sight, but it would have to do. Slowly, carefully, she sighted the arrow.

The man appeared completely unaware. At that moment, he had removed his glove and dug a finger into his nose.

Leiyn drew back. Breathed out. With her mahia, she quested to the soldier not in her sightline and subtly assaulted his senses. So long as her touch remained light, he would sense nothing of what happened.

She loosed.

The arrow whipped through the brush, whispering past leaves and branches before crunching into its target. The nose-picking Suncoat jerked, then withdrew his finger to stare at it, as if it might have caused the sudden jolt. Leiyn wondered how he still stood. Her bodkin arrow, designed to pierce armor, had gone through his helm and into his temple. Blood leaked around the shaft.

A moment more, then he collapsed with a metallic rattle.

Shouts sounded across the way, then agonized cries. Leiyn was already moving toward the final soldier, who remained oblivious to the entire affair thanks to her meddling. As he came into view, she saw he stared over the river in the wistful way of a man remembering a different time and place.

Your spirit touches mine, Leiyn thought as she drew and loosed.

It took two arrows to fell him. The first caught him in the back, but the chainmail under his tabard must have prevented it from driving in deeply. The soldier staggered and whirled around, released from her thrall to stare in pained and confused fury at where the missile had originated.

Leiyn took the opportunity to loose the second arrow at a more optimal spot: the opening in his helm. The man tumbled back, falling into the Radiante with a fresh clatter.

Fesht!

Leiyn glanced toward the opposite bank, her lifesense seeking the Suncoats stationed there. Their sudden movements showed they had noticed something amiss; all four congregated and moved toward the riverbank. Soon, they might spot their fallen comrade sinking into the water, or notice his absence from his post. Once they did, she did not doubt their first course of action would be to rally their fellows from Fort Ribereño.

Leiyn gritted her teeth and moved away. She could try scrambling their senses with mahia, but even if she succeeded, the situation would become plain soon enough. She would do better to speed up her party's crossing.

With all four Suncoats taken care of on their side of the river, she broke from cover to stand amid the muddy open clearing. Relief flooded through her when she saw the ferry remained on their shore—though "ferry" was a generous term to assign it. Made of a dozen logs lashed together, the stubs of their broken-off branches jutted up from the floor, and shoddily shaped oars lay across it. The vessel was large enough for their party to cross all at once, though not comfortably.

Leiyn raised her gaze to the opposite bank and saw soldiers staring back.

One pointed and shouted. The others turned to look at her as well. Whatever they said was swallowed by the river's roar.

Once, she might have mocked them with a crude gesture. But she had seen too much death to treat this as a game.

Isla and Batu emerged from the opposite side of the clearing, gazes cast warily across the river. A moment later, Isla's eyes widened, no doubt seeing the flash of the Suncoats' helms.

"They know."

"We'll have to move fast. Start preparing the ferry—I'll run back to fetch the others."

Leiyn was off and running before her friends nodded,

drawing on her esse to cast off her weariness and sprint back uphill to where Belen and her soldiers waited. In minutes, she reached them, panting and dripping sweat.

"It's done?" the captain asked as she looked over Leiyn's shoulder.

"Yes. But we have to hurry. They saw from the other side."

"Shit!" Belen looked over the men and women who followed her, then leaned in close. "Tell me we'll make it. I don't want more of them killed for nothing."

Why Belen believed she knew any better was beyond her. Still, Leiyn understood what the captain needed to hear.

"We can if we go now. Come on!"

Grabbing Feral's reins from a soldier, Leiyn mounted the mare. Together, they tore down the slope. Feral neighed as Leiyn pulled up short of the river. The rest of the company churned the earth behind them.

"You'll like this even less, old girl," Leiyn muttered as she leaped back to the ground and hauled on Feral's reins.

The mare fought her every step, but it was not until she tried to compel her to step foot onto the makeshift raft that she truly resisted. Tossing her head with eyes flared wide, she seemed on the verge of rearing and kicking Leiyn to the ground.

Leiyn reached into the horse's lifefire, soothing with a cool touch. "Spoiled princess," she muttered as she finally forced Feral onto the wood.

The mare still did not go without baring her teeth.

The others scarcely had an easier time with their mounts, yet one by one, they settled each horse onto the ferry. Isla and Batu had scooted the raft close to the shore, but it took their entire company to shove it into the water, and only with Leiyn channeling strength into her body.

The last aboard, she waded into the water, afraid of the ferry moving off without her. As it looked like she would be left behind, Batu grabbed hold of her and hauled her aboard, depositing her on the logs like a half-drowned mongrel.

When she gained her feet, Leiyn found every oar had been

claimed, and the Baltesian soldiers rowed furiously against the current, angling for the opposite shore. Leaving them to it, she quested around them to see the Suncoats reach the Ofean fort opposing Fort Ribereño. Their fears were realized as the blare of horns sounded up the river, warning of their imminent arrival.

"Row harder!" Belen roared over the tumult of the river and the whinnying horses. "Row if you want to live!"

The soldiers hauled against the water. The shore crept closer. The Radiante was wide, but the current was slow enough to labor against it. Leiyn watched the rapids flowing downriver, the rocks emerging from the seething white froth. She could not help imagining how those stones would punch through their feeble watercraft.

She tore her gaze away and focused on the dots of esse emerging from the Ofean fort's gate. *Focus, Firebrand. You have enough to worry about.*

A glance showed that Batu and Isla remained ready for a fight, bows in hand and arrows within easy reach. Leiyn gave them each a nod, which they returned.

Her gaze traveled to Arias. She did not think the desperation in his eyes was only her imagination.

She turned away, hardening her spirit. Now was not the time for empathy. She had to be the blade that cut through the Suncoat ranks again. The huntress born of hatred.

It was more difficult to remember her each time.

At last, the logs scraped against the muddy shore. Leiyn had to leap into the murky waters to wade onto the land. Hauling on the ropes with the others, they moved the ferry enough onto the bank for the horses to bolt, their riders barely catching them before they broke free.

Leiyn had to chase down Feral. Only her magic lulled the mare to a stop. "Take me with you!" she hissed as she climbed into the saddle.

Feral was beyond her hearing. She danced in place, the whites of her eyes showing.

"Fly!" Belen shouted, urging her horse forward. At once,

Feral leaped after the rest of the company. Leiyn reached back to see their pursuit was still a half-league away.

"Wait, damn you—*Catch him!*"

Leiyn twisted around at Belen's shout, even as her lifesense told her what her intuition already knew. Arias, unbound to ease the crossing, was breaking away atop his lent horse. Grown used to the Suncoat riding him, the beast was only too glad to flee.

The young man cast one last terrified look back. Their eyes briefly met. Then the thick vegetation swallowed him up.

Leiyn threw up an arm as the captain made to follow. "Leave him! We have to go!"

Belen glared at her, her horse shifting impatiently beneath her. "It better not be our graves."

The captain did not wait for a response, turning her mount westward and calling for her soldiers to follow. Swallowing her apprehension, Leiyn leaned low over Feral's neck and followed them into the thick of the Ofean woods.

24

OFF THE BEATEN PATH

othing still?" Belen asked, glancing over her shoulder.

Leiyn slapped at a mosquito and attempted to rein in her temper—another attempt that ended in failure.

"Don't you think I'd tell you if there wasn't?" she snapped.

The captain only grimaced and faced forward. Leiyn sighed and scratched at one of the innumerable bites up and down her body. Evening was falling as far as they could tell. Under the gloomy canopy, it seemed like the sun had sunk behind the horizon hours before. The vegetation grew even thicker here in Ore-Ofe than on the Baltesian side of the Radiante. She had heard it called a "jungle" back at the Lodge but had not truly known what that meant. Every step was a labor fit for a saint.

But though it grated on her temper, it was an exchange Leiyn was glad to make. An hour had passed since she sensed signs of Suncoat pursuit. Perhaps they did not care to make the effort, or their captain had realized the political ramifications were not worth the risk. Either way, Leiyn was relieved to be rid of them.

Belen, less certain of their safety, had requested that they continue trekking through the dark wilderness—a taller order than expected. Vines and creepers stretched between the trees.

Thorny bushes rose underfoot. Branches crowded out all but a hint of light. The soldiers had brought their blades to bear, but swords and axes were ill-suited for this kind of cutting.

Then there were the pests. Mosquitos and midges were only the first part. Moths fluttered into Leiyn's eyes a dozen times during their trek, though Omn only knew what for. Spiders and beetles caused more than one soldier to startle. Insects crawled over every surface, themselves included.

The jungle was alive and thriving. The brightness of the surrounding lifefire should have instilled in Leiyn a peace similar to what she felt in her own stretch of the Titan Wilds.

If only the buggy bastards didn't scratch and bite and spit.

Their pace slowed until a wearied Isla begged for a stop. The site they selected was poorly suited for their purposes, the vegetation still thick and the ground soggy, but they hunkered down all the same.

Night brought a deeper darkness. Leiyn had never been more appreciative of her mahia. The only one who could sense anything in the utter dark—not daring to risk the smoke from fire —she kept watch for most of the night.

She did not idle away the time. One of the first things a ranger learned was how to keep the mind busy during the many stretches where waiting was required. In a rare moment, Gan had told her, *It isn't the wilds that kills most—it's the quiet.* With a mind prone to wander to all the wrongs in her life, Leiyn had taken the lesson to heart.

First, she replenished her amber beads with esse, drawing from the plentiful life surrounding her. Then Leiyn quested out with her lifesense as far as she could. The wilderness continued in every direction. Only to the east, where the Via Austral ran, did it thin and fall away into the Torrent Sea. The only human life she felt was back at the forts on either side of the Radiante. For leagues on end, they were alone.

At last, she felt she could breathe.

When she had finished seeking, Leiyn reined in her life-sense and took to observing their surroundings. She noted the novel creatures that came to inspect them: birds and critters she could not name, at least not by their esses. She tried to distinguish ways to differentiate them, but it was too tricky a task in the utter darkness. Had she any light to see the creatures by, she would have pulled out her journal and set to sketching. It had been far too long since she had indulged in idle curiosity.

When she tired of the game, she focused on the day ahead and the problems it would bring. Most likely, they would make for the road, but leagues of jungle yawned between them and it. They needed a more efficient method of traveling.

An idea sparked in the gloom.

Leiyn touched a fern leaf, running her fingers along the smooth top and sharp edges. Xepi had taught her to influence animals. Perhaps plants were similarly susceptible.

Pressing forth her mahia, she tried to enforce her will on the fern. It felt like pushing against bark. Though there was some give to its lifefire, it was similar to the way a gust would make a candle flame dance. Devoid of intent.

She withdrew and considered the plant. Swaying creatures with mahia worked by instilling your notions into their behavior. While plants were alive, they were not sentient in the same way. They grew and moved but lacked even instinct. They responded to sensations, not to thoughts.

The answer came to her.

Again, she reached her magic into the fern, but now she formed herself like a gust of wind, then a downpour of rain. She made herself into the elements, a messenger of the sky. Not a person, but a storm, tossing aside all in its path.

The fern whipped free of her hand, so quickly it cut her skin, and stretched away as if blown by an unrelenting squall.

Leiyn smiled into the dark, then repeated the trick, whittling away the hours until dawn.

Isla blinked at her. "You can do what?"

Leiyn grinned wider as she crouched next to their bedrolls. Despite the lack of sleep the night before—or because of it—she felt giddy, even exuberant.

"I can move plants with my mahia," she repeated. "We don't have to cut through them anymore. I'll *will* them aside."

Isla exchanged a look with Batu, whose eyes were bloodshot and half-lidded. Their poor campsite had ensured no one slept well.

"I'd take easy trekking," he said with a weak smile.

Leiyn's legs protested as she stood, but she barely minded. "Come on—time to move!"

Soon, their company was up and wearing the same damp clothes as the day before. Leiyn stood at the fore, Feral's reins in one hand, the other dancing on her thigh. She felt as eager as a child showing their parent their latest discovery and could scarcely hide it.

"First," Belen said, bringing the attention of the company to her, "we should discuss our direction."

Leiyn reluctantly met the captain's gaze. "We should head for the road. Unless you're enjoying our trip through the jungle?"

Belen's mouth tightened into a hard line. "I don't think that's a good idea. With the Ofean fort taken, we cannot guarantee Ilberian soldiers won't patrol the highway. It's best if we continue to avoid it until we're farther from Fort Ribereño."

Not unwise words, but Leiyn was not sure she agreed. Still, when Isla and Batu looked convinced, she nodded.

"Fine. Let's get on with it."

She faced the forest again. Narrowing her eyes, Leiyn moved forth her mahia to touch all the vegetation before her. She pushed out esse in a burst.

Branches snapped. Vines retreated. Ferns blew aside.

A path lay bare, several paces deep.

Leiyn relented and glanced back at her friends. Isla's mouth had fallen open. Batu was shaking his head.

Belen's expression dampened Leiyn's excitement. The captain's brow knitted as she studied the path.

"Very well," she said at last. "Clear the way."

Leiyn turned away, trying to stifle her disappointment. She had forgotten how unsettling magic could strike those unused to it. Not so long before, after all, people like her had been forced into bondage if they were not killed.

But she refused to repress that side of herself any longer. Not for Belen. Not for anyone.

All that morning, Leiyn opened a way through the jungle. Their pace increased twofold for her efforts. It almost might have been comfortable but for the continued presence of mosquitos and midges. Though she tried blasting them away as she had the plants, they were too many and too insistent to keep off for longer than a breath.

But she soon realized this method came at a cost. Each burst of mahia borrowed from her own lifeforce. Though she could replenish her reserves from the jungle as they went, the ache of overuse was one pain mahia could not diminish.

"I need to rest," Leiyn said at last, leaning against Feral. The mare sidestepped, almost sending her tumbling to the forest floor.

Isla chuckled as Leiyn righted herself. She silenced her friend with a glare.

"Rest, then." Belen strode past without a sideways look. "We'll cut through as we did before."

Leiyn fell behind the company of soldiers as they hacked away at the undergrowth. The path was too narrow to walk side by side, but she was keenly aware of Isla and Batu just behind.

"She'll come around," Isla murmured. "It was just a startling way to start off the morning."

Leiyn glanced back and shrugged. "You're probably right."

Slowly, they whittled away the leagues, forging a path that was roughly parallel to the road. An hour proved sufficient for the aches to ebb away, after which she returned to the fore to resume her path-forging. Isla once more proved correct, for by the time the afternoon fled, the easy pace had warmed Belen to this novel display of magic.

With dusk oncoming, they continued until Leiyn sensed something ahead. Or rather, the lack of something.

"I think it's a clearing," she said, disbelieving. "A large one."

In all the time they had been cutting through the Ofean jungle, they had yet to encounter a place that comfortably fit two horses, much less their entire company.

They pushed forth with fresh vigor. The soldiers took their turn cutting through the forest, but Leiyn soon grew impatient and replaced them. Forcing aside the plants, she saw an end to the unrelenting verdure just beyond and hurried toward it.

When Leiyn stepped foot in the clearing, she sucked in a breath, taking in its fragrance. Isla stepped up beside her and did the same.

"Feels like I can actually breathe," her fellow ranger sighed.

"Almost." The humidity still made every breath heavy, but Leiyn was grateful for any lightening of the air.

The force behind the clearing became apparent as she turned her gaze ahead. An enormous tree, larger even than the dryvans' maple in Glade, spread from its center. Leiyn could not tell what kind of tree it was, its leaves and shape foreign to her. Its trunk was thick enough around that she doubted their entire party could encircle it.

There was still little light to speak of, for leaves crowded thick overhead. The congested canopy and the roots slithering from the tree seemed to choke out most other plant life. Those roots crossed the clearing, as thick and sinuous as giant serpents. But for the moss and dirt layered over them, they would have promised an uncomfortable night's sleep.

Not only was there little plant life, but the bugs disappeared as well. Leiyn smiled to be rid of the biting pests. More than anything else, they had been driving their company mad. She wondered if the tree possessed some natural defense. If so, it would be a fine one to plant back near the Lodge. While insects were not the worst problem they suffered, it might provide a stout defense against termites and garden pests.

Then she remembered.

A pang struck through her. The Lodge was gone. Yet here she was, pretending it could be as it once had been.

Can we not rebuild it?

It was a hope she barely dared acknowledge. Perhaps once the war was over, she could. If she survived. Until then, the dream hurt too much to hold.

"A fine spot." Belen strode past with her horse to examine the space, a hand propped on her hip. "We'll be comfortable enough here. Set to it!"

The soldiers hurried to their tasks, looking as eager as Leiyn felt to have a restful night. Leiyn moved Feral to the trunk of the majestic tree, seeking a place to tie her up. As they drew closer, the horse yanked on the reins, almost pulling them from Leiyn's grasp. Her hooves skittered on the mossy roots, eyes flaring wide.

"Damn it, Feral, what now?" Leiyn fought to bring the mare under control, but the horse's resistance was dragging her away from the tree. "Stop fighting me for one Legion-cursed moment!"

She reached out with her mahia to soothe her, then blanched as her magic flailed.

Always nimble and responsive, her mahia suddenly felt as clunky as a misshapen hammer. Disconcerted, she let Feral drag her back, tossing her head this way and that as she searched for the source of the disturbance. Instead of feeling revitalized by being surrounded by living things, their lifefires seemed to dazzle her lifesense. Like debris swirling in a river's eddy, tainting once-pure waters.

Panic spread as the other horses reacted to Feral. Shouts from her companions filled the air, muted by the dense foliage. Leiyn did not spare them more than a glance.

As if by some unseen force, the tree drew back her gaze.

Feral had been fine until they approached the giant tree. Leiyn had wielded her mahia competently all that day until they reached this clearing. And the lack of other life was... unnatural.

Too many signs to ignore.

Focusing as best as she could on the tree, she searched for idiosyncrasies with her lifesense. She scarcely knew what she suspected, only that this tree was at its center. The esse flowing under its bark was certainly brighter than the surrounding trees, but that was to be expected for such a paragon of its kind. Craning back her neck to peer into its branches, some twenty times her height, she squinted to pick out anything that might have been lurking among the leaves. She saw nothing.

Her eyes grazed over the branches, then landed on a large bough hanging overhead.

Her knees went weak with terror.

Only experience with magical camouflage allowed her to see it. The disguise was seamless. Its skin matched the pattern of the leaves, the branches, even the dappled fading dusklight. The shadowed forest hues melded smoothly into its surroundings.

But she could feel the miasma exuding from it: a shimmering pollen falling over her and her party. Each time one of those seeds hit her skin, fresh fear coursed through her.

Leiyn swallowed against her dry throat and tried to speak. The word came out as a croak, barely audible:

"Titan."

25

STALK THE SHADOWS

The jungle titan slowly revealed itself.

It stood on the bough at which she stared, pollen falling from its hide. Its lithe, powerful body had the shape of an enormous cat—a jaguar, like the symbol of Acalan's tribe. Even though it had cast aside its disguise, it still blended in with its surroundings, for its body was made of twisted vines and roots, from its powerful jaws to its swishing tail. Yellow blossoms opened along its length, the source of the pollen from all Leiyn could tell.

It would have made for a beautiful sight at another time. Now, even the flowers raised Leiyn's hackles. Peril pounded through her veins like poison. This titan was smaller than others she had faced, much smaller, yet still three times larger than the cat it resembled. And there was something in the way it slowly padded along the branch, in its unblinking, golden stare that screamed of a stalking predator.

She did not know of titans that hunted humans. But she had never encountered one like this before.

Leiyn swallowed, trying to work some moisture back into her throat. "Get back!" she hissed, hoping the others could hear. "We have to leave!"

She risked a glance at her companions. To a one, they stared up at the vine jaguar: faces rigid, bodies trembling, paralyzed by the pollen fear cascading from the titan. One soldier had even pissed himself, though the man seemed wholly unaware of it as he stared up at the titan.

Jerking her gaze away, she saw the jaguar had inched closer. Perhaps it was only her galloping imagination, but it seemed its eyes had settled on her and her alone.

Like it had selected her for its prey.

Leiyn tensed her muscles, striving against the terror that threatened to freeze them. Pressing esse through her body, it invigorated and strengthened where it spread. She released Feral's reins, then slowly reached down to the falchions at her hips, hands settling on the hilts.

She did not know what would come next. But a ranger strove to always be prepared.

The titan positioned itself over her. With a single bound, it could pin her to the ground and tear into her. Still, she did not move.

A notion broke through the torpor. One Gan would have called "deranged," and Tadeo would have forbade. But she had to try.

Leiyn rallied her mahia and drove at the vine jaguar.

Xepi and Zuma had taught her how to leash titans. She had bound Clouded Fang to her. She had turned aside the sand stampede assaulting Qasaar. She knew what must be done. And she needed to see if she could still do it.

Her magic collided with the creature—then slid along its hide.

Leiyn stared up, baffled. She could see it, but to her mahia, there was no titan there, only an impermeable barrier. It spread like oil over water, unable to push within. She could have been loosing arrows against a stone wall for all its effectiveness.

Camouflage. It hid not only from their eyes, but her magic. She needed a way around this armor to have a chance of commanding it.

Leiyn braced for a second attempt. She would have to bore into it to have any luck.

The giant branch creaked. A shadow shot through the air, plummeting toward her.

Leiyn threw herself aside.

Too late—claws cut into her back, rending the Iritu garments as if they had not a scrap of magic to them. Her flesh split open.

She screamed and tumbled across the roots. Agony spread through her. Her back was damp, her tunic sticking to it. Her esse had darkened in three long tears down the middle.

But she still had control of her limbs. Her spine was intact. She was alive.

She could fight.

Up, damn you!

Leiyn rolled to her feet and faced the titan, healing her wounds as she went. She flooded her body with esse from Xepi's amber beads, more than she had since her contest against Man'nah.

If the first exchange was any sign, she would need every scrap.

The vine jaguar was already bunching its legs for a second pounce. Not letting her recover, it sprang, soaring over the roots with frightening speed. Leiyn was barely fast enough to dive aside. The wind of its claws whipped against her legs.

She faced it again, swords raised against the inevitable follow-up. But something else had caught the titan's attention.

An arrow shot into its hide, gouging the vines.

Leiyn glanced over to see Batu drawing a second arrow. The others remained caught in the titan's thrall, but somehow, the former plainsrider had freed himself. With teeth bared and body trembling, Batu did not hesitate to loose a second arrow.

The jaguar turned toward him.

"Get out of here!" Leiyn shouted. "Don't be a *feshtado* fool— save the others!"

She could not wait to see if he obeyed. Remaining on the

defensive would spell their deaths, especially if Batu stood his ground. She had to strike back.

Even if it was futility itself to fight a titan.

Leiyn charged, feet flying across the root-riven ground toward the jaguar, falchions pumping up and down. The spirit beast turned toward her, baring wood-brown fangs. Lightning-fast, it lunged, jaws snapping at her head.

Leiyn dodged aside, striking with a falchion as she did. Though her aim had seemed true, the blade swung through air. The titan had all but melted out of the way, pivoting around to pounce at her again.

Another arrow from Batu bought her an instant as it pinged into the jaguar's eye. Any other creature would have been blinded by the blow, but the titan only seemed distracted.

Leiyn took the opportunity to thrust a falchion forward. Again, the jaguar dodged, but she had it backing away now. An advantage, however slight.

She pressed forth, timing her attacks with Batu's missiles. Each slice missed, but she was gaining on the creature. Learning the way it moved, its instinctual patterns. Reversing their roles, one exchange at a time.

With her shorter falchion, she feinted a strike. The vine jaguar fell for it. Its sinuous body rolled out of the way—directly into the follow up from her longer sword.

The titanbone blade scored across its hide.

A savage smile spread across her lips as she positioned herself for another blow. She had only managed a shallow wound, but it was a sign that they could do this. Keep this up, and she could take down a titan.

As she pressed forward again, the jaguar struck back.

She tried dodging but could not pivot swiftly enough. Heavy paws, hard as tree trunks, slammed into her shoulders and drove her to the ground. Leiyn thrashed, trying to lash out with her falchions, but it had pinned them to her sides. Her feet scrabbled against its underbelly, but she could have been kicking a tree for all it gave.

The jaguar paused, shining eyes staring into hers. Its mouth opened wide to envelop her head. The scent of moist moss and floral fragrance washed over her, jarringly pleasant.

She was pinned. Trapped. About to have her head torn from her shoulders. But the slash along its hide was bright to her life-sense. The camouflage barrier was broken.

Seizing the scant hope, Leiyn struck with her mahia.

She focused all her magic on that glimmer of esse along the vine jaguar, flowing into it, then through it. She felt its presence extend beyond the cat's body. It was the tree, the leaves, the roots hard against her back. It was the jungle itself, aware of its movements down to the last fiddlehead.

Leiyn spread herself through it all, seeding her lifeforce like the roots of an invading plant. She was small and fragile next to it, but she did not seek to conquer. This was a gift, a joining. A release from separation.

As she flooded in, Zuma's spark flared to life in her chest. Like her father's hands had once guided her in learning tasks, she felt the shaman's presence run alongside hers. She did not let it distract her.

Surrender, she commanded the titan. *As I surrender to you.*

A moment passed. She focused on her vision. The jaguar loomed over her, crushing her into the ground. Air froze in her lungs as it hovered in place, motionless as no living thing could be. Its overwhelming lifeforce surrounded her, an unrelenting reminder that it could still crush her.

She sent a thought along the roots connecting them. Querying. Testing.

The jaguar lifted one paw, then the next, setting them to either side of her. It raised its head and closed its jaws.

Coughing, gasping in a breath, Leiyn scrambled back on her elbows. She did not go far. She could feel the titan's compliance now. It was not like the connection she had with Clouded Fang, but it had obeyed. That would be enough.

Distantly, she heard her companions shouting. With effort, she drew herself away from the titan enough to listen.

"Leiyn!" Isla spoke in a strained way, like she tried to scream and whisper at the same time. "Get away from it! What are you doing?"

"It's alright." It taxed her to speak and maintain the connection with the titan. Leiyn had to force out every word. "I have it."

"Have it?" Belen spoke now, a note of hysteria edging into her voice. "We must go!"

Leiyn started to shake her head, then stopped, worried that even the small action would disrupt their tenuous link.

Batu came to her aid. "It's under her control. She's commanding it."

"Hells if she is!" the captain snapped back. "It nearly tore her apart!"

Leiyn knew she could not lie there any longer, lest fear further unhinge her comrades. Slowly, carefully, she positioned her knees under her, then rose to her feet. The vine jaguar never shifted its eyes from her. Even now, it had not lost its predatory cast. Only Zuma's thrumming presence layered over hers reassured her it would not attack.

Yet.

She would have tried ordering it away, but with their souls intertwined, she knew that would not work for long. This tree and its clearing was the titan's habitat. It would not abandon it, no matter how hard she tried to convince it otherwise.

This was like no merging she had experienced before. She had leashed a feral beast. As soon as she released it, the jaguar would attack them again.

"You're right," she managed to say. "We have to leave. Collect everyone and make for the road. I'll follow."

They needed no further encouragement. Within moments, they had gathered the scattered horses and fled. Only Batu and Isla lingered.

"Please, Leiyn. Come with us." Isla sounded as if she was weeping. Leiyn did not dare check.

"Can't yet," she responded through gritted teeth. *"Go!"*

She heard Batu muttering assurances to her fellow ranger. It took some convincing, but at last, the two of them departed with their mounts and Feral in tow.

Leiyn was alone with the titan.

For a long breath, she only stared across the root-infested ground at the jaguar. It crouched with preternatural stillness as it stared back. Only its lifeforce had any movement, pulsating through their surroundings like a heartbeat, sensations rushing back to it like a spider sensing the vibrations of its web.

Her control over it held, yet Leiyn knew it was a tenuous thing. Slowly, she backed away, not shifting her eyes from the creature, navigating by lifesense alone. The jaguar stayed put, though it observed her every step.

After many shuffling strides, Leiyn reached the edge of the clearing. Still, she did not turn away from the titan, but backed into the jungle. Creeping vines and roots caught on her heels, and she stumbled more than once. But never did she let her eyes fall away, lest she lose sight of the creature.

A few paces more, and only her lifesense could track the vine jaguar. Once out of sight, Leiyn turned away and walked as quickly as she could. She did not dare run; even with Zuma's assistance, her concentration would not endure that.

Night crowded in close, darkness swallowing her vision. Only by her lifesense and heightened perception of the jungle through the titan did she navigate it safely. She wondered how her companions fared. All she could sense of them was their continued, slow progress. At least other predators seemed to give the jaguar and its clearing a wide berth.

Slowly, she put distance between her and the titan. A quarter league; half a league; one full length. She closed in on the others, their progress hampered by their blindness.

When she heard their whispers, Leiyn called out, "Still alive up there?"

Isla and Batu's relieved shouts came back to her. Though the intense concentration required to keep the titan at bay made her head ache, Leiyn grinned. Soon, this ordeal would be over.

Emerging from the trees, she saw they had stopped to

fashion torches. Weariness and worry lined every shadowed face looming from the night. Their lifefires stirred with anxiety. Even having heard her approach, they startled as she came into view before sighing with relief.

"Are we safe?" Belen snapped. "Is it over?"

"Not quite." Leiyn waved a hand back in the direction of the jaguar. For all she could sense, it remained statue-still in its clearing. "I'm holding the titan at bay. As soon as I release it, it may come after us."

Necessary words, yet Leiyn regretted them as a moan of despair rose from their company. Isla bit her lip. Batu's face hardened.

"We need to press on," she continued. "Once we make it to the road and out of the jungle, we should be safe."

I hope.

The captain nodded. "You heard her," she barked at her soldiers. "Keep moving!"

No one outright protested, though there were plenty of grumbles. Leiyn gave Batu and Isla a tight smile, then took back Feral's reins to tail the rest of their company.

26

THE HIGHWAY

The sun peeked over the trees as they emerged from the jungle.

Leiyn climbed the rise to the road, then hunched over to catch her breath. Still, she clung to her connection to the vine jaguar, though the distance and sustained effort sought to rip it from her.

But, at last, the time had come to release it.

Stay away, she commanded the titan, then severed the connection. At once, her aching eased. Leiyn straightened and leaned back, cracking her spine. Relief rushed through her.

Isla sidled up next to her, Mottle in tow. "We're safe now?"

"I think so."

Batu gazed back toward the tree line, as if expecting the titan to come bulling out of it at any moment. Belen, meanwhile, looked up and down the road, a different threat on her mind.

"No sign of Suncoat patrols yet," the captain said. "Nor much other traffic. Still, we'd best push on through the day."

With the peril of the titan past, the soldiers openly objected. "The horses," one whined. "They cannot continue much longer."

"You worried about them or yourself?" Belen barked. "I know. I get it. We're all tired, and hungry, and footsore. But we have to stay alive to complete our mission. If we don't reach

Kunu, the war could be over. Your families will all be dead within the year."

The reality sobered them. To the last, they remained silent as they nodded and turned south. Leiyn exchanged a look with Isla and Batu, glad she was not on the receiving end of the captain's tongue. She was no happier than the rest to keep walking. But what other recourse did they have?

One, if she was not mistaken.

"Hold up!" she called as she moved to Isla and Batu. Feral, already in a foul mood, reluctantly followed.

Handing her reins to Batu, Leiyn took Isla's hand in hers. "This might feel odd."

Her friend's eyes widened. "Are you—?"

Leiyn did not let her finish. Closing her eyes, she drew on the remaining esse in the amber, then poured a measure of it into Isla. Maintaining control over the titan had taxed her, but this was a minor enough task for her to manage.

Releasing her, Leiyn turned to Batu. Isla quickly took the reins of their horses, her renewed vigor plain in her movements. The former plainsrider looked reluctantly at Leiyn's outstretched hand.

"Enough of your Kalgan prudishness," Isla teased. "We don't have all day."

Grimacing, Batu set his large hands over Leiyn's. Moments later, he stumbled back, staring at his palms, his esse burning higher within his body.

One by one, Leiyn gifted strength to the soldiers. She moved to Belen last, trying to remain casual as she took the captain's calloused hands in hers. Belen's gaze was steady on her, and her esse felt open to Leiyn in a way the others had not. Almost eager to accept the drifting of Leiyn's spirit.

Teya, she reminded herself, pulling away and turning from Belen's small smile.

Xepi's beads were drained, but the spryness with which their party moved was worth the tradeoff. She could regenerate their stores when they stopped to camp. Only the horses remained sluggish, but Leiyn had long ago learned the beasts were far hardier than their riders. They would last until that night, provided they did not ride them hard.

Their party set off again, keeping the horses to a walk as they headed southward. The Ofean highway was not as well maintained as the Via Austral on the Baltesian side. Nature waged a war to reclaim it, and by all measures, it was winning. Grass grew over entire swaths of the road so it was in danger of being swallowed by undergrowth. Despite that, the track was even and easy to follow.

With no one else in range of Leiyn's lifesense, her thoughts drifted. She thought first of the vine jaguar. The encounter represented both a victory and a troubling realization. Though she had commanded it, their connection was nothing like the one she shared with Clouded Fang. It had been a struggle to maintain, a contest of wills, rather than a joining of souls. She had not been able to draw strength from the jaguar, nor could she sense it now they had left its tree far behind. No thread remained between them as still existed between her and the ash dragon.

Perhaps it was due to their natures, unlikely as that seemed. Could a jaguar be wilder than a dragon? But perhaps titans were as individual as humans and horses, with their own thoughts and temperaments. They seemed to act on drives and instincts like animals, yet the few times she had connected with titans, their minds had felt intelligent, though so foreign and vast as to be incomprehensible.

What are you? she thought to the dragon slumbering deep in Unera's belly. *Why do you stay near?*

She may as well have asked the wind for all the answer she received.

Her luck remained equally as poor at coaxing a response from Zuma. The shaman had awoken when she needed him with the vine jaguar, but since then, he had fallen silent, his spark dim.

Why help me now and not with Clouded Fang? Please, Zuma. I need you.

Her pleading had as little effect as before.

Eventually, she relented and joined in idle conversation with Isla and Batu. A niggling question soon resurfaced.

"How did you throw off the fear?" she asked Batu. "No one else could move."

"And poor Zezé," Isla murmured, glancing back at the soldier who had soiled himself.

Batu winced and rounded his shoulders, appearing more like the young man they had first met. "I don't know. I just..." He shrugged, shaking his head. "Just found the strength for it, I suppose."

Leiyn frowned at him. She thought he had cast off his shyness. What brought it back now? But at a glance from Isla, she let it go, not wishing to make him uncomfortable.

The landscape changed little as they proceeded south. Only the disappearing peaks of the Radiante Slopes and the flattening of their path showed signs of progress. If the map Belen carried was correct, the highway would soon turn east, then travel the rest of the way south, nearer the coast.

As evening came on, a break in the forest soon revealed their path intersecting with one heading west and east. Belen called for a halt and dismounted to withdraw her map, gazing down either way with a frown.

Leiyn slid off Feral's back, eliciting a half-hearted whinny from the mare, and walked over. Her legs felt heavy from the labors of the past two days, yet she tried willing her mind back into motion.

"Shouldn't we be heading east?"

"Probably. But look here." The captain pointed to the system of roads drawn on the parchment. "There's a bend that goes west before turning back east."

Leiyn tried recalling the past day, but the road blurred together. "I think we might have passed that a half-league back. Can't be sure, though."

"Nor can I." Belen faced their company. "We'll camp at the crossroads tonight. Have to be sure we're headed the right way."

"Here?" one soldier asked, his expression pinched. "Thought we were trying to hide from Suncoats, not make it easier for them."

"They won't come this far into hostile territory," the captain countered. "And if Ofeans find us, they'll be able to point us in the right direction. Besides, there's been no better site for two leagues back."

No one raised further protests, Leiyn included. She felt she could have slept where she stood. Caution prevailed, however, so that she refilled the amber beads with esse before relenting to much-needed rest.

When she returned from drawing lifeforce from the jungle, the horses had all but collapsed around the perimeters of their camp. The rest of the company ate their road rations in silence. Leiyn joined Isla and Batu in chewing through hard bread and dried mutton before sprawling onto her bedroll. A few soldiers had started a fire and begun passing a flask around it. Their laughter was a backdrop, like the buzzing of insects rising from the forest, as Leiyn drifted to sleep.

～

"Can you see the strings? Can you feel them, Oldsoul?"

She opened her eyes. They were on a beach. He stood before her, posture unassuming, pitted eyes bright with amusement. Sand as black as his roughened skin spread beneath their feet. A constant wind whipped his robe and sash around his thin body and worked Leiyn's hair free of its braid.

She squinted through the sea spray at her adversary. At this devil swaddled in fine clothes. The architect of her misery.

"Sharo."

The lyshan smiled. "Is it a rope to raise you from a canyon? Or a noose? Do you grasp it, not knowing which it might be?"

She took a step forward. "Stop. Enough talking."

"Words only cease with breath. And if I know you at all, Oldsoul, you cannot help but try to survive."

"I said *stop*!"

Leiyn reached for her falchions, but they were gone from her belt. Grinding her teeth, she looked around her for a bow, but there was nothing but umber sand and dark water for leagues in any direction.

When she looked up, Sharo was gone. But his voice curled into her ear, coming as if from a distance.

"You are the fly dancing on the silk of my web. Why, then, have I not trapped you?"

She closed her eyes, pressed her hands to her ears, trying to drown out the noise—

"*Ugankazi!* No movement!"

Leiyn startled awake. For a frenzied moment, she stared around the dark camp, wondering if she had imagined the shout.

Then she sensed them: a pair of people, almost hidden in the gray pre-dawn, standing over two kneeling soldiers. The silhouettes of bows were visible against the sky, as were the whites of their eyes.

Ofeans, by the language and their accent. Their equipment further identified them. Only once had she met their kind, and then it had remained a distant interaction. But a ranger recognized their counterpart.

Skystriders had found them.

27

ARROWS OF THE STORMHOLD

*N*o movement," the skystrider repeated, his voice male yet high-pitched. "*Nphenle*: why are you here?"

Belen spoke first. "That depends on who you are."

"Skystriders." Leiyn had to clear her throat to continue as the strangers looked toward her. "You're skystriders of the Stormhold, aren't you?"

The man who had spoken gave a sharp nod. "You *ukweqa*. You... not where you should be."

"I'm a ranger of the Wilds Lodge." She pressed a hand to her chest to emphasize the point and sat up. "Isla Ogbi over there is also a ranger as well as an envoy of Baltesia."

"Yes," Isla spoke from behind Leiyn. "These soldiers are escorting me to Kunu on a diplomatic mission. *Sizo kothula.*"

Leiyn wanted to turn and stare at her friend. She could not recall hearing her speak Eyin before. She had not known she *could* speak it. Even after a decade together, her friend could still surprise her.

But she kept her eyes on the arrowhead, still aimed at their sentry. The skystriders' heads moved, barely visible in the scant light. She watched their esses for any flaring that might signal aggression.

"A *bala*, a... paper. You have?"

"Yes, I have a *bala*. The writ is here."

Isla rose and held up the oiled case containing the writ of diplomacy. Leiyn watched as her friend slowly approached the skystrider and extended it toward them. A moment passed, then the man eased the tension on his bowstring and snatched the writ, tucking it at his waist. His hand returned to the bowstring.

"How pass the river?" the other skystrider spoke, a woman with a low voice. "Ilberia hold, no?"

"We seized a ferry," Belen said. "By force."

The male skystrider made a clicking sound with his tongue that put Leiyn on edge. A disbelieving laugh? Or a gesture of approval?

"You come," he said. "To *Isphopho*, Stormhold. *Uphathi* know what to do."

"*Siwazi ukamba.* Kunu is where we must go." Isla's protests were soft, but firm. "Wait until dawn. You can read the writ then."

No, they cannot. The realization dawned on Leiyn. Their spoken Ilberian was already rudimentary; what were the chances they were literate in the written language? Likely only their master—the *Uphathi* if she guessed correctly—could understand the writ. She tried to think of a way to tell Isla without giving insult.

"You come," the skystrider repeated. "At dawn."

He jerked his head, and the female skystrider eased her bow and sidled up next to him. Both withdrew a few paces from the camp, but there they remained, bows in hand, eyes watchful.

Isla looked about to speak again. Leiyn pressed a hand to her arm. "Do as they say for now. I don't think they can read the writ."

Her friend stared at her, then let out a small sigh. "You're probably right. But Leiyn, we cannot afford to delay. Do you know how far out of the way the Stormhold is?"

"Likely a week each way, but what's our alternative? If we resist and it comes to blood, harming skystriders won't help our cause for an alliance."

Isla knew defeat when it stood before her. Still, she held out a moment longer before sighing and pulling away. "I hate when you're right."

Despite the watchers at the edge of their camp, Leiyn's smile stretched wide. "Only because it happens so rarely."

As soon as it was light enough to travel, they followed the skystriders north.

Belen was as unhappy with the change in plans as Isla. The captain glared at the back of the male skystrider, who led their company. His female partner followed at the rear. The soldiers, sensing their captain's mood, adopted it as their own. Sulky dissent spread through their ranks. Batu's brow was creased with concern, but if it was for Isla or their situation, Leiyn could not tell.

Strangely, Leiyn appeared the most at ease of them all. Perhaps it was from the kinship she felt with the Ofean counterparts to the rangers. Perhaps because part of her did not want to reach Kunu yet and welcomed the delay. Though the *eesuwé* there might have answers for her troubles with her mahia, enduring the discomfiture of another city, and this one belonging to a people she knew little of, hardly seemed worth it.

The fact remained that they were stuck with their lot. A ranger always adapted.

Observing both skystriders, she decided she stood a better chance teasing out information from the woman. Dropping Feral back, she fell in alongside the Ofean, though she kept a respectful distance. Isla glanced back, as did the others as she passed, all curious if not outright suspicious.

Leiyn ignored them. Keeping her stance easy but proud, she glanced sidelong at the skystrider. She had to look up at her as the Ofean's mount was a mulish beast two hands taller than Feral. The skystrider's hair was longer than Isla's but braided against her head in tight rows. On her neck were patches of discolored skin, pale pink against dark brown.

"What's your name?"

The woman only spared her a glance before staring forward again. Leiyn wondered if she understood the question. As she thought of a way to rephrase it, the skystrider answered.

"Odowa." She slid her gaze over. "You?"

"Leiyn."

Silence fell before Leiyn continued, keeping her voice conversational. "And him?"

Another hesitation. Then, "Joromi."

Already, Odowa seemed to warm to conversation. Her shoulders had relaxed slightly, and she seemed less wont to draw her bow at the slightest provocation.

"You and Joromi are far from the Stormhold." Leiyn squinted up at the mountains rising to their right. "I wouldn't have thought this was within your range."

"It is not when... *kothula*. In peace."

"Ah. So you're here for war. With the Suncoats."

Odowa jerked her head in a nod. Leiyn mulled over the information. It made sense. Though Ore-Ofe had a militia similar to Baltesia before the war, it did not have a standing army outside of the Eyin Empire's control. The skystriders were best equipped for reconnoitering in the absence of trained scouts.

"How far to the Stormhold?" she asked after a lengthy pause. "It isn't near, is it?"

The skystrider cocked her head to one side. "Four," she said, then raised and lowered a hand. "Sun up, sun down."

"Four days."

Odowa nodded. "Five when slow."

Her guess had not been far off then. Two weeks to return to the crossroads. Leiyn pursed her lips, wondering how they could turn this around. For Isla's sake, she had to try.

"Listen, Odowa. This is all a misunderstanding—a mistake," she amended, thinking it might be a more familiar word. "Our mission to Kunu is urgent. Could you not escort us there instead of the Stormhold? I'm sure someone there can confirm our writ."

The skystrider glanced at her with an inscrutable gaze. Just as she thought she was getting through, the woman shook her head.

"To *Uphathi*. Must when *impi*... war."

Leiyn sighed. "I understand. Thanks anyway."

She pressed her heels against Feral's flanks to urge her forward, but Odowa spoke again, halting her. "I am sorry, Ranger Leiyn. It is duty."

Leiyn turned back to find the skystrider's expression sincere. Her words were not simply air; she actually seemed apologetic.

Leiyn smiled. "Don't sweat it. We'll make it work."

With that, she spurred forward to rejoin her friends.

"No luck?" Batu murmured when Leiyn pulled between him and Isla, Feral none too polite in shoving her way in.

Leiyn shook her head. "At least their hearts are in the right place. Odowa seems an alright sort. Joromi, though..."

Isla stared at the male skystrider's back. "There must be a way," she murmured. "Some way to convince them."

Leiyn could only shrug. Sometimes, it was best to let the truth make itself apparent. Besides, she had stood in the way of Isla's ire enough times to know to avoid it.

"We'll see," Batu answered, sounding as convinced as Leiyn felt.

⌇

The rest of the morning passed in oppressive silence. The soldiers muttered among themselves, but not loud enough for Leiyn to overhear. She understood the drift of their conversation from Belen's expression alone. None were happy with the turn their journey had taken.

But though she had spent the hours turning the matter over in her mind, Leiyn could not see a way out. They could not fight them even if she had wanted to without ruining their mission.

Making a run for it would arouse too much suspicion. Odowa seemed the more amenable of the two, and even she had not been persuaded toward an alternate course of action. Joromi barely spoke with any of them. He only broke his silence to issue the occasional direction, never graciously received by those he "escorted."

Resigned, Leiyn focused on their surroundings. Their path, which had descended from the River Radiante, now moved uphill. In places, it followed a ridgeline, opening up the view to their right of the white-peaked Radiante Slopes. The Saints had blessed them with sun, and the ride would have been pleasant, but for their present circumstances.

Later in the afternoon, she discovered a more curious sight. Leiyn idly looked for creatures and plants she might wish to sketch when a break in the dirt and grass made her bring Feral to a halt. Disregarding the mare's haughty sniff, she dismounted and crouched, sweeping aside the dirt from the path to peer at it.

She had not imagined it. Along the road was a stone paver such as might appear on the promenades of Southport. But it was no ordinary stone.

From within it emanated the faint glow of esse.

"What is it?" Isla pulled up beside her. "Did you see tracks?"

She shook her head and gestured to the slab. "Something even odder."

Isla shifted Mottle closer. Feral bared her teeth at the gelding, and Mottle edged away. Isla ignored the horses as she squinted down at Leiyn's feet.

"A paving stone?"

"An old one." Leiyn rose and looked up and down the path. The rest of their company had continued on save for Odowa, who lingered behind them, leaving the land exposed so she could glimpse a few more of the pavers with her lifesense. "This was once an Iritu road."

Isla's eyebrows shot up. She pursed her lips. "It's difficult to imagine them needing roads. They seem to appear and disappear as they please."

"I don't think they were all like At—Foxfur, I mean, or Eld and Mooneyes." She had not divulged Ata's true name even to Isla, it seeming precious to the dryvan. She hurried on, hoping her friend had not noticed the stumble. "Those remaining have the strongest Inheritance—the Iritu form of mahia."

Her fellow ranger frowned, then shrugged. "We'd best press on. Wouldn't want our friend to get antsy."

Leiyn nodded and mounted Feral with an apologetic wave to the skystrider, then continued up the path.

Their assorted company fell into an uneasy truce throughout the day's march. Yet when Belen called to make camp, tensions simmered once more.

"No," Joromi said, crossing his arms. "We go to dark."

The captain had already dismounted. "It's nearly dark, and this is a fine spot. You think we'll find a better one in the next hour?"

If the skystrider understood her, his expression did not show it. Odowa came up on her large horse and positioned herself between her comrade and Belen. After a hushed conversation in Eyin, Odowa coaxed her horse back, and Joromi spoke again.

"Tonight, we camp. At dawn, we ride."

With that, the skystrider dismounted and studiously ignored the rest of them as he settled his horse.

Their camp split in two. Belen centered the small campfire within the circle of their bedrolls, leaving the skystriders out in the darkness. Leiyn contemplated the divide with pursed lips, but there seemed little she could do. Only once the necessity of what they did settled in could she hope to convince her fellow Baltesians to act more amiably.

They were tucking into a bland dinner when Joromi stepped within their circle. Spurning the others, he moved before Isla to loom over her, arms crossed once more.

"You are ranger."

"*Yeba.* I am."

"You speak as them." The skystrider waved a hand. "Act as them."

"Baltesian? I am Baltesian. My parents moved there before I was born."

Leiyn swallowed her mouthful and observed the exchange. She could tell where this was leading, and by Joromi's posture, it would not be a pleasant conversation. Casually, she lowered a hand to her leg, resting it near the hilt of a falchion.

Joromi stared at Isla for a long moment. "But you believe?"

"Believe." Isla repeated the word, her tone neutral. Neither committing nor denying.

Leiyn cleared her throat. "What do you mean, believe?" she said, feigning ignorance. "In what, exactly?"

The skystrider's eyes never left Isla as he snapped out a reply. "In *Odisi,* Sky Queen Kyaka Ndaye. In *Okulukulu,* Mother Goddess, Mistress of Stars. In way it should be." He slapped a hand against his chest.

Leiyn was preparing to stand when Isla replied.

"No—*angi kolwa.* I never have. Nor did my parents."

Joromi's eyes widened. His arms fell to his side. Leiyn was all too aware of the knife sheathed at his hip.

Her hand grasped one of her falchion. The grip warmed at her touch, the weapon readying for violence.

Batu stood first. He had always been tall, but never had he looked so intimidating, with his hands bunched into fists and eyes seeming made of flint.

"Joromi!"

Odowa stepped amid their circle as she spoke, the name sharp on her tongue. Joromi tore his gaze away from Isla to cast a disdainful look at Batu. He turned away, but not before spitting into their fire with a muttered word.

Heretic.

Among Ofeans and Eyins, who devoted themselves to their Sky Queen and the divine pantheon from which she was supposed to originate, the accusation of heresy was the most damning condemnation. It was why Isla's parents had left. Why Isla had never dared visit Ore-Ofe before. Leiyn wondered how it would compromise their mission once that information reached Kunu. If Mauricio's choice of Isla as the envoy had been so wise, after all.

Batu glared after the skystriders as they returned to their corner of the camp. Isla rose and set a hand to his arm.

"No need for anger, *kha-ir*," she murmured. "He's right—I am a heretic. I'm not ashamed of it."

The former plainsrider softened at her touch and words, though the anger did not completely depart his expression. As they returned to their seats, Leiyn saw Batu glance often in the skystriders' direction.

He need not have bothered. Leiyn kept a closer watch that night than any he could muster.

〜 〜

Despite Joromi's hostility, the night passed in peace. They resumed their travels without a word about the exchange the next morning.

The landscape continued its steady ascent. Only the weather changed, taking a turn for the worse as a drizzle settled over the company. Leiyn pulled the hood of her ranger cloak over her face, glad to have something to keep the moisture off. Feral's temper grew shorter still until she began snapping at air.

Mist veiled their surroundings and dampened sound but for the pattering of droplets. Leiyn let her gaze drift, keeping watch with her lifesense instead. Her mind wandered back to the problems they faced, her own the most pressing of all.

So withdrawn did she become that she did not notice the oddities until they were almost upon them.

Jerking her head up, Leiyn stared off to their left. From there came sensations against her lifesense, almost like the fog had grown heavy. Ahead, the trees broke away, and the land rose toward what appeared to be a craggy, misshapen hill. Closer inspection revealed it to be far more.

Threads of esse wended through stone. As if the broken buildings themselves were alive.

She looked over and caught Isla's attention, then gestured toward it. "I guess we know where that road led."

Isla followed her gesture. Her eyes widened. "An Iritu ruin?"

"Looks like it. Hold!"

Leiyn pulled a grumpy Feral around to stare up at the ruins. It looked similar to those that she, Isla, and Batu had taken shelter among with Zuma and Acalan on their first journey to Southport. Broken walls rose, uneven and jagged, like the spines along a draconion's back. They dripped with moss and vines, while grass and creepers stretched between the buckled paving stones. Where the drive had once led up an incline to the gate, there now stood a gap that framed the toppled tower beyond.

A castle, it had once been, or something rather like it. Having seen Qasaar, she could imagine its lost grandeur. But like most Iritu creations, this, too, had been torn down. Destroyed by the flaw of their kind, as Ata told it.

Hubris.

She continued to stare at it, ignoring Odowa and Joromi closing in on either side. Somehow, she could not tear her gaze away. The old stones sang a soft, gentle lullaby. The long centuries since their construction had failed to silence their voices. The murmurings held a curious tone, like they had a secret they wished to tell her, if only she would lean in to listen.

"Come," the male skystrider said, scowling toward the ruin. "Bad place. *Ukile.*"

"Haunted," Isla muttered in translation.

A smile broke free of Leiyn. They were right, in a way. Spirits lingered in the walls, pieces of the departed kept to honor their lives. But they posed no danger to her or any of them.

As far as you know, Tideraiser.

"Come," Joromi said, voice hardening. He turned away, expecting them to obey.

With a sigh, Leiyn followed. Then jerked Feral to a halt once more.

"Leiyn?" Isla paused beside her, looking around in confusion.

Leiyn held up a hand for silence. She stood still, reaching after whatever had made her hesitate. No more than a ripple had she felt, and now that she paid attention to it, she could not tell which sense it had hit. She saw nothing to cause alarm. Heard nothing. Smelled nothing. Felt only Feral shifting uneasily beneath her, and a gentle breeze against her face.

She reached out with her lifesense, scouring the area as she continued to ignore the alarm spreading through the company. She examined the dense jungle to either side. To their left, it rose to the ruins, while to the right, it descended into a valley before the mountains rose again. Sweeping her lifesense across the land, she tried to sense any being that might pose them danger, be it human, beast, or lyshan.

Nothing.

Only as she withdrew her mahia did Leiyn notice what it was. At the bottom of the slope, the lifeforce in the vegetation seemed... muted. Like a cloud descended to settle over it. Only, this cloud did not stay in one place, but moved, ascending the rise.

Coming toward them.

Disregarding her friends' questions, Leiyn moved Feral over to the right side of the road and squinted down into the dense vegetation. With the day shrouded, the canopy choked out the light. But her lifesense could feel that cloud nearing, now only two dozen paces away. Soon, if there was something there, she would see it.

Another titan?

The vine jaguar had showed that they came in more varieties than she knew. And there were spirit animals to consider, like Chispa, her silver fox; it stood to reason that some were malevolent as well as friendly. She almost hoped it was one of their kind. They were threats she knew how to deal with.

The leaves rustled. The branches parted. Eyes peered from the shadows.

A man's eyes.

Leiyn stared, disbelieving. A man stood in front of her, yet she sensed nothing of his esse. It took only a moment longer to understand how.

Veiled. Like Teya hid us in the Barren.

The sight of the man spurred the rest of the party into action. Leiyn reached for her bow, never shifting her gaze. She needed to see what kind of man this was who knew the Gasts' ways. Why he meant to ambush their party in the middle of the wilderness.

The man surged forward with a cry.

The brush parted behind him. He was not alone. Two dozen others, all on foot, charged up the slope after, their boots tearing up the earth.

A golden sun shone dully from their wet coats.

Leiyn had raised her bow and was nocking an arrow when two more figures emerged. One was cowled in a gray robe that hung flaccid about a thin frame. A man, by all appearances, though no ordinary one. She had seen the gray robe too many times not to know an odiosa on sight.

It was the other who drew her eye, for it was no man at all.

Its eyes were pits, its skin petrified wood. It rose two feet higher than the robed man next to it and moved with a lethal, unnatural grace. Its mouth was set in a rictus line like the smile of a skull.

Lyshan.

This one was not like the others she had fought. Hundreds of souls writhed within it, as they had in Man'nah, but these were plump with lifeforce. Before, she saw now, their kind had been malnourished, weakened by their long confinement to the Barren. This skin-walker had dined on life recently, gorged itself on it.

And it came prepared for war. The lyshan clutched in claw-tipped hands two weapons: a pale, yellowed mace and a barb-ended, black whip. By the esse shimmering from them, she sensed they were both formed of titans, the same as her falchions.

The scarlet armor it wore was of a strange yet familiar design. The helm hid much of its face, showing only a sliver under the aspect of a raptor. The breastplate had a titan's ribs wound around it. Pteruges, shaped to resemble giant feathers, fell down its legs to reach the greaves bound around its legs. Its arms, hands, feet, and knees were left exposed.

Leiyn knew this armor. She had seen it in the hidden barracks of Qasaar, mounted on a stand. Questions raced through her head.

There was no time for them.

The veil over their enemies' lifeforce fell away, bringing them into glaring focus. The Suncoats roared as they closed the last of the distance. The front rank held poleaxes, raised to skewer her company's mounts.

"Form up!" Belen shouted, wheeling her horse into line with the rest of her soldiers. "Meet their charge!"

Isla and Batu had their bows out and drawn, as did the two skystriders. As they loosed, Leiyn shot her own arrow into the throng. A few men fell, but not enough. Not nearly enough.

The lines clashed. Blood and rain showered down.

Then something rocked Leiyn back, and she tumbled from the saddle.

28

IN RUINS

*L*eiyn clawed at her attacker as she hit the ground.

The breath exploded from her lungs. Her back roared with pain. But though she lashed out, her hands met only air.

No one was there.

Gasping, she climbed back to her feet. As she did, she took stock of her body. Unharmed, for the most part. A fortunate turn when a fall like that could break her neck.

The battle came back into focus. Understanding of what had occurred flooded in with it. The blow had been against her mahia, not her body.

The odiosa had struck her.

Leiyn raised her mahia's walls and shut out the magic. It left her lifesense blind, but she could not afford another distraction. Patting Feral's rump, she moved her out of the way. The mare took to it with gusto, galloping down the road.

Then she drew on the esse in Xepi's beads, flooding her body with buzzing strength. She did not stoop to pick up her warbow where it had fallen, instead drawing her Iritu falchions. The enemy was already upon them. Blades would serve better than arrows now.

Stop staring and fight, damn you!

Leiyn raced around the line of rearing Baltesian horses. Two had fallen, their riders slain, but the rest of Belen's troops held against the Suncoats. On the far side, the pair of skystriders fought against twice their number, upholding their reputation as skilled and ferocious warriors.

But as she took in their enemy, she saw none of them would hold for long. Half a dozen Suncoats had fallen, yet four times that swarmed behind.

And then there was the lyshan. As of yet, it remained standing next to the odiosa, content to watch the battle play out. She doubted it would stay there for long.

"Leiyn!" Isla shouted at her back. "Don't!"

She ignored her friend and locked eyes with a Suncoat. Under her stare, he blanched. Leiyn smiled and advanced. He knew her reputation. *The Wilds Witch*, Arias had called her. She meant for them to have worse tales to tell after this day.

If any survive.

Bursting into a sprint, Leiyn lunged. She led with the long titanbone sword, stabbing through the sun on the Ilberian's coat and staining it dark. Her shorter sword swept aside his blade as his strength faded.

She kicked him off and into another soldier, then met the attack of the man behind. Parrying with one falchion, she slipped it around to cut at his arm. Metal parted like cloth to the enchanted edge. The soldier stumbled back and into one of his fellows, throwing both of them off balance.

Leiyn helped him find it again on the edge of her weapon.

Throwing the dying man off, she found a space had formed around her as the Suncoats sought easier targets. It allowed her to look beyond down the slope to where the lyshan and odiosa had stood. Only the gray-robed man remained there now, the lyshan having disappeared.

Fesht!

The odiosa's dead eyes bored into her as his magic attempted to do the same. Next to the strength of her walls, his attack was feeble. But he did not need to pierce them to fulfill his purpose.

So long as her mahia was veiled, she was blind to wherever the lyshan might reappear and attack.

"Isla! Batu!" She pointed a falchion downhill. "Aim for the odiosa!"

Hearing her friends' assents, Leiyn scanned the battle, searching for the skin-walker. Still, there was no sign of him. Snarling, she raced toward the thinning group of Suncoats again. Even if he was the most dangerous foe, she could not stand idly by while her comrades died.

As she raced forward, she saw arrows fly down the slope. The assault lessened against her walls, enough for her to lower them.

She sensed the lyshan a moment before its weapon slammed into her back.

Leiyn flew and crashed to the ground. Then she was rolling, all sense of orientation lost. Throwing out her arms, she felt one falchion rip free of her grasp and barely clung to the other. Fire raced along her back and through her body, but she summoned the strength to drive the blade into the dirt and bring herself to a stop.

Lifeforce flooded the injury as she tottered to her feet and looked up the slope. The lyshan stood at the top, two dozen paces up, watching. Blood painted the mace's spines. Her blood.

Her lips pulled back in a snarl as she raced up the incline.

Scooping up her fallen falchion along the way, Leiyn charged her enemy. Her shoes slipped in the muddy slope. Rain, blood, and sweat streamed down her face.

She ignored it all. Her enemy stood above, motionless amid the melee. Waiting.

Crossing the final stretch, she struck—and found only air.

Impossibly swift, the lyshan pivoted out of the way and stood three paces out of reach. As she reconciled with her opponent's speed, its left arm snapped forward.

Black blurred through the air.

Leiyn raised a sword even as she tried to dodge. The sinew whip wrapped around her blade, then snapped against her arm.

She burned, body and soul.

Leiyn barely heard the scream torn from her throat. She collapsed, utterly helpless as agony ravaged her. Desperately, she thrust up her mahia's walls, but the weapon ate through them in moments.

Her fight with Man'nah had shown her of the ravenous hunger of Iritu weapons. Leave it attached to her flesh and the whip would hollow her of life within minutes.

Frenzied, she writhed and lashed back. Her free left hand struck all around her with the falchion. But even when she managed to land a strike on the whip, it proved as strong as titan-bone, leaving only a shallow cut.

A blur of movement before her, then Leiyn was soaring through the air again, fire flaring through her side.

She crashed among a riot of esse. Disoriented, unable to make sense of the world except through her lifesense, she tried to differentiate friend from foe, but it was all madness. Her side felt as if it had caved in, but at least she was free of the whip. Without its ravenous teeth in her esse, awareness quickly returned.

Leiyn fought free of the melee, elbowing and shoving indiscriminately. She pushed out with her mahia, compelling those touching her to retreat, a command they complied with at once.

At last, she stood free and sucked in a ragged breath. The lyshan stood stark among the rest. Its esse writhed like a thousand worms tangled together, each burrowing into one another. As her black-spotted vision returned, she saw fresh blood painted its weapons.

A glance down showed where it had all come from.

Her Iritu clothes were torn and dead of life. Scarlet blood oozed from the wounds beneath. Fiery red marks spiraled around her right arm where the whip had touched her.

She sent lifeforce to the wounds, healing them, but already, her amber ran thin. She had little esse left. And a touch to her connection with Clouded Fang promised little aid from that direction.

Survival is the highest virtue.

"Damn you, Tadeo," Leiyn muttered as she glanced around. Isla was still atop Mottle and had caught and looped the reins to Feral and Saikan around her saddle's pommel. She loosed arrow upon arrow into the skirmish, and even mounted, most of them landed true. Batu was caught amid the fray, his axe dipping among the Suncoats. The blood and mud coating his face transformed his wrath into that of a savage beast. A few Baltesian soldiers fought next to him. Belen was not among them that Leiyn could see.

Beyond, the skystriders fared even worse. Joromi had already fallen motionless to the ground, an ugly gash split his face. Odowa looked ready to follow him. Three Ilberians harried her from all sides, and her movements were slowing, almost sluggish, as a dozen wounds wept red.

Leiyn had to face the hard truth: she could not save them all. Not without her titan's help. With a last glance at the lyshan, she snarled a curse—

—then turned and ran.

She dove as soon as she moved. Her instincts proved true as the whip scythed overhead. Scrambling, she regained her feet and kept going, lifesense tracking the lyshan's movements. To her surprise, it remained where it was, content to watch her retreat. As if she was reacting precisely as it wished.

She pushed the notion from her mind and made for Isla. "Go!" she shouted at her friend. "Get to Batu and go!"

Isla paused mid-draw to stare at her. "Where?"

Leiyn looked up and down the road. Suncoats had pushed onto the north-bound path. The armored lyshan blocked the way to the south. Despair lapped at her mind. She rose above it.

"The ruins! Get to high ground!"

It was unlikely to provide an escape, though in its tumbledown state, there was a possibility that a collapsed wall might provide an egress for the three of them. If not, it would give them an advantageous position against pursuers, given its narrowed entry and the ascent to the broken gate. Perhaps they could hold out long enough for her to figure out a way to fight the lyshan.

At the moment, it was the best she could do.

Isla nodded, then latched her bow to her saddle to wrestle the horses into obedience. Leiyn raced toward Batu and the surviving soldiers. Only two other Baltesians stood now, neither of them Belen. Corpses or those near enough littered the ground. She scanned the fallen for the captain, sorrow wrenching in her chest, but there were too many bodies to search.

Can't save them all, she counseled herself as she looked away. *Maybe not even yourself.*

"Batu!" she called. "Batu, come away!"

The former plainsrider seemed beyond hearing. His face frozen in a rictus of rage, he chopped his axe into the helm of one of the handful of remaining Suncoats, cleaving his skull in two.

"Batu!"

At Isla's shriek, he finally jerked around. His eyes looked startling white among the gore covering his face.

"Come!" Leiyn crossed the last of the distance between them to knock a fist against his shoulder. "To the ruins!"

He still did not seem to comprehend, but he moved toward Isla as if in a daze. Leiyn grimaced at abandoning the two remaining Baltesians, but the lyshan was stalking toward her and her friends. At any moment, it could put an end to them all.

She thrust every ounce of despair and frustration coursing through her into the curse. *"Fesht!"*

Then she left them to their fates.

Leiyn raced toward Feral. With mahia fortifying her muscles, she leaped atop her in a single bound. The horse took off before she had settled, nearly sending her tumbling off her rear. She wrangled the reins in one hand, still clutching a bared falchion in the other.

"Damn it, old girl!" she gasped, tightening her legs over the surging mare. "Don't get me killed now!"

Feral was beyond listening. She and the other horses took the only route available to them up the uneven pavers to the castle ruins. As the mare faltered, Leiyn was certain she would tumble down the rise to the ground far below. But Feral recovered and, with a ferocious neigh, went galloping into the courtyard.

Leiyn jerked her to a halt and turned back. Isla and Batu raced through moments afterward. Their mounts' eyes showed their whites and their nostrils flared, but they obeyed their riders as they directed them to stop.

Using her lifesense, she followed the movements of those below. The last of the Baltesians had fallen. The remaining four Suncoats advanced up the slope. The lyshan loped behind, his pace unhurried, almost plodding. Leiyn had hoped at the least the odiosa had died, but she felt his presence back down in the alley.

"Shit," she muttered under her breath. "Shit, shit, *shit*..."

"Now what?" Isla had her bow in hand again and wiped a sleeve over her brow. The rain fell harder with each moment. "Can we fight that thing?"

"Probably not. But I'll be damned if we don't try."

Sheathing her falchions, Leiyn reached into one quiver strapped to Feral's saddle and withdrew four arrows. Their fletching was colorful amid the drab surroundings. Their tips hummed with esse.

"Iritu arrows?" Her fellow ranger's brow furrowed.

"It's our best chance. If you can pierce its armor, the magic will do the rest for us. It's partly how I defeated Man'nah."

"Partly." Batu directed his horse close enough to accept the arrows, though he still had his axe in hand. "And the dragon?"

Frustration knifed through her. She bit off each word. "Not coming."

Rain fell in sheets. Almost, the worsening storm had a weight to it beyond the water. As she reached down to unstrap her longbow—her warbow lost during the fight—she darted a glance up at the dark clouds.

And froze.

They swirled and formed into a column that steadily descended toward them. The tip writhed like the head of a serpent. A tornado—she had occasionally seen them in the Titan Wilds accompanying the unruly awakenings of sky titans. Most often, one particular variety had spawned them.

Esse flared to life at the heart of the storm.

Exhilaration thrilled through her. Leiyn stood in the stirrups and reached up toward the forming titan. Her lips pulled back in a wild grin.

Only the echo of a memory brought her back to awareness.

Focus, Firebrand! Save your friends!

Even as Leiyn fought against the titan's influence, hope took root. She might not bond with this titan as she had with Clouded Fang, but she could command it to fight the lyshan on their behalf. Xepi had warned her once it would not work, that past shamans had attempted to use titans against lyshans and failed.

But they had no other option.

Her friends called to her, but Leiyn ignored them. Feral dancing beneath her, however, was a distraction too far. Slipping from the horse's back, she stepped onto a nearby mound of rubble and reached up again. Her lifesense felt the Suncoats gain the broken gate, a score of paces away. The lyshan approached behind them.

Their enemies, too, she pushed from her mind.

She sent her mahia soaring up into the funnel, touching upon the blazing spirit at its heart. It bristled at her presence and tried to shake her off, but she clung to it and sent a trickle of her lifeforce into it.

Surrender! she commanded the titan. *Surrender to me!*

Zuma's spark came to life, as she had hoped it would, steeling her will. But this titan did not respond as the vine jaguar had. The tornado swirled faster; its tip hovered above the ruins. The winds tore Leiyn's hair free of its bindings so it whipped about her face.

"Titan!"

She screamed with both mouth and mind. She alternated giving it esse and firming her mahia against it. It had to submit. Had to. There was no other way.

The titan vibrated. Its esse drew inward. For a moment, the tornado slowed, faltering.

Then the clouds burst apart.

From their heart emerged a bird whose wings spread as wide as the entire castle. Clouds formed its body, but its eyes were bright and sparking. Across it ran flickers of blue lightning.

The tempest hawk shrieked, and the world stilled.

Leiyn sank to her knees, but she did not let her arm fall. Her jaw clenched so hard she felt her teeth must crack. Still, she did not relent.

Surrender to me!

The storm titan's wings flared. Lightning coalesced around its beak.

It burst free, blazing down to the earth.

29

THUNDER'S HEART

The bolt struck with blinding force.

Lightning lashed Leiyn's hand, then crawled down her arm, a cruel parody of the lyshan's whip. It charged every pore of her being as it writhed along her body like a ravenous serpent.

The world burned.

Leiyn fought back. The attack was as much esse as energy. Even as lightning seared her, her magic stayed firm beneath the assault. She mended her walls, cracked by the initial blow, then shoved them forward.

The lightning pulsated and retreated—but only a fraction.

She could not only defend. Vaguely, she was aware of her friends drawing their bows as the Suncoats charged, and the lyshan's slow advance behind. If she submitted to the titan, her friends would die.

She had failed too many this day.

Leiyn raised her head. Using the lightning like a ship's anchoring line, she sent her mahia racing up toward the tempest hawk. It screeched as they made contact again and intensified its attack. The stench of burning flesh filled her nose.

She ignored it, the same as she ignored her friends' peril. With all her will, Leiyn drove against the tempest hawk.

Submission had not worked as it had with Clouded Fang and the vine jaguar. Perhaps domination was the key—if she was capable of it.

Born of a storm, this titan was not easily tamed. A heart of thunder thrummed in its breast, crashing across the ruins with each flash. But as Leiyn thrashed against it with every scrap of lifeforce she had left, she realized its nature alone was not the issue.

A leash of magic led away from the tempest hawk. It was barely perceptible, almost undetectable. Yet it was the same sensation she had felt from the sand stampede when she wrestled it from Patli's control.

Someone else commanded this titan.

The odiosa? No—she sensed the witch hunter down the slope, and the chain did not lead to him. Almost, it seemed to disappear, leaving only a vague impression of the master.

It was enough.

Leiyn left off the storm titan to race along the thread and seize the one at the end. Forming her mahia into teeth and claws, she rended them. As vague as their presence was, she felt them falter beneath her blows.

The tempest hawk shrieked. The lightning evaporated.

Freed of its agony, Leiyn redoubled her attacks. She felt the master's esse lapsing beneath her blows. They could have faded from her awareness if they released the titan, yet they did not, stubbornly clinging on.

She did not know who they were or their intentions. But their leashed beast had attacked and would have killed her.

Though they were a stranger, she would have no mercy.

Leiyn struck again and again, until she felt her victim buckle. At the killing blow, she hesitated. The titan echoed their master's agony as it soared above, wailing to the sky.

But the lyshan was almost upon her friends. Leiyn had only to glance its way to decide. Arrows bristled from its titanbone armor, blackening the magic imbued in it, but onward it came. Never quickening, never slowing.

She reared her magic for the final blow.

Before she could strike, another appeared beside her and launched themselves at her.

"Kasaru! La matar! Akki hanaqu akka!"

Already embroiled in battle, Leiyn tried to throw off this new assailant. They—she, telling by her voice—held no weapon that Leiyn could tell, but as the newcomer wrapped around Leiyn, a potent force washed over her.

Weariness, heavy as a lead blanket, traveled along a wave of magic.

Leiyn slumped, her body yearning for rest. Her speech slurred as she tried to shout, *"Fesht...* Get off me..."

But she had not submitted to the titan's attacks. She would not relent now. Fighting to keep her eyes open, Leiyn raised her walls, sealing off the woman's influence. As the fog faded from her mind, vigor returned.

She fought back in full then, writhing and throwing her elbows. Her captor's grip failed as Leiyn bashed her again, driving her back. The woman stumbled away holding a hand to her bloody nose. She was young, younger than Leiyn, and her eyes, a startling lavender, were wide with fear. But she did not retreat far. Her garb was strange and colorful, unlike anything Leiyn had seen before, yet somehow familiar. The pieces of stone embedded in her flesh reinforced her foreignness.

"Addan—Please, I beg you! Cease your attack!"

Leiyn almost did not realize the woman had switched to speaking Ilberian. She spoke with a strange, lilting accent that was difficult to follow. As the words sank in, she bared her teeth at the mysterious maha.

"Like hells I will!"

The woman's eyes darted to the titan above. "You do not understand. That man you hurt—" She broke off as she looked to the side, then retreated a step. *"Etaru anni!* They are here? Now?"

Keeping a wary eye on the maha, Leiyn followed her gaze to the lyshan. Isla and Batu had backed up before it, still mounted on their horses. Feral skirted back between the two, screaming at the lyshan with a ferocity that awoke a glimmer of pride in Leiyn. The skin-walker seemed unconcerned by any of its opponents. Almost, she thought she imagined a glimmer of satisfaction in its rigid expression.

"There's no time," Leiyn snarled. "Fight with us or stand aside!" She squared off against the lyshan, then raised her gaze. "I need that titan."

"That is what I am saying! It is bonded to Ab-Abi. You cannot command it."

Leiyn ignored her and sent her mahia soaring back up to the titan. She hoped its master had released it by then, but her stomach sank as she saw he stubbornly clung to it.

Then I have no choice.

Forming her mahia into a blade, she drove at the hidden maha again.

"NO!"

Leiyn did not have time to raise her walls. The foreign woman's mahia unfolded, extending all the way to her friends and the horses.

Then it tucked in, enfolding them in an elongated orb of shimmering esse.

She withdrew her magic to drive it at the young woman. "Don't, you Saints-damned—"

She never finished the sentence. The ground shook. Leiyn stumbled, barely catching her balance.

Yet, as her mahia trembled, she sensed this was not a true quake.

Leiyn whipped up her head, ready to fight. The sight that greeted her struck her into stillness.

"Wha—what is this?"

The lyshan was gone. The ruins had transformed.

She stood in a strange new world.

PART IV

GUARDIANS OF AEONS

30

SIXTEEN YEARS BEFORE

*L*isten," her father murmured. "Can you hear her *breathe?*"

Leiyn screwed up her face in a frown. Though her heart pounded at her father's words, she refused to let him see he was getting to her.

"That's the wind," she retorted.

He chuckled and shook his head. "No, lion cub. Out here in the Bone Hills, everything moves by *her* will. The wind, the stars... even the darkness."

A shiver stole through Leiyn. She wrapped her arms around herself and huddled closer to the bonfire, pretending only to shiver from the chill autumn air.

Her father's amusement sloughed off his face. "I'm only teasing, Leiyn. Maybe you're not old enough for this story."

"No, I am! I asked for it, didn't I?"

Their trip out to the Bone Hills had evoked the request. They had come to replenish the stash in the cave, as they did each season.

Each visit reminded her anew that she was a danger.

Living in Orille, Leiyn could almost forget she carried a deadly curse inside her. She had grown adept at stifling it, so much so that it rarely flared up, and only when she was at her most angry or afraid. Even when it did, odiosas did not travel through their town to discover her. Rare was the moment she felt unsafe.

But here at the hollow, the knowledge of what she was came flooding back in. Instead of turning away—her usual reaction— this time, her incurable curiosity flared.

She knew she could not ask about Gast magic directly. Forest witches, however, were a different story. Rumors of one haunting the Bone Hills had long spread among the children of Orille. Sniffing after fairy tales was less likely to provoke her father's ire, even if they did concern magic.

Her ploy seemed to have worked. Her father was eager to play the troubadour that night. If entertaining her pleased him, Leiyn was determined to be his obliging audience.

The firelight glinted in her father's eyes. "You did ask for it. Fine—I'll tell you about the Bone Hills witch. But don't crawl into my bedroll if you cannot sleep tonight."

She had not slept in his bed since she was seven. But, wanting the story, Leiyn kept her mouth shut and raised an eyebrow.

After another laugh, her father settled into a thoughtful expression. "It began with a young man too curious for his own good. He lived in a town close to here, near a Gast ruins." He spat with habitual disdain. "One day, he got the idea in his head to go poking around the old stones. Only, after he went in, he never came back out.

"Some said it was a *ferino* curse that got him, their Legion-born magic lingering in the stones. Others claimed it to be the work of skin-walkers, the witches that take on the appearance of trees and forest creatures. All agreed on one thing, though: the boy was lost for good.

"But his mother couldn't give him up. Each day after he disappeared, she went to the entrance of the ruins, as far as she dared go, and called to her son. In rain and sun and snow, she returned for two years, holding out against hope he would hear her voice and come running back.

"One day, the mother came with as little expectation as the day before when, to her shock, a young man sat amid the ruins. Only, he wasn't like the son she remembered. His clothes were more colorful than the beak of an Ofean rainbow bird. Gone was the incessant curiosity that kept him poking his head where he shouldn't, replaced by a look in his eyes like he no longer saw this world.

"His mother cried out to him and, unable to help herself, she ran into the ruins. The man that looked like her son startled and looked up at her, then fled. Like he didn't know her anymore. And before his mother's eyes, he disappeared into thin air.

"That glimpse of her son only drove the woman deeper into madness. She kept coming back to those ruins, year after year, until decades passed and she was bent and gray. When she came for what would be the last time, someone waited for her. But it wasn't her son this time, but a skin-walker instead—a dryvan.

"The witch looked as strange as any of their kind. It had a mane of feathers around its head and thick hair like a lion down its body. Its eyes were slitted like a devil's, and its grin full of sharp teeth.

"The woman feared damnation, but her desire to know if this creature was behind her son's disappearance was stronger. So she hobbled up to her and said, 'Have you taken him? Have you taken my son?'"

Leiyn giggled at her father's impression of an elderly lady. He smiled, then adopted his grave air once more.

"'No,' the Bone Hills witch answered. 'It was not I.'" His voice fell low and menacing as he imitated the dryvan. "'He lives in the stones now.'

"'The stones?' the old woman asked. 'He's my flesh and blood. How can he live in stone?'

"The witch smiled. 'Those who took him fear me. As well they should.'

"Only then did the woman notice that smile was familiar. Having looked for it for decades, she knew it at once as her son's smile. She fled, screaming, until she reached her bed, where she lay down to never rise again."

His words hung in the night air. Leiyn hugged her knees to her chest and rested her chin on them, staring at the dying flames.

"Is it real?" she asked at length. "Is there a witch out here? And children who disappear?"

Her father scooted around the fire to drape an arm across her shoulders. "Best to assume it is and avoid all things magic. In these wilds, you never know what might be waiting for you."

He squeezed her into his side, and Leiyn nestled into him. For a moment, she let a hint of her mahia peek through to feel the full warmth of his lifefire.

She knew she should avoid magic. But there, ensconced in darkness, the comfort it brought was worth the guilt.

31

THE HIDDEN

*L*eiyn held tight to her falchions as she took in their surroundings.

The castle remained in ruins, but there the similarities ended between her world and this new one. Where rubble and moss had dominated, buildings had sprung up in their stead. Immediately around them were tents boasting bright produce: pale green melons, scarlet apples, golden wheat abounding on stands. The fabrics were as cheery and colorful. Between the tents ran lines with fluttering blue and green banners.

A market. The courtyard had become a marketplace. There was no lyshan, no Suncoats, no corpses or comrades left to die. Not even rain fell.

Instead, strange people filled the plaza. They looked every bit as foreign as the young woman who had assaulted them—and brought them here, if Leiyn guessed correctly. They, too, wore a kaleidoscope of colors and in as bright of hues as the richest merchant lord could afford. Their eyes came in a startling variety of shades. Often, those of similar shades congregated together. There stood a few pinks; beyond, a spattering of golds and silvers. Blues, greens, more purples like the young woman— no hue was too extravagant for this crowd. All were nearly a head shorter than Leiyn, and she was far from the tallest woman she had met.

None bore weapons beyond a belt knife, and they flinched away from her and her companions. Many elicited small screams of surprise and fear. Citizens, not warriors, she had to assume.

Not only people were present, but a wide variety of creatures as well. A hummingbird flitted around the first young woman, feathers green as rain-fed moss and textured the same. A reptilian creature no taller than Leiyn's knees crouched atop a tent, head cocked, feathered ruff standing on end. Its hide resembled bark, its ruff, ferns. Hogs, dogs, and hissing cats hid behind the legs of the gathered, many with similarly bizarre appearances.

They seemed a peaceful crowd, yet Leiyn did not lower her blades. Peril could still abound here. Around each person—and many of the creatures—drifted clouds of esse. A telltale sign of the presence of magic.

Mahas and spirit beasts.

It should have been impossible, yet a ranger never denied her senses. Tadeo had taught her to trust what she saw, smelled, and heard. The same applied to her lifesense.

Barely had she oriented herself when a shriek came from overhead. She flinched and jerked her head up, expecting the titan to be diving toward them, but she only saw a flash of shocking blue before it vanished into the clouds above. Though it was out of sight, its presence reverberated throughout the sky. It lingered above, unseen.

Leiyn straightened and raised her falchions against the crowd. "Back!" she roared, turning slowly, heart pounding in her chest. "Get back, all of you!"

The young woman backed away with the others. The green hummingbird flew in a circle around her head, than vanished. The woman did not seem to notice. Her lavender eyes were wide, but she had clenched her hands into fists. The pearls embedded in her face formed the vague shape of a bird, Leiyn saw now, wings extending to her ears and tail feathers dancing along her jaw. Blood trailed from her nose from Leiyn hitting her, but already it dried, her magic healing the wound.

Stones were not only on her face—pink coral lined her arms and legs as well. Her clothes looked similarly foreign, despite feeling familiar before. Emerald webbing fell over one bare shoulder to her hip in a sash. Her chest was bound with a violet cloth that shifted to cream around her waist. The skirt fell to her knees, while her sandals lashed up nearly as high on her legs. Every garment had the ember-glow of imbued esse.

The woman did not stand alone. From the panicked crowd emerged other young and hale people. With stone-studded arms and legs bared, they showed themselves to be used to labor, if not combat. Their hard gazes showed little fear of her weapons.

Leiyn readied her walls and met their stares. The village seemed largely a peaceful place. Yet with wounds still raw and the threat of both lyshan and titan looming, she could not lower her guard.

"Leiyn," Isla murmured as Mottle edged her closer. "What in San Inhoa's name is happening? Who are these people?"

"That woman?" Leiyn nodded at the one with lavender eyes. "I think she brought us here. To a grotto."

Her friend uttered a noise of surprise. Batu, who had also approached from behind, asked in a cracking voice, "Like Glade?"

"Yes."

Her friends crowded close, bringing Feral with them. Her horse's esse churned as she issued a warning whinny. It was almost enough to make Leiyn smile.

Good girl.

"They seem harmless," Isla said.

"They're mahas, Isla. All of them. And magic creatures as well."

Leiyn's attention returned forward as the odd young woman took a step closer, hands raised.

"Who are you?" Leiyn demanded, pointing both falchions in her direction. "What is this place?"

"Please, lower your weapons." The woman spoke again in lilting tones, though her command of Ilberian had improved. "You do not wish to alarm the others."

Leiyn did not let her swords waver. "That isn't an answer."

The young woman stared at her in silence for a long moment. Around the edges of the marketplace, more mahas appeared. It might have been her imagination, but as many of those hard gazes seemed leveled at the woman as at Leiyn and her friends.

"I am Ketti Ta'Rul," she said at last. "I am the daughter of a powerful family here."

"And here is?"

"*Nehtu.* Solace, in your tongue."

Solace. As peaceful a name as the people seemed, but for their magic. Leiyn did not let it soften her.

"Is this a grotto?"

"Grotto..." Ketti Ta'Rul's brow furrowed, shifting the pearls embedded in her face so it seemed like the bird folded its wings. "I do not understand."

Leiyn grimaced. She was certain she was right; the air seemed to shimmer here, and even the stones felt different than the world they had left. Other grottos had felt the same: the dryvans' home, Glade; the barracks hidden in the walls of Qasaar; the ruined city where she had fought and slain Man'nah.

"Why bring us here?"

The young woman lowered her hands. "To save you from the Iritu."

Leiyn's pulse quickened. She had to fight the temptation to lower her weapons. "What do you know of the Iritu?"

"More than you ever could." Ketti's expression hardened. "They are our enemies. I believe they are yours as well."

Not all of them. But the woman was not wrong when it came to the lyshan.

Behind, Leiyn felt Isla dismount her horse and edge closer. "She brought us here?"

"Yes."

"And can you get us out?"

"Not yet."

"Then don't be a fool, Leiyn. Lower your swords and let me do the talking."

Reluctant but seeing her logic, Leiyn let her falchions fall to her sides, but she did not sheathe them. A ranger did not live long if they trusted easily. Except for Isla—but her friend was the exception to many rules in life.

"Our apologies," Isla said, standing beside Leiyn. "We have been attacked and are still afraid. Perhaps you could explain what is happening here."

Leiyn recognized the tactic behind the question. It was an old ranger move, to give few expectations of your own in order to tangle an interrogee in their own half-truths and lies. Isla pretended to be more trusting than she felt.

Before Ketti could respond, another stranger spoke, a young man whose clothes put on display the firm lines of his body. His words sounded as hard as he barked them at the young woman's back.

Ketti half-turned to them, her expression spasming with concern, and spoke a few short words back. Whatever conflict the words brought smoothed away when she once more faced Leiyn and her comrades.

"I must be brief. My people also require explanations."

Or demand them. Leiyn scanned them again. Judging by all she had seen, Ketti bringing them here had taken the villagers by surprise as much as it had them. A promising sign, possibly; it indicated no ambush had been planned.

"As I have said," Ketti continued, "you stand in Solace, the home of my people."

"And who are your people?" Leiyn cut in.

Those violet eyes met Leiyn's. "Etemans, we call ourselves. Though Etema is long gone from this world."

It was the final clue. The puzzle pieces of their identity tumbled together. A displaced people possessing mahia, hidden from the world in a grotto...

Guess not all the Gast ancestors disappeared.

Ketti spoke on, oblivious to Leiyn's epiphany. "Please, I beg of you, remain at peace here. I must speak with my people and see to my Ab-Abi." Her mouth tightened for a moment. "He is resilient, but you may have dealt him grave injury with your attack."

Leiyn tried to keep the flush from her face. The man commanding the tempest hawk seemed somehow related to the young woman—a father or uncle, perhaps. Hurting him did not make for a promising start to their visit. But what other choice had she had?

"Our sincerest apologies." Isla bowed her head, attuned as ever to etiquette. "We didn't mean to cause him harm, only to save ourselves. Of course, please check on him. We'll await your return."

Ketti nodded and turned away, but Leiyn spoke before she could leave.

"These others." She jerked her head at the surrounding Etemans. "They'll keep their distance?"

"Seeing you, I trust they will."

The woman hurried away then, two others joining her. By their furrowed brows and sharp tones, they did not speak kind words.

Leiyn cast another glance around, ensuring the villagers stayed well away, then tracked where Ketti went. She traveled down a lane of buildings, set in the shadow of where the great hall of the castle must have once stood. The buildings—houses, most likely—were as friendly in appearance as the marketplace. Red reeds lined their eaves, and more spirit beasts perched atop them, watching warily from afar. Yellow and white paint was drawn onto doors in swirling and dotted patterns reminiscent of Gast tattoos.

She examined the people again. While they did not boast

tattoos, all had precious stones embedded in their flesh like Ketti. Pearls and smooth coral fragments were common, but so were beads of amber and black jet. She guessed how they stayed in place even before she felt the pulse of esse originating from them.

Mahia.

Like how dryvans and lyshans molded their bodies, the Etemans had their own practices. Those stones were more than mere decoration; they were stores of lifeforce to be drawn upon in moments of need, like the amber Xepi had gifted Leiyn. Yet they could never be lost and were likely easier to access as well.

Despite the situation they found themselves in, a smile twisted her lips. For a moment, she almost desired some flesh stones for herself.

"Something amusing?" Isla whispered.

Leiyn turned to her friends. At a glance, they were mostly unharmed. Isla had scarcely a scratch on her. Batu, however, was awash with blood, staining his face and leather lamellar armor. Judging by the few cuts and bruises beneath, most of it was not his. More concerning was his silence. With his brow furrowed and his eyes downcast, Leiyn had to assume memories of violence cycled through his mind. She had faced it often enough to know.

Or maybe he mourns.

Grief crept up on her. She shook her head and refocused on the Etemans encircling them, still casting wary glances their way as they whispered among themselves. They remained in a precarious situation. She could not stop to remember that Belen was dead along with her soldiers. Even the skystriders' passing held its sorrow. They had been misguided in where they led them, but they had only been doing their duty, the same as Leiyn would have.

No. Not now. Not yet.

"Leiyn..."

She did not dare meet Isla's eyes. Her friend's tone told of her seeing what passed through her mind. No doubt the same thoughts crossed Isla's.

They had no choice but to drown them.

"We cannot think about that," Leiyn croaked. "We have to plot our next move."

Isla pursed her lips, the corners of her eyes crinkled with concern, but she nodded. "Right now, I see one option: hearing Ketti out. I don't trust her either," she added as Leiyn opened her mouth. "Not entirely. But being here is better than facing the lyshan, isn't it?"

"You won't hear me arguing with that. But we keep our eyes open and don't let our guard down." Leiyn glanced at the last of their trio. "Batu, you agree?"

Batu raised his head. His eyes were bloodshot amid the grime, and they seemed to have trouble focusing on her. He mumbled what might have been an affirmative.

"Are you alright?" Isla turned and placed a hand to the side of his head. "You aren't acting well."

Suspicion shot through Leiyn. Reaching out with her life-sense, she delved into his esse—and recoiled.

Black threads crawled from the top of his skull.

"Did you knock your head?" she demanded, stepping closer.

Batu's eyes rolled up. His knees buckled.

Then he toppled to the ground.

32

THE BAREST TOUCH

*I*sla was there, wrapping her arms around Batu to keep him upright, but being smaller than him, she could only cushion his fall. Both folded to the cracked pavers, Isla cradling her beloved's head.

"Batu!" Isla whispered, her eyes wide, then spoke louder. "*Batu!*"

"Let me see him." Leiyn fell to her knees next to the former plainsrider, then swept her gaze around at the Etemans, who watched with alarm and interest. "None of you come closer!"

She could only hope they would obey. Leiyn poured all her will into her mahia. With her hands, she felt along Batu's skull and quickly found the wound. It was beside his topknot and as long as her hand. When she removed her hands, her fingers came away red.

"Batu, please..." Tears welled in Isla's eyes.

"He'll be fine, Isla."

The words sprang to her tongue even as doubts assaulted her. Mending bone and muscle was one thing, the brain another thing entirely. She knew little about it beyond what the Catedrál said of the skull being the spirit's temple. Tadeo and Surgeon Arlo had recounted stories of blows to the head being far more catastrophic than it seemed they should be. Leiyn's experiences had confirmed it.

She could not flood Batu with lifeforce; she had only to look at how Isla kneeled on her half-healed leg to be reminded of her past follies. This healing would have to be precise, every movement as exact and intentional as if she loosed an arrow at a mark two hundred paces off.

Leiyn exhaled, attempting to steady her nerves, when she noticed a trio of Etemans creeping closer.

"Back!" she snarled, whipping her head up to stare at them. "I told you to stay away!"

Two of them sprang back, but a middle-aged woman stood her ground.

"*Tubu*. Peace, please. Your friend is injured of the head." She placed a hand on her chest. "I will heal."

Her accent was thicker and harder to follow than Ketti's. Like the young Eteman, this woman's face was dotted with pearls arranged in a bird's shape. Her features were thinner and more petite than Ketti's, and her curly hair was bound back by an ornate beaded tie, yet all was similar enough for Leiyn to notice the resemblance. Most telling were her plum-colored eyes.

"Who are you?" Leiyn demanded. "A relation of Ketti's?"

The woman nodded. "Nidinu Ta'Rul. Ketti's mother." Nidinu shuffled a step closer. "Please. I care wounds like this before."

Leiyn wavered, then shook her head. "I can do it."

She was bending back to Batu when Isla pulled her upright. Alarmed, Leiyn stared into her friend's frenzied eyes.

"Don't." Isla spoke in a harsh whisper. "Unless you're absolutely sure that you can heal him, don't fumble through his head. Or did you forget what happened last time?"

Her words pierced deep. Leiyn tried to steady her voice. "I—"

"Yes or no, Leiyn! *Are you sure?*"

Leiyn tensed her jaw, afraid of what might come next. Isla

was her oldest friend, her sister in all but name. She could only give her the truth.

"No."

"Then step back and let Nidinu Ta'Rul heal him."

"Isla..." Leiyn cleared her throat and fought down the shame roiling through her. Whatever hurt her friend inflicted on her, she still had to take a stand. "We don't know this woman or her abilities. How can we be sure she knows any better than I do?"

Isla was unyielding, her eyes slivers of petrified bark. "Her daughter brought us here, to a world hidden from our eyes. Something you cannot conceive of doing. If I must decide now, I'd wager she knows better than you."

Leiyn opened her mouth to protest, but what could she say? It was an assumption, but as sound of one as they were likely to get.

"And if she meant him harm," her friend continued, "then there are simpler ways to do that. Step aside, Leiyn. For once, you must have trust."

Trust. Had the situation not been so dire, Leiyn might have laughed. Now, of all times, Isla wanted her to trust strangers, foreigners with a mysterious grasp of their language, whose intentions they could not begin to guess at?

But Isla was right on one count. Even with all Xepi had taught her of healing, Leiyn doubted she could save Batu. She could not barrel ahead at his wound like at an enemy in battle, nor even as she had healed the odiosa's brand in a cleansing flood. This was something strength alone could not solve.

Step back, Firebrand, a voice in the back of her head mocked. *Have some trust.*

Clenching her jaw, Leiyn rose and sheathed her swords. Then she looked at the Eteman woman and jerked her head toward Batu.

Nidinu Ta'Rul did not hesitate. Hurrying to the young man, she folded smoothly to the ground, her dress whispering about her legs. Leiyn glimpsed a line of coral beads down the outside of her leg before the fabric hid it from view. The Eteman did not look at any of them, but set her hands to Batu's head, her touch gentle but firm. Leiyn could see she positioned her hand around the wound without touching it.

The woman closed her eyes. Magic surged within her and flowed into Batu.

Leiyn crossed her arms over her chest as she watched the woman work. Nidinu wielded her mahia in ways she had never thought possible. Leiyn's magic was like a bull charging headlong at her target; Nidinu's resembled a water spider, dancing over the pool of Batu's esse and entering it with remarkable precision. Splitting her mahia into tendrils, she worked them in tandem to smooth away the injuries, which spread like black spiderwebs throughout his skull.

The accuracy and speed of her mahia astounded Leiyn. It was beyond anything Xepi or Zuma had displayed. In some ways, it was even beyond dryvans and lyshans.

The marketplace fell even quieter. Hushed whispers rustled among the gathered. Isla had not moved, staring at her beloved's face and Nidinu's hands, unseeing of what occurred beneath Batu's skull. The healer's performance transfixed Leiyn. Though Nidinu never faltered or slowed, the mending was not swift, and judging by the dimming of her esse, it took a fair toll. Leiyn witnessed the precious stones in the Eteman's skin at work as, one by one, their light went dark, drained of the lifeforce they had held.

At last, the healer had burned away all the dark threads. Nidinu lifted her hands and sank back, exhaustion writ across her features. Other Etemans skirted forward, darting glances Leiyn's way. When she did not react, they advanced and lifted the woman to her feet, gifting her with lifeforce as they did.

Isla saw none but Batu. As soon as Nidinu moved clear, she leaned over him, cupping his cheek in her hand.

"Batu? Batu!"

Leiyn moved closer, peering at him from around Isla. Beneath his eyelids, his eyes moved, and small groans escaped his parted lips. She turned to Nidinu, determined to pry answers from her.

Batu speaking pulled her up short. "Isla?"

Her fellow ranger fell on him, shaking with sobs. And laughter, Leiyn was surprised to hear.

"Thank the Saints!" Isla gasped. "I thought I'd lost you."

Batu blinked slowly, then smiled. "Still here. Wherever 'here' is."

"Don't you remember?" Leiyn came closer, worried. "Do you recall anything that happened?"

The former plainsrider turned slowly to look at her. The vagueness in his gaze before had faded. "We're in Solace. I meant, where in the gods-damned hells is that?"

Isla laughed as she folded into his chest. Leiyn had to crack a smile.

"Well," she said, "if you still have your poor sense of humor, I guess you'll live."

Reluctantly, she looked up at the one responsible. Nidinu watched Batu with calm satisfaction, then met and held Leiyn's gaze. Not challenging, but neither yielding.

"Thank you," Leiyn said. "For healing him."

"Yes." Isla rose, wiping at her eyes and nose with a sleeve. "Thank you, Nidinu Ta'Rul. You saved his life. We are in your debt."

Leiyn winced, but there was no taking back the words. Who knew how much a debt might mean to Etemans.

The woman already seemed to be recovering her strength. Gracefully, she bowed her head in acknowledgment. "*Ama vu amatu.* It was my honor."

Before Leiyn could ask what that meant, she sensed people approaching from the lane of houses set within the great hall. She looked up to see Ketti Ta'Rul emerging from the crowd, a man of middling years at her side. The young Eteman's eyes flickered over the scene. Her brow creased.

It was the man who spoke first. Though the words were in Eteman, his concern was plain in his tone as he hurried forward.

The robe he wore was like the togas said to once be worn in the Ancestral Lands, and it flapped about his knees as he strode over to Nidinu and clasped her arms. Another relation of Ketti's, Leiyn had to guess by the stone outline on his face and his violet eyes. Perhaps her father or an uncle, judging by how he took Ketti's mother in his arms.

The young Eteman woman approached Leiyn. With Leiyn's swords sheathed, Ketti seemed to have lost her fear of her, for she came within striking distance. "Your name is Leiyn, no? Did something happen?"

"My friend fell." Leiyn nodded at Batu, whom Isla was helping to sit up. "He took a blow to the head. Your mother healed him."

Ketti murmured something in Eteman, then shook her head with a small smile. "She does as she is. My mother has always sought to help those in pain."

Leiyn remained silent, unsure how to respond.

The young woman grew serious again as she eyed Leiyn. "Ab-Abi wishes to see you. He awaits you in our family hold. Can your friend walk?"

"Looks like it."

As they spoke, Batu stood, one arm wrapped around Isla's shoulder. Though he had collapsed not a half-hour before, he seemed steady on his feet once more, even casting Leiyn a self-effacing smile at her look. Whatever wariness he and Isla had of Solace and its inhabitants had been cast aside.

I'll have to stay alert for all of us.

"We will look after your animals." Ketti's eyes showed uncertainty as they flickered over the horses. "Your bags will remain untouched."

It seemed another bitter draught she must swallow. The alternative to snubbing the extension of hospitality would displease Isla and make their situation more precarious. Swallowing her pride, Leiyn forced out the words.

"Thank you. Be careful with Feral, though. She has a bite for everyone, me included."

Another smile touched Ketti's lips. "That will not be an issue."

Leiyn had her doubts before she turned to Feral. Etemans had already stepped forward to take the reins of their mounts. As the handlers spoke soothingly, Leiyn felt their magic extend forth in a calming mist. To her surprise, Feral relented to the Etemans with barely a rolled eye.

Stifling a twinge of jealousy, Leiyn turned back to the young woman. "We'll go to your Ab-Abi. I think I have some apologies to make." She swept an arm toward the lane of houses. "Lead the way."

Ketti waited for Isla and Batu to signal they were ready, then led them deeper into the castle ruins.

FATHER OF THE TEMPEST

*S*olace was a place like no other.

Once Leiyn was certain Batu would not collapse again, she pried her attention away to take in the Eteman village. Everywhere she looked, unfamiliar sights and scents greeted her. Fires crackled and shouts rose from those cooking, oblivious to the newcomers to their village. In the chimney smoke she smelled spices unknown to her. She wondered if those spices existed in the world she knew, or if they had faded from memory.

Those who stood or sat outside their homes stared at Leiyn and the others with awe and fear. All were adorned in precious stones similar to the Ta'Ruls. Though the brightness and spread of their esses varied, their capacities for mahia exceeded her students back in the Order. Some even surpassed her own.

The spirit beasts that had fled before slowly returned. Golden hounds snuffed at their heels, curious and cautious. Night-dark cats hissed as they passed. The emerald humming-bird returned to flit around Ketti's head, whom she called "Biqqa." The flighty creature was the only one who seemed unafraid of them.

But it was the magic flowing through environment that put Leiyn on edge. It filled the air, the cobblestones, the walls of the houses. No object was too common to be imbued. She glimpsed ladles in cookpots with a sheen of lifeforce. The handle of a wood axe that was wedged into a stump glowed like a live branch. Every garment, whether worn or hung up on lines, shimmered like a starry night.

Even the sky was different. The roof of the castle had largely eroded, enabling Leiyn to see the storm clouds had been replaced by a shroud of gray mist. Flat to her eyes, her lifesense felt it spark with life, like a thousand fireflies winged through it.

Leiyn lowered her gaze, but her lifesense lingered on those low-hanging clouds. Almost, it felt like the desert titan of the Barren, a presence suffusing the fog. She wondered if it was the tempest hawk, ever-watchful, ensuring their good behavior.

Perhaps that watcher was why no one had tried to take away their weapons. Or perhaps it was because the sheer weight of magic possessed by their people would overwhelm them should they attempt to do harm. Whatever the reason, their confidence made her feel no easier about seeing the titan's master.

As she grew accustomed to their surroundings, Leiyn fell in step with Isla and Batu. The former plainsrider had regained his shrewd awareness, though he made for a ghastly sight, painted as he was in mud and blood. Still, she was glad to have him upright again, debt to the Etemans be damned.

Speaking so Ketti would not hear, she murmured, "I've been thinking about the attack."

"Hard to think about anything else." Isla kept her eyes on their escort's back. "I was wondering how they surprised us so thoroughly."

Leiyn winced. "The odiosa cloaked their lifeforce so I couldn't sense it, like Teya did during our expedition to the wardstones back in Qasaar."

Batu nodded. No doubt that ill-fated mission—ambushed by lyshans and half their party slaughtered—had left an invisible scar on him as well as herself.

"It hides the Suncoats from my mahia," Leiyn continued.

"Which means," Isla surmised, "that they can move undetected."

"Mostly. Unless odiosas are scrambling natural senses now—which they might do—sentries should still be able to see and hear them coming."

Her friend chewed her lip. "I'm more concerned about the lyshan with them."

They walked in silence for several paces. The implications were clear: if a lyshan fought on Ilberia's behalf—or, more likely, that Ilberia openly fought for Sharo—then Baltesia was in even graver danger than before.

And I still cannot reach that egreshti *dragon.*

Leiyn shook her head, as if that could dislodge the thought. "We'll worry about that later. For now, we need to figure out how to get out of here."

"Convincing this Ab-Abi seems like a good start." Isla nodded at Ketti's back.

"Though I could do with a rest before we leave," Batu muttered. "They don't seem the type to murder us in our sleep, do they?"

Leiyn set her jaw, keeping her suspicions to herself.

At last, the lanes of bright houses ended at a building larger than most, and one backed by a broken-topped tower. Leiyn craned back her neck to look at it. She sensed someone sitting at the top. They possessed great power, even if it was reduced at the moment. And she recognized their esse from when it had torn beneath her attack.

The tempest hawk's master waited above.

"Be welcome to Hold Ta'Rul," Ketti announced as she ushered them through a rounded door.

Despite the grand name and impressive exterior, the home's interior was modest. Leiyn scanned the surroundings, noting the herbs hanging from the rafters, the doorways to off-shooting rooms, and the unlit hearth. The mantlepiece drew her eye, where one object gleamed brighter than the rest. There, resting on ornate wooden prongs, was a sword, the first weapon she had seen in Solace. Its hilt echoed the style of her own falchions, a coincidence that gave her pause. Why would Eteman weapons resemble Iritu ones when they were supposed to be enemies?

Ketti gave her no opportunity to ask. "Come," the young woman said, moving toward a spiral staircase at the opposite end of the room. "He awaits us in the tower."

With rising trepidation, Leiyn ascended after the Eteman. Each step felt heavy, the battle and healing weighing her down. She did not want another confrontation, nor to face a man she had nearly slain. But as the tower room neared, she drew herself up straight, Tadeo's advice echoing from across the years.

When you face something difficult, face it head-on.

They emerged into a roofless chamber. The wind, deadened by the walls of the castle below, was frigid and alive this high up. Drawing on her esse for heat, Leiyn girded herself against it and strode toward the chair at the opposite end.

The Ab-Abi watched them approach.

As expected, he was an old man, hair and beard white and long. Both were tangled into braids secured by beads of jet. His eyes had a hint of milkiness to them, yet they were no less keen as they raked over Leiyn and her party. Like the other male Etemans, he wore a robe, his made of scarlet reeds that rustled with the slightest movement. Green fronds decorated his shoulders, while golden moss laced the hem. Atop his head sat a circlet of laurel, like a crown of a bygone aeon. A feathered staff leaned against his chair, topped with large feathers of startling azure.

Outwardly, he scarcely resembled that of a man who had been near death a mere hour before. But as she peered at his esse, she saw dark wounds threaded throughout—wounds she had given him. Even so, his strength cascaded over them like a warm wind, contrasting the cold gust against her skin. It well surpassed her own.

She wondered how she had overcome him.

The Ab-Abi's gaze never wavered as Ketti halted a dozen paces before him. The young woman bowed her head and splayed her hands out in front of her forehead, like the open wings of a bird.

"Ab-Abi. I present to you the three newcomers, as you requested." She turned back to them. "Leiyn, Isla, Batu, you stand before Oro Ta'Rul: patriarch of the Ta'Ruls, Father of the Tempest, the Guardian of Solace—and my great-grandfather."

Leiyn shifted, uncertain how to greet such formality. Isla took the lead and bowed.

"Thank you for meeting us, Ab-Abi. I am Isla Ogbi. This is Leiyn of Orille and Batu Khatas." Her friend straightened and cast a sidelong glance at Batu and Leiyn until they both followed her lead, murmuring their own appreciation.

The elderly man made a humming sound before speaking, his voice creaking like the boughs of an ancient oak. "Patriarch Ta'Rul will do. Ab-Abi is reserved for members of our family, as my great-granddaughter should have explained to you."

Ketti's expression did not shift, but Leiyn had the sense she flinched under the reprimand.

Oro Ta'Rul looked again at them for several moments. His eyes settled on Leiyn.

Then his esse swelled and shot upward.

Leiyn gripped her falchions, preparing to dash forward. Yet she hesitated, watching as his magic reached into the clouds and touched the countless sparks within them.

They reacted at once. Clouds writhed, then swirled together. In moments, a black thundercloud appeared above them, then surged down to the ruined tower wall behind the patriarch.

Leiyn bit back a cry. Her instincts screamed to attack. Still, she refrained, holding out against hope that this old man did not mean to claim vengeance against her. For Isla and Batu's sakes, she kept the peace.

The air splintered with a thunderous boom. The black clouds dispersed. In their place perched a bird.

To call it a "bird" felt wholly inadequate, for it dwarfed the size of any other she had encountered. Its wings stretched far along the castle walls to either side, a score or more times her height in length. Its feathers were a brilliant blue, the same as decorated the elderly man's staff, traced with deep violet and light green. A ruff flared about its neck, feathers standing on end. Violet eyes rested above a hooked, black beak. Its stench billowed across her, holding both the acrid edge of urine and the softened scent of petrichor. Magic rolled off its body to crackle across Leiyn's skin.

A tempest hawk. It was a titan, not of cloud and storm, but feather and flesh. Just as Clouded Fang had in grottos, this spirit beast also had a corporeal form.

Leiyn realized she had fallen into a fighting crouch as it emerged. She yearned to draw her falchions. Prey did not face predators unprepared. Like a threatened hedgehog, she meant to bristle with sharp ends.

The titan pulsed with overwhelming power, almost more than she could stand. Any resistance promised to be short-lived.

Yet she let her hands fall from the hilts and straightened. The tempest hawk revealing itself abated a measure of her terror. She was still a guest here. Why save Batu to kill him minutes later?

The patriarch's words resurrected her fear.

"You are strong, Leiyn of Orille. Stronger than most of my people. Few have the power to kill me, the Guardian of Solace. But you might have, if not for my great-granddaughter's... meddling."

Leiyn stiffened. She let the silence draw out the elder's point.

"You are not of our people," Oro continued. "You are not Eteman. Yet you have the *ilis*, the... vitality of one. Who are you, child? Who made you this way?"

34

TRAIL OF SPARKS

ho are you?

The patriarch's question demanded an answer. Leiyn barely tempered her reply.

"Many shaped who I am. But I don't think that's what you mean."

She did not know what he drove at, but she could speculate. Zuma had guessed her early exposure to mahia had awoken it strongly within her. Or that her mother's spirit within her was responsible. She had rarely thought long on the mystery. More than how she had attained power, she was concerned with how she wielded it.

Oro looked down at her in silence. His face might have been carved from wood for all it shifted.

"You were opened to the world from birth," he said, "as is our way. Someone formed you like one of our own. Yet you are not Eteman."

He made a gesture, and the tempest hawk shifted. Leiyn flinched as sparks crackled through the air. She did not dare look at it. A head-on gaze provoked many predators to attack. She would not risk finding out if the same went for this titan.

"You carry *ilis* that is not yours. Scars mar your body. Your weapons and bearing mark you as a warrior. You are not

Eteman," Oro repeated. "So I ask again: how have you come to be like one?"

He did not have to instill threat into his words; his leashed titan provided more than enough. Yet she remained loath to give him the answer he sought. Held at their mercy, she could not muster any trust, even if a Ta'Rul had saved her friend. The story of her birth, of losing her mother and the shaman who had preserved her life, was not his to know.

But silence would prove a poor defense. So she launched an offensive of her own.

"You ask to know my story, but we understand nothing of who you Etemans are." She swept an arm around them, the gesture stilted. Nothing felt casual with the titan's unblinking gaze upon her. "You've hidden here in this grotto for what, aeons? Stood by while the rest of your people suffered. You must have watched—how else could you know our tongue? Yet you did nothing. Before I give my answers, I would know who *you* are, Oro Ta'Rul. And how you explain your cowardice."

"Leiyn," Isla said. A sharp warning.

Part of her shrank from the admonishment, but Leiyn did not let her gaze waver from the patriarch. Her accusations were shot through with wild assumptions and wilder conclusions, but they were the best picture she could form. If any of her claims were off, Oro did not show it.

Ketti proved less composed. From the corner of her eye, Leiyn saw the young woman wince and look at her great-grandfather. Oro turned slowly to stare back at the young Eteman for a long moment before facing Leiyn once more.

"Defending one's home is not cowardice," he said at last. "Refusing to fight when we would fail does not make us uncaring. We have done what we must to survive. Can you claim any less?"

The words arrowed her chest. She could not suppress a jerk. Behind her eyes, she fled the armored lyshan again, leaving Belen and her soldiers to be cut down.

Leiyn tightened her jaw as her eyes burned. Danger still shadowed them.

My sins can wait their turn.

"Ab-Abi..." There was a subtle shift in Ketti's tone as she spoke a few sentences in the Eteman tongue. Leiyn let her eyes flicker to the young woman as she stared up at her great-grandfather with open imploring.

Oro Ta'Rul had seemed made of stone. Now, a sigh melted away the flinty exterior.

"My *at-iti* is correct. I should not hold you guilty where I do not hold us so. You must accept my apologies."

While Leiyn still processed what he had said, the distinguished man rose from his chair and folded his hands over his forehead.

Then bowed to them.

Isla stifled a gasp. Leiyn tried to hide her own surprise and suspected she did a shoddy job of it. After the hostility Oro had shown, she had not expected such a display of respect from him.

"This must come as a shock," the patriarch said as he sat once more, slow with the caution of the elderly. "And I have been a poor host. You do not seem to mean us harm, and we intend you none. I hope my poor manners can be forgiven."

Leiyn glanced at her companions. Batu appeared as baffled as she felt. Isla, however, was once more composed. Drawing herself up, she bowed in return.

"Nothing need be forgiven, Patriarch Ta'Rul. We are the ones intruding upon your sanctuary. We're thankful to you and your great-granddaughter for offering it, and to your relation, Nidinu Ta'Rul, for healing our friend. Had you failed to act, none of us would have survived."

Another score against Leiyn's pride. But could she deny it? She had been too slow, too weak, too frail without Clouded Fang. The lyshan would have torn her apart, then done the same to her friends.

Her hands clenched into fists. She pushed the horrid images away and forced her muscles to relax.

Punish yourself later, Firebrand.

Oro inclined his head. "Gratitude invites a gracious reply. I will relent to your demands and explain the situation in which we find ourselves. You are here because of Ketti's intervention. Though our tenets forbid leaving Solace, my great-granddaughter violated them to save my life, then yours. Our tradition has it that no outsider has ever set foot in our home. For as long as my memory stretches, this has held true."

Once more, Ketti winced. Leiyn wondered at such isolation, and how long it had lasted.

For as long as my memory stretches...

Telling by his esse, Oro was old, indeed. And if these people were related to Gast ancestors, could they have been here for hundreds of years? Thousands, even? Could people survive that long in a grotto?

She had too many questions to contain them all.

"How long have you"—*Hidden away*, Leiyn almost asked, but Isla's look made her adjust her words—"been here?"

The patriarch's chin rose. "Since the beginning of the *Palaq*. The Culling. Since our enemies discovered the passage of time was our greatest frailty. Since one people became two, and both wilted under the shadow of endless threat, the Gasts most of all."

The conversation's timbre had turned more cordial, and she was reluctant to turn it back. Yet she had no choice but to risk it.

"It's the Iritu, isn't it? The lyshans. They drove you here. They're the enemies you've evaded all these years."

Both Etemans flinched. For a moment, visceral fear flitted across their faces.

It was all the confirmation she needed.

Oro swiftly regained his composure. "Lyshans..." He rolled the word around his tongue. "What our brothers and sisters of old call those who linger beyond the *Maru Simmu*—the northern mountains, no?"

It seemed impossible he should know that. She could do nothing but nod.

"They are our enemies, yes, but also the others lingering in the southern forests. All Iritu spilled our ancestors' blood and sought to cull our *semah*, our magic. All bear the guilt of their crimes."

Leiyn kept her expression blank as her mind whirled. *All Iritu.* With each revelation, she became less certain of Ata's friendship. She wished she could summon the dryvan and speak with her. Perhaps there was a reasonable explanation. But she was as powerless to summon her as Clouded Fang.

Did you hurt these people, Ata? Hunt them into hiding?

The patriarch's expression hardened. "Your question troubles me, Leiyn of Orille. How do you know of the Iritu? Their true name is not spoken among your people. You call them woods witches, skin-walkers, Servants of Legion. Dryvans. They are but monsters in stories to most, a mystery to those few who have encountered one. Yet you speak with knowledge that has long been lost."

Without warning, the tempest hawk threw back its head and cawed. The sound thundered in Leiyn's ears, and a fresh wave of its scent burned in her nostrils. Threat crackled over her skin, causing her hair to stand on end.

She scrambled for an answer. Lies would not suffice here, but neither could she divulge the truth. Leiyn chose her words carefully.

"I've spoken with Gasts, both their chieftains and shamans. I've heard the legends of their people and my own. The war never ended for those living in Qasaar. Until recently, they had to ward constantly against lyshan attacks."

Oro cut in. "Again, you distinguish between them. Lyshans, dryvans—they differ only in appearance. They are all Iritu. They all bathed in blood."

Leiyn tried to ignore the shiver of apprehension running through her. She clenched her jaw shut lest she reveal more than she meant to. Any association with dryvans at this point seemed liable to land them in even more trouble.

Ketti stepped forward. "Perhaps we should focus on the matter at hand, Ab-Abi. Let the past lie in the past."

The patriarch cast her a sharp look. Then he nodded and relaxed back into his chair. "Forgive me. This day has been... tiresome."

"No forgiveness is needed," Isla was quick to respond.

Leiyn glanced at Batu and was glad to see his arms crossed over his chest. Clearly, he was inclined toward Leiyn's point of view that, despite being healed by them, they were not safe among these Etemans. If Isla was determined to embrace their captors, at least two of their party would remain on guard.

Oro gave Isla a thin smile, one that scarcely touched his eyes. His gaze shifted back to Leiyn.

"I have answered your questions. Now, I would have you answer mine. I wish to understand who it is we welcome into our refuge. Why is it that an Iritu hunts you? And, once more, how has your *semah* come to be so potent?"

Despite her maneuvering, he had corralled her into a trap. Leiyn looked at her friends, but neither offered a way out. Isla even nodded with an encouraging smile. There was nothing left but to tell the truth.

Unclenching her jaw, she drew in a long breath. "You're right. The Iritu are hunting us—hunting me." She paused, deciding where to begin. "I suppose it started with the Gast shaman who saved my life."

She told the story of her birth dispassionately, brushing over the death of her mother and the angry grief of her father, focusing instead on Zuma's role in her life. She spoke of her mahia, how it refused to be cowed, yet how she endeavored to hide it all the same. Breezing through all the losses and travails of her life, she arrived at the moment that had changed all: when she came back into contact with Zuma and went to Southport with him.

"He saved me again." Leiyn's throat seized at the mention. Touching upon his spark, she forced the guilt back down. "War was breaking out with Ilberia, Baltesia's ancestral homeland. I wanted vengeance for what they had done to the other rangers. So I tried commanding a titan." She remembered being sucked down into the kraken, darkness closing in. The relief of surrender. "But for Zuma, it would have killed me. At the cost of his life, he brought me back."

The others remained silent as she told her story. Leiyn felt it a struggle to move on, even as she little wished to dwell on the loss of the shaman and her failings.

"Before he died, he made me promise to help his people against the lyshans. Then he passed a piece of his soul into me, as is the Gast tradition among shamans." Her hand drifted up to her chest before she forced it back to her side. Her lifesense, however, lingered on Zuma's spark.

"Your mother and the shaman, Zuma," Oro said at last. "These are the lives you hold within you?"

"Yes."

What the patriarch thought of her answer, she could not tell. He merely gestured for her to continue.

"So we went to Qasaar, the Gast city beyond the Silvertusks. Another shaman trained me in mahia—*semah*, as you call it. We fought against the lyshans and won. I killed their leader, Man'-nah. Then I returned to my people to try to win our own war." She nodded to Isla and Batu. "We came to Ore-Ofe to seek allies but were ambushed before we could reach the capital."

"Man'nah?" Oro's intense gaze bored into her. "This Iritu leader—he called himself Man'nah?"

"Yes."

For the first time, the patriarch looked surprised. He settled back in his chair, a thoughtful expression stealing over him.

"You know of Man'nah, Patriarch Ta'Rul?" Isla queried.

His eyes flickered to Isla before returning to Leiyn. "All Etemans know of Man'nah. He was once the greatest among their kind. The greatest, and most terrible."

Ketti's head had fallen as she listened to Leiyn. Now it rose again, lavender eyes filled with fury. "But you did not kill all the Iritu," she said. "And so those remaining marked you for death."

Leiyn grimaced. "I suppose so."

"This cannot be."

She tensed at the patriarch's words. Yet at Isla's look, Leiyn held her tongue.

"I cannot believe it," Oro continued. "There is no victory against the Iritu. They drove our ancestors into hiding and rooted out magic from those who remained behind. You could not stand before one of them. You do not even know how to cross Solace's borders. How could you defeat even one, much less Man'nah himself?"

Leiyn's temper rose at that. "You asked for an explanation. I gave it." She tucked her arms against her sides. "It's up to you if you believe it."

Ketti bit her lip and looked up at her great-grandfather. Oro Ta'Rul continued staring at Leiyn. A moment later, she felt the touch of his mahia. She tensed but did not raise her walls. Though it was an intrusion, the consequences of denying him were too great.

As he withdrew moments later, the tempest hawk threw back its head and loosed another head-splitting screech. Leiyn winced but was more concerned with the patriarch's hardened gaze.

"You have bonded with a *kainox*."

Ketti gasped, her eyes flaring wide. Leiyn met the patriarch's look with an unflinching one of her own, even as the titan's power continued to spark behind Oro's chair.

"Yes," she answered, hoping it was not a lie. "The same as you have with the tempest hawk."

Oro pursed his lips. Leiyn suspected the questions running through his mind. If she had bonded, where was her titan now?

Before either of them could speak, Ketti stepped forward and placed herself between them and her great-grandfather. She faced him with her shoulders set.

"Ab-Abi, please listen to me. You have always taught me to keep my eyes open to the world beyond Solace. You have said again and again that though we hide, we must never be ignorant. Through you and the other elders, I have learned their languages, their histories, their cultures. You have taught me to be unafraid to ask questions."

The young woman's head fell for a moment. Leiyn shared a look with Isla, but her friend appeared just as mystified by what occurred. Batu watched with his arms crossed and brow creased.

"*Ama zabu akki.* I have betrayed your trust. I have invited danger into our home." Ketti's head snapped back up. "But it has stood upon our doorstep! Can it be a coincidence that two Iritu come to *Nehtu* within two seasons? They know we are here, Ab-Abi. We are no longer hidden or safe."

Another Iritu? Leiyn wondered who it had been. As Ketti implied, it made the ambush all the odder. She could guess how they had been found: after Arias escaped, he likely told of their location and intention to cross into Ore-Ofe. And if they knew of the skystrider patrols, perhaps they had even anticipated their being waylaid and taken to the Stormhold.

But the lyshan's manner had been peculiar. Though he had not withheld from violence, he seemed to taunt them more than anything. And he and his Suncoats drove Leiyn, Isla, and Batu into the ruins, as if that had been the plan all along.

Perhaps it had been. Perhaps Sharo had other priorities than hunting her down. Why else attack them here if not to draw the Etemans out?

"Ketti." The patriarch spoke her name like a reprimand.

The young woman hesitated, then backed up several steps, no longer standing between them. Oro looked back at them, lips pressed together. It was a long while before he pried them open.

"These matters must be discussed with the other elders. For now, what is done is done." He extended a hand. "Be welcome to Solace as its first guests. Eat of our food and drink of our water. Accommodations will be made for you here in Hold Ta'Rul. So long as you mean us no harm, you will be treated as one of our own."

Isla bowed, as did Batu. Leiyn half-heartedly followed suit.

"We cannot thank you enough for your hospitality, Patriarch Ta'Rul," Isla said. "I hope we may speak more later."

Oro nodded, then gestured to his great-granddaughter with several words in their tongue. Ketti nodded, then walked toward the stairs they had first ascended.

"Follow me," the young woman said, slowing beside them. "You may rest in my room until food can be found for you."

Leiyn cast one last glance back at the tempest hawk, which had begun preening its feathers, before following Ketti down.

35

THE CULLED

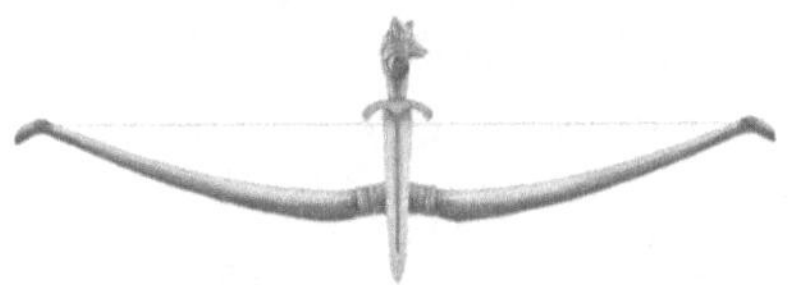

The stairwell hummed with silence and stirring thoughts. Their footsteps echoed throughout the stone tower.

Leiyn barely heard. Behind her eyes, she faced the tempest hawk and its master once more as she sieved through Oro's words. For all her inquiries, she left with more questions than she had arrived with.

Only once they reached the bottom stair did their guide turn back to them. "My chambers are this way. I will show you our washing room as well. We do not have inns, I believe you call them? This is the most we can offer. I apologize for the disorder —I did not expect guests when I rose this morning."

The corners of Ketti's eyes crinkled. Leiyn's lips quirked, unsure if their hostess meant it as a joke. Her mind was still turning over the idea that they had no inns here. The idea of such isolation made her itch to move around, even as her body dragged with weariness.

"That's perfectly alright," Isla rushed to say. "We're grateful for any shelter."

Ketti led them through the hold's dining room and kitchen to an entryway at the far side. In place of a door, there was a drapery of gold and purple beads organized in a flowing design. Ketti swept it open then stood to aside, inviting them in.

Leiyn stepped through first. The interior was tidier than the young woman had implied it would be. A bed, covered in ornate blankets similar in pattern to the doorway drapery, sat opposite under a window with open shutters. The covers were pulled up, though disheveled, as if someone had recently slept in them. Similar to the beds of Qasaar, this one was of hard wood without cushioning, yet promised comfort with the gentle pulse of esse. The desk and chair occupying another wall were also of enchanted wood. Atop the desk lay an assortment of items: beads of amber, half-carved wood figurines, white goose feathers. Most pulsed with varying degrees of esse; to what purpose, Leiyn could not tell.

Against the opposite wall stood a wardrobe, elaborately embellished yet worn and notched with age. Carpets spread across the floor, softening the hard edges of the stone. From wall to wall, it was only five strides—a tight fit for three people.

Ketti moved to the desk, hands tidying its contents as her gaze darted up to them. "As I said, it is a bit messy."

Almost, the young woman sounded shy as she busied herself with picking up the room. Leiyn tried to imagine how strange this must feel. Not only were they the first visitors to Solace—ever, if Oro was to be believed—but they now stood in her private sanctuary. She wondered where Ketti would sleep. Had the Eteman slept anywhere else in her entire life?

"Don't worry," Leiyn found herself saying. "We've been on damp, hard ground for the past month. Being dry and indoors will feel heavenly."

The young woman's eyebrows drew inward, but she nodded and set down the feathers she had picked up. "If you say so."

Sudden pounding shook the front door.

Leiyn whirled, hands finding her falchions as she faced the entrance. Until that moment, she had not sensed the pair of people standing outside the house. The glut of lifeforce filtering through the village dazzled her lifesense; she had to focus to see beyond it.

Yet another thing to be wary of.

Excited voices came from those standing on the other side of the door. Though they did not sound unfriendly, she could not make herself release her weapons.

"Please, do not worry." Ketti squeezed past them and cast a pleading look over her shoulder. "My friends bring your bags."

At a glance from Isla, Leiyn let her hands fall. Batu also released his axe, letting it settle back into the loop at his hip. Warily, she watched as Ketti opened the arched door and admitted two others, laden with familiar saddlebags, into the house.

Though the bags were far from light, the Etemans handled them with ease, their esses augmenting their strength and balance. They set them down near the entrance to Ketti's room, then the trio carried on a rapid conversation in their own language for several sentences. At last, Ketti burst out in Ilberian, "Do not be rude! In their tongue, both of you."

The pair of Etemans faced Leiyn, Isla, and Batu with darting eyes. They looked around Ketti's age; one younger, the other older. The younger one was male, with hair that fell like the boughs of a bush around his face. Amber was his stone of choice, though the pattern it formed on his face defied her immediate comprehension. It seemed to have the shape of a rooster, but with a reptilian head and tail. She wondered if it was the feathered reptile she had glimpsed earlier.

The older had a soft, feminine face, but a body more similar to a man's, with a flat, broad chest and narrow hips. Their hair was cut short, and their angled eyes, colored a startling pink, gazed upon them with steady consideration. Their gemstones were of jet and in the more recognizable shape of a many-antlered stag.

"Ah, apologies," the young man said with a jerky bow. "We, ah, mean no harm."

"He means offense," the other said, bowing with more grace.

Their voice was deep, further adding to Leiyn's uncertainty. "Be welcome, please."

"Better." A laugh danced in Ketti's eyes, but her mouth kept to a thin line. "Now, if you can remember your lessons..."

Leiyn shared a look with Isla and Batu. Before the trio's easy rapport, she could not help but lower her guard.

Ketti gestured to the male. "He is Isirat, and they are Zaki." She indicated the last member of the trio. "You two, meet Leiyn of Orille, Isla Ogbi, and Batu Khatas."

"*Burumu etak akki, basamu ersu akki,*" Zaki said with another bow. "The spirits honor me to meet you."

Leiyn murmured her thanks along with her companions before the question burst from her. "Do you all speak Ilberian?"

Ketti cocked her head. "Ilberian... Ah, yes. The name of your language. Strange, is it not? You were born in the place you call Baltesia, yet you speak the tongue of another land. It is as if you have no true home of your own."

Leiyn faltered before the strange observation, unsure if she meant it as an insult.

"And yet, are we different?" Zaki smiled, the jet embedded in their face shifting. "We live like..." They seemed to struggle for words. "...Like a leech on a hog."

The young man, Isirat, barked a laugh, while Ketti raised a skeptical eyebrow. "*Etaro,* what words! Do not let the elders hear you. You mix enough feathers as is."

"Ruffle," Zaki corrected, even as they shrugged in acknowledgment.

"Ruffle feathers." Isirat shook his head, muttering something under his breath in his own tongue.

"In Ilberian," Ketti reminded him.

Amusing as the three were, restlessness was growing in Leiyn. With tragedies and failures both fresh, her questions pressed with cutting need. Judging by Batu's shifting feet and Isla's strained smile, her comrades were in a similar state.

"Sorry to interrupt," Leiyn said, drawing the gazes of the three, "but we still barely know what's happening. Ever since you appeared in the ruins..." She shook her head, struggling to find where to begin.

Ketti's expression softened. "Of course. I am sorry. Please, would you like to sit while we talk? You must be tired."

"Thank you," Isla said with relief, all but collapsing into a dining room chair.

Leiyn sat cautiously, perching on the edge of hers. With her clothes tattered and her body layered in grime, she would be hard-pressed not to make a mess of their furniture. "Now, if you could explain where in all the Wilds-cursed lands we are?"

The Etemans shared a look. Ketti spoke first.

"As we said before, this is Solace, our home, and we are Etemans. Long ago, our ancestors created this place for us to live so we might survive the inevitable Culling at the hands of our enemies."

"The Iritu," Batu murmured.

"Yes." Ketti clasped her hands and wrung the air like Leiyn might have a condemned hen's neck. "Many aeons ago, our peoples warred. We believed we won that war. Our ancestors slew the strongest among the shapeshifters, took their cities and burned their groves. The few who remained little concerned us, for our civilization thrived.

"The elders say that for centuries, we prospered. Our people spread to every corner of *Alissu'Ba*—these 'Veiled Lands,' as you call them. But though we are a long-lived people, memories of our enemies faded with each generation. And as their absence continued, the shadow of their threat faded to myth.

"But they had not died, nor had their fury abated. I do not know that age can kill them. Their *semah* is strange, their bodies malleable. They thrive off of souls like crows on carrion."

All three Etemans wore disgusted expressions. Once again, Leiyn was glad she had made no mention of the aid they had received from dryvans. She could only imagine their welcome if she had.

"And so the Culling began." Ketti spat out each word. "They started with the patriarchs and matriarchs of the greatest holds.

Their deaths came in the dark of night, and in ways that made them seem accidental. Yet, with them stretched over decades, few suspected anything was amiss. They called it poor fortune to lose all these revered souls and their knowledge before their time. And for a time, that was that.

"As we came upon a century of these poorly timed deaths, however, our ancestors became aware that something was wrong. That legends had returned to haunt them. By then, it was too late."

Assassinations. A frosty hand clenched over her heart. Leiyn could all too easily imagine Ata doing what Ketti accused her of. Green eyes gleaming in the dark. Claws red with human blood.

Did you do this, Ata? Kill their elders in cold blood?

"Our ancestors hunted the Iritu," the young woman continued, "but our enemies proved elusive. Chaos and panic arose as our households were beheaded, our civilization left leaderless, and our ancestral knowledge drained. It came to a point where a decision had to be made: to continue fighting a futile war, or to flee from it."

Ketti gestured around, a bitter smile on her lips. Isirat bowed his head while Zaki stared solemnly at their friends.

"You know which route our ancestors took. The stories claim that those of us who hid were half of those remaining, and that we went to places we could defend: our palaces, sacred places, burial grounds. We split into factions, each led by one of the most powerful remaining families, we Ta'Ruls being one. Then we went where even the Iritu could not follow."

"Grottos." Batu stared at the young woman with an unwavering intensity.

"*Haru*, we call them. But yes."

Leiyn recalled all that Ata and the Gasts of Qasaar had shared of the grottos' nature. They were supposed to be like bubbles in the world's fabric: formed of the same threads, yet woven parallel to them so they did not touch. Some grottos appeared to be inaccessible to those not invited into them, such as when Sharo had isolated Leiyn and Man'nah in a grotto of his making. Others, like the grotto beyond the barracks wall, had been easily infiltrated by the lyshans, to Leiyn and the Gasts' sorrow.

She tried to articulate her thoughts. "So the Iritu cannot come here. Could other Etemans—or Gasts, maybe—enter if they knew of Solace?"

Isirat startled and looked at his friends, eyes begging for confirmation. Ketti shook her head. "No. This is a place commanded by Ta'Ruls. Only we can come and go as we please."

"Only you?" Isla looked at Ketti's friends. "Don't you both have magic as well?"

"Ketti." Zaki spoke her name like a warning. Leiyn's shoulders tightened. She watched their shared looks like a rat would two owls.

"Ab-Abi would not wish me to say more," Ketti said, turning back to them. "I am sorry. I will answer what other questions I can."

More secrets. Yet Leiyn had learned enough for the moment. She wondered what kept control of the grotto in the hands of a single family. Was it connected to the tempest hawk bonded to their patriarch? Could it be something in their bloodline? She knew too little of mahia's origins to say which was more likely, or if another reason was responsible instead.

"We understand," Isla was quick to say. "I'm wondering about something different. You said we're the first visitors to Solace. Is that really true?"

Another wince from their hostess. "It is."

Leiyn exchanged a look with Batu. His suspicion was written plainly on his furrowed brow.

"Why?" Leiyn blurted. "Why bring us here when it's such a risk to yourselves?"

Ketti's expression went as still as a forest pool. Her companions were less placid. Isirat muttered something in Eteman under his breath. Zaki pursed their lips and stared at the wall.

"'To save Ab-Abi," the young woman said. "It was the only way I could."

A lie, or a half-truth, at least. Leiyn kept her suspicion hidden. There was more to Ketti's actions than mere protectiveness. And until she knew their role in the young woman's plans, she meant to keep their hostess at a distance, no matter how kindly she acted.

Ketti stood abruptly. "But I am being a poor hostess. Please, allow us to fetch you food and drink. And to show you to the baths. And bring bedding since you cannot all fit in my bed."

"Us?" Isirat said, standing as well. "I bring the bags already!"

"Brought," Zaki corrected him as they rose. "But we will, of course, help settle our new friends."

"You're all very kind." Isla smiled, though it looked strained, to Leiyn's eye. "Refreshment would be more than welcome."

Leiyn touched her auburn tress, clinging to patience a while longer.

36

ONE OF OUR OWN

*S*he grappled with darkness.

Throwing it off, Leiyn bolted upright. She sat in her bedroll, trying to catch her breath.

Just blankets. Again.

Moments before, she had been fighting the armored lyshan and losing. Even awake, she had to touch her side to be certain blood did not run freely from her. Her heart hammered against ribs that, a day before, had splintered beneath the titanbone mace. Her right arm ached from the whip. Burns from the titan's lightning touched the rest of her body. She could feel the ridges of scars her injuries left behind, dark memories etched into her flesh.

Leiyn quieted her breathing, calming herself as Tadeo had taught her, then tried orienting to her surroundings. Ketti's room, given over to them for the night, was only visible by her lifesense, as were Batu and Isla huddled in their hostess's bed. By their still forms, neither were plagued by nightmares.

They have each other for comfort.

She thought of Teya holding her, their esses twining together, before it became too painful to imagine. Months still lay ahead before their reunion. No need to pick off the scab before then.

Leiyn rolled her head, using her mahia to ease the cricks in her neck. Even with the stone padded by rugs and enchanted like the beds of Qasaar, the floor made for a poor mattress.

Rising and stretching, she drew off the simple clothes they had been given and found her ragged Iritu clothes by the faint remainder of their imbued esse. Though they remained soiled and stiff from the previous day's battle, she preferred them to anything the Etemans had given them.

Dressed, she left the room. Leiyn sensed the rest of the household was still abed. Ketti's parents and great-grandfather slept in rooms on the floor above. Ketti was sprawled out in the dining room area. She did not stir as Leiyn padded past to the front door and eased it open. The hinges were well-oiled, for they made no sound as the door swung closed behind her.

Rubbing her eyes, Leiyn gazed about her. Solace lived up to its name at dawn. The silence, broken only by the small sounds of geese and sheep milling about yards, was welcome after the hubbub of the day before. She breathed in and marveled at the cleanliness of the village. No city smelled so sweet. Even Folly under Itzel's competent guidance could not match it.

The morning air nipped her skin, especially where the rends in her tunic exposed her skin. She set off at a stride. Her muscles quickly warmed as she wove through the broken stones, away from the houses and toward the exterior of the castle ruins. She, Isla, and Batu were prisoners to her mind, yet not one sentry stood watch. Leiyn wondered if the complacency was born from centuries of isolation. Or perhaps the tempest hawk was a more vigilant guardian than she sensed.

She kept an eye on the overcast sky, studying the sparks of esse within its misty folds. None seemed to stir.

For now.

Leiyn soon found a place through the crumbled castle walls and squeezed through. Mindful of the many tons of rock hanging above, she wasted no time sidling through several paces of crumbling stone until she reached the other side.

There, she was arrested by the sight spread below her. Like

in the world she had left behind, the ruins were set atop a hill, affording a view for leagues around. But the resemblances ended there, for where forest had spread before, now there were fields of crops and feeding grass, green with summer vitality.

She sensed people among the fields. Here as everywhere else, farmers rose before all others. But these were no ordinary farmers. As she watched, they moved between the even rows and pulsed lifeforce into the plants. Even at a distance, Leiyn detected how the burst of energy filled each plant, then shot it up in growth.

Grass reached inches higher. Plants flowered and produced their fruit. In moments, vegetables grew, ready to be harvested.

They never hunger. Never want for anything.

This was abundance. True wealth. And from what she had seen, it was available to all. The simple luxury of ample food gave time for all the decorations she had seen, the delicate weavings and carvings. It had allowed the Etemans to make their bodies, their clothes, and their homes into works of art.

Her head swelled with insight. Did this method of growth apply to animals as well? Did they have all the wool and feathers they could want? They did not eat meat, telling from supper the night before, but that seemed to be by choice rather than necessity. What could become of a civilization with such resources? She ached with the idea of the paradise. Even with the inevitable jockeying for power among the wealthy and noble, still, she yearned to believe it could exist.

The brightening world drew her attention beyond the fields. This isolated world ended there, and a thick bank of fog began. Ordinarily, fog would have choked out any light, but this cloud caught fire. Orange, red, and yellow grew from the east, spreading like a forest fire in a drought. Leiyn had to squint before its intensity, but she could not look away. The mist writhed, making it seem a wall of flames. Lifeforce stirred within, as if the inferno were a devil of Catedrál lore come to life.

"It is stunning, is it not?"

Leiyn did not startle as Ketti stepped up beside her. She had not been so captivated by the dawn as to fail to notice the Eteman's approach.

"Yes," she admitted. "Even more than sunrises in my world."

"Ah, yes. You do not have the *Kai'am*, the Shroud, there. Is it true that you cannot stare directly at the sun?"

The question brought her gaze around to the young woman. She wore a bare-armed, one-strapped dress, as colorful as her clothes from the day before, and did not seem to feel the dawn chill. Her esse glowed warm.

Leiyn spoke her realization aloud. "You've never seen the sun."

Ketti winced and nodded. "It must seem strange to you. Never leaving this place. Never stepping foot in the natural world. Almost never," she amended.

"A bit. But I've faced lyshans before. I can understand it."

They watched the light stretch all the way around them, setting fire to the entire misty dome over Solace. Then, as quickly as they came, the colors faded, returning the world to gray.

Ketti broke the silence. "You have caused quite the stir, you know. Not even when Laqip and Gemeti had a dalliance has there been so much... ah, what is the word?"

"Commotion? Ruckus?" Leiyn smiled. "It wasn't really us that caused it, though."

The young woman winced again. Her eyes darted to Leiyn, then away. "I could not stand by like we always have."

"I'm glad you didn't." She grimaced but forced out her next words. "We'd be dead if you hadn't come."

"And Ab-Abi, too."

At the mention of the patriarch, one of Solace's many mysteries rose in Leiyn. "Your great-grandfather said something I haven't been able to get out of my mind. That my mahia is like an Eteman's—'One of our own.' What does that mean, really?"

Ketti nodded as if she had expected the question. "Our

semah does not happen by accident. When a child is born, a midwife opens them to *Tlalli's* blessing."

"Opens them?"

"I do not know the precise method. But it involves touching the child's *ilis* with magic. The *dalah*—ah, what is the word?"

"Stimulation? Stirring?"

"It will serve. The *stirring* of their esse so early in life causes the magic to grow." Ketti cocked her head, considering Leiyn. "You said your mother gave her life for yours. And a Gast shaman made this occur. This is likely why your *semah,* your mahia, is so potent."

Leiyn looked back to the fields, blanketed now with a dimming golden glow. A strange hollowness filled her. *Happenstance.* It was mere accident that had shaped her and her abilities. Had she not needed saving at birth, had she been born stronger, she might never have possessed mahia. It certainly would not have asserted itself so she could scarcely repress it.

Magic had haunted most of her life. Part of her wanted to curse Zuma for those decades of shame and misery. But gone were the days she relented to mindless resentment.

Tadeo had sometimes said, *Think on what is, not what might be.* She could not dwell on a life that never existed. She had been born dying. Her mother had given her own life for Leiyn. Zuma did what he saw as right.

In the end, he had given her a gift.

Leiyn closed her eyes. A ranger did not cast aside her truest arrow. Mahia had saved her time and again. It had kept her friends alive. Without it, she could have never stood up to Man'nah and left the Gasts better off for her coming.

She delved inside herself to find Zuma's spark. *Thank you, old friend. For all of it.*

The piece of the shaman's soul warmed at her touch. An acknowledgment of her attention, if not her words. It felt a reassurance all the same.

"If you do not mind, I have a question."

Leiyn opened her eyes to find Ketti staring at her. There was something sharp to her gaze that put her on guard. She hid her alarm behind an arched eyebrow.

"Let's hear it."

A smile crossed Ketti's lips, but it was fleeting. "You have bonded with a *kainox*, a titan. I can sense this as Ab-Abi did. Yet even when the Iritu threatened you and your companions' lives, you did not call it to your side. Why?"

Leiyn looked away, lips pursed, wondering if it was wise to divulge her weakness. Yet she had seen the Etemans' mastery of mahia. Oro Ta'Rul did not struggle to summon and command his tempest hawk. If anyone understood her problem, it would be them.

"Yes, I bonded with a titan in my time of need. And I've only called him to me twice, the last time being when I killed Man'nah. Since then..." She grimaced. "He seems far away and our connection thin. It's still there, like you've sensed, and I can feel him, but..."

"You cannot reach him."

Leiyn looked back at the Eteman to find her staring over the fields, eyes narrowed. After a moment, Ketti returned her gaze.

"I am not bonded. Yet, to prepare for the day when I will become Solace's protector, I understand how it is done. Perhaps I can help you."

Leiyn tensed, waiting for the request that must follow. Rarely was aid given freely between strangers. Yet the young woman only ran a hand over her hair, smoothing it.

"But not yet. We must wait for a time when we may be undetected. Just now, it would attract too much attention, and that is something we both must avoid."

"A wise plan." Leiyn tracked down a thought prickling her mind. "You say you're not bonded. But what about that hummingbird who follows you?"

"Biqqa?" Ketti smiled. "We are not bonded. She has been fond of my company since I was a child."

"I know a creature like that. There's a fox, a silver one, that has followed me most of my life. I've never known why. Gasts speak of animals of our spirit in their myths, beasts manifested from our being. But Chispa doesn't seem a part of me. Or if he is, he walks his own path."

"Animals of our spirit?" The young woman frowned toward the dun horizon. "No, the *etaro* are not born of us. They are the children of *Tlalli*, the same as the *kainox*."

"*Etaro*. That's what you call spirit animals like Biqqa?"

"It is."

"Why do some follow us, then?" Leiyn gestured toward the village beyond the ruined wall. "Why do they gather and stay in Solace? They're not domesticated like horses or livestock—at least, my fox isn't. Surely, there must be some kind of bond."

"A bond, to be certain, but not in the way of titans. That is a chain, forged in dedication to one another, of mutual sacrifice. The *kainox* have been made that way. 'Broken in,' as you might say in your land."

"Broken in... You cannot mean tamed?" While not every encounter she had with a titan had ended in disaster, she could never call them tame.

"No. Not tamed." There seemed a wistful look to Ketti's far-off gaze. "Long ago, they were changed to suit my ancestors needs. *Nox'mekva*—the Tumult of Titans. When we broke the world."

Leiyn burned to know more, but the Eteman continued before she could ask.

"But that is a different tale. The *etaro* were not affected by the Tumult. They choose who they follow, should they follow any." Ketti looked sidelong at her. "It is the highest honor to be chosen by such a spirit. Most are creatures pure of malice and evil intent. For one to look upon your inner being and judge you worthy... It is not a privilege to be taken lightly."

Leiyn nodded. She had always been baffled by Chispa's attentions. Now, they humbled her as well. She wondered if he fared well, wherever he traveled with Ata. If indeed they still remained together.

"Regarding your issue with your *kamit*, your bonded," Ketti continued, "I will come to you when it is time."

"Thank you."

Leiyn's smile felt forced. She faced forward, hoping the woman would not see. Though she was beginning to like the Eteman, she could not fully trust her. And she did not want Ketti to see her hunger for that promise.

Soon, she might understand her bond with Clouded Fang. She could be the Prima Maha that Baltesia needed. She would not have to fear the red-armored lyshan or Sharo any longer.

But not yet.

Isla and Batu had awoken by the time she returned. As she stepped within, the mood of the room shifted. The events of the previous day came rushing back.

They were dead. Belen. The soldiers. The skystriders.

She had failed them.

Leiyn sank onto the bed and rested her elbows on her knees, feeling as ragged as the clothes she wore. Batu sat next to her. As cautious as if she were a rabid hound, he pressed a hand to her shoulder. His esse burned steady and true.

"We'll do right by them," Isla said, addressing their unspoken thoughts. "But perhaps we should discuss how we'll do that."

Leiyn raised her head to stare at a tapestry on the opposite wall, a pastoral scene of animals and ranchers woven into its face. "Killing that damned lyshan would be a fair start."

Batu let his hand fall away. "If anything can kill it."

"Ketti might help with that."

Leiyn told them what the young woman had said that morning. By the end, she was standing again, unable to keep still. She found she preferred the energy of anxiety to the torpor of mourning.

Isla let out a long sigh. "I don't know, Leiyn. Is that wise?"

"Probably not." Leiyn flashed a wicked smile. "But I've never been much for wisdom."

Her friend rolled her eyes while Batu spoke up. "Leiyn's right. If Sharo hunts us, she needs Clouded Fang. There won't be Etemans to save us the next time a lyshan comes."

Leiyn gave him a nod, trying to ignore the stinging of her shortcomings. "Exactly."

"Fine," Isla relented. "But as soon as you have your answers, we must request of Patriarch Oro that he release us. Our mission has been delayed too long as it is, and Southport remains under siege."

"Maybe we don't need to go to Ore-Ofe."

Leiyn and Isla both turned to Batu.

"Explain," Isla said.

Warning rang in the word, but Batu did not flinch from it. He leaned forward, eyes alight with excitement. "We were to make allies of the Ofean mahas, right? But that might not be necessary. Maybe we could find stronger allies right here."

"The Etemans?" Isla crinkled her brow. "Batu, I don't see how that would happen. They've hidden here for centuries. What could possibly draw them back into the world?"

Leiyn agreed. Except for Ketti, these people seemed too set in their ways to change them, even if it might be necessary for their survival. But she had no intention of intervening in what verged on a lovers' quarrel.

Batu held up a hand. "I know; it's a shot for the stars. But we're already here. Isn't it worth trying?"

"Maybe. Maybe not." Isla lowered her gaze to her hands, wringing them like she tried untying a stubborn knot. "Any delay might make us too late to return to Southport. You saw the assault when we were still there. More might have come since. All those people, all they've worked for... we cannot risk it."

As a sullen silence fell, Leiyn dared to speak. "Let's keep both options in mind. For the moment, we know what we need to do." She paused, then reluctantly said, "Besides, we've yet to see if they'll let us leave at all."

The ominous words rang through the room. Isla sucked in a breath, then let it out.

"We'll try to bring them around. But I cannot guarantee—"

Esse blazed into the room.

Leiyn was on her feet, falchions half-drawn, before her mind caught up. She stared at the creature before her, scarcely able to comprehend what she saw. But she knew him by his esse.

"Chispa?"

37

UPROOTED

"Chispa," Isla repeated. "Isn't that your silver fox?"

Leiyn nodded, her eyes remaining on the spirit beast. Had she lacked her lifesense, she might have never recognized him. He was still in the shape of a fox and had a silver sheen, but there, the resemblances ended.

In place of thick fur grew shining meadow grass undulating across him like a constant breeze flowed past. His tail was a braid of long leaves that twisted and untwisted together, as natural a movement to him as a dog's wagging. His eyes shone with an inner light. In place of the fiery bronze, they were now emerald all the way through, a shade somehow familiar.

His esse, too, had undergone a transformation. Where it had been kept coiled about his body before, now it flowed as freely as his grassy fur. He seemed at ease in Solace as he never had been in their world.

Releasing her falchions, Leiyn kneeled before him and held out a hand. Chispa padded closer to sniff her fingers, then nuzzled his snout against her palm. His lifeforce touched hers, as soft as his fur.

Leiyn repressed a shiver. She did not draw away, but allowed the silver fox to come closer, his esse intruding deeper.

"What are you?" she murmured as he investigated her inner self.

Chispa had always been a strange creature, but this transformation turned everything she knew of him on its head. In her world, he had resembled any other fox. Here, he appeared more like a miniature titan.

"Are you a little titan, Chispa?"

"He looks like it," Isla murmured. Neither her nor Batu moved closer, equal parts fascinated and wary.

"My people have stories of these creatures." The former plainsrider frowned down at the fox. "Spirits that play tricks on humans. Have care, Leiyn."

She knew it to be prudent, but it was impossible to distrust Chispa. She tried to put the thoughts into words.

"He's watched over me. All my life, when I needed him most, he's been there." Leiyn dared to brush the back of her hand over the fur behind his jaw. The meadowgrass was silky and fine like hair. She doubted she had ever touched anything softer. "Chispa won't hurt me."

"Leiyn..."

The shimmering fox stepped closer. His eyes drew her in. Was it her imagination, or did the light in them brighten? His esse seemed to expand, growing like the grass of a lea after a rainstorm. She longed to bury her face in his coat.

Slowly, carefully, Chispa nuzzled her stomach. Then, like he grew brambles, his lifeforce cut and lodged into hers.

"So. You survived."

Leiyn almost jerked away. Only recognition of the voice made her stop.

"Ata." She spoke aloud, unsure if the dryvan would hear her thoughts alone.

Her friends started speaking, but Ata's voice inside her skull commanded her attention. *"I see much. But this, I didn't anticipate."*

Her senses twisted. In place of Ketti's room, a different locale asserted itself, if in faint impressions. She smelled crisp rain on old stone, the heavy musk of jungle underlying it. Rain pattered in her ears. To her eyes appeared the gray ruins, the lines of it blurred.

A face came into view, one at once familiar and foreign. Only the bright green eyes had any clarity to them.

"How are you here?" Leiyn tightened her hands over Chispa's coat. The silver fox did not seem to mind, remaining still against her body. "Do we speak through Chispa?"

"You might call it that."

One enigmatic answer after another. Leiyn ground her teeth, heat spreading through her chest. But, frustrated as she might be with the dryvan, she knew better than to let her temper get the best of her.

"You have some explaining to do."

"Do I?" Leiyn could see her smile, her angular teeth white against the dark slash of her mouth. *"Something troubling you?"*

"You know damn well what is." Her control was slipping. Leiyn steeled her will and tried again. "The Etemans. Why keep them a secret? And why do they believe you to be their enemy?"

"Because I am."

Like a frigid gust blew in, Leiyn's anger was extinguished, replaced by creeping dread. She wondered if she should release Chispa and flee while she still could. But her curiosity had always been too rapacious for her own good.

"Explain, Ata. Now, or we're done."

Her companions' questions and the droning rain carried on in the background. As the dryvan failed to move, Leiyn wondered if Ata was on the verge of striking her. If barely restrained rage simmered beneath the surface of her acorn skin.

Ata closed her eyes, the green of them fading from view, then collapsed to the ground.

"Ata? Ata!"

Leiyn could barely tell what was happening. From the vague impressions she had, something seemed to extend from Ata, dark and sinuous. Serpents?

"Roots," Ata whispered into her mind.

She did not know what to make of it. The dryvan seemed more like a tree than ever before. Was she rooting in place like Eld had in Glade? What did it mean among their kind?

"We root when we feel... unsteady." Ata's head rose, a glimmer of emerald shining from her eyes again. *"When our world is uncertain. Perhaps from anger. Or from sorrow."*

Leiyn held her tongue. Her fingers dug into Chispa. The silver fox pressed hard against her.

"I have kept secrets for so long, Awakener. There is an inertia to sharing them. You kept your shame hidden for two decades. Mine have lain dormant for millennia."

The dryvan's eyes opened fully, capturing and holding Leiyn.

"Yet they must be dug up, like roots long buried in earth. These things... I should have confessed them as soon as you struck down Man'nah. I should have known you could have no master but yourself. Even so, I tarried. I made excuses. I sought to confirm what I had suspected all along. And I gave Sharo more time to consolidate his power."

Sharo. Another of the many mysteries plaguing her. But all Leiyn could do was sit and listen.

Ata spread her arms. Even with blurry vision, Leiyn detected the sharp tips of her talons. *"They do not lie, Leiyn of the Wilds. I and all Iritu remain enemies in the eyes of the Etemans. After the sins we committed against them, it could be no other way."*

"So it's true. You hunted them across centuries. You tried to cull them of magic."

"That was our intention."

Leiyn closed her eyes, reeling from the admission. To her surprise, the vision of Ata and the ruins did not disappear but sharpened behind her eyelids.

"Why?" she whispered. "How could you? Slaughtering innocents..."

"That is not the whole story."

"I think I have the gist of it."

Ata held up a hand. *"Peace, my friend. I do not call you that idly, nor do I retract it. And I do not mean to make excuses—there is no excusing what I have done. But innocence and guilt may not be as clearly drawn as you believe."*

Leiyn clenched her jaw. Though her gorge rose at the thought of Ata butchering humans, she needed to hear what she had to say. She needed the truth—the Iritu half of it, at least.

"Tell me."

The skin-walker sighed. *"My people struck the first blow. The Etemans' ancestors came to us, fleeing their homeland. Something had come over it—an unspecified disaster. I never bothered with the details, nor did the rest of the Kin. Such concerns seemed below us then.*

"The Etemans had suffered and sought refuge among our people. But, powerful as we sensed them to be, they were still mortals. The eldest and strongest among us decided to turn them away, leaving them to wander the northern wastelands and make their own way. I and most of the others agreed with this decision. What were the fleeting lives of a thousand mortals next to our great civilization?

"But a few objected, worrying that our derision would create powerful enemies should they survive the harsh existence awaiting them. Even then, the Etemans had leashed the Vast Ones, though they had not yet achieved the mastery they would. Among those speaking these warnings was Sharo."

"Sharo?"

A harsh laugh broke from Ata, rough as two trees rubbing against one another. *"Oh, yes, he was there. Sharo was very different then. Nothing like he is now. But then, we've all changed."*

Silence fell again, enough that Leiyn heard Isla's plea.

"Leiyn, please, answer us!"

She drew away from the dryvan enough to say, "I'm fine. Don't worry. I'll explain soon."

Releasing her hold on Ketti's room again, the scene of the

ruins reasserted itself more strongly than before. The dryvan's eyes were like green fires as they peered into her.

"*No one listened to him or the others,*" Ata continued, as if there had been no interruption. Perhaps, lost in memories, the dryvan had not noticed. "*We killed a few of the refugees to make an example, then sent the rest on their way. Before our wardstones and artifacts and heritage, they had no choice but to depart.*

"*Years passed, a great many. Decades, centuries? Too much time to recall. We tracked their movements throughout the frozen tundras we'd exiled them to, but few paid the Etemans much heed beyond that. Still, Sharo never stopped whispering of the threat they posed. His opposition pushed him ever further from the innermost circles of influence.*"

Ata bowed her head. Several long moments passed before she raised it again.

"*Then they returned. This time, they did not come with pleas for aid, but spitting fire and blood. Each one was like you, Awakener: warriors fueled by titans, their leashed Vast Ones come in a terrifying variety. They toppled our wardstones, slew our warriors, all without a word exchanged. When the first city fell, we sent emissaries to their leaders to sue for peace. None returned.*

"*So we fought. We slaughtered one another. I was on the frontlines of that war. In each battle, I bathed in Eteman blood...*"

The dryvan trailed off. Leiyn wondered if Ata sensed her revulsion. If she could see the horrific scenes playing out in her mind.

"*But we were losing. We Iritu never flourished in great numbers. For each one of us, there were a hundred Etemans. And their magic was potent, their command of titans masterful. It was a doomed war from the start.*

"*We couldn't flee, rooted to the land as we were. We had no choice but to fight. Even if it could only end in our destruction.*"

"What do you mean you were rooted to the land? Why couldn't you leave?"

Ata bared her teeth. With the uncertainty of the vision,

Leiyn could not tell if it was a smile or a warning. Knowing Ata, it was likely both.

"It is not a thing you can understand."

"Maybe not. But let me try."

The shapeshifter barked a laugh. *"Very well. This secret can harm us no longer."*

Yet still Ata paused, seeming to struggle to form the words. They came out of her with all the reluctance of a grub pulled from a rotten log.

"We were not born like humans or animals. We were grown. From our Ialadta—our Mothertrees—we sprouted and took shape."

Again Ata hesitated, then waved a clawed hand through the air.

"All the Mothers are gone now. But they were the reason we stayed. We fought to protect them. For if the Mothers were taken away, we would cease eventually. The Iritu would slowly grow extinct. As we have."

Leiyn tried to comprehend the concept. *Dryvans are grown from trees...* What kind of tree could form such creatures? Even more important was their role: that was how they reproduced. Now, they were the last of their kind. It was why they all seemed so ancient and so few.

No Iritu would ever be born again.

"I'm sorry, Ata." She floundered for words, then huffed out her frustration. "It's all... Omn above."

"Yes." The word whispered in Leiyn's head. *"My Mothertree was the last to fall. I meant to die protecting Her. But Sharo stopped me. 'It is too late for Her,' he said. 'But not for us.'"*

Again, Sharo intersected with Ata's life. The question of who he was to her tipped Leiyn's tongue, but again she refrained. Ata trembled with repressed emotion already. Push her too far, and she might learn nothing more of this history.

"And then... you did what Ketti said you did. You killed their shamans."

"We did. It was at Man'nah's command, but the idea origi-

nated from Sharo. He'd always been clever. Now, vengeance focused and honed his cunning. I... I didn't know what else to do. I preferred hatred to sorrow."

Leiyn winced. "I know the feeling."

Ata's eyes brightened, their intensity pinning Leiyn. *"It was wrong. The Etemans we killed were not the ones who had destroyed our people. They were their descendants, profiting from their ancestors' actions, but innocent of the crime we placed on them. Only as we neared our goal of expunging magic from their lines did I come to realize this. That our vengeance was as terrible as what they'd done to us.*

"Eld helped me see the truth. Under his leadership, we defied Man'nah and his followers, Sharo among them, and protected those remaining of the people who became the Gasts. That war killed many of those few who survived among us, but we fought it. No longer could I stand by and let these atrocities continue. And what other meaning did my life have by then?

"In the end, we won through resilience. Not wishing to weaken his followers further, Man'nah withdrew across the mountains, claiming the lands where we had once banished the Etemans. Since, we have kept an uneasy truce—or so I believed. Until Sharo's schemes showed it to be a farce."

"But when the Gasts were driven beyond the Silvertusks—you knew what awaited them."

"Yes. But long ago, we decided mortal affairs were best settled among yourselves. The fate of Etema's children was not our responsibility."

"Even if weakening them allowed their lands to be conquered?"

"Was it not your ancestors who conquered them? And whose lands were they before, if not my people's?"

Leiyn started. When had she begun taking the Gasts' part in that conflict? Ata was right: Ilberians had taken it from Gasts and the other native peoples. Should she not be on their side?

She contemplated all she knew of the history of the Veiled Lands. The bloodshed between the Iritu and Etemans. The

Titan War between the Ancestral Lands and the natives. And now Baltesia's own conflict with Ilberia.

Perhaps no side in war was innocent. But if she had to choose one, she would never support the oppressor.

"This is my home," she said. "But I wouldn't have slaughtered others to take it."

Ata grinned. "*I believe you.*"

A kindness, that reassurance. Its warmth swiftly fled. "There's still much I don't understand. Like why you're here now."

The smile faded. The light in her eyes waxed brighter.

"*Because the Etemans cannot continue to hide. This is their world as well as ours, though they have forgotten it. If they refuse to come to its defense, there will be nothing for them to return to. And they are not as hidden as they believe.*"

There was an edge of threat to the dryvan's words she could not ignore. Despite Ata's words, despite having seen her assist the Gasts against the lyshans and her saving Leiyn's life, she wondered if a sliver of old animosity did not still burn within her.

"They won't come out, Ata. There's nothing you or I could say that could convince them."

No. There is not.

"Then how?"

Ata rose from the ground. The roots that had dug in between the pavers around her retreated into her legs, leaving them the lithe shape they had been before.

"*How is a fox flushed from its den?*"

Before Leiyn could answer, Chispa leaped free of her arms, ripping the vision away.

"Wait!" Disoriented, Leiyn sprawled after the silver fox. But Chispa pressed against the back of the wall, grassy fur standing on end. The green faded from his eyes, returning to the burnished bronze they had always been before.

They did not stare at her.

"Leiyn..."

As her lifesense returned to Solace, Leiyn realized she and her companions were not alone anymore. Slowly, she rose to her feet to face the newcomers.

Ketti stood, her expression carved of ice. At her shoulders were her parents. Her mother's brow was creased, and she had a hand on her daughter's arm. Her father wore a grave scowl.

"Please," he said in heavily accented Ilberian. "Come with us. The elders request an explanation."

38

THE FINAL MARK

Explanation?

Leiyn glanced over her shoulder at her companions. Until she understood the situation, it was best to play innocent.

Turning back, she asked with forced calm, "Is something wrong?"

Ketti opened her mouth to respond, but her father spoke first. "All will be made clear before the elders. Bring the *etaro,* the, ah—"

"Fox," Ketti murmured.

"Yes, the fox."

Anger flickered through Leiyn. But with tension thick in the air, she snuffed it out.

"I don't command him. He comes and goes as he pleases."

Ketti's father narrowed his eyes. "*Burumu ek basa.* That cannot be for an Iritu pet."

Leiyn flinched as his mahia lashed out, but it was not aimed at her. A yawp from behind and the recoiling of Chispa's spirit made her realize his target. She whirled to find the fox trembling and hunched against the floor. At first, she thought the Eteman had struck him; then she saw the bright tether running from the fox to Ketti's father.

A leash.

She turned back, lifeforce bunched inside her as tightly as her fists. "Let him go."

"Leiyn, please." Ketti shrugged off her mother's hand and stepped toward Leiyn. "Do not resist. We simply wish to speak."

"Release the fox first. Then we can talk."

"No." Ketti's father spoke with unflinching resolve.

Gritting her teeth, Leiyn tried to think of a way out. She did not want to hurt any Etemans, nor could she take on the entire village even if she were willing. Even if she did overcome them all, what then? As long as she failed to summon Clouded Fang, they could not leave Solace. Chispa may have found his way here, but he had not brought Ata in. She doubted he could give them an escape even if he was not under the control of Ketti's father.

"Leiyn," Isla spoke from behind her. "Do as they say. Please."

What else can you do? part of her mocked.

Leiyn exhaled and settled her mahia. She let her shoulders fall.

Seeing her calm, Ketti's father nodded. "Come. We ask that you leave your weapons here."

He turned and departed. Ketti and her mother gave them a last glance, then followed. Chispa reluctantly rose from where he crouched and tailed them, head drooping. Leiyn burned with fresh fury as she watched the magic tug him along, but she freed her weapons belt all the same and let it fall to her bedroll. She heard Batu do the same behind her.

"Come on," Isla whispered, tugging on Leiyn's arm as she passed.

All she could do was let her friend pull her after.

The air outside sat heavy and cloying in her lungs. As Leiyn stalked after the Etemans with Isla and Batu, each breath came harder than the one before. Glancing at the cowed Chispa only heightened the feeling.

Breathe, just breathe.

Ketti's father—Arash Ta'Rul, as Ketti introduced him—led their party with a stiff back. He did not look or act like a warrior, yet Leiyn felt the powerful pull of his mahia. Not as mighty as the patriarch of the Ta'Rul family, but significant enough to tense her shoulders. A hound remained wary when facing a wolf. His anger rolled off him, as palpable as his magic.

Iritu pet, he had called Chispa.

They knew. That the silver fox associated with Ata. That Leiyn and her friends were not free of dryvan influence. How deep did their knowledge go? Had they heard the discussion held through the fox? They spied on the world—how could they miss a dryvan standing in their ruins? Or the maha using her magic in their village?

She had not meant to take a risk. Had not known what she was doing until it was done. But she could have pulled away. She could have ended the conversation before it was too late.

If only I weren't so damned curious.

The three Ta'Ruls led the way through the village. Curious eyes followed their passage. Leiyn kept her gaze forward and her chin up. Beside her, she sensed Isla looking around them with a nervous air, and Batu similarly wary.

They passed through the crumbling front gate. As with the area to the west, this differed from their world. Instead of a road cutting through the jungle, more fields proliferated there. The exception was a clearing at the bottom of the slope. A circle two dozen paces across, it was ringed with archways formed from tree trunks that twisted themselves into braids. Flowering vines draped between the arches. In the center was a still more startling sight: a platform made entirely of amber and pulsing with esse. How such a thing had been constructed defied her comprehension.

At the peripheries of the amber stage sat a dozen Etemans on benches. One of their number stood in the center. She guessed who it was before recognizing his ancient lifemark.

"Patriarch Oro Ta'Rul awaits," Arash said, beckoning them on.

They made their way down the winding slope. Leiyn fell back in step with Isla and leaned closer.

"If this doesn't go well—"

"We'll make sure it does," Isla interrupted. "We don't have any other way out of here, remember?"

Leiyn glanced back at the silver fox, who remained hunched down as he slunk behind their party. "Ata reached us through Chispa. Maybe he can show us a way out."

"Not until he's freed. Leiyn, promise me you won't be rash. For Tadeo's sake."

Leiyn grimaced. "You had to bring him up, didn't you?"

"Whatever makes you listen." Her friend pressed her arm, almost hard enough to hurt. "Please. I mean it."

"Fine. I won't strike the first blow."

She glanced at Batu, who strode on Isla's other side. His right hand hovered at his waist, as if ready to grab the axe he had left behind in the room. Even so, with a thunderous scowl on his face, she wondered if she was the one they needed to worry about.

The forum loomed. As they reached the break between the braided arches, the Ta'Ruls parted, their eyes urging them forward. Leiyn scanned their faces but saw no salvation among them. Even Ketti, the most sympathetic of the trio, wore a pinched look.

Setting her shoulders, Leiyn led her party into the clearing, stopping short of the amber platform. Those seated around the edges pinned her in place with their gazes. To the last, they were white and gray of hair. The elders of the community—likely the patriarchs and matriarchs of the village households if Solace functioned similarly to the Ta'Rul family. All were dressed in ornate robes and sashes, making her feel even shabbier with her torn clothes.

Chispa huddled against her leg. The fox's gaze darted about, and he trembled as Arash's leash continued to hold him. Leiyn was more than a little tempted to try and sever that torturous hold.

Don't be rash, damn you.

"You." Atop the amber platform, Oro Ta'Rul was high enough to stare down at them. "Leiyn, Isla, Batu—you have much for which you must account."

His words seemed to resonate; the stage beneath his feet pulsed. Something about it compelled her attention. Leiyn fought the urge to raise her walls against it, Isla's warning ringing in her skull.

"Patriarch Oro Ta'Rul." Isla bowed as Ketti had before, fingers spread before her face. "We intended no offense to you and your people. But what have we done that called for this meeting?"

"Is that not clear?" The Eteman elder gestured to Chispa. "The *etaro* is only the final sign. You three reek of our enemies to the last."

Leiyn did not want to say it aloud but she had to know. "The Iritu?"

Oro's flinty gaze gave his answer.

"I'm afraid I must protest, Patriarch," Isla said after a pause. "This fox has only been a friend to us, and to Leiyn especially. What does this have to do with the Iritu?"

Though Isla's manner was both sweet and diplomatic, her words failed to soften the elder. He stared at each of them, his bright gaze seeming to pierce through to their souls. Not far from the truth: his mahia probed each of them, perhaps searching for some sign of the Iritu in their esses.

Let there be none, she prayed to the Sacred Saints. *Please, if you care at all, don't punish my friends for what I've done.*

"Our ancestors had a name for her, the Iritu who has befriended the fox: Laughing Death." Oro pressed his lips together. "Would you like to know why?"

Leiyn remained silent. Isla took the bait.

"Tell us, please."

"Because she delighted in tearing my people apart."

Leiyn flinched. The dryvan's confessions were still fresh in her mind. How easily she could picture the slaughter. Blood dripping down Ata's talons. Staining her feathers. Spilling from between her teeth.

Isla looked at Leiyn as if asking permission. Leiyn shrugged. The path forward was as obscure to her as when they had trudged through the Ofean jungle.

"That is not the dryvan we have come to know," her fellow ranger said. "She has adopted many names—Hawkvine, Foxfur, Rowanwalker—but none so vicious." Isla paused, then continued in soft, conciliatory tones. "Is it possible you are mistaken? That she is not who you believe?"

"The error is not ours." The amber platform pulsed with the patriarch's conviction. Around the circle, other elders nodded their agreement. "Since Solace's founding, we have kept watch over our enemies. That one is Laughing Death. The annals do not lie."

In Leiyn's experience, every word, written or otherwise, could be a lie. She treated each with equal suspicion. But these Etemans clung to their beliefs. She doubted she could disavow them of any of their traditions, no matter how small.

And we'd thought to make them allies.

"But it is as I have said," Oro Ta'Rul continued. "The Iritu and the fox were the final signs of guilt, not the first." He gestured toward Isla as if presenting her with a platter. "You, Isla Ogbi, are infected with their *semah*." His hand twisted, a finger pointing at her legs. "You bear their mark within your flesh."

Isla's eyes grew wide and her mouth parted. Leiyn grimaced. If she paid close attention, she could sense the same from Isla.

I should have known.

Even if she had, what could she have done? It seemed now their visit had been like a horseless cart barreling downhill toward a cliff. There could only have been this one end.

Leiyn stepped in front of Isla, shielding her with her body. "Yes. They healed her. And we don't regret it. I tried to do it."

She clenched her hands. "But I knew nothing of mahia then. She would have died without their help."

Oro's embedded gems glimmered, as much a warning as a dog's bared teeth. She did not let her gaze waver.

"They are not what you believe, Oro Ta'Rul. What any of you believe." She looked at each of the elders. None looked convinced, though some lowered their eyes before her stare. "There are vile Iritu, yes—lyshans, we call them, as you know. But there are good ones as well. Dryvans like... Rowan."

She scarcely knew what to call Ata anymore. But that was the least of her worries.

"I didn't face Man'nah and his followers alone," Leiyn continued. "The dryvans fought beside me and the Many Tribes. Together, we drove them back from Qasaar, the ancient city beyond the Silvertusks claimed by the Gasts and other native peoples. Without them, we would have failed."

Leiyn took another step forward. Her toes verged on the edge of the amber stage. She wondered if it would strike her if she dared to set foot on it.

"Patriarch Ta'Rul, I understand why you mistrust them. Why you continue to hate the Iritu for the crimes they once committed. I know how deep hatred can go."

All the memories of slights from Gasts flashed through her mind. Guilt trailed close behind.

"But hatred is blind. Rage is irrational. You and your people must look beyond it." She spread her arms. "Or all of us are doomed."

Oro stood impassive before her pleas for a moment—then the platform blared into brilliance. Leiyn stumbled back into Isla, a hand raised against the flare. Only as it did nothing to block it did she understand the blindness was to her lifesense alone.

The patriarch walked slowly toward them. "You claim you know them. That they are changed. But I have seen what they did. I have borne witness to their crimes. *Akken hitu ek serru.*

The blood of guilt cannot be rinsed. Only punishment may cleanse the wounds."

Anger sent fresh resolve coursing through Leiyn. Standing on her own, she faced down the approaching patriarch. "Even if your revenge costs the world? You pretend to care for justice, but you've done nothing, *nothing* for it! You hide like mice in a field. But the eagle still circles above! It's only getting closer. And it will come for you. Every. Last. One."

"Silence!"

The command rode on a wave of esse, rattling through Leiyn's being. She firmed herself before it, slightly raising her walls to weather the blow.

Oro breathed heavily and leaned on his feathered staff. "Perhaps this will help you understand these *gallu* you believe to be good." He turned to Batu. "Do you know what lies within you? What was done to your ancestors long ago?"

Batu flinched, eyes darting to Isla and Leiyn. She gritted her teeth, helpless. Dread filled her as she waited for the accusation to fall.

"You are tainted, Batu Khatas. Their blood runs in your veins."

39

TAINTED

The patriarch spoke with such conviction she found it difficult to doubt him. Leiyn delved deep within her for a ranger's clarity.

It was Isla who spoke first.

"What do you mean, 'tainted'? You mean he's... part dryvan?"

The former plainsrider stiffened. She felt his esse quiver with uncertainty. The images of his lifemark, so clear before, grew murky.

Oro sounded weary, the vigor from moments before subsiding. "It came during the Culling. Before that, they had only killed. But during that time, they became more... *sakilt* is the word in our tongue."

"Barbaric," Ketti murmured.

"Yes. Some captives, they tortured. Some they... violated."

Violated. Leiyn swallowed, bile burning her throat. Could it be true? Could an Iritu have raped his ancestor long ago? If Oro could sense it, dryvans certainly could. Which meant they had concealed it.

Ata included.

"We believe this transgression had a purpose: that they sought a way to reproduce without their birthing trees. If they succeeded, we have seen no sign of it, for their numbers have only dwindled, spirits be thanked. When their experiments ceased, they released some of those impregnated back to our ancestors to bear the children. Why, we can only speculate. Perhaps only as another of their cruelties.

"Some of these ill-born were too twisted to survive. Others were ordinary in appearance, or almost so. It was not in our people's hearts to kill a babe, innocent of the crimes that brought it into the world. And so, those with tainted blood passed it down through generations."

Batu dropped his gaze to stare at the ground. Isla neared him, but though she reached out, she fell short of touching him. As if she did not dare.

Leiyn was lost, helpless. She did not know what he suffered or how to reach him. This changed nothing of who he was to her. Why would it? He was the same man he had always been.

And did I know who that was?

Memories flitted through her mind. Batu gifting of his esse as she lay dying but standing moments later. Batu defying the vine jaguar when all but herself were paralyzed by its pollen.

She shook away the thoughts.

"Even if what you say is true," Leiyn said, "even if he has Iritu blood—"

"It is true," Oro interrupted. "I have seen it."

It was a step too far.

"You cannot have seen these crimes!" she spat. "I don't know what you are, but you're not dryvans. You haven't lived for aeons!"

Doubts flickered through her before she squashed them. She had sensed the difference in age between these Etemans and the Iritu. If dryvans and lyshans were like trees, Etemans were mere saplings.

"I have," the patriarch repeated. "The annals do not lie."

"Every history does!" She threw out a hand. "Every *person* does! The only truth you can know is what you've seen."

"And I have. Our annals are not like yours, Leiyn of Orille. They are the memories of those long departed. Through their eyes, we understand history exactly. I have witnessed the Culling. I have seen the violence of the *gallu*, the Iritu. I have seen the destruction of our world."

Oro struck his staff against the amber. The platform resonated like a Kalgan gong. Around the edge of the forum, the elders of Solace rose to their feet. Leiyn sensed a ritual's beginning. Impatience for such formalities vied with her need to understand, twisting her tongue into knots.

"*Ganu ama ikri.* This I say," the patriarch declared. "These three did not know the demons with which they dealt. In this respect, they are innocent of the Iritu's crimes. Nevertheless, they are a danger to our home and our people. This matter requires further discussion among us elders of Solace. Until we have come to a decision, I ask that they be held under eye and storm."

The patriarchs and matriarchs responded as one.

"*Aman ikra akkir matu.* We hear your word."

As Leiyn parsed what Oro said, the meaning of it became all too clear. *Prisoners.* Now, they would be treated as she had expected all along. Defiance tightened her muscles.

Yet she would not fight. They had spoken too much truth for her to believe them her enemies. And with their knowledge and power, Baltesia—Saints, all of Unera—needed them.

If only they could understand.

But there was one thing she could not overlook. Glancing back at the cowering silver fox, she faced Oro again.

"What of Chispa?" She ignored the gasps of the elders as she spoke. No doubt they deemed it uncouth to interrupt the ceremony.

Oro narrowed his eyes at her. "The *etaro.* That is his name?"

"It's what I call him. Release him. Please," she added as Isla cast her a look. "He doesn't pose any danger."

The patriarch's eyes gleamed a brighter violet for a moment, esse concentrating within them. Then he nodded.

"*Ganu ama ikri.* This I say: the silver fox shall be freed. Even if it has aligned itself with the Iritu, the *etaro* are not ours to command or enslave. It remains innocent as only their kind can be."

The elders were more haphazard in their response, but all spoke the words. "*Aman ikra akkir matu.* We hear your word."

Leiyn felt Arash release his hold on Chispa. The fox bolted to its feet, grassy hair standing on end. His fiery eyes alighted on hers, then he turned and fled.

Before he had bounded thrice, his esse melted and he was gone.

Relief spiraled through her. Though she might have relinquished their one link to the outer world, she could not have borne the thought of Chispa bound a moment longer.

"My family will show you back to Ketti's room." Oro raised his hand, and the other three Ta'Ruls stepped up next to Leiyn and her companions. Leiyn stared Ketti in the face, her gaze challenging. The young woman turned away.

"Come," Arash said, then led them back up the slope to the castle ruins.

⌒ ⌒

Leiyn bowed her head and leaned her elbows on her knees. From the corner of her eye, she watched Isla speak quietly to Batu in the corner of Ketti's room.

Something had shifted. Like a tremor in the earth, she felt the change in their fellowship. The truth of Batu's lineage had formed cracks between them. It was not Leiyn's feelings that had changed, nor did she think Isla looked at her beloved differently.

Batu was the source.

He had remained withdrawn for the march back to the Ta'Rul hold. She had hoped the Etemans departing would change that, but his silence held. Isla had gone to him, eager to mend his wounds, but Leiyn suspected this was one injury that would be long in healing.

Tainted.

She wondered what it truly meant. Did it only mark a dark deed of the past? Or did he bear a hint of heritage, of dryvan magic, that changed his very essence? The questions plagued her, but she kept them to herself.

More urgent was what this meant for their alliance with Ata and the other dryvans. Leiyn stared at her hands, clenching and loosening them. Considering how the tainted blood had originated, it could not have been an oversight that they had not mentioned it.

But the more she thought about it, the less she viewed it as a betrayal. How often had she concealed her shameful past long after when she should have revealed it? Maybe Ata had been waiting for the right moment. Maybe it would not affect Batu's life, and the dryvan feared judgment of who the Iritu had once been.

Or are.

She forced her hands flat against her thighs. No. Until she spoke again to the dryvan, she refused to believe her capable of it. Ata had already confessed her sins. Leiyn had seen the dryvan's nature in the aid she lent again and again.

So Ata had her secrets. Who was Leiyn to judge her for that?

Leiyn looked at the curtain hanging across the doorway. The three Ta'Ruls had lingered in the main living space for some time, but all were absent then. She wondered if they were still being watched. After Oro's declaration of imprisonment, she had expected more overt guards than this.

Then she froze, staring. Before her eyes, the curtain lifted.

She stood with a falchion extended before the entrance fully parted. Her weapon only wavered a little as she saw who stood in the doorway.

"Ketti," Leiyn hissed.

The young woman stared at Leiyn's sharp blade with wide eyes, but she did not retreat. Nor did she drop the veil she had cast over her esse, hiding her approach.

By her lifesense, she felt Isla and Batu approach from behind. "Leiyn!" Isla gasped. "Don't threaten them now!"

"She's hiding her lifeforce. Why?" she demanded of the Eteman. "Why sneak up on us?"

"I do not hide from you." For all the fear in her eyes, Ketti's voice hardly warbled. "I cannot be seen speaking with you."

"You're hiding from your family?" Isla guessed. "From the other Etemans?"

The young woman nodded, her eyes remaining on Leiyn's sword.

Pressing her lips together, Leiyn sheathed the weapon and crossed her arms. "Explain."

Some of the tension went out of Ketti's shoulders. The young woman stood straighter.

"I wish to help you."

"Help us?" Leiyn could not entirely keep back a laugh. "You're holding us prisoner!"

"No—it is Ab-Abi and the elders who do that. I... I believe you are right."

She had been prepared for an ambush. She had not prepared for this.

"Right," Leiyn repeated. "About what, exactly?"

"My people cannot remain hidden here." Ketti's voice rose, though she still spoke in hushed tones. "Solace is not only our home; all of *Tlalli* is. If the Iritu mean to destroy it, I will not stand by. I cannot."

Batu laughed. "So you'll trust a tainted? Trust that the dryvans are our allies?"

Leiyn's hair rose at his bitterness. Ketti paled, but she did not retreat.

"I trust you," the Eteman woman said. "And I am willing to listen."

"How?" Leiyn could scarcely muster belief. "How can you trust us, now of all times?"

"Because I have seen into you. I know you, each one of you." Ketti rested her eyes on them one at a time.

Our lifemarks. Leiyn had not hidden hers, and Isla and Batu were incapable of it. That had to be what the Eteman meant. But could Ketti see enough to know they were truly trustworthy? It spoke to the qualities of a person's soul, but good people could be on the wrong side of a conflict. Much as she might wish to believe all Suncoats were evil, her brief time with the young soldier Arias had disavowed her of that notion.

Her only guess was that Ketti saw something in her the others did not. Perhaps it was all the similarities they shared. The resolve to protect, even if it meant flouting every rule of their societies.

The Eteman stepped into the room. "Let me show you. That I mean what I say." Her eyes fell on Leiyn. "Let me fix your broken bond."

More than anything, it was what she wanted, *needed* to hear. It made her all the slower to trust it.

Leiyn stepped closer. Only a pace separated them now, easily within reach of a knife. "First, we need a straight answer. Why are you doing all this? Why did you save us to begin with?"

Ketti's eyes flared. Her chest heaved for a moment before she spoke.

"I want... out."

The words, soft as they were, cut through the air. Before their eyes, the Eteman seemed to deflate.

"I want out," Ketti repeated, this time in a whisper.

Leiyn tried imagining her life to this point. One spent watching the world from afar by whatever magical means they used. It seemed an empty existence to lack all she had experienced, the good and bad alike. Like drinking from a cask of stagnant water.

That pain, that need—those she could trust.

"I'll let you help." Leiyn let her arms fall back to her sides. "Where do we start?"

She had suspected the kindest thing she could do was pretend they had not glimpsed inside Ketti's soul. Her suspicion seemed correct as the young woman straightened again.

"You know how to hide your esse? Good," she said at Leiyn's nod. "Do so and follow me. Isla and Batu, stay in case my parents return. Better if two of you, at least, are still here."

"You want Leiyn to go alone?"

Leiyn turned back, hearing the worry in Isla's voice. She tried on a reassuring smile.

"I'll be fine. I believe Ketti. And it's like you said: if they were going to harm us, why save Batu?"

Especially when he's tainted, she almost added. But it seemed too cruel to point out.

Batu still scowled, but Isla gave a terse nod. "Return as soon as you can."

"I will."

"Quickly," Ketti said, drawing Leiyn's gaze back around. "I cannot say how long we have."

Leiyn nodded, raised her mahia's walls, then followed the Eteman from the room.

40

A BROKEN WORLD

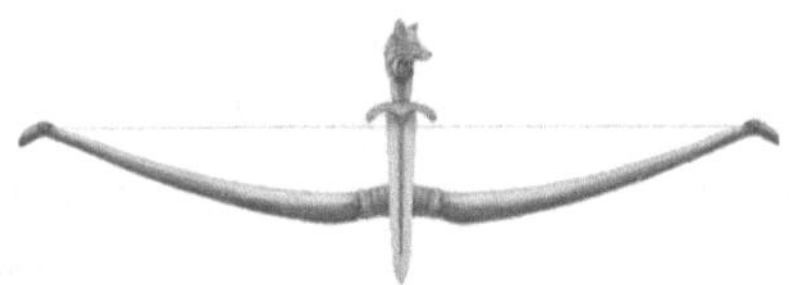

*L*eiyn felt like an apprentice again, stalking elusive prey with Tadeo out in the Titan Wilds, as she followed Ketti from Hold Ta'Rul. For the first time in Solace, her lifesense was blinded. That and the thrill of discovery seemed to heighten her natural senses. The quiet place came alive with subtle sounds.

"Remember the way through the wall?" Ketti whispered. "So will we go. Stay close."

They followed the outer wall from her family's residence until they came to the place where it had caved in, the same as she had found that morning. On the other side, Leiyn looked over the farmland again. The sunset colors had already faded, and with her lifesense closed, the magic in the plants and atmosphere remained hidden, leaving the landscape gray and flat.

Ketti gave her a moment to take it in. "The path down is narrow. Watch your step."

Having spent half her life trekking through rugged wilderness, the warning slid by her. Yet she soon discovered Ketti did not exaggerate. The path was little more than a run-off for rain, lacking even roots to reinforce the crumbling dirt. Facing the cliffside, she tentatively lowered one foot after another, often having to scrabble for a foothold. She had not done such daring climbing since she was a girl.

Despite herself, a smile stole over her.

The dusklight was fading by the time they reached the bottom, though the clouds gathered an ambient silver glow reminiscent of the moons. Her guide took a moment to brush off her hands, then gestured toward the cloud bank at the far end of the fields.

"Hurry!"

Leiyn matched her jog, keeping her eyes on the uneven ground to avoid tripping. The exercise felt good after the sedentary day. It was not long before her muscles warmed to it and her lope lengthened.

Soon, they reached the forest. Its canopy sheltered them from the rest of the scant light. Between the trunks, Leiyn could see where the vast cloud dome began, curling in and around the trees, possessive as a jealous lover.

Ketti stopped and turned to Leiyn. "We will try it here—No, not now, Biqqa!"

Leiyn flinched as the emerald hummingbird appeared from empty air. Unchastened, it happily fluttered around the Eteman's head.

"Will others notice?" Leiyn asked, watching the bird's revolutions.

"No." Ketti did not sound altogether convincing. "Ignore her. Drop your walls and try to summon your bonded *kainox*. I will hide us from the others."

Wondering what good it would do, Leiyn obeyed. The world came alive as her mahia was unveiled, dazzling her. Her companions burned brightest of all. A moment later, the outer light dimmed as Ketti's barrier fell over her.

Drawing inward, Leiyn focused on the thin thread leading away from her esse deep beneath Unera's surface. Though Biqqa's constant movement plucked at her concentration, as she followed it down, her mind filled with the image of the ash dragon, crowding out all other distractions.

Clouded Fang, come. Come to me.

Nothing. She could not even sense the titan. Had Ketti not stood there and risked so much to make this moment, Leiyn might have given it up for lost. But she knew she could not surrender so easily.

Come! Please, Clouded Fang—

The thread caught fire.

Flames raced up the bond, then through her. The ash dragon flared inside her mind. Even as she staggered, she tracked his progress as he raced toward her. His ascent was sudden and swift—too much so. He would break open the ground below her feet and blast her apart at such a speed.

As he touched the surface, she instinctively threw up her arms. Ash and smoke billowed up, inundating her. Leiyn coughed, but she kept her watering eyes open as the dark smog coalesced into a vast shape.

Wings grew first, then a head, a neck, a body. The whipping tail emerged last, swaying behind him.

With a flare of his wings, Clouded Fang became flesh.

Smoke spiraled off and ash fell away, revealing the dragon beneath. Burning cinders shifted to blue-fire reptilian eyes. Black scales gleamed up and down his sinuous length. A crest of horns and spines framed his long, fearsome face.

The dragon looked down on her from forty feet high. He was vast, unknowable, powerful.

He is mine.

Biqqa disappeared, prey fleeing before a predator. Ketti gasped something in Eteman and took a step back.

"That is your bonded? A *hulmitu*—a dragon?"

"Clouded Fang." Leiyn could not help smiling up at the majestic creature. His every breath steamed as if fire roiled in his belly. It felt as if it stirred within hers, too. Now that he sat there before her, solid and real, she felt months of anxiety slough off her shoulders.

For the first time in half a year, she felt light. Free.

Leiyn stepped closer, then placed a hand on his immense

body. She could reach only partway up his neck. A single scale dwarfed her hand. It felt hard as glass, yet rough as unshaped metal, and was almost unbearably hot to touch. She did not pull away.

Once, she had feared him. Now, she sensed the truth: Clouded Fang would do her no harm. His loyalty was absolute. She did not understand him or their bond, yet she knew that as surely as she knew the world would always be underfoot and the sky overhead.

That only reminded her of the strangeness of all that had occurred.

"Why now?" She spoke to the titan first, then she tore her gaze away. Her lifesense lingered on him, admiring his length like a merchant might a prized horse. No—more like a rancher might his beloved sheep dog. "I called him before and felt nothing. Yet this time, he came at once."

Ketti stood far back, staring with wide eyes, but her answer was coherent. "When and how did you summon him before?"

Leiyn thought it over as she ran a hand over the seams between the scales. They overlapped, leaving no gap for enemy claws, teeth, or nails to work between. The perfect armor.

"The first time came after the lyshans attacked." She hesitated, remembering the forum's discussion, but Ketti had come this far to help her. She doubted anything she said now could change things. "The dryvan you call Laughing Death protected me from them by sending me to a grotto, away from where we were attacked. I was badly injured. Likely, I would have died."

Even then, she did not want to admit she had no way of escaping grottos. With Clouded Fang here, that ought to have changed; with his aid, she had escaped grottos twice back in Qasaar. But how could she be sure of anything with titans?

Leiyn placed her other hand to the ash dragon. Clouded Fang had stood proudly upright to that point. Now, he curled his neck down to bring his head level with her. Leiyn's breath caught as one of his eyes, as large as her head, came beside her.

She moved toward him, entranced.

"I reached for titans deep in the earth, for I sensed none near. Perhaps I found him because I'd encountered him before. It took some convincing, but he came to me. And I felt our bond take root."

Heart racing, Leiyn touched her hands to the horns about his crown, then the finer scales of his jaw, which transitioned to rough hide around his mouth. His jaw looked capable of unhinging like a snake's. She marveled at the size of the prey he could swallow.

If titans even eat.

Clouded Fang closed the eye she could see. Almost like a hound might while enjoying his human's touch.

"The second time he came was when I fought Man'nah. I was alone with the lyshan, isolated in another lyshan's grotto. Without Clouded Fang, I would have died at once. But he fed me strength and life, and we overcame him together."

"Then you have your answer."

Leiyn blinked, tearing her gaze away long enough to stare at Ketti. "What do you mean?"

The Eteman woman crossed her arms. Instead of growing comfortable around the ash dragon, she seemed less at ease with each moment. Her voice, however, remained steady.

"Both times you summoned your bonded, you were within a *haru*, a grotto, as you are now. I assume you were not in one when you tried calling Clouded Fang before?"

"No, I wasn't."

The concepts felt as slippery as wet fish. Leiyn shook her head, trying to loosen the stupor that had settled over her mind.

Ketti nodded. "Here in Solace, when we practice summoning *kainox*, we do not need every step of the process. Yet all know, should we ever be in the outer world, we must call through a grotto."

"I don't understand." She looked back at her dragon and found his eye open and staring at her again. "Why? Why is that step so crucial?"

It seemed such a small thing to have tormented her all this

time. Not that she was any closer to fixing it. She would not be in a grotto when protecting Southport. Had Zuma known this missing step? Or did he not, and that was why his spark had remained silent throughout her struggles?

The young woman shrugged. "It is as it is. *Tlalli* follows its patterns. To some, these appear random and without reason. It falls to us to understand them." She gestured hesitantly at Clouded Fang. "But if that is not explanation enough, I would guess it is because this world is their home."

"This world?" Leiyn looked around. Solace seemed a small place with its dome of fog. Far too small for more than the tempest hawk to inhabit it. "You mean grottos? I thought they were..." She struggled to remember how Ata had put it. "Like pockets, caves, or clearings in dense woods. Not a world of their own."

"They are clearings to us, as you say. But *kainox* and other creatures of *ilis* are not bound by our rules. You saw how your bonded surpassed Solace's barrier as if it did not exist." Ketti gestured to the fog bank beyond the trees. "They enter the outside world with similar ease. They flow through the realities as we pass through water: with some resistance, perhaps, but too little to keep them out.

"What is more, you must have seen how they are shadows of their true selves out there. Here, they have substance. They are as they are supposed to be."

"Supposed to be..." Leiyn frowned at the sky. The clouds seemed thicker than before, the esse in them more active. But she could not yet tell if it was merely her imagination. "Then they are... wrong in my world? Broken, somehow?"

Ketti clutched her arms tighter around herself. "All *Tlalli* is broken. Perhaps beyond saving."

"No. We can still save it." She only had the vaguest idea what Ketti referred to, but the words burst free of her all the same. "I took an oath to preserve and protect it. I won't give up on that now."

"Even if this oath kills you?"

How often had it come close to doing that? A smile surprised her.

"Some things are worth dying for."

Ketti stared, her face smoothing to stone. "I would like to think you are right," she murmured.

Clouded Fang jerked upright, rising to his towering height. Leiyn came alert as well. Tilting back her head, she followed his gaze to the sky.

The clouds spilled open.

A familiar, blue-feathered hawk dove from them, wreathed in lightning. Thunder followed its descent, rattling Leiyn to the bone and nearly knocking her to the ground. Ears stinging with the boom, she steadied herself against her dragon.

Clouded Fang did not react before the descending titan, but only continued to stare at it, as imperious as if he could not be harmed. With those scales and his inferno of lifeforce, perhaps he could not.

The storm titan pulled up short. With each flap of its wings, the electrified air stood Leiyn's hair on end. She bared her teeth at it. Perhaps she could do little to harm it, but Clouded Fang's power filled her. She was not afraid.

Only then did she notice the people racing across the fields toward them.

"*Ketti Ta'Rul!*" Oro's voice boomed with all the force of his titan. "*What have you done?*"

The mob numbered a dozen; Oro outshone them all. The hawk instilled lifeforce in him, brightening his esse almost too much to behold. Her hands fell to her falchions. She did not wish to harm any Eteman, but if they attacked, she would show them the error of their choice.

Ketti stepped past Leiyn and her titan. Alone, she stood between them, a quavering figure illuminated by the lightning dancing across the clouds.

The sky rumbled. Leiyn flinched, waiting for what came next. She sent up a brief prayer. *Let Isla and Batu be alright. Saints, let them be unharmed.* It was all the thought she could spare for them. She had more than enough to worry about herself.

"Ab-Abi!" Ketti called. Her voice trembled, but defiance lent it sharp edges. "I demand my right to speak upon the Amber Altar!"

The Ta'Rul patriarch stopped a dozen paces away. At his back were young men and women from the village. Leiyn recognized one of Ketti's friends, Zaki, their brow furrowed as they stared upon the scene. None held weapons, but their esses spoke of a readiness she could not dismiss.

"No." Oro's denial whipped across the field. "You surrendered that right when you acted like a child."

Ketti stepped toward him. Her chin did not lower, though her eyes twitched at her great-grandfather's words. "It is not for you to deny. My words are meant for all. And I am Ta'Rul, heir to Mehu'Ra, the guardian of storms who defends us. This is my right."

Leiyn did not see how the man could be swayed. Like her, he was filled with a titan's power. It did not incline one to compromise.

Yet though his expression did not shift, his voice was soft as he replied. "And what would you say?"

"The truth." Ketti's chin raised a fraction higher. "The truth we have long denied."

Like an arrow striking a waterskin, the patriarch deflated. Pulling his gaze from his great-granddaughter, his eyes fell on Leiyn.

"Dismiss your bonded. We will go to the Altar together."

Leiyn did not move. "You first."

They matched stares. Then, with a sigh, Oro raised his gaze to the storm hawk above. Leiyn risked a glance up to see the titan's feathers fading to mist.

In a swirling gust, it dispersed.

Reluctant, but mindful of what Isla would counsel if she were here, Leiyn turned to Clouded Fang and rested a hand on his chest, pulsing her intentions along their bond.

"Time for you to go, old boy."

The dragon tilted his head to look directly at her with one smoldering eye. Then he began to fade into smoke.

It took mere moments. One second, hard scale pressed against her hand; the next, she felt it soften, then blow away. Leiyn's chest ached as the dragon turned to black smoke and white ash, then dissolved into the air.

"Come," Oro said, turning. His retinue followed, though not without many glances over their shoulders. Zaki looked at them longest, fear filling their eyes.

Leiyn turned to Ketti and, at her nod, set after the Ta'Rul elder.

41

HEIR

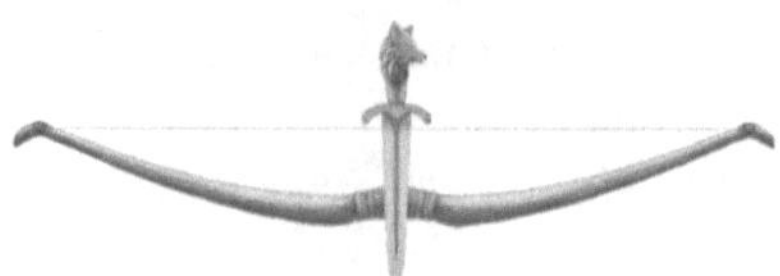

They circumvented the castle ruins to reach the forum.

As they walked, Leiyn looked up at the town, lifesense seeking her friends. To her relief, their lifefires still burned high within Ketti's room. With any luck, all of this would be resolved before they were inclined to leave it.

If there can be a resolution.

Her gaze traveled back to Ketti. She did not look from side to side as she led them alongside the fields but kept her eyes forward and her chin up. A woman on a war path, by all appearances. Leiyn was only beginning to glimpse what her purpose might be.

She quieted her thoughts. A ranger should anticipate the next moment, but there came a time when speculation served as distraction. Tadeo would have advised her to keep her eyes and ears open, prepared to face whatever came next.

When the twisted arches and glowing platform of the Amber Altar came into view, Leiyn perceived they were not the only ones heading to it. The other elders and Ketti's parents also trudged their way down the slope, Ketti having notified them of the conference through Biqqa. Their curiosity and bafflement was plain as they turned to gaze down at them. Leiyn wondered how often emergency councils had been called before she and her friends had showed up. The number of scowls directed her way gave her some idea of it. Arash and Nidinu Ta'Rul looked worried more than anything.

Entering between the twisted trees, Ketti stepped onto the amber platform. Her great-grandfather lingered at the edge, then shuffled back to lean on his feathered staff. Though the young woman had lost favor with her elders, it seemed she retained the right to speak.

Leiyn took a place several paces aside and kept a careful watch around her. The young Etemans who had accompanied Oro Ta'Rul spread out between the arches like guards protecting an arena. So long as they did not threaten her, she would remain peaceful.

And if they seize Ketti?

She caught her hand rising to her auburn tress before pressing it back down by her side. Her absent mother could not guide her. None of her mentors could. She would make this choice on her own.

A flare from the amber platform brought Leiyn's attention forward, brightening the forum.

"*Ikra ami matu.* Hear my words." Ketti turned as she spoke, gazing upon her fellow villagers. Her eyes alighted on Leiyn, then swept past. "Solace has been our home through two aeons. For two thousand turns of the seasons, it shielded us from our enemies. It has been a good home. Bountiful. Safe. But it is not where we belong."

The young woman swept out her hand, gesturing to the gray cloud bank rising beyond the fields. "The world is out there: *Tlalli,* our true home. Next to it, Solace is little but a fleeting dream. You, my elders, speak of the bygone days when we reigned across the lands. When our ancestors walked free and prospered. We did not live under a veil of fear then. We did not live for a tomorrow that would never come.

"Each generation prepared the next to enter that world beyond. We observed the customs of those people, those who walked upon our lands. We learned their strange tongues. The morphing geography, the perverted *semah*, the mourning *kainox* —all were watched so we could be ready. Ready for the day we returned."

Ketti faced her great-grandfather and took several steps toward him. Her next words seemed for him alone.

"I am ready, Ab-Abi. Ready to gaze upon *Tlalli's* true face."

Leiyn's heart raced. Ketti meant to turn her back on all she knew. Leiyn had never lacked for courage, but she doubted she possessed that same daring. That she could risk everything for a chance at something more. Something real. Especially if it meant leaving behind all those she loved.

Her hands tightened into fists. Had the Wilds Lodge not burned, she doubted she would have sought a life beyond it. She had needed nothing she could not find there.

Even as you denied yourself? part of her whispered.

Had all remained as it had been, Leiyn would have continued to repress her mahia. Would still blame Gasts for her mother's death and her fate. She would have been less than she was now. Stunted, like a tree trying to grow in a mountain's shadow.

Leiyn beheld Ketti anew. Her purpose resonated within her body and being. This was one they shared.

She would not let anyone deny Ketti of it.

Silence fell across the forum as the Ta'Ruls stared at each other. Ketti's mother trembled, tears trailing down her cheeks, but she said nothing as she watched her daughter.

At last, the patriarch cleared his throat and tapped his feathered staff on the ground. "You, Ketti Ta'Rul, are truly our family's heir."

Shocked whispers broke out around the circle. Even Ketti looked taken aback, though she tried to maintain her composure.

"Abi, you cannot mean it!" Arash Ta'Rul gripped his grandfather's sleeve, eyes wide and pleading. "You would bless this *mekva?*"

Oro's calm was untouched. "It is not madness, Arash. It is conviction. Yes, it breaks traditions that have stood for dozens of generations. Yes, it may spell the end of Solace. But your daughter speaks from her heart and head. She sees what she must do, and she is determined to do it." He waved his staff in Ketti's direction, feathers shimmering to Leiyn's lifesense. "It is not our way to prune the leaves of a growing tree."

Arash dropped the patriarch's sleeve and staggered back. His wife caught and held him, clutching him close like he was tossed in a stormy sea.

"Mother. Father." Ketti's voice cracked, but she spoke through it. "I will not leave forever. I will return. But this is something I must do."

"What is that, exactly? What will you do?" Her father flung his free arm around him. "What purpose could lie out there for you?"

"A duty we have long neglected." Ketti's jaw spasmed. "To mend the world our ancestors broke."

Again, the mystery tantalized Leiyn. For as much as she had learned of Etemans, she still muddled through darkness.

"Mend it?" A wild laugh broke free of Arash. "It cannot be mended, *ita*! It is broken beyond healing!"

"Then I will discover that!" The amber at Ketti's feet burned bright with her anger. "And I will know the truth. But if we never attempt it, how can we know what is possible? It is said the wingless bird never flies. Father, I will succeed or I will fail. Either way, I must make this flight."

Her father remained rigid a moment longer. Then, like a branch snapping in a gust, he folded back. Nidinu clutched both arms around him. She seemed the only thing keeping him upright.

Ketti trembled. Tears trickled down her cheeks. But she remained where she was.

"*Ganu ama ikri.*" Oro Ta'Rul stepped onto the amber platform. Lifeforce rippled out from his footsteps, intersecting with the resonance from Ketti. As he approached and placed a hand on her shoulder, they resolved into one pulsation. "My great-granddaughter has decided. She has done and will do what none of us have dared since the founding of Solace. She will step foot once more onto the face of *Tlalli*. An Eteman returned to our homeland."

"*Aman ikra akkir matu.*" The others' reply roiled with emotions. Unease, awe, joy, melancholy—Leiyn could scarcely track them all.

Ketti looked at her great-grandfather like she wanted to embrace him. But she stood as unyielding as stone even then, only saying, "You have my thanks, Ab-Abi."

"We will do all in our power to see that your journey is comfortable. I ask only one thing of you in return."

The young woman narrowed her eyes. After a beat, she nodded.

Oro continued, "You will not allow our enemies to reach Solace. If they find you, you will do everything you must to guard your home and people. Do you understand?"

Leiyn's breath caught. Ketti froze.

This, she had not predicted.

To Leiyn's horror—and admiration—the young Eteman took mere moments to reply. "I understand, Ab-Abi. I swear to protect you, even if it costs my life."

Ketti's parents sobbed louder. Leiyn understood their sorrow then: In their eyes, to leave Solace was to die. They could see no other fate awaiting an Eteman. And if a lyshan caught them, as one already had, that death might come from Ketti's own hand.

Oro Ta'Rul's eyes flickered to Leiyn, holding her. She wondered if he had spoken these words in Ilberian for her bene-fit. If she was meant to play a part in holding this secret.

But that was not the oath she had sworn at the Wilds Lodge. She preserved as well as protected. She would not kill Ketti to save them.

Even though you killed Patli to save Qasaar?

Leiyn closed her eyes, pushing away that moment. Trying to forget how his lifeforce snapped under her attack.

I'll protect her, she promised herself. *It won't come to that.*

Just as you protected Belen, and her soldiers, and the skystriders escorting you? Just as you protected Southport?

The Ta'Rul patriarch spoke again, rousing Leiyn from her torments. "We will prepare for your departure," he said to his great-granddaughter, "when you are ready."

"Tomorrow," Ketti snapped. "I leave tomorrow. With our guests, if they will have me," she added, eyes flitting to Leiyn.

"We'll guard you as our own." Leiyn doubted Isla and Batu would object. Even if they did, she had already chosen her path.

Ketti was part of their pack now.

Oro nodded. "We thank you, Leiyn of Orille. My great-granddaughter's trust in you compels my own."

"And mine," Nidinu spoke, voice choked with weeping.

Ketti quavered, her expression turning more fragile by the moment.

"For now," the patriarch said, "we must rest. The night is late, and we have much to prepare on the morrow."

Those around the forum muttered their assent. Leiyn shifted, uncertain where to go next. When the Ta'Ruls huddled together, however, it seemed best to give them a moment alone.

Turning away, Leiyn followed the Etemans streaming back up to Solace.

42

THE FIRST FAREWELL

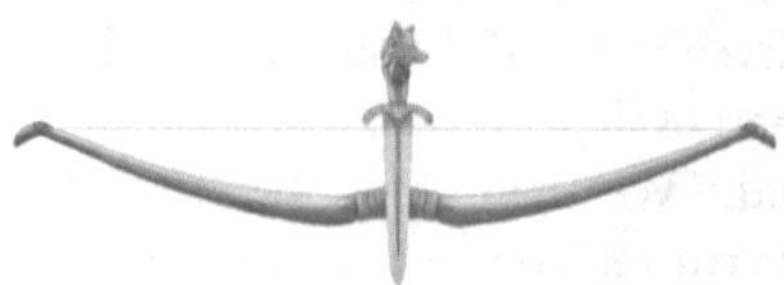

With Ketti's impending departure, the sleepy town of Solace blossomed into activity.

Leiyn beheld the whirl with a mixture of nostalgia and bemusement. As Ketti's mother fretted over her daughter's packing, and her father fetched this and that item from neighbors across the village, and the patriarch worked in a last word of advice—it reminded her of life at the Lodge when a newly cloaked ranger departed on patrol. Every stationed ranger would peck and nag until the one on patrol was almost glad to be leaving. Leiyn had felt that tolerant frustration often enough. No other time had they felt more like a frontier family.

Many of these preparations were uniquely Eteman. When Nidinu checked in on Leiyn, Isla, and Batu's supplies, she looked shocked at the state of their clothes, as if she had not noticed them before. "Give them to me," she insisted of Leiyn and her Iritu garb, still torn from the vine jaguar's claws. "I make them right."

Curious, Leiyn had surrendered them and Nidinu had swept them away to a backroom. When the woman returned them that night, she was astonished to see not only had she mended the fabric, but esse pulsed within their threads once again. Even the burns from the storm hawk's lightning had faded. The art of enchantment, it seemed, had not yet died from the world.

"They keep you safe." Ketti's mother gave her a fragile smile. The previous night's dejection was already lifting. Or, likelier to Leiyn's mind, she buried it under the flurry of work.

Leiyn stuttered her thanks, but Nidinu was already turning to Isla and Batu with a fresh pile of clothes cradled in her arms. "Our garments for you," she announced as she distributed the bright clothes. "To protect you protecting my daughter."

The conditions of accepting them were not subtle, but neither of Leiyn's companions hesitated. During their long discussions the night before, they had already resolved to accept Ketti into their party as an equal member. Isla thanked her profusely while Batu bowed with a small smile.

The imbued clothing was only the first of the strange gifts offered that day. When it came time to resupply their food and drink, Leiyn followed an Eteman to the fields, where they grew more plants through entire cycles to yield their crops. Vegetables and fruits made up most of their supplies. None of it was easy to transport like hard bread and jerky, but Leiyn expressed her gratitude all the same as their saddlebags were filled to over-flowing.

When golden light tinged the cloud dome, the prelude to sunset, the Ta'Rul patriarch summoned their party to his side.

"Come, and I will show your way." Turning, he shuffled off through Solace.

At Leiyn's questioning glance, Ketti only smiled. They had been coming easier to the young woman, the burden of farewells fading as anticipation grew. "You shall see," the Eteman told her.

They went through the marketplace at the center of town, stopping for Ketti to speak with people along the way, until Oro led them to a watchtower similar to the one joined to the Ta'Rul residence. This one had not been made a home, its outer wall caved in. Something shone against the ceiling, patterns shimmering like sunlight reflected off water. Its source was obscured by Ketti and Oro walking before her, but her lifesense could feel it. A font of esse, it seemed; still, yet constantly moving. Dead, yet alive.

For a moment, Leiyn paused at the entrance. The sensation was not threatening, but it was foreign and unfathomable. She did not know what to make of it.

"What is it?" Isla asked from behind. "What's wrong?"

"Nothing." Leiyn forced herself to move inside.

The sight that greeted her was less disconcerting than she had imagined. In the center of the round room lay an ancient tree stump, almost too large to have fit through the opening. Its gnarled roots were a faded pale pink in the gloom and were broken or shaved off a few paces from the trunk. The stump only rose as high as their waists, but it was large enough around to hint at a once gargantuan size. She wondered what tree this had come from. If its kind still existed, or if it was the remnant of a forest long departed.

The stump had a shimmer of life to it, but most of the esse she sensed stirred within its hollow. There swirled a liquid substance in a ceaseless eddy. It glowed with a gentle purple hue and was the source of the light upon the ceiling. Some plants and animals had the natural ability to produce light, but this did not come from living things. It emanated from the liquid itself.

Leiyn stepped back from the stump, an impulse to close her mahia's walls seizing her.

Oro's violet eyes flickered up to her. He stood on the opposite side of the stump. "Yes. The *ara'buru* is unsettling to behold. But it is vital to our lives in Solace."

"The *ara'buru*—the 'seeing pool,' you might call it—is how we visit the world outside." Ketti leaned on the stump with obvious familiarity, staring down into the radiant water. "It is the source of our knowledge."

"One source," her great-grandfather corrected.

Ketti glanced up at him and nodded. "Along with the annals."

"This is how you speak Ilberian so well." Isla moved around the edge of the stump with eyes wide. Even without mahia, she seemed hesitant to approach. "How you know what happens in our world."

The Etemans inclined their heads.

Leiyn glanced at Batu and noticed his agitation seemed to go even beyond hers. Wearing an open scowl, he pressed his back against the stone wall, crossed his arms, and glared at the enchanted pool. It was as if he expected a viper to rise from the water and strike them at any moment.

Pushing the mystery from her mind, Leiyn drew in a breath, stepped closer, and peered down into it. Though it could not have been more than a pace deep, she saw nothing of the bottom of the stump, only glowing, periwinkle liquid.

"How does it work?" she asked after a moment.

Oro pressed a hand to the edge of the stump, fingers lingering above the swirling pool, but not touching it. "Put your hand into the *ara'buru*. Reach into it with your *semah*. Then, in your mind, paint a picture of the place you wish to visit."

"How can you imagine a place you've never seen?" Leiyn waved toward the tower entrance. "None of you have left Solace, you said."

"Until my great-granddaughter did otherwise, that was correct. But each generation has shown the world to the next. I saw many places across *Tlalli* from my own Ab-Abi. Though they have changed shape—cities built, forests burned, *kainox* rising and falling—we recall enough to glimpse their new forms. And so we keep our eyes on the lands."

Leiyn wondered at the extent of this knowledge. Had any seen the Ancestral Lands? Did they espy the Catedrál? Or the old Iyshan cities—had they kept watch over Man'nah and Sharo?

She shook the questions from her head. They could be asked of Ketti later. Only one place mattered now.

"Show us the ruins," she said. "The ones in our world. Please."

Oro nodded, then dipped his fingers into the liquid. His eyes squeezed closed. Through her lifesense, she felt his esse flow and meld with the strange liquid. It spun faster, the edges of the whirlpool touching the rim of the stump, but never splashing over.

Leiyn stepped back, wary, yet unable to tear her eyes away.

A pulse of lifeforce, originating from the patriarch, shot into the pool. All at once, the water ridged into lines as distinct and precise as if drawn. The glowing violet shifted to white, then split into many colors. It took Leiyn a moment to realize she was looking upon a scene like any she might have depicted in her logbook. The details were murky, yet distinct enough to distinguish stone from plant from person. But they did not remain still, as they would have if drawn by pen or brush but moved.

For a moment, captivated by the display, Leiyn did not take in the meaning of what she saw. Ketti's sharp inhale woke her to the meaning.

"Soldiers." The Eteman glanced up and caught Leiyn's eye. "Like those who pursued you before."

"Suncoats," Isla whispered.

Tensing her jaw, Leiyn lowered her eyes back to the pool. She counted a dozen in the narrow view afforded by the pool. They had set up camp and seemed to have little purpose, milling about the grounds on aimless patrol. Yet appearances could be deceiving.

"They're waiting for us," she murmured.

"I fear so." Oro still had his eyes closed and his head tilted back. The deep creases on his face had smoothed as an almost euphoric trance overtook him. It reminded Leiyn of her experiences after drinking Xepi's mushroom tea. His voice was soft, his focus seeming distant. "They complain of waiting for nothing. They complain of the rain and their captain."

Leiyn shared a baffled look with Isla. Ketti addressed her question before she could ask it.

"The one who uses the *ara'buru* inhabits that place with all their senses. Ab-Abi can hear, see, smell, even touch his surroundings."

Batu made a small sound and hunched tighter against the

wall. Leiyn studied him for a baffled moment, but there were more urgent matters to attend to.

"They know we're here in Solace." She glanced at Ketti. "We have to reemerge back in the ruins?"

After a hesitation, the young woman nodded. "Within the borders of the old castle, yes."

"Not outside it?"

"It is not possible." Oro opened his eyes, his hand leaving the pool. Leiyn felt the magic in the stump settle as the water turned milky violet again and resumed its swirling. "We have extended our town's borders beyond in this world, but it only *zaqip*... what is the word?"

"Intersects," Ketti supplied.

"Yes, intersects with yours within Solace."

Leiyn frowned back at the pool, even though the scene of the Suncoat camp had disappeared. "How many did you see?"

"Eighteen men and women. Seventeen had armor and coats with yellow suns. The last was a man wearing a hooded gray robe. This one sat apart. The others spoke of a captain not present."

"Nineteen. And one an *odiosa*." Isla shook her head. "Too many to fight."

"We'll have the advantage of surprise." Leiyn stared at the opposite wall. The *odiosa* posed more of a problem than the Suncoats. If he made her close off her *mahia*, she would not be able to use it to their full advantage.

And there was the possibility of a *lyshan* lurking unseen. Biding their time. Her scars, only days mended, pricked with the memories of the whip and mace.

She looked at Ketti. "Can you teach me the missing step to calling my bonded here in Solace?"

The young woman glanced at her great-grandfather, whose expression hardened, then shook her head. "Not quickly enough. It is a technique learned slowly within another *haru*—ah, a grotto, I mean. And you do not have years, from what I understand."

"No," Isla murmured. "We don't, nor does our home." She looked at Leiyn. "Can we do it?"

The others looked to her. Their hopes weighed on her chest.

Leiyn sucked in a breath, then let it out slowly. Before she could speak, Oro intervened.

"Do not forget—you will have Mehu'Ra helping you."

Ketti turned to her great-grandfather. All their disagreements seemed to fade as she smiled. "Thank you, Ab-Abi. You are generous to share your bonded."

The patriarch offered a grave nod. "You are my great-granddaughter. I only hope to protect you. And Solace's protector will one day be bound to you. It is only right he watches over you while he still can."

Leiyn nodded, the tightness in her chest loosening slightly. A tempest hawk would go a long way toward evening the odds. Even if a lyshan materialized, it might fend it off long enough for them to make their escape.

"We should leave while there's still light. We'll have to move fast, and we cannot risk one of our horses breaking a leg." Leiyn looked around their small party and received their consent with nods.

"Then we must send you off." The patriarch never looked older as he gazed upon the youngest Ta'Rul. "Come. Your mounts should be waiting for you in the market."

⌒ ⌒

The color had faded from the clouds when they stood back in the marketplace.

Leiyn held Feral's reins tightly as the mare pulled against her. Somehow, she seemed less at ease now that they prepared to leave Solace.

Perhaps she enjoyed a break from you.

"Too bad, old girl," she muttered with a glare. "We're stuck together, you and me."

The horse rolled her eyes and tossed her mane.

They waited as Ketti gave her final farewells. No eyes remained dry for long. Ketti had resisted the tears for a while, but the sheer number of goodbyes broke down her will. Every person in the village, it seemed, had come to see her off.

Leiyn battled her impatience. Ketti was the first to leave Solace. It was the first farewell they had ever given. Seeing all that sorrow made her question bringing Ketti with them. If she should truly expose her to war.

Don't doubt. Not now.

She tightened her hands on the reins. Ketti had made her choice. And Leiyn needed Eteman knowledge and guidance. Without it, Clouded Fang would remain aloof until she next chanced to enter a grotto. And she doubted Sharo would give her that opportunity in their next fight.

Leiyn stared through the broken front gates, watching the sparks of esse flicker in the wall of fog, and waited.

At last, Ketti broke free from the villagers and approached them, wiping a sleeve across her face. Her eyes were puffy and red, but she looked determined as she stopped before them.

"I apologize for keeping you waiting. I am ready."

Isla murmured reassurances and gestured her closer. Etemans did not keep horses, not being needed for travel, so Ketti was to ride with Isla atop Mottle. To start, however, they would remain on foot. The transition from a grotto could be rocky, and none of them wished to begin their journey with a tumble to the pavers.

Leiyn met her friends' eyes. Their gazes were steady. She turned last to Ketti, who appeared more afraid, if no less certain.

"Whenever you're ready."

The young woman nodded, swallowed, and glanced over her shoulder to where the crowd of Etemans waited. Only Oro Ta'Rul was missing, having returned to his tower to prepare to bring down his bonded titan.

Ketti faced forward, drew in a breath, and exhaled. "I am ready."

Leiyn tensed, bracing for the shift. It still caught her by

surprise. Vision blurred and lifesense scrambled, she fell to one knee.

As she hit stone, the world settled.

Rain pelted her shoulders. Leiyn blinked against the droplets and raised her gaze. Above the drone of the storm, shouts sounded from the glowing shelters ahead. Shadows writhed in the gloomy courtyard. Weapons flashed in their hands.

"Flee! Now!" Leiyn roared the order while rising and scrabbling for Feral's reins. The mare screamed, but it was full of rage rather than fear.

A blur of movement in the corner of her eye stopped her short. Whipping her head around, Leiyn's stomach dropped. A horse lay on its side, legs kicking the air—Mottle. Isla and Ketti desperately pulled at him, trying to get him to rise.

In a moment, their plan had torn to shreds.

"Shit, shit, *shit!*"

Releasing Feral, Leiyn faced the courtyard and drew her falchions. They glowed like burning brands to her lifesense, alive in her hands. Eager to taste blood.

Suncoats charged toward them, a dozen of them. They came in a ragged line, but a veneer of order remained even when surprised.

She stood alone against them.

Leiyn bared her teeth and raised her weapons. She settled her balance and drew on her amber beads, instilling her body with vigor and power.

She threw up her mahia's walls as the odiosa struck.

He had been readying his attack behind the enemy line; peripherally, she had been aware of it coming. Like a soldier instinctively raising a shield, she met it with a barrier as hard as iron.

But the distraction cost her moments. The soldiers closed in, nearly close enough to strike. She was one against too many. Just before her lifesense was blinded, she felt Batu attempting to help the women get Mottle upright.

She would be enough. She had to be.

43

STORMFALL

Her blades danced up to meet the Suncoats and found their weapons.

Leiyn struck aside one pointed end, then another, then a third and fourth. She whirled along the line of soldiers, trying to keep the whole rank at bay. The titanbone blades lopped off the ends of the poleaxe shafts with each parry, to the surprised cries of the soldiers.

But as the poleaxe-wielders fell back, shields and swords pressed forward. Leiyn danced back from one charge, tripping the man as he went, but had to meet the second as Feral crowded behind her, negating other options. She whipped her blades against the upraised shield and was rewarded with a gurgle. The soldier fell, head tilting back at an unnatural angle, blood jetting from the gash in his neck.

Two more Suncoats with shields and swords closed in. With her lifesense blinded, she had lost track of the one she had tripped. Risking a glance over her shoulder, she saw Mottle had nearly gotten his hooves under him, but the soldier had risen from the pavers and charged them.

Just as he reached her companions, Batu flew at him, his axe rising and falling.

Her distraction cost her. Facing forward, Leiyn barely raised her falchions against a charging shield. Even her strengthened body was not enough to halt the charge in its tracks. The soldier grunted as he sent her tumbling to the ground, then tripped over her and sprawled past her.

She ached, but with lifeforce flooding her, her mahia already eased the wounds. Bolting to her feet, Leiyn found five more soldiers fast approaching, fresh poleaxes in hand.

Yelling and spitting, Leiyn brandished her weapons. These Suncoats were more cautious than those in the initial charge. Perhaps they had seen the deadly efficacy of her enchanted blades and were loath to feel their touch.

The true reason slammed into her shoulder a moment later.

Leiyn spun to the ground, disoriented. Only as her esse darkened and her arm numbed did she realize what had happened. Crossbowmen—they were the reason the rest of the Suncoats had not charged. Marksmen hid across the ruins, loosing from on high upon her and her comrades.

She rose. Her imbued clothes had repelled the quarrel, but her shoulder was stiff and aching, the esse beneath purpled from the impact. She shrugged the shoulder and ignored the pain. She could not afford to show weakness.

The poleaxe wielders spread out in an arc, encircling her. They knew she could not fend off attacks from every angle.

Another quarrel shot through the gloom, pinging on the pavers just past her.

Rain streamed into her eyes. Her shoulder throbbed. Leiyn snarled and raised her swords. Though they might believe her near dead, not understanding the armor she wore, this fight was far from over.

A cry echoed across the ruins, clapping like thunder. Light spilled from the clouds.

The sky split open.

Leiyn flinched from the tempest hawk tearing free of the clouds while the Suncoats screamed. Splitting apart, they bolted toward what scant shelter was to be found among the derelict stones.

It did little good. The creature of black clouds and crackling energy swept in low. Its power coalesced, then thrashed out. The top of a tower, where the figure had stood silhouetted against the sky, burst with lightning. Rubble fell as thick as rain.

Coughing, ears ringing, Leiyn turned away and spotted her comrades. She ran back toward them, her path weaving. She felt as tipsy as if she had overindulged in brandy. The tempest hawk's influence? Her walls still held, though cracks crept through them. If she could just reinforce them before—

An unseen blow sent her reeling.

"Odiosa!" She bit off the word with a snarl. The taste of blood flooded her mouth. Spitting, down on one knee, Leiyn scrambled to shore up her defenses. The odiosa was relentless in his attacks. Like water against a dam, his mahia seeped through every gap to infect her mind. His touch was unctuous, violating.

Relent, a whisper rode on the wave. *Cease your struggles.*

Rallying her strength, she thrust him out, then whipped around to face the witch hunter. Her lifesense bared, she picked him out from among the ruins, a cloud of mahia extending from him to reach toward her. Though he cringed under his meager shelter as the tempest hawk ravaged his company, she felt his single-minded focus on her. She had to deal with him before they could flee.

Sharpening her mahia, she readied to thrust it like a poleaxe. Before she could strike, a figure composed of brilliant light materialized next to the odiosa and seized him.

Even across the courtyard, she heard the squelch as his head was ripped from his shoulders.

Leiyn was staggering away before she recognized who it was. Ata—she had come.

Thank the Saints she's on our side.

The dryvan stared down at the man she had decapitated, then sprang after the next Suncoat. Leiyn did not have to wait to know the result.

Turning, Leiyn fled toward her companions, who lingered not far away. Another roll of thunder sent her lunging for Feral's reins as the mare screamed in fear. Isla shouted something at her, but she could not register the words. The rest of their party was already mounted, their mounts dancing to be off. Pulling herself into the saddle, Leiyn bent low over her horse's neck.

"Fly, old girl!"

Feral was off before she had settled in the saddle. Cutting in front of the others, mud flying from her hooves, they fled into the wet gloom, the screams of the dying following them into darkness.

PART V

THE THIRD COLONY

THIRTEEN YEARS BEFORE

Leiyn could not keep still. Though she knew she ought to conserve energy while she could, her feet danced with the jangling of her nerves.

It's a patrol, she reminded herself. *Just another patrol.*

But she knew better than to believe that. This was no ordinary jaunt through the woods—it was the Hunger Patrol. It left its mark, if you came back at all.

She banished the thoughts with a snort and turned to her companions. Isla stood nearby, staring toward the forest, hands cinching her pack against her back. That and the crease in her forehead showed she was as worried as Leiyn.

Both their packs were light. Carrying no food supplies— those being borne by Tadeo, both as a mercy and to negate any temptation to cheat—they had only their waterskins, a sleeping roll, and vital survival items such as tinder and flint. They each carried a rudimentary map of the Titan Wilds as well in case they became separated—though, having spent nearly five years at the Lodge, Leiyn figured either of them could navigate the land without it.

In addition to bows, they carried their respective weapons: Isla her spear, which she held like a walking stick, and Leiyn her long knives. As promised, Tadeo had customized them for her, carving foxes into the pommels. Their bows, too, were shaped for them by the lodgemaster's hand from the boughs of a favored ash tree.

Finding no words to lighten the mood, Leiyn looked in the same direction as her friend. Autumn had recently fallen. The aspens were green-gold, the mountaintops mostly bare of snow. The weather was pleasantly cool that morning. An ideal time of year for the march, if any time could be called "ideal."

Tadeo arrived at last, pulling in tow the horse coming on the expedition, a black stallion named Steadfast. Having taken a shine to him, Leiyn was glad to have him along. The lodge-master would keep possession of the horse, though he promised he only brought the beast for emergencies. This patrol tested a ranger's fortitude, both in body and mind. No one received their cloak without passing it.

Like that'll make me less nervous.

"Don't suppose we could set out in the evening and count it?" Leiyn said when the lodgemaster stopped by them, giving Steadfast a stroke in greeting.

Tadeo flashed his slight smile. "You're both prepared?"

"I think so," Isla said in a small voice.

"Then I see no reason to delay."

"You might not," Leiyn muttered. "But you get to eat every day."

While Tadeo would keep up his strength to protect them, Leiyn and Isla would be restricted to a single meal every three days. Already, having been forbidden their morning meal, her stomach was rumbling and she would have to endure this schedule for the next fifteen days. That she could drink as much water as she desired was only a slight consolation.

Though it's not the worst thing I've gone through.

Tadeo's eyes were full of sympathy, but his voice remained firm. "Once we begin walking, it will become better. Your body adjusts and your mind grows occupied."

Leiyn turned away. "Then let's get walking."

Their journey would take them around almost a complete

perimeter of the lands guarded by the rangers of the Wilds Lodge. They would first head west through the Coyote Fens before they turned south along Storm Lake. Then they would loop around to the east to edge the Robin Holts, and finally go north to the Tortoise Bluffs and along the Sierra Foothills. When Tadeo first told them this, Leiyn had joked that it was designed to give them mountain views while they suffered most. The lodgemaster had not disagreed, so she wondered if it was true.

The walk started off easily enough. Fueled by her nerves, Leiyn's stride ate away the leagues. The Coyote Fens smelled foul but were pretty enough to gaze upon.

The first day passed in easy banter that faded toward the evening. Hunger asserted itself then. A fanged deer they glimpsed in the distance tempted her to reach for her bow. She only just resisted. That night, Leiyn curled around her empty belly, trying not to listen to the quiet sounds of Tadeo eating, wondering how she could last another three weeks of this.

I can. I will.

The second day, she felt strangely energetic. Isla's head was bowed, but her smile was as brilliant as ever. Conversation came in fits and starts. Only Tadeo seemed to have the will to continue it, and he had never been the most talkative.

The third day, Leiyn woke to her stomach trying to digest itself. Groaning, she rubbed at her pounding head and squinted up at Tadeo, who watched with undisguised pity.

"Has anyone ever died on this *feshtado* march?"

The lodgemaster hesitated before answering. "Only once."

Leiyn stared for a moment longer. When no clarifications came, she looked at Isla. "He's joking, right?"

Isla shrugged. "Maybe?"

Their progress slowed that day. Breaks became frequent. Whenever they paused, Leiyn collapsed onto the nearest log or boulder and bowed over nearly double. Though incessant training kept her fit, even this idle pace left her winded.

Damn this patrol. Damn Tadeo for making us go on it.

But each time the lodgemaster called to continue, she rose.

This was the price of the cloak. Every ranger underwent this trial, even Yolant and Gan. She had to do the same.

At last, Tadeo bade they make camp, then supplied their first meal. Though it was only a few mouthfuls of smoked mutton and hard bread, Leiyn salivated as soon as it came into view. She barely refrained from snatching the food out of Tadeo's hands.

"Don't eat too quickly," he cautioned.

Leiyn scarcely listened. Mere minutes passed before it was gone. Her jaw ached, but energy already flooded back into her limbs. Her belly remained hollow, like the meal had been a coin dropped in a cavern, but for the moment, she clung to the savor in her mouth.

The feeling departed long before morning arrived.

The fourth day fell just short of miserable, particularly as they caught sight of Storm Lake, which made up part of the border between Baltesia and Ore-Ofe. Leiyn stared at the sparkling blue water as they climbed up and down the wooded ridge running alongside it, then up at the mountains beyond. On the far side was the territory of the skystriders of the Stormhold, the Ofean counterparts to the rangers. She wondered if any watched them, as wary of their intrusions as they were of the skystriders.

It mystified her that relations with Ore-Ofe were worse than with Kalga. The answer Tadeo provided was only marginally helpful.

"I think it's because they're bound closer to the Ancestral Lands than the rest of the Tricolonies," he said after a moment's consideration. "Their religion holds their Sky Queen as a step down from a goddess, and I believe that binds their loyalty to her even when they suffer similar mistreatment as Baltesia. Not that we don't remain loyal," he was quick to add. "It is for the Caelrey and Ilberia that we guard this frontier."

Leiyn nodded, but only halfway in agreement. Tadeo might be here out of patriotic duty, and perhaps Isla and the other rangers as well. Leiyn was not concerned over such distant things. It was for the Wilds Lodge and the other frontierfolk that she meant to fight. She protected people, not property. Even if it was in the Crown's name.

The vague sense of peril helped pass the time. After they left the lake over the next two days, the march became far more monotonous. The forest was beautiful, and Leiyn glimpsed a fern and a bird she had not yet seen, but she did not have the wherewithal to commit their features to memory for sketching. Only the prospect of another lean meal that night kept her going.

She also had to endure another assault from within. Either from the privations or her weakening willpower, the barriers she erected around her mahia were crumbling. Often, Leiyn would walk in a daze only to realize the world had come alive with tantalizing light. Each time, she managed to close off her magic again.

She worried for when she no longer could.

After the next meal and rest, the third trio of days were easier to bear. Even as they neared the Wilds Lodge, which their route brought them alongside, Leiyn only felt a distant impulse to end their torturous march early. Her body was adjusting, and while she could not be called energetic, each step was no longer a fight. Even maintaining her mahia's walls came simply enough.

Isla's trajectory looked the opposite of Leiyn's. Instead of adjusting, her fellow apprentice deteriorated with every league traveled. Thin to begin with, she looked skeletal to Leiyn's eyes, though it seemed too soon for such changes to be visible. Most of the day, she was asleep on her feet, stumbling on in a daze.

By the eighth day, Tadeo was walking beside Isla, ready to catch her should she fall. When Leiyn joined them at a wider part of the path, he murmured, "I may need to intervene if she grows worse. Remain vigilant."

Leiyn nodded, her head seeming to weigh far more than it should. "Perceive, preserve, protect. I know how it goes."

He smiled, but it was fleeting.

Yet Isla persisted, making it to their third meal and then

undergoing a miraculous recovery. The next day, when she walked nearly upright, Tadeo stopped hovering and returned to his place behind them, silent Steadfast in tow. Leiyn breathed a sigh of relief. The worst had passed, and they were more than halfway through the march.

But like the weather of the Titan Wilds, the situation could turn at a moment's notice.

When she awoke the next morning, Leiyn could barely sit up. Her chest seemed weighed down by an anvil, each breath little more than a gasp. An eternity seemed to pass between each heartbeat.

A shadow obscured the sky above her. She felt so weak that she barely had room for alarm. As a cold nose nudged her cheek, she realized who it was.

"Steadfast," she croaked. "Good old boy."

The black stallion made no sound, but he did not need to. His unshifting presence was an anchor binding her to Unera. Without him, she felt she must sink down into the world, never to surface again.

With the help of the horse, she gained her feet. The ground pitched underneath, tossing her this way and that. She felt Tadeo and Isla watching her, but she could not summon the energy to meet their eyes.

"Leiyn?" her friend asked. "Leiyn, are you alright?"

She managed a nod, then proceeded in a weaving walk as they set out for the day. Even as iron seemed to pool in her muscles and limbs, she persisted. A splitting pain worked through her skull, threatening to split it in two. She pressed a palm to it, but nothing could ease the pressure.

Slowly, despite her last, desperate efforts, her mahia's walls crumbled.

Though her eyes were closed, Leiyn sensed the world around her. The sparse plants along the trail. The roots buried beneath. The denser vegetation alongside fading into a glowing sea. The insects at their feet and along the tree trunks. The birds and small mammals in the branches.

Life surrounded her, its energy enticing. Esse could sustain her in the absence of food. She knew that from when it had brought her back from the brink of death following the Blush's coming, and after when it had sustained her in the wintry woods before the silver fox fetched her.

Her body was deteriorating. Her lifeforce faded, its glow dulled. But she did not have to die. She could survive.

No...

Little discipline remained to Leiyn, but she set every scrap of it toward fighting that urge. She was barely conscious of stumbling along as she waged her battle, hardly noticing Tadeo and Isla's concerned questions. Only when they tried to touch her did she respond, flinching away from the greedy grasping of her mahia and muttering, "I'm fine, I'm fine," until they let her be.

She barely slept that night, worried that while unconscious, she would draw on life-giving fire. Her esse was an ember's gleam when she rose for the next march. Only the prospect of food that evening gave her the courage to press on.

A little longer... Just a little longer... Just a—

Leiyn fluttered her eyes open.

The world came alive in sharp detail. She felt as if she had woken from a dream, and a pleasant one. Peacefulness flowed through her. Only the dirt sticking to her skin and Isla and Tadeo bent over her were alarms that all was not as it seemed.

"Good morning," Leiyn said with a wry smile as she sat up.

"Saints, she's awake." Isla's voice was strained, her eyes bloodshot. Only then did Leiyn realize she had been crying.

Her smile slipped. "What happened?"

Tadeo placed a hand on her shoulder. Leiyn flinched, but her mahia did not tug at his esse as she thought it would. Now that she noticed it, her lifeforce seemed much brighter than it had been for days.

"You fell," the lodgemaster said. "Just moments ago. Are you sure you're well?"

"I'm sure."

An uneasy feeling stirred her. Leiyn looked around. The surroundings were unfamiliar, and not only due to her lifesense being open. Delirious with hunger, she had barely noticed where they walked.

One odd thing drew her attention. Next to the trail, a tree looked gray and shriveled. Her hands pressed against one of its roots where it spread across the ground.

Fesht!

She reinstated her mahia's walls, but it was too late. The cursed magic had betrayed her, sucking the life out of another living thing to sustain her. Leiyn drew her knees up to her chest and curled her arms around them, shrugging off Tadeo as she did. The shame welled up inside her like a dark pool threatening to suck her down. She almost wished it would drown her.

"Leiyn..."

There was too much knowing in her mentor's voice for comfort. Rallying herself, Leiyn raised her head, then got to her feet and slung her pack over her back. Shrugging it into place, she took her bow in hand again.

"Are you sure you should be up?" Isla asked, biting her lip.

"I'm fine. We've lost enough time as it is."

That Tadeo nodded without objection only further grated on her. Without waiting for his consent, Leiyn soldiered on.

She partook of the meal that night, the final one they'd have on the trail, but without relish. They trekked through the foothills of the Silvertusks in the following days, new scenes of beauty spread out around, yet she found no joy in them. She would complete the Hunger Patrol; of that, she was certain. But it would not be an honest victory.

Only the fluttering of wind against her mahia's walls roused her from her mood.

Leiyn looked up as the forest canopy rustled with a stiff gust. Instead of fading, the wind grew stronger. Leaves spiraled off the branches and whipped into her face. Yet, with the sky nearly devoid of clouds and no sign of a storm, there could be only one conclusion.

"Titan!" Tadeo shouted over the rising gale. "Behind the knoll!"

They moved only a fraction slower for their starvation as they took shelter behind the squat hill. The wind still rustled about them, but without an edge. Leiyn braced herself against the battering that was sure to come, as it did with every titan's awakening. She bunched her hands into fists and clenched her muscles tight.

Yet the pressure on her walls never rose beyond a hard nudge. Whatever this titan was, it was not one she had experienced before. She had never thought an awakening might be tolerable.

Minutes passed before the incessant wind eased and the strain on her mahia followed suit. As soon as it lightened, Tadeo rose.

"Up the hill! We'll see if we can catch a glimpse."

Groaning, Leiyn and Isla followed him, their condition reasserting itself now that the danger seemed to have passed. Leiyn kept her gaze on Steadfast's rear as the lodgemaster made for the top of the squat hillock.

Once Tadeo stopped and looked east, Leiyn paused next to him, trying to catch her breath. Isla bent double on her other side, only raising her head after several moments. They still were not above the canopy, but a break in the trees afforded them a view for leagues afar. She squinted against the wind. It blew harder against her face now that they stood in the open.

"There!" The lodgemaster sounded like a boy as he pointed. "It rises from the forest!"

Leiyn caught sight of it then. Something was taking shape above the dancing canopy two leagues afar. It had no visible body but was outlined in swirling patterns by the green and gold leaves and wildflower petals captured by its winds. Two wings beat as it moved higher in the air, supporting a thick body. A pair of antennae emerged from its top, wide and striated.

"A wind moth," Tadeo murmured, a smile in his voice.

Despite all that had come before, Leiyn's lips parted. Titans might be a scourge to the colonists, but there was an unmatched majesty to them. Even starved, tired, and discouraged, she could not help but soak in the sight of the wind moth. The temptation to lower her mahia's walls and experience it more fully was almost too much to resist.

Almost.

It ascended clear of the trees and rose higher until it was a half-league in the air. Then, the captured debris dispersed.

The gale died. Its presence faded against her walled magic.

The titan slumbered once more.

Tadeo brushed back the hair from his forehead, which the windstorm had mussed. "I'll loop back to check on the damage later. With a wind moth, though, it should only be a few splintered trees." He smiled wide. "A fine way to end the patrol."

"I'll never forget it," Isla said, sounding as if she meant it.

Leiyn only nodded. The experience had lifted her malaise. It had been a reminder of what being a ranger was truly about. It was not about completing a trial to the letter. Her mandate was to maintain the splendor of the Titan Wilds.

Perceive. Preserve. Protect. That was the oath she was to take and uphold.

All the rest she could endure.

45

FAIR COMPANY

Gray light edged into the sky by the time they halted.

The night had passed in a long and tense tedium. Once they had left behind the carnage, they slowed to a trot to avoid injuries. Few words were passed between them, all listening for signs of ambush and straining their eyes against the darkness. Leiyn swept her lifesense around them in an ever-revolving circle, her vigilance so constant that her head ached. Behind her, Ketti kept a similar watch.

Only when morning broke did they allow their beleaguered mounts to rest. Descending from the saddle, Leiyn filtered a sliver of lifeforce to her battered thighs and rear to ease the soreness of riding. Stretching, she looked about them. Though the jungle was clear for several paces around the road, it was too poor for a campsite. Not that any of them were willing to risk stopping for that long. Finding a viable stone, she sat atop it, trying to ignore its chill dampness seeping through her trousers. She would have been surprised if any inch of her was left dry. Feral ambled off, grazing on the little grass to be found.

The rest of their party found their own perches. Only Batu remained standing. Leiyn leveled a raised eyebrow at the young man. His scowl did not lessen.

"We made it out," he said. "To Kunu, then?"

"To Kunu." Isla seemed close to crying, her eyes bloodshot and puffy from lack of sleep, and her voice was strained. "The fork in the road should be no more than a day's ride farther. We'll reach it, turn south, then be at the city in a few more days."

And hope Southport hasn't already fallen.

But Leiyn kept her objections to herself. If Southport had not already succumbed to the Ilberian siege, it would likely stand a week longer. They were far enough away that moving forward only made sense. Though, if she could manage to summon Clouded Fang again, she might shift the tide. And having an Eteman on their side could also balance the odds.

The answer did little to improve Batu's mood. With a terse nod, the former plainsrider walked to the edge of the woods.

Leiyn let him go. Isla must have decided the same. That, or she was too cold to rise. Her spare frame had all but collapsed in on itself as she hunched over on the rock and shivered.

Rising, Leiyn went to her friend and placed a hand on her shoulder. Gently, she sent lifeforce into her. Isla straightened with a gasp, the energy turning into heat as it entered her body. She cast Leiyn a small smile.

"Thanks. But shouldn't you save that for more important things?"

"I have enough." Her amber beads were halfway drained, but she did not mention that. No need to make Isla worry more than she already did. "Besides, we won't go far if you die of cold."

"Ha, ha."

From the corner of her eye, Leiyn observed their last party member. Ketti sat apart from them. Though the Eteman was nearly as slight as Isla, she did not shiver, her mahia warming her through, the same as Leiyn's did. Yet with her eyes downcast and her shoulders bowed, Leiyn could not help but wonder if she suffered more.

Isla noticed the direction of her gaze. "Think she's alright? It's not easy, your first battle."

Memories sprang to Leiyn's mind. The hating stares. The bristling weapons. She had stood alone before eight poachers and an odiosa intent on mining a hill tortoise, as improbable as that still seemed, with only her bow and knives to defend herself. Yet her mahia had found a way out, and though she had hated to admit it at the time, it had saved her.

As it so often has.

But Leiyn had been trained for bloodshed. She had prepared for that moment. Even minor acts of violence while hunting inured her to the horror of it all. Ketti had not butchered livestock, judging by the way Etemans ate. Perhaps she had never harmed another living being. And while she had not lifted a hand against the Suncoats who died back in the ruins, she had helped initiate it.

Ketti had killed them as much as Ata and the tempest hawk had. Their blood stained her hands, and the Eteman knew it.

"Give her time," Leiyn muttered. "It's something she has to work through for herself."

"It's easier with company."

"She knows we're here. Offering more will make it worse, the same as with other struggles."

Catching her meaning, Isla's eyes darted over to where Batu stood staring into the depths of the jungle. Sighing, she shook her head. Leiyn squeezed her friend's shoulder, hoping each of their burdens would lighten soon. Otherwise, the journey to Kunu would feel even longer.

❦

After the brief rest, they pressed on through the day. The skies took mercy on them, breaking from the unrelenting rain and allowing them to dry out in pallid sunlight. Their esse-imbued clothes absorbed the lingering moisture and soon dried out. Leiyn remembered past patrols carried out through stormy weather, how the dampness clung for days after a soaking. Though ranger cloaks were treated to be resistant to water, they could not hold a candle to magic.

Their constant surveillance turned up no enemies. Only the

reappearance of Ketti's hummingbird took them by surprise. Leiyn whipped her head around as she materialized over the Eteman's shoulder, but Biqqa scarcely noticed, fluttering rapidly around Ketti's head.

Ketti wore her first smile since leaving Solace as the spirit alighted on her outstretched hand. She murmured to Biqqa in Eteman before the hummingbird took off into the jungle.

"She will return," Ketti assured them, "after she's had her fill."

The hummingbird accompanied them the rest of the way, mostly flying near the Eteman, but often investigating the rest of them. Her presence made Leiyn think of Chispa and where he hid. For as often as he appeared near her, the silver fox had always kept aloof. She could not help but hope he would visit soon.

By evening, they returned to the crossroads where the skystriders had led them astray. Leiyn wondered at all that diversion had led to. Ketti was a stark reminder, the gently pulsing pearls in her skin never letting her forget her foreignness.

Whatever else had come of it, she had answers. And soon, she might solve the problem haunting her.

They moved off the road, not wishing to make camp where Suncoats could easily find them. Before they went far, however, a creature with blinding esse stepped into existence on the road.

The horses neighed and skittered away. Biqqa vanished in a flash of esse. Leiyn had halfway drawn a falchion before she realized who it was. She hissed out a breath. "Do you have to appear like that?" Leiyn barked as she slammed the sword back in its scabbard.

Ata donned a wild grin as she glided toward them. She did not wear Chispa's silver fur anymore, but had returned to her motley arrangement of vines, leaves, feathers, and talons. Her teeth, however, remained as sharp as before.

"No," the dryvan answered. "But I do delight in it."

Leiyn looked back at her comrades to see how they took the surprise. She had been concerned with Ketti in particular.

Despite Leiyn's claims and Ata proving her worth back in the ruins, it could not be easy for an Eteman to accept an old enemy as an ally.

But it was not Ketti who strode forth, but Batu. Hands bunched into fists, the young man approached Ata like she were a drunk offender in a tavern brawl. Leiyn did not think to step forward until he already stood before the dryvan.

Ata's smile shrank, but she drew up her considerable height to match Batu's. For a moment, human and dryvan met one another's stares.

"Batu..." Isla cautioned.

He was beyond hearing.

"What am I, *sach'aan?*" Batu spat in the dryvan's face. "What monster have you made of me?"

46

THE BEAST WITHIN

The accusation hung in the air. Leiyn inched forward, shoulders tight. If she had to, she would throw herself between them, but she had seen how fast Ata could move. If the skin-walker meant Batu harm, there was little she could do to prevent it.

But Ata did not strike. When she moved, it was to take a step back. Her height seemed to shrink, her lithe body bowing. Her clawed feet extended thin roots into the ground, holding her firm.

"So you know," the dryvan murmured.

"Then it's true? What they say I am?" The anger did not leave Batu's voice, but something else edged into it. A hollowness that made Leiyn's chest ache. "That I have your kind's blood?"

Sighing, Ata raised her head and cocked it to one side like a curious bird. "The hunter-children told you." Leaf-green eyes flickered to Ketti. "Perhaps it was you who spoke of it?"

The Eteman stiffened. Leiyn edged closer to the young woman. Ata was a friend; after all they had been through, she could assume no less. But there was too much bad blood between their peoples to rely solely on sentiment.

"Not her." Batu moved between Ata and Ketti. "But that

doesn't matter. I need to know what I am. What it means to be... tainted."

"Tainted?" Ata laughed, the feathers along her shoulders flaring. "Is that our legacy?"

At another time, the comment would have had the young man tripping over his words to apologize. Now, Batu stiffened his spine and held Ata's gaze.

Back down! Leiyn wanted to yell at him. She had been rash often enough to know how much trouble it could land you in.

But the dryvan did not lash out. Instead, she looked aside, a wheezy breath issuing from her wooden lips. "You cannot understand. What was done to your ancestors... It was a different era of the world. My people were different. The wars, different." Her bright eyes flickered to Leiyn. "The ills done to mortals seemed less dire. Especially when to fail to act would mean our end. Even still, all our efforts proved futile."

Leiyn felt her expression hardening and smoothed it. Playing the peacemaker did not come naturally to her, but with Batu's blood risen, she would have to try.

"Explain," she offered, taking a small step toward the pair. "Please."

The dryvan's head fell to one side, considering. Then she shrugged. "Very well. It is a scandalous tale. Suitable for a dismal night, I suppose."

Fluid as water, she pivoted away from Batu to stride around the edge of the small clearing. When she spoke again, she did not face any of them, but directed her words toward the jungle.

"You will know how it happened. We Iritu can shift our forms to suit us. While we do not possess your reproductive organs—nor would we wish to, with all their inconveniences— there was a time after losing the Mothertrees that we adopted them in an attempt to... procreate."

She halted mid-step, eyes scanning them, perhaps to assess their reactions. Leiyn was careful to keep her disgust concealed.

"We did not know how devastating such acts were to you. Lacking such urges ourselves, we saw them only as a way to further our lines. Once I knew..." The vines on her body twitched, like a snake disturbed among the grass. Ata shuddered, then continued her walk as if she had never stopped. "Nothing but regrets came of those attempts. That, and those with 'tainted blood.'"

Did you do it? The question needled her. *Were you one of the tormenters?*

Batu had fewer reservations. "So that excuses it. Your raping was an innocent mistake."

Ata moved faster than Leiyn could follow. Her hands fell to her falchions before she saw the dryvan had stopped short of Batu, her face inches from his. Her expression had transformed into one both foreign and feral. So monstrous she could almost believe the sins of her.

"*Confession.* The Catedrál is fond of it, is it not?" A mocking smile spread wide across the skin-walker's face. "Perhaps you wish for my confession? Why, child? So you may take vengeance against me?"

A quiver ran through Batu's esse. Leiyn released her breath at the sight. Reason had not entirely left him that he would attack a skin-walker.

Isla edged closer to them, hand outstretched to her beloved. She stopped short of touching him. "Batu, please. Just listen to what she has to say."

He did not shift his glare. Then, as if it pained him, Batu nodded.

The dryvan turned her back on him, almost disdainfully. "Some victims birthed children," she continued as if he had not interrupted. "The most changed didn't survive, but those resembling other mortals did. But like the hunter-children observed in you, their ancestors could sense the... wrongness about them."

Ata continued her revolution around the clearing, circling them. Leiyn tried not to feel like a deer stalked by a lion. She resisted the urge to keep her eyes on the dryvan at all times but let her walk behind until she came into view again.

"Tainted..." Ata spoke the word as if tasting it. "Yes, they were tainted. They carried Inheritance, the magic of my people, within their essence. Weaker than all but the least favored of my people, yet it conferred some of the Kin's talents."

Ata halted before Batu to narrow her eyes at him. Daring him to ask.

He opened his mouth twice before he muttered the words. "What could they do?"

Her smile was wicked. "Change. Transform. With the help of creatures like your Chispa"—Ata nodded at Leiyn—"these tainted became beasts both horrific and beautiful. Wolves. Bears. Birds. Fish." She waved a hand toward the sky. "There was no telling what form they would take."

Leiyn's imagination strained to picture it. *Beastfolk.* It was one thing for dryvans to change their forms, strange as they already were. But for humans to become other creatures...

Yet was it not similar to how the Kalgan gods were represented? Their goddess of horses had the head of a mare. The Gasts, too, had legends of spirits halfway between animal and human. Perhaps the stories held more truth than any of them had known.

Batu bowed his head. Leiyn watched the young man, chest aching. She was closer to him than she had been to most of those at the Lodge now, yet she did not know how to comfort him.

Even Isla seemed at a loss. Her hand raised toward him and this time, she dared to brush his arm. Batu jerked away without looking back.

"Will I do that?" he murmured to the ground.

"Slither out of your skin?" Ata laughed, the sound as rough as bark on skin. "No, child. Heritage lies dormant within you. And did you not listen? It takes more than an ordinary animal to inhabit its essence."

Leiyn breathed a sigh of relief. Until then, she had not known the shape of her fears. "Then he's fine. Batu will be fine."

The dryvan cocked her head at Leiyn. "As he always would be."

"The Etemans." Isla struggled to speak, each word pulled out like a rotten tooth. "They spoke of this taint, or whatever we should call it, like it was a curse."

"As they would." Ata came back upright, eyes glittering. "But you fear asking your question. I do not fear answering it. Why view it as a curse when it might be a gift?"

"Gift" was a stretch too far for Leiyn. But she had once said the same of her magic. Barely, she held her tongue, a terrible curiosity burning within.

The dryvan tapped a talon against the smooth bark of her chest. "It is enough that it came from us, their enemies. But you can answer this better, can you not, Eteman?"

This last she directed at Ketti, who stayed as far away from the dryvan as she could. The young woman startled at the address but held Ata's gaze.

"We have stories." Ketti spoke so softly that Leiyn had to strain to hear. "Tales told to children to remind them of the cruel world outside of Solace. They speak of monsters haunting full-moon nights. Men changed halfway into wolves. Women with wings like bats that develop a taste for blood." She hesitated, then continued, softer, "Of those who lost their humanity and joined our enemies."

Ata twisted her lips, her smile perverse. "So you see. Anything to do with the Kin is tainted in their eyes." Her eyes slid back to Batu. "Your kind have rarely suffered a just fate. Though their torment often came at the hands of those who called it a curse, did it not, Eteman? Did you not hunt and kill these 'tainted' for sport?"

Ketti's esse shuddered like she had been struck. "Not for sport," the young woman whispered. "Nor since Solace was established."

"Because none were allowed in, I think." Again, she looked to Batu. "Yet, as the Iritu mark in your blood persists, we can reason that your ancestors survived long enough to spawn more young. One of your parents included."

Batu looked away from Ata. Leiyn recalled what she knew of his lineage. His mother had been Kalgan, his father Gast.

Unless by an unforeseen twist of fate, the blood taint had surely come down through his father.

Isla, at least, seemed reassured. She went to stand at Batu's side. The young man seemed lost to his thoughts. Unpleasant ones, judging by the scowl he wore.

Leiyn knew she should say something, though she scarcely knew where to begin. Yet, in the wake of all they had learned, the silence felt unbearable.

Before she could find the words, Ata's esse vibrated.

The dryvan went still, her eyes as wide as Leiyn had ever seen them. Almost as if she felt something that made her afraid. Frantically, Leiyn delved into the dryvan's being, searching for any clue as to what was happening.

All she sensed was an overwhelming pain.

"Ata," she said, advancing. "Ata, what's happening?"

Batu raised his head. "What now?" he growled.

"Something happened?" Isla, focused on her beloved, had noticed nothing amiss.

Before Leiyn could reach Ata, the dryvan collapsed. Her head folded to her chest. Taloned hands pressed into the soil, barely preventing her from thudding to the ground.

Heart pounding, Leiyn stopped short. She did not dare come nearer. "Ata?"

The Iritu whipped her head up. Her eyes were wide circles, her pupils narrowed to slits.

"It cannot..." she whispered. "He cannot have..."

"Ata, what is it?" Leiyn demanded. "What's wrong?"

The dryvan looked up, but she seemed to see through Leiyn. Then the world rippled and folded the shapeshifter into it.

Ata was gone.

47

BEYOND

No sooner had the dryvan vanished than Leiyn spread her lifesense around her, scanning for threats. She felt nothing but the jungle's flora and fauna. Her mind raced, imagining reasons for Ata fleeing.

Feshtado *Saints, what's gone wrong now?*

"Leiyn, what was that?" Isla grasped her arm, bringing her focus back to the clearing. "Why did Rowan disappear? And did you call her 'Ata'?"

"Doesn't matter." Leiyn pushed down the guilt at the slip. Ata herself had not seemed to notice, stricken as she had been. "And I know as little as you. But it seemed bad."

"She seemed... *palhu.* Afraid." The idea seemed to frighten Ketti. Her eyes had not left the space Ata had occupied moments before.

"What could scare her?" Isla chewed her bottom lip as she peered around them.

A few possibilities occurred to Leiyn, none of them good. The most likely was that Sharo had gotten to her somehow. Struck her where it hurt the most. But they still knew too little of the Iritu to jump to conclusions. No doubt Ata kept more secrets from her than she knew. Perhaps something had happened to someone for whom she cared. There was more to life than war, including for dryvans.

Leiyn shook her head, trying to dislodge her misgivings. "Speculation won't change anything. It's late, and there's still something I need to do tonight."

"Which is?" Isla glanced at Batu, who had returned to the periphery of the clearing.

Leiyn answered by turning to Ketti. "I don't think it can wait," she said. "Whatever has Rowan concerned, I need to be ready for it."

The Eteman's eyes were wide, but her composure seemed to return. "You wish to reach your bonded."

"If you're still willing to help."

"Of course." Ketti cast her gaze around them. "Perhaps we should not stray far, though."

"That'd be best." Leiyn looked to Isla. "We'll be over there if you need anything."

Her friend nodded, then went to her beloved. Leiyn watched her go. She hoped some time with Isla was what Batu needed. Some truths cut deeper than knives. But it was better to be in pain than ignorant.

Leiyn turned to Ketti. "He'll be alright, won't he?"

The Eteman's eyes flickered to Batu, a small crease forming between her eyebrows and crinkling the pearl set there. "*Etaro siam.* It is left to the spirits now. I only know of those with tainted blood from myth. The truth of their condition... that, I cannot say."

It was as much as she could have expected. Leiyn jerked her head toward the opposite side of the clearing. "No point in dwelling on it, I suppose. Ready to begin?"

They went as far as they could across the small clearing. The jungle buzzed with nocturnal insects and other creatures, though none large enough to threaten them.

The Eteman faced Leiyn with arms crossed. "We know what you are missing in summoning your bonded: forming a *haru*, a grotto. I will teach it to you as it was taught to me."

Ketti closed her eyes. Leiyn followed suit. With her heart still racing, it was difficult to pull her attention from their surroundings. But if she was to learn anything, she had to devote her full concentration to this.

"Reach out with your *semah* to the world around you. Feel the lifeforce in all. *Tlalli netsu*: the world is alive."

Ketti spoke like a priestess reciting a litany in a temple, rhythmic and soft. Leiyn did as instructed. She noticed all the little details she had missed before. The curious creatures, five in all, that watched them from a nearby tree. She wondered at their long arms and tails curled about the branches. Fine subjects for sketching, at another time.

And the clearing—the roots from the trees around them dove underneath it, weaving together like the fibers of a basket. The grass on which their horses grazed had roots that went as deep, brushing against those of the grove.

"Do not focus on the individual pieces of your surroundings," Ketti said, drawing her back to her voice. "Feel the world as a whole. *Ammar ek ist*: all is one. You and I are not separate from one another, nor from our environs. We are all connected, our lives feeding into one another."

Though Leiyn tried to listen and obey, her objections interceded. "You've lost me."

Cracking open her eyes, she saw Ketti gazing upon her with a placid expression. "What do you mean?"

"I don't understand what you're asking of me. The world isn't one, and we *are* separate. Sure, we're all connected by the air and earth, the sun and seasons, but that doesn't make us one thing."

The young woman considered her for a long moment. "I understand your... ah, what is the word?"

"Hesitancies? Objections?"

"Yes, objections. When I was young, perhaps your age, I would question—"

"Wait? My age?" Leiyn screwed up her eyes at the Eteman.

"How old do you think I am?" Then, as another realization dawned on her, "How old are *you*?"

A smile stole over Ketti's face, the pearl hawk upon it seeming to take flight. "As you saw from Ab-Abi, we Etemans age slowly."

"That doesn't answer my question."

The woman inclined her head. "Forty-seven."

Leiyn blinked. "Forty-seven years old? Many women would kill to look like you do at your age."

Ketti laughed. "So I have observed." Her mirth slipped away. "But we are diverted."

"I think you mean distracted?" Leiyn held up her hands at Ketti's frown. "Never mind. You were saying?"

The Eteman nodded, lips pursed. "When I was younger, I questioned if *Tlalli* was one. I wondered if it was truly alive. I saw all things as connected but separate from one another. But Ab-Abi explained his perspective. 'If I breathe out, you breathe in my air,' he said. 'The water we drink once came from clouds, and the clouds from the earth, which we...'" A smirk curled Ketti's lips. "'We gift our water.'"

"I get the idea. But that doesn't—"

"I have not finished. He said to look at each animal or plant upon *Tlalli* like looking at the threads of a spiderweb. Apart, a thread cannot serve its purpose, for the wind will soon carry it away. Together, interwoven—only then is it correct."

Ketti held up a hand, forestalling Leiyn's objections. "You do not believe it, I know, but let me tell you this: without seeing the world this way, you will never open a grotto, nor summon your titan outside of one."

"Fine." Leiyn touched her auburn tress before forcing her hand back to her side. "I'll try again."

It felt like a tale for children, a story to convey some moral. Not truth. Not reality. She had always stood on her own two feet. When life grew tough, when she lost everything time and again, it had been down to her alone to carve out a new life.

And yet you were never whole, a part of her whispered. *Not until you opened yourself to the world.*

She remembered all those times when her guard had lowered and her mahia had slipped free. How she had lost herself in the wider world for a time and been happier for it.

Could she be right?

Leiyn wanted to deny it, to push away that thought. It felt threatening, somehow, like inviting a wolf to sleep in her bed. But she had to pretend to accept it for now.

For once, she did not close herself off, but opened up to the world.

She stopped looking for the details of her surroundings. Stopped worrying about what predator might watch them or what harm might come to her and her friends.

For a moment, she was content to be. To simply exist.

She spread herself wide, seeping into the plants and animals. She felt the jungle for what it was: thriving, ever-moving. Interconnected. Alive.

"I see it." The words felt as if they floated from far away, disconnected as moving fingers on a numb hand. "I understand."

"Good." Ketti's voice vibrated in her ears. She was as much part of the jungle as the rest; Leiyn's esse threaded through hers as well as the rest of the world. "Very good. Now, you must attempt the second step. Reach into *Tlalli's* web, then beyond it. Beyond the life you know. *Aman eken al*: we are more. Grottos exist beyond what we can sense. It is there you must go."

Leiyn tried. She pushed against the world. For a moment, the interconnectedness wavered.

Then, like a spinning coin hitting an edge, it toppled over.

Leiyn's lifesense snapped back into herself, a painful separation. She rubbed her forehead as it ached, then cracked open her eyes. Ketti watched her, lips pursed.

"I lost it."

"You did well. I myself did not achieve what you have for many weeks."

Leiyn nodded at the praise. "We don't have weeks. We might not have days."

Fear flitted through Ketti's eyes at the reminder. It took mere moments for her to master it.

"We will try again. Do not be discouraged. It will help that you have summoned your bonded before. We must be persistent."

Leiyn nodded and let her hand fall away. Persistence was one thing she had never lacked.

"Then let's try again."

48

OMEN

*L*eiyn kept at it until long past dusk, though she had made scant progress. Twice more, she felt the world as Ketti bade her, whole and integrated with herself. But she could not go further, much less form a grotto.

As she sat to rest, Leiyn mulled over the Eteman's instructions. "It is like pushing your hand into dirt," Ketti had said. "You still feel the world and remain a part of it, but you have reached beyond what you can see, beyond the outer layer, the crust. Your eyes will not serve you. Now you must *feel* your way through. Reach in deep enough and you might find a pocket of air, or a small burrow. That is what a grotto is: a burrow beyond this world. A hidden hole in *Tlalli's* web."

Though it seemed a useful analogy, it had not yielded results. Leiyn tried to push through the blanket of esse, but always found the illusion broke before the natural barriers did. Instead of reaching through, she ended up pushing against plants and bugs like she had while bushwhacking with Belen's company. The thought of all those she had failed further hampered her concentration.

By the time they stopped for the night, Leiyn's head pounded and her mahia felt stretched thin, like a wrist strained after too much practice on the bow range. Rubbing her temples, she made her way back to Isla and Batu, who still sat talking on a fallen log on the far side of the clearing.

Ketti brought her up short. "Thank you for defending me, Leiyn of Orille. Had you not..."

Leiyn turned back, noticing her downcast eyes. *Saints, she doesn't seem forty-seven.* Still, she doubted any number of years could prepare a person to weather the transitions she had undergone this past day.

"It's what I'm here for," Leiyn murmured.

The Eteman did not seem to hear her. "I... froze. I knew I must fight, but I could not remember how to move. I could not think of anything to do."

Leiyn squeezed Ketti's shoulder. "Everyone freezes their first time."

A lie, if a kind one. Rare was the time Leiyn had spurned a fight. For as long as she remembered, she had been all sharp edges, eager to cut. The gentle influence of friends and mentors had filed down those edges over the years, but she doubted they would ever truly dull.

Ever the damned huntress, she thought.

Aloud, Leiyn said, "You'll improve. If we have the misfortune of more battles, that is."

Ketti nodded in gratitude more than acceptance. Her shoulders slumped. "Until then, I will do what I can."

Together, they returned to Batu and Isla, hesitant and fearing they might be interrupting a discussion. But as the pair rose and faced them, Batu's expression had lightened, and Isla looked tired but relieved. Leiyn did not have to ask to know: their plainsrider would come through this revelation fine.

"Shall we?" Isla gestured toward the clearing.

They split toward their saddlebags, but Ketti brought them up short. "A moment, please."

Leiyn turned back with a frown. "What is it?"

"I may have a way to keep us safe while we sleep."

"Safety," Isla murmured. "I could do with some of that."

Batu stepped close and drew his beloved to his side. Isla

wrapped an arm around his middle, glancing up with a small smile.

Leiyn frowned. "What do you mean?"

"I could form a grotto. Just large enough for our camp." Ketti shrugged. "I have not attempted it before, but if it works, no Iritu could reach us."

The prospect was heartening, but Leiyn narrowed her eyes. "What if it doesn't work?"

The Eteman looked aside. "I do not know. Likely nothing will happen. But..." She only shrugged again. "If it is not stable, it may cease to exist, as will anything within it."

It was an awful risk to take. But every moment they stayed out in the dark jungle—within a day's ride of Solace, no less—brought its own perils. Leiyn could forgo sleep for one night, but she could not keep it up the entire way to Kunu.

"If you agree, I will attempt it first." Ketti held their gazes. "I would not endanger you unnecessarily."

Isla opened her mouth to answer, but Leiyn spoke first. "Try it. It's our best option."

Ketti nodded. When the others did not object, she murmured, "A moment, please," and closed her eyes.

Leiyn watched her carefully, her lifesense open and noting every movement of her esse. The Eteman was still for a moment; then, like a droplet hitting the surface of a pond, she expanded outward. She had not been paying close attention during their previous transitions in and out of Solace. Now, she understood what this meant: that Ketti experienced the world as an interconnected web of lifeforce.

For a moment, Ketti appeared suspended in that place. Then her esse stirred again. She pulsed, then pushed outward. It was not like a force against the plants and animals or their party; more, it was the lap of a wave against the sand far up the shore. A gentle touch, then seeping in.

The Eteman rippled faster and faster. Then her esse flashed.

Next Leiyn knew, Ketti had disappeared.

"Saints," Isla breathed. Leiyn blinked, her vision struggling to make sense of what she had witnessed. Even watching the transition on multiple levels, she found it disconcerting. It was one thing for dryvans, lyshans, and titans to vanish and appear at will. But humans? Even as she had been transported herself multiple times, it seemed a step too far into the unknown.

They stood there, looking at each other in silence. A minute passed, then two. Leiyn's impatience rose. She wondered what they would do if Ketti never returned.

Batu moistened his lips. "How long should we wait?"

"Time's different in grottos. I'm sure she's fine." An unfounded assumption, but Leiyn did not want to voice the alternative. "We can give it a few minutes more before—"

She cut off as Ketti winked back into existence.

Isla loosed a startled, "Oh!" Batu muttered curses under his breath in Kalgan. Leiyn bit back foul words and examined the Eteman. From all she could sense, she was unharmed.

"It worked?" Leiyn pressed.

Ketti nodded. "I hope I did not keep you waiting long."

"A few minutes, no more."

"Only moments passed for me."

Isla, overcoming her shock, edged forward. "Will that be a problem for us?"

"Only if we need to leave at dawn. I cannot know if it will be the same in *Tlalli* as the grotto."

"It's a risk we'll have to take." Leiyn looked at the others, ensuring they agreed. "Let's gather the horses."

Once they had corralled their mounts together and draped the saddlebags over their backs, they huddled close to Ketti. As before, it did not seem necessary to touch her, though Leiyn asked to be sure.

"I can do it," was all the Eteman said in reply as she closed her eyes, then activated her mahia.

Leiyn felt her esse viscerally this time. The sensation was not unlike hooks piercing her lifeforce; uncomfortable, though without pain or harm. She fought the urge to raise her walls and kept a tight hold on Feral's reins as the mare snorted her displeasure.

Paying close attention through her lifesense, she felt the moment of the transition. Like a gentle breeze, the world they knew swept away, a dust of esse passing over and through them. Her vision distorted for a moment, then settled. Her balance suffered greater, bringing her down to one knee on the loamy earth.

"Saints," Isla said again as she rose from where she had fallen. "We're doing this every night?"

Leiyn was too busy scrutinizing their surroundings. Like in other grottos, the air shimmered with flecks of formless esse. Otherwise, it was a mirror image of the clearing they had left behind.

"I would not stray far," Ketti said. The Eteman seemed most at ease, yet she resembled a rabbit out in the open, eyes darting from tree to tree. "Even when relieving yourself. It is a small grotto, and I do not know what would happen if you strayed beyond its bounds."

One more worry. Leiyn kept it from her expression and gave the Eteman a firm nod. "We'll stay close."

"It's late," Batu reminded them. "And I'm tired. Can we make camp now?"

With humorless chuckles, they dispersed and set to their tasks.

⌣ ⌣

Leiyn knew what it meant to sleep like the dead that night.

Upon waking, it barely felt as if she had slept on the ground. Her body had shed its aches and pains. Much of the weariness she had carried had sloughed off like dead skin.

Leiyn yawned, stretched, and listened to the songs of birds and insects echoing through the jungle. The grotto's shimmer became dazzling under the sun's golden glow. The air was cool and moist. The fresh scent of life filled her nose.

Then she recalled the events from the previous days, and the beauty hollowed.

For a moment, she was tempted to call Clouded Fang to see if she could, yet it struck her as rude to disturb him with no cause.

Rude?

The thought made her smile. She did not understand enough of titans to know if he *could* feel annoyed. Though it stood to reason; other animals could, after all. Saints knew how often Feral grew irritated.

He's there, she reminded herself. *You can reach him. Let that be enough.*

The others rose soon after, feeling just as rested. Even Batu's mood had lightened, and he smiled at their light banter throughout the morning meal. Almost, the shadow of battle and loss had lifted from their party.

They set to packing up camp but had not yet resettled their mounts' tack when Ketti drew Leiyn aside.

"Before we depart, I would mend your clothes. They were harmed, no?"

"I suppose I took an arrow or two." Leiyn shrugged off the Iritu vest, then hesitated. "You'll need them all?"

"Any affected."

Her comrades looked away as Leiyn stripped. Tossing the vestments to Ketti, she donned in their place the set of Eteman clothes Ketti's mother had given her in Solace. Like the other enchanted garments, they molded to her shape, but only to a point. The tunic still hung loose even after she bound her weapons belt over it, and the trousers slouched about the legs. The colors, aqua and violet, were garish compared to the Iritu garments. She neglected the sash that went with the set. As it was, the clothes were already appalling to her ranger sensibilities.

Better than going nude.

Ketti spread the Iritu clothes on the ground and kneeled next to them. One by one, she placed her hands on the fabric and, murmuring in her tongue, pushed esse into them. Curious, Leiyn watched her work. It required a delicate touch, nearly as much as Ketti's mother employed while healing Batu's head injury. The Eteman wove lifeforce in threads parallel to the fabric, then wound them together. Leiyn doubted she had the patience for the finicky work, or that she could wield her mahia so delicately.

After a lengthy stretch, the Eteman rose, dusted off her hands, and handed the articles back to Leiyn. When Leiyn made to change again, Ketti said, "Solace clothes will serve as well as those."

"And they could do with being aired out," Isla noted with a smirk.

Reluctantly, Leiyn packed them in her bags. "Then let's get going."

Ketti was swift in returning them to the world. When the ground settled and they had risen back to their feet, Leiyn scanned the surrounding area. No danger lay nearby that she could sense, though that meant little when their enemies could veil their esse.

All the more reason not to tarry.

Mounting, they carried on their way, moving south from the crossroads. The road carried them through the unceasing jungle. Leagues passed with little more change than the rise and fall in the road. Only when Leiyn glanced over her shoulder and saw the Radiante Slopes shrinking did she feel any sense of progress.

They encountered no passersby that day. When the forest refused to yield any viable clearings, Ketti formed their grotto on the road, though not before instructing Leiyn in forming her own. Several more times, she felt the world as a whole, yet even so, she could not reach through it.

"It will come," the Eteman reassured her. "You are doing well."

Leiyn tried quieting her doubts and nodded as if she believed her.

The next day, Leiyn requested that Ketti ride with her

instead of Isla, suspecting they had many topics to discuss. The Eteman agreed, though not without a curious look, as she mounted Feral behind Leiyn.

It felt strange to be so close to her with her mahia open. Leiyn was distinctly aware of Ketti's esse, which was never content to remain in her body, the same as her own. All she could do was shove down her discomfort and maintain an easy facade.

When Biqqa reappeared, Leiyn contemplated the emerald hummingbird for a long moment. "Do you intend to bond with one?" she asked at length. "With a titan?"

Ketti stiffened at the question, or perhaps only from Feral jolting on a bump in the road. Unused to riding, the Eteman was liable to tense at the slightest misstep.

"One day, yes," Ketti answered at length.

"One day soon? Even once I reach Clouded Fang"—she tried to think of it as a certainty—"two titans would be better than one."

"I... understand."

Leiyn listened to the clopping of hooves as she waited for an explanation. When none seemed forthcoming, she pressed, "I'm guessing there's a 'but'?"

Ketti's lifeforce whirled like liquid in a spinning cup. "I have left Solace for now, but I am still Ta'Rul. So long as Ab-Abi does not join the ancestors before my return, and thus needs to pass along the protection of our home to my father, I am the heir to Mehu'Ra, the Tempest of Solace, the *kainox* guarding our borders. I..." She trailed off for a moment. "*Ami bast ek ami balt.* 'My name is my pride,' as we say. I would not surrender that."

Leiyn nodded, glad she faced forward so her frown was hidden. She understood the sentiment, but it left them vulnerable until Leiyn succeeded in her own summoning.

If I ever do.

Seeming to sense her disappointment, Ketti added, "But I may still bid *kainox* to do my will. A bond is not necessary for that."

"I suppose that's true. It should be useful." Leiyn glanced back to see Isla and Batu riding side by side, carrying on a soft conversation. She hoped that would be enough to protect them.

"You did not know, did you?" Ketti seemed hesitant to speak but pressed on. "With your bonded. You did not understand what you did."

"No. At least, not the full extent of it." Leiyn lapsed into silence, following the gossamer-thin thread to the ash dragon slumbering far below. "Can't say I regret it, though. He saved my life. And a dragon doesn't seem such a poor companion."

The Eteman chuckled. "No, it does not."

That afternoon, Leiyn felt the first sensation of it at the edge of her awareness. She had to stretch her lifesense for dozens of leagues to detect the faintest glimmer, but the dichotomy of esse exuding from it—emptier yet stronger than the vast jungle they traveled through—made its identity unmistakable.

Kunu awaited them ahead.

When Leiyn informed the others, relief spread with the speed of a brushfire. Batu smiled; Isla laughed.

"About time we saw the Jewel of the Jungle!" her fellow ranger declared.

Only Ketti looked troubled. Leiyn could scarcely blame her. The precious gems in her skin and her lavender eyes would always mark her as different, even beyond their outlandish clothes. She could only hope it paled in importance next to their errand.

The road promised further trials before they reached the city. Leiyn detected the guardhouse positioned along the path long before it came into sight. Biqqa seemed to sense it as well, for the hummingbird darted off into the jungle and did not reappear.

A brief consultation among their party decided they would not try to avoid it. Isla still bore their writ of diplomacy, even if the case had been breached and rain had damaged it. Still, with their mission a peaceful one, it would hardly do to sneak in to try and gain an audience with the Ofean leadership.

They rode up to the guardhouse in plain view, only stopping when a soldier shouted a warning.

Leiyn remained atop Feral, tense and ready. The guardhouse was positioned next to a gate, which barred their way. She picked out archers to either side, four in total. Another four soldiers hustled from the guardhouse, long spears and oval wicker shields in hand.

Fanning out before them, they held their spears at a slight angle, ready to dip and thrust. Leiyn could not help but eye those sharp ends. Even if their Eteman clothes were supposed to protect them, she had no desire to put them to the test.

"*Tani ey?*" one soldier shouted, brandishing his shield.

"Who are you?" another said, eyeing their appearance. "Do you speak this tongue?" Her accent was thick, but the words easily understood.

Isla spoke in a ringing voice. "*Eti ma kun ora re.* I understand you, but my companions only know Ilberian. We are a delegation from Baltesia, sent by Lord Governor Mauricio di Siveña himself. I request an audience with the chancellor, Cloud Awera Talabi, to confer on matters vital to both our nations."

The second soldier, a woman with a white birthmark down one side of her face, flicked her gaze over them. "Proof. I cannot take you at your word. Do you carry the governor's seal?"

"We carry it upon his writ."

Isla dismounted and approached the soldier. The spears of the other three hovered over her. Leiyn watched with clenched teeth as her friend walked beneath them to hand over the bedraggled paper. The soldier shifted her spear to her other hand to accept it, then unfurled the parchment. Her eyes scanned the words before she let it roll back up.

"It has been damaged."

Isla genuflected in a way Leiyn had not seen before: arms crossed over her chest and eyes lowered. "We suffered poor weather and several misfortunes on our way here," she said as she rose. "I pray enough remains legible."

The soldier stuck out her lips, then offered the parchment back to Isla. "Very well. I am Talon Eghe Ilori, captain of this outpost. Come with me; I will bring you to the *Aafinsowa* —'Heavens' Reach,' I believe it is in your tongue. There, Cloud Awera will decide what to do with you."

Isla thanked the captain while Leiyn hid a frown. The spears lifted, but the soldiers came forward, demanding their weapons be handed over. Leiyn only relented at Isla's stern stare.

Once they were disarmed, Talon Eghe bade them to follow. Moving through the gate as it creaked open, four horses were revealed to be saddled and waiting on the other side. The captain and three of her soldiers each mounted one.

"Come!" the woman barked, leading the way forward.

Leiyn kept her lifesense trained on the guards flanking them. They were being admitted to the capital, but not with the fanfare merited by an emissary's visit.

A poor omen to start.

After their journey thus far, she should have expected no less.

49

JEWEL OF THE JUNGLE

*O*nly as Leiyn laid eyes upon the city did she understand why it was called "the Jewel of the Jungle."

Even from a distance, Kunu shone. Bronze lined walls that stretched out of sight inland and abutted the coast. Their size was impressive enough; that they were completed and constructed of stone put Southport's defenses to shame.

Their chaperoned journey had proceeded in tense silence. Though Isla attempted to bridge it, inquiring into how Ore-Ofe fared against the Suncoat incursions, Talon Eghe met her questions with impolite refusals. Still a two-day ride from the capital, they had spent a night at another guardhouse, where they were under constant surveillance by Ofean soldiers. They sat at separate campfires, eating their own food. Even the spices wafting from their meal felt foreign and hostile, though Isla sniffed after them with an air of longing.

They carried on the next day, moving ever south. The jungle ended to the east, where the Torrent Sea met the coastline. Leiyn spread her lifesense over the ocean, marveling at the relative emptiness, though those salty waters were rife with life. Fish, seaweed, and tinier forms of life rode upon the waves. The jungle was preferable to any city, but it had become nearly as claustrophobic to Leiyn's senses. Especially when hunters might haunt the shadows.

As they neared Kunu, the trees abruptly ended. Leiyn drew Feral to a halt to stare at the open view. Atop a rise, she could see for leagues afar. Terraced farms segmented the hills with rows of green crops and trees. She could identify some at a distance. Rice grew where the ground was flooded. Bananas, mangoes, and coconuts burdened the groves of trees. Cows, goats, and pigs strolled along the grasslands between patches of indomitable jungle.

"Come," Talon Eghe said, commanding their party back into motion.

Farmers and ranchers, more people resembling Isla than she had ever seen, watched as they passed. Most seemed curious, but some were openly hostile as they stared at Leiyn and her comrades. Yet they did not appear as people at war. Perhaps, beyond the river fortress, Ilberia had yet to infringe upon Ore-Ofe.

As they neared the capital, Kunu itself drew her gaze. Positioned below them by the shore, she could see it from above enough to notice its startling geometry, round except for where the walls met the harbor. Beneath the bronze walls was a wide moat, passable only by the bridges leading to and from its gates. Leiyn was hard-pressed to imagine the Ilberian Armada putting a dent in Kunu's defenses. The thought provoked an uncomfortable question:

Why should they fight when they could wait out the war behind their walls?

Afternoon waned by the time they reached the bridge leading inside. People departing the city crowded the way, those who had come in as day laborers or to trade goods. All parted before Talon Eghe, bowing their heads and crossing their arms to tap their hands to their biceps. That did not stop them from studying Leiyn and the others from the corners of their eyes.

Leiyn had been a foreigner many times in her life. As in

Qasaar and Solace, she felt her guard raising. That which was unknown, her instincts warned, could present peril.

Yet she forced a smile and nodded to the onlookers. Perhaps danger lingered here, but she refused to assume it. Treat them as enemies and they would inevitably become them.

Be like Isla for once.

A word from the captain saw them through the gates. A bronze-tipped portcullis loomed overhead as they passed within, points bristling like the teeth of a titan.

The city drew Leiyn from her thoughts. Like Solace, Kunu was a tapestry of colors. Many of them put her in mind of the sky: the aqua of a clear day, the yellow of the early and late sun, the oranges and pinks of dawn, the violet of rain clouds. They radiated from the tents in the streetside marketplace and were painted on the wattle-and-daub walls. They decorated the streets where tiles interrupted white cobblestone.

The people were adorned in eye-catching patterns, many in enveloping robes or with long shirts over loose pants and sandals. Their jewelry was unlike anything Leiyn had seen, even among the Gasts and Etemans. Some had earrings that had elongated and exaggerated their earlobes. Others had strands of beads framing their face or ringing their arms and legs.

Isla, riding next to Leiyn with Ketti mounted behind her, spoke about them in a quick, breathy murmur. "Those robes are *kentes*. They're preferred by the nobility. The shirts are known as *dashikis*. Either peasants or nobles might wear them. You can also differentiate between the classes by their ornaments. The richer you are, the more silver and gold and beads. Commonfolk can only afford ordinary materials."

The streets and people were not the only ones arrayed in dazzling hues. Rainbow birds, so-named for their iridescent feathers, infested the city like seagulls did Southport. Though stunning to behold, Leiyn soon adopted the Ofeans' low tolerance for them as they dove at their saddlebags, seeking the foodstuff kept within. As Feral whinnied warnings, she warded them away with both her hand and mahia.

Her sense of smell was similarly assaulted. Though there was the underlying quality of human waste endemic to every city, the riot of spices nearly overwhelmed it. Some were sharp enough to burn her nose. Others were sweet as honey. The ocean blew in a salty breeze. The air was thick with moisture, so she was sweating soon after entering, despite summer's waning.

Isla was unsympathetic in her tutoring, however, but kept up a steady string of explanations. Crucial as they might become, Leiyn did her best to pay attention.

"The chancellor, Awera Talabi, is the representative of the Sky Queen of Eyi, Kyaka Ndaye. Cloud Awera is her voice here in the Veiled Lands, so she is the one we must convince to gain a meeting with the leaders of the *Kekére*, who are known as the Wings."

"So the chancellor is like our governor," Leiyn supplied. "Mauricio's equal."

"Not exactly. Religion and state are more closely tied together for Eyi than in Ilberia. The *Odisi*—Queen Kyaka—is seen as a mere step from divinity. No major decision is made without the queen's consent. Cloud Awera may defer our request on that basis."

Leiyn frowned at Talon Eghe's back, bobbing with her horse's movements. "Then what of the *Kekére*? Are the Wings also under the Sky Queen's thrall?"

"Hard to say. The *eesuwé*—the Eyin variety of mahas—have always been an order unto themselves. They obey the *Odisi*, but likely act independently of the chancellor and the *Alufaa*, Ore-Ofe's head priest here in the colony."

"Perhaps they might be convinced to help?" Ketti said from her place behind Isla.

"Perhaps—if we can reach them." Isla turned her gaze forward. "First, we'll have to sway the chancellor to our cause."

While they spoke, the captain kept a punishing pace through the city, unafraid to force her horse through the crowds. Only before the litters, carried on the shoulders of a pair of bare-chested men, and in the sling of which a person in *kente* robes swung with imperious nonchalance, did she yield, respectfully touching her arms and bowing her head while they passed.

"Nobles," Isla confirmed at Leiyn's sour look. "The *tipoye* is their preferred mode of transportation."

Riding on the backs of the poor. Leiyn swallowed the spit that rose at the thought. Baltesian nobles insulating themselves in carriages was bad enough. Making humans into beasts of burden was an insult too far.

Her expression did not escape Isla's notice. "Leiyn," she murmured, "say nothing."

"You think I'm that rash?"

"Don't glare, either. We cannot afford to offend any Kunans, especially the most powerful of them."

Leiyn relented as she lapsed into sulky silence.

Her irritation faded as their destination became clear. Bronze-tipped spires rose above the concentric walls to the west. One tower soared above the others, a broad pillar of golden stone. Sky-blue domes, either painted or patinaed copper, garnished the rest of the sprawling estate.

There was no doubt to its identity: Heavens' Reach, seat of the Ofean government and religion.

"That tower?" Isla indicated the largest of them. "That is where the *Alufaa*, the high priest, resides. We won't meet him unless their gods visit him with inspiration."

Leiyn stared at her friend. Isla's words dripped with a rancor typically unknown to her. Leaning in, she murmured, "I didn't realize you resented them so much."

"I don't," Isla said. At Leiyn's look, she amended, "I try not to."

"Guard your tongue," Leiyn warned. "And you know it's loose if I'm telling you that."

Though her expression remained mutinous, Isla nodded.

Talon Eghe led them through gilded gates and down shining pavers to the stately manor. Pergolas and gazebos rose amid luscious gardens. Most of the flowers were still in full bloom. Trickling fountains contributed to the ambience. Less pleasing to Leiyn's eye were the gilded statues of jaguars, apes, and other animals common to these lands and the Eyin Empire. Amid the verdant beauty, they struck her as garish and lifeless.

Before the steps leading up to the entrance, grooms appeared to lead away their horses and saddlebags. Leiyn tracked them with her lifesense as they departed, making careful note of where the stables lay on the sprawling grounds.

Talon Eghe, who still carried their weapons, surrendered them to the guards at the palace door. "They will be returned," the captain assured them at Leiyn's watchful gaze. Still, she tracked where they were kept.

The atrium soon caught her attention. As they strolled down the cerulean carpet, narrow columns reached up to the lofty ceiling, featuring a dizzying display of colorful striations and diamond patterns. At the far end, a pair of colossal doors awaited, parted to allow a glimpse into the chamber beyond.

When they reached the doors, the captain consulted with one guard, who stepped inside. She heard voices echoing for a moment before the guard returned and said something in Eyin. Talon Eghe gestured for them to follow.

Had opulence not barraged Leiyn the entire way there, the sight of the audience chamber might have overawed her. Gold touched every surface: the floor, the columns, the ceiling. Windows soared nearly to the domed ceiling to cast the room in a shining glow.

Squinting against the radiance, she looked toward the opposite end of the room. There awaited a simple, if well-cushioned, chair flanked by a dozen more guards. In the chair sat a woman who could only be the chancellor.

"Approach with respect," Talon Eghe whispered, then stepped aside, eyes up and posture erect.

Leiyn exchanged a look with Isla, then followed her friend forward, Batu and Ketti trailing behind. Even with her Iritu clothes mended, she felt unkempt and uncouth in this room. No doubt it had cost more coin than all of Orille had ever seen. Her every step seemed to leave behind a film of grime, even though the magic imbued in her shoes kept them cleaner than most.

But as her gaze settled on the awaiting chancellor, old words of Tadeo's drifted into her mind. *We're all flesh and blood.* No matter the ostentatious surroundings and the Ofeans' pomposity, they were still people.

People who can damn your nation. Or save it.

Leiyn studied the woman. She wore azure robes in the *kente* style, thickly patterned with silver thread. Hints of gray struck through her black, tightly curled hair, suggesting she was in her middle years. Her lips were powdered white in contrast to her rich, dark skin. A copper hairpiece fanned out her hair like a draconion's crest. Bangles of silver and gold wire enwrapped her arms. The largest gemstones Leiyn had ever laid eyes on hung from her ears, brilliant indigo in hue. A many-layered silver pendant draped across her chest.

This was a woman unafraid to flaunt her wealth. Leiyn kept her shoulders from rising about her ears. Nothing made her warier than artifice.

Eyes and ears open, Firebrand. Trust nothing.

Isla halted their party ten paces before the chair, then bowed low in the Ofean fashion. Leiyn followed suit, Batu and Ketti doing the same next to her.

"Sky's blessings, travelers, and be welcome. How may I assist you this day?" The chancellor spoke with a lilting accent unlike those of the other Ofeans they had met. Leiyn wondered if she hailed from the Ancestral Lands, from Eyi itself, appointed here as Mauricio had been to Baltesia's governorship.

"*Orun ka ibukun,* Cloud Awera," Isla responded. "We thank you for granting us a swift audience. I am Isla Ogbi, emissary to Baltesia. Lord Governor Mauricio di Siveña sent me and my companions here to your glorious city to entreaty you on his behalf."

The chancellor did not react for a long moment. Leiyn wondered if she ever would when her lips parted.

"Ogbi... This name is known to me. Where were you born, child?"

Leiyn sensed the ripple in Isla's lifeforce. To call a foreign diplomat "child" represented an inexcusable insult. She was glad her friend kept a tighter rein on her emotions than she did. Already, Leiyn's temper strained to pull free.

Though Isla stiffened, her tone remained measured. "Baltesia is the only home I've known, Chancellor."

"As your first name would imply." Another slight disguised by a smile. "Ogbi, Ogbi..." The woman's eyes, lined with blue paint, suddenly widened. "Ah! Now it comes to me! The heretics condemned by my predecessor. Your parents, I presume?"

Fesht. Leiyn took careful stock of the room. Between the captain's escort and the chancellor's guards, over a score of Ofeans surrounded them. Beyond the audience chamber awaited more fighters—hundreds, perhaps—throughout the estate. And *eesuwé* might linger nearby, hiding from her life-sense. Even if she could call up Clouded Fang and still had her weapons, she doubted she could overcome so many. Without them, she did not stand a chance.

But she had spat in Legion's face for Isla before. She'd be damned if she let anyone threaten her.

"Yes." Still, Isla kept her composure. "So were my parents named."

Cloud Awera smiled, powdered lips curving like a crescent moon. "But you are Baltesian and not one of the Cherished. And an emissary of another colony! Do not fear, child. I could not hold such a sentence against you."

Even as her held breath whistled between her teeth, Leiyn sensed the barb tucked inside the words. The Cherished—it was how Ofeans termed themselves, couched in religious superiority. But though Isla did not believe in their goddess, it contained a poignant message:

You don't belong here.

Isla stood as still and unyielding as a stone slab. "Your generosity is overwhelming, Cloud Awera."

If the chancellor heard the thinly veiled contempt, she ignored it. Her eyes flickered to land on another in their party. "Ah! *Kiniun laarin awon odo-agutan!* Who is this fascination with whom you travel, child?"

It was Ketti's turn to stiffen. That she had be singled out had been inevitable; the gems embedded in her flesh were far too conspicuous. Yet the chancellor would not understand what they meant. Etemans had been hidden away for too long for it to be otherwise.

A passing curiosity, nothing more.

Isla glanced over her shoulder. "Ketti Ta'Rul, Chancellor. One of my companions."

Awera barely seemed to hear. The white was visible around her brown eyes as she stared at the Eteman.

"I see, I *see*. Sky's blessings, Ketti Ta'Rul. I would cherish some time with you, should you be willing."

That spoke more ill. Separate their party, and Leiyn would have a tougher time protecting them. But, seeing no other option but silence, she only gritted her teeth.

After a lengthy pause, Ketti stuttered a response. "O-of course, Cloud Awera."

The chancellor smiled again. Her eyes shifted back to Isla. "Now, child. You mentioned you came to... 'entreaty,' was it? What are your Lord Governor's wishes? We have spoken at length by message of certain matters that are quite settled. I must hope he would not send you all this way to waste your—or my—time."

The war. It had to be what she meant. A poor sign that she attempted to shut down the conversation before it had begun.

Admirably, Isla soldiered on. "Lord Mauricio understands Ore-Ofe's position on the Tricolonies' conflicts with the Ancestral Lands, and he does not ask you to reconsider it."

"Baltesia's war with Ilberia, you mean." Awera issued the

correction with sharp politeness. "But that does not answer my question."

Isla bowed her head, doing the only thing she could—acknowledging the amendment, but not accepting it. "I would not speak more where ears remain deaf, but to those who might still be willing to listen. With your permission, we would speak to the Wings of the *Kekére*."

"The Wings!" The chancellor's eyelashes fluttered. In surprise? Amusement? Leiyn could not tell. Her esse rippled with too much emotion to guess at.

Awera's expression soon settled back into bland benevolence. "Ah, but if only I could bless you with an audience. That is not within my power."

"Not in your power." Isla repeated each word as if unsure she had heard them correctly. "Are you not the chancellor of Ore-Ofe? The caretaker of the colony?"

"Ah, child, this is something an envoy should know! As chancellor, I am the mouthpiece of the *Odisi*, the Sky Queen of the Empire of Storms. Without her explicit permission, how could I allow something that might counteract her will?"

Leiyn narrowed her eyes. The logic was so twisted it was liable to strangle itself.

She's bluffing.

"I would not wish that," Isla said cautiously. "But surely, the *Odisi* would see little harm in a discussion."

"I cannot say, child. So I fear I must decline my blessing."

Isla's earlier lessons flashed through Leiyn's mind. An idea had scarcely formed in her mind before she stepped forward. Isla's eyes flashed a warning at her, but Leiyn kept her gaze leveled on the chancellor.

"Cloud Awera, forgive me for speaking out of turn."

The chancellor was slow to look at her. When she finally did, her gaze was weighty and difficult to bear. "And you are?"

"Leiyn of Orille. A ranger of Baltesia."

"A ranger..." Awera's eyes slid back to Isla. "Odd. I heard your kind had disappeared due to Ilberian sabotage."

Flames in the night—the scene flashed before her eyes. Leiyn blinked it away. "Not all of us."

"But you are not only a ranger, are you, Leiyn of Orille? What is it they call you in Southport? Ah, yes—*Tideraiser*." The chancellor nodded in mock somberness. "You are an *eesu* of your people. Or should I say 'odiosa'?"

"Mahas, we're calling ourselves." She thought of mentioning her recent title, but she doubted "Prima Maha" would have any meaning to this conniving woman. "That's not the point I wanted to make."

"Pray tell, what is it?"

"Leiyn..." Isla muttered, low enough that others might not hear.

Leiyn kept her eyes trained on Awera. "You don't have the authority to grant us an audience, right? Then I don't see why you'd have the authority to keep us away."

For the first time, the chancellor seemed off-balance. And, like many creatures, she only grew more dangerous. With eyes narrowed and her smile sharpened, acid dripped from her tongue as she spoke.

"That is... presumptuous, Ranger Leiyn." Her eyes flickered over Ketti before settling back on Isla. "I cannot guarantee the Wings will heed your words. But I would not arrest you for merely wishing to speak!"

The chancellor laughed and Isla laughed with her. All Leiyn could manage was a thin smile.

"Fair fortune to you," Awera said, waving a hand in dismissal as she settled back in her seat. "May the Goddess bless your ventures, as I cannot."

Isla bowed with crossed arms. It grated on Leiyn, but she did the same with Batu and Ketti. They had secured a victory, however small. No need to spoil it.

Not before the Wings of the Coterie Tower took that honor for themselves.

50

THE WINGS OF THE TOWER

The *Kekére* was impossible to miss. Looming above the wharves and warehouses lining the sea, it stood apart like a lighthouse upon an inlet. A courtyard of sky-blue stones widened around its base, and breakwaters weathered the high waves, rolling in from the Torrent Sea to crash into shimmering clouds.

Even if it had not protruded from the city into the sea, the Coterie Tower would have drawn Leiyn's eye. Shaped like a conical shell, it curled around itself to end in a pointed pinnacle. Just under the apex spread a platform that resembled a pair of wings. Hundreds of window panes winked in the daylight, the glass following the bronze ridge spiraling upward. No other building came near its height, the nearest no higher than two stories, while the *Kekére* rose at least six. An intentional choice, she did not doubt, to make it all the more striking.

No gates or walls protected the spire. From what Leiyn sensed, they scarcely needed them. Esse rose in a cloud around the building, seeping through the stone and into the ocean air. Did the *eesuwé*, the mahas of Ore-Ofe, practice their magic? Did they keep watch over those who ventured near? Or had Leiyn and her party drawn their attention, their foreignness apparent by their lifeforce alone?

Leiyn was tempted to investigate them in return, but she kept a tight leash on her lifesense. Though the chancellor was aware of her magic and most notable deeds, it was best to keep the extent of her abilities hidden. Easier resolved than done—with all the witchery in the air, her mahia felt as excited as a hound spotting hares in the brush. If her vigil lapsed, it threatened to stretch forth on its own.

Leiyn guided Feral across the spray-slick stones to the tower, her companions mounted around her. Isla stared at the top of the tower with a pinched expression. She had been quiet for most of the trip from Heavens' Reach. Their escort of soldiers, headed once more by Talon Eghe, trailed close behind. Hardly an honor guard, considering they kept their weapons.

She understood why Isla's parents had left this land.

The base of the Coterie Tower showed the first signs of defense. Two guards with winged helms and armor as finely detailed as Kalgan porcelain watched them approach. Leiyn was surprised to find both possessed a sliver of mahia. Their capacity was roughly comparable to Teya's, enough for minor tricks and a vague lifesense. Behind them loomed two bronze doors that matched the curvature of the spire.

As they dismounted, an older man with a scar puckered through his lips barked a word in Eyin and scanned their party. His eyes lingered on Ketti and Leiyn. She silently endured his probing lifesense, only warning him off after several moments with a shove of her walls. The guard's expression soured, but he said nothing as he turned to the captain. Eghe spoke a few words back before Isla broke in, also in Eyin.

Leiyn drifted closer to Ketti. "You understand them, right?" she muttered.

The Eteman nodded. "They are requesting an explanation for our visit. They wish to know what we want with the Wings." Her expression pinched as she concentrated on the conversation. "Isla's explanation does not seem to please them."

Leiyn had guessed that much by her friend's tense posture. "Are they turning us away?"

"Not yet. They go to seek permission."

The tower guards turned away to haul open one of the formidable doors. The second guard, a young man with two beaded braids hanging from his chin, slipped inside. As he went, she felt his mahia activate, reaching up through the tower toward the summit. There, she picked out two people, shining brighter than most in the *Kekére*, who accepted what she assumed to be a message.

Moments later, a shiver ran through her. Had she not been so wary, she might have missed the gentle touch on her esse. Feather-light, it seemed more like a cool mist than lifeforce. Instinctually, she raised her defenses against the invasion and felt the intruder retreat.

Who are you? Leiyn narrowed her eyes at the top of the tower. Now that she knew what to look for, she saw the nearly imperceptible shimmer of esse cascading out from the two near the apex. *The Wings that bitch chancellor mentioned?*

Glad they could not read her mind—that she knew of, at any rate—she crossed her arms and waited. Feral put on a show of impatience for them both as the mare snorted and shook her head.

The probing did not return, though Leiyn felt it continue over the rest of her party, lingering longest on Ketti. Despite Isla's attempts to converse with the soldiers, an uneasy silence fell.

At last, Leiyn felt the guard approaching the door again. Exiting, the guard strode up to his comrade and held a whispered conversation. The scarred guard returned to Isla and once more excluded the others by speaking in Eyin.

"They are admitting us," Ketti translated for Leiyn and Batu. "The Wings wish to meet."

"Really?" Leiyn studied both guards, but neither seemed liable to yield information. "I wonder why."

"You two," Batu murmured.

She wished she could disagree.

Isla finished speaking and waved them over. Leiyn handed

Feral's reins to one of Talon Eghe's soldiers, who accepted them with a wary look at the mare. Feral did little to reassure him as she bared her teeth.

"Be good, old girl," Leiyn warned, risking a pat on her snout and dodging the retaliatory bite.

The young man with the braided beard looked them over, then with a sentence in Eyin, led them inside. With a final vain wish for her confiscated weapons, Leiyn followed her companions in.

The atrium of the *Kekére* was no less impressive than its exterior. A center column rose to the ceiling, intricately painted in bright Eyin patterns mirroring reptilian skin and mammalian coats. Around the outer wall curled a stone staircase devoid of handrails. Every step echoed in the cavernous space. Light from the spiraling band of glass cast the room in glowing striations.

Like the chancellor's chamber, she knew it was designed to daunt its visitors. Leiyn lowered her gaze, determined not to let it as she followed their guide up the stairs.

The floors above served more practical uses. One seemed to be dormitory-style housing; another, a library, sprawling with books. A third was some kind of study area. These spaces were softened by rugs and tapestries, making them seem more homier than the atrium had.

Eesuwé moved about their daily routines on every level. Most watched them as they passed, distantly curious. Their mahia brushed against them, observant yet unobtrusive. They wore robes that draped over them like loose dresses; *boubous*, Isla called them. Blue, violet, and white swirled together in homages to wings, wind, and clouds.

Though the Coterie seemed far from poor and these Ofean mahas free—unlike their odiosa counterparts—all went barefoot. Isla had a ready explanation for this as well.

"It symbolizes both humility and ascension. They humble themselves by going without shoes or sandals, but it is only because when they walk, they are said not to touch the earth."

"Sounds painful," Batu said, walking behind Isla.

"Probably not." Leiyn noticed the esse the *eesuwé* concentrated within their feet. "They use mahia to prevent injuries, or maybe to heal them."

"And to walk lightly," Ketti added in a murmur.

The higher they went, the more the tower narrowed and its occupants thinned. As they neared the top, only the two brightest *eesuwé* remained. Leiyn felt the touch of their magic, noting their every step, as they cleared the final flight and the guard escorted them into the chamber.

The top floor of the *Kekére* echoed the design of the atrium. Windows extended from the floor to the ceiling, bathing the chamber in light. The platform they had seen from below extended in a bronze disc beyond, a pair of doors leading out to it. Columns rose around the edges, interrupting a ceiling ringed with countless ridges.

The Wings awaited them on cushioned chairs. Like the other *eesuwé*, they wore *boubous*, but their robes were threaded with cloth of silver so they shimmered with each movement. A ruff of feathers adorned their shoulders. The one to the left, a woman with short gray hair and a lined face, wore what appeared to be a cape of white feathers—from a gannet, a large seabird, Leiyn guessed at a glance. The rightmost Wing, a middle-aged man with long braids and prominent whiskers on his cheeks, had black raven feathers falling from his shoulders almost down to his elbows.

"Here they are!" the male exclaimed in fluent Ilberian, raising his arms like a priestess giving a benediction. "Our Baltesian envoys! Please, leave us to greet our guests."

This last he directed at the guard, who bowed with crossed arms and retreated down the stairs. Leiyn was relieved to see the guard go. Between the Wing's friendly manner and the lack of weapons in sight, she wondered if they might receive a friendly greeting after all.

"Be welcome," the woman spoke once the guard had disappeared from sight, her grasp of their tongue only marginally worse than her counterpart's. "I am Onah Salako, Wing of Moons. He is Samu Oyabola, Wing of Stars."

"Thank you, Highest Onah, Highest Samu. *Orun ka ibukun*—the sky blesses our meeting." Isla gave them each a deep bow.

Leiyn took the hint and followed suit, though she kept her bow shallow.

"The Goddess was generous to send you our way." Samu flickered his eyes over them, a shrewd look belying his merriment. "An envoy of Ofean blood. A young, strapping Gazian. And two strong in *Okulukulu*'s power!"

Leiyn tensed under his eager gaze, but she became more uneasy as he studied Ketti.

"You are a Gast shaman, perhaps?"

Ketti looked to Leiyn. She did not dare nod back. *Play along*, Leiyn willed her. *They cannot know.*

The Eteman looked back to the Wings. "Yes," Ketti lied. "That is correct."

Leiyn stifled her relief.

Samu's generous eyebrows rose, but he only smiled. "How enlightening you might be. But you must forgive me, I have not allowed you your introductions."

Isla gave their names and relevant positions. As she came to Leiyn, her stomach sank at the title she assigned her.

"Leiyn is our Prima Maha," her friend said. "It is a recently established position for our strongest maha and leader of the Colonial Order of Mahia."

Leiyn drew herself up straighter, trying to look more like the leader she was made out to be and less like a vagrant recently from the road.

"While we are grateful to have her," Isla continued, "the Order remains in its infancy. Its candidates have only begun their training and are few in number, for the Ilberian Union has stolen most who possess mahia and corrupted them into odiosas."

"Yes," Wing Onah said with a frown. "A foul practice. The

Goddess would never condone such barbarity against her Cherished."

Isla bobbed her head. "That is why we come to you for aid, Highest Ones. The support of the *Kekére* would bolster Baltesia where we are weakest. The Ilberian Armada sieges Southport even as we speak. Before we departed, they sent a titan to destroy our fleet and nearly succeeded. I fear what may have befallen the city in our absence."

"If your Prima Maha is here," Wing Samu noted, "then who protects the city?"

"The wisdoms of Altan Gaz. They have been gracious in lending their support."

As the Wings shared a look, Leiyn wondered if this was a mark for or against them. She struggled to keep that fateful night from mind. Absently, she rubbed at the scar in her chest before forcing her hand back to her side.

"Your plight is grave. Of that, you leave little doubt," the austere woman said.

"Yet," Wing Samu added, "we remain uncertain we can provide the aid you request. To stand against one of the Ancestral Lands may be seen as standing against them all."

"Ore-Ofe is, and will always be, part of the Eyin Empire." Wing Onah drew herself up to her full height, white feathers rippling behind her. "The Goddess has bound our nations together, and by her will, so it shall remain."

It should not have disappointed her. Leiyn had known all along this was as far a stretch as they could have hoped for. Yet the hard pit in her stomach was impossible to deny.

Hiding a grimace, she looked at Isla. To her surprise, her friend appeared unmoved by their refusal.

"You need not fight by our side. There are many ways you could support us and not violate your loyalties. Training our mahas, for one. Or warding against titans. Surely, defending the lives of colonists cannot be offensive to the Sky Queen."

"Only the Daughter of the Heavens could say." Wing Onah looked at her counterpart. "Without her blessing, I would not risk such a defense. But training... yes, perhaps we could reach an arrangement there."

Leiyn's eyebrows rose. Beside her, Batu also looked surprised. Ketti maintained her composure.

Isla smiled. "We would be most grateful. But we would not ask for a favor without providing value to you in return."

All elation faded as the Wings' eyes went first to Leiyn, then to Ketti. Leiyn firmed her jaw, wondering what they would request.

Without warning, the Wings extended their esses, brushing over them both. Probing, prodding, measuring. Leiyn tightened her fists and endured it. Rude as the inspection seemed, to refuse it might imperil all they worked toward.

After several moments, the Wings withdrew. Leiyn felt Batu and Isla's curious stares as they waited in silence.

"We feel," Wing Onah declared, "that we could learn much from a Gast shaman. Perhaps a private conversation or two with Ketti Ta'Rul would be illuminating enough for us to agree to your request."

Leiyn eyed the Eteman. Ketti hid it well, but her discomfort was plain in how stiffly she stood. Something about the request felt off to Leiyn as well, though she could not exactly place her finger on why.

Isla glanced back at Ketti, but if she caught her expression, she did not show it. "I must discuss this with her, but I'm sure we could—"

"Not private," Leiyn interrupted. "If you wish to speak with her, I must also be there."

All eyes turned toward her. The Wings raised their eyebrows and firmed their mouths. Isla wore an expression that spoke her thoughts plainly: *What are you doing?*

But seeing Ketti's shoulders relax wiped away Leiyn's doubts. She firmed her jaw and awaited their response.

Wing Onah broke the pause. "It is not necessary. The shaman would be safe in our care."

"Still. I would feel better for it."

"If that is your stipulation." Wing Samu spoke like a father disappointed in his daughter. "We must discuss this between ourselves before we arrive at a decision. We will give you quarters where you may rest until then."

Waiting us out. The tactic was plain as clouds heralding a storm: they were being punished for Leiyn's demands. Yet it made her all the more certain she had made the right decision. Maybe they needed the Ofeans as allies, but she had sworn to protect Ketti. Until she knew their intentions toward the Eteman, Leiyn could not step aside. Not for any cause.

"Thank you, Highest Onah, Highest Samu." Isla led them in bowing their way out.

51

A PRISON WITHOUT CHAINS

*D*id you have to insist?"

Isla propped her hands on her hips, wearing a look of profound disappointment. Leiyn tried not to feel ashamed. For once, she knew she was in the right.

"Yes, I did." Leiyn emphasized each word. "We don't know their intentions. And I swore to protect Ketti."

"I can protect myself." The Eteman murmured, as if unsure of it.

Leiyn pretended she had not heard. "Until we know more, we should stick together."

Isla waved a hand. "You'd like us to wait here, then? For how long?"

That such a wait would be uncomfortable was obvious at a glance around their furnishings. It would have been generous to call the room they had been given "humble." Cozy before their saddlebags were piled in—absent their weapons, as expected—there was scarcely room to walk, much less sleep, with only a pair of narrow cots provided.

It stated what the Wings thought of their guests. After the way their conversation had ended, it was an omen of worse to come.

Leiyn crossed her arms. "You know me—I'm not patient. All I'm asking for is time."

"Time. Ah, yes. A thing we have plenty of right now." Isla huffed out a sigh and sat on a bed next to Batu. The former plainsrider sat with his head bowed, no doubt wearied from the travel, arguing, and long day of meaningless meetings.

"Tell you what," Leiyn said. "I'll have a look around, see if I can stir up the hornets' hive a bit. Maybe I can smoke out some information."

"Or get stung," Batu said without lifting his head.

She cast him a droll look. "*Now* he speaks."

"Didn't you say we need to stick together?" Isla objected. "It's like you said: we don't know their intentions. Are you any safer than Ketti off on your own?"

Despite her continued arguing, Leiyn felt the switch in Isla's temperament. Her friend had already relented.

"I'll be fine," she said, mellowing. "Just look after the others while I'm gone."

Not waiting for further objections, Leiyn passed into the hallway. They had been relegated to one of the lower floors serving as dormitories. This late in the evening, most of the *eesuwé* had retreated to their rooms, but she sensed a few spread throughout the tower. The closest were cloistered in the library on the floor above.

She smiled as she set up the winding staircase. She was the wolf; the Ofean mahas, the sheep. In every flock, there was one straggler, slower or weaker than the rest.

Wherever they hid, she meant to track them down.

The library was dimly lit, only a handful of lanterns illuminating the long line of shelves. Between the rows, the darkness became nearly complete, only lifted by dusk spilling through the band of glass running around the tower. Unlike in Solace, where most every wall and piece of fabric was imbued with esse, the Coterie Tower was dark to her lifesense but for the sole seated figure.

Like a hawk circling a hare, Leiyn closed in.

As she neared the occupied table, the *eesu* looked up. He was a young man, perhaps a year or two shy of Leiyn's age, and lean from a life of scholarly leisure. His robe was sky blue patterned with white swirls and circles. His tightly curled hair was close shaven but for a small tail braided off the top of his skull. A large, cracked bead dangled at its end.

Despite her stealthy approach, he did not look surprised. Plainly, he had been aware of her through his lifesense. His eyes were deep pools as they stared up at her.

"Hello." Leiyn tried for her friendliest voice and found it did not suit her nearly as well as it did Isla. "Sorry to sneak up on you. Wasn't given a lamp."

The young man nodded. She wondered if he spoke Ilberian. If he remained where he was, she could fetch Isla to translate. Though it would pain her pride to come crawling back to her friend so soon.

"I'm Leiyn." She pressed a hand to her chest, then extended it to the Ofean. "What's your name?"

Again, the young man did not respond. Leiyn let her hand fall and pursed her lips. Just as she swallowed her pride and resolved to return to Isla, his words, spoken in competent Ilberian, pinned her in place.

"You're the one they speak of. Tideraiser."

Hiding her surprise, she nodded. "I suppose I am."

"Is it true? That you commanded a kraken against the Union?" He spoke in a precise, clipped way, as if every word was intentional.

"Yes."

"That you saved your capital and its people?"

"More like I almost doomed it. But it worked out in the end."

The *eesu* nodded, as if confirming something with himself. "I am Ekosa Siza. I have been wishing to speak with you."

"You have?" She spread her lifesense around, searching for a trap. If anyone was nearby, they had cloaked their esse, for she sensed nothing. Only two people moved about the study above.

"Yes. That is why I waited here." Ekosa rose and tucked his

chair back in. A ring, bronze set with a jade stone, flashed on his finger—an extravagance, from what she had seen of the other *eesuwé*. "Please, follow me."

Leiyn glanced at his lifemark, wondering what kind of man she was dealing with. His actions were strange and inexplicable. If she knew his character, perhaps she might understand...

He gently rebuffed her probing. Taking the hint, she withdrew her mahia. Her resolve, however, remained unshaken.

"Why should I go with you?"

"Please, we cannot speak here. You must come somewhere safer."

Leiyn propped a hand on her hip. "No offense, High Ekosa, but I'm not doing that."

The young man displayed the first sliver of emotion, eyes darting in either direction. She wondered if his stiffness had not been a mask to cover a nervous disposition.

Maybe he has reason to be nervous.

The Wings could have instructed him to lure her or her companions into a trap. It would worsen relations with Baltesia, certainly, but if Ore-Ofe had already chosen its side, perhaps that was not a concern.

"You do not understand," he said. "Your companion is not safe."

"Who? Who isn't safe?" Her voice rose with her temper. "Tell me. Please."

"The ancient of Etema."

The words sliced through her.

Leiyn stared at the *eesu* with fresh wariness. His eyes danced before her look, and his hands as well.

No warrior, this one.

But it took a different kind of courage to tell her this. Drawing in a breath, she settled her ire.

"What do you know of Etemans?"

"Much. Of their lore, at least. But we have never—"

The young man jerked around, staring toward the staircase. Leiyn sensed what he had a moment later: someone descended the stairs. Coming to the library, or moving past? It was clear which Ekosa suspected.

He looked back at her, eyes wide. "Please. I will try to return here tomorrow. You must come with me then. There is a place where we may speak in private."

The other person had almost reached the library landing. Leiyn gave a curt nod. She did not know if she meant to keep her word, but it was best to keep her options open.

"I'll see you then."

With that, she strode toward the staircase. On the slim chance Ekosa was on her side, she could not risk getting him into trouble. The dim lamplight flashed on metal as the newcomer stopped at the landing; a guard patrolling the tower. Leiyn halted a few paces short.

"Honored Guest, you should be resting," the guard said. A woman, judging by her voice. "Please, return to your room for the night."

"That's where I was headed. Sky's blessing." With a stiff smile, Leiyn slipped by and onto the stairs.

She felt the guard's lifesense following even after she was out of sight.

She slept poorly that night, worse even than on the road. Having given Ketti the bed while Isla and Batu squeezed onto the other one, Leiyn tossed and turned on the floor, the rug doing little to soften the stone. When the *Kekére* roused, she was more than happy to rise and shake off the night's sores, a sliver of mahia chasing away both pain and bruising.

The day passed as slowly as the night had. When she and her companions were not discussing Ekosa's cryptic words or arguing over whether she should seek him out the next night, they ate meals in their room brought by Coterie servants. The times that Leiyn ventured out to explore, either an *eesu* or a guard soon approached to encourage her to return to their room.

Her inquiries into the Wings' decision were met with empty assurances.

"They're waiting us out," Leiyn grated. "Like hunters around a foxhole."

She paced as she complained, though the small space meant she could only walk a few strides in any direction. The chamber was beginning to feel too much like a cage. She wondered if they had become prisoners. If they could leave the *Kekére* without risking a fight. After their time in Solace, it was a feeling all too familiar. She only hoped it would have as happy a conclusion.

"Didn't I say they'd do as much?" Isla said. "They know we cannot wait long. We should give in to their demands sooner rather than later."

"I am not afraid." The warble in Ketti's voice told otherwise.

Leiyn gave the Eteman a flat look. "They know what you are. And Ekosa sounded genuinely afraid. We cannot risk it."

"And why should you risk going with that *eesu?*" Isla countered.

"I can take care of myself."

"I could go with you." Batu straightened from where he had slumped on the bed. "To watch your back."

Leiyn shook her head. "I'd prefer you watch over Ketti."

"I do not—"

"Please," Leiyn cut off the Eteman's protests. "Let me do as I swore to your Ab-Abi. Trust me—all will be fine."

She pivoted the conversation to their plans for after Kunu, a topic the others took to reluctantly. Keeping her doubts to herself was tantamount to meeting with Ekosa again. It was perilous to go wherever he wished to lead her, but she had to admit he had hooked her curiosity.

What do you know? she railed silently at the young man. Often, she sought him out in the tower by her lifesense, a habit of which she assumed he was aware. *What do you intend?*

Once sunset arrived, she focused on the *eesu* and ignored her companions' hushed conversations. Before long, he returned from his room to the library, only he was not alone. For hours past dusk, other *eesuwé* moved about past him. Were they watching him? Did others suspect Ekosa? Or was it to entrap Leiyn, should she appear? Perhaps it was all happenstance.

Leiyn had grown weary of waiting when the last of the other occupants left the library. Holding out until the staircase cleared, she rose to her feet and headed for the door.

"You're going now?" Isla sat up in her shared bed. "It has to be near midnight."

"He sits alone," Ketti murmured.

Leiyn nodded. "This might be my only chance."

"I can still come." Batu sat up as well, still fully clothed despite reclining in bed with Isla.

She gave him a tight smile. "Noted. But I'll be fine."

"You'd better be." Isla gnawed her lip before waving her away. "Hurry back as soon as you can."

"I will."

Slipping out the door, Leiyn put up her walls and ghosted down the hall. Though it blinded her lifesense, if the Coterie posed a danger to them, she preferred that no one tracked her movements. Though, if they watched as she disguised her esse, that might be warning enough.

Can't worry about that now. Focus.

She padded up the stairs and into the library. Once more, Ekosa sat alone amid his pool of light, books spread all about the table. Silently, she proceeded toward him, then waited for him to look up.

When he did, the *eesu* nearly knocked the lamp over as he scrambled to his feet. The oil flame sputtered in protest.

"*Orisa!* Ah, it is you." Ekosa bobbed a bow. "My apologies, Leiyn Tideraiser. I admit, you frightened me."

Leiyn smiled. "I tend to scare people. And Leiyn is fine."

The young man nodded, his expression uncertain as he studied her.

"We need to talk." She jerked her head toward the stairs. "You said you had somewhere safe?"

"Yes. But it is this way."

Taking the lamp in hand, he walked deeper into the library rather than toward the stairs, the only exit that Leiyn knew of. Wary, she followed, peering between rows of shelves as she passed. With her lifesense blinded, the gloom felt more threatening than the night before.

Ekosa stopped midway across the floor to stand before the center column. Leiyn walked up next to him, keeping out of arm's reach. Like its base in the atrium, the pillar was painted with expert precision. In the figures and scenes, she imagined the pieces of history interred in the mural and wondered at their stories.

She looked sidelong at her guide. "It's beautiful. But I don't see how it'll stop eavesdroppers."

The Ofean maha glanced all around before meeting her gaze. "Please, do not speak to anyone of what I show you."

"Of course."

Her curiosity flared as Ekosa drew in a breath, stepped up to the pillar, and splayed both hands over it. Even with her walls up, she could almost sense his mahia delving into the stone. Leiyn frowned, wondering if it could be as she suspected.

A moment later, a seam appeared in the stone where none had been before. On silent hinges, a door swung inward.

Not all stone, she realized, eyes scraping over the door's edges. *Ancient wood imbued and hidden.*

"Follow," Ekosa breathed, eyes wide as he stared around them. "Swiftly, please."

Leiyn did as asked, slipping past him and into the pillar. By the scant light of the lamp, she saw a landing beyond. Leading up and down from it was a spiraling staircase.

"A secret stairwell?" she breathed.

The *eesu* did not answer as he entered behind her. Slowly, he pressed the stone door shut. As the wooden edge met the rest of the wall, the seam disappeared once more.

But she had greater concerns. She had let herself be trapped inside this stone pillar with no obvious way out. She was at Ekosa's mercy.

Here we are again, Firebrand.

"You may reveal yourself," the young man whispered. "Within the central pillar, none outside will see, nor will you see without."

Eager to no longer be blind, Leiyn dropped her walls and saw the door outlined in esse. Invisible from the other side, the enchantment was apparent from within. Other doors glowed faintly up and down the tower, but true to Ekosa's claim, she could sense nothing outside the pillar. The *Kekére* laid empty for all she could tell, as did the city beyond. Even the Barren beyond the mountains had not lain so dark and dead.

"How do you open it?" She nodded at the door.

Hesitancy played across his expression. Leiyn did not let her stare waver, pinning him like she might a strawman with a dozen arrows.

"With your *idan*—your magic. Press a hand to the stone, push into it. It will open. But not now," he added as she moved to make the attempt. "We would not wish to draw attention."

Leiyn withdrew her hand but she frowned at the young man. "What's going on, Ekosa? What are we doing here?"

"Not yet. Please, Leiyn, follow me. There are rooms below where we may speak."

The *eesu* moved past her, but Leiyn seized his arm, drawing him up short. His esse was strong, but nowhere near as potent as hers. Ekosa's eyes were wide as he looked down at her grip, then up into her face.

She wondered what he saw in her hard expression. After the stories he had heard about her, his imagination would be more potent than any threat she might say.

Only after several breaths did she speak. "Let me see your lifemark."

Ekosa opened his mouth, but hesitated. He turned his head aside. "To look into another's *emi*, the soul... It is not our way."

"Your Wings did it to us," she noted. "And I need to know if I can trust you."

"Do you not already?"

"Not enough to follow you down there blindly."

The young man looked back, his expression pained. "There is no other way?"

"None."

"Then look. I will not stop you."

The *eesu* was tense. From fear? Anger? Affront? She could not let speculation or mercy hold her back.

Pressing past his natural defenses, Leiyn peered into his soul.

The images of the lifemark rose. The first began with small, smooth hands, fingers clutched around something. As they parted, she glimpsed it: a wooden bead, large and cracked down the middle. Its paint was flaking and faded, but the green still showed through.

The bead on his braid.

Then the image faded and another replaced it. A different hand, larger and lined, reached down. On one finger gleamed a bronze ring set with a jade stone.

The ring Ekosa now wears.

A small hand, the same as in the first image, reached up to grip the larger hand. As they clasped, the image dissipated and a third roared into its place.

Leiyn nearly withdrew as a wave surged upward, dominating her view of Ekosa's esse. It was taller than any she had seen, towering like the kraken of Anchor's Refuge. A single figure stood silhouetted against it, arms raised like they meant to stop it with their bare hands. With a ring gleaming on their hand and a bead bright on the braid, she understood it was meant to be Ekosa himself.

Breath held, she waited for the wave to crash down on him and crush him. But though the water churned, it seemed to climb ever upward, never crashing down.

Blinking, Leiyn withdrew her lifesense and met the *eesu's* eyes. Ekosa stood as still as the statues in the courtyard of the chancellor's estate, but he did not flinch from her stare.

She glanced at the bead on his braid, then the ring. "What are they?"

The young man pressed his lips into a thin line. "Memories."

"Memories," Leiyn repeated. "Of those you've lost?"

"Yes. The bead belonged to my mother. Sometimes, if I hold it tight..." He grimaced and lowered his gaze.

Leiyn pressed her mahia toward the bead. At first glance, it had appeared as dun as the rest of the tower surroundings. But if she looked at it closer... Did she imagine it, or did it have a faint glow of its own?

She took a risk. "You can still feel her. Your mother."

He startled, staring at her with wide eyes. The lamp glow pooled shadows under his brow. "How did you...? You cannot... sense her, can you?"

The hope in his voice pained her to hear. Even for her benefit, she knew she could not lie about this.

"Maybe. I don't know. Could have been a lucky guess."

His gaze fell, but only for a moment. When Ekosa looked up, resolve had replaced the confusion.

"Thank you for being truthful."

Leiyn shrugged. "I'm not known for being subtle."

They shared a brief smile, then she gestured down the stairwell.

"Lead the way, Ekosa. I trust you."

Nodding, the *eesu* set down the stairs. Leiyn followed.

HEART OF STONE

For all Leiyn could sense, she and Ekosa were alone. Twin pools of light in a sea of darkness.

It was unsettling, knowing a city full of people spread around them, yet unable to sense anyone. Only the impressions of the hidden doors, outlined in esse, appeared to her mahia.

Being isolated did not make her fear for herself more; after viewing his lifemark, she felt as certain of Ekosa as she could after their short time together. Yet not being able to watch over her friends worried her. She kept checking to see if, by some chance, they would appear to her lifesense. Outside of the column, though, the world remained dark.

"How does this work?" she asked Ekosa after descending several flights. They had to be coming level with the atrium soon, if they had not already descended past it. "Blocking life-force outside the column."

"It is the same for those within as those without." Ekosa gestured around them with the lamp. "I cannot say how it functions. I have not studied the *eesu's* role in architecture as of yet. From what I know, this is the smallest of the wonders we *eesuwé* have built. In Kaiam and the Eyrie, there are said to be buildings as alive to the senses as any living being."

She had glimpsed the Eyin Empire's capital on maps of the

Ancestral Lands before, along with the island territory of the Eyrie to the east. Her knowledge of either, however, was too thin.

"The Sky Queen's palace is as rich with magic as it is gold and jewels," Ekosa continued. "The *Oris Orun*, the Sanctum of Heavens, can transport you to times long past. There are defenses against titans, enchanted spires of stone that keep them at bay."

Wardstones. She wondered if that could be true, if Eyins constructed them as the Iritu once had. Though, with such similarities between them, how could she doubt it? The same went for the temple that showed "times long past"; the Etemans had spoken of similar powers within Solace's archives.

Thinking of Etemans reawakened her wariness. Questions pressed upon her with increasing urgency. "Are we nearly there? I shouldn't be away for long."

"Yes. We are close."

True to his word, the staircase rounded the central pillar with a final turn before opening into a rudimentary hallway. The ceiling was rough-hewn stone, though the walls had been smoothed. No color or paintings graced this corridor, a stark contrast to the rest of the *Kekére*. For as far as she could see, ordinary doors lined the way, fading into the gloom beyond their lamplight. By her lifesense, she sensed nothing more.

"What is this place?" Her voice fell to a hush.

"Somewhere the people of my order can practice without prying eyes." Ekosa started forward again, only moving as far as the first door. "In here, we may speak."

Reluctance dragged at her. The darkness, the ground pressing around, the isolation—she felt like she was back under the First Temple of Baltesia, locked in her cell and slowly starving. Her lungs froze, as immovable as iron. Her vision blurred.

Not this. Fesht, *not now.*

Anger followed on fear's heels. Leiyn pressed a fist against the wall to steady herself. Only after her knuckles crunched into stone did she realize she had lashed out harder than she had meant to. In her panic, she had drawn esse into her muscles, strengthening them.

It woke her from the trance. Ekosa's alarmed stare caused shame to smother her sudden anger.

Keep it together, Firebrand. At least a little longer.

"I'm fine," she said in answer to his unspoken question. "Just not fond of dungeons."

Uncertain still, the man nodded. He tarried outside the door a moment, then led the way in.

Leiyn trailed behind, stopping in the doorway to take it in. The chamber was smaller than the living quarters given to her and her party. It was a match for the corridor without, all barely tamed limestone. Only a round table in the center and a single chair gave it any sense of civility.

Cautiously, senses straining for any signs of ambush, she stepped inside, then moved aside while Ekosa closed the door. Backing up to the wall and trying to repress her panic, she watched as he reached into a deep pocket of his *boubou* and withdrew a worn iron key. This he pressed into the door's lock, turning it before replacing it in his robe with a deep sigh.

"We may speak now." Ekosa moved to stand opposite her, his back nearly to the wall. His eyes held as much wariness for her now as she had for him.

Leiyn drew in a steadying breath, then exhaled it. As Tadeo had always promised, breathing helped calm her nerves and refocused her on her numerous simmering questions.

"How about we start with why you think Ketti isn't safe. And why you think she's Eteman in the first place."

The *eesu* looked at her almost reproachfully. "She shows all the signs of one. The precious stones embedded in her flesh. The strength and complexity of her spirit. Even her name is known to us. The Ta'Ruls were an influential family long ago. Perhaps, since Etemans have not died out, they are still." He cocked his head, as if hoping she might provide the answer.

Leiyn only pursed her lips, thinking. His depiction was so accurate and precise there seemed little point in denying it further. "How did you learn all this? In Baltesia, Etemans are unknown."

"The Coterie has studied the ruins and civilizations of these lands ever since our first landfall. Some of our answers came from the stones themselves. A few hold memories, like those in the Eyrie are said to, for those who know how to reach them." Ekosa hesitated, then admitted, "Or so the elders and archives claim. I have not been privileged enough to witness these myself."

"That doesn't explain why Ketti's in danger."

The *eesu* edged closer but stopped short at Leiyn's warning look. "It is simple. She is the only known living Eteman. This is not an opportunity the Wings would let pass. They will wish to speak with her, learn from her. Study her."

Ice crawled through Leiyn's veins. She crossed her arms tightly over her chest. "They're welcome to try."

Ekosa gave her a weak smile. "I would prefer not to give them the chance."

"So that's why they wished to speak to her alone. To... what? Experiment on her?"

The *eesu* winced. "Nothing like that, I hope. But I do not think they would let her walk free. She would be a prisoner in all but name."

With Ketti's ability to enter grottos, Leiyn doubted they could keep her confined against her wishes. Still, she had not known about the hidden column and dungeon within the *Kekére*. Who knew what deadly arrows might still remain in the Wings' quiver?

She focused back on Ekosa. "Why tell me any of this? You're going against your Wings and the rest of your Coterie. I'm guessing the consequences won't be light if you're caught."

"At best, I would be exiled. At worst..." He waved a hand. "Death, or as good as."

Ekosa did not flinch as he spoke but stood tall. He had known the risks and accepted them with admirable courage.

"Then why?" she pressed.

The young man's eyes fell. Silence crowded into the small space, stifling. Leiyn barely held her tongue as she waited.

Ekosa raised his head. The tongue of lamp-flame reflected in his dark eyes.

"It is not the first time I have faced death, nor endured the scorn of those with authority. Those with enough not to starve was how I once thought of them." He blew out a breath. "I came here by stealing from the wrong person. Or the right one, it turned out. I did not know much of *eesuwé* or magic then. I only knew I must find enough for my mother, who lay dying, to eat."

Ekosa touched the bead on his braid before letting his hand fall. Leiyn guessed what it meant. She had a similar habit of touching her auburn tress, the legacy of her mother written upon her.

"I had tricks," he continued. "Tricks that made thievery simpler. Ways to make people turn the other way, or not see me, or feel a distracting prick. To see and sense things that are not there. None of these worked against the *eesu*, of course. He saw right through them."

Leiyn noticed Ekosa twisted the ring on his finger. Another memento, judging by his lifemark, from a long-gone mentor. She resisted the urge to touch a hand to Tadeo's fox figurine, always tucked into the pouch on her weapons belt.

"High Ituah did not turn me into the guards, but took me in. He trained me, formed me into an *eesu* like himself. But it came with... a cost." He looked at her sidelong, not quite meeting her gaze. "Fearing his intentions, I did not tell him of my mother at first. By the time I realized his regard was genuine, it was too late."

Her chest ached, his loss an echo of her own. She knew well the dreams he must have indulged in his head. How a different choice could have saved the ones they had doomed.

Pada. Patli. Zuma. Belen. Tadeo and the Lodge.

"That's a heavy burden," Leiyn murmured. "I'm sorry."

He waved a hand. "It is an old guilt. I do not seek to change the past, but the future." Shadows cast across his face, masking its nuances. "I learned two things then. That the Sky Queen's yoke—unyielding and punishing as it is—must be thrown off for the sake of those worst off. Those such as my mother and I, kept in poverty by benefit of our births. And I learned to extend trust early to those who are worthy of it."

She nodded, the tidal wave of his lifemark in mind. The whole of the Eyin Empire—that was what he had placed himself against.

"That's a lesson I've been slow to learn," Leiyn admitted. "But with you, I'll try."

Perhaps Ekosa lied. Perhaps *eesuwé* knew how to change their lifemark any way they saw fit. But if that were true, he was the most devious manipulator she had ever met, Sharo included.

At some point, she had to set aside her doubts and believe. Just like she had with Ketti.

Leiyn thrust her hand across the table. She did not know if the gesture was familiar to Ofeans. But after a moment, Ekosa gripped her arm back, long, spindly fingers wrapping about her forearm. With their mahia brushing against one another's, the gesture resonated deep within her.

"As long as you're willing," she said, "I'll accept your aid."

Ekosa smiled and pressed her arm back. "You have it."

She still held his arm when two things flashed against her lifesense.

The first was the outline of a door higher up the column staircase. For a moment, it flared brighter, then opened inward. Her awareness of the *Kekére* and Kunu flooded in through the doorway, blinding and overwhelming, almost obscuring the figure who stepped inside the hidden stairwell.

The second came closer at hand. A creature, small and hovering, buzzed into being a foot in front of her face. Its green feathers were bright to behold, its esse even more so.

"Biqqa?" Leiyn said, staring at Ketti's hummingbird.

Ekosa released her arm and raised his head to the ceiling. As the stairwell door closed, Leiyn's lifesense deadened but for the figure descending the stairs. They appeared to be an *eesu*, esse drifting outside their body. She felt the tendrils of magic as the newcomer focused on them.

His eyes followed the spirit creature now flitting around Leiyn's head, but he remained surprisingly calm before it. "What is—no, it does not matter. We are out of time. You must return to your friends at once."

As she stared at the hummingbird, Leiyn hoped it was not already too late.

53

FLEETING

$\mathcal{W}$hat are you doing here?" Leiyn demanded of the hummingbird. "How did you find me? Is Ketti alright?"

She did not know what she expected. Biqqa could give her no answers. The room hummed with her rapid wingbeats as she flew around Leiyn's head. If she was more familiar with the spirit beast, perhaps she could have understood its purpose from its esse. As it was, it seemed to burn as brightly as ever.

"You must go," Ekosa urged, bringing her back to their other conundrum. Scooping up the lamp, he moved to the door, unlocked it, and swung it open.

Leiyn strode into the corridor, Biqqa following. "What do we do about the *eesu?*"

"I will handle it. Here, take this." He held out his lamp.

She accepted it, unsure what he planned.

Ekosa turned away before she could ask, taking the lead forward. Though his eyes and esse betrayed his fear, she did not countermand him. They had clasped arms. He had expressed trust toward her time and again. She would not insult him by questioning him now.

And Biqqa's presence gave her pause. It was possible the hummingbird was merely curious. Perhaps she had taken a shine to Leiyn. But with her friends beyond her senses and enemies lingering nearby, she could not take further risks than she already had. The mere thought of losing them made her breath come quicker.

Reaching the stairwell, Ekosa started up it first. The *eesu* was two flights above them. Leiyn kept her eyes trained on the bend ahead, the lamp illuminating the way, waiting for the inevitable encounter. Another pool of light signaled their visitor's approach, as did their echoing footsteps.

"Ekosa? *Kini ose isale?*"

An unfamiliar male voice. As he turned into view, the lamp held before him, Leiyn saw she did not recognize him. He was short, middle-aged, and balding around the pate. A pair of spectacles gleamed on the bridge of his nose.

"Otsu." Ekosa did not slow, even as the other *eesu* stopped several stairs up. "I apologize for startling you."

The man's eyes flickered between Leiyn and Ekosa. Though he must have known she was Baltesian, he spoke again in Eyin. Excluding her and not bothering to hide it.

"To have a conversation," the younger *eesu* replied in Leiyn's tongue.

As Ekosa came level with Otsu, Leiyn hesitated, unsure how to proceed. The older man was far from intimidating, but she could not provoke him lest she be forced into harming him. He was innocent as far as she knew, and relations between Baltesia and Ore-Ofe were bad enough without her worsening them.

Ekosa did not slow, clasping Otsu's arms too suddenly and firmly to be friendly. A glance over his shoulder told her what to do.

Leiyn skipped forward, slipping past the pair on the narrow stairwell. Biqqa flew after her.

"*Orisa rami lowo!* What are you doing?!"

Heart pounding, she ignored Otsu and sprinted up to the floor containing the dormitories, trying not to spill the oil in the lamp as she went. As far as she could tell, Ekosa only held the older man back while she fled. No one would be hurt.

She put their struggle from mind as she reached the stone door and pressed her free hand to it. Around the edges, the imbued wood inlay responded to her mahia's touch as she willed it to open. The door complied. Silently, it swung toward her.

Unera flooded her lifesense.

Leiyn stood before the open portal, unable to do more than adjust to the onslaught for several moments. When she could think clearly again, she quested forth with her mahia, searching for familiar esses.

She quickly found her friends. They appeared unharmed, but two others were there with them. One appeared powerful, though their esse writhed with pain. Nestled next to the bright one was a small, dimmer figure. She recognized them both.

Ata. Chispa.

Leiyn set off at a run.

She did not think to close the column door until she was halfway down the hall. Still, she did not turn around. Her trip into it with Ekosa had already been discovered. There was little use in hiding the evidence now.

Behind the doors she passed, she felt the *eesuwé* stirring, no doubt wondering at the commotion. Some reached for her with their mahia. She rebuffed them out of hand. Just then, she could not dredge up worry about causing offense or raising an alarm.

Her lifesense flitted between her friends as quickly as Biqqa flew, seeking answers and finding none. Rounding a corner, she came nearer the room until at last, the door appeared.

Leiyn threw it open and, panting, stared down at her feet.

Ata lay spread across the floor. Her body had always been formed of plants and animal parts but kept nearly a human shape. Now, it was like someone had pulled her apart and strewn the pieces around the room. Roots burrowed into the stone, splintering it at the seams. Leaves hung shriveled and brown. Flowers wilted and shed. Her feathers had molted in a halo around her deconstructed body. Her talons cut into her bark-like skin, beads of amber ichor tipping them.

As Leiyn stood in the doorway, the dryvan raised her head,

the only part of her still recognizable. Leiyn could barely hold her gaze. Her eyes were a sickly yellow at the edges with threads of green shot through, like a rot had taken hold within. Her pupils were yawning chasms.

"Leiyn," Isla breathed. "Thank the Saints you're back." She stood on Ata's other side, clutching Batu's arm like it was the only thing holding her up. The former plainsrider had positioned himself before her so his body was between her and the dryvan.

Ketti had pressed against the back wall, eyes wide, chest rising and falling with shallow breaths. Biqqa flew to her, the flitting pattern about the Eteman's head now unmistakably anxious. Chispa, who was pressed against what remained of Ata's torso, shone with a similar feeling, his lifeforce feverishly bright.

"What happened?" Leiyn demanded, venturing a step into the room. Any farther and she would trample on Ata's roots. Instead, she kneeled where she stood, level with the dryvan's face. "Ata, what's wrong?"

The Iritu stared at her, lips parted. Still, she did not move or speak. Her esse pulsed with unmistakable agony.

"Ata, answer me!"

It did not matter that she used her true name before the others. Just then, Leiyn needed to pierce the dryvan's stupor. She needed to understand. A nameless terror gripped her, and she feared it above all else.

Setting down the lamp, she reached forward, took the dryvan's head in her hands, and touched her esse.

Barely had she made contact before Leiyn had to release her. The union held nothing of a friend's touch. Where their lifeforce met were only torturous flames. The dryvan had become like a cornered, feral animal, foaming at the mouth, snarling and biting at any who approached.

Yet the excruciating truth had also seared into her mind.

"Glade is gone? *All* of it's gone?" She looked between Ata's diseased eyes, hoping to see some sign that she had misunderstood. That the scene of the broken bodies and burned trees and smoke-filled sky had not been a memory, but a nightmare, as untrue as any dream.

In the dryvan's pained gaze, she saw only confirmation.

Distantly, Leiyn heard Isla speaking. "How can Glade be gone? Are all the dryvans...?"

Leiyn forced herself to stop listening, focusing her attention on the Iritu. "Ata, speak to me. I cannot help if I don't know what happened."

A rasping note, nearly a death rattle, issued from the skin-walker's throat. Leiyn thought she had missed some injuries, but no darkness stained Ata. This was an inner pain made manifest.

"I... I..." Each syllable creaked like old dead wood. "Killed them... I killed them all..."

"You?" Leiyn pictured the dryvan tearing apart Eld. No—it was too much to believe. "You mean it was your fault?"

She was not sure Ata heard her. "Alone..." the skin-walker muttered. "All alone..."

Leiyn reeled. Eld. Mooneyes. The others who had stood with them at Qasaar. Who had protected the Veiled Lands from Sharo and his lyshans.

All dead.

Who would fight on their behalf now? Who would stop lyshans from appearing anywhere they pleased and doing as they wished?

Nothing. No one.

They were on their own. Sharo would find her. Sooner or later, he would come.

Yet as fear rose, it was not him she pictured, but the armored lyshan from the ruins. Her scars pulled as the memories rose. She shivered and pressed them back down. They would surface again when she slept, but they would have to wait until then.

Ata needed her.

Leiyn held her hands up, afraid to touch the dryvan even as she wished to shake answers free of her wooden lips. "Ata, talk to me. Tell me what happened. Did the lyshans find Glade? Is Sharo behind this?"

A hint of fury rose at the thought. Leiyn latched onto it. Anger would not drown her like sorrow might.

"Sharo..." The green creepers in Ata's eyes retreated. Her pupils narrowed to slits. The mass of roots shifted, easing a bit out of the stone, pulling closer together. *"Sharo...!"*

Her voice, creaking like an old tree in a storm, rose with the furor of her esse. Leiyn had never seen her burn so bright. Only Man'nah would have been a match for the strength rolling off her.

"Ata, please." Leiyn put one foot beneath her, ready to rise at a moment's notice. At the peripheries of her awareness, she felt the *eesuwé* amassing in the corridor outside along with the Coterie guards. Closer at hand, her companions backed away, pressing against the walls as if they tried melting into them. Leiyn felt Ketti's esse held in preparation, ready to whisk them off to the safety of a grotto.

"Please, Ata, speak to me. I need to understand!"

The dryvan continued to rise, her body twisting back together. Yet it seemed wrong, how it merged. Like she had forgotten what shape she wanted to be midway through forming it.

Leiyn rose and backed up a step. "Ata!" A hard edge crept into her words. "Don't ignore me!"

"Leiyn," Isla said, her voice small, "maybe you shouldn't—"

She cut off as something snapped in the hall.

A being blazed into Leiyn's awareness.

Her chest squeezed tight. Her heart beat frantically against it. Leiyn whirled to the open door, fists raised, mahia braced. The thought of what she faced nearly sent her back to her knees.

Her nightmare had returned.

The lyshan in scarlet titanbone armor stood in the hallway. Its pitted eyes stared out from under the raptor helm. Its esse writhed like bloated termites in rotten wood.

For a moment, they stared at each other. Still. Waiting for the other to make the first move.

Chispa and Biqqa broke first. Both spirit beasts flashed from existence with barely a whimper.

Then a scream slashed the air.

"KHAMO!"

With a tearing as loud as her thunderous voice, Ata ripped her roots free of the stone and flung herself at the lyshan.

54

REND

*L*eiyn narrowly dodged the leaping dryvan, knocking the lamp over as she did. It shattered on the stone, spreading oil and flames across the floor.

She barely spared it a glance. Just in time, she whipped her head back up to see the Iritu collide.

The force of it sent her stumbling back toward the fire.

The lyshan, Khamo, was like a mountain ensconced in his armor, but Ata was a flood. The dryvan screamed, filling the tower halls with the horrid noise as her roots twisted around her enemy. She rained strike after strike down on him, each more furious than the last.

Yet the lyshan fought with equal vigor. Twisting to get at her, Khamo tried to strike Ata with the whip and mace clutched in his hands. His wrath was expressed in silent violence. Their blows landed on each other with dull thuds, war drums underlying Ata's shrieks.

Leiyn was caught in awful fascination for several moments before her ranger training kicked in.

Weapon. I need a weapon!

Her blades and bow were locked away elsewhere in the tower. Vaguely, she sensed their location on the ground floor.

Even if she had the key required to retrieve them, she had no time. Ata needed help.

Her only remaining weapon was her mahia. Without Clouded Fang, though, she doubted it was enough to distract the lyshan, much less harm him. Their kind's protections were too solid, subtle, and strong for her to penetrate on her own.

She needed her titan.

But how, Legion damn it all!

Though she had made progress, she had not formed a grotto. Attempting it now verged on pointless. She required a better solution, one she could implement in moments.

By her lifesense, she felt the scrapping Iritu trample farther down the hall, but they remained within a score of paces. The *eesuwé* fled before them, but she sensed them not far off, like carrion birds waiting for a corpse to pick clean. Whirling, she commanded the gazes of her companions, stiff with shock and illuminated by the flames now spreading across their bedding.

"Ketti!" Leiyn snapped. "Can you transport us all to a grotto? The Iritu included?"

The Eteman roused from her stupor. "N-no. Not the Iritu. They are too..." She trailed off as her eyes darted to where the shapeshifters fought, their weaving path leading them back toward their chamber.

Not the answer Leiyn had hoped for. If the fight could be moved to a grotto, she could have summoned Clouded Fang. She would have to find another way.

"Fine. Take Batu and Isla."

"Just them?"

"No, Leiyn! You're coming with us!" Isla stepped forward, though a hand still clutched Batu's arm. The former plainsrider remained where he was, hands bunched into fists, horror and loathing battling across his features.

Leiyn leveled a hard stare at her fellow ranger. "Ata never abandoned me. I won't leave her to die."

Not like I left Belen.

Isla reached for her, but Leiyn stepped away. Her friend kept her hand lifted between them.

"Stop and think for a moment. The lyshan almost killed you last time. Now you don't have a weapon!"

Fear for her friends fed Leiyn's anger. Fury gave her focus, as it always had. "There's no time to argue," she snapped. "Ketti, do it now!"

The Eteman needed no further prompting. Leiyn felt her mahia expand out, then seize the other two. Isla's accusing stare was the last thing she saw before all three sputtered out of existence.

Alone, Leiyn turned back to the brawl.

Once more, the Iritu neared the door. Ata seemed to hold her own. She hoped the dryvan would last a little longer.

Sweat coated her skin, only partially from the flames at her back. Her heart raced, quick as the tempo of their strikes. All the same, she closed her eyes, tried to calm her breathing, and focus as Ketti had taught her.

Connected. It's all connected.

Herself. Ata. The lyshan fighting the dryvan, killing her. The *eesuwé* lingering down the hall, their lifeforce tumultuous with terror and indecision. Each drop of ichor flying from immortal claws, each scream of rage and pain.

She tried to see it as one, as united and interwoven. Tried, then tried again.

And failed.

"Damn it all!"

Choking on the smoke, Leiyn opened her eyes. Panic settled in, hard and immovable in her belly. If she could not reach Clouded Fang, how was she supposed to help? Even with mahia strengthening her, human fists would do little against titanbone.

By her lifesense, she felt the lyshan fling Ata away. She soared down the hall until she met the stone with an audible crash. Her furious groans sounded softer, and her lifeforce was dimmed, yet she rose once more to rush at her enemy.

But Ata would not last much longer. It was not a question of if she would lose, but when.

Leiyn drew on the amber beads nestled at her waist, sucking all their lifeforce into herself. The rush was heady, intoxicating. For a moment, she felt invincible.

Stepping outside the door swept the delusion away.

Khamo had pinned the dryvan against a wall, the fist holding the whip pressed against the side of Ata's head. Her claws and roots had twisted around his arms, straining to keep him from crushing her skull. Stone cracked beneath the force of their struggle.

Leiyn started toward them, then noticed one of the *eesuwé* behind her stepping forward. She knew who it was even before she turned to face him.

"Get back, Ekosa! This isn't your fight!"

But the young man pressed on. He approached at an awkward lumber, burdened by the items clutched to his chest.

Her weapons.

Leiyn sprinted toward him and ripped them free of his grip. With lifeforce filling her to overflowing, every movement packed deadly strength. Ekosa gasped and flinched away at her rough treatment.

She winced, but there was no time for apologies. *"Go!"*

He needed no second warning. With a hurried nod, the young man stumbled back to where the other *eesuwé* waited.

Leiyn turned to find the deadlock worsened. Ata's head had begun to cave in. Ichor leaked from her eyes. Her lifeforce dimmed to gray. She had moments left of survival.

Only then did the onlookers act.

The concentrated magic of thirty *eesuwé* shot toward the pair. For a split moment, Leiyn feared they would finish Ata, not knowing their true enemy, but the Ofean mahas struck the lyshan instead. Their combined mahia pierced his esse like metal would flesh.

But their weapons were like needles. Together, they had wounded him, but only in the way of gnats biting a lion. Yet, like pests, they were too irritating to ignore. Khamo's head swung away from Leiyn toward the offending Ofeans. His grip eased on Ata as he ripped free one arm and brandished his mace.

The dryvan was not finished yet. Seizing the opportunity, Ata wheezed out a shriek and dug her roots under the lyshan's helm. As silent as ever, the armored Iritu swatted away her attack and drove an elbow into her neck. Her esse grew darker still. One more blow, and Leiyn feared she would break.

Too far for a charge, Leiyn dropped the sheathed falchions, slung her quiver of imbued arrows over a shoulder and, drawing one, nocked it to her longbow. If she could land one on his flesh, its enchantment could turn the tide of the battle. Yet even at two dozen paces, Khamo moved so swiftly it would be easy to miss.

Pick your moment, Tadeo whispered in her mind. *You will only get one.*

Baring her teeth, Leiyn drew. Aimed. Released.

The arrow whistled, arcing down the hall. It flew true, plunging toward the opening in his helm.

Khamo twisted.

Instead of finding stony flesh, the arrow pinged off titan-bone, though it gouged the red armor. The lyshan spared her a glance.

Leiyn reached for another arrow.

Before she could draw it, Ata's esse brightened. With a last surge, the dryvan seized against the lyshan. Yet she did not strike him but pulled him toward her, as if in an embrace.

They careened against the stone wall—then tumbled through it.

Leiyn stared at the gap left in their wake. The wall looked to have been gnawed through; Ata's roots had dug into the stone as she was pressed against it. Helpless to do anything else, she followed their fall with her lifesense.

They never reached the ground. Halfway down, both winked out of existence.

"Grotto," she growled under her breath.

Had Leiyn gone with them, she could have summoned her

ash dragon and helped Ata. As things stood, the dryvan was on her own.

She wondered if the last benevolent Iritu was already dead.

But the rest of them were far from safe. As soon as he had killed Ata, Khamo would return. He was here for Leiyn as well as Ketti. Sharo had already come for her twice. He would not stop until she was dead.

Leiyn stared down the hallway at the *eesuwé* crowding the other end, feeling their regard in return. She could spare them no more thought. Slinging her bow over her free shoulder, she stooped to pick up her swords and looped them onto her weapons belt along with her quiver. Up and down the hall, the Ofean mahas crept ever closer.

"Prima Maha!" one called from behind, a vaguely familiar male voice. "How have you brought that fell creature here? And where are your companions?"

Leiyn turned to see both Wings of the Coterie striding toward her. They were clad in little more than nightgowns, yet their expressions were as severe as if they wore their articles of office.

"Get out of here!" she snarled at them. "He'll be back soon, and you'll be no help to anyone dead."

Leiyn set down her bow and drew her falchions as she spoke. She doubted Khamo would allow her a second shot. Dread settled in her gut as heavy as iron as she recalled how poorly the last fight had gone.

He's weakened this time. And the eesuwé will distract him. There's a chance.

The Wings ignored her warning. "I demand answers!" Samu grated, his face darkening. "An attack by the Iritu demands it!"

Leiyn broke off from examining the lay of the corridor to spare him a surprised glance. Ofeans, it seemed, knew about more than Etemans.

"Answer us, Leiyn of Orille," Onah said. "Do not force our hand. Why did that *anjonu* come here?"

They would not relent until they had answers. Leiyn was no

lyshan. If all the *eesuwé* attacked her, she would not withstand the onslaught.

"Fine." She turned to face them. "Some of the Iritu—most of them, now—want me dead. That one in red armor? He attacked us before. The other, the dryvan, was trying to stop him. But I don't think she'll—" Leiyn bit off the sentence with a shake of her head. "The armored one will be back soon. So if you don't want him to kill you, I'm warning you one more time—get far, far away from me."

"Highest Ones, please, heed her words." Ekosa approached from behind the Wings, unwisely drawing their attention. Though he came with arms crossed and head bowed respectfully, his boldness would undoubtedly be seen as insolence. "She travels with an Eteman, as you saw."

"And why should we listen to you, High Ekosa?" Samu snapped. "You, who have repeatedly betrayed the *Kekére* this night, from what I understand? When this is over, you will be fortunate if we allow you to remain one of us!"

Or alive. Leiyn remembered the consequences the *eesu* had outlined earlier. Though she despised it, she knew she had to intervene.

"Ekosa has done nothing but help. Without him, the lyshan might have already won. But all this can wait. Right now, you need to—"

A creature appeared before her.

Had it been taller than her knees, Leiyn might have struck. As it was, she sank to a knee and stared in amazement at the silver fox trembling before her.

"What are you doing back here? You have to leave! It isn't safe."

But Chispa did not go. Instead, he crept closer, eyeing the sharp blades in her hands. She spread them to either side, not wishing to scare him, but neither daring to sheathe them.

"Please, Chispa. I cannot worry about you, too."

The fox was inches away. She felt his esse tugging at hers, like a child wishing to show their parent something. Almost, she pulled away. But she remembered all the times the spirit beast had helped her. Swallowing her impatience, Leiyn waited.

Chispa pressed his snout against her knee. His lifeforce touched hers, then pressed into it.

Then she saw it. All of it.

Unera as one.

The web of lifeforce spread from her and the fox, out to the *eesuwé*, stretching across the entire city and into the world beyond. Leiyn beheld it all, broader and more majestic than a titan. And still, this was only a fraction of reality. Its entirety, she could scarcely imagine.

For a moment, she was lost in wonder. Then one thread asserted itself over the others. A connection not lost or weakened by the others surrounding it but strengthened.

Come to me, Clouded Fang.

The ash dragon was slow to rouse. The magma blanketing him was warm and comforting, lulling him to drowsiness. Yet his presence hummed along their bond, her urgency stimulating it.

At last, with a rumbling of the earth, he rose.

Sensing the awakening titan, the Ofean mahas stumbled back and shouted at her, but Leiyn was beyond hearing. She pressed the back of one hand to Chispa's soft fur, reinforcing their connection.

Outside the tower, she sensed Clouded Fang taking shape. The *eesuwé* appeared to as well, retreating farther still. Even Ekosa did not dare remain near her.

Leiyn rose to her feet. The world around her wobbled, vibrating to her lifesense. She had to tread carefully, like a spider on a weakened web, lest the slightest movement break the silk. Chispa remained nestled against her leg, holding the connection between their souls. Had he parted, she doubted she could have maintained it.

Now fully formed, the ash dragon beat his wings. She could only sense him by her mahia, but through the gap in the tower's side, his scent wafted in, all smoke and hot stone. The longing to see him gripped her. Ever so carefully, she edged forward, Chispa shuffling with her.

They had traveled three strides before another tore through the web.

Leiyn raised her falchions. Fear pulsed through her and cascaded along the web, weakening them. It took every ounce of focus to maintain Clouded Fang's bond as she faced the Iyshan.

Khamo stood alone. His armor had been battered and split, and the opening around his helmet was chipped and cracked from where Ata's roots had torn at it. Yet he remained upright and whole, his thousand-soul esse still strong. Ata, on the other hand, was nowhere to be seen.

Fury washed away the fear, its heat just as dangerous to the web. Stifling her anger, Leiyn drew upon her bond and felt life-force flood into her. She burned as too much filled her, like Clouded Fang had breathed dragonfire within her.

"Leave," she said, her voice distant and strange in her ears. "Leave us now, or I'll kill you."

The Iritu did not move. His mahia brushed her, as if in evaluation. She wondered if she had become the predator or remained prey with a titan's uncertain power. Wondered if he recalled her killing Man'nah, his onetime leader.

Did he know how tentative her bond was? That a single strike might snap it?

She pointed the falchions at him, titanbone tips mere paces away. "This is my final warning."

Khamo did not acknowledge the threat. He neither raised his weapons nor retreated. Only then did Leiyn wonder if he understood her. If any powers of speech remained to him, or if they had eroded with the rest of his identity.

Before she could decide on her next action, a slow rumble issued from his mouth. A word, barely intelligible, ushered from it like the first tumbling stones of an avalanche.

"*Eteman...*"

Suspicions flashed through her mind, connecting like Unera was around her. This was not about killing her or her companions. It never had been. Sharo wanted to eradicate Solace and its Etemans. It was why he had sent Khamo to ambush them at those ruins, to draw them out.

The lyshan had come for Ketti. Either Sharo needed her to enter Solace, or he wanted to ensure none of his ancient enemies slipped his vengeance. But it was plain now that she was their primary quarry.

Leiyn forced a smile. "She's gone, *sach'aan*. You'll never reach her now. Leave, and you might get another chance. Stay, and I'll make sure you don't."

The lyshan remained still but for his thrashing souls. Then, without warning, he winked back out of existence.

Leiyn stared at the space Khamo had occupied. When he did not reappear after several breaths, she lowered her swords. Disappointment slivered through her. With lifeforce overflowing, she itched for the fight, even when she knew it was better to avoid it.

Greater concerns pushed to the fore. Ignoring the *eesuwé* shouting fresh warnings at her, she lowered herself to one knee and looked at Chispa. With their esses joined, eye contact was unnecessary, but it helped her focus on him amid the life swimming all around.

"Can you find them? My friends?"

If the silver fox understood her, he gave no sign of it. Thinking it through, Leiyn tried picturing them in her mind instead, focusing on their little defining attributes. Isla's warm smile. The pattern of gems on Ketti's face. The firm regard in Batu's eyes. She threw in Ata's image as well, and her forest scent—far more constant than her shape.

Chispa's esse pulsed with recognition. Lifting his nose, he sniffed the air, then nudged against her. A welcome sign.

Leiyn looked toward where Clouded Fang hovered outside, smoke and lifeforce wafting from him with every beat of his wings. "Bring us to them."

She felt the titan behold her for a long moment. Then he tilted his body forward and glided toward where she and Chispa crouched on the tower floor. Stone posed no barrier to him; the ash dragon flowed through the rock. His snout reformed inches away from her.

She raised her hand, falchion still clutched in it, and settled upon it.

For a moment, Leiyn spread across the world. Then she folded into it.

55

VOW

Obsidian scales. Sulfurous breath. The bite of salty wind.

Blinking away her blurred vision, Leiyn beheld a new world. She no longer stood atop a tower, but on solid, rocky ground. Her fist remained pressed to Clouded Fang's snout.

Tentatively, she withdrew it. If either movement disturbed the dragon, he did not show it. He moved with ponderous weight as he straightened his neck and turned to look about him, taking in the lay of this new land.

Leiyn looked with him. The Coterie Tower had disappeared, yet they stood upon an inlet recognizable as the one on which it had been built. Though it remained night, both moons lifted the darkness. Young Chiuni was a crescent, while Great Teyao waxed slightly larger. Ambient lifeforce sparkled in the air, further revealing the landscape. Crude and unshaped, the inlet was little more than a rocky outcropping jutting out into the sea. Tall stones kept thunderous waves from crashing over the shore and sweeping her into the powerful swell.

She and the titan were not alone. Chispa was there as well, a step apart, watching the flying spray with curious apprehension. Other, familiar presences lingered farther back.

Breath catching, Leiyn turned to her friends. All three were there: Isla, Batu, Ketti. They stood in a circle, looking down at something with a faint life of its own, spread in an unfamiliar shape. Yet she knew the esse running through it.

Ata.

She took off at a sprint. At her approach, the others startled and cried out in alarm, but Leiyn only shouted, "It's just me! Move aside!" Her knees jolted with the impact of falling next to the dryvan, but she scarcely felt it. Isla threw questions at her, and Batu added his urgent queries.

Leiyn ignored them both as she focused on the dryvan. Healing came first. The rest could wait. She moved her hands forward, then hesitated.

Ata was dying.

Khamo had ripped her asunder so she spread over the rocks, like a bush with its branches pried apart. Faint, wheezing gasps issued from what remained of her face. Her jaw had been broken and twisted sideways, her skull caved in. One eye had been squashed, while the other rolled up so only white shot through with yellow veins showed. Her aroma before had always been pleasant, earthen and vital as plants, but it now reeked of pus and sour wounds. Worse still were the injuries to her esse. Black canyons gaped throughout her body. What remained was like the last sluggish water in a drying riverbed.

"Shit," Leiyn breathed as she moved her lifesense along the dryvan. "Shit, shit, *shit.*" Where to begin? She was a poor healer for humans; how could she hope to help an Iritu? What wounds should she try to heal first? What parts of her were most vital? Did she have a heart? Lungs? A brain? Organs of any kind? Did she need any of them to survive?

Esse. They live on esse.

It was the one thing she knew of that sustained them. The lyshans she had killed had only succumbed when she had cut into their essence. Their shape did not matter, only the strength of their being.

Just give her lifeforce.

It was the best plan she had. Clenching her jaw, Leiyn gingerly set her hands to the writhing roots.

She pressed esse in.

Instead of staunching the oozing wounds, Leiyn tried bolstering the shapeshifter's flagging strength. She started slowly. When it seemed to cause no harm, she pushed more in, faster. Lifeforce brimmed inside her, both Clouded Fang and her amber beads contributing, yet in moments, she devoured her reserves.

A groan rose from Ata, the sound like an old stump being uprooted. Not a healthy sound. Her vitality seemed only marginally brighter. She needed more, far more. More than Leiyn could gift alone.

To me, Leiyn thought to Clouded Fang as she accessed their bond.

The ground rumbled as the dragon approached. Here in the grotto, their bond had returned to being simple and intuitive. Leiyn felt the others flinch away, but she could not spare a moment for a reassuring word. At another unspoken request, the titan seated himself behind her, looming overhead and blotting out the little light from the moons. With scales black as midnight, his silhouette was like the night sky devoid of stars.

To her lifesense, he blazed as bright as Omn Itself.

Leiyn let his lifeforce cascade in, then funneled it through to the dryvan. Even while fighting Man'nah and healing from fatal wounds, she had never drawn in so much esse. The bounds of her body strained. She felt first bloated, then flayed open. She scarcely knew where she ended and the titan began.

Yet it was working. The sallow parts of Ata's esse brightened; the black fissures became threaded through with gray strands that thickened with each passing moment. Leiyn could see the changes as well, the dryvan's parts twisting together, drawing back into a vaguely human shape. The cratered flesh pushed back out. Her eye socket opened, and within it formed a new eye, pale and undeveloped.

A long, agonized sigh issued from the dryvan, growing louder with each moment.

"Leiyn, be careful... Don't go too far..." Isla's warning came as if from a distance. Leiyn ignored it.

More, she told her bonded titan. *She needs more!*

Ata was nearly whole again. Not recovered, not hale like she had been before, but neither fractured. She had to hold out longer. Just a little—

The world throbbed. A dark wave crashed over her.

She sank beneath it.

Hands, blisteringly hot, pressed against her skin.

Leiyn gasped at the sensation. Her eyes fluttered open. It was difficult to focus, and her vision danced and swayed, yet she sought after the one hurting her.

At her movement, the burning hands lifted away. Leiyn perceived enough to know to whom they belonged.

"Ketti..."

"Rest, Leiyn." The Eteman's voice was calm and soothing. Like she imagined her mother's might have been. "Just rest."

"She's awake. Saints be good, she's awake!" Isla spoke somewhere to her right, a sob choking her.

"Still Firebrand," Batu noted wryly from above.

Leiyn managed to rise to one elbow. Clouded Fang was gone, her connection to him severed. She wondered if she had dismissed him or if he had left by his own volition. Either way, it had probably saved her. Her body felt loose as a limp waterskin, her command over it tenuous. She doubted she would have survived more lifeforce funneling through it.

"Ata," she slurred. "Is she—?"

"I'm here."

She turned toward the voice. The dryvan stood over her, appearing as she had at their first encounter. Her esse was scarcely brighter than a human's, and there were still threads of darkness showing lingering injuries. But after the way she had appeared before, it was a marvel that she stood at all.

"Ata." Leiyn let her weary smile speak for her.

Atastimina kneeled, bringing her face close enough for Leiyn to see her clearly through swimming eyes. The dryvan's skin had smoothed to acorn bark once more, seams indicating where Khamo had cracked it open. Her eyes differed; one kept its original green, but the other was entirely white, devoid of pupil and pigmentation.

"You attempted too much, Awakener," Ata murmured. "Even for you."

Leiyn shook her head and regretted it. All of Unera seemed to shift with the movement. Her stomach bucked so she had to swallow back a mouthful of bile.

"I had to," she eked out.

"No, you didn't." Ata bent down and gripped her arms. Her touch did not burn as Ketti's had, but felt pleasantly cool, like shaded stone on a summer day. "You chose to save me."

"We're friends. You said so yourself."

The dryvan held perfectly still. Then a deep, shaking laugh trembled through her.

"Odd and odder. The passion of mortals... That's what I require now." Ata lifted her gaze to stare back toward the sea. When she lowered it, all amusement had fled. "I would have thrown away my life. Would have let Sharo win." Her talons pressed into Leiyn's arms, uncomfortably tight. "My sorrow grows no less, but my hatred is stronger. I cannot rest until he is stopped."

As if realizing she was hurting her, Ata released Leiyn's arms but her intensity did not flag, nor did she blink, steady as a hawk's.

"For saving my life, for giving me this chance, I owe you a debt that cannot be repaid. To you, Leiyn, I swear this: where it does not interfere with my mission, I will stay by your side. Where you go, I go. Your fights are my fights. When you rest, I will watch over you and let neither you nor those you call friend come to harm. By my *Ialadt*, may Her spirit rest in eternity's embrace, as one seed-sister to another, I vow to keep true."

Leiyn squeezed her eyes shut. A dryvan's oath—it was too much to take in. Yet she could not ignore it. Blinking her eyes open, she struggled into a seated position and, with the world swimming around her, grasped for the right words.

"Thank you, Ata. But I'm not sure—"

"I am." The dryvan settled a hand on Leiyn's shoulder, gentle now as she helped keep her upright. A glimmer of her old fey humor twisted her wooden lips. "Better to accept it now."

Leiyn glanced at Isla, then at their companions. They stared blankly back, as lost for a path forward as herself.

"Then I do, I suppose." Swallowing against her rising nausea, Leiyn scrambled for some measure of focus. "And, for what it's worth, I still mean to fight Sharo. You'll have my help, and the rest of ours, I'd guess."

Looking up at her companions, she found them nodding at her words.

"Whatever you need," Isla murmured. "Sharo has stolen from us as well."

"All of us," Batu said, his brow furrowed.

Ketti pressed her lips tightly together, but gave a single, abrupt nod.

"But if we're to help," Leiyn continued, looking back at Ata, "then we must know the full truth about Sharo. Who he is to you."

The dryvan froze. Only an Iritu could hold themselves so unnaturally still. When at last she moved, it was to release Leiyn's shoulder and rise as fluidly as if she were water given shape.

"Yes," Ata said, voice deadened. "It is time you knew."

The skin-walker looked out toward the sea again. Isla moved to sit next to Leiyn and coaxed her to lean against her shoulder. The worst of her overuse of mahia seemed to have passed, for Isla's esse was comforting rather than painful. Chispa, unseen by Leiyn until then, padded over to curl against her other hip.

Salt-tinged wind sighed past. Leiyn watched the dryvan. Waiting.

Ata began to speak.

56

ONE

Once, Sharo and I were one.

"We Iritu aren't born like you mortals. We are... grown. The fruit of the *Ialadta*—our Mothertrees. All burned away now.

"When the time came for a new Seeding, each branch of a Mothertree would sprout many Iritu. During my creation, only two germinated on our branch.

"We grew next to each other, us two. My memories of that time are thin and grow thinner with each year. Yet I recall being aware of him, feeling him sprout beside me. Somehow, it was a comfort. A sense that I would never be alone in this world.

"Once we blossomed and left our Mother's shade, we took our first shapes together. He wished to fly; I followed him, growing wings and trailing his tail feathers. We had few cares then. Sustenance was plentiful and our existence free of peril and predator. We roamed where we pleased, took different forms as suited our fancies. We grew and grew closer together.

"But we couldn't remain in our adolescent forms, no more than humans can. When it came time for our change, I didn't wish to return to our Mothertree. It struck me then as a cage, of sorts. I reveled in the freedom of childhood. I didn't wish to limit my shape to... this. Yes, we Iritu retain great control over our bodies. But in our infancy, we were unbound.

"Only by Sharo's coaxing did I enter my chrysalis. Only by his spoken visions for our future did I consent. Perhaps, without him, I never would have relented. But he was my seed-brother, and the elder of us two. I trusted him, essence and limb.

"The transformation was nothing like I expected. It was simple, natural. When I emerged in my mature form, I felt more... myself.

"It was the opposite for Sharo. He crawled free, dripping of ichor and drained to the last of his heritage. I went to him and found our roles had reversed, for it was I who comforted him.

"'Why?' he cried as I held his fragile form together. 'Why did She ruin me?'

"My reassurances were in vain. Every change was different, and if the Mothertrees had purpose in how they enacted them, we never learned what they were. Yet I cannot help wondering if She knew what destiny awaited him. If She deemed killing her son a worthy trade to spare the world a greater pain.

"In time, he recovered, and we both grew into our new forms. Our civilization was young at our creation, but already, it spread and developed. I was eager to be part of it. Strong in our Inheritance, inflated with power and a sense of importance, I pursued ambition. And none were more ambitious than Man'nah.

"Sharo, before the elder and stronger of our pair, had emerged weak and hesitant. He cautioned me against the path I trod, for he looked upon our expansion and aggression toward *kainox* as akin to a mortal prodding a bear. 'They will destroy us,' he said. But I and my comrades laughed until he slunk back into seclusion. We deemed his words the small fears of the weak, unworthy of those with ample heritage.

"He only returned when the first invaders came. Those ancestors of Etema were pitiful, fleeing a disaster that had claimed their homeland. Sharo warned against this callous course of action, but we spurned him the same as them.

Following Man'nah's lead, I helped turn them away with scorn and threats, sending them back across the sea to their wasteland.

"Sharo was right to fear them. When the Etemans returned generations later, they were different. Hardened. Dangerous. Each was a warrior with a bonded Vast One, as you are, Awakener. Each a match for the Kin.

"They didn't waste time with words but struck. Few Iritu had died to that point, time and environment posing us little danger, but many succumbed in those initial attacks. Only then did we know Sharo's fear.

"Even before the war, we had never numbered many. The Mothertrees often went decades between Seedings. The loss of a single Iritu rippled throughout our society. That we could lose hundreds to mortals seemed an impossibility. But they came with mighty titans leashed and in overwhelming numbers. Soon, it became apparent even to the most stubborn among us we were losing this war.

"Only when they discovered the Mothertrees did we truly despair. One by one, they located them and burned them down. We threw away our lives toward protecting our creators, but it was never enough.

"My Mothertree was one of the last to fall. Sharo had been absent for much of the war, but for Her defense, he returned. The battle went as poorly as the others had. Soon, we began to fail.

"I was determined to die there, to never see the fall of the Iritu, and I threw myself into the thick of the fighting. But though distance had grown between us, Sharo never left my side. He protected me the same as he had when we were young and flew free. I couldn't seem to die.

"Yet neither could we save Her, our *Ialadta*, nor the others. When our Mothertree burned, Sharo dragged me away from the battle. 'We will make them bleed,' he told me. And so I began to live for vengeance.

"The rest you already know. I won't recount those shames

again. But whereas I grew weary of killing, Sharo only seemed to need more.

"'They're ants,' he told me once. 'Their lives, their suffering, their deaths—all meaningless.' And when I asked him what satisfaction he took in torturing ants, he smiled. 'To see if any still bite.'

"So he remains: callous to killing, consumed by hatred. And yet who he is to me is the same. We were one, him and I, once. The only two blossoms on our branch."

57

UNTIL THE LAST

$\mathcal{A}$s Ata fell silent, a hush spread across the grotto.

Leiyn drew in a deep breath. She felt light-headed, like she had not breathed the entire time the dryvan spoke. All she had learned crammed inside her skull, clamoring for attention. She could not decide where to start.

One question rose to the top. The one she least wished to say.

You followed Man'nah?

Isla was the first to break the silence. "Thank you for telling us, Ata. We will guard your secrets as if they were our own."

The dryvan turned toward Isla. A smirk stretched across her face, but there seemed little humor in it. "Your loyalty is appreciated, Isla Treeleg."

Isla blinked, the epithet catching her wrong-footed.

Leiyn finally found her voice. "I think I understand. And we needed to know this. But for now, we have to set it aside. We have more immediate concerns."

"Ekosa," Ketti murmured.

Leiyn nodded. "He risked his place in the Coterie to help us. Perhaps his life. We cannot let them hurt him."

She grimaced, knowing what else she must say. But she had never been one to back down from a hard thing.

"We have to return for him," she finished.

"Rescue him." Batu crossed his arms. "And it must be now." Neither his expression nor tone betrayed what he thought of the suggestion.

"Of course we must." Isla placed a hand on Batu's shoulder. "It's not unlike what you did for us, is it?"

Few could remain firm before Isla's gentleness. Leiyn knew she could not. Batu proved equally malleable as he cast his beloved a small smile.

Ata's grin faded as her mismatched eyes moved to each of them. "This man—he will assist us?"

"I don't know," Leiyn admitted. "This isn't his fight. But we still owe him a debt."

The dryvan stared at her before bowing her head. After the oath she had given, Leiyn knew she understood the depth of debts.

"We must return for more than him." Batu touched a hand to his empty belt. "Our weapons and mounts remain in their custody."

Leiyn was glad she bore the weight of her falchions and the Iritu arrows. She hoped her longbow had not been damaged following the fight. Along with Tadeo's figurine, the ranger's seal, and her cloak, it was one of the last remaining items she had from the Wilds Lodge.

"We'll retrieve them as well," she said. "But then we must return to Southport. We've delayed too long as it is."

Ata drew herself up taller. Her body creaked like a branch moving in the wind. "When that time comes, I may be of assistance."

Leiyn suspected what she intended. The dryvan's use of grottos differed from Etemans, theirs twisting both time and distance. Remembering how disorienting her experiences with them had been, she little looked forward to it.

Focus. Plenty to handle now.

She staggered to her feet. Blood rushed to her head, and her vision fizzled to white. Isla and Batu gripped her arms, though, and after a moment, her sight returned.

"I'm alright." With a queasy smile, Leiyn freed herself from her friends and looked at the last two members of their party. Both Ata and Ketti watched her: the dryvan with her head cocked as if intrigued by the moment of weakness; the Eteman with a worried frown.

Leiyn thrust her doubts from her mind. There was no time to delay.

"Ata, can you return us to the tower? To the top," she added, thinking of the many flights of stairs. "Where the Wings are likely to be."

With a coy smile, Ata nodded.

"Wait." Isla turned to Ketti. "I think you should stay behind."

The Eteman blinked at her before bowing her head. "Perhaps you are right."

Leiyn frowned, not liking to split their party, but she found it hard to disagree. Ketti might prove a distraction for the conversation to come with the Wings. And if she came with, would it provoke Khamo to return? Did he still watch the Coterie Tower, unseen, biding his time?

"Look to Biqqa." Ketti gestured to her hummingbird, who had taken to the air around her head. "She will guide you back."

No sooner had Leiyn nodded than Ata's esse flared outward. Though dimmed, it had regained much of its former vigor.

"If that is decided," the Iritu said drily, "shall we proceed? I advise that you keep your feet under you."

Barely had she finished speaking before the world lurched away.

As stone sprang up around them, Leiyn's tenuous balance gave way, pitching her to the floor. She caught herself as her senses reoriented to the natural world.

"*Orisa rami lowo!* You are alive! But how have you...?"

She looked up. Dawn peeked over the ocean, bathing the chamber in orange light and backlighting the Wings, who stood before their chairs. Their lifefires danced about, showing their alarm and readiness to defend themselves. Leiyn struggled to her feet, her companions doing the same. Only Ata remained upright, the transition scarcely affecting her.

Once she was standing, Leiyn raised her empty hands. "We won't harm you, Highest Ones. We came to talk."

"To talk! After you fight an Iritu in our tower and nearly get us all killed? Then bring another of their kind into our midst?" Samu barked a humorless laugh. "What have I done for *Okulukulu* to so mock me?"

Onah held up a hand, silencing her counterpart. Her dark eyes flicked between their companions. "What is it you seek, with an Iritu among you?"

"You need not worry about me. I'm sworn to assist." Ata cast the Wings a droll smile. Leiyn wondered if she was the only one to see through the brittle fey facade.

Casting the dryvan a warning look, Leiyn faced forward. "Has the other Iritu returned? The one we fought?"

Onah pursed her lips. "No."

"Not yet," her fellow Wing added.

"All the more reason to hurry. Highest Onah, Highest Samu, we must leave for Southport. We've been away too long, and this attack changes everything."

Isla stepped forward. "We would be grateful if you returned our equipment and horses to us. And I must beg for the *Kekére's* aid once more. Name your price, and I will do all in my power to meet it."

The Wings looked at each other, silent communication passing between them. By her lifesense, Leiyn felt their esses drift out and intertwine. She wondered what they exchanged. Ideas? Thoughts? Words?

Several long moments passed before their eyes returned to their party. Even the oft-cheerful Samu was inscrutable as he stared at them.

"In such troubling times, it is unwise to act with haste," the Wing of Stars said. "I regret we must—"

"Enough."

A single, disdainful word from the dryvan was enough to

silence the Ofean leader. Ata ambled forward, her lips pulled back to bare her sharp teeth.

"You wish to cower in your tower, hoping this war won't find you. *It already has.* Your enemy is not other humans and their empires. It is my kind, the Iritu—those few who remain. They who have forgotten all but what they should have forgiven."

She began a slow stroll around the Wings. Samu and Onah turned with her. With their feathered garments, they resembled a pair of hens stalked by a coyote.

"Your tower won't protect you," the skin-walker continued. "Your magic won't protect you. Nothing can. Had I not been here, had my companions not, could you have stopped him? Or would he have torn you apart, one by one?"

Ata completed a revolution and reversed direction. As she circled them, she drew closer, driving them back so their legs bumped against their chairs. Leiyn heard the smile in her voice as she continued.

"We are not a threat you can ignore. The one who leads the Iritu won't stop until every mortal with an Eteman's talents is slain or enslaved. *Every. Last. One.*"

Her final words came out in a growl that made Samu shudder and lean away and Onah stare wide-eyed at the dryvan. Leiyn glanced at Isla, wondering if they should intervene, but her fellow ranger only watched with eyebrows raised.

After a tense silence, the Wing of Stars spoke, his voice gathering a slight warble. "May the Goddess forgive us, Great Iritu. I understand your position. But there is much to consider. To make such weighty decisions without pondering our position—"

"Our agreement need not violate your trust with the Empire," Isla interjected. "I ask only that you provide training to our mahas. Teach them magic. Help Baltesia defend itself. That will be enough."

"Even that may be too much." Onah's eyes did not leave the dryvan as she spoke. "Assisting you may be considered an alliance."

"Or a check on Ilberian overreach," Isla countered. "Please,

Highest One. You have seen what we face. We cannot delay now at this critical juncture."

A hush fell. Leiyn shifted, barely reining in her impatience. Khamo might reappear at any moment and they still did not know what fate had befallen Ekosa. While the others spoke, she had been seeking after his esse, yet could find no trace of it.

Hidden within the pillar? Or already dead?

"Very well." Onah finally tore her eyes from Ata to glance at her fellow Wing. "I would comply with their request."

"But Highest Onah..." Samu broke into Eyin, urgency pushing his words together.

"The war has already found us," Onah responded in Ilberian. "They are correct. To fail to act would be a choice as well. One I do not wish to make." Onah raised her gaze to Isla, then shifted to Leiyn. "It is not only Baltesia we assist, but you. To fight these enemy Iritu."

Ata turned and ambled away. Already, she appeared bored with the proceedings. But Leiyn sensed the ripple through her lifeforce. No matter the strong front she put on, under the surface, she was barely holding together.

"Sky's blessing upon you both, Highest Ones." Isla bowed with arms crossed. "Baltesia is indebted to you."

"I would discuss that debt further. But another day, perhaps."

Though Isla's posture remained demure, her words were firm as she spoke again. "And when should we expect this aid to arrive?"

Onah's expression soured. "By the end of autumn," she relented, "five *eesuwé* shall arrive at Southport to instruct your Order. Provided Baltesia has cleared a path through by then, with both river and sea captured."

"I am sure we will. I thank you again, Highest Ones."

Leiyn could restrain herself no longer. "One more thing. Ekosa. What have you done with him?"

Onah's eyes narrowed, while Samu sighed. "Ah, young

Ekosa. I do not know what you said to him to make him act so... rash."

She hid a grimace. "He was doing what was right. Did you kill him for it?"

"Leiyn!" Isla hissed, grabbing for her arm, but Leiyn stepped away. Batu hovered nearby as if also ready to seize her. She ignored him as well.

"Kill him?" Onah shook her head and muttered something in Eyin.

"Of course we have not executed him," Samu clarified. "He is being confined while we decide the best way to deal with such behavior."

"So you're keeping him in the central pillar." Leiyn's gaze fell to the floor, finding the place where the pillar ended at the level below. She could rescue him now that she knew the secret of the hidden doors. But it might require battling *eesuwé* along the way and violating the agreement they had endured all this to make.

Isla managed to seize her arm and tightly gripped it. "I understand that High Ekosa acted in a manner unbefitting your Coterie. But he helped us in a time of duress. Perhaps there might be room for leniency?"

"Leniency." Onah dropped the word with all the weight of a stone. "Tell me, Envoy Isla, if you would be lenient to a traitor?"

"Ekosa isn't a traitor." Leiyn took a step toward the Wings but was yanked back by Isla.

Ata was not so restrained. The dryvan, drawn back in by Leiyn's ire, approached the Ofean leaders, no trace of a smile on her parted mouth now.

"I have a proposal." Isla's eyes flickered to Ata as the words spilled forth. "Perhaps Ekosa could accompany us as the first tutor to our Order of Mahia. You may determine any necessary punishment in the meantime. Would this be amenable?"

Samu watched the dryvan, full of fear. Both Wings prepared their mahia. After seeing Khamo wreak havoc upon their tower, they had to know it would be of little use against one of the Iritu.

Ata was several paces short when Onah spoke. "Very well, take him. But he will not represent the *Kekére* as an *eesu*, and he may never return to this tower, nor any place in Ore-Ofe."

Exile. Leiyn felt the gut-blow as if it were her own. All too easily could she imagine being banished from the Wilds Lodge. She had spent long nights awake, worrying that she had failed to hide her mahia. Fearing she would be turned away and never again see the place that had become home.

That nightmare was now Ekosa's reality.

Did I do this? Did I force their hand?

Ata, satisfied by the answer, drifted back to the peripheries of the room. Isla seemed to understand what this meant judging by her tightened grip on Leiyn's arm, yet her tone remained measured.

"Very well. If Ekosa accepts, so will we."

"Fine, fine." Samu collapsed in his chair and pressed a hand to his head. "Goddess shelter me, this is not the day I expected."

Nor I, Leiyn mused.

⁓ ⁓

Afternoon was coming on as their agreement was carried out. The Wings of the Coterie did not seem to want them to linger any more than they did, and they deployed their ample resources to send them swiftly on their way. Within hours, their company stood outside the tower, horses saddled and laden with bags rescued from their burning room, weapons strapped back on their persons.

While they made ready to leave, Ekosa was brought out, escorted by a pair of tower guards. The *eesu* carried a small bag, but otherwise appeared unharmed and as he had been before. Only his expression had changed. Lines furrowed his brow, and veins shot through his eyes. She wondered if he had been weeping.

A dozen paces short, the guards stopped, leaving Ekosa to

amble forth. Dragging Feral's reins, she stepped forward to greet him.

"Ekosa." Leiyn grasped for more words, but none seemed sufficient.

"I heard what you did." The young man dipped his head and pressed his free arm to his chest in an approximation of an Ofean bow. "I am grateful you thought to spare me."

"Of course. After what you did for us, I had to do something. But Ekosa, I'm—"

"Please. Do not." The fragility in his voice silenced her more quickly than any anger could have. "We must hurry, no? Then let us leave."

He walked past her to stop near Isla and Batu. Leiyn tried to harden herself to guilt as she watched.

Later. Look ahead for now.

Biqqa appeared from thin air to flit about her head. Opening her hand, she was pleased when the hummingbird settled on a finger. At least the spirit beast welcomed her company.

"Can you lead us back to Ketti?" she murmured to it.

The twitchy creature fluttered her wings and cocked her head. A response? How could she know?

"You'll need me for that."

She glanced up to see Ata sauntering closer. Holding out a hand, the dryvan waited for Leiyn to move the hummingbird over to rest on one extended talon. Esse pulsed from the tiny green creature as it complied. The skin-walker smiled.

"Are we ready?"

Leiyn had barely gathered assent from the others before the world once more tipped beneath her feet. This time, she kept upright. Feral was not so fortunate. Neighing, the mare fought to rise back to her hooves, nearly pulling Leiyn to the ground as she did.

"Serves you right," she muttered as the horse panted with frustration.

"You are safe." Ketti rushed over to them, pearls winking in the afternoon light. Her eyes scanned their party, catching on

Ata before resting on Ekosa. "And you are High Ekosa, I believe."

"Ketti Ta'Rul." The young man stared, seeming dazzled at the sight of her, his malaise momentarily banished. Then he blinked and bowed in his people's fashion. "The Goddess blesses me to meet you."

The Eteman looked as if she could not decide between being amused and flattered as she nodded back.

"We cannot delay." Ata strode into their midst. "Khamo's attack signals an acceleration in Sharo's plans. Your city may soon fall. We must travel swiftly."

Leiyn saw questions dance in Ekosa's eyes, but he kept his lips pressed tightly together. She had her share of things she wondered about. Foremost was what exactly Sharo had been thinking to send one of his lackeys to brazenly assault the Coterie Tower. It had been the impetus that pushed the Wings into assisting them. Without it, she doubted they would have understood the severity of the threats facing the Tricolonies. Surely, one as cunning as the lyshan would know that.

Does he want Ore-Ofe to assist us? But why?

There was no time to wonder. If the Saints were good to them this day, she could mull over it later. But if she understood what Ata had in mind, they would have to be merciful indeed.

"Travel swiftly?" Leiyn pressed.

Ata smiled; her eyes laughed. "I will keep you together. At least, I will try. Are you prepared?"

Leiyn's mouth had gone dry. She caught each of her companions' gazes and saw comprehension dawning on them as well. Only Ketti blanched. She, most of all, understood what this meant.

Barely did Leiyn feel whole after the events from the sleepless night before. Yet she tensed her jaw and faced the dryvan. "We're ready."

Ata's laugh was the last thing she heard before a torrent ripped them away.

PART VI

NO SAFE HARBOR

58

ADRIFT

*T*he seas weep, red and black...

Sea. It was all around her, *in* her. She spun in a current, tossed from wave to wave. The water was dark, lightless. The pressure against her eyes cast the world in scarlet.

The sky shatters, storm and sorrow...

Words hummed through the churning, disembodied and faint. Were they only in her head? Saltwater filled her ears, tinged her tongue. The only other sounds were the discontented sighs of the ocean.

'Ware, comes the Wither...

A wave crushed her chest, reminding her of her need for air. Her lungs burned. It was all she could do not to inhale water.

Swim, Firebrand!

Her voice. One to heed. She moved her limbs, fighting against the swell. Which way was up? Darkness spread in every direction, no hint of light penetrating from a faraway surface.

She struck out, hoping she was right, knowing the price if she was wrong. Panic endeavored to make her freeze. Unable to breathe through it, she struggled to keep it at bay.

SWIM, damn you!

The current shifted, strengthened. Against her weakening

strokes, she was swept backward. She did not give up, did not stop swimming.

Her mouth parted, and a stream of water poured down her throat.

Then there was light all around, blindingly bright. The water pulled her free and threw her into the air. For a moment, she hung in it, suspended.

Then she crashed to the ground.

Leiyn gasped, trying to breathe in blessed air, but coughed instead, water rising from her lungs. When the fit passed, she lay on the ground, exhausted. With hazy vision, she noticed a golden shore leading away from her into unbroken blue. Grains of sand stuck to her cheek and coated her face. Heat bathed her cold back.

Her body ached and her limbs had gone limp. But she was alive.

"The final part—speak it again. Leave out no word."

That voice. That damned voice. She knew it. Had often heard it in her dreams. Though they had only spoken twice, she could never forget it.

Sharo was here.

Terror and rage spurred strength back into her muscles, enough to push herself upright. Her vision remained blurred as she stared down the shore. There, the pair of figures were silhouetted by directionless light. One was seated in a vast ornate chair at odds with their surroundings. The other circled the first like a predator. That was Sharo, if she knew the lyshan at all.

"Very well," a feminine voice said. *"'The undying rise for the final feast. The Titans awaken from the depths. For any to survive, all must be sacrificed. Life begins—'"*

"'—with death.' So you have said, so you have said. But do you understand what it means?"

"Do any understand those who have glimpsed Omn?"

Her legs felt as strong as leaves of grass, but Leiyn forced herself onto them. Wavering, she stood, then took a halting step forward.

"I understand. Would you like to? To know your tomorrow?"

"I serve the Undying."

She felt so weak, but she could not turn back. Here was Sharo, her enemy, revealed at last. She had to kill him, here and now.

Even if she died trying.

Sharo's laugh cut across the sand. *"'All must be sacrificed,' Ayda, my loyal servant. All. With death, we bring life."*

"The Saints bless our mission."

"As you say, as you say."

Leiyn had crossed half the distance, but each step stole more from her than the one before. Faltering, she sank to a knee, only to rise again and stumble forward another stride.

"This... Wither," Sharo continued. *"Long has it fallen. First, it claimed my people. Now it will claim yours."*

"For a greater purpose."

She fell to her knees, then raised her head. Now that Leiyn looked again, Sharo and the seated woman seemed farther away than before. Despair threatened to rob the last of her strength.

Not yet. Not until he's dead.

Leiyn clambered back to her feet.

"Yes. Far greater." The lyshan's voice slithered through her ears. *"One beyond your comprehension. Mortal minds have ever been small. You believe yourself preserved, do you not? Protected by some higher power?"*

"Omn works through me, as It works through you."

"Of course 'It' does." His words had a singsong, mocking lilt. *"But that will not keep you from harm. None are safe. Any may die at any moment."*

"Except you, Deathless One."

A laugh broke free of him, only to cut short. Leiyn stood, swaying, as Sharo faced her. Though he remained silhouetted, his eyes blazed with a sudden fiery light.

"There you are, Oldsoul. Come for me at last."

Leiyn bared her teeth, a wordless snarl rising in her throat.

She was weak, so weak. Her legs threatened to buckle. She made to advance all the same.

Something grabbed her arm.

She struggled to win free as she tried to see her attacker. They blazed as if aflame. The hand wrapped around her arm seared into her. Nails dug into her flesh.

"*NO!*" she tried to roar, but she was already being swept off her feet. A blinding light filled her eyes, her chest, her head.

Sharo's laugh followed her into the drowning light.

59

DELUGE

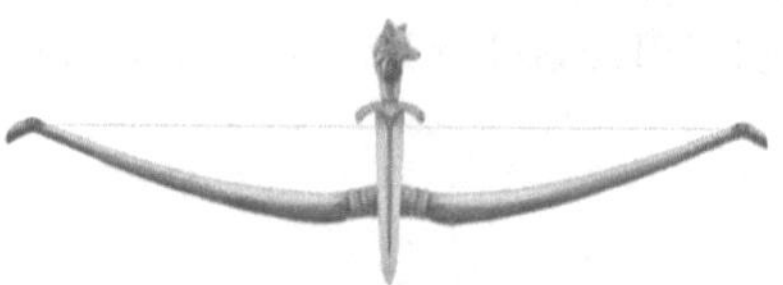

A wave swept away the light, leaving behind cold darkness. Leiyn opened her eyes to the sting of salt. *Saltwater. Ocean.*

Lungs straining, she paddled upward. She had a vague notion she had just done this, but now, she saw muted light above. Her body obeyed her sluggishly, sapped of strength. Yet slowly, she rose.

She broke the surface and sucked in a ragged breath. A poorly timed entrance—a wave washed over her so she breathed in as much water as air. Choking and spluttering, Leiyn snuck in a breath before the next wave toppled over her.

Blinking to clear her eyes, she treaded water and took in her surroundings. All seemed a hazy confusion of esse to her life-sense as it threaded through her surroundings. Her eyes were clearer. Before her spread a shoreline rife with civilization. Docks thrust out over the water. Behind them, weathered build-ings defied an overcast sky. They had a familiar design, one distinctly Baltesian.

Only one city in her homeland had such an extensive harbor. Ata had done it. She had flung them across the Veiled Lands.

All the way to Southport.

Her mind scrambled to understand how it was possible as more water washed over her. The wave brought more immediate concerns to the fore. Her lifesense resolving into stark clarity, Leiyn jerked around to stare up in horror behind her.

Hundreds of feet high and thrice as many away, a kraken towered over the bay.

"Fesht!"

She threw herself toward the shore. Only then did she recognize the swell bringing her back toward the monstrous creature. Against a titan's power, she stood little chance of making it. But what other choice did she have?

Her only saving grace was that the titan paid her no heed. Swaying where it rose, its bulbous body and tentacles were formed of surging, foaming water. Despite the violence of its formation, it seemed content to remain in place. She knew better than to rely on its complacency, though.

Its presence alone was a danger. The ocean alone had enough power to drown a woman; with a titan added in, it became deadly and unpredictable. Waves poured off its body to pound against her head, yet underneath the surface, an irresistible current sucked her toward it. With every stroke, Leiyn felt herself being drawn back toward its core.

Don't think. Don't worry. Just swim, *Firebrand!*

She was not stranded alone. Five others treaded water around her, all being drawn into the kraken. One lifefire sputtered as the riptide sucked them beneath the surface.

Drowning.

It was death to swim toward the titan. Leiyn did it all the same, heading for her endangered companion. Ketti—she was the one flailing and sinking into the ocean. Potent as her mahia was, it could not keep her afloat.

Wheezing, Leiyn thrust against the water. Waves crashed into her, blinding and choking, but the undercurrent swept her on. In moments, Ketti was before her, now entirely underwater.

Leiyn sucked in a watery breath, then grabbed her under the arms and heaved her upward.

The Eteman came up spluttering. Her limbs lashed out, nearly knocking into Leiyn's head.

"Stop!" Leiyn tried to bellow, but seawater splashed into her mouth as she spoke. She pressed her intentions toward the woman with her mahia, then added in a choked voice, "Kick with your feet!"

Either her words or magic instilled the message. Ketti sagged against her chest for a moment, then feebly began kicking. Her foot caught against Leiyn twice before she shifted out of the way.

With the first crisis alleviated, Leiyn twisted around to stare up at the titan. They had already crossed half the distance toward it, and as they neared, their speed only increased.

"We have to swim!" she shouted in Ketti's ear. "Move in my direction!"

She knew it was hopeless before they tried. The Eteman did not know how to swim—that much was obvious in the way she thrashed about. Having lived all her life in Solace, Leiyn doubted there had been any opportunity or need. Now, her inexperience was likely to get them killed.

Her mahia might have expanded their odds, but it remained inconstant. Like her lifesense, it suffered from their erratic journey and the titan's presence. Though she tried pushing strength into her muscles, the best she could achieve was a trickle.

Desperately, she quested after her companions. Batu had gotten ahold of Ekosa; they appeared to be faring better than her and Ketti. Isla swam on her own but seemed to be treading water. And Ata...

Ata was transforming.

The dryvan's esse writhed as it reordered itself. Her body, always malleable, took on a different shape. Some parts retracted. Others grew.

In moments, Ata was shooting through the water, moving as fast as any fish. Coming for them.

Hope surged in Leiyn's chest. She kicked her leaden legs

with renewed vigor, trying to move toward the Iritu. Ata was a flash of silver among the dark gray waves. Turning around next to them, Leiyn glimpsed a fin before something snagged her arm and jerked her forward. It was all she could do to keep her grip on Ketti as they were dragged through the water and away from the titan.

They did not move as swiftly as Ata had coming toward them, but it was enough to overcome the undercurrent. Relief washed through Leiyn as the dryvan angled her trajectory toward the other three bobbing in the water. As Ata seized them, she glimpsed one of the dryvan's limbs: a sinuous root, slimy with seaweed, but tough and implacable.

With each additional burden, their pace slowed until it came almost to a standstill. Leiyn kicked, trying to help move them forward. Between the waves, she instructed Ketti to do the same. Ata's esse, always so bright before, was rapidly dimming. At this rate, they would never make it.

"Help her!" Leiyn spluttered, then sent esse traveling up through the root that held her.

It was a paltry offering, her stores already depleted, yet Ata seemed to respond to it, moving forward with a fraction more vigor. Ketti sent more lifeforce traveling through Leiyn, and she pushed it along to the dryvan. Ekosa, sensing what they did, also made contributions.

Ata's lifefire surged; their momentum increased. Through spotty vision, Leiyn saw anchored ships towering over them, straining at their ropes, and the docks nearing. Relief remained far away; she had to continue to channel lifeforce into the dryvan even as she felt near the end of her own. But with each stroke away from the titan, the undercurrent grew weaker, and their speed increased.

A hundred paces out, Leiyn could maintain it no longer. Focus faltering, she concentrated on keeping her hold on Ketti. The Eteman sent a fresh surge of esse into her, perhaps sensing Leiyn's weakness. Tasting the panic lacing it, she tightened her grip.

A dock rose above them. As Ata reached for the pillars, Leiyn glimpsed more of the changes wrought upon her body. Webbing had grown between her elongated talons. A fin had sprouted from the vines atop her head. Her eyes, too, had changed, pupils dilating and orbs thrusting out like a fish.

Clinging to the dock seemed as much as the dryvan could do. Summoning the last of her resolve, Leiyn thrust Ketti toward the closest pillar, then kicked them toward it. Only once the Eteman had grabbed ahold did she release her and seek a perch. The beams were too slimy to climb, but they provided enough support to keep her from drowning.

For several moments, they clung to the dock and caught their breaths. With their lives out of immediate peril, Leiyn spared a mournful thought for their horses. Their gear had been lost with the mounts, her longbow included. Later, she would ask Ata what had happened to the beasts.

But they had to survive first.

"Ata," Leiyn called over the crash of the surf. "Can you reach the pier?"

The dryvan raised her head and met her gaze. Even that seemed to tax her. Ata's lifeforce burned nearly as low as when she had lain dying. Yet she obliged, the long roots that had grabbed them slithering up to wrap around the top of the posts. Seaweed sloughed off them like a bird molting its feathers.

"Up!" Leiyn shouted at the others.

They scarcely needed coaxing. Ekosa went first, then Isla. Batu helped each of them along before ascending himself. Leiyn did the same for Ketti, giving her a supporting hand until the Eteman wrapped her legs around the thick root and began shimmying up it. Once she reached the lip of the dock, Leiyn followed. Dragging her body skyward felt as difficult as any trial she had undergone at the Lodge. Her limbs threatened to give way with every tug.

But rarely had she let a physical challenge best her. It seemed by stubbornness alone that Leiyn reached the top of the pier, where her comrades helped drag her onto it. She sagged onto the boards, spent, while the others turned back for Ata. The dryvan, however, had enough energy to leverage herself onto the deck before she splayed out across the planks.

Leiyn's eyes caught at the sight of her again, silver-scaled and finned, before her lifesense alerted her to turn away. Hurrying up the pier were a dozen soldiers wearing tabards of Baltesian blue. Half carried pikes, which they lowered as they stopped a dozen feet back.

One man, stout and with thin dark hair oiled back against his skull, stepped between them, staring down with undisguised suspicion. His air of authority denoted him as a captain even if she had not seen the patch stitched into his uniform's chest.

"Who are you?" he barked. "How did you come to be here? Don't move!" he added as Batu started rising. "Answer me!"

Leiyn was still scrambling for an explanation when Batu answered. "Captain Tomas, it's me, Batu Khatas."

"Batu?" The captain narrowed his eyes. "The former plain-srider? Legion take me for a fool if I believe that."

"It's him, Captain," one soldier said. "Don't know how, but it is."

The captain rounded on the young man who had spoken. "Are you certain, soldier? Don't give me half-measures!"

The soldier grimaced, but he did not back down. "That's him, alright. Trained next to him for weeks, didn't I?"

The captain's glare did not lessen as he turned back to examine them.

Isla spoke up then. "Your soldier speaks true, Captain Tomas. I'm Isla Ogbi, named an emissary of our country by Lord Mauricio. And I'm sure you've heard of Leiyn Tideraiser."

Leiyn scarcely had the wherewithal to cast her a look. The shadow of a smile passed over Isla's lips.

"Tideraiser? Her?" Tomas seemed even more skeptical at this. "What in Legion's hells is going on here? And what kind of devil is *that*?"

She did not have to look to know where the captain pointed. Knowing there would be no simple explanation for Ata, Leiyn stumbled to her feet. The pikes bristled at her movement, but none attacked. She mustered every scrap of authority left to her.

"Captain Tomas, I know this looks strange. But there's no time for this." Leiyn pointed at the kraken, still looming over the bay. "Southport's under attack. And it looks like you could use our help. Or don't you remember what I did with the kraken last time?"

Doubt flickered across the captain's gaze. She waited, knowing he had to weigh the evidence of their identities against the oddness of their appearance. Yet it was with admirable decisiveness that he gestured for his soldiers to stand down. The pikes raised to point at the sky.

"If you can command the titan away," Tomas instructed, "do it. Until it's gone, we stay on this dock."

Leiyn nodded and turned away, trusting they would not strike her in the back. Soul-deep weariness left room for only one concern.

Escaping the kraken's tide made it no less intimidating to face. Eight watery limbs rose from its towering body. A strike from any could kill them as easily as it had once crushed Lord Conqueror Armando Pótecil and his ship at her command. The saltwater that made up its form moved with dizzying speed. Had she and her companions been sucked into it, the pressure alone looked sufficient to have slain them.

But the true danger lay behind the titan. Leiyn sensed them, the pinpricks of light betraying the odiosas who commanded the titan. There were four of them, all on the same ship, working in tandem to assert their authority.

Perhaps four would not have been necessary but for those standing against them. From various places within the city, high in watchtowers and balconies, four Gazian wisdoms pitted their wills against the odiosas. Thus far, they appeared locked in a standstill, neither side giving way.

This was no accidental deadlock. Leiyn sensed dozens more odiosas scattered throughout the Armada. If it suited them, they could join in at any moment to press the kraken into the city. Thus far, they had refrained.

They're wearing them down. Whittling away our defenses.

Leiyn firmed her jaw. If that was the Ilberians' intention, it was working. The wisdoms felt nearly as drained as her and her party. Even if they held against this invasion, it was unlikely they would withstand another.

She felt as thin as paper and as likely to tear, but she had taken an oath to earn her ranger's cloak seven years before. That did not end with the Wilds Lodge burning. Only death would release her from it.

Perceive. Preserve. Protect.

Leiyn quested forth with her mahia, searching for her opening. One more person trying to control the titan would not make much of a difference, not with her presently paltry strength. More likely to yield results was a direct attack. She firmed her will and reached farther. The odiosas were leagues out to sea, but she had attacked Patli at a similar distance. Commanding a titan left mahas vulnerable. Perhaps she could strike a killing blow, even now.

But her magic fell short. She could not reach them, much less harm them. After attempting to push farther, Leiyn let her mahia lapse and bent over, panting. Her esse felt stretched to the point of tearing. Could it suffer injury as her body could? Wounds that would not heal?

She scarcely noticed her companions until they stepped up beside her. Jerking back upright, Leiyn stared at them and tried to hide her surprise. She had expected Batu and Isla, but instead Ketti and Ekosa stood there. They looked as tired as she, their arms wrapped around their shivering bodies, but determination shone in their eyes. She recognized it, having often felt that same need. To prove her worth.

"Let us help," Ketti said. "Together, we can reach them."

Leiyn stared at her. Though her words remained vague, the warble in her voice told all. Ketti knew what Leiyn meant to attempt. Knew the violence she would enable.

"Please, Prima Leiyn," Ekosa said on her other side. "Allow us to assist you."

She hesitated a moment longer, then nodded. They understood and accepted what they did. They could make their own decisions. And it was not like she had any other option.

"Alright. When you're ready."

Ketti set her hands on Leiyn's right arm. Ekosa followed suit a breath after on her left. Burning esse shot into Leiyn. She gasped as her lifefire burned higher and higher. Almost, she felt renewed. Yet the strain of all they had endured still permeated her person.

No weakness. Not now.

Gathering every scrap of her willpower, Leiyn drove her mahia forward. It soared swift and sure as an arrow from her bow. She crossed the leagues, moving past the blazing titan, as she aimed for the four bright stars sitting atop the shimmering ocean.

She did not slow as she crashed into the first.

The odiosa staggered beneath the attack. Though he and his fellows had flinched at her approach, each ceding enough control of the kraken to ready a paltry defense, it was not enough. Leiyn blew past the half-formed walls, tunneling into her enemy's esse and tearing into it with the savagery of a snow ape. Dark threads coursed through the odiosa's soul under her attacks. She did not have to look long to know it would be a fatal blow.

Leiyn moved to attack the second, then faltered. At first, she thought she had reached the end of her strength. Then she noticed one of her sources of lifeforce had lapsed; Ketti had drawn back. Only a heartbeat later, her hands were back on Leiyn's arm, her magic bolstering Leiyn's flagging strength once more.

Homing back in on her quarry, Leiyn saw the damage was already done. The odiosas had walled themselves off too stoutly for her to break. But to do so, they had been forced to release their hold on the titan.

That was all she had needed.

Leiyn let her mahia lapse and gazed upon the titan. The wisdoms were pushing it back, sending it surging toward the Ilberian Armada. But though the three odiosas commanding it remained walled off, others opened themselves to surge against it. Leiyn flirted with the idea of another attack but dismissed it as the kraken sank back into the ocean. The assault was over.

For now.

Carefully, she moved her arms free of Ketti and Ekosa's grasps. As the flow of esse ceased, fatigue spread through her.

The world went dark.

When it cleared, Leiyn discovered she was on her knees, head cradled in her hands. Distantly, she heard shouts from her companions. She pried her hands away and felt around her. Even that was almost beyond her.

She never saw the wave that knocked her flat.

Coughing and wheezing, Leiyn lay against the dock as water flushed over her. The final farewell from the kraken, she had to presume. Even as it dripped away, she remained on the sodden planks. She imagined staying there forever, never mustering the effort to rise. A pleasanter thought than expected.

Sleep. Must sleep.

"Saints! Leiyn, are you alright?"

Isla. Her friend touched her shoulder and brushed a hand across her forehead. Comforting and warm when she felt so cold. Leiyn cracked open her eyes to look up at her.

"Never better," she croaked.

A beat passed before her fellow ranger sighed. "If you can joke, you can stand. Come on. Before you embarrass yourself more."

The last thing she wanted was to rise, but like most people, she had never been able to refuse Isla. Groaning and cursing, Leiyn let her friend wrap her arms around her and got back to her feet to face the soldiers. The wave had knocked them out of line and bedraggled their armor and tabards, but under their captain's gaze, discipline quickly reasserted itself.

"Tideraiser. Envoy. Soldier." Tomas addressed each of them as his eyes flitted over the other three. "I assume you had something to do with this occurrence."

"Yes. As did our companions," Isla offered, gesturing to Ketti and Ekosa. "And please, do not fear the dryvan. She is our ally."

"Dryvan." The captain's face was stony, but he could not hide the shudder through his esse. "They're real, then?"

"Oh, I should say so."

Leiyn twisted around to see Ata rising to her feet—or flippers, rather. The shapeshifter's aquatic transformation had robbed her of her usual grace, or perhaps that was due to sheer exhaustion. Her shoulders, scaly as well as feathery, were bowed, and she did not seem able to stand straight. But the brightness in her eyes was enough to reassure Leiyn that her long-lived friend was far from dead.

Ata speaking seemed to further unsettle Tomas rather than reassure him. Muscles twitched on his face as he stared at her.

"Captain," Isla said, tone gentle, "perhaps you could escort us to the Lord Governor's villa. We will clear up any uncertainties with him and the Lord Conqueror."

The captain hesitated, then gave a jerky nod, seeming relieved to follow orders. "Form up around them," he commanded his men. "To the governor's villa, as the envoy said."

Leiyn stifled a sigh and, with Isla's help, shambled down the pier after them.

60

BEFORE THE BREAK

Southport had suffered in their absence.

There were signs of it everywhere Leiyn looked as she shuffled next to her companions toward the governor's villa. Docks, splintered and torn down to their pilings, as if decades had passed rather than weeks. Houses with roofs and walls caved in as if by strikes from titan-sized fists. The presence of soldiers and the absence of civilians. She wondered how many times the kraken had risen since they had left. How many had died in the invasions.

Fewer than you'll save, she reminded herself, *once you form that damned grotto.*

The docks were not far from the villa. As they turned a final corner, the white walls of the compound rose above the street, the wrought-iron gate midway through. Too far, it seemed. Leiyn had long stopped trying to hide her shivers. She curled her arms about her middle, trying to hold in what little heat remained in her. The constant breeze off the sea and the overcast sky conspired to turn her drenched state into misery. Ordinarily, she would have warmed herself with esse, but with her mahia overtaxed, she could not muster the effort. Her companions fared little better—even Ata, who trailed the rest in an unsteady lope.

Captain Tomas escorted them through the gates and up to the villa doors. There, he left them with the guards as he and his company returned to their patrols along the shoreline. The guards stared at Ata, vacillating between apprehension and fascination, until the dryvan gave them a smile fit for a shark. At another time, Leiyn would have found their fear amusing, but she had no doubt the dryvan was the reason they were left to wait in the rain. Leiyn shook her head and huddled under the sparse shelter outside the doors, trying not to look as miserable as she felt.

It was not long before the mayordomo came breezing through the manor doors. His only sign of distress from the recent siege was a slight tilting of his white wig; otherwise, Dinis Sorje remained as pristine and collected as ever as he took in their strange company. He could not hide a startle, though, as his gaze touched on Ata. His eyes soon darted back to Leiyn and Isla.

"Envoys," he said with admirable composure, "it is my pleasure to welcome you back to Southport, and a fair welcome to your esteemed companions." He bobbed his head to each of them before looking back at Isla. "The Lord Consul will be ever so pleased to see you, Envoy Isla."

"Lord Consul?" Leiyn searched her mind for who that might be, but Isla gave her a hard look.

"I trust the election went as planned, then?" her friend replied. "Lord Mauricio is now the Elected Consul?"

"Verily, Envoy Isla." Dinis bowed his head. "Without hiccup or hitch."

Elected Consul. At another time, she would have dwelled on this late development and its portent for the former governor's ambitions. Just then, however, politicking felt as frivolous as the costumes in which they dressed.

Titans in our harbors, and they wear wigs. Only for Isla did she swallow the spit building up in her mouth.

"We'll be pleased to see the *consul* as well," Leiyn said, her acerbic tone undermined by her chattering teeth. "Where is he?"

The mayordomo narrowed his eyes. "The Lord Consul is with the Lord Conqueror in his solarium. Shall I show you to some rooms for refreshment? I do not know precisely when my lords will be available for a conference."

"I'm afraid we don't have any changes of clothes," Isla said. "Our horses and saddlebags were... lost."

A fresh pang cut into Leiyn's chest. She blinked, surprised by the burning in her eyes as she thought of Feral never nipping at her hand again.

To think I'd ever miss that nag.

"Perhaps not," Ata spoke up, turning all eyes toward her. "The titan and the distance complicated matters. I had to release them early, but only just. They may be alive. With rest, I may find them."

Leiyn barely dared harbor the hope in her chest. Isla and Batu looked in a similar state.

"We'll search for them when you're ready," she assured the dryvan.

The mayordomo cleared his throat. "I understand. If your search proves fruitless, I am certain I could locate some clothes to suit you." The mayordomo turned his gaze back on Ata. "My sincerest apologies, but I must ask: who is your, ah, companion?"

"Oh, her?" Leiyn gave him a sharp smile. "That's Rowanwalker. She's a dryvan. Perhaps you've heard of them?"

"A... dryvan." Dinis was turning nearly as pale as his wig. "I see. I am afraid, Mistress Rowanwalker, that I must ask you to remain outside the villa until I can ascertain Lord Mauricio's wishes regarding your occupancy."

"Mistress." A ragged laugh won free of Ata. "That's the first time a mortal has flung formalities at me."

The mayordomo blinked. His mouth parted twice before he recovered his composure. "My apologies, Miss... ah, Rowanwalker. I mean only the utmost respect. You'll pardon me for my clumsy manners—you are the first dryvan to which I have had the delight of being introduced."

Ata cocked her head far to one side. "Will I pardon you?"

"She's pulling your strings," Leiyn interjected at the manservant's bafflement. "Go fetch the gov—consul," she amended, catching herself, "and the conqueror if he wishes. We'll wait here."

The mayordomo all but fled, failing to object to Leiyn's imposition. Isla gave Leiyn a long-suffering look, but she seemed as glad as the rest of them to be out of the wind and rain.

It was almost warm in the atrium once the guard shut the doors. Leiyn took to pacing, fearing she would fall asleep on her feet. Where she walked, her clothes dripped on the polished marble floor and the sapphire carpets slashed across it. Batu and Isla huddled together, while Ekosa and Ketti stood near one another, though with some distance separating them. Ata cared nothing for their mortal decorum, if she was even aware of it. She slumped to the ground, roots spreading out around to keep her upright, and closed her eyes. Leiyn thought Isla must be relieved that her roots did not burrow into the fine tiles.

Leiyn's lifesense had dulled with exhaustion, but not so much that she could not seek out Mauricio and Luca's esses. Focused on observing them as Dinis reached the solarium, she did not notice who stood at the villa doors until the guards opened them.

She turned, baffled, as Acalan Tikau strode into the consul's villa.

By all appearances, the pressures of war had yet to touch the war chieftain. He remained as solid a presence in body and spirit as he ever had. His esse was undiminished, its scarlet hues more pronounced in the months since she had last seen him. His bald head shone with rain, highlighting the pale green tattoos splayed across his skull.

Only his clothes had changed. Gone were the heavy Gast stylings of leather, cloth, and fur, replaced by an extravagant Iritu garb. Seeing the chieftain in a garish gold gambeson and aqua trousers almost pulled her stiff lips into a smile.

She hid her surprise behind a stony stare. "You're early."

The Toa'Yao gave her as much a smile as he ever did. "You sounded like you needed the help."

"And here I thought things were going well."

Acalan stopped several paces off and looked to Isla and Batu. "Envoy. Young Bear."

"It's good to see you, Acalan," Isla said with genuine warmth.

Batu strode forth to grip the chieftain's arm in a warrior's shake before stepping away. In Acalan's presence, he stood taller.

The Gast's eyes hardened again as he scanned the rest of their comrades. Ekosa, he gave a cursory glance. His gaze lingered longer on Ketti, trailing over her embedded pearls and Eteman attire before he nodded a greeting to her as well.

Then he turned to Ata.

"*Sach'aan.* I did not expect your kind to be here."

"My kind." Ata levered herself back up to standing. "I *am* my kind now. They go where I go."

Acalan's frown deepened, but he turned back to Leiyn, not seeming to wish to know the answer to her riddle. "You are recently returned?"

"More or less." Leiyn jerked her head toward the bay. "Took care of a titan first."

"Of course that was you. *Tideraiser.*" Amusement glimmered in his dark eyes.

"It was too much to hope you hadn't heard that one. Don't suppose you'll let it go?"

He shrugged. "A name does not change who you are. Only deeds."

"But bringing it up changes my mood." The question that had been bubbling up inside Leiyn finally spilled out. "Is Teya here, too?"

One corner of Acalan's mouth curled up. "She guards the southern shore. I expect her to report later this evening."

This evening. Having already spent seasons apart, it should not have felt so far away. Yet the closer they came to reuniting, the longer the intervening time stretched.

"Good," she managed, turning aside.

The chieftain's gaze lingered on her before shifting to Isla. "I go to confer with Lord Mauricio and Lord Luca. Will you come with me?"

"We're hoping they'll come to us." Isla looked pointedly at Ata.

"Ah. They are wise to be wary."

"One thing upon which we agree." The dryvan punctuated her statement with a wide smile.

Acalan met Ata's stare with a hard one of his own. Leiyn repressed a sigh. They had fought together against a common enemy, yet still, they were slow to trust one another. Even Leiyn shifted her outlook faster.

And that's saying something.

"I will go to them, see if I can hurry their progress." Acalan started to turn away, then pressed a calloused hand to Leiyn's shoulder. "It is good to see you. All of you." He swept his gaze across their party.

"No need to be weepy about it." Leiyn softened the words with a smile.

The corners of his eyes crinkled as the Gast chieftain departed for the stairs.

They were not made to wait long. Minutes passed before Leiyn sensed the three men heading their way, the mayordomo and several others in tow. She raised her head and tried to clear her mind of Teya as they came into view.

"Ah! Most loyal servants of Baltesia, be welcome home!" Mauricio di Siveña seemed as merry as if he attended a ball as he descended the stairs, arms spread wide. Yet, looking beyond the smile, Leiyn saw the strain of the siege etched upon him. Dark bags lay under his eyes, and more gray struck through his generous head of curly brown hair. Even his clothes suffered, if the rare wrinkle in the fine fabric could be called "suffering." Yet the cape of Baltesian blue spilling from his shoulders looked new and rich enough to compensate.

A sign of his ascension, she guessed, lips twisting at the thought.

The odd conqueror appeared less changed. Clad in full shining silver armor but for a helm, he gave no greeting as their small company stopped at the bottom of the stairs, but let his eyes wander over the ornate walls and ceiling, hands held behind his back. He almost seemed bored, as if sieges were of as little concern as an afternoon rain shower. Behind him came a retinue of messengers, responsible for bringing the conqueror news and issuing his orders across the city.

"Lord Mauricio. Lord Luca." Isla led their group in respectful bows. "I apologize for the timing of our arrival, but we have much to report."

"I would hope that you do." The consul's gaze was as sharp as ever as it raked over their assorted company. "You return with both fewer and more than you left with. Pray introduce your new comrades?"

Leiyn balked at the task, but Isla handled it with admirable grace. "Lord Consul, Lord Conqueror, Toa'Yao, this is High Ekosa Siza, an *eesu* of the *Kekére.*"

Or was. Leiyn had the sense to keep the thought to herself.

"He has been kind enough to volunteer as a tutor to the Order of Mahia," Isla continued. "The first of six such tutors, come the end of the season."

Ekosa bowed in the Ofean fashion. "*Okulukulu* Herself blesses our meeting. I thank you for your welcome, my lords."

"*Orun ka ibukun,* High Ekosa. We are glad to have you. I trust we'll have more to discuss when there's time." Mauricio layered the words with intent. Weary as she was, Leiyn could scarcely muster the energy to worry about how they would explain their misadventures in Kunu. Much less all that had come before.

Isla moved them on. "And this is Ketti Ta'Rul. She is a powerful maha whom we met along our travels and has pledged herself to our cause."

"Has she?" The consul squinted at her as he smiled. "That is most generous of you, Mistress Ketti. But forgive me, is that a name from the Many Tribes? I must confess to being unfamiliar with your markings."

Ketti's eyes darted to Leiyn. Swallowing a sigh, Leiyn obliged by speaking for her.

"Close enough," she said. "We'll explain later, Lord Consul."

Acalan's gaze was hard on Ketti. Leiyn wondered how much he suspected. How much knowledge the Gasts had retained of their ancestral traditions. But until she decided how much to share with the consul and the conqueror, it was best to leave them all in the dark about her Eteman origins.

Mauricio gave her a look that spoke of his awareness of the omission. "Very well, Prima Maha. I trust your judgment on the matter."

Prima Maha. Her stomach sank at the reminder of the duties awaiting her here in Southport. After her earlier defiance of the consul's wishes, she doubted she had the leeway to slip them a second time.

Even if they prove a noose.

"Besides," the consul continued, "we cannot neglect our final guest." He turned to Ata with a bright smile, which the dryvan matched. Only, to Leiyn's eye, Ata's had more than a hint of the predator in it.

"You may call me... ah, what name should I be now? Silver-fish? Finvine?"

"Rowan," Leiyn interjected. "It's as good as any."

Her forwardness drew Luca's gaze. Ata's smile cut through the unease that fell. "Rowan will serve."

"Mistress Rowan, then. You are a dryvan, if I'm not mistaken?"

"Most insightful of you, m'lord." Isla took back the conversation with her usual tact: honey and balm. "Rowan has been a staunch ally and champion against the varied threats facing us."

"I think I have some idea about which threat." Mauricio had a glimmer in his hazel eyes as he winked at Leiyn. She met it with a grimace. It would not have been her reaction at the mention of Sharo and his lyshans. Khamo still loomed large in her mind. All they had experienced since his assault did little to dull the memories of him tearing Ata apart—and herself before.

The consul continued. "Your support is most welcome, Rowan of the Drvyans. I fear the circumstances in which we find ourselves are most dire. But with your return"—he included all their company in a sweeping gaze—"I am confident we shall prevail."

Mauricio's declarations touched few of them by their expressions. Luca appeared as unaffected as the rest as his intense gaze fell upon Isla.

"Captain Belen," the conqueror said. "She traveled with you and twelve soldiers. Only two returned. Where are the others?"

Even her name pricked Leiyn, as much from the loss as the reminder of failure. She felt an urgency to be out with it and spoke before Isla could.

"She's dead. They all are."

A crease worked its way across the conqueror's well-lined face. "How did they perish?"

"A Suncoat ambush. Killed two Ofean skystriders traveling with us as well. If not for Ketti here, they might have done us in, too."

Mauricio's eyebrows shot up so they nearly disappeared beneath his generous locks. "It must have been a mighty company indeed to overcome the Tideraiser and her companions. You have much to report, Prima Leiyn. But I hear you have had a trying return. Unless you must divulge something at once, I will allow you to rest this night, then tell of your varied adventures in the morning."

Relief washed through Leiyn. An interrogation was more than she could endure just then.

"Thank you, Lord Consul," Isla answered. "You are most gracious."

Leiyn wanted to slink away to her room, but one matter could not wait. "Our horses. We... lost them on our way here, and our saddlebags with them." *Only lost,* she told herself as her chest squeezed tight at the thought of not seeing Feral again. "But they may still be in the surrounding area. Can you put out the word to watch for them?"

"Lost them, did you?" Mauricio hid his bafflement at the prospect well. Not knowing the path they had taken to arrive here, it would seem odd to misplace their mounts. "Very well. Lord Luca, if you would?"

"It is done." The conqueror motioned to a messenger, who went scurrying off ahead of him, then strode from the villa without a farewell.

Leiyn stared after him. "Doesn't he need us to describe them?"

"I'm sure he recalls their look." Mauricio tapped his skull. "A mind like tree sap, has our Lord Conqueror. I wonder if he forgets anything."

She balked at the thought. To remember all seemed more a curse than a blessing. Especially in war.

"But I won't delay you any further," the consul continued. "Dinis, please return Prima Leiyn, Envoy Isla, and Batu Khatas to their rooms, if they remain available. And find suitable accommodations for our other guests as well."

"Pardons, m'lord," the mayordomo said. "But I am uncertain how best to, ah, satisfy Mistress Rowan."

The consul turned a keen eye on the dryvan. "Perhaps she might enlighten us?"

Leiyn mistrusted the fey light that winked in Ata's eyes, but she did not intervene.

"The gardens will do," Ata replied. "I trust they're merely decorative?"

Without waiting for a reply, the shapeshifter peeled her roots from the floor, heedless of the grime she left behind, and ambled through the villa as if she knew precisely where she was going. Leiyn supposed she did—with her powerful magic, sensing the location of the gardens would be simple even at her most depleted.

Mauricio watched with undisguised fascination as she left, then shook his head. "My, my, she is novel. I shall be terribly eager to hear about your journey. But go now—I will delay you no longer. Until the morning."

Murmuring their thanks, Leiyn moved with the others up the stairs after the mayordomo.

61

REKINDLED

She could not sleep.

Leiyn was as tired as she had ever been, wearier than after the most punishing training at the Lodge. Even the Hunger Patrol had not weighed on her so heavily as the day's events. Though the bed given to her by Mauricio was as sumptuous as any she had slept in, soft with goose down, she found it a comfort rather than a hindrance that night. Darkness had long since fallen, only scarce moonlight peeking through the clouds.

None of it could compel her to sleep. Not when Teya could return at any moment.

Leiyn compulsively scanned the compound for any sign of the scout leader's appearance. She felt nothing of her by her life-sense. Acalan had said she was due to report to him that night, but what if something had held her up?

What if the Suncoats had killed her in the siege?

Fear and anticipation boiled within her. Were she not so weary, they would have had Leiyn pacing the length of her quarters. As it was, all she could do was wait—until she could wait no longer.

Leiyn sensed the moment she approached the compound's gate. Watched as she strode across the courtyard, entered the villa, and ascended the stairs. Leiyn sat up, futilely brushing at her braided hair. Too late, she wished she had mustered the energy to bathe before, self-conscious of how her dip in the sea had not improved her aroma.

It's Teya, she chastised herself. *She's a* situal. *She won't care.*

But self-assurances did little to assuage her fears. They had been apart for months. Feelings such as these could change as readily as the seasons.

What if Teya's had?

Teya brushed her with her sparse mahia, and Leiyn fought down a shiver. She reached out, trying to capture her ghostly touch, but the scout eluded her, drawing away as soon as she had come.

She did not make for Leiyn's room but headed toward where Acalan waited.

Doubts resurged. Reason did little to temper them. *She has to report. She's Acalan's soldier first.* Leiyn squeezed her eyes shut and clenched her fists. As she hated how much of the smitten girl she acted, she could not help it. The emotions arose on their own.

It took mere minutes, yet it felt like hours before Teya left the chieftain and returned to the corridor. Then she walked toward Leiyn's room.

Fighting to regain her composure, Leiyn faced the door. She remained seated for a moment, then thought better of it and rocked up to her feet. Noticing how dark the room was, she scrambled to light one of the beeswax candles provided to her. She had just lit the wick when her door eased open.

Leiyn came upright and stared at the woman in the open doorway. Her breath caught as she beheld the full force of Teya's lifefire, burning as bright a blue as ever, with that same mesmerizing movement.

"Redlock."

That endearment. That slanted smile. She forgot her insecurities and fears and closed the distance between them.

Leiyn wrapped her arms around Teya and buried her face into her neck. Her chest tightened so she could not breathe. For a moment, it felt as if she never would again. Finally, she sucked in air as tears pressed free.

Then she was sobbing.

"Hush, hush. I have you. You are safe. I am safe. We are here."

Teya brushed a hand along her head, her voice as soothing as Leiyn's imagined memory of her mother. Embarrassment and anger at her weakness rose for a moment, but the scout's presence tamed them, and she let them fall away. For the moment, she let all be.

When at last she settled, Leiyn drew back and cuffed her eyes dry. She was reluctant to look up, but the prospect of seeing Teya's face was too alluring.

She raised her head.

Teya smiled, eyes creasing at the corners. In the gloom, she appeared much the same as when they had parted. Her dark braids draped over her right shoulder, opposite the shaven side of her head. Her ruby pendant hung over an Iritu vest that made her glow even brighter to her lifesense. Her pale red tattoos—the lines on her forehead, the spirals on her cheeks—almost caught their own glow.

"You stink of the sea," the scout murmured.

A surprised laugh broke free of Leiyn. "You don't smell like roses yourself."

"No, I suppose not. I hope you do not mind a *situal's* scent."

Teya looped an arm around her hips, drawing her closer. Leiyn went willingly. Heat spread through her, a fire sparking low in her belly.

"No," Leiyn breathed as Teya kissed her neck. "I don't mind."

◦◦◦

"Looks like that one hurt."

Teya traced a finger along one of her scars, a hand propping up her head. Morning light streamed in through the curtains behind her.

Leiyn sat up. She had lain at ease with Teya since waking, but the reminder of past injuries stiffened her spine. Looking down, she stared at the seam of flesh between her breasts. It lay next to a second, longer scar. She saw again the assassin's knife lodged in her chest, then the sword that had first endeavored to kill her, all those seasons ago.

"Not the first time I've been stabbed," she said ruefully.

The scout pursed her lips. "The Suncoat the night your Lodge burned?"

Leiyn crossed her arms over her chest, hiding the marks. "The same."

Teya's eyes fell to her outer arm and the red blemishes winding around it. "Another nasty one."

"Hurt like hells, too. Got it from a lyshan. Khamo, Ata called him."

"Ata. Another name for your *sach'aan* friend?" Teya wrapped her hand over the rough red lines, covering part of it. Her touch was gentle, as if afraid of harming her further. "I regret not being there to defend you."

"I don't." She wondered if she should have confessed the dryvan's name. Then again, it was only to Teya, and "Ata" was the shortened version. "He almost killed me. Would have, but for Ketti stepping in. I don't like to think what might have happened to you."

"Mm. Perhaps. But do not forget I have killed their kind before." Teya smiled, reminding Leiyn of a jaguar's snarl. "I am getting a taste for it."

Leiyn snorted a laugh and shoved her playfully. Teya captured her hand and nibbled a finger before her expression grew serious.

"Your *kainox*—it was not enough to fight this Khamo?"

Hesitation caught in her throat. But this was Teya. She had already broken down before her once. This admission was slight next to that.

So she told her of the troubles she had experienced since

leaving Qasaar with summoning Clouded Fang. Teya listened with her brow furrowed.

"Taht Xepi would have insights into this. A shame you did not realize it until leaving."

"I suppose." Privately, Leiyn doubted the shaman could have helped more than she had. Then again, the aged woman had often been full of surprises.

"I am no shaman," Teya continued, "but I will think on this. This view of the world, of *Tlalli* united as one—it is not so different from the Gast way of seeing things. Perhaps I can help."

"I hope so. Chispa won't always be around." She wondered where the silver fox had gone off to. If he would return when she needed him, or if she was on her own in the coming fights.

Teya brushed a finger along Leiyn's jaw, ending along her bottom lip. Leiyn smiled and pulled her hand away, her touch tickling.

"For now," the scout said, smiling, "we must go. Before your consul sends someone to drag you out of bed and Acalan tans my hide."

Reluctantly, Leiyn obliged. Servants had brought her a clean pair of trousers and a tunic when they took away her Iritu and Eteman garments for washing. Though ordinary clothes felt limp and ill-fitting after so long wearing enchanted ones, she had little other choice in the matter. Pulling on shoes that were soft and flimsy enough to be slippers, it felt ridiculous to loop on her weapons belt around her waist. But she had already lost her bow; she'd be damned if she went anywhere without her falchions and knife.

Teya, dressed in her scout armor, departed with a final kiss and press of hands. Isla and Batu joined Leiyn outside their room. The former plainsrider was dressed similarly to Leiyn, while Isla wore a simple but winsome green dress. Catching Leiyn's brief frown, her fellow ranger gave her an exasperated look.

"We cannot go around in armor all the time," Isla pointed

out. "And we'll have our other clothes back soon enough. Let me have a few moments free of them."

"Yes, m'lady." Leiyn gave her a mocking bow.

Isla rolled her eyes.

"What of Ekosa and Ketti?" Leiyn looked down the hall to where their companions remained in their rooms.

"Not invited," Batu supplied.

"I wouldn't worry about them." Isla wore a mischievous smile. "I asked Ekosa to spend some time with her. Get her acquainted to another new place."

Leiyn knew that look. "Back at playing matchmaker—you cannot help yourself, can you?"

"Why stand in the way of a good thing?" Isla laughed. The sound of it was lighter than it had been in months. "They have more in common than you might think. Besides, the companionship will do them both good. They've been through a lot these past few days, beyond what any of us have."

She could not argue with that. One was self-exiled, the other outright banished. They were foreigners in a war-torn city. They could do worse for company. Still, she shared an exasperated look with Batu, who appeared as bemused as she was.

Isla tried to convince them of the necessity of her interventions while leading them to the Elected Consul's solarium. Only at the sight of the guards at the entrance did their bantering cease.

Mauricio was leaning over his desk when they entered, papers spread out before him. Hair falling free, he had a disheveled appearance at odds with his usual manner. Only as they stopped in the middle of his office did he look up.

"Ah, there you are, my friends! Please, come in, come in. Have you eaten? Have a pastry—the servants always bring too many."

Her stomach rumbling at the sweet, buttery scent, Leiyn took up the offer, ignoring Isla's chastising gaze as she swallowed it down. Batu, mindful of his beloved, contented himself with small bites around the edges, though he grimaced and tried to hide the crumbs falling into his hand.

"Have as many as you like." Mauricio glanced out the window. "At least one of your guests has helped themselves to my fare. Did you know the dryvan's intentions with my garden?"

Leiyn stifled a groan. "What'd she do?"

"You would know better than I. But where it was flowering and verdant yesterday, now it lies entirely fallow. Alas," the consul sighed. "It is but the smallest price to pay in this war."

A quick questing showed the truth of the consul's words. None of the plants had died, but their lifefires had been reduced to whispers. Amid them lay Ata, her esse blinding once more. Somehow, she seemed as smug and satisfied as a satiated cat as she sprawled on her back amid the desolation.

"Ah, but I have not told you!" Mauricio continued, drawing her back to the room. "You were correct about your horses—we found them in the fields south of the walls."

All thoughts of Ata fled her mind as her heart lurched. *Feral, you stubborn old girl!*

"They were?" Isla said, sounding as eager as Leiyn. She had grown attached to Mottle over the past year. "And they're unharmed?"

"On that point, I'm afraid I have worse news. One has suffered a broken leg, a ghastly injury that my grooms say requires us to free it of its torment."

"Don't do that!" Fear made Leiyn's words come out harsh. Only as she thought better of it did she moderate her tone. "That is, I can heal them. Which horse was it?"

Mauricio brightened. "Ah, of course! Our Prima Maha would be able to. I trust we will not come too late—I ordered that they be spared until I spoke otherwise. It was the blonde with white spots."

Saikan. Leiyn turned to Batu. "He'll be alright," she assured him. "He'll be hale as a titan once I see to him."

The plainsrider nodded, his expression pained. Even

knowing Saikan would survive could not make it easy to bear knowing his horse lay in agony.

She looked back to Mauricio. "Can someone lead us to him?"

"I will do you one better—I'll have the horse brought here."

The consul summoned a servant. While they spoke, Isla cast decorum aside and wrapped an arm around her beloved in a brief hug.

Once the serving man scurried away, Mauricio turned back. "While we wait, I must ask that you give your report. Time is a luxury we have far too little of at the moment."

"Of course. We understand, my lord." Isla glanced at Leiyn. "Do you want to start, or shall I?"

"Go ahead."

Leiyn suspected she would need to step in when it came time to truncate the truth. She trusted Mauricio. If she did not, she would not have told him about Sharo and their greater war.

But some secrets might not be theirs to tell. How would he react to a people hidden across the countryside with magic beyond any of the colonies? Would he see them as a threat? A resource to be mined? Allies to be won over, or enemies to be eradicated?

Mauricio was a good man, kind and gentle, but he was Baltesia's ruler. And rulers often trampled ideals for what they deemed necessity.

Isla covered their journey up to the second ambush near Solace's ruins. From there, Leiyn took over. She spoke of Khamo, making clear he was a servant of Sharo's, then introduced Ketti with no mention of her people, describing her instead as an eccentric hermit. If the consul harbored any doubts to the story, he gave no sign of them.

Upon reaching Ore-Ofe, Isla spoke up again, the better authority to speak on the happenings in the colony. Only with Ekosa did Leiyn see the need to put in a word.

"Then he is a proper *eesu*," Mauricio mused when she finished. "But exiled?"

"So it seems," Leiyn replied.

"I wonder if harboring him will sour our relations. But you said they were to send more from their Coterie to train our mahas?"

"So long as the path to Southport is clear," Isla said. "I believe them to be sincere in their desire to aid us. Rowan was persuasive when convincing them of the danger lyshans pose to the Tricolonies—all of the colonies."

"That is a fair sign for a future alliance. However, in this embargo, it does little to ease our situation." The consul turned to the window, tapping his chin with a finger. "If High Ekosa is willing, we shall make use of him now. Any consequences can be dealt with later."

Leiyn wondered how much use the *eesu* would be. She did not know the extent to which their order was taught magic for battle, but Ekosa did not seem much of a warrior. While his esse was strong for the average maha, he paled in comparison to Ketti and herself.

"We might place him with Wise Jegu and the other wisdoms," she suggested. "It's likely he knows how to repel titans."

"Let's be certain to check." Mauricio turned back with a shrewd look. "But there is one explanation missing from your narrative: how you came to be here so quickly after leaving Kunu. Unless I'm mistaken, even if you left at once, you should have still been absent at least a month longer, if not two."

Leiyn hesitated, again wondering if this was a power she dared divulge. Isla decided for them.

"Rowan. She brought us here. I don't understand how, but... dryvans can appear in another place almost at once."

"It's not pleasant," Leiyn added, hoping to deter any plotting by the consul. "And I doubt Rowan'll do it for anyone else. She's loyal to us."

"Indeed." Amusement shone in Mauricio's eyes. "I would not wish to impose on her, then."

Did he suspect her attempts to curb his hold over her and her companions? Leiyn let none of her unease show through.

Let him wonder. He needs us.

It was a truth neither of them would deny. But he was not only the governor now; he was the Elected Consul of Baltesia. The war had yet to be won, but already, he solidified his authority. Little made her more suspicious than the hoarding of power.

"Regardless," the consul continued, "it does not change our immediate goal: driving back the Ilberian Armada from our shores." He rocked to his feet and sauntered over to a window. Leiyn followed his gaze to the ships dotting the bright ocean horizon. Scores of them spread there, far more than Baltesia could ever hope to match, especially with the kraken harassing their harbors.

"How?" she asked baldly.

Mauricio eyed her, a smile playing on his lips. "The question that has haunted me. All my life, I have slept like a babe. But these past few months, I've hardly had a wink."

He chuckled. Isla gave him a tentative smile. Leiyn did not think his levity warranted it.

"Regardless," he continued, "those decisions shall await tomorrow's council. This day, the Lord Conqueror and I shall have our hands full, so you may use it to rest and recuperate. And see to your horses, I suppose. Just be sure to attend us tomorrow morning. Envoy Isla, I trust you remember the way?"

"Of course, Lord Consul."

"Then enjoy the sunshine." Mauricio turned away. "It is, perhaps, the last moment of peace any of us will have for some time."

62

UNION

Other tasks stood in the way of Mauricio's exhortations to make the most of the day. After a brief reunion with Feral—during which the mare did not snap at her, an almost sweet gesture from her—Leiyn turned to the horse lying prone upon a cart in the middle of the villa's courtyard. Batu whispered some words in Saikan's ear as he stroked his snout, then rose and nodded at Leiyn.

It was a simple enough matter to heal. The break in the bone was clean, and the intervening hours had not much complicated the injury. Horses took more lifeforce to heal than humans, though, as she discovered when she staggered upright. She had not needed to draw on her amber beads, but as she swayed on the cobblestones, she was sorely tempted.

The sight of Saikan standing banished all thought of weariness. Batu laughed as he charged forward, clapping his hands to the gelding's broad neck. The horse nudged his master, then cast one dark eye at Leiyn. Almost, she sensed a glimmer of understanding, as if he knew she had healed him and was thankful.

She gave the pair a final smile before staggering back over to Feral, leaving them to their reunion.

After spending some time with their horses, they led them to the villa's stables. Upon leaving, Leiyn caught sight of a familiar crowd streaming out from the First Temple of Baltesia. She did not need her lifesense to tell her who they were: her mahitas, departing from the afternoon's training. She remained their Prima Maha and knew she should go to greet them.

Instead, she turned and slipped inside.

It was too much to hope none of them had sensed her. They would already know of her return. Yet it was not wholly out of cowardice that she fled. Leiyn had yet to form a grotto and call upon Clouded Fang alone. Failing to summon her bonded could prove fatal for all of Southport. She had failed too many of those she loved. She refused to do it again.

If I can help it.

Making her excuses to her companions, Leiyn retreated to her room, curtained her windows, and sat in the cushioned chair tucked in one corner of her bedchamber. She closed her eyes and breathed as Tadeo had taught her, settling her mind and clearing it of intrusive thoughts. Then she tried seeing the world the way Ketti had described, whole and unified.

Cities had always clouded her mind when her lifesense was open among them. This moment proved no exception. It seemed impossible that she could view the chaotic movement of its citizens as all part of the same organism.

Focus, Firebrand, damn you!

She thought of seeking counsel from the Eteman but gave up the idea as soon as she had risen from her chair. Ketti had done all she could to guide her. The rest remained to her.

I can do this. I have to.

The chair suddenly seemed too comfortable. Instead of returning to it, Leiyn folded onto the floor, sitting cross-legged with her spine straight and her eyes closed. Again, she returned to the task at hand.

Her efforts proved as futile as before.

Sharo will kill you, a voice whispered from the recesses of her mind. *He'll kill all of them. Isla. Teya. Batu. Do you think he'd spare any after what he did to the dryvans?*

Thinking of Sharo brought back another intrusive memory,

one that gave her pause. When Ata had cast them across the continent, she had seen... something. A vision, perhaps, though it felt more like a dream upon recollection. Saints knew her nights were filled with nightmares involving the lyshan.

Yet there had been a tangibility to the scene that no dream had possessed. And the woman with him on that beach, the words they spoke to one another—she could not prise them from her head. Somehow, they seemed like words she had heard before, though none of the phrases she recalled were from any book she knew, few as those might be.

'Ware, comes the Wither...

When she could endure the torment no longer, Leiyn rose, shook out her aching limbs, and made for the villa gardens. Having never visited them before and seeing little point in wasting time in leisure, she lost her way several times. Ata's presence among them, however, acted as a beacon to guide her.

"Awakener!" the dryvan called when Leiyn came into view. "I wondered when you would grace my domain with your presence."

"Because you've made it such a delight." Leiyn took in the gardens' destruction. Mauricio had not lied: the dryvan had all but decimated the plants there. Leaves had fallen from trees, wrinkled and gray. Flowers had wilted on stems. A sight that must have once been beautiful to behold now seemed like the derelict remains after an army's passage.

"And," Leiyn added as she strode toward Ata, "what did I say about calling me that?"

The dryvan rose with a mischievous grin. She had been reclining where the garden paths crossed next to a tinkling fountain, sprawled like a thorned lion after a substantial meal. Her roots had twisted back into her usual shape. Leiyn was relieved to see the fins and scales of the day before had disappeared, replaced by vines, feathers, and moss.

"My apologies, *Tideraiser*." Ata gave her so deep a bow that her head almost touched the pavers.

Leiyn rolled her eyes. Privately, she was glad to see the

dryvan in high spirits. It had not been long before that she had lain in utter despondency. She wondered how she could bear the destruction of all the other dryvans so easily.

She has faced it before, she reminded herself. *She's borne the sorrow of her fading Kin for centuries. Aeons, even.*

Leiyn stopped several paces off and crossed her arms. "You were watching me."

"Aren't I always?" Ata cocked her head to one side. "Or would you prefer I not protect you? But come, my ephemeral friend—that is not why you sought me out."

"No, I suppose not." Part of Leiyn always blanched at asking for aid, but there was no way around it. "I'm having trouble forming a grotto to reach Clouded Fang."

"Ah. The summoning of your titan is the issue? I had wondered why he so rarely appeared."

"You form grottos easily enough. Is there a trick to it? Some step I'm skipping?"

"Would not your Eteman be better positioned to answer that?"

Leiyn touched a hand to her auburn tress, then pulled it away. "She did. But I'm still having trouble. This city..." She waved a hand inarticulately around.

"Ah, yes. It is quite *noisy*, isn't it?" Ata straightened her head and stretched, her body creaking like a tree in wind, and sighed with relief. "Nothing like the quiet I've grown accustomed to."

Lowering her arms, dryvan's gaze went distant and her height shrank several inches. Only a moment passed before life returned to her eyes.

"But we cannot cleave to the past." Her voice fell low, growing sharp as the edges of fern leaves. "It is where our roots grow, but our branches must reach beyond it. I cannot help you, Leiyn, though I wish I could. Moving between this world and that... it is simple to me. Natural. The way a plant does not need to learn to soak in the sun and the rain—it *knows*.

"But this I will say." She thrust a taloned finger at Leiyn. "You know how to do this. It is in your being. It is *who you are.* I knew you as Awakener from the first moment I beheld you. Don't hide from all you can be."

Ata meant well, Leiyn knew. But her rallying speech struck her as upside down, a capsized boat. *I don't know!* she wanted to rail at her. *That's the problem!*

But she silenced her frustration. If that was all Ata could give, she would have to seek answers elsewhere.

The dryvan tilted her head to the side. "I have disappointed you."

"No. I'm disappointed in myself."

A hum vibrated from Ata's chest. "Impatience," she murmured. "Always in a hurry, you mortals."

"Aren't you?"

More bitter words burned on her tongue, but Leiyn bit them back. *Be careful where you throw stones*, her father had once warned her after she had fought with a girl who had been her friend. It was a lesson she had often ignored, but with Ata, she could not afford to.

Already, it seemed too late. The dryvan had lost her gaiety, her feathers falling limp about her shoulders.

"I wish you good fortune, Leiyn," she said. "For the sake of this world."

Leiyn jerked her head in acknowledgment. Then, unbidden, another question rose to the fore.

"I saw a vision while we traveled here. Of Sharo."

Ata stiffened. Her feathers stood erect. Both her white eye and green one seemed to pierce Leiyn like quarrels would a stuffed target on a bow range.

"What vision?" she asked, each word clipped.

Leiyn tried not to feel threatened before her—difficult, when the dryvan seemed liable to pounce at any moment—and dredged up the memories. "I was drowning, then I washed upon a shore. Everything was... hazy. Vague. But I heard voices all the while, reciting lines of... poetry, I think. 'Ware, comes the Wither'—I remember that one."

"'Ware, comes the Wither," Ata repeated, her gaze peeling

from Leiyn to look out toward the compound wall and the sea beyond.

"Then I saw two figures. One was seated in a chair—a throne, maybe. A woman. Ayda, the other called her."

"Gran Ayda," the dryvan murmured. "The Altacura of the Catedrál?"

Leiyn nodded, stunned. How had she not realized that might be who was referenced? And if Sharo and the Altacura were conferring together, did it not confirm everything he had hinted at? That he had spawned this war? That he pulled the strings of Ilberian power, and perhaps beyond?

If the damned vision's real.

"That other," she continued, trying to fit the pieces together as she spoke. "It was Sharo, walking around the seated woman. They both spoke of the poetry. Or prophecy," Leiyn amended, realizing it for what it was. "They discussed the words as if they would come to pass."

"Prophecy." Ata started to pace in that smooth, eerie way of her kind, her eyes downcast. "Once, it was practiced among the Kin. Even among mortals, it is not unknown, though it is a path to madness."

"Madness?"

"Oh, yes. Many seers have raved in the wake of their glimpses into the world's heart." The dryvan paused and tilted her head as she peered at Leiyn. "Ah, but you do understand. This prophesying—it is not true-seeing. It's less a seeing into the future than a seeing into the *now*. Their divinations are predictions, keenly made through the collation of an expansive view of present events. Their augury is *farseeing*, like the hunter-children use to spy upon the land... except it spreads their minds thin as ice and makes them equally brittle and liable to break. Not unlike how you experienced your vision, as a matter of fact."

Leiyn stood in stunned silence. She had never dwelled overlong on fortunetelling. Those claiming to peer into the future were not infrequent in Southport's seedier quarters, despite the Catedrál's condemnation of any kind of magic. What little thought she had spared for the profession was tainted with disdain. Few could see the here and now clearly, in her estimation. That some might glimpse what was to come seemed beyond the reach of mahia.

"Then you think my vision was real?" she asked. "That their... prediction will come to pass?"

Ata smiled, putting all her teeth on display. "Was it real? Likely. But, real or not, I would not dwell on it or the prophecy. Nor should you risk such visions again. Overreach, and who can say if you shall return in your right mind?"

Leiyn crossed her arms. "I'll try to avoid it. Though you'll have to stop flinging me across the continent."

The dryvan chuckled, viny hair slithering with the movement. "But there is one lesson we may glean. Like prophecy, farseeing is a communing with the world. Is this not what you seek to do in forming a grotto?"

"I suppose it is."

Ata spread her hands wide. "The ability lies within you, my hasty friend. If you can manage to dredge it up again."

Leiyn mustered a smile. It was a note of hope, and they sorely need any shred of hope they could find. But it did not offer a solution. Head full of all they had discussed, she started to turn away, but another thought made her look back at Ata.

"If you're feeling better, you might restore the gardens. I think it's bothering our Lord Consul more than he lets on."

A measure of mischief returned to Ata's eyes. "What, like this?"

Without warning, energy spread from the dryvan like wind-fed wildfire. The garden, near lifeless before, awoke from the dirt. Withered stalks brightened and straightened. Wilted petals were shed in place of fresh blossoms. A frenzy of aromas flooded her nose. Pollen glimmered golden in the air.

Everywhere Leiyn turned, life flourished.

When she faced Ata again, the dryvan wore a small smirk. Her flat, horizontal pupil dilated as she beheld her creation.

"Almost an analogy, wouldn't you say?" Ata noted. "Where there seems no hope, it may still flourish, perhaps?"

"A bit heavy-handed, if you ask me." Leiyn did not have to force her smile this time.

———

Back in her room, Leiyn closed her eyes and tried once more to see the world as unified. Again, the task she had achieved several times before Kunu eluded her.

Frustration mounting, she took to pacing. *What am I doing wrong? What's missing?* She was conscious of Ketti in her room not far away, but something kept her from going to her.

Will you let pride get your friends killed?

The prod was too great to ignore. Moving down the hall, Leiyn stood before the Eteman's room and raised a hand to knock.

"Enter," Ketti called before she touched the door.

Bemused, she did as requested. Ketti sat on her bed, hands in her lap. She appeared not to have moved at Leiyn's approach, though what she had been doing, Leiyn could only guess at. The Eteman's room was much the same as the one Leiyn had been given when she first arrived in Southport: comfortable, but smaller and less luxurious than her present quarters. She almost wished they could swap.

As soon as she closed the door, Ketti spoke. "You are having trouble calling your bonded."

"With seeing the world as one, specifically." Her hands clenched until Leiyn forced them open. "Can you do it here, with all these people?"

"Yes. I have been ensuring I could. I thought that was what brought you to me."

Leiyn had not noticed. It did not speak well to her vigilance, a sting to any ranger. But she could not heed that now.

"What am I missing?"

Ketti rose to stand before her, face crinkled in sympathy.

"Nothing, Leiyn. All you require is further practice. I mastered the formation of grottos over decades. It is not reasonable to expect to do so in days."

"I *have* to."

The Eteman's eyes went wide at Leiyn's snarl. Almost, she looked frightened. Leiyn closed her eyes and concentrated on her breath.

Breathe. Air does not know worry.

When her eyelids fluttered open, her vexation had dampened to a simmer. "I'm sorry," Leiyn murmured. "I'm angry at myself, not you."

"It is nothing. I understand."

Despite her words, Ketti still seemed wary. Leiyn had no choice but to ignore it. She stepped closer and pitched her voice low.

"If I cannot do this, the war is lost. Do you understand? The lyshans will win. Sharo will kill or enslave every Eteman he can find. You, Solace—others we don't know about, maybe. I doubt he'll spare any maha in the end." She paused, letting her words sink in. "Please, Ketti. If there's anything you can do to help, I need it now."

Her chest was tight. Asking for help once was hard enough. Asking twice in the space of an hour was unbearable. But Ketti did not seem to notice, a thoughtful expression softening her features.

"Before, at the *Kekére*, you reached your bonded. How?"

Amidst the flurry of events, Leiyn realized they had hardly spoken of it. "Chispa helped me. He touched my esse and... I don't know. Showed me his perspective on the world, I suppose. It's all hazy now."

Despite the muddled explanation, Ketti smiled and held up her hands. "Then that is what we must do."

Leiyn stared. "What?"

"I will do what Chispa did for you before. I will show you the world as I see it."

Leiyn's breath caught, comprehension dawning. "That might work."

"Only one way to know."

The intimacy of the proposal made Leiyn think of Teya. When they made love, their souls entwined in a way not dissimilar to what Ketti suggested.

Don't be stupid, she chastised herself. *This isn't the same. And do you have a choice?*

She took Ketti's proffered hands. At once, her lifeforce hummed with the nearness of the Eteman's mahia. Her hesitation reared higher, but Leiyn fought it back down.

Before she could doubt again, she seized hold of Ketti.

The other woman recoiled, perhaps surprised by the ferocity of Leiyn's grip. A moment later, Ketti firmed her will and strove against her. With strength rivaling Leiyn's, she guided Leiyn's esse so it enwrapped hers, like vines around a tree trunk. So closely melded, the Eteman's thoughts came into Leiyn's mind almost like they were her own.

The dozen images of her lifemark became too much to ignore:

An emerald hummingbird alighting on a finger, fluttering its wings with pleasure...

A figure kneeling before a tempest hawk, body wreathed in lightning...

Clouds crowding overhead, then tumbling down like boulders in a landslide...

Here.

A voice resonated through her being, commanding. Ketti's voice. Leiyn heeded it and let the Eteman pilot her again.

They burst across reality.

It felt like they were insects perched on the surface of a pond, light enough not to break it, but feeling the ripples in the water. Every person, every pest in the sewers, every fish in the bay were like specks in the vast ocean of their souls.

Through, Ketti reminded her.

Leiyn turned her gaze from around them to look into the

great depths beneath. Anchored by Ketti, she pressed in. The surface resisted her efforts. She pressed harder. A glimmer emerged, esses awaiting on the other side.

Zuma's spark blazed into awareness within her.

The resistance fell away. With Ketti uniting with Unera and Zuma steering her movements, Leiyn reached through reality. The bond tethering her to Clouded Fang felt as strong as a ship's rope. She tugged on it.

Come to me, Clouded Fang!

The ash dragon, burning in fiery rivers far below, turned up at her call. At once, he began rising, flying through stone as easily as air.

Come!

As the titan breached the surface, Leiyn opened her eyes. Smoke filled the room, making her lungs strain for air. She heard distant screams and the shouts of soldiers rise from elsewhere in the villa.

Outside the window, Clouded Fang beat his murky wings, his burning eyes steady upon her. His esse burned with all the force of the volcano from which he had first erupted. His power flowed into her.

A chuckle rose from her belly. Before she could suppress it, wild laughter burst free.

Ketti, still entwined with her, was infected. They sank to the ground, shaking with mirth, while panic spread on the streets below.

The dragon watched on.

63

EYE OF THE STORM

Following Clouded Fang's awakening, Leiyn moved about the villa, trying to settle the fear evoked by his presence. Filled with the elation of victory, she scarcely minded the duty.

She had not summoned him on her own. Perhaps she never would. But if she required a friend's help to access this power, what of it? Rangers had always been strongest when they stood together.

For a time, she was reluctant to let the titan return to Unera. She tested releasing Ketti to see if she could maintain the link on her own. To both their surprise, she could, though not entirely of her own power. Once more, once she reached Clouded Fang, Zuma's spark helped maintain the bond. It remained tenuous, but with the shaman's lifetime of expertise on her side, Leiyn trusted it would grow easier with practice.

Mauricio was exasperated by the incident, yet his pleasure at her success outweighed any concern. "Just wait until the proper moment next time, if you would?" he requested before dismissing her from his solarium.

The greatest fallout came from an unexpected angle. Leiyn waited on her bed, barely repressing a grin, when Teya entered. At the scout's somber expression, her elation faltered.

"What's wrong?"

The scout made a noncommittal noise as she slumped into the chair. For several moments, she stared at Leiyn like she were a tool she could not find a place for in an overstuffed shed.

"You caused quite the stir," Teya said at last.

"You noticed, did you?" Satisfaction seeped back in. "Ketti helped me reach Clouded Fang, like Chispa did."

"I noticed that as well."

The words crystallized into an insight. Leiyn went to kneel before Teya, taking the scout's hand in both of hers.

"You saw our... joining, didn't you?"

Teya looked aside. "It was difficult not to."

"Teya, please. She only did it to help me. It wasn't anything like when you and I—" She coughed, suddenly timid. "Well, you know."

The scout turned back to her, a hint of her old humor returned to her eyes. "Oh, I am not certain I do."

"Don't make me say it."

"Has my little ranger become bashful?"

Leiyn rose to her feet and crossed her arms. Teya grinned, relaxed once more.

"Maybe I should show you." Leiyn could not stop one corner of her lips from lifting.

"I would welcome that. But in a moment." The scout straightened, eyes serious. "You are right—it is nothing. I know you must do it. But it does not mean I must like it."

"Of course not." Leiyn stepped closer and offered her hand. "No one could replace you."

Teya took it and drew her closer until they pressed together. Leiyn's esse reached out eagerly, and Teya's reciprocated.

"That," Teya breathed, "is one thing I do not fear."

～ ～

Teya had dressed and left before the sun rose. Leiyn was not far behind her. After fetching food from the feast hall, she returned to her room, attempting to form a grotto on her own, but the morning's obligations were too distracting to make progress.

Relenting, she turned her focus to the ships floating at the edge of her awareness, then to the brighter sparks among them. Counting the odiosas and noting their positions, she mulled over their best approach. On land, she could have plotted an ambush, a tactic rangers were well-versed in. At sea, she would have to resort to other methods.

A plan started to weave itself together.

When the time finally came for the Council meeting, she rose and sought her companions. Isla and Batu stood outside Ketti and Ekosa's open doors. Moments after Leiyn approached, the two newest members of their party joined them. Their nervousness reflected Leiyn's, though she tried not to show it.

"Follow our lead," Isla advised them. "We'll make sure no plans are made for you without your consent."

Ekosa crossed his arms and bowed his head, while Ketti murmured, "As the spirits will."

Isla led their small party to the Council Domo. Even having witnessed the wonders of Solace and Kunu, Leiyn still had to stifle apprehension at approaching the bronze dome and marbled columns. Far from the only ones attending the meeting, they were swiftly admitted along with the rest of the audience.

Leiyn paused at the entrance to the Freedom Chamber and took in those seated around the central table. The wisdoms Jegu Qayag and Qara Gegeen drew her eye first. While Jegu's attendance was obvious, Qara likely represented the Order of Mahia in Leiyn's absence. Her chest tightened at the reminder.

Her breath grew shallower still when the Gazians looked up and stared at Ketti and Ekosa. Their esses expanded, prodding her companions like ranchers buying new stock. Leiyn resisted the urge to retaliate. In this, they had to fend for themselves.

Taban Khyan's presence only heightened her dread. The moorwarden's back was to her, a fact for which she was grateful. She could imagine his smirk if he had seen her flinch at the sight of him.

Mauricio occupied one end of the table. Luca was seated to his right, the conqueror marginally less armored than the previous time she had seen him.

"Saints' fortune," Isla whispered in Leiyn's ear, squeezing her arm before leading the others to the general audience stands. Swallowing, Leiyn made her way to the table.

As she neared, the consul caught her eye and gestured to an open seat to his left beside Wise Jegu. Leiyn avoided the others' stares and took it, trying to hide all that stewed beneath her skin.

Impatiently, she waited for those in attendance to get settled. When the doors to the chamber boomed closed, Mauricio stood and raised his arms with a wide smile. "Thank you, loyal and brave Baltesians and our allies, for attending to our country this day. It will not be news when I say that we stand on a precipice, one from which we must now step foot. The manner in which we do this is tantamount to our success..."

As the Elected Consul acknowledged the challenges facing them, then thanked particular individuals for being present, Leiyn's attention drifted back to the problems they faced.

How do you defeat an empire?

Titans lay at the heart of any sensible strategy. Only two of the mahas at their disposal knew how to command the spirit beasts as far as she knew: herself and Ketti. If Ketti could turn the kraken of Anchor's Refuge against the Ilberian Armada, it might be enough to break them. But the Eteman could not stand alone against thirty odiosas. Even if Leiyn pitted her strength alongside her, it still would not be enough.

The odiosas had to be dealt with. And she was beginning to understand how.

"Prima Leiyn."

Leiyn startled and looked up. Every eye in the chamber was on her.

Her cheeks turned hot. Though her tongue felt thick in her mouth, Leiyn forced it into motion. "Apologies, Lord Consul. Did you say something?"

Mauricio waved a hand with airy nonchalance. "It was nothing, only an invitation to give your greetings. But I am sure many vital affairs occupy your mind."

Inexperienced at statecraft as she was, Leiyn knew the thorns hidden in words. Others around the table shifted. Taban smiled at her like a tusked jackal spotting its next meal. Her resentment bubbled to boiling. She grasped onto it. Anger had always sharpened her focus. She would need every scrap of wit she had to get through this unscathed.

The consul swept his gaze over the gathered. "Prima Leiyn's return brings us more resources than her own might. Members of the Council, I present to you Ketti Ta'Rul, a powerful maha generous enough to offer her aid to our cause, and Ekosa Siza, an *eesu* recently of Ore-Ofe's *Kekére* who has risked all to come to our defense."

Murmurs filled the lofty chamber as, at Mauricio's invitation, both of her companions stood. Though many of those sitting in the stands appeared surprised by the news, none of the councilors were. Still, few could hide their intrigue as they stared at the outsiders. No doubt they wondered at the terms given for this "generosity," as Mauricio phrased it.

Leiyn's lips curled before she caught herself.

Thanking the pair, the consul invited them to return to their seats. "In addition, a most novel ally has come to our lands, one which I am certain you have heard rumors regarding. I am here to tell you they are true: a dryvan of legend has joined our cause."

The whispers grew into exclamations. A few scoffed aloud. "A forest witch?" one of the merchant lords Leiyn did not know spoke up from the Council table. "You must be mistaken, Lord Consul! They're mere myth, Gast stories spread to inspire fear in good Baltesians. Surely, everyone knows that!"

Acalan's face hardened, but he was disciplined enough to hold his tongue. Leiyn had no such qualms when her blood was up. Leaning forward, she spoke with the same precision as she would loose an arrow.

"Should I call her? I'd like to see how much of a 'story' you think Rowan is then."

The merchant, a richly dressed fellow with a blotchy complexion, colored a deeper red. Before he could bluster a response, Mauricio stood with his hands raised.

"Members of the Council, please! We have enough enemies without making more among ourselves. Mister Cadel, I assure you, our dryvan friend is real. We may need to summon her before this session is over. If she is amenable to such a request," he added with a deferential nod to Leiyn.

She imagined the mischief the dryvan would cause. Considering how little she had respected those Many Tribes chieftains that formed the Tetrad, it would be more than enough to satisfy Leiyn's appetite.

"She'd be delighted." Leiyn leveled a grim smile the merchant's way. Cadel turned away with a pinched look.

"Now then," the consul continued, not bothering to hide his exasperation, "Prima Maha, I would ask that you appraise us of your professional opinion on the use of our new allies. Where might we position them for our success? If you would prefer Lord Luca to recount any aspects of the siege, I am certain he would be willing."

The conqueror's gaze fell from the ceiling at this, an eager light in his eyes. Remembering his crystalline mind, which no fact seemed to escape, Leiyn thought quickly of how to answer. Her eyes alighted on Isla for a moment, and her friend gave her a nod.

They both knew what they must do.

"That won't be necessary, Lord Conqueror." Leiyn looked at Mauricio. "Lord Consul, you know as well as I do that this siege cannot continue. We must break the Ilberian Armada as soon as we can. I believe I have a way to do it."

The chorus of mutters was cut short by Mauricio seating himself and raising a hand. "Please, Prima Maha. I am sure we would be delighted to hear your plan."

So careful, those words. Did he mean them? Either way, they left Leiyn no choice but to barrel forward.

"The true power of Ilberia isn't in their number of ships or the soldiers aboard them—it's their command of titans. We've witnessed this each time the sea kraken that slumbers in the bay rises against the city."

A poor admission to come from the lips of the "Tideraiser," perhaps, yet someone had to admit it. And no one had more authority on her shortcomings than Leiyn herself.

"Two-and-a-half score odiosas are spread out across six ships," she continued. "That means those six out of their hundred ships—"

"One hundred and twelve," Luca interrupted.

Leiyn buried her irritation. "Six out of a hundred and twelve are critical to hit. Take out the odiosas and we can use titans to sweep away the rest."

The councilors exchanged looks with furrowed brows. She could see their lack of comprehension. They did not know the potency of mahia even with the continual attacks against Southport.

One way or another, they soon would.

Mauricio cleared his throat. "Be that as it may, how do you propose reaching these odiosas? I assume the Union understands their vulnerability as well as we do."

It was a question she had pondered. How far would Sharo go to protect them? Would he send Khamo or another lyshan to defend them? If he did, was there anything they could do but meet the threat head-on?

Problems for later. Worry about now.

Leiyn raised her chin higher. "I'm sure they do, but they won't be able to stop us. Our dryvan ally, Rowanwalker, can take a small group to these ships."

"How?" Luca spoke up. With his expression placid and his head cocked to one side, the conqueror seemed genuinely curious.

There was only one answer to give. "Dryvan magic."

The merchant lord, Cadel, scoffed and crossed his arms. Few other councilors looked more confident, the Elected Consul included. Leiyn's heartbeat quickened.

"I have experienced it several times, as have my companions," she hurried to explain. "With it, we reached here from Kunu in a single day. Or does the timeline of our journey make sense any other way?" Leiyn asked of Mauricio.

The consul shook his head, a hint of a smile touching his lips. "No, Prima Maha, it does not."

Sensing the turning tide, Leiyn forged on, sweeping her gaze over the recalcitrant Council. "I will go with Rowan and a few strong warriors. We will kill every odiosa we can. Then we will raise titans to destroy the Armada." She turned to Luca. "Lord Conqueror, if we are to succeed, the Suncoats must be distracted. Can we rely upon our fleet to lead an assault and draw their attention?"

The conqueror looked impassive, untouched by her revelations. She wondered how much Mauricio had told Luca of the threats facing them. Could a man as odd as he fall under Sharo's sway, or was Luca di Eño Vasara as incorruptible as he appeared?

"Yes," Luca said at length. "Twenty-one ships are seaworthy and equipped for naval combat. Their capacities vary, but they can be supplied with sailors and archers sufficient for this purpose." Luca pursed his lips. "We cannot afford to lose them. This assault must succeed."

"It will." Leiyn gave the conqueror a nod, hoping it conveyed her gratitude, and looked back at Mauricio.

Taban stood, and everyone in the room looked toward him.

"With the Lord Consul's blessing," the moorwarden said, drawing out each word, "I volunteer my men to assassinate these odiosas."

Leiyn turned to face him. *Assassinate.* It felt repugnant when spoken that way, coming from his lips.

Taban met her gaze. His expression remained impassive, but

his eyes danced with too much cruel delight for the phrasing to be accidental.

Mauricio sounded as taken aback as she felt. "That is a generous offer, Taban Khyan, but are you certain Altan Gaz wishes you to take this step?"

"I am certain."

What are you plotting? She would have flayed him open then and there if it would give her answers. *Why risk this?* Taban had plotted against them before. Even if the conqueror he had consorted with now lay at the bottom of the sea, she would never be certain he would not turn on them again.

Suspicion stabbed cold daggers through her. One explanation, the worst possibility, surfaced above the others.

Sharo.

He had reached into the heart of the Ilberian Union. What would stop him from influencing key figures in Altan Gaz or any other country? Taban would be simple enough to sway. Men like him craved power above all else.

"Very well," Lord Mauricio at last replied. "If we proceed with this course of action, you may accompany Prima Leiyn in this task. I thank you for your courage."

Taban nodded and seated himself, letting slip a smug smile before he reclaimed his air of impassivity.

The last man she wished to accompany her was Taban. But that was a battle for another time. She refused to give him the satisfaction of seeing her uneasy.

All she could do was focus back on the task at hand. There were details to smooth out, so many she scarcely knew where to begin. Before she could decide, another rose and spoke from behind.

"My pardons for interrupting, but I have a proposal."

Leiyn turned to face Ketti. The Eteman stood with her narrow shoulders back and her chin set. Never had she looked as much like an exotic princess as she did then. Her esse blazed with such conviction that Leiyn could not find the will to intervene. By Isla's look, she felt much the same way.

Mauricio recovered first. "Please, Maha Ketti. We would be delighted if you informed us of this proposal."

Ketti nodded as if unhearing of the sardonic edge to the consul's invitation. "You speak of the titan in your waters. This one, this *kraken*"—the word, apparently unfamiliar, came out jarringly sharp—"will not serve us. It will be difficult, perhaps impossible, to influence it while these odiosas remain."

"Very well. Thank you for bringing this problem to our attention." Mauricio's gaze flickered to Leiyn, a question in his eyes, before settling back on Ketti. "Might I inquire into whether you have a counter-proposal?"

"I do." Ketti swallowed, then brought herself up straighter. "I will not try to raise that titan but seek one elsewhere."

Leiyn wished they'd had this conversation in private beforehand. Now, she had no choice but to openly speak against her.

"Where would you find it?" she countered. "The kraken in Anchor's Refuge is the nearest titan outside the Titan Wilds. Except a stray Gorge spider, if you can find one."

"There are titans at Breakbay," Isla interjected. At Leiyn's look, she flashed an apologetic smile.

"Breakbay is weeks upcoast," Mauricio reminded her. "Unless Rowan can transport you there—"

"Nothing would delight me more."

Leiyn startled the same as the others as Ata appeared beside the table. The dryvan almost looked her old self from before the tragedy befallen Solace as she flashed them all a grin.

"Mistress Rowan." Recovering, Mauricio rose from his chair and bowed. "I am pleased you could join us."

Ata cocked her head. No doubt she, too, heard the false ring in his greetings. "I'm sure," she said drily before turning her attention back to Ketti. "I will take you there, if you can trust me."

Leiyn had to stop herself from gritting her teeth. While she believed Ata was an ally and a friend, pairing her with the Eteman was asking for trouble. Yet Leiyn could not go with them, not when she still had issues to overcome. And the others had to remain here in case an Ilberian assault turned into an invasion.

Ketti looked past Ata rather than at her, but she gave the dryvan a jerky nod. "If we must."

Mauricio looked back and forth between them, a look of consideration falling across his face. Of the others, only Luca looked uncowed by the appearance of a mythic being, instead staring at her with open fascination.

At last, the consul broke the spell with a clap of his hands. "Lord Conqueror, Prima Maha, I would discuss these details further in private. But with the blessing of the Liberty Council, I propose we move forward with these plans."

Leiyn knew how the vote would go before the assents sounded. With a dryvan overlooking the assemblage, how could it go any other way? Yet Taban remained too smug for it to feel like the victory it should have.

THE SMALLEST PEBBLE

*A*ta and Ketti left that evening.

Barely had the plans been set before the dryvan could be made to wait no longer. A nervous Ketti shuffled toward her through the chaotic gardens, while Ata stood like a queen in her palace, commanding mortals like they were her servants. From another of her kind, it might have been a concerning display of conceit. But Leiyn understood Ata now: this was for idle amusement alone.

Flashing Ketti a reassuring smile, Leiyn approached Ata and spoke in a low voice. "Don't let any harm come to her. We need her and the titan she brings."

The dryvan bared her sharp teeth. "Would I compromise my vengeance and break an oath for petty diversion?"

"I'd be more certain of it if you said as much."

Ata threw back her head with a laugh like a raven's caw. The others in attendance jumped at the sound.

"Settle your fears, Awakener—she is under my protection as surely as any seed, sapling, or kit. But you cannot deprive me of having fun."

"I couldn't, even if I begged."

"Correct. Now..." Ata waved a dismissive hand. "Run along until we return to save your sordid city."

With no other recourse, Leiyn rejoined her comrades and hid her lingering worries.

"*Okulukulu* watch over you," Ekosa called to Ketti. Isla and Batu echoed the sentiment while Leiyn held up her hand.

The Eteman nodded with a slight smile. The pearls along her face pulsed as she looked to the dryvan.

"Be vigilant!" Ata shrieked. Then the pair was gone, the air rippling in their wake.

Leiyn blinked and turned to the others. As stunned as she, they still recovered in moments. Even the strangest things could become familiar, as Leiyn had often experienced of late.

"And now?" Isla queried.

Leiyn bit back a sigh. "Now, we wait."

⁓ ⁓

Waiting proved more eventful than Leiyn expected.

She dedicated as much time as she could afford to recreating what she and Ketti—and Chispa, before—had done to reach Clouded Fang. Sitting cross-legged on the floor in her room, she spent hours with her eyes closed, willing the world to merge into a cohesive whole. Sometimes, she glimpsed how it was supposed to appear, but the moment was always fleeting, the clamor of the city chasing it away.

Seeing her struggling, Teya offered to act as Ketti had for her, sharing her esse and perhaps expanding her worldview, and Leiyn accepted. Even if the offer came from lingering jealousy, she had to venture down every avenue she could.

To her relief, some success came from their merging. Thrice during the session, Leiyn saw Unera as an interconnected web of life. Yet she could go no further. Every time she reached beyond it or tried to coax Zuma into doing so for her, the illusion dissipated.

It's not an illusion, she chastised herself afterward. *It's true. It must be.*

A fantasy would not allow her to access the power of titans.

Even if Leiyn did not see the world this way, it did not make it any less valid or true. Tadeo had advised her to open herself to other perspectives. The least she could do was try.

Still, she was making progress. Even if it was too little to assuage her fears.

She visited with her other companions during mealtimes. With Isla occupied by her duties as an envoy, Batu gravitated toward spending more time with Ekosa. At first, Leiyn suspected it was out of a sense of duty, but the more she saw them together, the more she realized their camaraderie was genuine.

Only when she stopped to mull it over did she realize how much they had in common. Both were orphans and outsiders among their people. Though quiet, they showed unbreakable resolve when need called for it. Batu might dwarf the *eesu* in size, and Ekosa might never have touched a weapon, but both possessed a warrior's spirit.

Looks can lie. Yet another of Tadeo's sayings came to mind as she watched them converse over dinner one evening. *The keen ranger pierces through to the heart.*

The routine was not to last. After a day of seclusion, a messenger boy came by Leiyn's room with a missive from the Elected Consul.

Do not forget, it read, *that you remain my Prima Maha. Use your mahitas well.*

Leiyn sighed and sent the boy away. She was no politician, but the implications would have been clear to the dullest mind. Painful as her failures were, the prospect of facing the Order of Mahia promised to be even more so.

But first, she had another matter to which to attend.

Squaring her shoulders, she made for Mauricio's solarium. The guards hesitated to admit her at first, but she was soon escorted within.

"Prima Maha," the consul greeted her, not looking up from his scattered papers. "Did you come for clarity on my missive? I thought its implications abundantly clear."

"They were, Lord Consul. We need to discuss something else. Preferably in private."

He finally looked up at that. After studying her, Mauricio gestured to the servants standing in attendance about the chamber. They departed, closing the door behind them.

The consul leaned back in his chair and steepled his hands. "What is it you wished to discuss, then, Leiyn?"

"Taban Khyan cannot come on the invasion."

Mauricio pursed his lips. "You are aware he has offered to fight on our behalf? It is a great demonstration of faith on part of Altan Gaz, one I would not easily turn away."

"We cannot trust him, no matter what he offers."

The consul stared a moment longer before lapsing into his chair with a chuckle. "Come, my good woman! You cannot still suspect him of duplicitousness. We all err. I could hardly find fault in complying with an Ilberian conqueror for one in his position. Saints know I committed such a sin often myself."

"It's not that. It's *him*."

His smile faded as silence yawned between them. "I had a hound growing up," he said at length. "Ugly thing with a squashed face. He always drooled on the rugs when I snuck him inside. I loved him dearly. My only qualm was when he would bite one of his bits of rawhide and not release it, no matter how I tugged on it." Mauricio peered at her, one corner of his lips turning up. "You hold onto grudges in much the same way."

Leiyn raised an eyebrow. "Is that your way of calling me a bitch?"

Mauricio broke out into a startled laugh. "It wasn't, actually! Though I almost wish it had been. Perhaps I'll tuck that insult away for a particularly intractable dignitary. No, my dear ranger, I only mean to say what I uttered often to that dear ill-favored dog of mine: Let it go."

Let it go. The night they escaped the Gazian Greathouse flashed through her mind. The mad race through the meadows. The shadows emerging from the darkness with killing intent. The arrows raining down on them on the riverbank.

She forced a smile. "I might be fairer than your old dog, but I'm every bit as stubborn."

"So I have learned." Levity fled his expression. "But you will bring the moorwarden and his plainsriders with you on your raid. That is an order, Prima Maha, and you know I do not issue those lightly to you."

It was what she had feared. But Leiyn had never held out much hope of convincing him otherwise.

"Lord Consul," she said with a bob of her head. As he issued her a bemused dismissal, she turned away.

"And Leiyn," he called as she set her hand to the doorhandle, "look in on your mahitas, would you?"

Grimacing, she looked back. "If I must."

Then she strode from the office, the consul's sigh following her out.

It was past noon by the time she reached the First Temple. The Order was well into their daily practice as she approached. Leiyn dredged up the names of the students and ran them through her head. After weeks of only the occasional thought of them, it was no mean feat. Some came back easily: Genevieve, Izan and Reyna, Estel. Others, she could only picture their faces, no hint of their names remaining.

But she could not tarry any longer. Striding across the courtyard, Leiyn entered the temple's nave. All present looked around at her entrance, but none looked surprised. Their grasp of lifesense had plainly progressed since she had departed.

The flush of pride that warmed her chest came as a surprise. Especially since she could not claim credit for their progress.

"Prima Maha—I welcome you back." Qara Gegeen, the wisdom teaching the Order in Leiyn's absence, bowed her head in acknowledgment.

"Thank you, Wise Qara." Leiyn approached to stand by her side, then faced the watching mahitas. "Sorry to interrupt."

"It is nothing. We are practicing the channeling of essence into one another."

The wisdom kept her expression carefully composed, as she did her esse. Leiyn could not tell what she thought of her long absence, though her stillness alone was a sign.

"Good." Ignoring the undercurrents from Qara, Leiyn faced the mahitas. "It's a skill I use often. It'll serve you well."

She felt like a false priest facing them, speaking as if she had enough experience to warrant her authority. The expressions of many of her students made it clear they thought the same. Some frowned. Others smiled, eyes full of pity.

She resented that most of all.

Chin up, she scolded herself. *Spine straight.* Like in any battle, there was only one way through.

"Estel and Simó," she said as she scanned the assembled. "I don't see them." She hoped remembering their names would lead the others to believe she recalled them all.

"They have been dismissed, Prima Maha," Qara supplied. "Or hope to be. Estel has brought, ah, *litigation* against your government, seeking to be released from service to the Order. Simó, I am afraid, has been imprisoned for theft."

Neither came as a surprise, though the pang of regret surprised Leiyn. For Simó especially, as the youth had held much potential, if only he could have left behind his old ways. Perhaps, if she had remained, she could have helped him.

Can't save them all, Tideraiser. No matter how you try.

"I'm sorry to hear it," she voiced aloud. "We'll have to make do without them. Lord Mauricio has requested I make you ready for what's coming. To see where you might best aid in defending Southport."

"Is that why you're back, then?" Genevieve—Evie, Leiyn corrected herself—spoke innocently, but her eyes said otherwise. It seemed the girl had learned guile in her time in Southport. But insubordination was one thing Leiyn knew how to deal with.

Leiyn held her gaze in silence until Evie looked away. Only then did she speak.

"To know that, I need to see how far you've progressed. Wise Qara, if you wouldn't mind, I'd like a demonstration of what they've learned."

"It would be my pleasure, Prima Maha."

They spent the next two hours watching the mahitas use their mahia. Leiyn tried not to show her impatience and weariness as the wisdom ran the students through one drill after another. She strode up and down the line, observing each with her lifesense, judging their strength and skill and weighing it against what she had seen from the Union. Her conclusions were inauspicious.

Still too clumsy. Too green. Hindrances more than assets.

They had progressed since she had left Southport, but their mastery and strength was nowhere near what was required to take on fully trained odiosas. She tried to hide her evaluations from her expression, but as the afternoon dragged on, their suspicions came out in many small ways—darting glances, quirked eyebrows, downcast looks.

At last, Qara completed the final exercise and turned to Leiyn. The silence dragged on as Leiyn decided how best to phrase what she had to say.

The first mahita to speak surprised her: Nestor, the young soldier who resented being recruited into the Order. "Prima Leiyn, you must use us. There's to be a battle, isn't there? We're taking the fight to the Suncoats."

Murmurs sprouted up and down the line. The older couple, Reyna and Izan, looked at each other with furrowed brows. Some of the younger ones, Genevieve included, brightened with anticipation.

Little point in hiding it now.

"Yes," Leiyn said. "There'll be a battle, and soon. But you're not ready for it."

Objections broke out at once. Nestor's were the loudest. Stepping forward, the young man bristled from head to boot.

"You cannot keep us from protecting our home, Prima Maha. If I cannot help here, then I request you release me back to where I can."

"What about us?" cried the gangly teenage girl whose name Leiyn could not recall. "We want to help, too!"

"Perhaps there are other ways of helping," another young woman said with obvious nervousness. A mother of three children, if memory served. No doubt she sought to protect them however she could.

Leiyn held up a hand, expecting silence to fall, but these were not ranger apprentices. The chattering grew louder, both sides of the debate rising in heat and volume. Her temper started rising with it, and she felt her tether on it fraying.

"*Quiet!*"

Stunned into silence, the mahitas stared at Leiyn. Evie looked frightened. A tendril of shame calmed Leiyn, but only slightly.

She swept her gaze across the room before speaking. "Look. I understand you want to help, to fight. I would feel the same way in your shoes. But I cannot send you against the Union. You're not ready, not yet. In a few more months, perhaps you would be. But we don't have that time."

Her hand rose to touch her auburn tress. She forced it back to her side. No need to show them she was as on edge as they were.

Be decisive. Certain. Like Tadeo always was.

"This won't be the last challenge that faces Baltesia. Far from it. We'll need proper mahas before this war is through. So, for your sake and our country's, you have to stay out of this fight."

"Prima Maha." Nestor bowed his head. She could not tell if it was from frustration or acquiescence that he spoke.

"Please, Prima Leiyn." Evie had tears in her eyes. "There must be something we can do?"

"Hush, child." The grandmother, Tecla, shifted over to place her hands on the young girl's shoulders, kneading them. "Let her do as she sees fit."

"But we want to help!"

Qara Gegeen, silent to that point, approached from where she had been standing in the corner and leaned in close. "Prima Maha, if I may."

The last thing Leiyn needed was another opinion. But considering the favor this woman and her compatriots had done Baltesia, she hardly had any other choice but to humor her.

"Of course," Leiyn said through clenched teeth. "What is it?"

If the wisdom noticed her lack of receptivity, she did not show it. "I believe there is a capacity in which they may be of assistance. As you may recall, I and my fellow wisdoms have protected Southport night and day since your departure. We have turned back every *avaga* the Ilberian Union has raised against us."

"And we're grateful for your service," Leiyn hedged, unsure of Qara's angle.

"That is not why I speak of this. My proposal is that those of the Order could assist us by supplying us with essence as ours falters. We do not have artifacts to bolster our strength as you do."

Thrown by the wisdom's knowledge of her amber beads, it took Leiyn a moment to realize what Qara meant. "You want to use them for their esse?"

"Yes. Only as much as they can withstand. And only if it is permissible by you and the Lord Consul. Even the smallest pebble may break a wave."

Leiyn looked to one of the stained glass windows lining the temple walls. Gifting esse could be dangerous, as could standing near the wisdoms as they strove against the Union. Odiosas might target them, and with the paltry strength of the mahitas' defenses, it was unlikely they would be able to defend themselves.

Yet Qara was right. She did not have to delve far into the wisdom's esse to see the depths of her weariness. They needed help, and the Order needed to feel useful.

Leiyn turned back, meeting first the eager eyes of those

awaiting her decision, then the reticent ones. "Wise Qara has a way you could help. It isn't without risk, and I won't force anyone who wishes to remain safe to do it. But it would be useful."

"I will do it, Prima Maha," Nestor said. The other young members of the Order chimed in shortly after him, except for the young mother, who continued to gnaw on her bottom lip.

"Let me tell you what it is first." Even exasperated, she had to admire how quickly they volunteered. "You are to support the wisdoms by supplying them with esse when they request it."

The soldier seemed disappointed. All the rest looked relieved. Even those who had been skeptical started nodding then.

"We will be grateful for this support," Wise Qara said. "You will be vital to Southport's defense."

Her words seemed to further bolster their spirits. Evie and Celia whispered to each other excitedly. Izan and Reyna clasped hands, quiet resolve in their shared look.

"Don't give too much. And do nothing beyond what the wisdoms tell you." Leiyn paused, making sure her warnings were heard. "Do you know where the wisdoms are posted?"

Nods came from all around. "And we can sense them!" Evie piped up. "We'd find them anywhere they go."

"Good. We don't know when the battle will begin, only that it will be soon and may come at any time. Be ready. When the alarm sounds, move to attend your assigned wisdom. Wise Qara, would you mind giving them their assignments?"

As the wisdom moved among the mahitas, Leiyn stood back and watched with arms crossed. She hoped that, when the time came, they would not be as rash as she used to be.

Or still am.

A small smile curled her lips.

65

A BLOODY DAWN

*E*ven before she opened her eyes, Leiyn sensed it coming. Like a tidal wave rising from the edge of the world, its presence felt inevitable as it grew nearer with every passing moment. It was a prophecy for the day. A harbinger of war.

A titan crested the horizon.

Eight days.

Eight days since Ketti and Ata had disappeared from the gardens to fetch a titan from Breakbay. Eight days of practicing and failing to open a grotto on her own. Of counseling her mahitas in their role in the upcoming battle. Of keeping her body and mind sharp by training in the yard.

It was several days longer than she thought she would have to wait. And yet the day still came too soon.

She threw off the covers and climbed out of bed. Red light pressed through the curtains. She watched the day brighten as she secured her weapons belt. *A bloody dawn,* Gan would have called it.

Not so amusing a thought now.

Teya rose moments after her. Having also slept in her clothes—Iritu ones to match Leiyn and Acalan's—only her *situal* armor remained to be fastened on over them. "Ah," she said after a moment, her eyes unfocused. "So that is what awoke you."

"Didn't feel it coming? Thought you prided yourself on your sharp senses."

The scout afforded her a slight smile, but the teasing fell flat. Silence followed as they readied for battle.

Teya took her spear in hand, then turned to face her. "Redlock?"

"Hm?"

"Try to not die."

Looking up from settling her scabbards, Leiyn met the scout's gaze. Fear rarely filled those eyes, but it overflowed from them now. And she knew Teya did not fear dying.

The space between them felt unbearable. Crossing it, Leiyn wrapped her in a tight embrace. Teya smelled of old leather, sweat, and lilac soap from the bath they had shared the night before. She breathed it in.

"Don't worry," Leiyn murmured against her neck. "You'll be there every step of the way. What harm could come to me?"

Teya laughed and buried her lips in Leiyn's hair. Heat flooded Leiyn's chest.

"Don't be rash."

Pulling away, Leiyn swatted at the scout, then pecked her cheek with a final kiss. "Come on. The others are waiting."

❧

Salt-gnawed wind whipped her hair free of its braid as Leiyn squinted toward the horizon.

The titan was still many leagues off, but it ate at the distance with each powerful lash of its tail. Try as she might, she could not identify what kind it was: shaped like a fish, but writ in grand proportions. And there was something different about what formed its body as well.

You'll find out soon enough.

Turning away, she scanned those around her. They had assembled where the pier met land before it jutted out into the unsettled sea.

Most she was glad to see. Teya and four of her scouts. Isla and Batu. Even Ekosa had tagged along to ward against odiosas and titans they might raise against their invasion. *Eesuwé*, it turned out, were every bit as capable as odiosas in commanding titans. Their Ofean friend might prove vital should the battle turn against them.

Acalan would have been another welcome addition, but other duties intervened. The war chieftain had to remain behind to command the Gast warriors.

Others, she was far less pleased to bring. Taban and four of his plainsriders stood to one side, clad in their lamellar armor. Their expressions were of stone, but their eyes flickered often to Batu, disdain plain in every look. Only Taban seemed devoid of malice toward their kinsman. Yet the smile that curled the moorwarden's lips was more unpleasant still as he stroked the meadow grouse fletching of his arrows.

She looked away but kept her lifesense trained on them. Mauricio was convinced they were allies, but she knew Taban's nature. Yet another thing to keep watch for.

Only two were missing from their ranks now. The two most vital to this plan.

Where are you? she thought to Ketti and Ata.

The sun had risen behind a veil of clouds. Rain was promised along with blood, a curtain of it already darkening the horizon. The Ilberian Armada had pulled up anchor and positioned themselves against the oncoming storm. The odiosas had surely sensed the titan by now. Left unhindered, they would be more than enough to turn back Ketti's giant fish. The Gazian wisdoms and the mahitas of the Order would not be able to help against that; only if a titan drove toward the city would they enter the frey.

A hand on Leiyn's arm turned her back to her companions. Isla gave her a wan smile. She was back in her Eteman garb and had slung her bow over one shoulder, a short Gast spear strapped over the other. Batu was similarly equipped, though with his axe at his hip instead of a spear. Ekosa wore the sky blue *boubou* of his Coterie. Even as an exile, he preferred them to any true armor. The only weapons he carried into battle were his belt knife and his mahia.

Their bright enchanted clothes clashed with the day's purpose, yet it was as good of protection as they would get. She was grateful they had that much defense. Once they were among the Ilberians, they would need every scrap they could get.

And Omn's luck if we're to all survive.

"Be safe, Leiyn." Her old friend squeezed her arm. "And don't be—"

"—rash, I know. Someone already reminded me today." Leiyn flashed Teya a look, receiving a cocked eyebrow in return.

Isla followed her gaze and nodded. "Good. You need as many level heads surrounding you as you can get."

Before the approaching titan, Leiyn's amusement dwindled. "Keep close. We need to stay together and watch each other's backs. Once we clear a ship of odiosas, Ata will move us to the next one, but she can only do that if we're not too spread out."

Her friends nodded at her words, as did Teya's scouts. Taban only lifted his chin, eyes narrowing further. Leiyn ignored him.

Stray as far as you like, you two-faced bastard.

Looking back to Isla and Batu, she drew them in and muttered. "If I don't come out of this—"

"Leiyn," Isla cut in. "Don't talk like that."

"Just listen. If I don't, make sure Teya and her people are taken care of."

"Nothing's going to—"

"We swear it," Batu interrupted Isla's placations. He gripped Leiyn's shoulder, his esse steady with purpose. More than friends, now, they were comrades-in-arms.

Isla sighed. "Yes, of course. But no one is dying today, alright?"

"Right."

Leiyn turned away. Stare too long, and fear for her friends might shatter her. She had not bothered to ask them to remain behind; she knew what their answer would be. Now, she needed to be strong, as strong as she had ever been.

Even when this day might rob her of all she loved.

Though she knew it to be futile, she felt along the thin thread to Clouded Fang. *Heed me*, she pleaded with the titan. *When I call, you must come.*

But she had not learned to form a grotto. Unless Chispa showed up, or Ketti became unoccupied with controlling her titan, she had to rely on her wits.

With her attention drifting, Leiyn startled when someone blazed into being next to her. She had halfway drawn a falchion before she recognized them.

"Ata," Leiyn hissed, sheathing her weapon. "What in Legion's hells are you wearing?"

The dryvan grinned and spread her arms to do a quick spin. "How do I look?"

Terrifying was the only response Leiyn could think of. Titanbone armor covered the shapeshifter from head to toe. Similar in style to the red armor Khamo wore, Ata's was patterned in aqua and violet. Some creature's ribs cradled her torso, while broad scapulas projected from her shoulders. Horns erupted from a helm that only left a narrow opening for her eyes and mouth. In one hand, she carried a weapon with a handle and curved blade off the end that resembled a farmer's scythe. Of all her terrifying guises, Ata most resembled a devil then.

Good thing she's our devil.

Aloud, Leiyn asked, "Where's Ketti?"

"Can you not sense her?" The dryvan aimed her scythe toward the horizon, where the titan neared.

"What do you...?" The epiphany hit with the force of a titan's awakening. "She's *riding* it?"

Ata loosed a laugh. "Of course! How else could she shepherd it all this way? But we'll leave that for another time," she added, seeing Leiyn's incredulous expression. "The reef whale nears. Should we not be cutting the strings to our enemy's army?

Perhaps *before* they stop our Eteman friend from capsizing their ships?"

Though Leiyn flinched at the dryvan's casual divulgence of "Eteman," she stifled both questions and reprimands. *She's right. Now's not the time.* She set her mind on their task. The moment had come for the final preparations.

Leiyn reached for the dormant huntress within her.

Her edges had dulled and her anger diminished, but she needed to be the warrior she had once been, for which Acalan had named her. The one she abhorred.

Only the huntress could survive what came next. Only a killer that reveled in the slaughter.

Like a spark fanned to flame, fear blossomed into fury. Her senses felt sharper and fuller, her reactions quicker. Leiyn looked to the messenger boy standing nearby, shifting from foot to foot and staring with wide eyes at the armored dryvan. Her words snapped out like the nearby Baltesian banner did in the wind.

"Go to the Lord Consul and Lord Conqueror. Tell them it's time."

The lad bobbed his head and took off at a run.

Leiyn turned back to the others. It took an effort not to bark at them as well. "Remember: stay with Ata. She'll take us where we need to go."

Her friends nodded, as did the Gast scouts. Taban was the only one who spoke.

"We will keep close, Ranger, do not fear."

With her blood up, it took every ounce of will to ignore him. Leiyn turned away, shrugging her longbow into her hands as she did and nocking an arrow. Behind her, she heard the others ready their weapons.

Leiyn looked to Ata. "Ready when you are."

The shapeshifter's grin twisted with deep-seated rage. "Keep your feet. It won't be an easy landing."

Even as Leiyn nodded, the ground ripped away.

PART VII

IN THE STORM

TEN YEARS BEFORE

Wooden walls rattled as thunder shook apart the sky.

Leiyn hunkered down on the bench, knees drawn to her chest. The rest of the rangers and staff in the great hall of the Wilds Lodge should have been reassuring. For most of the evening, easy chatter and laughter had filled the space. But they quieted with every protest of the squall, each attuned to signs of peril. Yet when no lightning struck the compound, and no titan materialized from the dark clouds, they soon returned to their lighthearted conversations.

Storms did not frighten her—it was the thought of what might lie behind them. While the others took advantage of a night free from chores, Leiyn curled in on herself, waiting for a titan's awakening to tear down her defenses. Fierce as the storm was, it seemed the only possible cause.

As if hearing her fears, Gan gave voice to them. "Wonder which one's behind it," he mused from farther down the table. "A rain elephant? A tempest hawk? Or could it be... Winged Death?"

Some of the rangers groaned. Tadeo, who stood in a far corner, shook his head and cast Leiyn a scrutinizing look. She ducked her head, feigning weariness.

"What's Winged Death?" Isla asked, brow furrowed.

Inwardly, Leiyn lamented her friend falling for what was clearly bait. But she could not rouse herself enough to head off the jester.

"You don't know Winged Death?" Gan leaned across the table and pitched his voice lower. "Be glad you've never met it."

"Gan," Marina said from Leiyn's other side, "leave her be."

Gan ignored the older ranger, eyes intent on Isla. "You think ash dragons are terrifying? They're nothing next to Winged Death. They sweep in like a bank of fog, a thousand mouths thirsting for your blood. Wherever they pass, they leave skeletons in their wake, bodies gnawed to bones." He shuddered. "There's no more terrifying creature in all the Titan Wilds."

"Truly?" Isla raised her eyebrows. "Doesn't sound like any titan I've heard of."

"It's a myth," Marina cut in. "No one's actually seen it. And call it by its name: a fog swarm."

Leiyn repressed a shiver. Somehow, that name made it sound worse than Gan's elaborations.

Distracted by the conversation, she failed to notice the person standing behind her until a hand clamped down on her shoulder. Startled, she almost slapped it away before she noticed who it belonged to.

"Ranger Nathan," she said, hiding her surprise.

Though he was "Old Nathan" to everyone behind his back, something in the gray man's severe disposition awoke profound respect in Leiyn—enough, at least, to address him by his proper title.

For a long moment, Nathan only looked at her, his gnarled hand holding her almost painfully tight. His eyes screwed up, seeming to burrow into hers. Around them, conversation quieted.

At last, he spoke. "Storms pass. Always."

Simple words. A meaningless platitude from any other. Yet Leiyn felt the knots in her chest unwinding. She straightened under the elder ranger's grip and nodded.

"Right. Thanks."

His thin lips tweaked into what might have passed for a smile. As soon as it appeared, it was gone. Old Nathan released her and moved on down the line, heading for where a barrel of festival ale had been set up for all to enjoy.

She stared after him. *Storms pass.* More than any song from Yolant, joke from Gan, or advice from Tadeo, Nathan's words had given her something she had needed. Pushing down her fear, she summoned a bracing smile and leaned toward Isla.

"Shall we see if we can sneak in another ale?"

Isla smiled, eyes crinkling. "I thought you'd never ask."

67

BUTCHERS

Her shoes pounded against planks. The world righted around them.

Leiyn raised her bow and tried to gain her bearings.

Her vision pitched along with her balance. A ship spread around them. Ocean lay to either side. Alarm spread like fire across the deck, chaos erupting where it touched.

Her senses settling, her footing unsteady, Leiyn tried picking out friends from foes. All around, her fellow infiltrators struggled to do the same.

"Kill them!" a shout came from behind. A roar rose from the Ilberian crew.

No time for weakness. Relying on her lifesense, Leiyn found the closest Suncoat and whirled toward him. Her draw hand found her jawline, her bowstring taut and arrow nocked. The soldier had a shield raised as he charged, eyes peeking over the rim, sword ready to stab forward.

Her arrow shot over the shield and under his helm. At once, his esse went dark.

Death clawed into her, frigid fingers raking against her lifesense. She did not shut it out now. Death was what she had come to bring. Every kill brought them closer to victory.

Her turning stomach told her otherwise.

Gritting her teeth, Leiyn nocked another arrow and picked out her next target. With her vision finally resolving, the surrounding pandemonium came into clarity.

Her companions fought desperately to keep the ship's crew back, outnumbered three to one. Teya jabbed her spear through a soldier's neck, lips pulled back in a snarl. Her scouts matched her ferocity, each striking with unflinching resolve.

Isla sent arrow after arrow into their enemies' midst. Batu stood before her and Ekosa, axe gripped in both hands, swiping at any who came too close. Taban and his plainsriders clashed with more Suncoats nearby.

Ata stood in an arena of her own. She spun like a frenzied dancer, cutting down any foolish enough to stand too near. Where her scythe slashed, a red mist rose into the air.

Peering beyond the dryvan, Leiyn caught sight of the odiosas. Their mahia surged forth from atop the forecastle of the ship, but another was countering it.

Ekosa—the *eesu* had his eyes closed as he grappled with their enemies. Alone, he would not be enough to overcome them, but that he had held them at bay this long was impressive.

Even as she watched, esse built among the odiosas, then surged forward, pummeling as a tidal wave. Where it washed over Leiyn's companions, they staggered, while the Suncoats remained untouched. Only hastily erected walls kept Leiyn upright.

The Ilberians took full advantage of the moment. One hacked into a Gast scout, sending him falling to the deck with a pained shriek. Batu took a long cut down his arm. Bellowing, he stumbled back and clasped a hand to it, blood leaking between his fingers.

Rage drowned the last vestiges of her guilt.

Leiyn sent an arrow flying across the ship to pierce one of those gray robes. A dark patch sprouted around the arrow as the odiosa collapsed to the deck.

Five more.

She loosed another arrow, then another. Only one hit its

mark as the odiosas scattered before the assault, sending another to the ground.

Four.

Then Ata appeared among them.

There was no fleeing the Iritu's wrath. Her scythe whipped through one, then another, then a third. All their magic could not save them now.

The last one tried taking the only path left to him. Leaping overboard, he fell the dozen paces into the sea. No sooner had he entered the water than Leiyn sensed him knocking into the ship's hull. A killing blow. His essence faded to darkness moments after.

The dryvan turned back with her weapon raised. Blood dripped from the blade to coat the shaft.

"Onward!" Ata shrieked.

Barely had the word left her lips than the world upturned once more.

Leiyn fell to her knees, head swollen and aching. They were on a new deck surrounded by fresh enemies. Suncoats swarmed the ship, interspersed between her companions. Each threatening to kill.

The dormant huntress seized her in its talons.

She surged to her feet, her senses adjusting more quickly this time. Spotting three soldiers turning toward her, she whipped her longbow around to bash two in the face before shoving the last one back.

The stave of the bow struck as hard as a club. The Suncoats were staggered for long enough for her to toss aside her bow and draw her falchions. In the breath before they attacked, Leiyn touched the amber beads nestled against her hip. Like inhaling air, she sucked in power from two of them.

Energy swelled through her, quickening and strengthening wherever it flowed.

The trio of Suncoats seemed almost slow as they struck. She rebuffed them all, falchions moving in concert. As they tried for another strike, she moved between their rhythm in a dance to which only she knew the steps. Her blades dipped in and through their armor, titanbone slicing apart steel, skin, and tendon without discrimination.

Limbs parted. Men fell.

By the time she paused to catch her breath, the three Suncoats lay dead or dying on the deck. Blood soaked her shoes. Darkness leaked into their lifefires, like a bonfire sputtering under a rain shower. Their pain oozed in through her lifesense. She felt every death like it was her own.

Their deaths or mine.

Steeling her nerve, she looked for the odiosas. Again, Ata had beaten her to them, again atop the forecastle. Four had fallen, and the rest were not long for the world.

Leiyn looked to her friends. All remained alive, to her relief. A plainsrider had fallen, his legs cut out from under him, and wounds spread among the rest, but they were alive.

Leiyn had just retrieved her bow from the deck when Ata crooned, "Two done, four to go! To the next feast!"

"*Wait!*"

The dryvan, wreathed in esse, looked as ethereal as a Saint. Eyes wild and bestial, they were devoid of any empathy as Ata looked down at Leiyn. Instinctual fear thrilled through Leiyn. She did her best to ignore it.

"What, Awakener?" the Iritu roared back.

"Hold on a damned moment!"

Leiyn weaved through the pitched battle to look out over the railing. The Ilberian Armada infested the surrounding waters. Her party had slain a third of their odiosas, but thousands of soldiers still occupied those ships. These shouted at them and shook their weapons. Archers nocked arrows, awaiting commands to release. For the moment, they were out of range, but that would not last for long.

But they did not fight alone. From the distant city docks came two dozen ships, cutting through the water toward them. Baltesian soldiers dotted the decks. Soon, they would engage the enemy and draw away the Armada's attention, at least in part.

An immense pressure against her lifesense brought her whirling around to stare in the other direction. Peering around swaying bodies, she beheld Ketti's titan with her own eyes. The "reef whale," as Ata had called it, more than justified its name. It surpassed anything she had encountered before, as large as an entire fifth of the fleet. Still a half-league away, she saw part of it cresting the ocean surface. Unlike other titans of the rivers and seas, it was not formed of water, but a coarse, pink substance.

Coral, she realized, as irregular shapes rose in spires from the reef whale's back.

A spout of water brought her attention to a point midway down its back. As the water shimmered into the air, Leiyn saw her: Ketti, crouched atop the titan, hands pressed to its rough body. Even seeing it, her mind balked at the impossibility of it. Riding a titan! She wondered how long Ketti had traveled to bring the titan here. How exhausted she must be.

Ata took shape next to her. Ignoring Leiyn's startlement, she barked, "We must go now! Or do you wish them to strike back?"

A glance showed her companions' fights to be finishing or drawing to standstills. It was as good a chance as they were going to get.

"Do it."

The world peeled away again. Like a curtain revealing a play, a new ship awaited them.

Mayhem erupted once more.

Leiyn barely had time to raise her drawn falchion before a poleaxe descended toward her. Her surprise was sufficient that she could not keep hold of the blade as it was ripped from her hand and tossed aside. It felt as if a limb had been torn from her as it slid across the deck.

She stumbled back. The unwitting move saved her life: an axe thudded into her shoulder instead of her head. Ranger greens would have parted before the steel wedge, and armor might not have withstood it, but the strained enchantments in her Iritu garb held.

Only her longbow in hand, she lashed out with it, battering

any enemy within reach. Most blows fell uselessly against shields. Three Suncoats pressed forward, shields pushing her back against a railing. Soon, she would have nowhere to go but into the water.

Back!

She sent a wave of lifeforce pulsing from her, tumbling like an avalanche into their minds. The soldiers staggered, but so did those behind them, her companions among them.

A sword dipped toward Isla. As Leiyn watched, it scored against her side, piercing deep enough that her friend's vestments could not stop it.

Isla bled.

Her rage rose to a full blaze. Leiyn ripped free her remaining falchion and hewed into the soldiers between them. Shields fell in splinters. Bodies hit the deck. The Suncoats' screams for mercy went unheard.

As the first three fell, she charged the Suncoats attacking her friends. Barreling into one, she sent him sprawling, then cut out the legs from the one who had struck Isla.

He fell with barely a gasp and tumbled onto his back. For a moment, they locked eyes.

She thrust down.

Her falchion buried into his chest to the hilt, then lodged in the deck under him. Wood, flesh, and steel clung to the blade. Leiyn tried dragging it free, but for a moment, it resisted and defied her efforts.

The world tilted.

Her feet slipped out from under her. Clinging to the hilt, Leiyn watched as the deck turned into an incline. Bodies slid under the railing and into the sea. Men and women who had not secured a grip crashed after them, screaming until the water swallowed them. None of those who fell were of her party, though she kept searching for them, afraid she had missed one.

Her lifesense told her what was happening moments before she heard the crash. Ketti and her titan had arrived and begun barging through the Armada.

Only knocked by a wave, the ship Leiyn and the others occupied righted itself as the reef whale passed. As they pitched back and forth, Leiyn accounted for those remaining. Batu had one arm looped around the railing, the other holding both Isla and Ekosa against his chest. Teya had her spear around the central mast, locked in place next to two of her scouts. Taban still had three plainsriders with him at the far end of the ship.

Three odiosas still lived and congregated by the ship's wheel, but their lives promised to be short. Ata crawled toward them, her progress slow but implacable as roots extended from beneath her armor to drag her across the tilting deck. Her esse burned brighter than ever before.

The dryvan was draining her victims of their lifeforce.

Somehow, it seemed worse than outright slaughter. Leiyn shook her head free of the thought.

Worry about it later. You need her.

When the ship was finally steady enough, Leiyn clambered to her feet and, channeling a surge of lifeforce, yanked her sword free. She looked for her discarded weapons, fearing the worst, but the Saints smiled upon her: both her longbow and the second Iritu falchion had tangled in netting in one corner of the ship. She moved toward them, trying not to hear the terrified screams as the dryvan closed in on her prey.

No sooner had she reached the netting than he appeared.

Like the sun emerging from behind a cloud, his esse blinded her. Leiyn recognized him a breath after. Ripping her falchion free of the netting, she turned to face him.

Khamo had come at last.

RED

Khamo stood in the middle of the deck. The battle opened around him, humans instinctively flinching away.

For a moment, all on the ship grew still.

The lyshan appeared much as he had before, though he somehow seemed to loom larger. The same scarlet armor covered his hulking frame, the damage to it mended. Only thin seams and the shadow of lighter esse told of where Ata had broken apart the titanbone before, yet they seemed vulnerabilities, if she could find a way to exploit them. Only his barren eyes and his gray, scaled limbs remained exposed.

Yet while he held that cruel whip and heavy-headed mace, no part of him seemed vulnerable. Memories of wounds sent phantom pains running through Leiyn.

But she had never been one to run from fear.

She hefted her falchions into a guard position and advanced. Clouded Fang still would not heed her call. The deck under her feet was slick with blood and saltwater. Exertion and the horror of slaughter conspired to send her to her knees.

She had killed lyshans, but none like him. The others had been emaciated mongrels by comparison, their bodies starved of esse. Even Man'nah she had only overcome because his will was split among his countless souls. Because part of him had wanted to die.

Khamo was not starved; he was an alpha wolf in its prime. He was not divided in purpose and mind; he was unified with a single intent—to kill.

This fight promised death. Still, she went.

The lyshan paid her no heed. His gaze was only for Ata, his head tilted up to where she stood at the helm. The dryvan, for her part, seemed to be cast in stone. Only a slight quiver and her roiling esse betrayed the emotions locked within her still frame.

Enemy and ally alike were locked in this moment, trapped like flies in sap. Beyond their silence, the ocean stormed in the wake of Ketti's reef whale. The distant sound of splintering ships and shouting soldiers echoed across the waters.

"Still, you serve him!" Ata's hissed words carried across the deck. "Though you know all he intends?"

Khamo appeared unmoved. He only continued to stare up at his fellow Iritu. Leiyn wondered if any emotion remained to him, or if he was as desiccated on the inside as he looked from without.

"He cares nothing for you, Khamo, *nothing*! He uses you. You're a weapon he'll discard without care or thought. Why do this? Why throw away your existence for... this?"

The dryvan spread out an arm. The carnage surrounding them spoke for itself.

At last, the lyshan stirred. His parched lips turned up in a smile, more unsettling than his glower. A single word issued from his chasm of a mouth.

"*Red...*"

Unbidden images flashed through Leiyn's mind. Flames shooting up a massive golden tree, consuming its cerulean leaves. Human bodies split open, their innards spread around them. Clawed hands raised, scarlet blood streaming down corded arms. The cloying silence that followed the slaughter.

Red. She knew what it meant. How Khamo burned from the

wounds of the past. How he reveled in the mortal blood he spilled.

How vengeance never seemed to quench the flames.

A gust fluttered through the sails. Ata hefted her scythe in both hands and lifted her helmeted head. She stood as tall as Leiyn had ever seen her as she stared down at the lyshan.

"You always were a brute."

Then Ata disappeared.

A flash of lifeforce and the clank of bone on bone had her head whipping back to the lyshan. In the time it took Leiyn to draw a breath, the dryvan had appeared behind the lyshan and struck. Khamo met her attack, his mace effortlessly holding off the curved blade.

A feral shriek burst from Ata as she unleashed a flurry of attacks. Khamo looked every bit her match. Dryvan and lyshan moved with blinding speed and wove in and out of grottos. Their battle was all but impossible to follow.

Their clash ended the lull. The remaining ship's crew rose with a roar, bearing down on Leiyn's companions.

"Fesht!" Leiyn whipped her head around, looking for where she was most needed. Her friends seemed a match for the soldiers facing them. As for Ata, Leiyn was as likely to strike the dryvan as Khamo if she intervened in their duel.

The flaring esses from the three remaining odiosas snagged her attention a moment before the surge crashed into her.

She staggered and fell to the deck. Her senses scrambled like she had taken a blow to the head. Her stomach kicked. Bile sat bitter on her tongue.

These ones have you! a chorus echoed in her skull, as delighted as boys in their mischief.

Saints damn you all! she threw back before slamming up her walls.

Even the trio of them could not prevent it. Defenses built over decades rebuffed and cut off the odiosas' intrusions. Her mind reclaimed, Leiyn rose to her feet and scanned for danger.

With her lifesense blinded, she could bring only her natural senses to bear.

The Saints blessed her this time—no Suncoat lingered nearby to take advantage. Only an unlucky blow from the fighting Iritu put her in danger.

She raised her gaze back to the ship's wheel and saw the odiosas cower back out of sight. Lips parting in a bitter smile, she made for the ladder.

Next that she knew, she was plastered against the wall, body frozen with shock and pain.

"Khamo!" Leiyn hissed when she caught her breath. He had caught her in a blow to the back she had never seen coming. Hoping Ata had made him pay for it, she whirled around to keep track of the lyshan and sent lifeforce cascading to her wounds. Even having splintered the wood, they appeared minor. Her face felt as if it had taken the worst of it. She hoped she had not chipped a tooth.

Worry about that later. The odiosas!

Leiyn compelled her body back into motion, grabbing the ladder and scrambling up it. She went over the lip with a falchion raised.

An Ilberian waited for her.

Snarling, the soldier chopped at her with a sword while his shield battered into her side. Leiyn knocked the blade aside and took the blunt hit. She nearly went back over the railing but managed to get a foot on the shield and kick the man back far enough to gain her feet.

The Suncoat did not stand alone. A second one charged as the first recovered. Behind them, the odiosas pressed against the railing. She felt their attacks against her walls, as futile as children tossing stones at a cliff.

The second soldier's shield thrust forward, trying to knock her down. Leiyn sidestepped and hacked through both the metal and the arm behind it. As the soldier collapsed, gasping in shock, his comrade threw himself forward. There was no cunning to the assault, no hope for victory, only a reckless need to be done with it.

She granted his wish with sharp twin strokes.

Dispatching the injured Suncoat with a thrust of her falchion, Leiyn faced the odiosas. If fear was ever to appear in their eyes, it should have been then. Still, she detected no emotion.

Yet she knew the truth. They were lambs before a lion, innocent of the crimes they had been forced into. Helpless. She could save them, given the chance. Could break the brand that enslaved them.

But Khamo raged on the deck below. The other odiosas raised titans and drove against the wisdoms and her mahitas as well as Ketti. There was no room for mercy. No time for hesitation.

Us or them, Firebrand.

She forced herself forward. One step. Another. If they begged for their lives, would it be harder? She would never know. The odiosas only watched her approach. Their bodies flinched back, but their eyes remained steady. As if she were nothing more than a squall coming off the shore.

It's nothing you haven't done before. This is war. Is it different from hunting in the forest? From butchering livestock?

She struck before doubt could cripple her.

Her body seemed to move of its own volition. Falchions parted cloth. Flesh. Bone.

One by one, the enthralled men fell to the boards.

"Leiyn!"

She spun around. Teya stood at the top of the ladder, face splattered with scarlet but seeming unharmed. Leiyn's heart pounded as if she were an enemy. The rent bodies behind her burned into her mind like an odiosa's brand.

The scout flickered her eyes across the victims, but her expression did not waver. She strode up to Leiyn and pointed over the water.

"Lower your walls and *look!* Your Eteman will drown if we do not help!"

Leiyn obeyed. As she unveiled her lifesense, the battle came back into excruciating awareness. She tried to ignore the snuffing of lifefires and observe what Teya indicated.

Ketti sank into the sea.

She still rode atop her leashed titan, but the whale was descending into the ocean. No, being *pulled* into it—she noticed then the watery limbs enwrapping the giant beast. The kraken had awoken once more, leashed by the magic of a dozen odiosas. Even the Eteman's prodigious strength could not hope to match that, nor could the wisdoms and the mahitas give assistance enough to change the tide.

Leiyn felt a glimmer of Ketti's desperation as she commanded her whale to the surface. She had moments before the waves tossed over her and dragged her into the water.

And Ketti did not know how to swim.

The ice over Leiyn's mind thawed. Sheathing a falchion, she seized Teya's free arm.

"Give me esse," she ordered, then arrowed her mahia out to the nearest odiosa. As the scout obeyed, the force of her magic redoubled, speeding all the faster across the distance.

The first odiosa died as she speared through his essence.

Distantly, she was aware of her body shuddering, paying the price of the kill. Trying to ignore it, Leiyn drew on the remaining amber beads to reinforce her lifeforce, then went for the next odiosa.

This one met her with his defenses. For a moment, he fended her off, but could last no longer. With mahia formed as sharp as a blade, she punched into the core of his being.

As his lifefire sputtered out, her mahia faltered. Leiyn sank to her knees. Blinking, she saw the world spinning about her. *Too much.* Each killing stroke stole too much of her strength. Life-giving flames coursed from Teya into her, but the scout's esse was faltering as well.

Get up, Firebrand! Ketti's not safe yet!

Leiyn struggled to her feet, breaking Teya's hold as the scout collapsed. She could not take more from her without endangering her life. Firming her splintering will, she prepared to strike the next one.

The odiosas' counterblow caught her by surprise.

She staggered. Vaguely, she was aware of her feet scrabbling on the slick deck, her body slamming into the ship's railing. Did she still hold her falchion? Had she dropped it in the sea? She could not bring enough attention back to know.

She threw up her walls. Too late—the odiosas battered down her paltry defenses with another blistering wave.

For a moment, she hung suspended. Weightless. Unmoored from the world. By a thread, she clung to reality.

Cold water battered her, breaking her free.

69

RISE

The seas weep...

Words—disconnected, devoid of meaning—tossed through her mind like the waves tossed her body. All was cold and dark.

Swim. You have to swim.

It was beyond her. All strength had left her, body and mind. No will remained to struggle.

Broken.

Had her spine snapped? Her soul splintered? She tried to extend her senses and failed. Even that much awareness was gone. All that remained was the cold, the darkness, and the vague sense of fleeting sparks darting around her.

Am I dying?

She regarded the notion dispassionately. She did not fear death. The pain that accompanied it, certainly, but death itself? That last step was often a mercy. An end to life's agonies.

That, she could welcome.

But she was not dead yet. Dying? Perhaps.

She felt pressure on her chest, a burning in her lungs. Painful sensations reasserted themselves across her body.

Still alive, for now.

Those she would leave behind tormented her then. *Teya.*

Isla. Batu and Ata, Ketti and Ekosa. They were still in danger. Until Ata overcame Khamo—*if* she could—they were stranded among enemies. And Ketti—did she already drown as Leiyn did? Had the kraken forced her titan beneath the surface?

You have to swim.

She tried. Tried with all that remained in her. Yet her efforts were like those of a fish flailing on dry shore. Swiftly, she weakened, knowing they would amount to nothing.

Only one hope remained.

The idea would have made her laugh had she still had air for it. Reaching Clouded Fang when she could not reach the ocean's surface—it was too far a stretch to call "hope".

But what other choice did she have? She was drowning and beyond the reach of any other. Feeble a hope as it was, this was her last chance.

She tried to find the thread connecting to her bonded titan. *Clouded Fang,* she whispered into the vast emptiness. *Clouded Fang, come to me.*

The supplication fell as flat as words spoken into water. Nothing resonated with her call. No one heeded them.

Clouded Fang...

The grotto. She had to reach through a grotto. But how she could see Unera as unified? She had never felt more disconnected.

Alone.

She drifted. Her focus fizzled. As the life faded from her body, she noticed again the sparks around her. Fish, perhaps, or smaller forms of sea life. One spark felt different than the others. To her surprise, it nestled warm against her hip.

Leiyn grasped toward the paltry heat, numb fingers searching for the source. It was a distraction, likely. A figment of her imagination.

It was all she had.

Her fingers brushed the pouch ever secured at her hip. Disappointment threaded through her. *The beads.* Of course.

Some vestiges of esse remained after draining them. That was it, nothing more.

Then why does it feel like more?

She was growing weaker, her need for air ever more urgent, yet instead of trying to swim, she fumbled at the pouch's ties. Pulling them loose, her fingers darted in and pressed against that candle flame in the vast darkness.

Not amber—wood. A familiar carving. The only one she always kept with her.

Shock, deeper and more profound than anything she had suffered that day, wended through her. The figurine—the fox Tadeo had carved her. Somehow, in some small way, it was alive.

Tadeo?

She reached for him in the journey-worn wood. Pressed her thumb hard to its pointed snout. Beyond the small sting, she felt it again. A flutter of...acknowledgment.

Is it truly you?

It was not like Zuma's spark, or her mother's, both buried in her essence. She could not have said it was truly him. Yet he had held it while he died. Had still clutched it when she found his still body.

His face opened in her mind. Once more, she saw his small, almost shy smile as he gazed fondly at her.

Leiyn smiled into the cavernous dark. She was not alone. She never had been. Tadeo was here. Even in death, he never left her. And Zuma, and her mother—they were always within her.

They did not make her whole. Her soul was as fragmented as the world around her. Yet nothing lived long without gaining scars.

Not even the world itself.

Unera was not whole, but fractured, conflicted. Its parts constantly clashed. They always had.

Just like me.

The thought jostled something free inside her. *Conflicted.* She had thought that for something to be whole, it must be unified and peaceful, working in tandem toward a greater goal. But when had she known anything like that? People went against their interests all the time. Nature pitted creatures and plants against each other in a war for survival.

Conflict was as inherent to life as cooperation.

All of it. It's all of it.

Her lungs burned afresh. Water rushed inside her. A great heaviness settled over her limbs. Leiyn did not fight it. That battle was already over.

She delved into her mind, trying to expand it as she never had before. This time, she did not claw the world into her senses, but let the sensations usher in their own ideas. What did she know? All this time, she had been as ignorant of Unera's nature as any other.

Show me who you are.

They appeared as flickers. Beasts so tiny her eyes would never see them, her skin never touch them, flitted about and around her. Like leaves on the wind, the ocean currents moved them at their will, and they did not fight against it.

One.

Seaweed. It tried to root against the waves far below, but currents inevitably pulled strands free. A raft of it drifted near her, clinging to each other, though they were already dying. Yet under the raft congregated a small school of fish, finding shelter in their sacrifice.

All of it, one.

And her? She was a body waiting to feed those fish, if a greater predator did not steal her from them first. A log in a fire burning away. If she were consumed, what did it matter? Other flames would rise in her place.

I am nothing. Everything.

It took no effort to see it now. To reach and touch it and feel it firm beneath her grasp. Unera as it truly was—she sensed it now.

She *was* it.

She saw the thread that trailed beyond its surface. Grasped

it with her being. And, like a ship's anchor thrown overboard, she let it pull her down.

In moments, she felt him—*truly* felt him, as she never had before. He was far away from the shore and deep inside the earth, where stone became fire...

And fire burned eternal.

The dragon unfurled at her touch and looked at her. His wings spread. His nose snuffed. His eyes pierced countless leagues.

We are one, she told him, then let go.

⸻

Rising.

There was the pressure of holding on. The pain of release. Cold relented to warmth, wet to dry. Wind tousled clinging clothes. Locks of hair pulled free of their braid.

She had become ice. Fire melted it away.

Leiyn spasmed, then retched. Water expelled from her lungs, bile following close behind. Agony spread through her every limb.

The agony of living.

Her body railed against it, this resurrection. As its revolt faded, her senses revealed the world around her.

The ocean fell away. Her hands and feet dangled over low-hanging clouds. Her stomach, already fragile, bucked again at the sight.

She soared through the air.

Leiyn grasped for understanding. She twisted her head around, looking for what lifted her. Salt and hot stone filled her nose. Something gripped her about her middle, hard and strong, yet careful not to crush. Tilting her head, she saw enormous feet tipped with wicked, curved claws and lined with obsidian scales. Reaching out with her lifesense, it confirmed what she already knew.

Clouded Fang carried her. He had come.

It should have come as a relief. Instead, she beheld the realization with detached interest. The distinction between living and dying did not seem as important as they once had. They were two sides of the same coin, and all the world flipped back and forth between them.

She lived now. Someday, she would die.

But not now.

A glimmer of her old self resurfaced. The person she had been. Or who she was. If she was living, she remained Leiyn of Orille.

She tried to remember who that was.

My friends.

Their faces flashed through her mind. Isla smiling. Teya halfway into a laugh. Batu quietly bemused.

My enemies.

Khamo killing Ata—the image cracked through her numbness. Leiyn firmed her jaw and grasped after her hatred.

Sharo.

That was what she needed to return for. To stop him from taking any more of the people she loved. To protect humanity from him.

The result bore no weight for Unera. The world moved on no matter who claimed victory. But it was everything to Leiyn. Though she knew now how little she mattered to the whole, it was still her part to play.

"Clouded Fang." His name came out in a croak, too quiet to hear, yet she felt his burning presence shift in recognition, responding to her thought sent along their bond. "We must return."

To my world, she added in her thoughts as her voice failed.

Even now, his mind felt vast and unknowable. Her requests fell like rain into an ocean.

Yet every wave started with a ripple. Even droplets might turn into tidal waves.

The ash dragon shifted his wings, adjusting his course. They turned, circling as they descended back toward the sea. Leiyn twisted to stare across it. But for the gray waves tossing over it, its wide surface was devoid of the ships she knew lay on the other side.

Stay with me, she told him as the water closed in. *No matter what comes.*

The surface rushed closer. She tensed and prepared to meet it. A gust of wind blew over her, so intense it threatened to rip off her skin.

Flames rippled across her being, robbing her of her senses.

As vision returned, a fresh scene appeared beneath her. The battle between Baltesia and Ilberia continued in full force. Ships spread everywhere she looked. Her lifesense was overwhelmed with the presence of mahia and titans.

But as the claws holding her lost their grip, she snapped back to her immediate problem. Clouded Fang was melding back into smoke and ash, unable to remain in the flesh outside of the grotto. The ship below—the same as she had fallen from—rapidly approached.

Twisting, she tried to get her feet below her. The little good it would do her—she was falling too far, too fast. At best, she would break both legs. More likely, the impact would kill her.

But she did not fall alone.

The titan's undiluted esse filled her, forceful as a waterfall. Even though they had left the grotto, Zuma's spark held their bond in place, a small bonfire in her chest.

Leiyn grasped after the dragon's lifeforce greedily, sending it to her legs and body. She reinforced her bones, toughened her muscles. She quickened her reflexes and sharpened her mind.

Her feet met the deck.

The impact splintered wood and rippled through her body. But as she rolled across the planks, Leiyn came to her feet and found herself still whole, the black threads of injury already mending.

For a moment, she felt like how she imagined Ata must as she stood among mortals. Powerful. Invincible.

The Iritu, the only two who could rival her, paused their

fight to behold her. She matched their regard with her own. Then, she looked to her ally.

"Go, Ata. Save Ketti. Kill the odiosas."

Leiyn knew she spoke the words, but her voice felt separate, disconnected. She was more than her body; she was the fire that burned within her. The flames that soared in Clouded Fang overhead. The life that spread across the ocean waters.

"Awakener..." Almost, there seemed a touch of awe to the dryvan's voice. Amber ichor spotted her armor where it had cracked under Khamo's blows, and her esse sputtered with injury, but she remained strong.

"Go," Leiyn repeated. "There's no time. I'll handle him."

Ata hesitated a moment longer, glancing at the lyshan. Then she vanished from sight.

Khamo never shifted his stare from her. Leiyn matched it. The lyshan had not come through the fight untouched. Golden blood trickled over the red armor, proving he was not as impervious as he seemed.

He'll die. Just as Man'nah did.

Leiyn drew the falchion that remained at her hip. Her life-sense sought after the other to find that Teya carried it to her from behind. Halfway turning, she gave the scout a slight smile as she accepted it.

Only then did she see the tears tracking down Teya's face. Tears for Leiyn, still wet on her cheeks. But her expression was as fierce as a diving hawk's.

"Kill the *sach'aan*," Teya whispered.

"I will."

With a final look, Leiyn turned and ran toward the edge of the main deck. Hefting herself easily over the railing, she dropped to the deck below.

Her feet had scarcely touched the planks when Khamo charged.

70

WITHER

*L*eiyn twisted to one side, narrowly dodging the wicked spikes of the mace. As the lyshan's whip flashed from the other side, she held up a falchion to intercept. The cord wrapped around the blade, falling short of her body.

Then Khamo wrenched back, yanking the sword free of her grip.

"Fesht!"

She tried for a counterstrike, but the lyshan had already melted away. Before his speed and grace, she felt as clumsy as a bear next to a dancer. Even Clouded Fang's power coursing through her body could not close the gap.

Look for weaknesses, not strengths!

There was no time to dwell on either. Khamo exhibited another advantage as he winked out of existence. Leiyn scarcely had time to spin around before the lyshan's mace clapped her shoulder.

Her Iritu garments were scant protection before the blow. Pain obliterated all sense of self. Sailing across the deck, she crashed into the railing, splitting it wide. Only a quick grab for its splintered remains kept her from tumbling into the sea.

Yanking herself back aboard, she sent lifeforce coursing to her shattered shoulder. Khamo gave her no time to heal. The lyshan flicked the whip, snapping it out with enough force to fracture bones. Leiyn skirted away, quick enough to allay the brunt of the blow.

A second lash came at her face. Seeing the pattern to the movement, Leiyn ducked. The cord cracked above her as she stumbled away from the railing to open ground.

As she faced the lyshan again, an angry hiss stole from her lips. Though her mahia healed her wounds quickly, the pain of them flared her frustration into a blaze. Clouded Fang roared from where he circled above, her fury traveling along their bond. Around her, humans flinched at the sound, like the rumbling of a mountain.

Think, Firebrand, think!

There was no time for traps or clever ploys. The lyshan came at her again, and again, and again. When the whip was not attacking her from a distance, he was stepping from a grotto behind her. His mace crashed into her body twice, too swift to avoid, ravaging her defenses and straining her mahia as she healed.

Her breathing ragged, Leiyn squared off against him once more. Her garments had torn, the esse in them growing dim. She herself felt stretched thin; she was using too much of the titan's power too quickly.

An opening. I need an opening!

An arrow shot across the deck.

Khamo spun to avoid it, but too late—the arrow sank into his back, finding a chink in his armor and lodging there. Far from a killing blow, but it did not need to be.

Darkness started eating at his lifeforce.

Isla was already lining up another shot, the glow of an Iritu arrow at the sharp end of it. Beside her, Batu nocked an Iritu arrow as well.

Leiyn dashed forward. Her mouth fell open, a wordless scream rising in her throat. Fear of what must come next flooded through her, chilling the dragon's lifefire.

The lyshan lunged at her friends.

They scattered to either side, but with mortal slowness. Khamo caught Batu with his whip, the vicious cord wrapping around his neck. The mace only nicked Isla's bow, but with enough force to send her spinning to the ground.

Leiyn wanted to curse and yell at them to leave off the fight, but it was too late. The lyshan knew they were a threat, however slight. He would not neglect them again.

All she could do was take the advantage they had given her.

Batu was entangled in Khamo's whip, choking. Impossibly, he struggled against the lyshan still, wrapping his muscled arms around the whip as if to pull it from the lyshan's grasp. But his considerable strength was still only that of a human. Even with Iritu-tainted blood, he was no match for a true skin-walker.

Yet it served as a distraction. Springing across the deck, Leiyn stabbed her falchion into Khamo's back.

Titanbone scraped against titanbone, but her sword's enchantments remained intact. The tip pierced the scarlet armor, finding a weak point.

It drove into the lyshan's desiccated flesh.

Khamo whirled, mace leading, whip pulling free of Batu to leave him sputtering on the deck. Leiyn was already rolling away. She left her sword lodged in his back, allowing the esse-eating magic to continue its ravenous work.

The lyshan bared his teeth, long and razor sharp, before driving at her again. Weaponless, Leiyn could only try to dodge.

The mace caught her in the chest.

She slammed to the deck. Planks cracked beneath her. Her chest felt wrong. She could not breathe. Her vision dimmed. Her lifesense scrambled.

Clouded Fang!

Through their bond, the titan sent a fresh torrent of lifeforce cascading into her. Her bones pulled free of her organs and began stitching back together.

Too late. A silhouette stepped over her. A weapon raised.

"She's mine, *sach'aan!*"

A second shadow darted forward, stabbing at Leiyn's

assailant with their spear. Even wounded, Khamo batted aside the attack almost lazily, then dealt a blow in return. The whip cracked forward.

Teya went sailing back.

NO!

Leiyn sucked in air. Agony flooded her, but her body had repaired enough to gain her feet. She sensed her other falchion halfway across the deck, too far out of reach. But her longbow, visible to her lifesense by its Iritu string, only lay a few strides away. With a few moments' reprieve, she could reach it.

Another enchanted arrow flashed from behind Khamo, narrowly missing the lyshan. It still caused him to turn back that way.

Isla, you fool!

Still, Leiyn seized her chance, scrambling across the deck to seize her bow. Out of the corner of her eye, she saw another bow *thwack* as an arrow loosed, aid coming from an unexpected source: Taban.

His plainsriders had fallen, yet the Master of the Greathouse stood alone, face lined with a determined scowl. Lacking enchanted arrows, they would do little harm to Khamo, but every moment bought was a chance for Leiyn to end this.

And end it, she must. She felt the flagging esse of her companions, their wounds taking a heavy toll. Her strength was a quickly fraying rope.

Her hand met the familiar leather grip. Spinning, Leiyn raised her longbow and nocked an arrow from the quiver, still miraculously secured at her hip. The titanbone tip gleamed as she drew the fletching back to her cheek.

Khamo turned as she loosed.

The lyshan bent out of the way, dodging, but the movement drove her falchion deeper into his back. The shapeshifter staggered, his esse spasming. His thousand captured souls seemed to scream as the weapon devoured them into nothing.

Leiyn nocked and drew a second arrow. As she did, she sent a call ratcheting up her bond.

At him, old boy!

Clouded Fang pivoted midair. In moments, he descended, a cloud of ash and smoke and burning eyes. Esse rolled off him in blistering waves.

Khamo looked up, as she knew he must. It did not matter if Clouded Fang could harm him or not.

All she needed was a moment.

Aiming for the crack in the faulds falling over his thighs, Leiyn loosed. The enchanted arrow struck the compromised armor and pierced his flesh. Yet another point where his life-force was being eaten away.

Khamo sank to one knee. Death was a deluge, dark as blood in water. Clouded Fang banked close overhead, issuing forth a roar like the rumble of a restless volcano. A cry of triumph.

But no lyshan was harmless until they lay dead.

Leiyn swiftly retrieved her fallen falchion and stalked forward. Khamo raised his head as she approached. The life in his pitted eyes flickered against her lifesense. Cracked lips moved in a single, breathy word.

"Wither..."

It jolted her back to the half-forgotten vision of Sharo and the Altacura. To the prophecy that had begun with that word.

She pushed the mystery back into the recesses of her mind. It would have to wait.

"Damn you," she said as she stood over him. "You and your master. I hope you rot in whatever hells birthed you."

His mouth parted. A slow smile spread across his face.

Leiyn struck.

Her falchion dug into a cavernous eye. Khamo convulsed, darkness spreading from the titanbone. She threw her weight into it, driving it in deep until she felt the resistance of the helm on the other side.

The lyshan jerked one last time. A hoarse gasp ushered from his throat.

Then, at last, his body went dark.

Breathing heavily, Leiyn withdrew her blade and toppled

the shapeshifter's body with a kick. The edges of the lyshan fell off in a spattering of dust, its form already disintegrating.

Only once she had ensured Khamo no longer moved did she look up.

The little that remained of the Ilberian Armada sailed away from the city, barely a third of the strength they had begun with. A few odiosas remained aboard those ships, fleeing with the rest. The kraken they had commanded had subsided back into the sea. Ketti had survived; she sat atop her coral titan, now surfaced and facing toward the departing ships. Leiyn did not have to reach for the Eteman to sense her soul-deep exhaustion and know she would not be pursuing them. But she did not need to.

We won.

A smile claimed her lips. Even with a titan's energy flowing through her, Leiyn felt weary to her core. The stench of blood mixed with the salty air. Her clothes were saturated with it, both her enemies' and her own. The scars added to her flesh were the least she had gathered that day.

All worth it, she promised herself.

A strangled scream brought her spinning toward the aft of the ship.

She spotted him at once. *Batu.* He was on the ground, rocking back and forth. Checking his esse, she recoiled. It was riven through with injuries, but the disarray in it was more painful to behold.

Then she saw what he clung to.

Something—no, someone. But no life emanated from the body. They were as dark as the dead.

She blinked away her lifesense and froze.

Their face, wide-eyed, a rictus of pain and panic. The arrow erupting from their chest. The blood soaking their clothes. Pooling on the planks. Dripping through the cracks.

Leiyn could only whisper their name.

"Isla?"

PART VIII

REMAINS

ELEVEN YEARS BEFORE

I could stay here forever."

Leiyn fluttered open her eyes. The dappled sunlight was blinding as the leaves shifted so it fell on her face. Turning her head, she gazed at Isla, similarly reposed beside her.

"I'm already bored," Leiyn lied.

Her friend cast her a droll look. "Then why are you still here?"

"Too lazy, I guess."

"You can say that again."

Leiyn would have given her a playful shove were she not so comfortable. Nestled under one of the few trees dotting the hill around the Wilds Lodge, she let the beautiful day soak in. Meadowgrass, still green with spring, filled the air with a fresh scent and the quiet susurrus of rustling stalks. Two birds and a squirrel nattered in the boughs above, debating their ownership of the elm. Leiyn followed their progress around the tree until her eyes drifted back shut.

It was a rare afternoon free of their usual schedule. Pushing hard each day to learn and train as ranger apprentices drained them to their core. Leiyn's muscles were sore from the hand-to-hand combat they had engaged in earlier that day. Tadeo had thrown her to the ground enough times that her backside ached with bruises.

Some quiet time spent with her closest friend was all she could have wanted.

She felt the pressure of Isla's head resting on her shoulder as her friend nestled against her side. "Wake me when you cannot stand it anymore," she murmured, words thick with lethargy.

"I won't."

She felt Isla smile, then relax into slumber. For a long while, she listened to her friend's breathing grow heavy.

Then Leiyn let her vigilance lapse. She drifted off to green, sunny dreams. For this day, content to have only this.

Just the two of them.

72

AMBER

*L*eiyn drifted forward. She longed to look away, yet she could not. Could not stare anywhere but at Batu and the body he held.

This is a dream.

How could it be otherwise? Her eyes saw things that could not possibly be. Her body felt a thing separate, disconnected from her will. A puppet without strings. Why else would she approach this macabre scene, stare at her worst fear, if this were not a night terror finding her in her sleep?

Her mind was locked in amber. The truth, stark and ugly, pierced it.

Those eyes, acorn-brown, open and staring. Those lips, flecked with scarlet. That chest stained and unmoving. They were hers, all hers.

Isla.

Above, a dragon split the sky with a mourning cry.

Her eyes traveled to the arrow, up from the stained shaft to the fletching. The feathers were brown striped with white. The feathers of the meadow grouse native to Altan Gaz.

Fletching she had recently seen.

Leiyn looked back the way she had come. Taban stood next

to the ship's railing, clutching it. He held his bow in his other hand. His hip was bare, his quiver gone.

Yet she had seen the arrows it held before. Tipped with those same brown-and-white feathers.

The moorwarden flinched as he met her eyes. Then he was moving, pitching over the side of the ship and disappearing. By her lifesense, she felt him enter the water, then struggle against the waves, swimming for the shore.

She considered him a moment longer. Wondered if she should claim his life then and there.

But Isla still lay at her feet.

Leiyn turned back to stare at her friend. She searched for any sign of life, the barest spark remaining in her body. All lay dark. There was no hint of her soul, no trickle of esse.

She kneeled next to her and placed a hand on Isla's shoulder. Her body was warm, still warm. If she walled off her lifesense and closed her eyes, she could almost believe Isla was still alive.

"Is she...?" Batu choked out the words between sobs. "Is there any...?"

"No."

Part of her railed against the finality in that word. *Try! Why don't you try?* But that voice was tiny, its words muted in the vast emptiness spreading through her. The evidence weighed it back down to the black depths.

Leiyn squeezed her eyes shut. Should she be doing something? What was she supposed to do? What was left?

Around her, the boat creaked. Batu wept. The ocean lapped against the hull of the boat. The wind rushed against the unfurled sails.

Within, all lay still. Empty but for a quavering silence.

"Isla..." the young man whispered. "Gods, how can I...?"

Others gathered around them. By her lifesense, Leiyn identified them. Teya. Ekosa. One of the Gast scouts. She did not raise her head to acknowledge any of them.

Teya pressed her shoulder. Her esse reached for Leiyn's,

touching it tentatively. Leiyn could not find it in her to reach back. After a moment, the scout withdrew her mahia.

"Leiyn, I—"

"Don't. Please."

A fragile edge emerged from those murky depths. Just a glimmer of a need to be left alone.

"As you wish." Teya peeled away her hand and stepped back.

Batu's sobbing had quieted. Tears still glistened on his face as he stared at Leiyn. His voice cracked as he whispered, "What do we do now?"

Amber coated her thoughts, thick and unyielding. Trying to peer through it, Leiyn glimpsed a vague notion on the other side.

"We bury her. It should be at the Lodge, not here. With Tadeo."

"The Wilds Lodge? Yes, but... that's leagues away."

"Then we'll preserve her body." Another edge of anger, aimed at one undeserved. Leiyn pressed it back down. "Or Ata will take us. It's what we must do."

"I guess. Yes." Batu's hands bunched in Isla's clothes. He shook with fresh sobs.

Someone flashed into being behind Leiyn. She did not startle. It made no difference that it was Ata standing there on the deck. Even if it had been a lyshan, she was beyond caring.

"*Victory!*" the dryvan crooned as she sauntered forth. "Sharo's army, cut to the root! Now, we shall visit vengeance upon him wherever he hides, burn him down to the seeds of his power. As you did Khamo! But why do you kneel? What are you...?"

Ata trailed off into silence. Leiyn felt her regard for a long moment before the dryvan spoke again.

"Treeleg. They took her while you fought Khamo?"

"I didn't know." A memory stirred. "I saw the arrow. I should have known."

Taban had not aimed at Khamo. How could she have missed it? Missed the moment Isla slipped from this life? She had felt connected to all of Unera, but none of that mattered.

Not without her.

The dryvan's murmur sounded closer. Her esse burned over her shoulder. "Leiyn... This pain. Losing a friend. A sister. You cannot contain it. Grief must be expressed. Release it. Let it be free."

Grief. Was that what she felt? She knew she should, but emptiness spread as far as she could see. Absence. Darkness where bright life had once reigned.

"Leiyn, I am sorry, but we must leave." Teya spoke again, her voice firm. Returning to the Spear she had to be. "The remaining ships flee, but danger may still be near."

Only the prospect of leaving the gore-strewn deck could compel her to stand. Leiyn looked at Batu until he raised his eyes.

"Do you want to carry her or should I?"

Fiery lines wound around his neck, chest, and arms, burns from where the whip had lashed him. His lifefire smoldered low. Yet Batu nodded and scooped up Isla's body. The limp way it sagged in his arms stabbed fresh pain through Leiyn's chest.

"She's lighter," he whispered. "Why is she so light?"

"Her spirit has departed, young one." Ata's hands, still caked with blood, were gentle as they guided Batu toward the center of their small group. "Gather close. Leiyn, you must release the Vast One."

A simple enough task. Her hold on Clouded Fang had been slipping as the world splintered around her. Zuma's spark, holding the bond fast, settled into complacency at her request. Within her soul, all grew subdued. As muted as the surrounding ocean.

She did not resist as Ata dragged them across reality.

Leiyn stumbled as her feet met cobblestones. Her first thought was for Isla. Moving swiftly, she caught her friend's body as Batu nearly spilled to the ground.

"I can do it," he grunted, climbing back to his feet and clutching her body to his chest.

Leiyn stepped away. Anger gleamed through her. Why

should he bear her body? Leiyn had been closer to Isla than he could ever know.

But this fury was not for him. Others were far more deserving of it. Though she could not maintain the flames.

Looking up, she saw they stood in the courtyard of the consul's villa. Guards startled at their appearance, but seeing who they were, they kept their distance. Their procession was nearly silent as they made their way inside the estate.

The brightness within was dazzling. Here they were, smeared with blood and sweat and salt, and the marble floor gleamed as bright, the gilded ornamentation shone as golden. Somewhere up the stairs, she heard laughter and the clinking of glasses. The celebrations following victory had already begun.

"Where?" Batu croaked.

Leiyn glanced at Isla's slack face before she had to look away. "The consul's solarium."

The stairs were challenging for the former plainsrider, but he labored up them with repressed grunts. Leiyn walked beside him, watchful for any stumbles. The others trailed behind.

When they reached the corridor above, Teya stepped up next to her. She carried Leiyn's weapons, which Leiyn had neglected to take herself. She could not muster the energy to accept them back.

"What do you intend to do?" the scout said, her tone even.

"Bury her." Fire spurted through her chest, momentary and brief. A flare in a frosty night. "And avenge her."

"By killing who? The moorwarden? If he did not drown, he will be long gone before we find him."

"He didn't drown." Part of her tracked Taban's progress across the bay. The man was stubborn; that much she would give him. Even weighed down by plainsrider armor, he did not sink. He would continue to swim so long as he had strength.

"But how do you know it was him?"

Leiyn did not answer, only continued striding down the corridor. The sounds of laughter grew louder. The source of the festivities became increasingly clear.

The guards stared with open alarm as she and Batu strode past them and into the consul's solarium.

Mauricio stood from where he had been leaning on his desk, a fluted glass of red wine held loosely in hand. His clothes were ruffled, his tricorn hat sitting rakishly atilt. With him stood Wise Jegu, the conqueror, Lord Luca, and Acalan. Only the Gast war chieftain did not hold a glass but stood with his powerful arms crossed over his chest. He, too, looked to have avoided combat.

At their entrance, the small assembly turned. The consul's eyes were sharp as they darted over the scene. His smile disappeared as he set down his glass.

"Tell me what happened."

"Taban Khyan. The Moorwarden of the *Baishin*." The old fury flamed up. Leiyn did not tamp it down. "He's swimming the bay. Find him."

Mauricio considered her for a long moment before gesturing to a servant behind her. "Of course, Prima Maha. Shall I have him brought here when we do?"

She nodded, the movement somehow unnatural and jerky.

As the servant hurried from the room, a tense silence fell. Acalan was the first to break it.

"Young Bear, Huntress... I hurt for your loss."

An intense desire to laugh filled Leiyn. All she allowed it was a brief smile. She would not punish those who did not deserve it.

"I couldn't rise." Batu trembled; from the effort of holding Isla's body or all that wracked him, she could not say. "I saw the arrow fly, then... hit her. But I was too weak."

Acalan crossed the space between them and put his arms under Batu's, supporting him. His voice was hard. "You could not have saved her. Remember that. Do not take the guilt that belongs to another." The war chieftain looked first at Teya, then Leiyn. "Taban Khyan is responsible?"

She gestured to the bloody arrow, still lodged in Isla's body. She had not had the heart to pull it. To feel it stick in her friend's stiff flesh.

"His fletching," she said. "His arrow."

His gaze lingered before he nodded. "Then he will pay."

Mauricio stepped forward. "I will ensure justice is dispensed through the proper channels. But if Taban Khyan is truly responsible, this represents a delicate diplomatic situation—"

"If?" Leiyn rounded on him, then jabbed a finger at the killing arrow. "That is *his* arrow—I know the fletching. Batu knows it," she added, drawing out a dazed nod from Batu before turning back. "Taban betrayed us. *He murdered her.*"

Her vision swam. She swallowed hard, holding back the rising hot tide threatening to shake her apart.

No. Not yet. Later. Once it's done.

"Prima Leiyn." The consul did not flinch from her. Somehow, he sounded both firm and gentle. "I do not doubt your evidence. But we cannot punish the moorwarden without ramifications. Altan Gaz would not look kindly upon the plainsrider leader being executed without their say." His eyes flickered to the Gazian wisdom, who watched from a corner with eyes hard. "Most likely, they will wish us to hand him over to mete out a sentence as they see fit. You must understand the situation for what it is." He gestured to Isla's body. "Envoy Isla would have understood this. Please, try to see it as she would have."

His words rolled off of her—all but the last. She stepped close enough to smell the wine on his breath. The guards' armor rattled as they closed in, but Mauricio held up a hand. He never looked away from Leiyn.

"Don't pretend you knew her," she hissed. "You didn't. She was a tool to you, like all of us are. You didn't know *her.*"

Almost, she could have believed the hurt in Mauricio's eyes. "Is that what you think of me? After all we've been through..." He stepped back, shaking his head. "No. Never mind what I say. You are in mourning. But please, Leiyn. Do not act rashly."

Don't be rash. She could almost feel Tadeo's spark in the fox figurine at the words.

She pushed them away, stepped back, and crossed her arms

tightly over her chest. "Set her down, Batu," she said without looking over. "We might be waiting a while."

73

JUSTICE

For a time, she became ice. Frozen. Unhearing of the others' murmuring as they shifted around the solarium. Unseeing of their frequent glances. A sculpture waiting for fire to thaw.

She did not want to look at Isla. She could scarcely look anywhere but. Her body drew her gaze like carrion would scavengers. Did she imagine it, or did she already grow fragrant?

No. Not yet. Not until it's over.

At last, Leiyn felt them coming. Heat spread through her then. Having taken back her falchions—Teya relinquishing them with obvious reluctance—Leiyn rested a hand on one hilt.

A guard came first, announcing the imminent arrival. Then, flanked by two more soldiers, Taban shuffled in.

He was still bedraggled and looked weary from his long swim. His hair had come loose of the topknot to hang in dark, thin strands resembling dead seagrass before his face. His eyes darted about the room, taking in the others. He was not bound, but neither did he seem wholly free.

"What is this?" he asked, tone imperious. As if he were the one being wronged.

Leiyn drew her sword.

The soldiers shouted and drew their own. It only made the flames inside her burn higher.

"Leiyn," Mauricio murmured, "please, refrain from doing anything you might regret."

"Taban Khyan is my countryman," Wise Jegu spoke up, breaking his silence. "I would see him brought to justice under Gazian law, should any be necessary."

She did not heed either of them. Her words were for Taban alone.

"Did you kill her?"

The moorwarden's eyes flickered to the corner where Isla's body lay. Batu stood over it, his hands bunched into fists, his breathing ragged.

"Who? I only killed those required by our allies, as deemed by your consul." He nodded his head respectfully to Mauricio.

Leiyn stepped closer. The guards held their weapons at the ready, but she only pointed back at Isla's body. At the shaft rising from her chest.

"That arrow belongs to you."

Taban barely looked before shaking his head. "I do not recognize it. No, it is not mine."

Lies. Did he only ever speak lies? She saw the futility of words then.

Yet the questions burst forth all the same.

"Why? How could you take her from me?" Cracks trembled through her. Pain spilled in through them, worse than any wound. She trembled as her foundations crumbled. "Was it Sharo? Did he do this?"

Another flicker of his eyes, then Taban stilled. Too late. She saw the truth of his deception.

"She raves!" he spoke, looking around at those gathered. A corner of his lips curled up. "I know nothing of what she speaks! Please, Wise Jegu, Lord Mauricio, put an end to this madness!"

"Prima Maha." The consul's voice steeled with command now. "I order you to sheathe your weapon this moment. *Stand down*, Leiyn of Orille. Or I won't be able to protect you from the consequences."

"Leiyn, please." Teya spoke now. "Do not do it. Not like this."

She ignored them—all but Batu. Pain radiated from his bloodshot eyes as he met her stare. All the permission she sought was in that hopeless look.

There was only one way this could end. Left to the machinations of politics, Taban would escape, his hands still stained with Isla's blood. And that was something she could not abide.

Leiyn unleashed her mahia.

All save for Ata reeled under the staggering blast. Even Jegu was not prepared for the blow. Many lost their balance and tumbled to the floor. As the guards regained their feet, Leiyn crossed the distance between her and the moorwarden.

Her falchion pierced Taban's heart, so smoothly it scarcely seemed real.

His head fell back, eyes wide with pain. Life leaked from his body, falling dark in mere moments. The smirk he had always given her in life slumped from his lips.

This was no dream.

"Damn you to the hells," she whispered, letting his body slide free of the blade and topple to the floor.

The room erupted into pandemonium. The Gazian wisdom shouted protests into the tumult. The guards shouted and moved to attack.

All halted at the consul's cry.

Slowly, reeling as if drunk, Leiyn looked over at Mauricio. For once, he appeared truly disheveled. She could not find it in her to be amused.

"Ah, Leiyn. I wish you had not done that." Instead of angry, he sounded sorrowful. "I should have you killed for this, you know. It is likely the only thing now that would appease Altan Gaz."

Again, he glanced at Wise Jegu as he spoke. The gray wisdom nodded savagely, affirming Mauricio's words.

"You could try." There was no boast to it. Leiyn was far beyond that.

"Would that you thought better of me. But it cannot be overlooked." Mauricio drew in a deep, trembling breath, then sighed it out. "Go, Leiyn. Leave Baltesia. You must, for all our sakes. After all you've done for your homeland, I cannot banish you. But should you stay, we will find ourselves in the midst of yet another war. Who can say what will become of the Tricolonies then?"

Leiyn stared at him, hearing the words, but feeling nothing from them. Some distant part of her—the part trained to a ranger's discipline, perhaps—took them in stride and calculated the next step.

She turned to Ata. "Will you take me from here?"

"Of course." The dryvan moved from the corner she had occupied to Leiyn's side. She alone defied the mood of the room, her stride proud and strong.

Others moved toward her. Leiyn looked each of them in the eyes. Batu, hefting Isla in his arms again. Ketti and Ekosa, shoulder to shoulder, equal parts disoriented and determined. Teya, Leiyn's longbow still slung over one shoulder, regret swimming in her eyes.

"I won't ask you to come with me." Her voice was lifeless, as dead as she felt within.

"We're coming," Batu grunted. The guards parted before him, reluctant to stand in the way.

"We're your allies," Ketti affirmed as she stepped after him. Ekosa nodded and followed.

"I would not leave you." Teya glanced back at Acalan. The war chieftain only watched with an unyielding frown.

It would cost Teya, cost all of them, to go with her, wherever that might be. But Leiyn did not have the strength to leave them behind.

"Where to?" the dryvan murmured. Roots spread from her body, encircling their party and creating a barrier from the others. The governor's sorrowful look was quickly blocked from sight, as was Jegu's accusatory stare.

Leiyn looked down at the blood dripping from her falchion onto the carpet, then met Ata's gaze.

"Home."

The dryvan flashed her a small smile, then whisked them away.

EPILOGUE

Atastimina watched the mortals bury their friend.

She stood in the collapsed archway of the ashy ruins. Though the Wilds Lodge had burned the prior year, it still lay largely dead to her senses. The animals that might have lingered about it had been driven away by the presence of the plainsriders who had made their camp there. Even insects seemed wary, congregating in far greater numbers in the surrounding meadow and forest beyond.

An appropriate site for a grave.

The plainsriders lingered farther down the hill, beyond where Ata stood. Oblivious to their moorwarden's demise at Leiyn's hands, they had vacated the premises at the ranger's request. Word of the events in Southport would take a long while to travel by human methods; weeks and months, though such measures of time seemed much the same to her. But when it finally reached them, Ata wondered what they would think of this day. If they would regret not striking Leiyn down as she mourned.

Batu—her Kinblood, to her mind—shoveled at the dirt next to the ranger. They had found tools in a ramshackle shed to quicken the work, but it had still been an hour in the making. Ata was content to wait, as were their other companions, who stood not far away. The *eesu*, the hunter-child, and the Gast had offered to help, but those two had insisted on burying their friend themselves.

Isla Treeleg. Her eyes settled on the body lying beside the expanding hole, draped in the dark green cloak worn by Baltesian rangers. Ata remembered that day she had found the mortal dying, Leiyn desperately trying to save her by cramming her full of aspen esse. How amusing their efforts had seemed then to stay alive. It had been a whim to extend her aid, a curiosity to see how their efforts would play out.

That had been before she felt the sharp cut of loss once more. She did not smile at death any longer.

Shovel in, shovel out. Dirt moved from one place to the next. So much effort expended to inter a corpse in the ground. And why? Burial had always struck her as an odd custom. Why protect a body from jackals and crows only to let the worms and maggots have their feast?

Yet she understood the need to honor the fallen. Ata had felt that same compulsion upon finding the last of the fair-hearted Kin butchered on the ground.

The memories haunted her. Always, they lingered behind her eyes: The noble maple, shattered and toppled. Eld torn in two like a lightning-struck tree... only trees did not bleed. Awidan plucked of every feather, his owlish head twisted farther than he had been capable of.

All her companions, her brothers and sisters over untold years, gone.

She had returned each to the roots of their Mothers. Though the *Ialadta* had long been dead, Ata could not help believing some part of them remained to cradle their children into eternal rest. It brought comfort to her, at least, scant as it was.

As the sun dove toward the ground like a hawk at a fish, the diggers laid aside their tools and lifted the body. The others came over to assist. By rope and cautious effort, they lowered what remained of their friend into the hole, then drew the ropes back up.

Ata joined them around the grave as they spoke their final words. She remained content in her silence. The dead did not listen once their spirit had departed, and she could sense Isla's had long since left her corporal form. Her mourners spoke those words for themselves.

When the final tears had been shed, Leiyn and Batu took up their shovels again. After heaving the last of the dirt over her grave, the two dallied before her marker, a simple stone Teya had etched while they waited.

The horizon bled with sunset when Ata approached. She waited for the pair to turn toward her, knowing they were aware of her, but neither raised their heads.

"Come," she said at last. "You must rest, and so should she."

The Awakener looked up then, and Ata froze. Her pain was a mirror to her own, always burning inside.

Leiyn nodded, then led Batu away. Gathered with the others, Ata dragged them once more across the world.

⌢

She remained afar to watch the mortals stagger up to their refuge.

All but exiled from the lands claimed by the peacockish consul, Ata had brought them to an old oasis, a place belonging to her people deep in the jungle beyond the knowledge or reach of humanity. According to the Eteman with them, it was within the boundaries of the colony known as Ore-Ofe. Ata little knew or cared about that. All that mattered was that it was safe and would provide for them while they healed.

Then the next phase of the war would begin.

An emergence by her side drew her from her brooding. Ata kneeled and grinned at the creature who had appeared.

"Welcome back, little friend," she murmured. "You are a ray of moonshine among the shadows."

The silver fox trotted up to nestle against her legs. Their esses melded as they touched, their greeting warm and familiar.

Then Chispa came alert, his nose pointing toward the five humans exploring their new refuge.

"Yes." Ata stroked his soft coat as she looked in the same direction. "I fear she will need you in the coming days. It is not in your nature to remain in one place, but if you could linger by her side for a time..."

The fox looked up at her, cocking his head. It was as much a sign of his question as the shimmer through his spirit.

"Life and death are one; this, I know. Yet it is a difficult cycle to accept. Even for my kind."

Chispa nuzzled her again, with head and spirit both, then loped down the grassy lane. As Ata watched, the silver fox went up to Leiyn and pressed against her leg. The ranger—the last of them, now—bent to ruffle his head.

Ata sensed no pleasure in the reunion. The young woman seemed incapable of such feelings. Blood—her own and her enemies'—still stiffened her clothes. Black tendrils shot through her body from wounds still healing. Dirt from digging the grave caked her hands and boots. Her lifefire burned as low as she had ever seen.

Yet she would survive. If Ata knew nothing else of the Awakener, she knew she would continue on.

Turning aside, Ata looked to the east and stretched her senses as far as they could reach. Her heritage could sense all the way to the coast in impressions, but nowhere did she feel the one she sought. Still, she spoke to him as if he stood there before her. As if he would heed her, even if he did.

"Why, Sharo?" Her whisper was as soft as the rustling leaves. Her thoughts rippled through the vegetation, causing them to shiver as if in a chill wind. "Why force me to this? You must know what you've done. That there can be only one end now."

Ata closed her eyes, tilted back her head, and let in the world. Her Inheritance remained strong; her will, stronger still. She could do what needed to be done.

She could kill her brother.

AUTHOR'S NOTE

Thank you, kind reader, for picking up *The Hidden Guardian*. I very much hope you enjoyed it.

Ranger of the Titan Wilds has been a turning point in my writing career. *The Hidden Guardian* continues and expands that journey. Personally, I think it is my best book to date. I can only hope you agree.

I'd love for you to be part of this series' story. One way you can pitch in is by leaving a review.

Reviews, as I'm sure you know, help other readers take a chance on a new author and book. In an age of an overwhelming amount of choices, including when it comes to picking your next read, an enthusiastic review can often be the thing that breaks through the noise.

If you're convinced, fantastic! There are several places to leave reviews for *The Hidden Guardian*. The primary ones are Amazon, Goodreads, and Audible.

And if you haven't left a review for *The Last Ranger*, you can also do so on those same sites.

If you're really loving this series, consider sharing it with a friend or two! Word of mouth is my favorite way of finding new books, and it's the strongest recommendation any book can get.

The journey doesn't end here—not for Leiyn and her friends

(most of them, anyway...) and I hope not for you. The series will continue in the fourth book, *The Wilds Exile*.

Keep an eye out for its Kickstarter near the end of '24 and for the retailer launch following that. To be sure not to miss it, follow me on Amazon or sign up for my newsletter on my website, *jdlrosell.com*.

Thanks again for reading this book, and if you take any of the above actions, a double thank you.

Until the next story, take care!

Josiah (J.D.L. Rosell)

APPENDIX A

THE CHARACTERS

Acalan Tikau - Chieftain of the Gast tribe the Tekuan, which translates to "Jaguars." Also now Toa'Yao, or "War Chieftain," of all the Many Tribes.

Altun - A plainsrider of the Gazian Greathouse. Has a contentious history with Batu, Leiyn, and Isla.

Arias di Carille - A young Ilberian soldier stationed at Fort Ribereño.

Arlo - The surgeon of the Wilds Lodge.

Armando Pótecil - A now-deceased conqueror, or general, of the Ilberian military.

Arash Ta'Rul - An Eteman of Hold Ta'Rul. Father to Ketti, grandson-in-law to Oro.

Ata - Also known as "Hawkvine," "Rowanwalker," "Rowan," and "Foxfur." True name is "Atastimina." A dryvan who fights on the side of Leiyn and humanity.

Awera Talabi - Title: "Cloud." The chancellor of Ore-Ofe.

Awidan - Also known as "Mooneyes." An owlish dryvan of Glade.

Ayda Santidad - The Altacura, or spiritual leader, of the Catedrál.

Baltesar Veda IV - The current Caelrey, or ruler, of Ilberia.

Bane - Teya's draconion.

Batu Khatas - An older plainsrider pupil of the Gazian Greathouse.

Belen of Wharfhaven - A wall captain of Southport.

Biqqa - A spirit hummingbird of a brilliant emerald hue. Often seen around Ketti Ta'Rul.

Carles Collon - A middle-aged servant in the governor's villa. Also a mahita of the Order of Mahia.

Celia of Quay - A teenage daughter of fisherfolk, now a mahita of the Order of Mahia.

Chispa - The silver-furred spirit fox who has tailed Leiyn after different points in her life. Sometimes merges with the dryvan Ata.

Clouded Fang - The ash dragon (a variety of titan) bonded to Leiyn. First encountered at the erupting mountain in the Titan Wilds known as Nesilfo, the Clouded Fang.

Dinis Sorje - The mayordomo to the governor's villa in Southport.

Eghe Ilori - Title: "Talon." Captain of an Ofean outpost outside of Kunu.

Ekosa Siza - An *eesu*, or Ofean maha, of the *Kekére*.

Eld - A dryvan whose shape resembles a young elm tree.

Emilio - A smooth-talking rancher living in Carmenar, a Baltesian frontier town.

Estel of the Fifth Quarter - A reluctant mahita of the Order of Mahia. Also a successful merchant.

Feral - The unruly, brown mare that once belonged to Lodgemaster Tadeo, and is now Leiyn's loyal steed.

Francesc - A Baltesian youth from Carmenar hung for having sympathies for the Ilberian Union.

Gan - A ranger of the Wilds Lodge. Originally from Altan Gaz.

Genevieve of Orille - Also known as "Evie." A mahita of the Order of Mahia. Named after the author's niece.

Isirat Fai'Don - An Eteman friend of Ketti's.

Isla Ogbi - A ranger of the Wilds Lodge. Leiyn's best friend.

Itzel of Folly - The mayor of Folly and premier over the Baltesian portion of the Titan Wilds. It is a widely known secret that she had a long-standing romantic relationship with Lodgemaster Tadeo.

Izan of the West Woods - A mahita in the Order of Mahia. Husband to Reyna.

Jegu Qayag - A wisdom of Altan Gaz. Leader of the wisdoms assisting in Southport.

Joaquin - A ranger of the Wilds Lodge.

Joromi - A male skystrider of the Ofean Stormhold.

Ketti Ta'Rul - An Eteman of Solace. The youngest member of Hold Ta'Rul and heir to Mehu'Ra.

Khamo - A lyshan often seen wearing red titanbone armor with seemingly malevolent intent.

Kyaka Ndaye - The current Odisi, or ruler, of Eyi.

Leiyn of Orille - A ranger of the Wilds Lodge. Protagonist of the Ranger of the Titan Wilds series.

Luca di Eño Vasara - The conqueror, or general, in charge of Baltesia's military. Named after the author's nephew.

Man'nah - Deceased leader of the lyshans. Once said to have been the strongest among them.

Marina - A ranger of the Wilds Lodge. A middle-aged, no-nonsense woman.

Mauricio di Siveña - The Elected Consul of Baltesia (formerly the governor).

Mehu'Ra - The tempest hawk bonded to Oro Ta'Rul. Guards the borders of Solace.

Mooneyes - A dryvan whose shape resembles a humanoid owl.

Mottle - The horse of Isla Ogbi.

Naia of Southport - A mahita of the Order of Mahia. Formerly a serving lady in a merchant lord's manor.

Nathan - Sometimes called "Old Nathan." A curmudgeonly ranger of the Wilds Lodge.

Nestor of Saints' Crossing - A former Baltesian soldier, now a mahita of the Order of Mahia.

Nidinu Ta'Rul - An Eteman of Hold Ta'Rul. Mother to Ketti, granddaughter to Oro.

Noemi of the Docks - A mahita of the Order of Mahia. Also a young mother of three.

Odowa - A female skystrider of the Ofean Stormhold.

Oktai of the Spears - The current Hesh Jin, or ruler, of Kalga.

Onah Salako - Also "Wing of Moons." One of the two leaders of the Kekére.

Oro Ta'Rul - Also "Ab-Abi." Eteman patriarch of Hold Ta'Rul. Bonded with Mehu'Ra and primary guardian of Solace.

Qara Gegeen - A wisdom of Altan Gaz. Temporarily the head of the Order of Mahia in Leiyn's absence.

Reyna of the West Woods - A mahita in the Order of Mahia. Wife to Izan.

Rúben of the Docks - A Union sympathist guard in the governor's villa and would-be assassin.

Saikan - The horse of Batu Khatas.

Samu Oyabola - Also "Wing of Stars." One of the two leaders of the Kekére.

Sergi of Southport - A mahita of the Order of Mahia. Son of a cobbler.

Sharo - A lyshan with malevolent aims.

Simó of Lake's Edge - A youthful vagrant and mahita of the Order of Mahia.

Steadfast - Leiyn's black stallion. As loyal as his name implies, he barely makes any sound, not even a whicker.

Taban Khyan - New moorwarden of the Gazian Greathouse.

Tadeo of Lake's Edge - The lodgemaster of the Wilds Lodge.

Tecla of Wharfhaven - A grandmother and widow, now a mahita of the Order of Mahia.

Teya of the Hunt - A Spear, or leader, of the *situali*, or Gast scouts. Also Leiyn's lover.

Wynn of Saints' Crossing - An odiosa briefly freed from his brand before succumbing to a titan attack in Southport.

Xepi - A shaman of Qasaar who teaches Leiyn about magic.

Yolant - A ranger of the Wilds Lodge. Fond of singing for the Lodge and playing her stringed gourd.

Zaki Gol'Tor - An Eteman friend of Ketti's.

Zezé - A Baltesian soldier under Captain Belen's command.

Zuma Apisi - A Gast shaman of the Tekuan tribe.

APPENDIX B

THE WORLD

An overview of the locations in the world of Unera.

THE VEILED LANDS
The three colonies of the Veiled Lands are also called "the Tricolonies."

Baltesia
Former colony of Ilberia.

Southport - Capital of Baltesia.
Orille - Leiyn's home village.
Folly - A Titan Wilds town.
Saints' Crossing - The bridge town that spans the Gorge de Omn.
Lake's Edge - Lodgemaster Tadeo's hometown.
Breakbay - An abandoned city ringed by titans. Ruined during the Titan War.
The Wilds Lodge - The Titan Wilds stronghold of the rangers.
Carmenar - A town in the Titan Wilds along Frontier Road.
Wharfhaven - Coastal town near Southport.
Quay - Coastal fishing village near Southport.

Altan Gaz
Colony of Kalga.

Orolt - Capital of Altan Gaz.
Helkist - Fur-trading town.
The Greathouse - Also called the *Baishin*. Stronghold of the plainsriders.

Ore-Ofe
Colony of Eyi.

Kunu - Capital of Ore-Ofe.
Lamayo - Fortified trading city; acts as a secondary capital of Ore-Ofe.
The Stormhold - Also called the *Izul*. Stronghold of the skystriders.
Solace - Hidden Eteman village in the Ofean jungle.

The Titan Wilds
Borderlands spanning the Tricolonies. In Baltesia, these lands extend beyond the Gorge de Omn.

The Barren - Arid wasteland beyond the Silvertusk Sierra.

Qasaar - Capital of the Gasts and other indigenous tribes.

THE ANCESTRAL LANDS
The continent is also called "Forye."

Ilberia
The Ilberian Union.

Vasara - Capital of Ilberia.
Refugio - Stronghold of the Catedrál; also considered a holy city.

Eyi
The Eyin Empire.

Mumsi - Capital of Eyi.
Kaiam - Important city of Eyi.

Kalga
The Kalgan Dominion.

Galkhir - Capital of Kalga.
Betgol - Important city of Kalga.

APPENDIX C

BESTIARY & BOTANICAL

BEASTS OF THE TITAN WILDS

Draconion - *Axolto* to the Gasts. A large lizard that resembles the monitor lizard of the Ancestral Lands, they have been domesticated over eons to be riding animals to the native peoples of the Veiled Lands. Docile unless threatened, they have spines along their backs except where a rider is seated. Draconions typically appear in four colors: orange, yellow, red, and black. They sometimes combine variations of these and have striped or mottled patterns.

Rainbow birds - Birds common to the Ofean city of Kunu. So-called for their iridescent feathers. Much like pigeons or seagulls elsewhere, they make themselves a nuisance and thrive near the city congestion.

Snow ape - A large ape with a shaggy white coat, a red snout, and blue around its eyes. An apex predator of the Silvertusk Sierra. It can be incredibly aggressive when provoked or when hungry.

Spirit animals - Little is known of the creatures that appear as animals, yet also seem to be more. Travelers through the Titan Wilds have reported being assisted by creatures who are often of silver or golden coloring. These have taken the forms of wolves, large cats, foxes, deer, and all other manner of beasts. Many believe them to be spirits from Omn, sent by the Saints to keep their followers safe. Others have reported the native peoples have stories of them as little gods taking forms that humans can understand, and that often their favors granted will someday need to be repaid.

Thorned lion - One of the largest predators in the Titan Wilds, it typically poses little harm to humans unless starving. They have been known, however, to prey on livestock. The rangers of the Wilds Lodge have learned torches burning fennel are sufficient to drive it away from human populations. With a mane of spines, it is deadly to contend with. Engagement should be avoided whenever possible. Thorned lions typically travel alone, though females will care for their cubs until they are several years old.

Titans - Also called *"kainox"* by the native peoples of the Veiled Lands. Straddling the line between beasts and spirits, they appear as enormous animals or mythical creatures that ravage the land. Titans are not always present in the landscape; they "awaken" or materialize in cycles that can vary from months to years. Many appear to be tied to a certain feature in the terrain, but this does not appear to be accurate in all cases. Following is a list of the titans known thus far:

    Ash dragon - Volcano titan.

Gorge spider - Rock titan.
Hill tortoise - Earth titan.
Mirror swans - Lake titan. Always appear as a pair of swans.
Rain mammoth - Rain titan in the shape of an elephant.
Reef whale - Ocean titan made of coral.
River serpent - River titan.
Sand stampede - Desert titan in the shape of stampeding wildebeest.
Sea kraken - Ocean titan. Also called "The Wight on the Tide."
Tempest hawk - Storm titan.
Vine jaguar - Jungle titan.
Fog swarm or "Winged Death" - Fog titan. Said to take the form of a swarm of flesh-devouring bats.

Tusked jackal - An aggressive canine species known for their destruction of other animal habitats. Tusked jackals travel in packs of thirty or more and bring down their prey through numbers and ferocity. As they pose significant threats to humans and livestock, they are best driven away

Wolfdeer - A species of fanged deer that appear to be particularly aggressive. Unknown if they are carnivorous or not. Like other deer species, they travel in herds. Stags compete for the rights to mate with a herd's does. Fights have been known to be to the death. Mateless young stags often travel in a herd of their own.

PLANTS OF THE TITAN WILDS

Drybrush - A fern-like plant that shrivels upon a touch, then slowly stretches back out its leaves and limbs, regaining color and moisture and seeming to come back to life.

Echinacea - A pink flower whose extract is often used as a natural antibiotic.

Everscent - A flower that changes its aroma throughout the seasons, and sometimes over the span of a few moments. Usually, these scents are quite pleasant. Its blossoms have long, sky-blue petals streaked with white around a fuzzy red pistil, from which long, pink tendrils emerged.

Firefruit - Aubergine berries that burn one's skin for hours. There are stories among the Gasts of using firefruit to incapacitate one's foes.

Hangman's vine - A carnivorous plant that strangles any creature unfortunate enough to be snared by it. Known by the red coloring of its vines and leaves, it is exclusively found wrapped around full-grown broad-leafed trees.Travelers are advised to be wary of which trees they rest against.

Nacatl - A mushroom found in the caves on the northern side of the Silver-tusks. Has hallucinogenic qualities when ingested as a tea.

Peyotl - A cactus whose flower is used for a hallucinogenic tea by the Gast tribes.

APPENDIX D

GLOSSARY

Many of the terms not defined in previous appendices can be found here.

Akan'Oala - Translates to "Those Who Came Before." This is the name given by Gasts to their ancestors. Legend has it that they came long ago to the Veiled Lands and conquered them by benefit of their superior magic. In the eons since, time and war have robbed the Gasts and other indigenous peoples of many of these secrets, leaving their history shrouded in mystery.

The Altacura - The leader of the Catedrál. Addressed as "Gran" or "Her Sanctity." The Altacura has always been female. Many of those who reached Ascendance to become one of the five Saints have previously been the Altacura. Though officially a religious leader, by benefit of her station and the Catedrál's resources, the Altacura has traditionally wielded great power both in Ilberia and in the world at large.

Ara'buru - The Eteman scrying pool located in Solace. Used to observe and learn from afar about the peoples, languages, and events of the Veiled Lands.

Ascendance - The process by which a person is made into a saint. Often, saints have arisen from a previous Altacura, though not exclusively. Holy miracles must be attributed to the person in order to achieve Ascendance, as do revelations of morality as divinely inspired by Omn. Only five individuals have thus far Ascended in the Catedrál's history.

Bond(ed) - *"Kamit"* to Etemans. References to either the mutual attachment of a maha to a titan or to the attached titan itself.

The Caelrey - Also known as "the World King." The political leader of Ilberia. In practice, often has to share power with the Altacura and her Catedrál. Reigns from Vasara, the capital of Ilberia.

The Catedrál - Also called "the Holy Catedrál." A sprawling religious institution worshiping the prescience of Omn and the god's revelations. The Catedrál has largely acted as a matriarchy, with precedence given to women for positions of power. Though officially a religious institution, its significant resources and moral sway often translate to geopolitical power that its leaders are unafraid to wield.

The Cherished - The name Eyins and Ofeans have for themselves as worshippers and believers in Okulukulu, the Mother Goddess.

Cloaking - The induction of a ranger apprentice into a full ranger by giving the apprentice a ranger cloak, a resilient and warm article dyed a forest green. Inducted rangers are also referred to as "cloaked rangers" by benefit of this ritual.

The Cloudholder - Leader of the Stormhold, the home of the skystriders of Ore-Ofe.

The Colonial Order of Mahia - The arm of government relegated to the training and deployment of mahas within Baltesia.

Conqueror - A general of the Ilberian military. In the colony of Baltesia, conquerors wield authority only surpassed by the Caelrey and, contentiously, the Altacura.

Council Domo - The building where the Liberty Council confers.

The Culling - *"Palaq"* to Etemans. The long period during which the Iritu winnowed magic from the Etemans' and Gasts' ancestors. These events led Etemans to hide within grottos and Gasts to lose their most powerful shamans and forget the deepest secrets of magic.

Dryvan - Also called "skin-walker" and "forest witch." Known as *"sach'aan"* to the Gasts. Among themselves, dryvans refer to themselves as "the Kin." Dryvans are shapeshifters. Though often possessing shapes approximately human, they are changed with attributes of animals and plants. Rarely seen, it is unknown what their disposition is toward humanity, for stories have been told of both boons and harms.

Eesu(wé) - The magic wielders of Ore-Ofe and the Eyin Empire.

Elected Consul - The leader of Baltesia. Elected by a host of representatives from across the former colony.

Epochs of Unera - According to the Catedrál, the first age of Unera was the Epoch of Sin, when all of humanity was mired in ignorance and transgressions. During that time, those with mahia were worshiped as gods, and all quailed at their power. Then, with the founding of the Catédral came the Epoch of Epiphany, the current age, which began with the miracles of the First Saint, Inhoa the Merciful. This is believed to be a time of civilization and virtue, when the truth of the Saints will be spread to the far corners of the world and all will be saved from their sins.

Esse - Also called "lifefire," "lifeforce," and "essence." Known as *"ilis"* to the Gasts. Esse is the vital life energy of a being. Invisible to most, those who possess mahia see it as bright life, often moving like flames throughout the body. Each individual possesses a unique esse, and those with an attuned enough lifesense may identify any being by it. Though mostly isolated to a being's body, mahia allows one to either draw it out of individuals or manipulate it to different effects.

Etaro - "Spirit" in Eteman.

Etemans - A people related to Gasts and their ancestors. Etemans now only exist in isolated pockets within grottos.

The Eyrie - A substantial island that forms part of the Eyin Empire. Believed by Eyins to be the birthplace of humanity.

Ferino - Translates literally to "feral" from Ilberian. A derogatory term used by Ilberians and Baltesians toward Gasts and other indigenous peoples.

Fesht - An expletive common in Baltesia referring to an aggressive sexual act. Thought to have originated from an indigenous tribe. Similar to the Gast expletive *"egresht."*

Gasts - Refer to themselves as "The Many Tribes." Though perceived by colonists as a cohesive group, Gasts entail various tribes bonded by cultural and spiritual beliefs held in common. During the colonization of the Veiled Lands, the Gasts resisted the Ancestral Lands, which led to the Titan War. Following their capitulation, the Gasts largely retreated to beyond the Silvertusk Sierra to the arid lands beyond the mountains called the Barren.

Ghosts - Called *"timili"* by Gasts. These ghosts are typically found in ancestral ruins and manifest as whispers and a lingering sense of esse.

Great Teyao - The larger of Unera's two moons.

Grotto - The Iritu term for a space outside of the ordinary world, created and sustained by magic. Also called *"haru"* by Etemans.

Heavens' Reach - *"Aafinsowa"* in Eyin. The luxurious estate of the chancellor and the head priest of Ore-Ofe.

The Hesh Jin - Also called "the Ocean Lord." Leader of Kalga.

Inheritance - The Iritu term for magic. Also "heritage," depending on the usage.

The Iritu - The original name for the species that separated into dryvans and lyshans. Shapeshifters with potent magic they call "Inheritance" or "heritage."

The *Kekére*, or the Coterie Tower - The tower in Kunu where the eesuwé live and train. The center of magic within Ore-Ofe.

Kha-ir - "Beloved" in Kalgan. A term of endearment used by Isla and Batu.

Lakti - The western cliff of Qasaar.

Legion - The force of evil to the Catedrál, opposing the good force of Omn and the Saints. Seen as a fragmented being with many faces on account of the tormented souls it has captured screaming for release. Some believe Legion manifests demons in Unera to serve his purposes. For some, titans and dryvans are a few of these demons, while others see them as natural manifestations akin to animals and plants.

The Liberty Council - The ruling council of Baltesia.

The Lodgemaster - Leader of the Wilds Lodge, home to the rangers of Baltesia.

Lualli - The eastern cliff of Qasaar.

Mada - A familiar term meaning "mother" to Baltesians and Ilberians.

Maha - A user of mahia; specifically, one located in Baltesia.

Mahia - Known as *"semah"* to the Gasts. Mahia is a magic of life and death, allowing its user to manipulate esse to various effects. These effects include healing, killing (by draining an individual of esse), and strengthening or energizing one's body. Mahia also seems to have something to do with titans, as the creatures appear to be at least partly magical in origin. While seen as having come from Omn by the Catedrál, it is also seen as a tool by which Legion could exploit human weakness and lead people into sin. The other Ancestral Lands have higher levels of tolerance, though most view it with distrust. Among the Tricolonies, these attitudes are often passed on, though more leniency has evolved.

Mahita - A pupil of the Baltesian Order of Mahia. I.e., a maha-in-training.

Makayo - Translates to "Unity." The Gast afterlife, in which an individual merges with the world. The losing of oneself to the great whole of being is anticipated with eagerness.

The Moorwarden - Leader of the Greathouse, home to the plainsriders of Altan Gaz.

The Mothertrees - *"Ialadta"* to the Iritu. Also called simply "the Mothers." The great magical trees that gave birth to the Iritu. Now extinct, burned by the ancestors of Etemans and Gasts.

The Murmuring Canyon - A ravine near Qasaar where the stone is alive with spirits.

Odiosa - A witch hunter of the Catedrál. By virtue of possessing mahia, odiosas sense out those with magic and either recruit them to their cause or have them executed. It is unknown how people become indoctrinated as odiosas, though their odd temperaments allude to some sort of torturous process that addles the mind.

The Odisi - Also called "the Sky Queen." Leader of Eyi.

Okulukulu - Also "Mother Goddess" and "Mistress of Stars." The central goddess of the Eyin and Ofean peoples.

Omn - Also called "the Unknown" and "Omn Almighty." The god honored by the Catedrál. Most often depicted as a faceless, genderless orb of astral origin, similar to the sun and the moons, though distinct from both. Omn is believed to be the creator of all, including magic and titans.

Pada - A familiar term meaning "father" to Baltesians and Ilberians.

Plainsrider - A protector of the Tricolonies dwelling at the Greathouse in Altan Gaz. Akin to rangers and skystriders.

Premier - A provincial governor in Ilberia or Baltesia.

Prima Maha - The leader of the Baltesian Order of Mahia.

Ranger - A protector of the Tricolonies dwelling at the Wilds Lodge in Baltesia. Akin to plainsriders and skystriders.

The Ranger's Lament - An invocation spoken by a ranger after taking a life. Often spoken to alleviate guilt at the killing. The phrase is as follows: "Your spirit touches mine."

The Ranger's Oath - An oath taken by rangers at their cloaking ceremony, which they vow to uphold during their service. The oath is as follows: "Perceive. Preserve. Protect."

The Sacred Saints - The five individuals in Catedrál history who have Ascended from mortals into divine representatives of Omn. The Saints are seen as intermediaries between the faceless god and humanity, and interpret what is good and what is sinful. The Saints and their associated virtues are as follows:

San Hugo of Resolution and Equity
San Luciana of Sincerity and Candor
San Jadiel of Grace and Beauty
San Inhoa of Mercy and Quietus

San Carmen of Loyalty and Justice

Shaman - A magic wielder and religious leader of the Gasts. As those possessing mahia, shamans serve many vital functions within Gast society, including healing the sick and wounded, communing with the ancestors and the spirits of the world, and warding against titans. They are often highly educated and serve as advisors to chieftains. By benefit of magic, shamans have also historically been reservoirs of indigenous history. Unfortunately, if a shaman dies before they can pass this knowledge on, it is forever lost, a problem that became particularly difficult during the Titan War and was one factor that led to the Gasts' retreat.

The Shroud - *"Kai'am"* to Etemans. The protective barrier erected around Solace.

Skystrider - A protector of the Tricolonies dwelling at the Stormhold in Ore-Ofe. Akin to plainsriders and rangers.

The Stormhold - *"Isphopho"* in Eyin. The stronghold of the Ofean skystriders high upon the Radiante Slopes.

Taht - Meaning "father" or "mother," it is a respectful address for shamans.

Talisman - Also called *"periaptu"* by the Iritu. Items imbued with magic that produce various effects.

Tekuan - A Gast tribe with a reputation for being continued aggressors since the Titan War. Their name translates to "Jaguar" and their people are tattooed with this symbol.

The Ten Virtues - The ideals upheld by the Catedrál as being good and worthy of pursuit. All are associated with one of the Sacred Saints. The virtues are resolution, equity, sincerity, candor, grace, beauty, mercy, quietus, loyalty, and justice.

The Tetrad - The council of four chieftains that leads the Many Tribes of Qasaar.

Titan's awakening - The event when a titan first emerges from a natural body, such as a hill or river, and forms its body. It is believed titans may lie dormant in places for years before rising. Upon their awakening, those with magic perceived it as radiating very strongly from them, often so much so that it is impossible to resist their pull.

The Titan War - The war over the colonization of the Veiled Lands, fought between the Gasts and other indigenous peoples against those coming from the Ancestral Lands. After years of failed negotiations, the Gasts finally pushed back against the people invading their lands. Using magic, their shamans sent titans against the colonial settlements, devastating them and killing thousands. Though those possessing mahia from the Ancestral Lands did not know how to control titans, they used their magic against the shamans themselves, leading to the deaths of most of them. Following the loss of their shamans, the Gasts and other natives retreated beyond the Silvertusk Sierra to the lands known as the Barren. Only a few remained behind, and these were discriminated against, often to the point of violence.

Toa - Translates to "chief," the title given to a Gast chieftain.

The Tumult of Titans - "*Nox'mekva*" to the Etemans. The event during which Eteman ancestors are claimed to have "broken" the world.

The Uman - Another of the indigenous people of the Veiled Lands, and included in the Many Tribes.

Unera - Called "*Tlalli*" by the Gasts. Unera is the planet, the world at large.

The *Uphathi* - Also "the Cloudholder." The master of the Stormhold.

The Veil - The misty boundary that separates the Veiled Lands from the Ancestral Lands. Once penetrated by a wisewoman from Kalga, it allowed for the conquest and colonization that followed.

Whisperspire - *Tepe'laka* in the Gast tongue; the tower where the Tetrad meets in Qasaar.

Wisdom - Also "wisemen" and "wisewomen." A wielder of magic in Kalga and Altan Gaz.

Young Chiuni - The smaller of Unera's two moons.

READ THE FREE PREQUEL

If you would like more of Leiyn's adventures, you can find a free short story about her contending with a company of titan trappers on my website at: *jdlrosell.com/ranger*

BOOKS BY J.D.L. ROSELL

Sign up for future releases at jdlrosell.com.

RANGER OF THE TITAN WILDS

1. The Last Ranger

2. The First Ancestor

3. The Hidden Guardian

4. The Wilds Exile

LEGEND OF TAL

1. A King's Bargain

2. A Queen's Command

3. An Emperor's Gamble

4. A God's Plea

THE RUNEWAR SAGA

1. The Throne of Ice & Ash

2. The Crown of Fire & Fury

3. The Stone of Iron & Omen

THE FAMINE CYCLE

1. Whispers of Ruin

2. Echoes of Chaos

3. Requiem of Silence

Secret Seller (Prequel)

The Phantom Heist (Novella)

⁓

GODSLAYER RISING

1. Catalyst

2. Champion

3. Heretic

ACKNOWLEDGMENTS

With each new book, the list of people who helped shape it grows longer. To wit:

Kaitlyn, my wife, first reader, and patient listener to my every half-formed idea. Even when you're fed up of my prattling, I'm grateful for how much you humor me.

Sarah Chorn, my editor and a talented author in her own right. Thank you for both your work on this book and the inspiration you gift through your fiction.

Félix Ortiz, the illustrator behind the cover art and three of the interior pieces. Your work is as incredible as ever.

Shawn T. King, the cover designer responsible for making Félix's art look so good. I appreciate you fitting these books into your insanely busy schedule! Your work continues to be stellar.

Joemel Requeza, the immaculate artist behind the other four interior pieces as well as the new chapter icon. I'm so glad to have found you! (And thanks to Eileen Mueller for the recommendation!)

Rachel St. Clair, the designer of the new Ranger of the Titan Wilds logo (the fox with the arrow seen on the title page). As with all the work you do for me, it's just what I was looking for.

Keir Scott-Schrueder, the artist behind the gorgeous world map of Unera. I never get tired of looking at it!

Shawn Sharrah, the incredibly gracious and speedy proofreader. I hope I didn't make a mistake failing to ask you to look over these final pages!

My patrons on Patreon, who give their support above anything I can repay. Thank you Debbie, Ruth & Tarris, Nick, Ben, Don, and GhostCat.

Julia, the first staunch champion of Ranger of the Titan Wilds. I hope you find the amount of archery in this installment up to your strident standards!

And a massive round of thanks to all the *Kickstarter backers*! I couldn't have made *The Hidden Guardian* up to the standards of the previous two books without all of the following people:

Astridd | Azi | Bruce | Grimteef | Jezza | Neil | Qavee
Tristan A. | Emma Adams | Joseph W. Aguiar | Joel Allan
Peter Allen | Kristen Altmann | Walter E. Alvarez Jr
Gregory Amato | Jerome Anello | Amelia Armstrong
Boyd Atkinson | Jon Auerbach | William Cody Austin
M-H Ayotte | Francesca B. | Marino Barcos | Steve Batezel
Cassandra Baubie | Dave Baughman | Polina Bazlova
Angel Becerra | Jan Birch | Brett Blakley | Christopher Boisvert
Bradley Bolt | Lorraine Bondi | Kurtis Boulianne
Kyle Boureston | Jason Bowden | Chad Bowden | Virgil Bower
Kaleah Brewster | Justise Briones | Robert Brown
Corinne Brucks | Philip Buck | Ryan Buell | Ashley Byrd
Bridget C. | Ryan Cahill | Kodie Caldwell | Joshua Callahan
Gabrielle Camassar | Franchesca Caram | Meredith Carstens
Lori Case | Scott Casey | Gabriel Casillas | Garret Castle
Pepe Centineo | Tyler Cheek | Cliff Chen | Scott Chisholm
L. J. Christie | Gianna Christopher | Vivian Cicero | Lee Clark
H.M. Clarke | Andrew Claydon | Christopher Clayton | CMT
Andrew Cobble | Cynthia M Coffman | Paden Cogswell
Jonathan Cole | Christopher Colón | Caitee Cooper
Matthew Corbin | Alexandra Corrsin | Eric Cotti
Patrick Couch | Timothy Cregar | Sarolta Csik
James Cunningham | Faelyn Curtis | Travis D. | Connor Daley
Susanne Daniels | David Daughhetee | Joanna Davis
Michael DeCuypere | David DeHaan | Michael Delaney
H. Deur | Aaron DeWaard | Riley DeWert | Z.S. Diamanti
Daniel Diez Blazquez | Heather Dow | Katie Dresel
Gabrielle Duncan | Tammy Dziuba | Tassilo E.| Richard Earl
Kristopher Ecklof | J. Eliason | Mark Erickson | Doug Erling

Hugo Essink | Andy F. | Randall Fickel | Miguel A. Fidalgo
Richard Fierce | Stephanie Fischer | Marie Fisher | Russell Fisk
Emma Flaws | Wizard Flight | Mychal Ford | J.R. Forst
Scott Frederick | Kallen Frieling | Christopher Froebe
Darren Fry | B. S. H. Garcia | Kim Garcia | Quinn Giguiere
John Gilligan | Drew Gohmann | Alex Goiea | Mike Gonzales
Elizabeth Gorman | Lorenzo Goyer | Alex Grade | Falk Gräpel
Chelsea Greathouse | Miranda Green | Martin Greening
Joseph Greentree | Justin Greer | Vickie Grider | Mark Griffith
Marie Grimaldi-Clermont | Michael Grovenburg | Kris Guthrie
Ryan H. | Taylor Haddock | Chelsea Hammink
Kristian Handberg | Michael Haney | Matias Hansen
Dylan Harney | Debbie Harris | Hot Hawks | Michael Hayes
L. Haymond | Shane Heaton | Deborah Hedges
Jackalope Heelein | Kristin Hendrick | Billye Herndon
Alicia Hintzen | T. Hise | Thomas Hodges | Austin Hoffey
Karin Holt | Christian Holt | Patricia Horton | Neil Houston
Terry M. Hulett | John Idlor | Ellie Ilieva | Ryan Scott James
E. Jennings | Zachary Jennings | Jay Johnson | Jennifer Johnson
Jeffrey M. Johnson | Jacob Joseph | Jessica Juby | Kevin Kastelic
Kenneth Kauffman | Christian Kegley | Katie Keith | Boe Kelley
Dan Kenner | Dominik Kessler | Matt King | Thomas Kjelsen
Laura Klaine | Heiko Koenig | James Kralik | Reinier Krouwer
Angelika L. | John Ladley | Paula Lafferty
Samantha Landström | Steven "Waffles" Lane | André Laude
Gayle Lazur | Joe Lee | Mathieu Lefebvre | Kyle Leubka
Yael Levy | Micheal Li | Richard Libera | Nicolas Lobotsky
Jason Lovell | Sean Lovely Ramsey | Ron Luck | Alex Luco
Karen M. | Lorenzo M. | Megyn MacDougall | Johnny
MacIsaac
Tommy Maguire | Nick Mandujano | Lahman Marcel
Kris Marchesi | John Markley | Jason Martin | Krista Marx
For Marykat | Charli Maxwell | Connor Mayo | Rory McCabe
Gerald McDaniel | James McGinnis | Karl McGurty
Cathy McLoughlin | Agnès Metanomski | Christian Meyer
Annarose Mitchell | Michael Mitchell | Benjamin Molina

Matt Mollo | Tyler Montgomery | Rochelle Moore
Tristan Morgan | R. A. Morley | Destinee—Mother of Children
Kyle Mowatt | King Father & Queen Mother | Julianne Nash
Brandon Neal | Jared Nelson | Korbyn Nelson | Kai Nichols
Matthew Nimmo | Richard Nimmons | E.S. Nisan
Brendan Noble | Hank Nordic | Charles Norton | James
O'Brien
Angel Ocampo | Tyler ODonnell
In loving memory of Basil Martin | Mike Olson
Joshua Oplinger | Chip Orlikowski | Darren Pallant
Scott Palmer | Crystal Palumbo | Daniel Papke
N. Scott Pearson | Steven Peiper | Jeff Pena | Gelar Phahla
Sarah Phillips | B. Plaga | Duane Powell | Wayne Priddle
Jason R. | Rhianne R. | Ian Rankine | James Rao | Tana Reeve
Ryan Reeves | Austin Regan | Håvard Jacobsen Reigstad
Sean Reilly | Vincent Kenneth Resullar | Xiomara Reyes
Tyson Reyes | Mark Riis-Cordsen | Joe Rixman | Todd Roark
SaraBeth Roberson | Caitlin Roberts | Will Rodd
Chris Roeszler | Wutthichai Roongkham | Matthea W. Ross
Lindsey Rubini | Robert Rush | Tomas Rydland | Sarah S.
Mishelle S. | Wilma S. Murphy | GhostCat | Josh Samples
Erik Sapp | C. Saulter | Jesse Schonau | R.M. Schultz
René Schultze | Stephanie Schwab | Brad Searing | Baird Searle
Nathan Seaward | Shawn Sharrah | Katherine Shipman
Sunny Side Up | Kindreth Silverwing | Em Sipprell
CJ Skowronek | Andrew Smith | Paul Smith | Heather Smith
Derrick Smythe | Keino Somers | Justin Sorensen
Sarah L. Stevenson | Sarah Stewart | Blake Strickland
Burt Struble | Michael H. Sugarman | Justin Swift | Melissa T.
Jason T. | C. Taormina | Greg Tausch | Carlos Tautimer
Rosa Thill | Lloyd Thistle | Vancil Thomas | Andy Thompson
Joni Toivonoja | Amanda Trumpower | Johannes Tuchscherer
Taylor Tudisco | Nathan Turner | Arild Tvedt | Alex Valdiers
Mike Vance | Eric Vilbert | C.V. Vobh | Jordan Waid
Andrew Wainwright | Thomas Walcher | David Walters
Tryston Webb | Ben Wehner | Floyd Weitzel | Mike Welch

Adam Weller | Kenyon Wensing | Duncan Wilcox
Nicola Wilkinson | Dexter Wilkinson | Kyle Wilkinson
Charles Williams | Blaine Williams | Debra Ann Wilson
C. Wilson | Anora Wilson | Carly Winchell | Lia Winnard
David Wolfson | Jonathan Woodman | Alex Wrigglesworth
Spencer Wright | Keelyn Wright | Nena Yochim
Peter Younghusband

Once more, I must say how grateful I am to each and every one of the above people. Thank you—*The Hidden Guardian* wouldn't be the same without you.

Finally, thank you, dear reader, for taking this journey with me. I hope it was everything you wished it to be.

Josiah (J.D.L. Rosell)

ABOUT THE AUTHOR

J.D.L. Rosell was swept away on a journey when he stepped foot outside his door and into *The Hobbit*. He hasn't stopped wandering since.

In his writing, he tries to recapture the wonder, adventure, and poignancy that captivated him as a child. His explorations have taken him to worlds set in over a dozen novels and five series, which include Ranger of the Titan Wilds, Legend of Tal, The Runewar Saga, and The Famine Cycle.

When he's not off on a quest, Rosell enjoys his newfound hobby of archery and older pastimes of hiking and landscape photography. But every hobbit returns home, and if you step softly and mind the potatoes, you may glimpse him curled up with his wife and two cats, Zelda and Abenthy, reading a good book, or replaying his favorite video games.

You can learn more about him and his books at jdlrosell.com or contact him at josiah@jdlrosell.com.

www.ingramcontent.com/pod-product-compliance
Lightning Source LLC
Chambersburg PA
CBHW030834190726
48285CB00004B/1213